Maxim Jakubowski is a London-based novelist and editor. He was born in the UK and educated in France. Following a career in book publishing, he opened the world-famous Murder One bookshop in London. He now writes full-time. He has edited many acclaimed crime collections, and over twenty bestselling erotic anthologies and books on erotic photography. His novels include *It's You That I Want to Kiss, Because She Thought She Loved Me* and *On Tenderness Express*, all three collected and reprinted in the USA as *Skin in Darkness*. Other books include *Life in the World of Women, The State of Montana, Kiss Me Sadly, Confessions of a Romantic Pornographer, I Was Waiting for You, Ekaterina and the Night, American Casanova* and his collected short stories *Fools for Lust*. He compiles two annual acclaimed series for the Mammoth list: *Best New Erotica* and *Best British Crime*. He is a winner of the Anthony and the Karel Awards, a frequent TV and radio broadcaster, a past crime columnist for the *Guardian* newspaper and Literary Director of London's Crime Scene Festival. In recent years, he has authored under a pen-name a series of *Sunday Times* bestselling erotic romance novels which have sold over two million copies and been sold to 22 countries, and translated the acclaimed French novel *Monsieur* by Emma Becker.

The Mammoth Book of
The Adventures
of
Professor Moriarty

37 Short Stories about the Secret Life
of Sherlock Holmes's Nemesis

Edited by
Maxim Jakubowski

Skyhorse Publishing
A Herman Graf Book

Skyhorse Publishing books may be purchased in bulk at special discounts for
sales promotion, corporate gifts, fund-raising, or educational purposes. Special editions can also be created to specifications. For details, contact the Special Sales Department, Skyhorse Publishing, 307 West 36th Street, 11th Floor,
New York, NY 10018 or info@skyhorsepublishing.com.

Skyhorse® and Skyhorse Publishing® are registered trademarks of Skyhorse
Publishing, Inc.®, a Delaware corporation.

Visit our website at www.skyhorsepublishing.com.

10 9 8 7 6 5 4 3 2 1

Library of Congress Cataloging-in-Publication Data is available on file.

Cover design by Laura Klynstra
Cover image: iStock

Print ISBN: 978-1-5107-3461-6
Ebook ISBN: 978-1-5107-0950-8

Contents

xi
Introduction
Maxim Jakubowski

1
Moriarty and the Two-Body Problem
Alison Joseph

20
A Good Mind's Fate
Alexandra Townsend

30
Everything Flows and Nothing Stays
John Soanes

50
A Scandalous Calculation
Catherine Lundoff

66
Dynamics of an Asteroid
Lavie Tidhar

82
The Importance of Porlock
Amy Myers

99
How the Professor Taught a Lesson to the Gnoles
Josh Reynolds

114
The Swimming Lesson
Priscilla Masters

128
The Malady of the Mind Doctor
Howard Halstead

146
Obsession
Russel D. McLean

160
The Box
Steve Cavanagh

178
Jacques the Giant Slayer
Vanessa de Sade

191
Rosenlaui
Conrad Williams

203
The Protégé
Kate Ellis

218
A Scandal in Arabia
Claude Lalumière

232
The Mystery of the Missing Child
Christine Poulson

251
The Case of the Choleric Cotton Broker
Martin Edwards

269
The Last of his Kind
Barbara Nadel

282
A Problem of Numbers
David N. Smith and Violet Addison

303
The Fulham Strangler
Keith Moray

323
The Adventure of the Lost Theorem
Julie Novakova

343
The Last Professor Moriarty Story
Andrew Lane

362
Quid Pro Quo
Ashley R. Lister

376
The Jamesian Conundrum
Jan Edwards

393
The Caribbean Treaty Affair
Jill Braden

408
The Copenhagen Compound
Thomas S. Roche

426
The Shape of the Skull
Anoushka Havinden

444
A Function of Probability
Mike Chinn

462
The Perfect Crime
G. H. Finn

478
As Falls Reichenbach, So Falls Reichenbach Falls
Alvaro Zinos-Amaro

492
A Certain Notoriety
David Stuart Davies

503
Fade to Black
Michael Gregorio

519
The Skeleton of Contention
Rhys Hughes

531
The Fifth Browning
Jürgen Ehlers

542
The Modjeska Waltz
Rose Biggin

559
Moriarty's Luck
L. C. Tyler

567
The Death of Moriarty
Peter Guttridge

Introduction

It is said that the devil has all the best lines and who are we to contradict this?

Heroes come, triumph against terrible adversity and eventually end up in the land of happy-ever-after, but you and I know that the baddies are more often the ones that stay in the mind. In books, movies, comics and, less seductively, also sometimes in real life.

Of course, we all remember James Bond's exploits, but it's the larger than life figures of Auric Goldfinger, Ernst Stavro Blofeld, Doctor No, Oddjob, Jaws and other representations of evil who come to mind. Think back: Hannibal Lecter, the Joker, Lex Luthor, Hyde on the dark side of Jekyll, Jack the Ripper, Fu Manchu, the Deaf Man in Ed McBain's 87th Precinct police procedurals, Long John Silver, Captain Hook, Tom Ripley – Patricia Highsmith's chilling but suave killer and manipulator – Bill Sykes, Sauron, Patrick Bateman – the anti-hero of 'American Psycho' – Dracula, Voldermort, the list could prove endless.

I rest my case.

No one will object to my stating that Sherlock Holmes is the most legendary of fictional sleuths and still captures our imagination like no other through renewed interpretations, impersonations and tales still being spun well beyond Conan Doyle's initial canon. But what would Sherlock be without his arch foe: Professor James Moriarty, a man whose fate and life is intimately entwined with his and who automatically comes to mind whenever we evoke the denizen of 221B Baker Street?

But unless you are a learned Holmes expert, did you know that Moriarty actually only appears in two Holmes stories? Respectively, 'The Adventure of the Final Problem' and 'The Valley of Fear'.

Holmes, or rather his chronicler Doctor Watson, evokes Moriarty in passing in five other tales but the master criminal, whom Holmes described as 'the Napoleon of Crime' doesn't in fact appear in the stories ('The Adventure of the Empty House', 'The Adventure of the Norwood Builder', 'The Adventure of the Missing Three-Quarter', 'The Adventure of the Illustrious Client' and 'His Last Bow').

Doctor Watson, even when narrating, never meets Moriarty (only getting distant glimpses of him in 'The Final Problem'), and relies upon Holmes to relate accounts of the detective's feud with the criminal. Conan Doyle is inconsistent on Watson's familiarity with Moriarty. In 'The Final Problem', Watson tells Holmes he has never heard of Moriarty, while in 'The Valley of Fear', set earlier on, Watson already knows of him as 'the famous scientific criminal'.

On such thin foundations was a legend born!

And scores of readers starved of further stories about Moriarty (and by extension Sherlock Holmes) have incessantly called out for more and writers have obliged. Prominent amongst these have been Michael Kurland, the much-missed John Gardner, and Anthony Horowitz, all of whose novels featuring the master criminal have provided a renewed light and insights into his nefarious, if clever activities.

Which is where this collection comes in.

Aware of the fascination Moriarty casts, I thought the time had come for our criminal mastermind to have an anthology of his own, and the submissions came flooding in, enough to fill several volumes of our size! So many admirers of crime out there!

The short stories I had the privilege of assembling prove so wondrously imaginative and challenging. Not all feature Holmes or Watson, and not all see Moriarty as the pure incarnation of evil we had previously assumed he represented, and the twists and adventures on offer are often a thing of beauty. The variations on display are both subtle and far-fetching, filling the gaps in the Doyle canon or opening up whole new cans of worms, which I found as delightful as they were challenging.

Inside these pages you will find well-known crime writers, and lesser stars too, as well as courageous interlopers from other popular fiction fields such as science fiction and fantasy and even erotica (albeit with their libido switched off for the occasion), all seduced by the attraction of Professor James Moriarty's criminal mind.

Never has evil been so fascinating and its fruit so exciting.

The game's afoot yet again.

Relish!

Maxim Jakubowski

Moriarty and the Two-Body Problem

Alison Joseph

It seems rather odd now, looking back, that I didn't see the shape of things. Given that, as a mathematician, seeing the shape of things is what I do, finding order instead of chaos, a pattern where once was randomness. As Professor Moriarty might have said – but, no, I must start at the beginning.

They were happy times. It was a small college in London, and I was embarking on my research under the supervision of Professor James Moriarty. My father, a pharmacist in Norwich, couldn't understand what had made me leave the security of Cambridge to end up in London, working with someone no one had heard of. But I'm working on Gauss, I tried to tell my parents. Carl Friedrich Gauss, who charted the path of the comet Ceres where everyone else had failed. I knew that Professor Moriarty had been feted in his day for his influential work on the dynamics of an asteroid. And now here he was, tucked away in London, in a small room in St Dunstan's College, still knowing more about Gauss's calculations than anyone other than Gauss himself.

'I can't imagine why you've come to me, young man,' were his first words when I introduced myself. 'Once, long ago, I might have had some influence, but we're in the twentieth century now. My work no longer carries any weight. Where once my name struck fear into my enemies, why now, no one has heard of me at all.' Then, with a brief, thin smile he said, 'I have no enemies now.' His gaze had somehow gone beyond me, into the distance, into the past.

Above him hung a portrait, and my eyes were drawn to it. It was clearly the Professor himself, as a younger man. Even now one could see the similarities. He looked more distinguished, older, of course, but the grey hair was still thick, the same domed forehead, the same rather stiff, upright posture. Next to it there was a charming painting of a boy, sitting at a table upon which lay various mathematical instruments. Moriarty's gaze followed mine.

'*Le Petit Mathématicien,*' he said.

'French?' I said.

'Greuze,' he said.

'I'm afraid I don't know who that is,' I said.

He laughed. 'It's a copy. I do have an original Greuze, but in the past certain people made rather, shall we say, unfortunate judgements about me for having such a valuable thing, so I keep it to myself. Now, young man, tell me why you're so keen to allow an old has-been any kind of influence over your work.'

I began to describe my work. I talked about orbits within solar systems, the measurement of the angle between two planes, and the measurement of the arc intercepted between the poles of the curves, and, as I talked, I noticed how his expression carried a blankness, almost a sneer. I wondered whether perhaps my parents were right, and that staying in the confines of Emmanuel with a tutor I knew well might have been a more rational decision.

But what my parents didn't yet know was that I had encountered Angela, a lovely librarian who worked in the university and lived with her widowed father in Harrow; and I had resolved that, if staying in London gave me the chance to see more of her, then London it would be. What they also didn't know was that I had taken a part-time job in a printers' warehouse in Holborn just to keep a roof over my head. I occupied two small rooms near Chancery Lane, where at night I would lie in bed listening to the rain dripping from the broken guttering and the shouts of unruly law students in the streets below.

I had reached a point in my paper where I describe the

calculations for the two points on a sphere that correspond to any given point of the curved line upon a curved surface.

'Hah!' Moriarty's exclamation interrupted my musings. 'This is all very interesting to me.' The flickering sneer had gone, replaced by an intense, dark gaze. 'It's not often people ask for me by name these days,' he said. He leaned back in his chair, glancing upwards at the portrait on the wall. 'Mathematics,' he said. 'The purest of the sciences. Gauss charted the path of the asteroid, not by looking outwards at the skies, but by looking inwards at the numbers. That's what we mathematicians do. We find the glory of the heavens in the pure, abstract truths of calculation.' He turned to look at me again. 'The workings of numbers,' he said. 'So much more reliable than the workings of the human heart. I shall be happy to tutor you.'

And so began our collaboration.

Moriarty was not a warm person. There was something hidden about him, a coolness, a distance. But his brilliance was indisputable. He was often occupied with his own writings, a reworking of his early work on the binomial theorem. 'Mere footnotes to Plato,' he said to me once with a wry smile. 'The balance between positive and negative, almost Manichean in its dualism.' Sometimes he'd say to me, 'Mr Gifford, I'm an old man. It's 1921. We have a new mathematics, we have general relativity, we have Hilbert and his unsolved problems. Worse than that, we have the legacy of this terrible war, the world turned upside down . . .' An air of weariness would cross his face, and his eyes would appear hooded, almost blank. But then something in my calculations would awaken his interest again, and we'd be off, and I would once again be impressed at the quickness of his mind, and his deep love of his subject.

It was a friendly department. The tutors' common room was oak-panelled and convivial, full of smoke and conversation. There was a fellow who had joined at the same time as me, a young Oxford chap named Roland Sadler, working on quadratic forms, and we used to share a pot of tea together most afternoons.

I noticed that Moriarty was rather left alone. One of the tutors, when I said I was working with him, simply said, 'Poor you.' 'Ah,' someone else chipped in, 'the arch nemesis, or so he likes to think,' and there was laughter, not altogether kind. I was glad that the Professor wasn't there to hear.

The head of the department was a Scotsman, Dr Angus McCrae. Amongst the other tutors was a new star, a woman named Dr Eveline Brennan. She had made her name at Girton, and had worked with the famous Isabel Maddison, teaching at Trinity College Dublin before joining our department. Some of the men were wary of her, but I liked her directness, her disregard for the social niceties. She called herself a New Woman, and rumour had it that she had studied martial arts with the suffragette Edith Garrud. She also was alone in being kind about Moriarty. 'It's thanks to him I got this position here,' she confided in me once. 'He said he admired my work on c- and p-discriminants.'

One can always see a pattern in retrospect, of course. But, at the time, to a mere observer, the unfortunate events unfolded in a succession that appeared to be entirely random. It all started in such a peculiar way. It was a sunny Monday morning, and we were variously engaged with our teaching, enjoying the sense of spring in the air, when there was a terrible noise from the quad. We ran to the windows to see two men fighting, right in the middle of the neat lawn. Real punches were being thrown, and we could see that one man was getting the worst of it, with a nasty cut across his jaw.

We ran down to the quad, Eveline ahead of us all. 'Stop that now,' she was shouting.

'It's the college porter,' someone was saying. 'Old Seamus.'

'Who's the other chap?'

'No idea.'

'Stop.' It was Eveline's voice ringing out. 'Stop that. Stop that now.'

Her words had an extraordinary effect. The punches stopped. The strange man was standing, panting, staring at her, his fists clenched at his side. He had a shock of black hair, a cheap ragged jacket. Seamus the porter began to crawl away, one hand across his bleeding jaw.

Still the man's dark eyes were fixed on Eveline. Then he spoke. 'I came to find you,' he said. 'I'd heard you were here. But I didn't dare to believe it.'

She was standing, illumined in the May sunlight, upright in her long black skirt, her starched white blouse. She spoke to him quietly, but, as I was nearby, I heard what she said. 'I thought you were dead,' she said. Then she turned and strode away into the college, without looking back.

Roland had gone to help poor Seamus. The rest of us stood, awkwardly. The brawling man had slipped away. People began to drift back to their teaching. I was aware of someone standing at the windows above, and I looked up. Moriarty was staring down at the scene. I could see him, framed by the window of his room. And I could see that he was smiling.

That evening I went to meet Angela at the library. We would often go to a little Italian restaurant and I would buy her dinner, even if it meant eating nothing but toast for the rest of the week. This evening she insisted on paying for her own dinner. 'You're a New Woman,' I teased her. 'Like Eveline. You'll be learning ju-jitsu soon too.' Angela laughed in her sweet, shy way, her brown eyes half hidden behind her dark curls. I almost asked her to marry me there and then.

The next morning was damp and drizzly, and the atmosphere in the college was rather muted too. People whispered in corners. Roland told me that poor Seamus was clearly terrified, even though the strange man seemed to have disappeared. Moriarty too was distracted. I had come to show him my calculations on the isometric simplification of the two-body problem, but his gaze was often drawn to his own papers. 'Dualism, Mr Gifford,' he said to me, suddenly. 'In Manichean terms, there is always the opposite. For every positive, the negative. The force that reaches upwards towards heaven is always balanced out by

Lucifer, the fallen angel.' Then he gave a strange, short laugh, reached for my calculations, scanned them with a glance and said, 'Ah, but you see, remember your Kepler – given that we know the value of "M", here, you still need to calculate the eccentric anomaly, here . . .'

And we were off again.

The next odd thing that happened was that later on that morning, while I was still with Professor Moriarty, we were interrupted by a knock on the door and Seamus appeared, carrying a large parcel of papers. 'These were left at the lodge for you, sir,' he said.

'Hah!' Moriarty seized the brown paper bundle. 'Very good. How are the bruises?' he asked.

'On the mend, thank you, sir.'

'You knew your attacker?' Moriarty watched Seamus closely as he replied.

'Oh yes, sir. Never thought I'd see him again though.'

'An old grudge, perhaps?' Moriarty yawned, and his eyes drifted back towards the newly delivered papers.

'You could say that, sir.' Seamus, seeing that Moriarty's interest had waned, gave a brief bow and departed.

Moriarty placed his hand on the papers. 'An explanation, Mr Gifford,' he said. 'I have a brother. Well, I have two, but this concerns my younger brother. He's a stationmaster in Dawlish. There's an old family matter outstanding that he's trying to clear up. He always was the guardian of these things. A mild-mannered, moral sort of man, never leaves the West Country, but he has deemed this business sufficiently important to visit the capital. Our other brother is a colonel and mostly overseas.' He flicked briefly through the first of the files then turned back to me. 'Enough. To work, Mr Gifford. Kepler's equation awaits us.'

That afternoon I went to my paid job. Loading boxes was dull work, but freed my mind for my calculations. An hour or so passed pleasantly enough, until I was amazed to see one of the shop-floor lads appearing, breathless, in my packing station. 'Your college has sent for you, Owen – they say can you come quickly, a terrible thing has happened.'

I hurried through Bloomsbury, barely aware of the abating drizzle, the thin sunlight breaking through the clouds. At the college lodge, there was a crush of people, and I could see the uniforms of police officers amongst them.

'He's dead,' someone said.

'Who—' I tried to ask.

'Seamus.' Roland was standing at my side. 'He's been killed. Felled by a punch to the throat. They found him in the alley behind the old staircase.'

After that, we all had to give statements. We were corralled into the porter's lodge by the sergeant, and one by one dictated what we knew to a young police officer. Indeed, we knew very little, apart from our witnessing the strange fight of the day before. Roland and I looked up as Professor Moriarty emerged. His expression was fixed, his eyes dark pools against the pallor of his face. He gave a brief nod in greeting, then headed back to his study.

At this point Eveline appeared, ready to give her statement. She seemed hesitant and nervous. I thought of the conversation I'd overheard, and wondered if she would tell the police about it.

Eventually, I escaped and went to meet Angela, luckily only a few minutes late, and my excuse was so dramatic and interesting that she forgave me instantly. We passed a pleasant evening, with a bowl of soup for supper and a walk in the warm twilight. She told me that she'd met her father for tea that day, as he had business in town. 'We met someone who knew your professor,' she said. 'A friend of my father's, a retired doctor. They were in the same tennis club once and they've kept in touch.' But I was only half listening, distracted by the charm of the City at dusk, and the disturbing events of the day.

The next day a strange calm had descended upon the college. The police were a quiet presence in the common room. 'There was a brawl,' the young sergeant said, when Roland and I had gathered for a morning cup of tea. 'It concerns a man named Edmund Sweeney, an Irishman, who was apparently known to the deceased.'

We agreed we had seen the fight, but we knew nothing of this Mr Sweeney. I assumed that Eveline must have told them.

'Fenians.' Dr McCrae spoke up. 'London is awash with them.'

'The Rebellion,' someone said. 'Thank God for our Army.'

'And it's not over,' Dr McCrae said. 'I reckon there'll be war in Ireland by the end of the year.'

'Fellow feeling, perhaps, Dr McCrae?' It was Moriarty who spoke. He had appeared in the doorway, and now helped himself to a cup of tea from the urn.

'Not at all, Professor. Not at all. No love lost between the Scots and the Irish.'

'At least these Fenians have had the good sense to have a mathematician at their helm.' Moriarty stirred sugar into his tea.

'You mean Eamon de Valera.' Dr McCrae raised a bushy eyebrow.

'Indeed. Rockwell College Tipperary. Isn't that so, Dr Brennan?' Moriarty turned to Eveline.

She flashed him a look. Then she shrugged. 'I'm afraid I wouldn't know, Professor.'

'The fallen angel,' Moriarty said, amused. 'One always needs one's Lucifer.' He turned on his heel and left, his cup and saucer balanced on one hand.

I spent an hour or two in my room, working on Cartesian co-ordinate systems for describing three-dimensional space. 'Show your workings,' Moriarty would always say, and I was trying to make sure that I'd written everything down, that it all made sense. But the figures swam before my eyes, distracted as I was by these terrible events in the college, and in the end I gave up and went for a walk.

I passed the porter's lodge, now occupied by a new chap, a war veteran with blinking blue eyes and a shock of white hair. He sat uneasily in Seamus's place, nodding silent greetings to those who came and went. As I started down the lane that led out to the back of the college, I heard raised voices.

'You must get away.' It was a woman's tone.

'I came here for you. I won't leave without you,' a rough, male voice replied and, as I rounded the corner, I could glimpse Dr Brennan and the man from the brawl, half hidden by the kitchen dustbins.

'You're risking your life,' she said.

'I'd risk anything for you, Bren. You know that.'

'I thought you were dead. That night by the barricades, when they dragged you away . . . and now all this time later you appear in my life . . .' She took a step towards him, and he enclosed her in his arms.

After a moment, she said, 'But, our porter—'

'Seamus O'Connor.'

'I'd heard of him,' she said. 'He went over to the others—'

'So he did. And, when he was interned, he held me responsible. Swore vengeance ever since.'

'So, when you came in here—'

'He set about me. Took me by surprise. Luckily I know how to defend myself.'

'Oh, Edmund.' She put her arms around him. 'But, you're not safe.' Her eyes searched his face. 'They'll arrest you for his murder. You must go.'

'But I didn't do it, Bren. I swear to you. You know, on Monday, after picking that fight, he came to find me. Invited me for a drink. Took me down to the river for a pint of cockles and a glass of stout. The Old Red Lion, where your Starry Plough boys always used to drink. I thought it odd, but I didn't want trouble.'

They stood a while, her head on his shoulder. After a moment, he smiled at her. 'So, is this your life, then? Sitting up there doing your sums?'

'It's what I've always wanted,' she said.

'You were always one to get what you wanted,' he said. 'Tougher in battle than any man.'

'Don't be hard on me, Edmund,' she said. 'We've all suffered.

We've all seen comrades shot dead before our eyes. You can't blame me for wanting peace.'

'Then come with me, Bren,' he said. 'Come back to the farm. I've been running too long.'

She shook her head, staring at the ground.

'You should have been a wife, a mother—'

'Not now.' She faced him, her fingers soft against his collar. 'If not with you, then with no one.'

He took a step back from her, stumbled a little. His hand went to his eyes.

'Edmund? Are you all right?'

'I'll be fine.'

'You're ailing – you look dreadful.'

'I'm fine.'

Another embrace, then she said, 'I had no idea. I had no idea that our college porter was the self-same O'Connor who swore vengeance on you.'

A brief laugh. 'We Irish. We get everywhere.'

'Edmund – you must go. They'll arrest you.'

He shook his head. 'Whoever killed Seamus O'Connor, it was sure enough not me. Even though the world is a safer place without him.'

'No one will believe you, Edmund.'

'People saw us drinking together—'

'From what I've heard of that man, he'd pour you a drink with one hand and poison it with the other.'

He gave a weary smile, took her in his arms.

'It can't be, Edmund.' She broke away from him. 'We both know that.'

He took her hand. 'One more day. One more day together. And then I'll leave you to your numbers.'

He put his arm around her, and they walked away, out of the college towards the square, where the white blossom of the trees dazzled in the sunlight.

I stood, wondering about what I'd seen, what I'd heard. I walked back slowly, into the college, hearing the bell strike the hour, aware that I was due at Moriarty's rooms.

I found him standing, gazing at the wall, at his own portrait. He turned to me as I came into the room.

'Mr Gifford – what is the matter?'

I explained that I'd just seen our main suspect in conversation with Dr Brennan, and that they'd left together. 'Should we tell the police, Professor?' I asked him.

He smiled. 'I think we should get on with our work, Mr Gifford. The police have their methods, after all.'

That afternoon Angela finished her work early, so she came to find me at Moriarty's rooms. I introduced them, and she greeted him with her shy charm. He shook her hand with formal politeness.

'My friend here knows someone you know,' I said.

'Oh, hardly,' she said. 'My father knows him. We went to Baker Street, called at his rooms.'

The words had a peculiar effect. 'Baker Street?' Moriarty was staring at her intently. 'Who? Who was it?'

'My father's friend was a doctor—'

'But Holmes? Did you see Holmes?'

'I think that was the man, yes.'

'You met him? You met Sherlock Holmes? And what did he say?'

'We hardly spoke, sir. It was only because my father was talking to Dr Watson, at the doorway there—'

'But Holmes? Did he mention me? Moriarty?' He waited breathlessly for her reply.

Angela answered timidly. 'I had in passing told my father that Mr Gifford here was a member of this college. Dr Watson turned to his friend, and said, "Did you hear that, Holmes?" I think that's what he said. Really, I wasn't paying much attention, my father and Dr Watson were comparing notes on the Maida Vale Tennis club . . .'

'Still there.' Moriarty shook his head. 'Still there. After all these years.' He looked up again. 'Reptilian, that's how he describes me.' His voice was harsh. 'Did he say that? Mr Holmes?'

Angela appeared flustered. 'Really, Professor, I had no reason to—'

'Peering and blinking . . . Weaving my head from side to side, did he say that? Oh, and the rounded shoulders.' He straightened himself. 'What do you think?'

He was addressing me directly, standing stiff-necked and upright.

I didn't know what to say. 'Really, Professor, Miss Blunt hardly saw this man—'

'I hold Dr Watson partly responsible. His account of things, he over-eggs it all in my view. A drama of equals, both of us brilliant, one good, one evil. Of course, real life is never like that. And, as for this tussle on the edge of the cliff that was supposed to carry me off . . . Watson should have known that I would never have engaged in hand-to-hand combat in that way. The truth is, we were just men. Flawed, as men are.' The rage seemed to have left him, and he sank wearily into his chair. 'Mr Holmes was very clever, of course, and captured something of the imagination of his time. But we've had a war since then. We're tired. The jubilant escapades of Empire, it all seemed a game. But not now. We've seen a generation lost in pointless battle, the boundaries of Europe redrawn.' He looked grey, and somehow flattened. His gaze went to Angela. 'How is he, Mr Holmes? Does he seem tired too?'

'I don't really know.' Angela glanced at me. 'I hardly saw him. He was standing in the shadows, trying to light a pipe.' She tugged at my sleeve.

'We really must be going,' I interjected. 'Thank you for your help today. I'm returning you those Göttingen papers on the Kepler equation.'

'Ah. Yes. Thank you.' He didn't look up, but gazed towards the window, a faraway look in his eyes.

'Baker Street,' he murmured to himself, as we left the room. 'Baker Street,' we heard him say.

The next morning was a Thursday, and I had hurried into the college in the hope of catching a few words with Professor Moriarty before I embarked on my teaching for the day. But there was no sign of him. I was standing outside his locked door, when a man approached along the corridor. 'Ah,' he said. 'Not in yet?'

He was short and stocky, with a lined face, blue eyes and still-dark hair. 'Come all this way to see him and he's not even there.' He flashed me a warm smile. 'I'm Jack. I'm his brother.'

I took the proffered hand. 'Pleased to meet you, sir,' I said.

'Well, when I say Jack – we have a joke we're all called James. All three of us. So I had to choose another name.'

We stood in comfortable silence. The sunlight flickered along the wood panels of the corridor.

'Not the sort to be late,' Jack Moriarty said.

'No,' I agreed.

'Can't be late in my job.' He smiled. 'Them trains don't wait for no one.' He tapped his foot against the floor. 'I'll be back home tomorrow. Thank goodness.'

There was another silence.

'I think these events have disturbed him rather,' I said.

'Oh, ah.' He nodded. 'I'd heard. He always spoke well of that porter. I think he got him that job in the first place. He has his networks. Anything you need, he'll find it for you. A hunting rifle. A particularly fine tea. A rare medicinal remedy . . .'

Again, he retreated into silence. Around us, the sounds of the college – footsteps along corridors, a snatch of conversation, the wheeling of the kitchen trolleys from the refectory below.

Jack Moriarty spoke again. 'Takes a lot to disturb my brother, mind you. The things that man has seen, and all you get is that blank smile.' He was still tapping his foot, gazing down at the polished parquet. 'I suppose I was the lucky one,' he went on. 'Being the youngest. After our mother died . . .'

This time the silence was awkward. 'I'm sorry to hear that,' I said.

He spoke slowly. 'Jim joined the Army as soon as he could. Oldest brother, see, I always thought it was like family for a boy who'd never had a family. But James here . . .' He looked up at me, his blue eyes clouded. 'How can a man love, who's never known love? That's what I wonder.'

He said nothing more. After a moment I spoke again. 'You had no parents?'

He sighed. 'I was only a baby when she died. I was given away. Kindly couple, childless, showered me with affection. But James here was left with our father. And, let's just say, he didn't manage things very well. One day, he upped and left. Never saw him again. James came home from school as usual, he must have been about six or seven, a shy, quiet boy . . . and the house was locked up. Empty. His home, taken from under him. I heard later he was found, hours later, just standing there in the street, freezing cold, staring at the darkened windows.'

We were silent, thinking our own thoughts. Then, the sound of steps striding along the corridor.

'Heavens, is that the time?' Moriarty's voice rang out. 'I became entangled in a Manichean puzzle,' he said. 'I had no idea how late it had got.' He greeted us with his characteristic smile. 'You heard about our troubles here?' he asked his brother, as we followed him into his rooms.

'I had heard, yes. That poor porter of yours . . .'

Moriarty gestured for us both to sit down. 'They're hunting for his killer, I gather. An Irishman. Always the Irish, eh, Jack?' He threw his brother a cheery smile.

'Don't we count as Irish, then?' Jack sat down stiffly next to Moriarty's desk.

'A long time ago, perhaps. A long time ago. Now, where do you need me to sign?'

Jack opened one of the files and pulled out a document, cream foolscap tied with tape. 'I hope this settles it once and for all,' he said to his brother.

'Oh, I'm sure it will,' Moriarty said. 'I know you have our best interests at heart.'

'Jim has written to me. He's in Afghanistan, apparently.'

'Good luck to him. Those Pathans are nearly as bad as the Fenians.' Moriarty laughed, and I wondered at his restored good humour.

'Jim has affirmed that he supports our claim to the legacy.'

'Good. Good.' Moriarty nodded. He had taken a pen and now signed his name with a flourish. 'And now, if you don't mind, I must get on.'

Jack and I found ourselves outside his rooms once more, the door firmly shut.

'A man of few words,' Jack said. 'He's always preferred numbers.'

'He seemed grateful to you. In his way.' We began to walk together along the corridor.

Jack gave a nod. 'What it is, see, is that our mother's family owned some land, in Galway. Her brother allowed it to slip from his grasp, and now we've got the chance to get it back. It's not for me, but I have a daughter, a sweet girl, newly married. I'd like her to have the proceeds. And James there, he's always been keen to see justice done. In his own way. Mind you,' he added, as we reached the main entrance, 'it's not solved yet. We're in dispute with the son of the former owners, who's determined to keep it at all costs. And now he's disappeared. Only the odd threatening letter to show us he's still in the fight. Well . . .' He turned to me. 'It was nice to meet you. I'm glad there's someone in James's life who can make him feel . . .' Again, his gaze went to his feet, to the golden stone of the old steps. 'He's not an easy man, as I'm sure you know. He don't need the money neither. No . . .' He offered me his hand. 'It's about righting a wrong, all this. That's the only thing that matters to him.' We shook hands, and then he turned and walked out into the quad towards the porter's lodge. I watched him go, thinking that whether he knew it or not, my professor was lucky to have such a brother.

That afternoon I went to find Roland in the common room for our customary cup of tea. The quad was peaceful, and I wondered about this trio that had somehow come to be here, this angry murderous man who had come here to find Eveline, only to risk his life with our quiet porter who seemed to want revenge. We were just pouring our tea when—

'What the hell's that?' Dr McCrae ran to the window, as a terrible wail came from below.

In the middle of the quad stood the figure of Dr Brennan, motionless in her long skirt, her blouse pure white against the clipped green grass, her brown hair pinned up on top of her head.

Her hand was across her mouth, and she was making an extraordinary noise of pure distress.

'He's dead,' she began to wail. 'Poisoned.'

Again we raced downstairs. She was standing, stock still, repeating the cry, the word, 'Poisoned.'

It was then that we saw him, Edmund Sweeney, lying on the steps by the porter's lodge. He lay in an unnatural pose, his body twisted, his eyes wide open, his mouth a grimace of horror.

'So trusting,' she was saying. 'A pint of stout down by the river. That's all it took.' She was shaking, crying, and Roland went to her and led her to a seat next to the lodge.

'I was too late,' she was murmuring. 'I was too late.'

Someone had called the police, and now they arrived too, and a doctor, all of them examining the body of Edmund Sweeney.

'I was too late,' Eveline said again, louder now. 'The betrayal of Seamus O'Connor,' she went on, 'to pretend to make up with him, while slipping something into his drink . . . And after all I'd done to make sure that the man I loved was safe. I caught Seamus alone, off his guard, just behind the lodge here. One move, and he was down. And I thought, the man I love will live.'

Her words hung in the air. The gathered crowd quietened, all eyes upon her.

She was calm now, and looked up at us all with a strange, empty smile. 'Oh, I have nothing to lose. A punch to the throat,' she said. 'A ju-jitsu move, it's lethal if done well.'

The crowd appeared to slow, to freeze. We stared at Dr Brennan, and she gazed back. 'I killed Seamus to protect Edmund. But I was too late.' Her words rang out in the silence.

The police officer took a step towards her. 'Madam . . . am I right in understanding what you say? That . . . you . . . that the porter here . . . ?'

Again, the thin smile. 'I had it all worked out. His enemy would be dead, he would be safe in Ireland, and I would take refuge in my calculations.'

She raised her hands to the policeman, who, red-faced and clumsy, locked his handcuffs around her wrists and led her awkwardly away.

We drifted back to the department in ones and twos,

fragments of conversation along the corridor. 'Always the worry with these Irish . . .' 'Never should have hired a woman . . .'

That night I slept fitfully. I arrived in college next morning hoping to find some solace in parabolic differentials. Moriarty's door was locked. As the morning went on, there was still no sign of him. The department was abuzz with gossip and police. The body had shown signs of arsenic poisoning, someone said. 'A slow death,' someone else replied. 'Two days. Most unpleasant.'

Later that day, Roland and I were together in my room when Jack Moriarty appeared at the door. He was out of breath and seemed upset. 'No sign of him,' he was saying. 'I've got a spare key from the lodge.'

Roland and I hurried with him to Professor Moriarty's room.

The room was bare. All books gone. Just the desk, two chairs, the empty shelves.

On the desk lay the Greuze painting, and next to it the Göttingen papers. They were labelled: 'For Mr Gifford'.

We gazed around the empty space.

'Gone,' Jack said, at last.

'How strange.' It was Roland who spoke. 'How odd to bail out like that. I know some of the chaps were a bit harsh on him. But I always liked him. You know, the other day, the day after poor Seamus was killed by our unreliable Dr Brennan, that other man was looking for her, skulking about downstairs, the police after him. And Professor Moriarty brought him in here, calmed him down, gave him a drink, sent him on his way. Didn't give him away to the police at all.' He pulled out his watch. 'Well, students await. Toodle-pip.' The door closed behind him.

Jack was staring at the painting. 'You know,' he said, his eyes fixed on the image of the boy, 'I heard this morning, our claim to the farm has been settled. The one descendant left who was opposing our claim was found dead, yesterday. In this college.'

I touched the Göttingen papers, tracing my finger along the pages. 'Kepler's equation,' I said. 'Relating to the Two-Body problem.'

Our thoughts seemed to whisper in the silence. 'Mathematics,'

Jack said, after a moment. 'It asks for nothing back.' He surveyed the empty room. 'It's always like this. He comes, he goes. Sometimes here, sometimes there. I'll tie up this Galway land now that poor Mr Sweeney is out of the way. My brother's share will be paid into his bank account.' He turned towards the door. 'I'm sure I'll see him again when he deems it necessary.'

I picked up the painting under one arm, the papers under the other.

In the corridor, we shook hands. 'Well,' Jack said, 'I don't suppose I'll see you again.' He sighed. 'Back home, see. A place of safety. A warm fire. My wife at my side.' He shook my hand again, and we parted.

I walked out into the London afternoon. I thought about the two killings. Edmund Sweeney was the one man standing in the way of Moriarty's inheritance. Seamus the porter had sworn to kill Edmund. And Moriarty, having made sure Seamus was installed in his porter's lodge, then championed Eveline's appointment. Knowing, all the while, that Edmund would find her, would follow her to the ends of the earth, thereby placing himself in the vicinity of Seamus – who wanted him dead.

A simple calculation.

But he hadn't factored in one important thing: that Eveline loved Edmund so much that she would kill Seamus before Seamus could kill Edmund.

He hadn't prepared for the workings of the human heart.

One thing I knew, from my father's work: that arsenic would kill someone in half a day, not three. Whatever was making Edmund look so green on Wednesday, was probably nothing more than the cockles in the Old Red Lion.

And now, a year later, I am sitting in our little house in Greenwich. That autumn, Angela did me the honour of becoming my wife. We're expecting our first child at the end of this year. Her father found me a rather good position as a clerk in a law firm, and it seemed only right that I should provide for my family. I catch myself thinking about Moriarty from time to time. The Greuze boy is on the wall of my study here. I look at his angelic blond curls and wonder if he, too, finds the glory of the heavens in the pure abstract truths of mathematics.

As for my work on the orbits of celestial bodies – one of these days I shall write it up. I shall give Professor Moriarty an acknowledgement. And, who knows, perhaps one day he'll read it. Wherever he is.

Author's note:

The author would like to acknowledge Carl Murray, Professor of Mathematics and Astronomy at Queen Mary, for his scientific advice.

A Good Mind's Fate

Alexandra Townsend

It was a rare man who had the courage to ask Moriarty about his past. It was an even rarer man whom Moriarty would bother to answer. In his opinion, courageous men were most often fools. Not that it made them special. Almost everyone was a fool.

But then there was the occasional moment when the wind blew southerly and the moon was exactly half full, in short when it struck his fancy, that the great Professor could be bothered to answer some questions.

Molly was a charming girl. She was a child on the cusp of becoming a lady. She delivered occasional messages within his criminal network. She was good for work that required a face that would be underestimated. Moriarty liked to tutor her in advanced mathematics sometimes.

"Professor," she asked one day, as they haggled their way through cosigns and imaginary numbers, "why did you decide to become a criminal?"

It was a bold question, but she asked it without accusation. It was a simple quest for information. Molly didn't judge morals. She judged facts. Moriarty had hopes that he wouldn't have to kill her one day. It might actually be a waste.

That night the wind and moon and so forth must have been right. For once, Moriarty was pleased to tell the story. "Molly, have you ever read *Crime and Punishment*?" She shook her head. "Well, you should. Add it to your reading list. I expect you to finish it by next week."

"Yes, *Professor*," she said with a hint of humor. He glared and she balked. "I mean, yes, sir. By next week."

"Good." He watched to make certain she showed no further signs of insubordination, then continued. "It's an involved story that goes on longer than it should and ends with a compulsory preachy moral. All the same, it quite captivated me as a lad. It's about a man who commits murder simply to prove that he can, to prove that he is more important than all the morals in the world."

In his mind, that sentence was filled with qualifiers and footnotes, but he'd said what was necessary to get Molly's attention. She waited, now seated notably closer to the edge of her chair. Good.

"I believe I was about your age at the time. I was young. I hadn't given much thought to the future, my career, or the nature of crime. That book opened my mind to many things.

"It taught me that there are ranks of men in this world. And I don't mean the ones you're taught about: the rich and the poor, the brave and the cowardly, the saintly and the wicked. No. Those are the simple categories a world of children plays with. The only real distinctions worth noting are those very few who can master the rules of the invisible games of the world, and then rise above those rules themselves. Those, dear Molly, are the only men worthy of respect."

"And what about women, Professor?" Molly asked, with something dreadfully akin to hope in her eyes.

"Women," Moriarty said with a severe look, "are governed by the most insipid fluff of all, the scraps that the idiot men of the world leave them. Keep up with your maths, Molly, and perhaps you'll be able to keep a brain under all that cotton the world will stuff in your skull. Now, no more interruptions."

Molly looked confused, but nodded solemnly.

"It gave me such ideas, *Crime and Punishment*. It made me question every rule I'd ever heard. I already knew I was a genius, of course. It's impossible to have an intellect like mine and not know it. And yet there I was, letting my magnificent brain be constrained by the laws and policies written to herd the masses into line. It was absurd! It was . . ."

He shook his head. "My work truly began when I was fifteen. There was a book I wanted. An excellent edition of Euler's *De fractionibus continuis dissertatio*. I wanted it, but didn't have enough money for it on hand. All I had was my schoolmate Timothy and the knowledge that he liked to play games of poker with the other boys. Gambling was forbidden at our school. He might have been expelled. It didn't take much to convince him to steal the book for me."

Moriarty grinned in that very way that chilled brave men to their bones. Memories could be so sweet. "But I think that is enough for tonight, dear Molly. Now, show me what you've learned."

A week later, they met again, a surprise but not an unpleasant one. The Professor had expected to be in Rome. Pressing matters in Dublin had come up instead. There was an art-smuggling operation that had suddenly spiraled out of control. Moriarty sorted it out within hours, but he was still irked it required his presence at all. Another maths lesson was a good way to soothe his ruffled mind.

Molly's progress was good. He could see she had a grasp of mathematics in a broader scope than most did. She understood the formulas and theories as more than arbitrary rules to be followed. Anything less would have been a waste of his time.

"Do you speak Russian, sir?"

He paused over a note he was about to make. "I speak twenty-three different languages, child. But yes, Russian is among them. Why?"

"How *long* have you spoken it?" she asked with an odd insistence. "When did you learn it?"

Moriarty frowned with impatience. "Nearly fifteen years ago. Now stop trying to be mysterious. You aren't clever enough for that."

For once Molly didn't seem stung by the strike against her intelligence. "I read *Crime and Punishment* like you asked me to, sir. As far as I can calculate, it wasn't published when you were a boy. Unless you're much younger than you look." She glanced at him nervously, but he allowed her to continue. "And it was only translated into English a few years ago." A pause. "Why did you lie to me?"

Again, he appreciated the lack of hurt in her voice. It acknowledged where they both were in the pecking order. He had the right to lie to her at any time about anything and they both knew it. Whether he answered her now was merely a matter of courtesy.

"There was a time when I saw crime as a sort of charity, you know," he said. He leaned back in his chair with a small smile on his lips. "I was more religious then. I had a sense of my actions bearing importance in a larger cosmic game. To my mind, both nobles and stable boys deserved the chance to climb up in the world. But the laws of men are imperfect and so often hold that poor stable boy back. The only option was to break those laws."

Molly watched him steadily. "You became a criminal to fight against class discrimination?"

"Of course. I had to do what was right." He looked away. "I was so naïve in those days. Sometimes I wish I could be that hopeful about the world again." He sighed painfully and went back to correcting her worksheet. It seemed logarithms were still giving her trouble. He got three problems in before she spoke.

"I think you're lying to me again, Professor."

"Good. Then you have an eye for details and you can recognize a pattern. Keep it up and I'll train you to spot forged artwork."

She nodded. It seemed like a fair trade. She also thought she sensed another challenge in his words. "Were you ever really a professor, sir?"

Moriarty snorted. "I taught for several years at Durham. That much is public knowledge. Learn to do a little research."

"But that assumes that Moriarty is your real name." She spoke reasonably, with only the slightest shiver. No one said the Professor's name lightly. "If it were me, I wouldn't go by my real name."

"Not all of us get the choice, poppet." He tweaked her nose. A little harder than necessary. He was losing patience. "Now get back to work. I refuse to discuss any more with an idiot whose proofs are this sloppy."

They worked strictly on her maths for the next three hours. Moriarty's drive was so fierce, he may as well have had a whip in his hand. It was hardly the best learning environment, but it relaxed his enormous mind just a bit. There was always a comfort that came with the simple logic of numbers and the satisfaction of frightening those around you.

Molly didn't see Professor Moriarty again for months afterwards. She ran the occasional message for members of the gang. From the snatches she overheard, she knew the Professor was busy. Very busy. With every message, the men who gave and received them looked more and more worried. Business was becoming difficult. The Professor was not pleased.

There wasn't much more to gather from the gang members. They knew the penalty for not guarding secrets. Still, the air grew quiet and tense around them. Slowly, Molly's work dwindled until there were no messages to run at all, at least none that she was trusted with.

In the meantime, Molly focused on her reading and did a lot of thinking. Was the Professor really who he claimed to be? True, there *was* a record of a Professor James Moriarty at Durham University. The dates even lined up with the Professor's apparent age. But that could be a ruse. There was nothing the Professor wasn't capable of.

In the end, she decided to dismiss any conspiracy theories. The man obviously enjoyed teaching. The background of the publicly known James Moriarty was probably close enough, if not the Professor's exact identity. Besides, the question was obviously a distraction from her real enquiry, the one the Professor had challenged her to answer for herself. Why was he a criminal?

Molly pushed herself to understand books on criminal theory and dismissed every obvious answer that came her way. Crimes were committed for money and power or out of passion? They echoed an inherently sinister aspect of the criminal's bloodline or mind? It was all nonsense. Maybe a common criminal was simply evil by nature, but the Professor was not common in any respect.

Though he wasn't there to speak to her, Molly could hear the tales he'd weave in her mind all the same.

"I was a poor boy from a poor family. I grew up seeing my own mother starve before my eyes. I began to steal to help us survive."

"I was an honorable professor, devoting my life to shaping the minds of our nation's youth. One day, I was framed for an unspeakable crime and I realized my honor meant nothing."

"You stupid girl! I'm a smart man and crime made me rich and powerful! Why else would I do it?"

Each fantasy was like a fresh phantom that would haunt her for a day or more. One by one she banished them. They didn't fit the facts. Moriarty was brilliant. Smart enough to overcome any poverty or tarnished reputation. Smart enough to gain riches and power without needing to be troubled by the law. There had to be something more.

She got her first hint of what was causing all the gang's problems when she snuck into the back room of one of their favorite taverns to get everyone's lunch orders. She interrupted a game of darts. The gentlemen involved only had a second to glance at her before the game was interrupted far more dramatically. A crashing sound came from the back of the room and suddenly a flood of police officers came swarming in. Within the gang there were many things Molly wasn't allowed to know. However, one lesson had always been thoroughly impressed on her: when the police arrive, it is time to be somewhere else. She took a quiet step back into the tavern, sat down, and played with a length of string until the fuss died down.

Police filed out. Men she'd worked with for years walked past her in handcuffs. No one looked at her once. She stared, but only because that's what a spectator would do. A dozen entwined strings of fate were snipped in an instant and no one said a thing. It could be worse, she mused. They might have died. And, although it was dangerous, she allowed herself to be grateful for that much at least.

She heard a chuckle as the last officers left. "It looks like they knew who to be bitter about. Not that it did them any good!"

When they were all gone, life at the tavern continued. The

owner had been arrested for harboring criminals, but the barmaid, Antonia, was still taking orders. She came over to Molly. "Anything for you, love? I'd give you tea for your nerves, only you don't look like you have any."

"Thank you." Molly smiled. "Can I have it in back? I think that will be my last chance to see the place."

Antonia nodded, not so much because she understood as because she'd long since learned not to ask questions about these things. Molly got her tea and walked back into the ransacked room she'd only ever seen for minutes at a time before.

She righted a chair and table and wondered what sort of plans had been made there. Would this room ever host crooked games of cards again? Ever hear the elaborate details of the most nefarious plots in England? Maybe the tavern wouldn't even be in business by the end of the week.

This was a place he built, she realized. Professor Moriarty had hundreds of secret dens throughout London. As far as Molly knew, this one wasn't particularly special. But the police *had* gotten some significant members today: Giles, Crane, Moffey. Men who did good work for the Professor. And now they were gone. Arrests happened sometimes, but the police weren't normally this lucky.

Or was it luck?

There was an article, almost waiting for her, on the dartboard. The headline read "Consulting Detective Helps Unravel String of Robberies". The paper was full of holes from the darts. It took a bit of time to piece the story together.

There was a man who helped the police solve crimes. It sounded like he was good at it too. The robberies mentioned in the article weren't Moriarty's so far as she knew. They weren't amateur work either. The detective had put together some very subtle clues to solve the case. He sounded smart. He sounded brilliant. So why was he *fighting* crime where Moriarty *caused* it?

Molly's tea grew cold as she sipped it and pondered.

The detective was more famous than she'd realized. Soon, she seemed to hear his name everywhere. She read his stories. The writing was overly sensational, but it was easy to see why he captivated people. He was like a magician, one who could explain his tricks and still keep the audience mystified. He was a genius and yet he was also loved. Perhaps he wasn't rich or exceptionally powerful but Molly suspected he could have those things if he wanted to. (Particularly if the rumors about his brother were true.)

Why one thing and not another? Why become any one thing with a mind that could choose and pursue any fate in the world? What would she choose if she could have and be anything?

She pictured kingdoms kneeling at her feet. She saw visions of herself revolutionizing any field, no, *every* field of science. She imagined having the chance to vote, to go to university.

But the Professor didn't worry about such common things. He would always want what was bigger, what was impossible. So, for his sake, no matter what fantasy she brought before herself, Molly pushed past it to ask, *But what next?*

And eventually there was no next. Molly's mind was too small to realize the grandest possibilities.

She wandered home in defeat, barely noticing how barren her flat was. She usually lived with two women. They were card sharps at a local gambling den, known for their high-pitched laughter and their low-cut dresses. Both things were distractions. It made them good at cheating drunkards out of their money. They too were part of Moriarty's wide-spread network. And now they were gone. The flat was empty of all their possessions. Molly had a fleeting thought of hope that they were alive and not arrested, then used the opportunity to sleep in the largest bed for once.

What comes after having everything? Molly thought in a dream-like state. In her mind, she saw the Professor. She saw him reading *Crime and Punishment* as a boy, saw him convince a classmate to steal, saw him weep at the evils of the world then laugh just as hard. He was a professor and a gentleman. He was a criminal and a monster. Her final vision was of the sneer he always gave her when she became tedious. Then she awoke and he was gone altogether.

Police were questioning other tenants of the building when Molly left the next morning. They saw her, but didn't say anything. Why would they? She was just a young girl. She didn't mean anything. Coming from a neighborhood like this, she probably never would.

She wove through the streets of London, dodging traffic as adeptly as she had her whole life. She knew where she was going, though she had only ever been there once. That had been an important day, when she had delivered a very important message. Molly still didn't know what the message had been. She only remembered handing it over as she had taken a look at the great Professor Moriarty for the first time.

It was a public office. It had his name on the door and everything. That was why few members of the gang were ever allowed here. Molly didn't expect him to be there. The Professor could be anywhere in the world right now. Still, she knocked and was somehow not surprised at all when he answered the door.

His face was red. His clothes were dirty. He looked like he wasn't sleeping properly. Molly had never seen him look so uncomposed. He stared at her blankly for a moment like he didn't recognize her. Then her face snapped into place and he scowled. "Molly. What the devil are you doing here?"

"I . . . I figured it out," she stammered. He was more frightening than usual, like an animal in a cage. She cleared her throat and made her voice steady. "I think I know why you're a criminal."

He stared at her even longer, clearly having no idea what she was talking about. The weeks must have been long for him indeed. The Professor never forgot anything. "I don't have time for this!" he snapped. He turned away and went back to throwing things into a large suitcase.

But he didn't tell her to leave and that was as good as an invitation to come in where the Professor was concerned. Molly stepped inside and kept speaking. "I kept thinking about what I know about you. You're incredible, a genius. I think . . . I think you can do anything. And then I realized how awful that must be."

He kept moving. It was impossible to tell if he was even listening. Molly took the chance that he was. "I think you *had* to become a criminal. Because if you can have everything, what's the point of anything? You had to become the best villain so that the best hero would come out to find you. It was the only way you could ever find your equal. The only way you could ever be challenged. Maybe—" she said the last part quietly "—maybe if another villain had come first *you* would be the hero."

James Moriarty was quiet. He filled his suitcase and shut it with an audible click. "Is that it then? Thank you, Molly. I'd been wondering why I did it." He looked at her and his face made a twitch. She decided it was a smile. "Goodbye, dear Molly. Keep up with your studies. Don't become a waste of my time."

And he left. Somehow Molly knew she would never see him again. She turned to the bookcases of the office. They were filled to bursting. In a few minutes, she found what she had come for in the first place: an excellent edition of Euler's *De fractionibus continuis dissertatio.* It was still in pristine condition. Molly took it under her arm and left the office, ready to see just what her meager mind could accomplish.

Everything Flows and Nothing Stays

John Soanes

The others filed out of the room, glancing back with barely concealed smiles; they knew what was coming, and were relieved they weren't going to be on the receiving end.

"You know why I've asked you to stay behind, don't you? You had very specific instructions, and you failed to follow them. Instead, you decided to—"

"I thought that—"

"You 'thought'? You *thought*? Oh, dear me, that won't do at all. You're not expected to *think*, as well you know, and you will be punished. What do you *think* about that, young Master Moriarty?"

Moriarty met the tutor's gaze, and took a deep breath. "I know I was supposed to complete the exercise from the textbook, but I thought you'd be more interested in the work I handed in. You did understand what it was, I presume?"

"Understand?" the tutor's face reddened. "Did I 'understand' the nonsense you handed in? What precisely was there to understand, boy?"

Moriarty shook his head slightly. "Sir, please, hear me out. You asked me to do some basic Pythagorean calculations, but I gave you much more than that, don't you see? I gave you the solution to Fermat's Last Theorem."

Moriarty folded his arms and smiled, but his mathematics tutor did not smile. Instead, he looked increasingly angry.

"Fermat?" the older man said. "Are you insane, boy? Are you seriously telling me that in half a page of foolscap, you solved—"

"I solved it, yes. I solved the final problem."

The tutor's face flushed a full shade of red, and he stared at this boy who stood in front of him so casually and made such unlikely claims.

"I should say," Moriarty went on with a shrug, "that the explanation I gave was only a summation, because I had only a limited amount of space on the page, but I—"

"Silence," the tutor growled. "You will be quiet, boy. Your insolence is . . . is staggering. I have heard many excuses from many boys over the years, but yours is surely the most brazen. Such misbehaviour cannot go unchecked. You *will* be punished."

"But—"

"You have gone too far already, Moriarty," the tutor warned. "Do not try my patience beyond its limits."

Moriarty said nothing more.

The punishment was quite specific; of all the boys in the school, Moriarty would be the only one forbidden to take part in the visit to London Zoo to see the hippopotamus Obaysch, recently arrived from Egypt and already attracting vast crowds. Moriarty would instead be made to stay in his dorm room and consider what he had done, and the importance of doing as he had been instructed.

His dorm room was a poor environment in which to consider these matters, or indeed to think at all. He'd made a limited effort to personalise his living environment, merely affixing two pictures to the wall near his bed (drawings given to him as a going-away present by his family: one of a soldier, the other of a steam train), and the furniture had been scratched and battered by the room's previous occupants, which in itself annoyed him; his predecessors at the school seemed to have aims that extended only as far as carving their names on the surfaces of desks, drawers and doors, whilst he was increasingly feeling that, with appropriate discipline and focus, a person could carve their name across the surface of the known world and become a byword for achievement, like Alexander or Napoleon.

Moriarty had, then, given scant consideration to the topic of obedience and its importance, and instead had thought about the cold smile on the tutor's face as he had stated the punishment; a near-sneer, as if the tutor derived some pleasure from exercising the power he had over his pupil. Moriarty could only conclude that the authority the tutors had over him and the pupils – indeed, the power all adults had over boys of his age – derived from the concept of "might makes right", a phrase he had read recently. The tutors had control over him solely because of their age and perceived seniority, he concluded; even their limited intelligence was not a hindrance, as they had the physical ability to force the pupils to obey orders, should the need arise.

Moriarty spent a full four minutes considering the imbalance of this – that lesser individuals should be able to manipulate those whose thinking was demonstrably superior – and then he had pulled on his coat and set about disobeying the terms of his punishment. Easily bypassing the groundskeeper who was supposed to be ensuring he remained within his dorm, he exited the school building.

And then he left the school grounds, and headed into London.

Whilst the others were at London Zoo in Regent's Park, Moriarty spent a little time in Hyde Park. On the south side of the park, wooden hoardings had been erected, ahead of the Great Exhibition, which was scheduled to take place the following year. Beyond the edge of the park, horse-drawn carriages passed by in a constant creak of wheels and clip-clop of hooves. Nearer to him, a stream of people passed by the work in progress, couples and nannies pushing baby carriages made of wood and wicker. He watched them pass by, and felt no connection with them at all.

Moriarty stayed in Hyde Park for a while, standing on the Serpentine Bridge and musing about the flow of the rivers through London, how vital they were for the city and yet how they were for the most part unseen, like the blood flow Descartes had written about. As he stood on the bridge and watched the wind playing over the face of the water, a butterfly landed a short distance from him, a dash of colour against the stone of the bridge.

It occurred to him that lingering in one place might prove to be a mistake; if the school party was unable to see the four-legged attraction in Regent's Park, the masters might decide to take the boys for a walk elsewhere in the capital, and he might be discovered. One single person too many in the queue ahead of the pupils might lead to undesirable consequences, and he did not intend wasting his time explaining himself to the older but lesser minds of the school simply because a conjunction of unlikely events had led to him being discovered. He decided to move on, to head towards the East End, generally following the route of the rivers of London, the city's hidden circulatory system.

He set off towards the park gates and, as he walked past the butterfly, it flew into the air, wings beating frantically.

He walked at a measured pace – he knew the length of his stride and the distance he could cover before he needed to get back to the school – and though he was still young, his height, his thin face and his high forehead made him look older. His long arms, and the subtle vertical striping of his coat, made him look even taller, and he stood out from the crowd both in appearance and bearing. His head moved from side to side as he took in all the details of his surroundings, and, as he made his way past Hyde Park Corner and on to the edge of Green Park, he realised that he was moving through the crowd unimpeded, the surrounding people leaving a space around him.

Moriarty allowed himself a flicker of amusement at this; he was happy for people to avoid him out of suspicion if not out of fear or respect, but, as he felt an east wind pick up and blow the thin strands of his hair back from his forehead, he found himself almost wishing to experience the normal Brownian motion of a body through a crowd, as others standing closer by might have afforded some protection from the wind that even now pulled at his coat.

As the carriages passed by and kicked up mud, he stood and looked across Green Park, at Constitution Hill, which was not a hill but a road; the road where Peel, the founder of the Metropolitan Police Force, had sustained a fatal wound after falling from his horse, but where all three of the attacks on Queen Victoria had failed. The moral, if one was to be sought, appeared to be that accidents were more likely to be fatal than assassination attempts, and less likely to attract further investigation.

Moving through the crowd as if in a bubble, Moriarty walked along Piccadilly, following the edge of Green Park.

Always keeping at least ten paces between them, the older boy followed, confident he had not been seen.

The crowds grew denser on Piccadilly, and Moriarty considered entering a shop to escape the throng. There was a bookshop there, and he had money enough to afford to make a purchase – having read of the recent premiere of Wagner's *Lohengrin*, he was minded to see if he could find a copy of the source material, preferably in the original German – but he also knew it would be difficult to hide a new book upon returning to the school. Any new item attracted the attention of the other boys, and would lead someone to hide the book by way of playing a prank, or, worse, news of the acquisition would reach the ears of the tutors.

So Moriarty did not enter the shop, despite the appeal of the items in the window display. Instead, he stood for a few minutes, carefully looking at the titles and authors of the books on show beyond the glass of the windows. He noted the presence of new novels by Dickens and Hawthorne, and of the older, taller boy who had been following him since Hyde Park.

And then he set off walking once again.

Moriarty varied his pace now, and stopped often, ostensibly to look in shop windows, and it was clear the boy was indeed following him. A game, perhaps, or some more sinister intent, but he did not feel he had time spare to consider the matter, as he must be back at the school before he was missed.

He had vaguely decided to make his way to the Bank of England and spend some time outside the building. There, should anyone ask, he would say he was admiring the architecture, but in fact he would be considering the Walbrook River which ran beneath the area, and how its route, if accessed, might allow one to enter the Bank from beneath. This was a thought experiment, of course. Nothing more.

But now his attention was diverted by the older boy, who walked when he walked, stopped when he stopped, and held his distance no matter the direction Moriarty turned, as if in orbit around him. Time was now becoming the crucial consideration, and Moriarty wasted a full minute standing before an art dealer's premises just off Haymarket, not even noticing that the picture he was staring at was called *Le Petit Mathématicien* because he was preoccupied using the glass of the window to observe behind him.

And the older boy was still there; he had produced a cap from a pocket somewhere about his person, and turned his collar up as if to protect him from the wind, but this was no disguise, and he was clearly following Moriarty. If this was some sort of game, the boy seemed intent on pursuing it. Moriarty had, however, played enough games to know that you stood a stronger chance of victory if you knew the rules. Or if you created them.

He nodded slightly to himself, then set off walking again, expecting the boy to follow; this expectation was met.

Moriarty walked at a casual pace until he reached a corner and knew he was out of sight, and then he broke into a half-run for a short distance, increasing the distance between them. As he passed through the crowds in Trafalgar Square, he paused near the base of Nelson's Column, apparently looking at the two bronze reliefs at its base, and, yes, the older boy was still there.

He moved on, down towards Whitehall. Once more, other people seemed instinctively to clear a path for him, which gave him an advantage over his follower, and Moriarty was soon on Whitehall, just across from the headquarters of the Metropolitan Police.

He ducked into the doorway of a nearby building, and waited.

As he'd calculated, less than thirty seconds later, the older boy came along, frowning at the apparent disappearance of his quarry. He stopped and looked across the road, but when he saw Moriarty was not there either, he took off his cap and rubbed his head, as if to summon an explanation of the situation. He was staring at the police building when the voice came from the doorway behind him.

"If you're going to keep following me," Moriarty said, "maybe I should speak to the police about it. What do you think?"

The older boy turned round, looking both surprised and annoyed. As he struggled to form his response, Moriarty realised that the boy was tall, but not as old as he first appeared; he carried himself with an adult's bearing, but his bright eyes suggested that childhood was not so far behind him.

"Don't – look, no need for that," the older boy said. "I was looking for someone to . . . someone to help me with something. There could be money in it."

"You want me to help you?" Moriarty narrowed his eyes. This sounded unlikely, but he was willing to play along, and the other boy seemed sufficiently off guard that he'd struggle to formulate a lie. "Help with what?"

The older boy glanced over his shoulder at the police building, and then looked back at Moriarty, weighing up how he should answer the question.

In that instant, Moriarty deduced that the boy was telling the truth about having an enterprise in mind, and it was clearly one that, at the very least, pressed hard against the limits of activities permitted by the law.

"There's a card game," the boy said. "I'm part of it, but I need someone else to—"

"I don't have money," Moriarty cut in, "if that's what you—"

"No, no," the boy said firmly. "I have money, but I need some-one else to be there, to help me, er . . ."

"To help you gain an advantage?"

"Something like that, yes," the boy replied, looking serious. "Well?"

"I . . ." Moriarty paused. He had his own vague plans for the day, but was intrigued to see what the boy was talking about. It would, after all, give him first-hand experience of the world of gambling; and the money was an additional inducement.

He reached his decision, his gaze flicking across the road to the police building.

"What's the game – and where is it?" All other considerations aside, Moriarty had to return to school before his absence was noticed.

"The game's called Twenty-One," the boy said, with a hint of a smile. "The Yanks are starting to call it Blackjack, I think. The aim is to—"

"To make twenty-one," Moriarty said. "Or as close as possible to it. Yes, I've heard of it." He'd read of it in Cervantes, where it was known as *ventiuna*.

"Good, good," said the boy, and he stroked his chin thoughtfully. "Well then, you'll see how a player would have an advantage if someone was giving him clues as to the cards the other players were holding."

"Yes," Moriarty said, nodding. More than an advantage; it would make victory almost certain.

"So I need someone in the room with me."

"And where is this game?" Moriarty asked again.

"Clerkenwell – do you know it?"

"Only slightly," Moriarty said. "Which part?"

"The part with the building work." The boy grinned. "Farringdon Street. You know it?"

"As I say, only slightly," Moriarty replied, nodding. Farringdon Street was being created as they constructed tunnels to cover and divert the River Fleet, one of the city's largest waterways. It seemed he might yet follow his intentions for the day, to an extent. "I've heard about it. What would I have to do?"

"Look, if you're *in*, we can talk on the way there. Come on, we need to make our way east." He put his cap back on his head, and looked at Moriarty expectantly.

"You mentioned money," Moriarty said, not moving.

"I did," the older boy said with a sigh. "I'll share my winnings with you. A quarter for you, three-quarters for me."

Moriarty hesitated for a moment and, taking this as a sign of reluctance, the boy rolled his eyes and tutted.

"Oh, very well – a third for you," he said. "Is that good enough?"

"That will do," Moriarty said, aware that his receiving anything was likely to be dependent on the success of the other boy's plan, whatever it might be.

The two of them started walking towards the Strand.

"If we're to be partners in this," Moriarty said, "will you at least tell me your name?"

"Of course," the boy said. "My name's Martin, but they call me Smiler. What's your name, then?"

"Moriarty. They call me—"

He hesitated. After his arrival at the school, the boys had taken less than a week to find a nickname for him, and it was the obvious one given his high forehead and solemn way of talking, but he had no intention of encouraging Martin to call him *Professor*.

"—they call me Moriarty," he said firmly, and Martin smiled.

"Is that a Paddy name?" Martin asked, after a moment's thought. "Did your family come over here because of the famine?"

"So, this game," Moriarty said, allowing a hint of exasperation to his tone. "If you want me to help you, we should discuss how to do it. My family is of no importance."

"Blimey, don't get all worked up," Martin said, clearly amused by this reaction. "So, about the game. I heard about it from a builder friend of mine who lives in Norwood. The men who are working on building the Farringdon Road often stop early and play Twenty-One, and they're playing today. You need a good sum to buy into the game, but that means the winner can take home a good amount, too."

"What kind of amounts do you mean?" Moriarty asked, glancing at the building they were just passing: Coutts Bank, known for the large sums it handled for its illustrious clients.

"Not those sorts of amounts," Martin said, having followed Moriarty's gaze, "but the builders are being paid well, and so the smallest wager a player can make is a florin."

"A *florin*?" Moriarty said in surprise, and Martin looked round to see if anyone had overheard him.

"Keep it quiet, will you?" Martin snapped. "Perhaps approaching you was a mistake."

"No," Moriarty said firmly. "No mistake. But that amount, it . . . do you have enough for more than one round of the game?"

Martin nodded, and Moriarty thought for a moment. A florin was not a small amount and, having only been introduced in recent times, the coin had a certain exotic novelty about it. If Martin was telling the truth, then there was much more to this enterprise – and indeed more to Martin himself – than one might initially have imagined.

"Where did you get the money?" he whispered, and Martin smiled slightly and shook his head. "Did you—"

"Don't worry about that," Martin said.

Moriarty deduced that this meant the money was not his, and Martin was the operative for some unseen person or persons, away from the scene of the crime and therefore apparently uninvolved if it failed or attracted police attention. This idea intrigued him, that a person might engineer events and yet be invisible.

They neared the end of the Strand, and passed a theatre called Punch's Playhouse and Marionette Theatre; Moriarty recalled that the unseen men who manipulated the puppets whilst remaining hidden during a Punch and Judy Show were known as "professors".

"And what do I have to do?" Moriarty asked. "I doubt I shall be playing Twenty-One with your money."

"You're right," Martin said, nodding. "No, the game is held in an empty house near the building works at Farringdon, and we need someone to keep watch for the local bobbies."

"I see," Moriarty said. He nodded, but his tone betrayed him.

"You seem disappointed," Martin said. "Or is it that you don't understand me? When I say 'bobbies', I mean police. What is it you call them in Ireland? Peelers, is it?"

"I understand you perfectly well," Moriarty said coldly, "but I expected you would need more from me – is this why you followed me halfway across London, and now would have me walk the other half? To be a watchman for a card game?"

"Let me finish," Martin said, and his smile took on a sneering look. "You're to be the watchman, yes, to make sure that no one interrupts the game, but standing at the window of the room, watching the street outside, you will also be able to see the cards of the other players, and to signal me about their hands. So, I can—"

"Will I be able to see all the other players' cards?" Moriarty asked.

Martin looked surprised. "There will be four players," Martin said slowly, "and I shall sit facing the window. From your position, you should be able to see at least two of the other hands, and you can signal to me—"

"And the other player? If he has a good hand, which I cannot see?"

Martin said nothing to this, and they walked in silence through Temple Bar, the gate-like structure at the point where the Strand joined Fleet Street. They were close to other pedestrians, but Moriarty knew this was not why Martin had suddenly grown so silent.

Beneath their feet, the River Fleet flowed, and only one person above it on the street that bore its name gave it any thought.

"You have a better suggestion then?" Martin said eventually.

"Yes," Moriarty replied, "in fact, I do. Have you heard of card counting?"

"What?" Martin said, frowning. "Are you telling me you can—"

"Yes, I can," Moriarty said. "Mathematics is my strongest subject. After a handful of rounds of Twenty-One, I will know which cards are yet to be played, and can give you an indication whether you should 'hit' for another card, or . . . is it 'stick'? Is that the word?"

"Yes," Martin said, sounding doubtful. "Are you certain you could keep count in that way?"

"I have done it before," Moriarty said, and this was true: whilst watching others playing cards, he had little difficulty in calculating what the next card dealt or revealed would prove to be. "I would merely need to cough, or make some other agreed signal, to indicate whether you should take a card. And I would have no need of seeing the other players' hands, just your cards."

"So I would sit with my back to the window, and you would look at my hand?"

"Precisely."

They walked down Fleet Street, closing in on Farringdon, and Martin was quiet, thinking about this proposal. He knew of card counting, but had never been able to do it. And the younger boy's notion did remove the element of doubt about visibility of the other hands . . .

"We could try your suggestion," Martin said, and in that moment Moriarty felt the balance between them shifting, as if a moon had suddenly become the focus for the rotation of a planet, or there had been a reversal in an asteroid's dynamics. "It *might* work."

Moriarty nodded, as if he was ambivalent to the approval of his proposal, despite the sensation he had of how easily one could go from being followed to leading, from puppet to professor; all one needed, it seemed, was knowledge of a particular sort, applied at the appropriate point.

"We're nearly there," Martin said, and they turned north off Fleet Street. Ahead of them Moriarty could see the signs of the digging and building works that were underway. "What signals should we use then?"

"A cough for hit," Moriarty said, "and a sniff for stick? How does that sound to you?"

"Cough for a card, sniff for stick," Martin said, nodding. "Yes, that sounds reasonable."

They walked on, and soon started stepping round holes in the paving and road surface. In several places, there were holes big enough for a grown man to enter, carelessly covered with pieces of wood or other items. As they walked past these larger holes, Moriarty could hear the sound of water running, the river, and this reinforced that there were forces at play beneath the everyday world.

"Before we go in," Moriarty said to Martin, "tell me, why me?"

Martin frowned at him, not understanding.

"Why did you pick me? Out of all those in Hyde Park today, why did you think I was most suitable for this – and likely to agree to it?"

Martin laughed, but it was a sound lacking in warmth or mirth.

"I saw you in Hyde Park," Martin explained, "standing there, without family or friends. And I saw the way you looked at the people passing by – you were frowning, almost sneering, as if watching them from a distance, even when they were close by. You looked at them as if they were—" Martin shrugged "—animals in a zoo. I knew then that you were more like me than the others in the park. I guessed at your age, too, and thought that the money might appeal."

Martin looked at Moriarty, and the sly smile on his face suggested he thought Moriarty might be disappointed by this explanation, that he might have preferred to have been told that he looked more intelligent, or even more devious, than the others in the park. But Moriarty merely nodded, his expression unreadable.

"This is the house," Martin said, pointing to a large and dilapidated house. In truth, it was more absence than building: the top floor was lost beneath a collapsed roof and the structure had caved in, though in the mess and disruption of the surrounding street the missing three-quarters of this house was unremarkable.

The front door, its wood burned in places and scratched in others, looked as if it would prove impossible to open, but Martin stepped to the door and pushed it inwards with ease.

Martin gestured inside, and Moriarty hesitated.

"Oh, very well," Martin said with a smile. He tugged his cap from his head and tucked it into one of the pockets of his coat – pockets that, Moriarty noted, seemed to go down a long way – and stepped over the threshold into the hallway.

Inside the house, there was a strong smell of damp plaster, and from the walls came the sound of mice, or possibly rats. Martin took a few steps down the darkened hallway, then pushed a door, and the two of them stepped into the room beyond, their footfalls noisy on the wooden floor.

The flickering of a number of candles revealed that the room had long since ceased to be a parlour, and was now devoid of furniture save for the small table and four chairs that sat at its centre. Three men stood in the room, and it seemed to Moriarty as if they represented a series of stages in an advertisement for a combined facial hair tonic and weight-loss patent medicine; the first man was clean-shaven and fat, the second man had a moustache and was stocky of build, and the third man was bearded and thin. They were all talking in low voices when Martin and Moriarty entered.

"Ah, the younger generation!" the bearded man said, and laughed. "Welcome."

"Good afternoon, gentlemen," Martin said. "Apologies if I have kept you waiting."

"No apology is needed," said the clean-shaven man, in a voice that was higher-pitched than Moriarty expected. "Who do you have with you this week?"

"This young man was recommended to me by an acquaintance," Martin lied smoothly. "I did not ask his name, nor did he offer it. I told him of our game, and of our need for a watchman, and he agreed to assist."

"He has no . . . shall we say, *qualms* about gambling?" the bearded man asked.

"None," Martin said. "I promised him a small fee for his time, and—"

"As long as I get my money," Moriarty growled, "I don't care what you do here."

"Splendid," said the man with the moustache. "Shall we play?"

The others murmured in agreement, and sat down at the table, Martin stepping quickly to the chair with its back to the window.

Moriarty went to his position by the window. It was boarded up in places and blackened with candle smoke in others, but by perching sideways on the windowsill he could see out into the street and by turning his head also see over Martin's shoulder. He sniffed as the first cards were dealt.

"You must excuse our watchman," Martin said, with a vague gesture. "He has a cough and a cold. But he assured me he will not breathe his bad air in our direction."

The three men laughed, and the game began.

Moriarty watched the first rounds without making any attempt to assist Martin, being careful to cough and sneeze only when the other men were making their plays.

After the first six rounds were complete, an impressive number of florins lay on the table in front of the men. Even without assistance, Martin was playing well, and appeared to be breaking even, though the bearded man had lost much of his money, and was attempting to distract the other players with a limerick he claimed to have heard the previous evening.

". . . told her when needs and seeds must, a man must go and sow – though his very first may be in Baker Street, and his last, Bow!"

No one thought this either clever or amusing, and the cards were dealt again.

Moriarty watched carefully, and could see over Martin's shoulder that he had a two and an eight for a total of ten. Moriarty had kept track of the number of jacks and tens in play, and assessed that there were more of these yet undealt than any other cards – as well as two aces – and so he coughed, and looked out of the window.

Martin took another card, the other players made their choices, and the round ended. Moriarty heard Martin laugh and the sound of florins being pulled across the table to be added to his pile. Only then did Moriarty look back at the game.

The bearded man looked to have been comprehensively bearded, as he had a single florin in front of him, and a scowl on his face. The clean-shaven man had what appeared to be two coins in front of him, and Martin and the man with the moustache looked to have equal piles of coins before them.

The mood in the room was tense and, not wishing to draw attention to himself and a possible connection between his presence and Martin's good fortune, Moriarty looked out of the window again, seeing no policemen.

The cards were dealt in silence. Moriarty glanced over Martin's shoulder. He had two tens, which was so close to twenty-one that taking no more cards might have seemed the wisest option, but the combination of these two cards and the tens that the other players had drawn in the previous round left, Moriarty knew, two aces yet to be dealt, and so he coughed, and then peered out of the window.

At the table, Martin hesitated, but took another card. The

others made their decisions and, as the round ended, Martin laughed triumphantly, and Moriarty heard the sound of coins being drawn across the table, accompanied by muttering from the other players. A quick glance revealed to Moriarty that both the bearded man and the clean-shaven man had no coins left, and the man with the moustache had one single florin left. Martin, for his part, had a large, uneven pile of money in front of him.

"I think I shall move these out of the way," Martin said, with undisguised amusement, and swept a heavy handful of the coins off the table into the pocket of his coat, where they clinked loudly. "Shall we play one last round?"

The moustached man paused for a moment, then Moriarty heard him grunt in unhappy agreement. Moriarty, looking out of the window, frowned at Martin's insistence on playing on. The pile of cards to be dealt was too small to make a round now, so the moustached man, dealing, shuffled the discarded cards with those yet to be dealt, effectively meaning the two players were being dealt from a fresh deck of fifty-two cards. Moriarty was now unable to derive any benefit from counting, but this fact only appeared to occur to Martin when his cards had been dealt, and Moriarty heard him shift awkwardly in his chair.

Moriarty glanced at Martin's hand: two eights for a total of sixteen, arguably the worst hand he could have in his uncertain position. Martin hesitated.

"Well?" the moustached man prompted. "Another card?"

"I . . ." Martin muttered, and then forgot himself, for one critical moment. He glanced over his shoulder at Moriarty, his eyes wide and pleading. This did not go unobserved by the other players.

"What's going on here?" demanded the bearded man.

"Nothing," Martin replied, unconvincingly.

"Why did you look to the watchman?" the clean-shaven man asked.

"I was making sure he was still keeping guard," Martin said, casually. "He had been so quiet – none of his usual sniffs or coughs – and I was afraid he had fallen asleep."

"Do you not think one of us would have noticed that, if it had happened?" the bearded man snarled. "We may be unfortunate with cards, but we are not blind."

"Of course not," Martin said, smiling warmly. "I did not mean—"

"You looked at him as if asking him a question," the moustached man said, firmly. "As if seeking some kind of information."

"Not at all," Martin replied. "As I said, I—"

"What information could the watchman have?" the bearded man asked.

"Nothing, I assure you—" Martin started to say, but he was cut off by the clean-shaven man asking a question.

"Are you two confederates? Is that what is going on here? Is the watchman monitoring the cards as well as the street outside, to ensure your victory and his fee?"

Martin said nothing.

"Well?" the moustached man said, his hand going to his last florin. "Are you two—"

Martin's nerve deserted him, and he jumped from his chair and ran towards the door. Moriarty was taken aback for a second, but then followed him, and the two of them ran out of the room and down the hallway of the house, with the three men in close pursuit, yelling threats.

Martin and Moriarty sprinted down the pockmarked Farringdon Road. The three men gave chase and, though the clean-shaven man was held back by his corpulence, the others seemed about to catch up with them, until Martin suddenly scrambled down one of the holes in the surface of the road. Without pausing to consider, Moriarty followed.

It was like being in a cave system, but it smelled like a sewer; the stench was nauseating, and Moriarty's senses revolted from it.

He took a few seconds to allow his eyes to adjust to the darkness and, when he could see properly, he realised Martin was a short distance ahead of him, the florins clinking noisily as he moved.

"Are they following?" Martin demanded, breathlessly.

His heart racing, Moriarty glanced up and back at the way

they had come, and could see no one behind them. He could hear voices, shouting, but no sounds of approach.

"No," Moriarty said.

"Good," Martin replied, and walked on.

Martin had clearly been down in the tunnels before, and Moriarty once more noted that one might move and act, unseen, beneath the surface of things. He allowed himself a smile in the semi-darkness.

"I know the way," Martin said, and then added, in a more sinister tone, "it's like the valley of the shadow of death, isn't it? Like in the psalms they taught us at school."

Moriarty thought that, in the close, dark environment, fear was more of a concern than the shadow of death.

Underfoot, the surface was treacherous and slippery, and Moriarty stepped with care. Martin seemed unconcerned how closely he was following, and it occurred to Moriarty that Martin would not care if he slipped and fell and was swept away. He had the money from the game, and that was as far as his interest went.

"When will I get my share of the winnings?" he asked.

Martin glanced back at him, and Moriarty could not see the expression on the boy's face, but his tone made it clear he was scowling.

"Later," Martin said. "When we're back above ground."

He said it without conviction. Moriarty frowned slightly, but still he followed, and they stepped around a corner, and came to a point where the tunnel system opened up and the flow of the Fleet dropped some twenty or so feet, like a miniature waterfall. The sound was very loud now, and the stench even more pungent and close. Moriarty tried to breathe through his mouth, but it made little difference.

Ahead of him, Martin had slowed down, and was peering over the edge of their narrow walkway into the maelstrom below.

"Quite a drop," Martin shouted. "This path leads to the way out."

Martin started to make his way carefully along a narrow brick ledge, and again the florins clinked in his coat.

"You could give me my share of the money," Moriarty said, giving Martin a second chance. "It would be less heavy for you."

Martin turned and looked at Moriarty then and, even in the near-dark, Moriarty could see the glint of his teeth as he smiled, though it was not in friendship, or even as between business associates. It was jarringly similar to the smile of the mathematics tutor as he stated the nature of Moriarty's punishment; the smile of someone who believes he has the upper hand, and will win the argument by virtue of age and position. My might, the smile seemed to say, will serve to make me right.

And, as he recognised this and realised what it meant for his prospects of obtaining the money he had earned, Moriarty knew what he had to do.

The smile fell from Martin's face as he saw Moriarty coming at him with his long arms outstretched. Instinctively, Martin stepped away, but this took his left foot over the brink, and his arms whirled in space for a few seconds. With the florins clinking in his pockets, he lost his balance, and over he went.

Moriarty had stopped advancing after a few steps, but was still close enough to see Martin fall back into the filthy deluge. He hit the surface with a splash, and quickly came up again, choking and spluttering, but then the current took him and bounced his head off the tunnel wall with a muted crack, and he was borne away by the tide.

Moriarty watched, seeing the unconscious boy first bobbing on the surface and then slowly sliding under, the weight of his winnings taking him down, until distance and darkness conspired to make it impossible to see any more.

After a moment of standing and looking and feeling nothing at all, Moriarty started walking once again, following the ledge in what he judged was a southerly direction. He knew he would have to surface soon, but was confident that the three men would have given up the chase by the time he did so. As he walked, he thought about what he had learned this day: that items and events which went unseen might yet have influence, that accidents could be made to happen, and that one might manipulate others through well-chosen ideas and well-timed words whilst remaining unconnected to the events that transpired.

And, he mused, fast-flowing water could swiftly remove a hindrance, leaving no trace.

Half a mile further down the road and observed by no one, Moriarty emerged from beneath the city street, and started making his way back to school. Despite going home without his share of the winnings from the card game, he knew he had gained much this day, that the lessons he had learned would prove more valuable in the years to come than anything that might be taught in a classroom.

A Scandalous Calculation

Catherine Lundoff

The old man, his back bowed and hunched, rested one trembling hand against a lamppost. From his expression, his rheumy eyes might have seen nothing at all. Or, perhaps, he merely watched the Whitechapel crowds that eddied and flowed on the dirty cobbles around him. But an astute observer, had there been such to study him, might have noticed that his venerable head tilted a bit and his gaze grew sharper when a dark-haired lad, cap pulled low over his face, approached.

The lad looked like any tradesman's apprentice, albeit cleaner than most. His pants bore only a few scuffs and patches and his hand, when he moved it from his pocket to pull his cap down lower on his forehead, was pale and nearly clean. He walked briskly past the old man and down a side street, as if bound on an errand for his master.

The man unbent slightly and walked after the lad, shedding a few years with his strides as he moved. The two might have been nothing more than two men hurrying on errands, or looking for a pint before nightfall. There was no reason for the old man not to walk down that particular street in the London dusk and settling fog. No reason for him to take a different direction from the lad's, if such was not his destination.

Ahead of him, the boy stopped to look up at a nondescript shop, a former tailor's establishment with rooms above it. His movement exposed an expanse of pink cheek, one still too young to have known a razor's edge. Then, as if he knew that he was being watched, he spun on his heel and began walking briskly away, his strides stopping just short of a run.

The man followed, his walk still slow and a little unsteady. The youth might have outpaced him easily enough, vanishing into the fog that was drifting to cover the end of the street, if another man hadn't stepped out in front of him. The boy went to dodge around him, but was stopped by heavy hands on his collar and his arm.

"I've been looking for you, Miss Adler. Or, should I say, Mrs Norton?" The old man's voice was deep and hollow, with a touch of the sibilant. That voice alone might have been enough to halt a brave man in his tracks.

The boy struggled against his captor, his expression shifting swiftly from annoyance to fear, then that abruptly smoothed over with a bland, puzzled expression. "You got the wrong lad, guv. I ain't no Miss Adler or any Mrs Norton." His voice was nasal with an accent that echoed London's backstreets and poorer quarters. "Chilton, apprentice to Master Carragher, the printer, that's who I be."

"Let us not waste time with these games, Mrs Norton. You have something that I need, and I fancy that I have something of yours." The old man gestured and they heard a distant whistle. Shortly thereafter, a black coach rolled up to the cobbles next to them. The horse snorted and tossed its head, making the harness jingle, and the boy jumped, his face at once a painting of fear and suspicion.

He, or rather, she, looked at the old man, "Who are you?" Looking at the erstwhile lad now, that same astute observer might have seen a lass in boy's clothes, as her confidence ebbed away. Or, perhaps, he would have seen just a very frightened boy, though he might not understand the reason for that fear.

"You may call me Professor. More than that you do not need to know." He glanced at the coach and the driver stepped down and opened the door. He gestured at the step and the big man hauled the woman up into the coach as if he was manhandling a puppy, for all that she kicked and struggled. The old man climbed in after them and placed his stick against her back, like a knife's edge, and she went still and limp, dropping into one of the padded benches inside. He made another gesture as he sat across from her and the big man left them to climb on behind the coach. The door closed and latched behind him.

A moment later, they were being rattled over the cobbles. "Where are you taking me?" Her voice quavered, then steadied.

"So many questions, Mrs Norton. One might think that the answers would be useful to you in some way. You will not escape me, nor will I release you until you are no longer useful to me. Do I make myself clear?" His eyes were no longer rheumy and there was little that suggested extreme age in his bearing. Now, he seemed a man of just above middle years, intelligence and a certain ruthlessness written on his lean face and sharp features.

Irene Norton's dark eyes narrowed a moment, apparently taking his measure, and she sat up straight, shedding all suggestion of an impoverished apprentice. "Why are you abducting me then, Professor? What is it that you want of me?" She studied him in a series of quick glances, taking in the coach as well as her companion, as far as he could determine.

The Professor sat back, putting his face in shadow and thus making his expression harder to read. "Mrs Norton, you have returned to London seeking someone, someone quite close to you. But you are concerned about encountering some individuals from your past, one being Sherlock Holmes and the other a member of a royal family from a foreign nation, hence your disguise. You received information, a note, I believe, informing you that news about the person you were seeking was to be obtained at the address you were looking at when I approached you."

She shifted slightly in her seat but her face portrayed no astonishment that he had known these facts about her and her purpose in London. Instead, she tilted her face and looked at him sidelong. "How long have you been following me?"

"I had little need to follow you, Mrs Norton, as I knew that you would be unable to resist responding in person." He glanced out the window before he looked back at her. "We are very nearly at our destination so I will speak plainly. You wish your husband returned unharmed, do you not, Mrs Norton?" This time, he had the satisfaction of seeing her expression shift, her lip tremble. She would do what he wanted now, without protest or argument.

He waited in silence for her to speak, to confirm what he already knew. Women broke so easily. Here was something that he shared with his erstwhile foe, Sherlock Holmes, that same casually voiced contempt for the weaker sex that broke through even Dr Watson's carefully edited accounts from time to time in *The Strand*. But then, his erstwhile rival had held so many of his fellow beings in contempt that it had led to his downfall. The Professor blinked away a memory of fast-moving water pouring over sharp rocks.

"Yes." Her voice was low and soft, yet sharp enough to cut through his memories and drag him back to the present. "Yes, I want my husband back, as unharmed as he was when you seized him. I want to leave England with him, to never return if necessary. You will have nothing to fear from giving him back to me and giving both of us our lives, Professor." Her dark eyes brimmed with tears under her cap until she rubbed them away gracefully with one bent wrist.

"That remains to be seen, Mrs Norton. I will require you to renew an old acquaintance, as well as to perform in your former profession tomorrow evening. I trust that you can still sing. You will follow my instructions exactly or there will be consequences. Do you understand?"

She flinched a little at his words, or perhaps, his tone; her mind was not as quick as his, of course, but it was fast enough to grasp the implications of his words. She might have heard the rumors about Holmes's death as they had spread like wildfire through the criminal underworld after Reichenbach. But there would be no need to abduct her husband to persuade her to confront the detective; she had crossed swords with him in the past and won. So she must realize that he was speaking of the new King of Bohemia.

But her tone sounded neither surprised nor apprehensive, despite what must be the state of her thoughts. "Yes, I can still sing. But why?"

He studied her from the shelter of the shadows and thought that he would have preferred tears, pleas, some open display of weakness that told him that she was in his power. Inwardly, he cursed Holmes for sowing the seeds of doubt, seeds that grew up despite the certainty of his own survival and the demise of the detective.

He had returned from Reichenbach to find his criminal empire in shreds and his closest henchman, Colonel Sebastian Moran, about to flee England as the false news of his own demise circulated. Now he would have to rebuild, and for that he needed tools like the woman who sat staring at him, unblinking despite the coach's jostling. Yet, he would succeed and this time there would be no detective to attempt to stop him. He reached into his jacket pocket and produced a card, which he passed across the coach to his companion.

The coach creaked to a halt as he spoke again, "You will perform at that address tomorrow night at eight. Prepare yourself. Put on the dress and jewels that you will find in your room; this coach will arrive to take you to your destination at seven. You will receive instructions then. Speak to no one and make no attempt to escape in the meantime, Mrs Norton. Your disobedience would be most damaging to your husband."

Her mouth twisted, as though she bit back a response or a refusal, but she said nothing and rose obediently when the coach door opened and she was handed out. She glanced back once, then away as she mounted the worn steps of the small hotel where the coach was stopped. As they drove away, the old man noted that she did not look back again.

Professor James Moriarty sat back on the coach cushions with a curl of his lip. It was by no means a smile, but it radiated a certain self-satisfied pleasure. At last, a plan was coming together. Once the opera singer obtained what he wanted from the King of Bohemia, he could access the funds that he needed from the King's own treasury. Those would be sufficient to finance his recovery, to restore him as the Emperor of London's underworld again.

As to what would happen after that to the opera singer and her husband or to the King of Bohemia himself, it was of little moment to him. They might continue to be of use to him, particularly Mrs Norton. He would enjoy making the woman who had outwitted Sherlock Holmes one of his tools. The coach rattled on through the fog as he lost himself in his thoughts.

It felt like only a few moments later that the coach stopped, its progress halted by some sort of traffic obstruction that he couldn't see from where he sat. A sharp rap from his cane on the coach's ceiling caused a panel to open behind the coachman's seat. "Dray overturned, sir. Should I look for a way round or wait for 'em to clear it, sir?" He flinched a little as he spoke, as if fearing a blow, but stayed where he was, uncertainty on his features.

Professor Moriarty bit back a blistering oath. This was something outside his calculations, a variable where he had not expected one so soon after his recent success, and it filled him with a brief surge of uncertainty that surprised him. He regained his composure with an effort. Very well, then he would have to adapt. "Yes, find another route." He checked his pocket watch. "I do not intend to be late for my next appointment."

The man must have caught the edge of menace in his voice because the panel closed abruptly and the Professor was gratified to hear a shout and the crack of a whip from the box. The coach lurched forward and he had reason to be grateful for the new springs he had had installed as it rattled around him. The driver made good speed, urging the horse to a teeth-rattling trot where he could and the Professor lost himself in thoughts mathematical, pondering a theorem that had recently occurred to him.

He allowed himself an instant of icy rage, one not given voice aloud, at how much the late Holmes had inconvenienced him. His theories would make him the toast of mathematics scholars the world over once they understood his brilliance, and would have done so by now if he had not been distracted by minor obstacles.

Crime was useful in its way, sparing him a life of scholarly privation as it did, but it could not replace the beauty of mathematics. Still, his lips twisted a bit at the picture of himself in a garret. Crime was also more of a challenge than the labyrinth of academic pursuits at present. He permitted himself to speculate on whether or not the singer would succeed in liberating the King's signet, before dismissing his concern. If she failed, he had other tools in place. Less amusing ones to be sure, and possibly less effective, but available if he chose to use them.

The carriage lurched to a halt, nearly throwing him across to the opposite bench. He glared up at the roof before throwing open the window. "What is it now?" His tone froze the air around the coach, but that wasn't enough to stop the fleeing boys who had halted their progress with a cart they had rolled across the narrow street. One wore a jacket and cap that looked somewhat familiar. The Professor's eyes narrowed; he had left a man to watch Mrs Norton as a matter of course, but he could not dismiss the notion that she might have given him the slip. Or the equal possibility that he might be mistaken about the running boy in the fog.

He dismissed this as a distraction. Regardless of who planned it, this delay must be deliberate. Someone had an interest in delaying his progress or perhaps ensuring that he missed his afternoon appointment. As to who that might be, he could think of a dozen enemies, the list coming to him as easily as breathing.

The realization that he had so many foes to choose from brought the understanding that he was vulnerable. His men were fewer and scattered and his present position was unshielded. Someone knew this coach, possibly had blocked his way with the overturned dray as well. He swung the door open and gestured to his man perched on the box. "Come with me. We will find another conveyance. This one has become too . . . noticeable." He gestured to the driver with his right hand, two fingers against the brim of his hat that might have been a dismissal or might have meant nothing at all.

He turned and walked away without waiting for an acknowledgement, his man at his heels. The square was not a familiar one and, for the first time in decades, he had a sense of being exposed, hunted. This was unacceptable. "I need a bolt-hole. Fetch the Colonel once you have escorted me to . . . ?" He ended with a question, his tone expectant. His companion murmured a response, too low for any passers-by to hear.

The Professor grimaced and gave a cold chuckle. "If that is the closest haven, then it must needs suffice. Lead on." He gestured and the man led him through a warren of twisting streets to a nondescript warehouse. The cobbles milled with drivers loading and unloading their wagons from each establishment on the street.

The Professor eyed the few scattered gentlemen in the crowd, attired as much as he was himself, and caught himself before he could nod approvingly. He would not stand out here, not for anyone who was not looking specifically for him. His man had chosen well.

Still, he reflected, as they entered the building, his companion in the lead, it might be as wise to take a page from the book of his foes and don a disguise before he left this place. But there would be time to consider that once he dispatched messages for his lieutenants. Such a list of petty details accompanied vulnerability! He promised himself that he would not know this feeling again, not once he had regained all that he had lost.

His mood was not improved when he found himself overseeing the kind of foolish, yet necessary tasks that he once might have delegated to his underlings. Only the lack of more competent tools to hand left some of his men alive, however temporarily.

After several incidents calculated to undermine his faith in his new organization, he determined that he must himself attend the reception for the King of Bohemia. It could not be entrusted to anyone else, not if he wanted to ensure that all would go as he planned. He scowled ferociously at one of his new lieutenants. "I will attend tomorrow's reception myself. I shall also need evening clothes; send my valet to me tomorrow."

He gestured dismissively and his men scattered to do his bidding. Professor Moriarty scowled at the barren room around him, wishing he'd returned to his comfortable apartments instead of going to the nearest safe hole. A bed had been found and assembled for him, at least, so he would not have to sleep rough in the bargain, but this was not the luxury he had grown accustomed to.

He closed his eyes and pictured the night to come, calculating the outcome of all the possible interactions between Irene Norton and the King. This was the kind of planning that had guaranteed his success in the past and, as he ran through the probable outcomes, he was certain that it would do so this time as well. That assurance was enough to ensure that he fell into an untroubled sleep before midnight.

When his men greeted him in the morning, they were in the company of his valet. The latter had brought both a portmanteau of his evening wear and breakfast, both of which contrived to make him composed and coldly confident once more. His men felt the shift in his mood, too, and responded to commands he had merely begun to formulate, almost predicting his every wish and request, until it was time to leave.

The Professor was soon dressed and as ready for the reception as if he had planned to attend it all along. He dispatched two of his men with instructions for Irene Adler, the name she would be performing under tonight. Let the King think her husband dead, the marriage dissolved, her still in love with him, whatever was necessary in order for her to get close to him again.

It would be enough. He pressed a napkin to his lips, wiping away the grease from the last of the cold meat and the pie that made up his supper. Colonel Moran was outside, dressed as a coachman and ready to drive him to the reception. His lieutenant could back up his plans in the event of a miscalculation, another piece falling into place. The signet would soon be his, and the forgeries that followed would set all his other plans in motion.

Once this step succeeded, he had only to defeat his foes, wipe them from the chessboard, and he would have his empire again. Visions of that success filled his head as he climbed into the coach, warming him against the slight chill of the night air. Yet even these jolly thoughts were not enough to completely distract a predator like him and he contemplated the details of all that he would need to do to solidify his success.

The mathematical precision of even his most shifting plans spread out before him until he felt the coach slow, then stop. A glance out the window told him that they had arrived at their destination and he straightened his cravat and adjusted his hat. Tonight, he had discarded the idea of a disguise, opting to attend as a version of himself. He was Professor James Moriarty, a mathematics professor from some local college or other, no one could ever remember which, a scholar with a passing interest in Bohemia and his fellow scholars there, not the "Napoleon of crime," as Holmes had dubbed him, not tonight. No one would suspect otherwise, with the exception of Mrs Norton and he had sealed her lips effectively.

He moved up the stairs with the quiet, fragile dignity of one whose studies have made his eyesight unreliable and any time spent away from his books a burden. The footman at the door had little difficulty believing his story about a lost invitation, particularly when a sovereign for his continued cooperation accompanied the tale. Achieving the ballroom was a matter of moments and little trouble.

He surveyed the crowd inside with a glance, nodding to several acquaintances and preparing himself to the appearance of the event's hosts at his elbow. A noble government functionary and his lady wife, vaguely familiar with some of his better connections, were as resigned to his presence at this event as he was to their polite chatter. Only their enthusiasm for the mysterious opera singer who had requested to perform for the King and the presence of the King himself were evident and certainly far more fulsome than their interest in a mere scholar of mathematics.

They amused him a little, but he was glad to see their backs once he had been safely escorted to the card room, far from the dancing and any young ladies he might opportune or any important guest he might bore; so he interpreted his host's actions. It was useful to be underestimated from time to time. He buried himself in commonplace conversations and pleasantries until an announcement from the door sent them all to the ballroom. The most important guest had arrived.

The new King of Bohemia was large, loud and florid. His attire and that of his guards sent a shock of barbaric splendor of furs and scarlet through the otherwise temperate attire of the other attendees. The Professor watched him critically as he swept down the stairs, a nod for each bow and a smile for each lady. His fingers flashed with rings, but at this distance none of them appeared to be the one that Mrs Norton was taxed with retrieving.

As if his thought had summoned her, the singer appeared on the heels of the King's entourage, the extravagance of her emerald-green gown subdued plumage in comparison to his party's brighter hues. She was pale, but her head was high, her expression resolute. The Professor gave her a thin smile that she could not see and vanished back into the throng, out of sight. He could watch her easily enough, but saw no point in providing a distraction by letting her see him.

Instead, he turned his attention to the other attendees and had a moment of what he might have recognized as shock, had he been familiar with such a sensation. A solid gentleman, tall and fat, without medals or uniform to signify his station, caught his eye. The man's nose was hawk-like, his eyes hooded but gleaming with dark intelligence. Yet it was not that which had caught the Professor's eye. There was something familiar about that countenance, but he was certain that he had not seen the other before.

It shook him, this recognition that was not one. The other man glanced at him, then elsewhere, as if indifferent to his presence, but somehow, the Professor still felt the urge to deflect his interest. He shifted away, seeking the shelter of the refreshment table in the next room. There, he found a moment's respite, an eddy in the crowds where he could overhear the gossip around him. Opinions were split on whether or not the reappearance of the opera singer or the King was the most exciting thing occurring at this particular reception.

It did not entirely please him, Irene Adler-Norton's notoriety in these circles. His plan hinged on her being able to approach the King and rekindle his affections enough to distract him. She was his best chance to steal the signet easily, as long as she was not the focus of undue attention. Moving another piece on his chessboard would take more time, delay his plans. His bankers would be expecting an influx of funds from the Continent soon, funds that would be freed by what he could do with the King's ring and his forged signature. There must be no delays; of that, he was determined.

He obtained a cup of tea and moved carefully toward the wall where he could observe the crowd. Across the room, the King started at the sight of the opera singer, while she cast her eyes down demurely. The Professor was too far away to hear what they said to each other, but then it was of little moment. What they did next would be of far greater significance.

There! The King gave her a lingering glance and reached for her hand, then pressed it to his lips. They stood in that posture for a breath too long, then parted as she moved toward the pianoforte. A few words to the accompanist and a hush settled over the assembly. Mrs Irene Norton parted her red lips and the voice of an angel poured out.

Her audience hung on each note, the King's gloved finger in mid-stroke of his substantial mustache. For a wild fanciful moment, the Professor contemplated picking his pocket or slipping the ring off his hand. But it might be simpler to remove his finger, if it came to that. He filed that idea away in the portion of his planning that involved last resorts, then dismissed it for the moment. Unable to resist obtaining a closer view, he inched nearer to the singer.

Mrs Norton sang several arias from popular operas, then a song in what appeared to be Bohemian, judging from the reaction of the King and his men. If nothing else, the Professor thought cynically, he had ensured Mrs Norton's successful return to the operatic stage. Perhaps she would be grateful, though he suspected that she would not.

Not that such concerns mattered. She commanded the King's attention with every tilt of her head and he hovered near her as if he could not pull away. If she felt uncomfortable with so much regard, it was not obvious to any who watched them. Rather, she seemed shyly to accept his adulation while responding no more than propriety might allow. This reserve unnerved the King, clearly accustomed to a more enthusiastic response and it captivated him. This much, the Professor could observe with little effort, but much impatience.

Someone jostled his elbow, causing him to spill his tea, and he whirled with a snarl, a smothered exclamation clamped behind his teeth. The young fool who had bumped into him looked simultaneously pained and annoyed, as if he had been incommoded by the Professor's presence in that part of the room. But he summoned both a servant and a passable apology then insisted on procuring another cup of tea to replace what he had spilled.

The Professor wanted nothing of the kind, but it was harder than he expected to lose the persistent young gentleman, who remained solicitously at his side. His vacuous and continuous conversation occupied several critical minutes, and it was some time before the Professor turned his attention back to the King and Mrs Norton.

They had vanished, at least from immediate view. He glanced around the ballroom, checking the visible alcoves and exits for his quarry. They were not in sight, though the King's men were still visible in the throng. He parted from his new companion with no small effort and circled the room. In truth, the singer was doing no more than he had commanded. If it were necessary for her to lure the King into a more private setting, it should matter little to him as long as she was successful. Still, he would have felt greater reassurance that his plan was intact if he had seen them leave together.

He gestured, a small, subtle movement with his left hand, and one of the waiters paused by his side with a polite bow. "Do you require refreshment, sir?"

"Information, if you please. Where is he now? Did he leave alone?"

The man fiddled with the glasses on his tray, as if trying to find the right one. He didn't ask which "he" the Professor meant, instead indicating a distant staircase with a slight tilt of his head. "We— I don't believe he was alone, sir." He handed the Professor a glass and turned away at his nod of dismissal. The Professor made note to ask Colonel Moran where he had found this paragon and how they might call for his services again. They would make good use of him in the future, of that he was sure.

He stationed himself near the foot of the staircase that the waiter had indicated and waited. His instructions to Mrs Norton had been quite clear; once she secured the signet, she was to make a wax impression of it, then slip it back into the King's possession. Failing that, she must steal it. How she was to do either was not his concern. He cared only that she reappeared with it soon and gave it to the man who signaled her. After that, she could wait upon his pleasure for news of her husband.

A brief stir at the top of the stairs caught his attention and he looked up in time to see Mrs Norton and the King on the landing. He looked angry, while she appeared to be most distraught. He saw her wrench her hand from the King's grasp and propel herself down the steps as rapidly as was feasible in her emerald gown. Her cheeks were flushed and she dashed an angry tear away as she descended. When she reached the bottom of the steps, she reached into her reticule, clearly searching for something.

A gentleman bowed and handed her his handkerchief. She thanked him and, after a moment of holding it in her hand, pressed it back upon him without seeming to use it. Any words exchanged between them were too swift and low for the Professor to hear, but that didn't matter. That had been the prearranged signal and Mrs Norton had provided either the signet or its copy. Biting back a smile, Professor Moriarty exited the room without waiting to see her departure or her host's reaction to it, happily assured of the success of his plans.

It was time to retrieve Godfrey Norton and prepare for his next steps. He thought it best to show Mrs Norton that her husband was still intact. Otherwise, she might be tempted to warn the King before he had the opportunity to use the ring, and that would be most unfortunate.

As he anticipated, Colonel Moran was waiting for him outside and he entered the coach with a brief nod to his lieutenant. They went by a roundabout path down several thoroughfares to a building on the outskirts of Whitechapel. There, the Colonel stopped and handed the reins to the guard before disembarking from the coach. The same man who accompanied the Professor earlier met the Colonel at the door and ushered him inside.

A few moments later, they emerged with another man held between them. He had a hood over his head and he hung limply from their grasp as if he were asleep or drugged. They hauled him toward the coach, only to be intercepted by a gentleman riding down the street on a smart hack. He slid his horse smoothly between them and the carriage. "I say," he said, "your friend a bit worse for the drink? He might do better without that bag on his head, though."

The Colonel reached a hand toward his pocket, his expression menacing. But another coach had appeared on the street and stopped next to the Professor's. Professor Moriarty, had he chosen to appear at the coach window at that moment, might have recognized the gentleman on the hack as his tea-spilling acquaintance from the King's reception.

Certainly, the two men who emerged from the stopped coach would not have been in attendance at that same gathering. "My friends from Scotland Yard would like a look at this chap's face," the gentleman on the hack continued serenely, as if he had not seen the Colonel's hand move toward his pocket, then fall away. The big man clenched his fist and dropped their burden before lunging at the men from Scotland Yard.

The Colonel released the man to fall limply to the cobbles and embarked on a lunge of his own, this one calculated to take him away from the detectives and down the nearest alley. He nearly collided with the hack. The gentleman now held a pistol in his hand, with the barrel most unequivocally pointed at his heart. Colonel Moran froze and held out his hands in a gesture of surrender. His companion was being subdued with truncheons and it was some moments before anyone had the opportunity to check the inside of the Professor's coach.

In the end, it was a new arrival who flung open the door and swore softly at the sight of the empty cushions. The lady with him turned away and swept over the cobbles to free the fallen man's head. She applied some salts from her bag and, a moment or two later, Mr Godfrey Norton, barrister, coughed his way back to life, if not immediately back to health.

Mrs Norton looked up at the large gentleman standing next to the coach and murmured in a choked voice, "Thank you, Mr Holmes. I am eternally in your debt."

The gentleman's hooded eyes appraised her and her husband for a long moment before Mr Mycroft Holmes favored her with a bow. "I believe that England may be in yours, madam. You have foiled a plot against one of Her Majesty's allies and kept our government from losing face. Allow me to have you escorted to your lodgings and a doctor fetched for your husband."

The Professor moved out of earshot after that. He didn't need to hear more; the details of how the clever Irene Adler and her allies had wrecked his plans could wait. The accompanying painful loss of faith in the mathematical precision of his plans, the precision that should have guaranteed his success, was overwhelming. But it would pass quickly enough. Holmes's brother was a variable that he had not accounted for in his calculations and he had underestimated Mrs Norton. These were not mistakes that he would make again and, when he returned from this Elba, his empire would once again be his. The Napoleon of crime disappeared into the fog.

Dynamics of an Asteroid

Lavie Tidhar

1.

They'd strung up the boy, Twist, from a gas lamp outside and left him there for us to find. Moran carried him in: a limp, pale bundle of broken bones encased in pinched, scarred skin.

Moran laid him down on the kitchen table, as gentle as a serving maid. He stood there looking down mutely on the boy. His face was a mask of anger and hate.

Remarkably, the dead body still tried to move. Moran jumped back with a cry. Twist's limbs flopped on the kitchen table. His mouth opened and closed without words. His eyes sprung open and glared at us, and I saw the evil, alien flame of intelligence behind the eyes.

The phenomenon only lasted for a moment. Then the flame went out and the body collapsed back and was still, the last vestiges of animated life gone from it. It had not been one of them, only a sliver, just enough for them to deliver this message, let us know they knew where we were, that they could reach us if they wanted to.

'They want us alive,' I said, and Moran turned on me and said, 'No, they want *you* alive, Professor. They couldn't give a f—k about the rest of us.'

The ratter, Fagin, looked up balefully from the corner. His face was as white as a skull.

'Where do we go now?' he said. 'We're trapped. There's no way out, not any more. Maybe there never was—' He was babbling, half crazed by now. He'd lost half his boys to the other side and the rest had run. Twist had been the last boy standing.

I stared at him coldly.'Remember, Fagin. This is still my city,' I told him. 'I ruled it from the shadows and I will rule it yet again.'

'Jack rules it,' the ratter said. 'This is Jack's town now.'

I was on him in a fraction of a second. My fingers tightened on his throat. The ratter's face turned even whiter. His eyes bulged.

'F—k Jackie Boy,' I said. 'This is *my* turf.' I stared into his eyes. 'Do you understand me, Fagin? Do you *understand*?'

'Yes!' he choked. 'Yes, yes!'

I released him and he slumped to the ground, massaging his throat. I looked around me, at our bolt-hole. The wallpaper was ghastly. The windows were covered in makeshift blackout blinds. Twist lay on the table. I turned my eyes from him.

'If they want us,' I said, 'then we shall go to them. We shall go to see Jack.'

'But that's suicide!' Moran said, stirring.

I laughed. 'Do you think me a fool?' I said. 'I have studied them, from the very start. I know them better than anyone alive. You are a hunter, Colonel Moran. And it is time for us to hunt.'

He looked at me wanly. The fight wasn't in him. Six months since it'd all begun. Six scant months since the world changed for ever. And we have fought them, in the streets and alleys, in the shadows, every day and night. And still, we were losing.

I checked my gun. Before, I had no use for guns. I believed in the mind, in pure mathematics. It was that which led to my infamous lecture, before the Royal Society, about the dynamics of that d—ed *Marsian* asteroid.

2.

I knew, even as I was speaking, that they did not believe me. They heard the words but the meaning did not register.

No one would have believed in the last years of the nineteenth century that this world was being watched keenly and closely by intelligences greater than man's and yet as mortal as his own, because, of course, this is complete and utter poppycock.

I would not have called them intelligent, not exactly. They had a species' predatory hunger, a need to survive. Intelligence was secondary. As for being mortal – they could be killed, yes, but with difficulty. But they were coming, even though, back then, I did not yet know the extent of it.

The Royal Society was packed that night but no one was listening any more. A man in the second row from the front was the only one paying attention. He was dressed in a seersucker suit, with mutton chops down his narrow face and a sun hat, which tried to disguise his bright fevered eyes, and failed. He had always taken ridiculous pride in his disguises, which I never understood – he was never very difficult to spot in a crowd.

'Gentlemen,' I said, 'your outrage does you no credit. This is science, simple and inevitable mathematics. There is a Marsian asteroid heading directly to Earth. If my calculations are correct – and my calculations are never wrong – it will hit somewhere to the south-west of London in approximately six months from today.'

The man in the seersucker suit raised his hand. 'Professor Moriarty?' he said.

'Yes, Holmes?'

He flushed red under the fake sideburns, mortified his disguise did not fool me.

'What do you mean, alien life forms?' he said.

'I mean exactly that. It is my determination that the course of this asteroid is not random. It has been *aimed*.'

'You consider it a hostile act?'

'I don't know what else we can call it, Detective.'

'But that means . . .'

'That the British Empire is under attack.'

'Your empire, you mean. The secret criminal empire of which you are master!'

'Like a spider in the centre of a web,' I said, tiredly. 'What was it you called me when we last met? The Napoleon of crime? I am a mathematics professor, Mr Holmes. A good one.'

The truth was I rather liked the old boy. Of course he liked to claim he was the top of his field, but then he was the only one *in* his field. Mostly, he did divorce work, much as he tried to deny it. All around us the distinguished members were booing and shouting. Only Holmes understood, and yet he misunderstood profoundly.

'They could be emissaries,' he said. 'Ambassadors from the red planet. If you are right—'

'I am never wrong—'

'*If* you are right, then this is marvellous,' he said. 'A first meeting with an extraterrestrial race!'

He thought he understood people, you see. He had that trick where he guessed where you came from or what you did by the type of cigarette you smoked. He was an idiot.

'I am quite sure that a man of your intelligence will see that there can be but one outcome to this affair,' I said.

'You speak of danger,' he said.

'Yes.'

'Danger is part of my trade.'

'That is not danger, you fool!' I said. 'It is inevitable destruction.'

He smiled, thinly and without charm. 'Then I propose a wager.'

'Oh? I did not have you pegged as a gambling man, Mr Holmes.'

'Only when I can be sure of the outcome,' he said, smugly.

I wondered if I should not let Moran shoot him. The Colonel was eager to play with his latest toy, some sort of air rifle used to hunt big game. It would have been wasted on Holmes. A knife in the ribs would have been quicker and quieter, and cost less to boot.

'Speak your mind,' I said. No one else was listening. They were still ranting and raving, calling me delusional, a madman and a flake. It had become a sort of sport. To them I was a nobody, a provincial mathematician, and they were, or so they thought, the grand men of their day. Unbeknown to them, most were in hock to me already. The others would be blackmailed or robbed, perhaps murdered. I do not suffer fools.

'You say it will hit in six months,' he said. 'Let us meet then, and go to welcome these life forms of yours. These *Marsians*. And we shall see who is right.'

I smiled at him pleasantly enough.

'Gladly,' I said. I had my own plans for the landing. By having Holmes along, I thought, I could kill two birds with one stone.

Though, as it turned out, I had underestimated our strange visitors from another world. And it had cost me: it had cost me dearly.

3.

The trajectory of the asteroid's fall led me to conclude that it would make landing somewhere near Woking, Surrey. It seemed unlikely to be a coincidence. It was far enough from urban habitation to be discreet, yet close enough to London to make any kind of attack a swift one. It was visible now in the night sky, a red, baleful eye, which had drawn a crowd and some members of the constabulary, trying to keep the peace, including that buffoon, Lestrade, of Scotland Yard.

When we arrived it was night. Holmes was already waiting, smoking a pipe, leaning against a fence with a nonchalance that didn't fool me for a minute. He was a hopeless addict, and I could see by the shaking of his hands and the feverish look in his eyes that he had taken enough cocaine to give an elephant a heart attack. What he was seeing in the night sky was anyone's guess, at that point. It must have seemed a magical fireworks display to him, some ethereal wonderland in the night.

To me, that red glare meant nothing less than a declaration of war.

'Stand back, stand back!' Lestrade shouted.

The observers gaped at the sky in a bovine fashion. Holmes gave me a nod and I nodded back, guardedly. I had my own plans for this extraterrestrial invasion.

My men had surrounded Horsell Common. They were hidden in the trees, drawn from the mean streets of London: heavy men, with heavy guns. My plan was simple. As soon as the asteroid – meteoroid, now, and soon to be a meteorite – landed, my men would open fire. Anyone who got in their way – a certain detective, say, or a dim-witted Scotland Yard inspector – would be blasted to kingdom come. I quite relished that thought.

'I wonder what type of cigarette tobacco they smoke,' Holmes said, dreamily. I saw his man, Watson, emerge from the trees then, fumbling with his belt.

'This is no time to go to the loo,' Holmes murmured. Watson shrugged. He was a small, stocky man who moved with a slight limp in bad weather.

We watched the sky, and that hateful red glow coming nearer and nearer.

4.

Now there were only the three of us left, Moran and Fagin and I. The boy, Twist, we left behind. He was no use to anyone any more. We crept through the city's dark curfew.

We had taken shelter in a maze of alleyways in one of the East End's most notorious slums. It had been Fagin's hinterland in the days of my empire, his base of operations, where the children were trained as fine-wirers and cutpurses. We had been retreating by degrees as the enemy, quietly and insidiously, grew in power. Now the streets were dark, deserted. The only shapes that moved did so jerkily, with a stiffness of limbs and a vacuity of eyes, and we avoided their patrols, hiding until they passed. Jack. Jack was somewhere out there, a spider in its web – what had Holmes called me? I missed Holmes. I missed all of it. The great game we used to play.

'Where are we going?' Fagin whispered. I exchanged a glance with Moran, who grinned in savage amusement.

'Do you know how to catch a tiger, Fagin?' I said.

'Professor?'

'The way to catch a tiger is to offer it something it wants,' I said. 'Hunters, like our friend Colonel Moran here, would tie a living goat to a tree and lie in wait nearby. The goat would cry in fear, until the tiger came. Do you understand?'

I could see the confusion in the poor man's eyes. 'But where will we find a goat at this time of night? In the East End?'

I sighed. I liked Fagin, he was a good worker, and he had no morals of which to speak.

'Not a goat, you fool,' I said. 'A man.'

Something must have finally registered. His eyes flashed. He began to turn towards me and there was a knife in his hand. Then Moran knocked him on the back of the head with the butt of his air rifle, and Fagin slumped unconscious to the ground. Moran picked him up, grunting at the weight.

'Do you know the place, sir?'

'The church,' I said. 'By the old Ten Bells. That's Jack's point.'

He nodded wordlessly. He hefted the unconscious Fagin over his shoulder and we began to make our way towards the church on Commercial Street.

The night was thick with silence. They were close. I could feel them, watching, sniffing, waiting: waiting for me.

5.

Holmes died first.

I took savage satisfaction from the fact, even as the world I knew was coming silently to an end.

The meteorite streaked across the sky. From this close I could see its malevolent evil, the malformed shape of the rock spinning as it burned through the Earth's atmosphere. Who could survive such a journey? All my planning, all my notes and schemes, have revolved around an enemy immeasurably powerful, yet fundamentally *known*. They would have machines, great and terrible machines to protect them from our hostile, alien environment. They'd have great tripod-like machines to scour the land, and death rays to cause unbearable destruction. All tools I could use, myself. Once my men had killed the invaders, using the power of surprise, I would have their technology, I thought. I would rule not from the shadows, but from the throne! And the British Empire – *my* empire – would rule the entire world – perhaps even beyond!

The meteorite streaked across the sky and burst towards us like a fist. I heard screams, onlookers running. I expected the jolt of impact, the shock of an earthquake, yet I stood my ground. Then, impossibly, the meteorite seemed to slow as it passed through the air. For a moment, it hovered above us. It felt – as irrational as this may seem – as though that misshapen lump of rock was *grinning*.

Then it floated down and settled on the ground, as gentle as a feather. Nothing moved. There was no sound.

No hatches opened. No terrible machines emerged. Against the fence where he was leaning, Sherlock Holmes began to laugh.

'Why aren't they shooting?' I said. I was speaking to Moran. 'Why aren't they *shooting*?'

Of my men there was no sign!

'Why won't they *shoot*! *Shoot*, you d—ed c—ks—s, shoot!'

Holmes's laughter grew in volume and intensity. The man was quite deranged. Hysterical laughter spilled out of him and he shook, helplessly. The silent meteorite sat there on the ground of Horsell Common, still glowing red as though from some inner source of light. As I watched, thin tendrils of smoke, like questing tentacles, rose out of the rock and into the air. The red mist thickened, spreading in all directions away from the rock. One questing tendril reached Holmes. It seemed to tickle him, behind the ear, and Holmes giggled girlishly.

Then, it entered him – penetrated him! – and Holmes screamed, a horrible, wordless cry.

I saw his man, Watson, bolt and run. Holmes began to shake, the questing tentacle rummaging inside him, studying him, *knowing* him.

Until it'd had enough.

Abruptly, and with a soft, wet popping sound, Holmes exploded.

Wet bloodied pieces of Holmesian matter flew everywhere like whale blubber; a piece of kidney hit my cheek and slid sadly to the ground. I wiped my face with my handkerchief.

'Professor?' Moran said.

I stared, dumbfounded, at the silent rock. The bloodied miasma of that unnatural, evil fog continued to rise. Its tendrils reached the trees and *pulled*. I saw my men emerge from the cover of the foliage, their faces blank, their motions jerky, uniform. They were led by red trails of smoke that were, I realised, like leashes around their necks.

An eerie silence had fallen over Horsell Common. And I realised I had underestimated these Marsian invaders.

Then, hovering out of the mist, I saw a great big sucker form. It darted towards me with a sinuous motion, as though coming for a kiss.

'Run, you fools!' I said. 'Run for your lives!'

And so, all dignity forgotten, and the remnants of Holmes's internal organs still on my face and clothes, I ran. I, James Moriarty, Ph.d., FRS, Chair of Mathematics at the tender age of only twenty-one and, since those long gone days, the greatest criminal mastermind the world had ever known – I ran!

6.

There were lights behind the windows of the Ten Bells pub. They were a wan red colour, and moved with some inhuman, yet intelligent, purpose. Fagin had recovered consciousness by the time we arrived. Moran tied him securely with a rope to the gates of the brooding church. What priests there were inside this grand edifice no longer worshipped God as any human could conceive it. Poor Fagin cried most bitterly. As we left him there, he began to hurl insults and curses at our backs.

We took shelter in the fallen-down remains of Spitalfields Market across the road, and waited. Moran had his air rifle out, and aimed the sights at poor Fagin's forehead.

'I never liked him,' he said.

'I know.'

'Poor Twist.'

'Poor all of us, when you come to think of it,' I said.

We lapsed into silence. It felt as though we were intruders in some dark, alien world, of the sort that philistine fool, Wells, wrote of in his little stories. Here and there bands of possessed creatures, barely human any more, moved about their masters' unfathomable business. Fagin had stopped screaming. He must have realised he would only draw the tiger to him quicker. He now subsided into muffled moans, more eerie than his shouting had been. His was the sound of a trapped and wounded animal. The sound of the human race itself, I thought, in a rare moment of fancy.

Make no mistake – it was the Martians' final goal: to rule us all, to control the world! Only Moran and I stood in their way – unlikely defenders of humankind.

We had been running the Resistance for six months, yet we had been thwarted at every turn.

Moran and I were now all that remained.

7.

The morning after the Martian landing, Moran went to collect the papers while I reclined in bed. When he returned, his face was troubled. I looked at the front pages, yet there was no mention of the meteorite strike of the night before; no mention had been made of Woking, of Horsell Common, not even of that oaf, Holmes, and his untimely – if personally, to me, quite satisfying – death.

'What is the meaning of this, Professor?' Moran said.

My mind worked rapidly. I had expected a technologically advanced species, yet my mistake had been to assume that their technology followed *our* path – the path of factories, parts, *machines*.

Theirs, I realised instantly, was a technology of the *mind*: who knew what dark practices and terrible experiments these Martians performed on their native world?

I was a fool to expect tripods and death rays! These were *parasites*, creatures of pure mind!

I almost laughed, in giddy exhalation. It was as though creatures such as Holmes and myself had transcended even the limitations of the flesh, had become beings of pure reason. At last, I thought, I had a worthy adversary!

I had sent men back to Woking, but all remnants of the asteroid were gone, and nothing remained on the clear, clean surface of the common to suggest any foul play. Inspector Lestrade, I learned, was back at work, as though nothing had happened. My gunmen of the previous night had disappeared as though the ground itself swallowed them; which, I suspected, may have been the literal truth.

There was nothing for me to do but bide my time, and organise, and wait.

In the next few weeks, the newspapers began reporting increasingly strange, troubling events. Key members of trade and parliament mysteriously disappeared, only to return as though nothing had happened, with strange new policies in place. 'It was like I went to sleep with my husband,' said one tearful woman to the *London Illustrated News*, 'and woke up with a stranger wearing my husband's face. I don't know him any more, he is someone else, someone completely alien.'

The same affliction spread elsewhere, even to the lower classes. It may have affected the aristocracy from the very beginning, but no one was able to tell: they had always been strange and aloof in their ways.

More troubling still were the stories, soon circulating, of the man they called *Jack*. A ruthless killer, he – if it were a he, if there were only one of them, and not an army – moved swiftly and silently through the night, brutally slashing his victims to death. He operated mostly in the East End of London, leaving a trail of corpses in his wake, so that the newspapers began to refer to a 'Spree of Frenzied Killings' and 'The Ongoing East End Massacre' before, finally and abruptly, they ceased from making any mention of any unusual events, and began instead to promote the new government line of *Obey, Produce, Conform*.

They – whoever *they* now were – had also began to hunt me down earnestly.

My organisation was being infiltrated from without. My banker, Scrooge, had set up an elaborate scheme to capture me on a visit to the vaults. I escaped with Moran's help, capturing the mean old man in the process, though not without having to kill about a dozen jerkily moving, Marsian-animated corpses. We locked Scrooge in a safe house and tortured him. The malevolent spirit housed in his body laughed in my face even as Moran got busy with the pliers.

"Step away from my banker's body, you Marsian bodysnatcher!' I screamed in frustration. Tendrils of red mist rose out of Scrooge's nose as though mocking me, and the man's eyes opened and stared straight at me. His mouth moved, but the words that came were spoken by another, alien intelligence.

'Join us . . . Moriar . . . ty. Obey . . . Con . . . form!'

'Never!' I said, and brought down my knife, hard, stabbing the reanimated corpse in the heart. The body shuddered and was still – yet the red mist continued to rise out of the body, and now it was making its way to me!

How we escaped that room – those clutching red, ethereal tentacles! – is not a story to be lightly told. When at last we departed, running down the wharf side of Limehouse with Scrooge's hobbling dead corpse in pursuit, I had sworn that I would take the war directly to the enemy.

I, Moriarty, would not be defeated so easily!

8.

The story of the Resistance is a long and glorious one, yet, ultimately, futile. In six months, the world had changed for ever. My men were dead or subverted, the Resistance broken, and I was on the run. Our dear Queen, it was said, was safe – had departed the palace in the midst of night, to regions unknown. French ships stood watch in the Channel, to stop anyone from escaping to the shores of Europe and bringing the plague with them. The French were only waiting for a chance to step in and invade us in the guise of saviours.

And then Jack ran wild.

We watched from the shadows. Somewhere nearby a clock struck midnight. But now, it was always midnight in London.

A dark shape materialised on the steps of the old church.

Resolved into the features of a blank-eyed man, and then

another, and another. Slowly, they came down the steps, and I almost laughed.

For they knew I was there. They had sent my own men down those steps: Roylott, the poisoner; the German spy, Oberstein; Gruner, the notorious sadist; Beppo, the Italian snatcher; even that red-headed confidence man, John Clay!

Good men, ruthless men, dedicated men, who once feared and obeyed me – now lifeless shells, animated by the malignant force of these Marsians.

They fell on the bleating, hapless Fagin. His screams tore the night. The shadows gathered behind us. Hands reached and grabbed Moran and me. We struggled against them in vain.

'Was this part of your plan, Professor?' Moran hissed, in pain. They pushed us along, towards the church steps. My feet stepped in poor Fagin's remains, leaving a trail of bloodied footsteps, pulling along trailing entrails.

'We have not lost yet, Sebastian,' I said.

He shook his head. His shoulders slumped and he let them push him forward. The fight was no longer in him. Colonel Moran had given up. It was a pitiful sight to see.

I followed along. I had no choice.

Up the stairs and into the church.

Ethereal red lights and fog, drifting . . . the air was humid, with an unearthly stench. Was this what the air of Mars smelled like? I pictured a world inhabited by spores, by leeches floating in the fetid air, carried on the winds. The mists parted and merged. We were pushed along, deeper into the church. Down the ancient steps to the cellars, no sound but the beat of my heart in my chest, the thrum of blood in my ears, air flowing in and out of my lungs, in and out through nose and mouth, and I was aware, more than ever, of my own weak flesh and blood, my mortality.

Down to ancient catacombs, the carved space of sewers underneath the city. They must have preferred it down there, I realised: slowly the under-city was being converted into a Marsian landscape. I saw with horror the glowing green moss spreading along the walls, smelled the fetid corruption of slowly rotting bodies.

Our descent ended. Down there, in the dark, it was impossible to tell where we were. Somewhere deep under London.

This was Jack's point.

I waited. Moran stood beside me. My men – what remained of my men – stood around us in a guard. I wondered if we were to be welcomed or executed. Perhaps both, I thought. I heard the tread of soft, unhurried footsteps. A small, tan figure, with only the hint of a limp, emerged from the thick foliage of creepers and vines.

It wore a familiar face, but it took me a moment to place it, until he smiled: I had last seen him at Horsell Common, running.

'Hello, Moriarty,' Dr Watson said.

9.

I said, 'Hello, Jack.'

He smiled. He had nothing of the softness of the old Watson about him. A greater intelligence animated this being, a pernicious, alien mind, bent on destruction.

A mind, if I were being honest, not entirely unlike my own.

'A merry dance you led us, Moriarty,' he said. I saw the red flames behind his eyes. 'But all joy must sooner or later come to an end.'

'So this is it?' I said. 'What will you do, kill me? You think yourselves invincible?'

'But my dear Moriarty,' the alien said. 'You completely misunderstand our position. We read of your work with great interest. Your *Treatise on the Binomial Theorem*! Your *Dynamics of an Asteroid*! Your mind is a great and precious thing! We could use a man such as yourself.'

'What do you mean?'

'We are beings of the mind. Bodies are merely an inconvenience, don't you think? Tools, to be used and discarded. Join us, Professor! And we would make you immortal.'

I stood still. Beside me, Moran stirred. He looked up with dull, defeated eyes. I pitied him then. I pitied Twist, Scrooge, Holmes and all the others. I stood alone before the alien mind.

'What would I have to do?' I said softly.

Watson's grin was a wet, grotesque thing. His tongue snaked out, a red, obscene thing. It spooled out of his mouth and kept on coming, like a snake. When it touched the skin of my cheek, it stopped, and I felt him shudder. I stood still, hating him, hating them all. The tongue found my ear and entered it, and the world changed forever.

10.

You may remember that day. The day the Marsians died. The day you returned home, through streets strewn with the corpses of those you once knew, those who had been taken. Host bodies, empty of the malign influence that had animated them during the Marsian occupation. The Regent's Canal was choked full of these corpses, and red, dying Marsian weeds rose from the subterranean depths in which they had found shelter, questing helplessly for the sun.

There were mass funerals held that day, and in the days to come. The host bodies were carted south of the river, to Blackheath, and were burned and buried in a common grave.

Bacteria! that fool, Wells, wrote, in his chronicle of the war.

Yet there is a word, an old Latin word, which I like. It is *Virus*.

I remember emerging from the subterranean depths, somewhere near Simpson's, where I often dined. The sky was streaked with red. Moran was by my side. I am not sure how we got there. Moran carried me, perhaps. I was both there and not there.

I was everywhere!

My mind had been sucked into the aliens' consciousness matrix. For a moment, I saw through their eyes, distributed all across London and beyond, extending even to the Midlands (though why anyone, human or alien, would wish to go there I'm sure I don't know). In their memories, I saw the red planet, its sandstorms and dust, its crawling, patient life forms, living in abject terror of the telepathic fungal leeches of which I was now, myself, a part!

Yet I saw beauty, too, a strange sort of pride of these aesthetic beings, who saw themselves as warrior-monks, separated from the great Marsian mind to launch themselves all but blindly at our planet. I saw, and was for a moment tempted.

Yet I am Moriarty, and I serve no manner of man or leech.

Within their matrix, I began to reproduce. To replicate. My consciousness spread like a sickness through their telepathic web. I was everywhere, I was everything! By the time the Jacks realised what I was doing it was already too late. I was replacing their mind with my own, rewriting their being with mine. I would not become the Marsians' puppet – they would become mine!

You may remember that day. Perhaps you were never there, but only heard of it later. The day Jack fell. The day the body-rippers died.

Later, there had been all kinds of stories. How bacteria killed them, or a bomb, or Sherlock Holmes. Each one as ridiculous as the other.

For myself, I came to, blinking and confused, my head pounding as from the worst imaginable hangover. I could not contain their great mind. I had destroyed it, and then withdrew, back into my own skull, diminished.

I am still the Chair of Mathematics at the university where I teach. With the death of that fool, Holmes, there is no one left to know my name, or my occupation. My web of influence spreads everywhere, from the lands of the Zulu to the great courts of the Raj. My name is whispered in awe and fear in the gutters of London.

Yet sometimes, late at night, I raise my eyes up to the sky, searching in the mesh of stars for that alien red planet. There is a longing in me now, new and unsettling. Sometimes I wish they would come back. Sometimes, I think, if they'd only ask me again, I would like to go with them.

The Importance of Porlock

Amy Myers

No chain is stronger than its weakest link... Hence the extreme importance of Porlock.
                    The Valley of Fear, Sir Arthur Conan Doyle

It was in the summer of 1887 that I first realised my own importance. My name, as I presented it to Mr Sherlock Holmes, was Fred Porlock, which pleased me as an invention. In that year I interfered with the plans of the most sinister villain ever known to the vast heaving London underworld, just as the gentleman from the village of Porlock once interrupted the flowing pen of the poet Samuel Coleridge. Adopting the name of Fred also pleased me. A name of no importance in itself, it smacks of greatness, of kings, emperors and heroes: Alfred, Frederick and Siegfried.

Later I knew this villain to have been Professor Moriarty, in whose evil empire I was a humble messenger, the fleeting shadow in the fog beyond London's gaslights, the whisper before the knife. I took my orders from the link above me in his devilish web and relayed them on to the next. That web controlled all that was vile, spinning its malevolence far beyond London, far beyond the shores of England itself, eastwards towards the great powers of Europe, and even westwards towards the mighty States of America. At its centre sat the Spider, manipulating and sucking in its prey in pursuit of its own ends, regardless of the human life it destroyed in the process.

Until the summer of '87, I performed my tasks without concern. I saw not their beginning, I cared not about their end. I knew nothing about the Spider, but now the very thought of Moriarty brings back the fears and terrors of that time.

My story begins with blood.

The blood of a flower girl spilt in the grey dawn of Covent Garden's market. She lay in a corner of the new glass-covered flower market. I saw her black dress and shawl with the red blood still streaming over her, as red as the rose she had handed me yesterday as she cried her wares in the Strand.

'Know her, mister?' asked a uniformed beadle curiously.

'No,' I lied.

'Elsie Bracken, her name is, God rest her soul. Her man sells matches outside St Bride's. Soldier once, he was. Out there in India.'

Bracken! I knew that name. I felt myself shaking as I sank to my knees at Elsie's side, despite the crowd around me. It was then I realised she still breathed, though near to death. Her eyelids fluttered, perhaps aware of my closeness to her, and her eyes opened. Did she recognise me? I doubt it, but she struggled to make one last desperate attempt to speak. Her dying breath was trying to form a word and I leaned over her as though this poor gesture might help.

'Hurry,' I heard her say, but then no more.

Flowers are too rare in this world for their passing to go unnoticed. Besides, the coincidence was too great. One of my few talents is an interest in codes and ciphers, as Mr Sherlock Holmes can testify, and the last message I had been ordered to deliver to my link, Bill Butcher, had indicated its next recipient: Jesse Bracken.

The name had meant nothing to me then, but now a terrible suspicion seized me. The message had indicated he was to present himself at the Tilbury docks and, caring little, I had deciphered no further, no time, no place. It was whispered in the taverns that the Spider tolerated no departure from his order of complete silence on those who worked for him. Any peaching or blabbing would result in death and, if circumstances warranted it, that sentence would include those near to him. If Jesse had dared to trespass beyond his orders, not only could he be doomed, but also Elsie, his innocent wife, the girl who'd handed me that red rose yesterday.

I'd heard her cry: 'Roses, red roses. Red roses for your sweetheart.' I had no sweetheart but I had bought one nevertheless, and, as she handed it to me, she had said: 'You look as if you need a rose, mister.'

I had been of no importance, a mere shape drifting past, but she had *looked* at me and cared. I might have been the unwitting messenger of her death. In vain I told myself I was not guilty of her murder, but I felt I was.

You'll not go unavenged, Elsie, I silently promised her. I would hunt down the Spider sitting so smugly in his web and make him pay by foiling his fiendish plans.

Brave words. How to find him, however? I knew only the identity of the person to whom I passed the message. Messages were delivered to me by the same anonymous man but in a different location on every occasion. It would mean my own death if I were discovered attempting to find the beating heart of the web, the Spider himself, but to descend it might be of no avail. I was at a crossroads: which way to travel? Climb the web or seek out Jesse Bracken? I felt a surge of power. I alone could choose. If I trod carefully, even this most elusive of spiders might not notice this insignificant fly. Yes, I would climb.

But then Elsie's cry echoed in my ears: 'Red roses, red roses . . .'

Few hear the cry of those whom the metropolis's uncaring ways trample underfoot. But I did hear it, and I knew I must answer it.

'Hurry,' had been Elsie's last word, and so my first step must be to find Jesse Bracken before he too was killed. To have left the army, Bracken must be an invalid. If, as was likely, another order along a different chain had been issued for his and Elsie's death, his killer might already have acted – or be about to act.

I had been early abroad as sleeping comes hard to me, and it was not yet six of the clock. No time to waste, however. I could see the police constable coming towards us now, but in the crowd around Elsie, it was easy to melt away with my usual anonymity and then *run*.

I ran from the market towards Wych Street and then down into the Strand, through the arch of Temple Bar and into Fleet Street where lies the great church of St Bride's. London's working world was already coming to life, and I hoped to find Jesse Bracken at his post.

There was no sign of any match-seller by or near the church, when I arrived, panting for breath. Where did Jesse live? No one could tell me. I must find Bill Butcher – who being the link above Jesse would surely know – but the taverns, whose company he sought more than that of toil, were not yet open. Then I saw a coffee stall by the cab stand and, to my relief, I could see Bill slumped against it.

He was a street entertainer, a one-man band, whose raucous music offended the ears of London. He jokes as passers-by drop halfpennies and farthings into his cap, but his eyes can turn into the coldest of weapons to those who cause him trouble. I had one advantage, however. Bill Butcher did not know who I was, just as I did not know the link above me. To him I was just another anonymous fly caught in this web.

Another of my talents is impersonations to dodge recognition; I can be an afflicted beggar, a chimney sweep, a fisherman, a jack tar, a night-soil man or even a toff as it takes my fancy, but there was no time today for such precautions. I could change my voice, but otherwise I was my own unimportant self with a fortunately unmemorable face.

I ordered tea and a muffin and stood next to Bill for a moment or two, then remarked gruffly: 'Heard there's a girl murdered in the Garden.'

'What's it to me?' he growled.

'Hard for her man. Invalided soldier, I'm told. Know him, do you? They're looking for him now. Sells matches round here.'

I feared I had gone too far, but he showed no signs of recognition, as he sniggered, 'He won't fret. Pulled out of the river last night by them River Police. Down by the big ship docks. Knifed,' he informed me, with much satisfaction.

My face changed not a whit, but inside I was very cold. 'What was he doing down those parts?'

He turned away, without bothering to reply, but I'd heard enough. 'Hurry,' Elsie had said less than an hour ago. Jesse must already have been dead, but Elsie might not have known that. Perhaps, however, her 'hurry' referred to something else. Could that be the Spider's planned crime in which Jesse and I had been links? My heart pounded within me. I must act – but how?

At that moment a police van passed, possibly carrying Elsie's body away. I doffed my hat and, as I did so, glanced upwards. There I saw flags of red, white and blue flying from every window. I live my own anonymous life, but how could I have not considered what was exciting most of the world, even though I had dismissed it as being of no relevance to me?

On the morrow, 21 June, Her Majesty Queen Victoria would be celebrating her Golden Jubilee. She would have been on the throne for fifty years and London was already crowded with visitors. Its ports, especially those with water deep enough to take the new large passenger ships, were greeting princes and crowned heads from as far afield as Persia, Japan and Siam; from India came maharajahs bearing gifts of jewels and servants for the royal household, and bringing gifts from Hawaii was Queen Kala Kaua. Most talk, however, was of Her Majesty's many German relatives, including the Crown Prince Friedrich, his wife, the Queen's eldest daughter, and their son Prince Wilhelm, later to be Kaiser himself and who was a far from popular gentleman, so the rumours went. The pomp of their arrival on the destroyer *Blitz* and accompanying flotilla of torpedo boats had demanded one of the newer docks.

Tilbury, I thought, where Jesse Bracken must have lost his life. The death of a flower girl seemed far removed from such grand matters of stage, and yet . . .

'*Hurry*,' Elsie had said.

Surely not even the Spider's plans would reach as far as Her Majesty's Jubilee Day, even to the Queen herself? It had to be considered, however, for in the past there had been failed attempts by madmen to assassinate Her Majesty, and the next might succeed. There were some foreign powers who might welcome the Queen gone from the throne of England and its empire. This very day Her Majesty was arriving by train from Windsor Castle to make her way to Buckingham Palace for the celebrations on the morrow. What could I do even if such an outrage were being planned by the Spider? For all my spurt of confidence, I was a person of no importance. I could not spill out my fears to Scotland Yard without appearing a madman myself and such a move would undoubtedly sign my own death warrant from the Spider. But I could try to climb the web even at this late stage. My very unimportance might enable me to move unseen.

And so my climb began. I went first to the dark and smoky tavern in the Strand near the Lowther Arcade; it was here that the message about Jesse had been handed to me by my anonymous link. I had little hope of finding him, not least because this was only one of the taverns where I had met him. Good fortune favoured me, however. My link had grown careless, for he was drinking here now. He failed to recognise me in the gloom, especially since my assumed accent and my cap identified me as a costermonger from the east of our city. It was surprisingly easy over the next hour or two for me to supply him with enough liquor to acquire a clue to where he had met the link above him.

'Must be a toff,' I then joked, as he had referred to a public house near to Eaton Square.

He spluttered with mirth. 'Him? His servant more like.'

Whose servant? I wondered, but could take it no further, for my link belatedly realised that loose tongues led to voices silenced for ever.

The information both heartened and depressed me. Eaton Square was a neighbourhood where the Spider might himself dwell and his servants might indeed spend time in the local taverns. What depressed me, however, was that by the time I had clad myself appropriately and found what I thought to be the right tavern, the day was advancing fast and tomorrow was

21 June. The chances of finding Spider, learning his plans, and foiling them were very remote, even if his servant were here.

The barmaid was eyeing me curiously. 'New round here?' she asked.

'Work for tomorrow evening. Up at one of them big houses in the Square.'

The Queen would be holding a splendid luncheon and dinner at Buckingham Palace after the procession and service at Westminster Abbey. She was related to so many of the crowned heads of Europe that they alone would dine at the Palace, which meant that the British aristocracy were planning to hold similar splendid gatherings in their own grand homes. My story passed muster with those around me.

'Sooner it's over the better,' said my neighbour, a morose-looking man, albeit smartly dressed, in his thirties. 'Dress uniform his nibs wants laid out tonight. And he's only off to his club.'

Uniform? That sounded interesting. 'Must be meeting Jubilee visitors,' I said wisely.

He snorted. 'Only a dinner with one other chap. Important, he says. Everything has to be important for him.'

'I'm thinking of joining a club myself,' I joked, knowing my workman's gear hardly put me in that class.

'You wouldn't get past the Albion door,' he said, grinning.

One of the famous clubs in Pall Mall. There was a slim chance that his employer might be the Spider, but I hesitated to arouse suspicion by asking more. I was in luck again, as my neighbour decided to continue the joke. 'Give it a try,' he urged me. 'Turn up there, ask for Colonel Sebastian Moran and say you're dining with him.'

'I'll do that,' I assured him.

He roared with laughter, the barmaid joined in and I followed suit. When he'd wiped the tears of mirth from his eyes, he clapped me on the back. 'I likes a man who likes a good joke.'

Anticipation filled the air that evening, crowds already gathering on the streets, talking of the great event on the morrow and of those dignitaries who were known to have arrived. The glorious weather was holding and much beer was drunk that night in the Queen's honour; many the working men who staggered home even more bung-eyed than usual.

I was not among them. I was sitting on a stool at the roadside near the foot of the Albion Club steps in Pall Mall and practising my newly acquired trade of shoeblacker. My companion, the regular shoeblacker, had been easy enough to square, once he had been informed that I was a detective from Scotland Yard, one of the many guarding the Queen's peace that evening; there was, I told him, an expectation of trouble with so many important people in the city. My shoeblacker friend was especially pleased to help on receipt of a whole shilling.

'Between you and me,' I told him in confidential tones, 'I'm looking out for a Colonel Sebastian Moran. Know him?'

'Not 'arf,' he told me eagerly. 'That's one geezer everyone steers clear of. You don't cross him. Yessir, nossir, that's what he wants and if he don't get it you're in trouble.'

'Tip me the wink when he comes,' I said.

'Right-ho, sir.'

I waited about an hour, filling in my time learning to buff an evening boot and, I admit, enjoying the task. Nevertheless, I was conscious that the hours were ebbing away like sand through an egg timer and I might be pinning my hopes on the wrong man.

'That's him now, sir,' my companion whispered. I looked up from my improvement of an evening pump shoe to see the most chilling face I had ever had the misfortune to encounter. Huge white drooping moustache, glaring eyes and a sharp jaw that would quell the fiercest of warriors all combined to convince me that this was my man. The Spider, resplendent in his army uniform, was before me.

'Indian Army,' my confidant said in awe. 'That's what he said once. The First Bangalore Pioneers.'

I rejoiced: Jesse Bracken too had been in the Indian Army – perhaps a coincidence or perhaps he had been chosen for his role at Tilbury for that reason.

Then I sobered. What came next? Even though I knew who the Spider was, how could I tell his plans? And, if I did not,

how could I avenge poor Elsie's death by scotching them?
With whom, I wondered, was he dining? Would that give me
some clue?

'Does his companion for this evening dine regularly with him?'
I asked.

'Once a week,' he replied. 'Some geezer he knows, a professor
or something. He's a good 'un, that one. Give me a tanner over
what he owed for his boots once.'

My hopes fell. A regular guest was less likely to be here for
final details of a master plan. And yet the Colonel had told his
valet that it was an important occasion. My hopes rose again.

'Here's that chap now,' my informant told me ten minutes
later.

The evening seemed suddenly chilly, as a figure descended
from the hansom, paid the driver, then paid him the unusual
courtesy of lifting his top hat to him.

'Thank you, cabbie,' he said.

I heard the voice quite clearly. It was like none other I could
remember, with its peculiar mix of softness and steel. He paid no
attention to us, as he climbed the steps, and I heard the doorman
greet him: 'Good evening, Mr Moriarty.'

'*Professo*r Moriarty,' he gently reminded him. Then he turned
round before entering the building. I could not tell what made
him do so. All I know is that I felt the presence of evil so power-
fully that I had to look away. Imagination, I told myself, but I
knew it was not. He must be the Spider's chief of staff, as tainted
as the Spider himself.

I sat at my post in despair. What had I learned? Nothing for
sure, save evidence that I was surely right about the Spider's
diabolical plans for the morrow.

Two hours later, the Professor returned alone. He stood at the
top of the steps looking out towards the roadway – or perhaps he
looked at me. Certainly a shiver ran through me. Then Colonel
Moran joined him and they walked down the steps together,
pausing not far from me for a whispered conversation. The
Colonel was laughing, a sound so alien that I trembled. There
was no mirth in it, just a maniacal triumph.

'Every crowned head of Europe will be with the Queen,' I heard him say. 'They and those who guard her.'

'Certainly,' the Professor agreed. 'Her Majesty will be served well by her Indian guards.' The politeness of his voice made his words more sinister than the Colonel's.

They were bidding each other farewell and I hastily concentrated on my current employment, a pair of button boots for which the owner waited expectantly. Yet I sensed the Professor was looking at me. I felt his eyes boring into me, as though they seared through to my very soul. If the Devil had sent his messenger then this was he.

With a great effort of will, I did not glance up at him, as my fellow shoeblacker took my customer's payment.

What did he want of me, this Professor? Had he understood my purpose for being here, *seen* my true unimportant self? Panic filled me, and I was on the point of running for my very life, when he spoke to me: 'My shoes, if you please.'

He addressed me, but fortunately my companion seized the opportunity of another tanner and took over the task of polishing the Professor's laced leather footwear. I felt he watched me, however. I thought he would speak to me, but he did not. I reckoned my ordeal would never end, and it was with great relief that I watched him hail a hansom and disappear from our sight.

Then a terrible suspicion came to me and, try as I might, it turned into certainty. Colonel Moran was *not* the Spider I had sought. The Spider was Professor Moriarty and I was now within the reach of his carnivorous tentacles.

I felt near to tears, but this was no time for weakness. What did this insidious Spider have in mind for the morrow? 'Every crowned head of Europe will be with the Queen . . . Indian guards.' I shivered. I had read that the Queen's carriage would be preceded by her Indian Army as well as the Household Cavalry. One of them was a traitor.

What could I do to wreck the Spider's plans? Nothing.

Then I realised that I was wrong. There *was* a step I could take, even now. Scotland Yard would take no notice of me, but they would pay heed to Mr Sherlock Holmes, the greatest

detective in London. Should I telegraph? Deliver a letter to his
Baker Street lodgings? My head spun with indecision. I might be
followed, watched, killed, the message destroyed. I must take
that risk. There must be no way that Mr Holmes could trace me.
I must invent another false name, use a code . . . It must be a
letter, delivered by myself to Baker Street. I hurried to the nearest open post office in St James's Street to acquire paper and ink,
and scribbled the best I could think of on the spur of the moment:

  Golden rosebay clive bilberries: Fred Porlock

I had partly used the language of flowers. I had not forgotten
poor Elsie.

The whole of London, the whole world rejoiced as kings,
emperors and potentates gathered under a cloudless blue sky to
celebrate fifty years of Victoria's golden reign. Like Atlas,
however, I felt the whole weight of that world on my shoulders.
I had delivered my letter and then slept overnight in St James's
Park, as if by my physical presence near to Buckingham Palace I
could protect Her Majesty from harm.

  The processional route to Westminster Abbey was a long
one from Buckingham Palace through the streets of London,
Hyde Park Corner, Regent Street and Whitehall, and thence
to the Abbey. At some point, a mounted guard would turn
assassin. There would be no attack in the Abbey itself, I
reasoned. It was too enclosed a space for such an outrage.
Along the processional route, troops lined each street, an
impressive sight with their red uniforms and black bearskins,
but they would provide little defence against a sudden move
by a mounted assassin.

  What to do? I was ignorant, I was helpless, I was of no importance. My letter to Sherlock would be of no use. Even he could
not watch the whole route.

  I chose to stand at the foot of Regent Street on its corner with
Pall Mall to wait for the procession to pass me. Perhaps I thought
being near to where I met the Spider last evening might help me
read his evil mind and even now prevent his planned crime.

  At last, I heard the sound of cheering above the noise of the waiting crowds. It grew louder, then the sound of the horses became audible.

'Here she is, God bless her,' someone roared, words taken up by the entire crowd. 'Here she is . . . here she is . . .'

I could see the troops' horses now, seeming to make straight for me as the noise began to deafen me. I forgot the Spider; I forgot the danger. I was caught up with the spectacle. Behind the mounted guard, six cream horses pulled an open landau in which was seated one small figure: Victoria. Did she wear a crown? No. Did she hold swords of state? No. There was no need of either. This was majesty. This was Victoria. She wore a simple bonnet that sparkled in the sunlight. The empress of a quarter of the world did not need a crown to boast her majesty. My eyes filled with tears of emotion, as the sound of the hooves and the cheering merged in one excited roar.

'Keep on going, duck,' shouted one daring man.

Hats flew in the air, cheers rang in my ears, and then she had passed us, followed by her sons and other family riding on horseback, including the Prince of Wales, the Crown Prince of Germany and his son Prince Wilhelm, withered arm or not. Her Majesty's grandson was said to have a great love of all things English – but a great envy of his grandmother's power and graciousness had led him to a wilful insistence on his own prerogatives and rights. He was twenty-eight now, but not, it was said, beyond playing practical jokes, the kind that are not jokes.

'Every crowned head of Europe will be with the Queen . . .' I had heard the Colonel say.

The procession was passing and I craned my neck to see it to the very last.

'It will not be here,' murmured a voice in my ear.

'The Abbey?' I instinctively blurted out, before terror at this unexpected companion silenced me. Then I relaxed. It was a tall, lean clergyman at my side, who seemed to offer me no threat. I must have been mistaken over what he had said. There was no doubt about his next statement, however.

'The Palace, Mr Porlock. I am sure of it. But how? That is the question. Do you have no other information?'

I shook with fear now. I was followed last night, I must have been. 'None,' I stumbled out. 'The guards, the Indian Army.'

'I think not. Come, man. What does that embodiment of evil have in mind?'

I could not speak for terror, but, as I looked at him, with his shrewd eyes and air of coiled tension, I calmed myself. He had called me Porlock. 'Mr Holmes,' I breathed, hardly daring to hope.

'The same. Think, man, *think.*'

'I know not,' I cried in despair. When I next looked, Mr Holmes had gone.

Hurry, I thought despairingly. The service at the Abbey would last an hour and then the procession would return this way to the Palace. Surely Mr Holmes must be wrong. How could the attack come there, where there could no longer be a threat from the guards?

I could not rest. I must see the procession on its return journey, watch it at a point where I could see it safely reach the Palace itself. And so I ran along Pall Mall, down past St James's Palace to the Mall which led up to the Palace. But my plan was to cross Green Park and wait at Hyde Park Corner. Here were the stands specially built for the Jubilee and full of quality folk. Beneath them, crowds blocked the entire road to the west as well as lining the road to Piccadilly and the point where the roadway sweeps round to join Constitution Hill. The island of green in the middle of the roadways was equally full of excited onlookers waiting for the return of the procession after the service in the Abbey.

Here, surely, was where the attack would happen. It was another hour and a half before the procession could be heard once again, and my head was dizzy. This vigil began to seem a mere dream and I was lulled into a conviction that all would be well as the procession passed and the Queen remained safe. I followed it with the cheering crowds down Constitution Hill to the Palace gates and saw the Queen's procession pass safely inside.

The Palace, Mr Holmes had said. Perhaps I had been wrong

and he right. The attack would come now. I was pressed far back in the crowds as the Queen came out on the balcony of the Palace and the cheering began again. How could they cheer when the Queen would be assassinated? Someone in the crowd shouted that the Queen was watching a parade of Blue-Jackets in the courtyard, but so thick were the crowds I could see no sailors. Every moment I expected the sound of a rifle.

None came.

Where now, as the Queen went back inside the Palace?

'Hurry,' Elsie had said.

'Think,' said Mr Holmes.

Other snatches came back to me . . . 'Well served . . .' 'No, but his servants may . . .'

What about the Queen's servants who guarded her and not her Army guards? The Queen's *Indian* servants. They were newly arrived and . . .

I must find Mr Holmes immediately. But where? How? I forced myself through to the front of the crowds, to the gates of the Palace courtyard. I could not enter them; they were too well guarded, not by police, who would recognise the name of Holmes, but the army. I was turned back.

Think, man, *think*. The servants' entrance! Perhaps there, or the mews. These were in Buckingham Palace Road, so yet again I found myself running, so fast now that my heart hurt with the strain. But what could I do? Leave it to burst with grief if I failed Elsie, if I failed my Queen?

This time it was uniformed police at the gates, but they turned a blank face to me when I asked for Mr Holmes. They told me to be gone.

I stood back and I howled to the skies: '*Fred Porlock!*'

Instantly, it seemed he was there, with half a dozen men in plain clothes who seized me, dragged me inside those gates as though I had wanted to escape them. And there was Mr Sherlock Holmes, looking strained and grim.

'Indian servants,' was all I could gasp out.

He groaned in disappointment. 'I was there before you. Two new ones arrived yesterday; we hold them already, but I fear we are too late. The mischief is done. Tell me their plan. The Queen's life may depend on it.'

'I do not know,' I sobbed. This had all been for nothing.

Mr Holmes did not reproach me, but looked at me kindly. 'Mr Porlock, you are a person of importance. *Think*. Where came your earlier information? From that murdered flower girl?'

So he knew about Elsie. I nodded. 'I was with her when she died.'

His eyes brightened. 'She spoke?'

'But one word, *hurry*, and I have been too late.'

He brushed this aside impatiently. '*Think*. Relive that moment, if you please. Speak as you do so.'

I closed my eyes, conscious of all these people around me waiting for me, hoping, demanding . . . Elsie was with me again, I took one breath and was back with her in the flower market: 'She is dying,' I whispered. 'I am putting my head close to her, trying to help, to hear if she would speak. She tries her very best, gasping, breathing out sounds from her throat . . .'

I sensed quickening interest around me, but I was with Elsie and must not lose her. I subdued the temptation to force the word from her. 'Tell me again, just as it was,' I whispered to her.

I listened and spoke: 'She is trying and it comes so softly like a breath itself, *hurry* – but she has no strength left, only the breath that comes as "hurry" because she can no longer form the proper sounds in her mouth . . .' And then I had it:

'*Curry!*' I cried.

One of the duties of Her Majesty's Indian servants was to prepare curry for Her Majesty, to which she had taken a liking. By the time they were apprehended in the Palace that day, so Mr Holmes told me later, the curry had already been prepared only for Her Majesty at the formal dinner that evening. It was found to be poisoned. The two Indian men who had come to join her household the day before the Jubilee were not those intended for the Palace staff, but assassins. Jesse Bracken had been ordered to meet the two genuine new Indian servants at Tilbury, but he had met his death. They were abducted by others of

Professor Moriarty's web, taken to Sussex and held in captivity. The plan had been to hold them there until their replacements had finished their perfidious work at the Palace, and these two genuine Indian servants had been fortunate not to be killed. On 23 June, two days after the Jubilee celebrations, Abdul Karim and Mahomet had been presented to Her Majesty and taken up their lawful appointment on her staff.

'But who would plan such an outrage?' I cried. 'Why would the Professor wish to kill his monarch?'

Mr Holmes frowned. 'That man's malignant intent would have daunted even Machiavelli. There are no lengths to which he will not go in pursuit of his own corrupt power. To those who do not know the truth, he is a brilliant and respected mathematician, a scientist of the first order. To those who do, he is the epitome of everything that is vile, but he brings to that the same brilliance with which he writes his learned tomes. His evil services are sought at the highest levels in kingdoms and empires far beyond this one.'

'By the Indian maharajahs?' I asked.

'I believe the plan we have foiled began much nearer our homeland than India. You have heard that the ruler of a certain European state is far from well?'

'The German emperor?'

'Please, no names. It is not generally known that the heir to the throne is also in bad health, and it is probable that his son will within the next few years bear the title of Kaiser.'

'The prince with a withered arm? But he would not wish to *poison* his grandmother.'

'You speak plainly, Mr Porlock, but you are correct. I fear the people he employs to perpetrate the practical jokes of which he is so fond are not all loyal to him. Instead of the mild emetic he had plotted to be added to her curry at the dinner that evening, a strong poison was substituted. There is a powerful circle in his country whom it would suit both to rid themselves of the Queen of England *and* to cast doubt over this Prince's suitability to rule over their nation and empire. And who, indeed, is to say that they are not right in that latter respect?'

'And the Professor's purpose?' I ventured to ask.

'Think of the power he would wield had this foul plan succeeded, of the great European monarchs he would have at his mercy. Why, he would have been an emperor himself, but of a sinister underworld that never seeks the light and wreaks only evil.'

'What will happen to the Professor now, Mr Holmes?'

'He and I will clash on more occasions I fear before my evidence is complete and he and that chief of staff of his, Colonel Sebastian Moran, are unmasked so that justice may take its course. If Moriarty is the core of all evil, then Moran is its physical presence. But it is for me, not you, Mr Porlock, to break Moriarty's power. As for you, forget the name Porlock, forget the Professor and his web, and take up some toil far from London.'

How greatly I wanted to follow his advice, but I could not. There would be other Elsies, innocent flies caught in a web whom I might manage to free. Roses, red roses . . .

'I cannot do so,' I told Mr Holmes in anguish.

Sherlock Holmes smiled. 'I see you wear a flower in your buttonhole, Mr Porlock, and I understand. Very well, *forget* we have ever met, as I shall forget both you and my involvement in this case. As long as you feel it is safe to do so, however, you will be of extreme importance in my quest.'

I was greatly moved. 'I will try to be so.'

He smiled. 'I shall not seek you out, so avail yourself of an appropriate means of communication between ourselves – you might consider Camberwell Post Office as a neutral channel. Use the name of Fred Porlock *only* to me. Pray continue, if you please, your invaluable role as a person of no importance.'

How the Professor Taught a Lesson to the Gnoles

Josh Reynolds

For Dunsany and Doyle

"A most peculiar problem, Mr Nuth, I do agree," the Professor said, in his sibilant way, as I sipped at his bitter tea. It was of his own devising, or so he assured me, brewed from the leaves of a certain flower that grew only on the most remote crags of the Scottish Highlands and mixed, improbably, with a jelly culled from the nests of wasps. "And they snatched him right through the knotholes, you say?"

"So I perceived, Professor Moriarty," I said, setting the tea aside, somewhat gratefully. It was not to my taste, but I had drunk enough, I thought, to avoid insult. It was not wise to insult the Professor, or to otherwise cross him. For as I was, in my own sphere, so too was he, in his. And even cunning Nuth knew better than to test the patience of the Napoleon of Crime, in his own apartments, no less. "They were . . . quite swift. Poor Tommy barely had time to scream."

"Such things often are. I have heard of the gnoles, though never have our paths crossed, for I do not much venture out of the city and, when I do, it is often to the continent, rather than the countryside." The Professor twitched his head. "I do know something of their methods, of course, and the fear that they incite in others, though they rarely leave their little dark house, in their dark woods." He looked at me. "You say you recorded certain details in your notebook? May I see it?" He held out one pale, thin-fingered hand, and I drew my notebook from the pocket of my waistcoat.

I was not surprised that he knew of it, or of my habit of recording my impressions, though writing was a task for which I had little patience. The Professor was a keen one, and sharp as an adder's fang. He took the notebook and flicked through it one-handed, his long thumb stabbing each page in turn. At certain points, he paused and his head oscillated slightly, as if in consideration of some point or other.

Eventually, he tossed the notebook back to me. "A problem, yes," he said, drawing out the sibilants in a peculiar manner. "But not an insurmountable one, I think." He met my gaze. "Your name is known to me, Mr Nuth. You are well spoken of, in certain circles. You do not advertise, for like my own, your skills are consummate."

I nodded, accepting the compliment. Moriarty smiled. "I seem to recall some outrage in Surrey, of late. The pilfering of Lord Castlenorman's shirt studs . . ."

I said nothing, for there was little to say that would not be viewed as boasting. And I am not, as a rule, inclined to the boastful. I am Nuth, and Nuth is me and all men know Nuth. Even the gnoles know Nuth, and I daresay that thought has kept me up at night.

"Tell me again," the Professor said. He leaned back in his chair, his hands clasped together before him. "Spare no detail, however inconsequential."

And so, I told him again of Tommy Tonker and how the youth's mother had brought him to me, in order to apprentice him so that he might learn a worthy trade. Moriarty nodded at this, for to him, the trade of thievery was an old and honoured one, with a storied history. After all, do we thieves not trace our lineage to Slith, and before him, Prometheus? The history of thievery is as storied as that of any noble house in Ruritania or Cephelais, and Nuth is said by some to be its grand culmination; though not me, for I am not, as I have said, inclined to the boastful. Tommy was a likely lad and he learned quickly how to cross bare boards without making a sound and how to go silently up creaky stairs. The business prospered greatly while Tommy was apprenticed to me and, after the affair of Lord Castlenorman's shirt studs, I judged it was time to try something more . . . extravagant.

To burgle the house of the gnoles had long been a going concern of mine. And not just mine, for the rumour of the great emeralds that the gnoles were reported to possess had drawn thieves of all stripes and reputations to that dreadful wood. Of course, none save Nuth had ever returned from the attempt.

The Professor smiled thinly as I spoke of young Tommy's hesitation as we entered that dreadful wood, and took the crooked, unmapped path to that narrow, lofty house where the gnoles and their fabulous, possibly fabricated, treasure waited. It was not a pleasant journey. One did not trespass twice in the dells of the gnoles, if one was caught, and there were many grisly memorials to those who had fallen afoul of them, nailed to the unwholesome trees. At those words, Moriarty snickered, as if at some private jest.

He leaned forward as I drew to the climax of my tale, his eyes bright with interest as I described how Tommy had climbed up to the old green casement window. And then how, as I watched from the corner of that dreadful house, young Tommy Tonker came to his predestined end. The gnoles had watched his approach through the knotholes of the trees that loomed close about the house, and they had taken him, even as he reached the window. Finished, I sat back. The Professor licked his lips. "How many?" he asked.

"How many what?" I replied, though I knew well what he meant.

The Professor held up a finger, as if in warning. I sighed. "Tommy makes four," I murmured. Four times I had tested the defences of the gnoles and four times I had come away empty-handed and lighter by an accomplice. Thus, rather than waste a fifth likely lad, I had come to the Professor in search of a solution. For he was considered, among certain parties, to be a man who could provide solutions to even the thorniest problems.

He gave a peculiar titter and shook his head. "I am in awe at your audacity, Mr Nuth. To sacrifice one, or even two young men on the altar of chance takes a chilly soul. But four? Ha! My respect for you grows in leaps and bounds." He leaned forward, his hands clapped to his knees, and chuckled wetly. When he had calmed himself, he looked at me expectantly.

"Half," I said, without hesitation.

He laughed, and my spine tingled. No, it was not wise to insult the Professor in his lair. Better still to steal the jewelled eyes of the spider god, or lean close and hear the words of the sphinx than risk the wrath of Moriarty, who was both sphinx and spider in equal measure, and more terrible than both, when roused.

"Two-thirds," I amended, spreading my hands. "I must have something, or else what for my reputation? Were I to receive less than a third of the potential proceeds from the proposed endeavour, Nuth needs must step aside, and allow some other to take his place at the top of the pyramid of thievery – shall I allow the foreigner Rocambole or the dissolute Raffles to wear the crown that is rightfully mine, then?"

Moriarty gestured sharply. "Your pride does you credit, Mr Nuth. It is a vice allowable only in great men, I think. A third, then, for you, and two-thirds for the grand old firm." He held out his pale hand. I took it, and tried to hide my wince at the sudden, albeit brief, crushing grip that enclosed my fingers. In my trade, fingers were everything. Moriarty knew that, and his grip was equal parts agreement and warning to me to play straight with him. Moriarty taught lessons with even the most innocuous gestures.

"When do we begin?" I asked, as I surreptitiously rubbed my hand.

"Why, my dear Mr Nuth . . . we have already begun," Moriarty said, as he sank back into his chair like a cobra back into its basket. He closed his eyes and tapped his prominent brow with two fingers. "The problem, such as it is, is threefold. To wit, how to approach undetected, how to enter safely and how to depart unmolested. You have accomplished the first, and the third—"

"Not without cost," I interjected.

One round eye cracked open, and I fell silent. A smile twitched at the corners of his mouth, and the eye closed again.

"Cost is subjective," he murmured. "A pound for one man is but a pence for another. No, it is to the second prong of the matter that we must attend. That particular house is guarded more ferociously than any bank, and more cunningly than any museum. Subtlety will avail little, I fear. Thus, we must turn to the brute arts. The gnoles . . . what do we know of them, Nuth? What is their shape, their mien, their physiognomy? How many limbs, and their allotment?"

"No man knows, for no man lives to say," I said.

"But you observed them in action, did you not? And you have done so more than once. You are the best man to hazard a guess," he said, and motioned as if to a hesitant student.

I chewed my lip, considering. Then I said, "They are not large, or else are possessed of protean proportions. The swiftness of their movements put me in mind of an octopus I saw once. But they have eyes, and need very little light. They also have an . . . odour."

The Professor nodded as I spoke, and his finger twitched in the air, as if scratching out calculations. "Strong too, I should say," he added, when I had finished.

"I thought that went without saying," I said.

"Mm." Moriarty leaned back, eyes still closed. "What of their nature? What drives them? Is it hunger alone, or are they possessed of more than their share of malevolence? Why lurk in a black house, in the black woods, so far away from their chosen prey? Answer that, and we may have them."

"I cannot speak to their nature, I fear," I said. "Only to mine."

Moriarty's head bobbed. "Of course, of course. It is of no import, not for this trifling matter. We do not need to understand them to burgle them." He twitched his head towards the grimy single window of the Soho flat in which we had chosen to meet, and looked out, over the wilds of London. "Still . . . to understand a thing is to own it," he said, after a moment, in a musing fashion. "I understand London, Mr Nuth. As you understand the ways of property and its redistribution."

"Your ownership is not in dispute," I said. "I am content with my fiefdom, small as it is."

"Yes, the finest house in Belgravia Square, save the pipes, I am informed."

I tensed as the words left Moriarty's lips. Was it a warning? Or more akin to the unsheathing of a cat's claws, as it stretched in contentment? In the end, I decided it was neither. It was merely Moriarty amusing himself, and again, teaching me a lesson. I inclined my head again, and he smiled.

"Leave it with me, Mr Nuth. I shall have your solution by week's end, I feel. And then, together, we shall take a trip out of town, into the country, and these old dark woods of yours. We shall visit the gnoles, Mr Nuth, and teach them a lesson that they will never forget."

And, true to his word, and warning, it was by week's end that one of the Professor's aides, an inconsequential man by the name of Parker, arrived at the house in Belgravia, and slipped in through a second storey window. Parker, a garrotter by trade, or so he proudly informed me upon arrival, had brought news – the Professor had solved my problem.

We caught the train from Victoria, Parker and I. As the iron snake wound its way towards a certain village, on the edge of a dark wood, Parker provided entertainment of sorts, after proving himself to have remarkable skill with the Jew's Harp. When we reached the station nearest the village that backed upon the forest of the gnoles, we found transportation awaiting us in the form of a horse and trap.

It was late afternoon by the time we reached that peculiar village, where all of the houses face away from the raw, untilled fields that separate it from the grim forest. Not a window or door is allowed to open on those trees, for reasons best left to your imagination. Having some small experience with the forest in question, and its masters, I found myself in sympathy with the dull-eyed villagers, who watched the goings-on in their market square from behind half-closed doors, and curtained windows.

The Professor had made the square his classroom and workshop, and stood atop a long-dry fountain, gesticulating with his cane, as his men scurried about a cumbersome cauliflower of iron and brass. As Parker and I drew closer, I saw that the cauliflower was anything but, for what member of the Brassicaceae family had ever possessed great grinding treads and an armoured shell the likes of which to put any crustacean to shame?

"A borrowed design, of course," the Professor called out, over the noise of the preparations. "A stew, you might say, from the hands of several cooks – a bit of Da Vinci and Brunel, a dollop of Archimedes and a smidgen of Oriental know-how from a certain Sikh of my acquaintance." The Professor slithered over to meet us, head bobbing in excitement. "Parker, distribute the firearms – one to a man! – and get aboard." Moriarty extracted a pocket watch from his waistcoat and eyed it, and then the sky, suspiciously. "The sun sets quickly here, Mr Nuth. Dashed quickly, but we shall make good time, once we are under way."

"Under way," I exclaimed. "You cannot mean—?"

"Oh but I do, Mr Nuth, I do indeed. Get aboard with you, man," he said, gesturing with his cane towards a round hatch in the great monstrosity's side, where the ever-gregarious Parker was waiting for us. "Our time draws short."

The interior of the beast was as uncomfortable as I had imagined, a cattle car of hard surfaces. Most of the space was taken up by the wide bank of controls – levers, pistons, cords and the like, the purpose of which I could scarcely fathom, set beneath a reinforced and barred slit, which allowed one to see what lay directly in front of the machine. Moriarty took up a position before this odd conglomeration like a captain at the helm of his vessel and signalled for Parker to seal the hatch. Behind us, the men Moriarty had hastened aboard took their seats on the hard benches that had been provided for just that purpose. "I took my inspiration from the Bohemian Hussites, who waged war from armoured wagons," the Professor said. "History, of course, is full of such lessons for those with but the wit to learn."

"An armoured wagon," I said, as a great rumbling roar set the whole conveyance to shaking. From somewhere within its depths, I heard the telltale gurgle of a boiler, and knew that the machine was powered by steam and coal, like a train compacted into a third the size and twice the mass. "Surely we cannot think to sneak into the house of the gnoles with such a device," I said, as the world gave a lurch and a rattle and the great machine began to move. Like a snail, at first, and then with a tortoise's lumbering pace.

"I told you, the problem was threefold," the Professor said, over the noise of the great engine. "How to approach undetected, how to enter safely, and how to depart unmolested. The answer, of course, was to do none of those things, but to plan for the reverse. As I said, subtlety will not serve in this instance . . . thus, the way of the brute, the basher, and the bagger." He reached up and hauled on a dangling whistle cord, filling the open field before the forest with a keening shriek. We were moving faster now, at a wolf's lope.

"You think they will hear us and leave?" I shouted, fighting to be heard over the infernal engines. "That they will flee, leaving us free to pick their lair clean?"

"Ha! No," he said. "Cast your mind to my second question, Mr Nuth . . . why do they live where they do, so far from their preferred source of sustenance? The answer, when considered carefully, is simple – they cannot go anywhere else! No, they will not flee, because they cannot. It is often the way of such folk. So they will muster their defences, our gnolish foes, and prepare for war. For war is what I intend to wage – total and unrelenting. I shall teach them the lessons of Troy, of Sarnath and of Peking. Where guile fails, force prevails. We shall smash through their knotty walls and shoot, stab and burn them in the best piratical tradition." He swung out a hand, indicating Parker and the others, all of whom were armed and certainly fierce enough for the comparison, I judged.

"That answers the first two parts of the problem," I said. "What of the third part? How will we escape? Unless you intend to exterminate them root and branch?" The thought filled me with no small amount of trepidation. Even armed and armoured by the monstrous engine, I felt the forest bearing down on me as we drew near to it. It was old and hard and wild in a way that not even Moriarty's diabolical sciences could defend against. And from the look that passed quickly across his face, I knew the Professor felt the same way.

"The third part," he said, "is well in hand, Mr Nuth. Such is the guarantee of the grand old firm." Then he turned away and leaned over his levers and cranks, urging his war wagon forward. For some time afterward, the only sound, besides the gurgle of the boiler and the growl of the engines, was the crash of falling trees and the noise of their splintering beneath our remorseless treads.

It took us little time to smash a path through those close-set and unruly trees. When one moves without care, dark paths do not take so long to tread. As we drew close to the narrow house of the gnoles, Moriarty hissed an order and his men lurched to their feet to man the narrow firing slits that lined the armoured hull of the machine. Carbines were aimed, and Parker played a cheery tune on his Jew's Harp. My palms were damp, and my throat dry. The Professor, for his part, hunched over his controls like a conductor over his sheet music.

A pair of crooked trees, blistered with knotholes, were ground under and suddenly the house came into sight through the viewing slit. Moriarty released one lever and pumped another, bringing the machine to a slow, onerous halt. The boiler audibly shuddered, and the whole contraption shook like a man afflicted with ague.

There was no sign of life from the house. There was no bird-song in the trees, not even the hum of insects, only the steady, dull grind of the engines and the breathing of the men in the rear of the war wagon. Nevertheless, I knew that we were being watched, sized up and somehow found wanting. I glanced at the Professor, and I saw that he knew it as well. His lips peeled back from yellow, thin teeth and his eyes sparked with an ugly light as he reached for the lever that would propel his construct forward. He hesitated, head cocked, as if listening. With every moment that passed, I expected some reaction from the gnoles, but none was forthcoming. It was as if, knowing of the Professor's expectations, they had decided to confound him by simply staying hidden.

His head oscillated, his eyes scanning the house, the green casement window where poor Tommy had met his fate, and his thin shoulders shook with what I suspected to be frustration.

I wanted to speak, but held my tongue. This was the Professor's pitch, and I was but an observer. "Fine then," he said, so softly I almost missed it. "If you will not come out, we shall come in."

The great machine groaned as he threw the lever, and it lurched forward, at all speed. Wood cracked and splintered as the war wagon crashed into the house, rupturing its aged face in a single, titanic motion. The uppermost levels swayed drunkenly as the Professor jerked and slashed with the arrangement of levers. Roof tiles, covered in centuries' worth of moss, pattered across the hull of the machine like hard rain. Old furniture, mildewed and puffy with mould, burst like toadstools as the war wagon forced itself deeper into the house, like a wolf gnawing on the innards of a deer.

When the first gunshot came, it was a surprise. I whirled, hands clutching uselessly at nothing. There was nowhere to hide within the belly of the beast, and I had not brought a weapon. Nuth is not a man for conflict, but the Professor's crew seemed to thrive on it. Parker led the others in a rousing hymn of repeating fire that would have done the South Wales Borderers proud. I spun in place, searching the nearby gun-slits for any sign of gnoles, but, if they were there, they were moving too swiftly for me to see.

I turned back to the Professor, where he stood before the controls, and saw that his attentions were fixed upon something ahead. He muttered to himself – calculations, I thought. Then, I heard the sound of wood creaking, and the war wagon lurched in an unpleasant fashion. Moriarty threw a lever and stepped back, straightening his waistcoat as he did so. "As I suspected," he said, as he made his way towards the hatch. "Mr Parker! It is time to disembark."

The Professor caught my arm and shoved me towards the hatch. "We have only a few moments, Mr Nuth. Best be quick."

"What is it? What's going on?"

"This house is but a shell – an overgrown knothole, if you will, in a thoroughly rotten tree. And we have cored it out and put much strain on the roots. So, now . . ."

"The tree is coming down," I said, as I squeezed out of the

hatch and dropped to the ground. The Professor followed me, walking stick in hand. As I stood, I looked about, keenly conscious of the fact that I was at last in the house of the gnoles. In many respects, it was a normal house, save for the damage caused by the wagon. A rotten house, a house that had seen better years, but a house.

That, if anything, only added to the strangeness of it. Moonlight pierced the trees and sagging, shattered roof, pinning the shadows in place. In that darkness, as deep as Roman wells, things moved. Things without shape, but more substance than I was comfortable with. They were humanoid at first and then rather like Jerusalem artichokes and, as they humped and slumped and slunk about us, their shapes billowed and shrunk like shadows cast by a fire. One of these shadows detached itself and slithered forward on too many legs, or perhaps too few, and I had the impression of many teeth and eyes winking like emeralds.

I leapt, and rolled, avoiding the claws I felt, more than saw. The gnole turned on a dime, eyes blinking, and then one went out as the Professor taught it its first lesson – never come within arm's length of a man with a walking stick. I had not seen him draw the thin blade from its sheath of walnut, but, as he swept it out, it caught the moonlight and drew the gaze of the gathered gnoles. They learned their second lesson then, about not ignoring men with carbines in favour of a man with a sword.

At Parker's cry, the disembarking criminals fired a ragged salvo, and gnolish eyes winked out as the dark was pierced by tongues of flame. Over the sound of this fusillade came the eerie groan of oft-abused joists and popping nails. The war wagon heaved, shimmied and then . . . fell. All at once, and promptly, as the floor gave way beneath it. It took men with it, down into the dark, and their screams trailed up and up, much as poor Tommy's had done.

The gnoles came in a rush then, a tide of slavering shadows that seemed to blend together into one. The Professor rattled off firing solutions with chill precision, and, where he gestured, gnoles died, or at least fell. But there were so many, boiling up out of the dark like ants; I had never, even in my most extravagant fantasies, conceived of such numbers and I knew then that the rumours of emeralds in the house of the gnoles were just that. I knew then that what men had claimed to see had been nothing more than the eyes of the gnoles themselves, watching from the corners and casements.

Parker caught my arm, his face as white as flour, and the Webley in his hand smoking. "The Professor says to run, Mr Nuth – run!" And, as if to lead by example, he did so, bounding away from me like a rabbit. I did not need to be told twice, and I too took to my heels. I was not alone. Men streamed past and around me, running for their lives, all thought of plunder forgotten in the mad rush of fear. They scattered through the crooked woods, but I kept to the path, running for the free field and the village beyond.

As I ran, the night was punctuated by screams and cries as men were taken, one after another, by the gnoles. I am not ashamed to admit that I leapt over one such struggling knot of fell shapes and anguished cries, and did not look back. I ran and ran, and, all the while, something kept pace, following me unerringly through the trees. Gnoles, I knew, were very fast, and I heard them slashing through the trees on either side of me, their emerald eyes glinting at me. No man had ever caught Nuth, but gnoles were not men, and I wondered, in those moments, whether my legend was to end like Slith's, in grandeur and painful mystery.

Then, within sight of freedom, calamity. A root, or perhaps a claw, caught my foot and graceful Nuth, catlike Nuth, went end over end in the dirt. As I scrambled upright, a black shape flowed towards me, teeth shining like stickpins. There was a flash, and a sound like a boiling tea-kettle, and the shape receded, dripping something foul.

"Up, Mr Nuth," the Professor intoned, sword-stick extended. Sweat creased his withered features, and I realised that it had been he who had been on my heels. He glanced down at me and smiled, as if he'd read my thoughts. "You have been here before, Mr Nuth. I am no fool, to wander in the dark without a guide."

As I got to my feet, I saw that we were barely a hair's breadth from the forest's edge, but I knew that if we made for it, the gnoles would surely pull us down. The Professor knew it as well, and made no move to run. Instead, he said, "Quite something, that."

"What?"

"The house – it is not theirs. Or, not their lair. No, they live beneath it, beneath this whole dratted wood, like rats in the walls, or worms in the earth, burrowed down deep in the soil. They stretch down as deep as the tree roots, I expect." He paused and raised his sword-stick as a gnole drew too close. "Back away, sir. Thank you. But they go down, not out. Only to the circumference of this wood, else all of London would be as a molehill. Curiouser and curiouser." He looked at me. "There are no emeralds."

"No," I said.

"A shame. But treasures are a trifle, compared to knowledge."

"What of survival?" I asked hoarsely, as the gnoles closed in on us, hemming us in.

"Ah, even better." Moriarty eyed the gnoles the way a hyena might eye a circling lion: wary respect, tinged with cunning calculation. Moriarty, as I had come to learn, was always calculating. Always thinking, always weaving his schemes, plots and stratagems. That was his art, as thievery was mine. He held up two fingers, and gestured curtly.

The shot, when it came, made no sound. I heard it nonetheless, for I have long practised the skill of hearing what is not there. In the empty space between the breeze and the rasp of creaking branches, I heard the whisper of the bullet as it passed over my shoulder. And then, more loudly, I heard the pumpkin-groan of the lead gnole's head as it split open and spilled out its dark contents on the forest floor. I blinked in shock, and I fancy the gnoles did as well.

Moriarty held up his hand. "Mr Nuth, take one step back. You are in Colonel Moran's line of fire, by several millimetres."

I hesitated. The gnoles watched me. Moriarty watched me. Then I took one step back. The gnoles began to move. Moriarty gestured again, and another indistinct shape slumped, strange skull split by the passage of a bullet.

"There is a line, gentlemen," Moriarty called out. "A line you cannot cross. I have moved it by several paces, as you can observe. It will return to its original place when we are safely away. You understand?" He twitched his hand. It was the gnoles' turn to hesitate. Then, as one, they shuffled back. His smile was more terrible than any undulation of the gnolish physiognomy I had yet observed. He nodded. "Yes. You can be taught. Good. Perhaps there is a future for you yet in this world." His smile faded. "Then, perhaps not." He lowered his hand.

A third and final shot stretched out from the unseen shooter's weapon and struck a branch, dropping it at the feet of the gnoles. Moriarty held them with his gaze, slightly stooped, hands behind his back, his sword-stick held loosely. Then, without a word, he turned away and strode past me. "Come, Mr Nuth. It has been a tiresome day, and I would be done with forests and the things that creep within them."

We did not have far to walk. A trap and horse was waiting for us, a man holding the reins. He tipped his cap to Moriarty, as the latter climbed aboard. He ignored me. I did not speak until the horse had plodded along for some time. "What of the others?" I asked.

"I fancy there will be no others. If I am wrong, they will seek me out and I will compensate them accordingly," he said. Something of my feelings must have crossed my face, for he said, "Cost is subjective, Mr Nuth. And treasures but a trifle. You know that as well as I, I fancy."

"You knew that they would defeat your machine," I said.

Moriarty oscillated his head towards me. "I planned for it, yes. That is what I do, Mr Nuth. I plan," he said. He tapped his veined brow for emphasis. "The devil, as they say, is in the details."

"You knew that they would pursue us," I continued. "You wanted them to. You practically taunted them into it, with all your crashing and shootings. Why?"

Moriarty cocked his head. "You tell me, Mr Nuth. You are observant, sir. Surely you have come to some conclusion of your own."

I met his gaze. He had the air of a tutor, waiting for a student to unravel some theorem. The Professor, at his art. Then, I had it. "You wanted to see if your theory were correct," I said, slowly.

He smiled, and I knew instantly that I had guessed wrong. He patted my shoulder, as if comforting a particularly dull-witted child. "Stick to your trade, Mr Nuth. And I shall stick to mine."

And so I did.

And, you may ask, did I ever discern the true motivations behind the Professor's lesson to the gnoles?

Oh no, my friend.

No one ever learns what the Professor does not wish them to know.

The Swimming Lesson

Priscilla Masters

It was Uncle James who taught me to swim. He underlined how important it was. Pointed out that one day it might even save my life. My father, who is a pragmatist, argued with him. He insisted that, as we lived inland and I was not in the habit of frequenting lakes or rivers, it was an unnecessary skill to acquire. 'Far better for the child to learn to read and perhaps to sew,' he grumbled, challenging his brother for once. 'And certainly to cook,' he added, looking slyly across at me. But already I felt rebellious. I slipped my hand into Uncle James's and he bent down and winked at me, patting my head. I treasure that memory now. I believe I was eight years old at the time and I knew that if it came to it Uncle James had a stronger character than my father. It would be my father who would back down.

And so it proved. Little more than a week later, my father silently handed me a bathing suit and Uncle James winked at me again. 'Come, Cicely my dear,' he said to me. 'Shall we now go for a drive in the country?'

My father grumbled again and made weak objection. 'She should be helping her mother. There is work to do around the station, beds to be made, weeds to be lifted, platforms to be swept.' Uncle James silenced his babble with a stare. It was then that I first realized that my father was not simply in awe of his brother. He was afraid. He soon dropped his eyes and contented himself with bustling importantly around the station, waving flags and strutting up and down the platform.

Uncle James watched him for a moment, almost pityingly, then we left.

He drove me to a nearby lake and left me discreetly in the carriage while I donned my bathing dress and the horses grazed. He himself was soon handsomely attired in a black woollen bathing suit. Tall and thin with a large domed forehead, (an indication of his outstanding mathematical ability) and the bowed shoulders of an academic, he still looked as though he could swim the length and breadth of the lake. I looked up at him, trustingly. He then led me to the water's edge. It was a warm day but I shivered. I was anxious for Uncle James not to perceive my anxiety and so masked it with a smile, trying to display a confidence I was far from feeling. Of course I wanted to learn to swim, even if only to please him, and yet I was seized with fearfulness as I looked over the lake. The waters were calm, but, as I watched, a small wave lifted and tossed white foam into the air before dropping back into the surface with a loud and threatening splash as though to scare me away. Was this perhaps a premonition? If it was my uncle did not seem to recognize it as such, merely taking a step or two towards the water's edge and scooping deep breaths in in preparation for the exertion. The lake was near our house and but a short drive away. It would have been easy for me to escape the swimming lesson and run back home. But, as I glanced back along the track and heard the sound of a train puffing into the station, I knew that I could not let my uncle down by showing cowardice. He believed in me. I had to learn to swim at least a stroke or two before I returned to my home.

'Come, Cicely,' he said, perhaps understanding my apprehension. 'Do not be afraid. It is merely a matter of confidence and trust.' He paused, looking at me intently. '*Do* you trust me, Cicely?'

For answer, I stepped into the water and moved steadily forward until it was waist deep. He then held my chin while I kicked my legs and that afternoon I believe I did manage to stay afloat for a few seconds before sinking to the bottom and spluttering beneath the water's surface. Uncle James laughed and showed much amusement but some tolerance too. We resumed our activity. After about an hour of splashing, he put his face near to mine. 'Have you had enough, child?'

Slowly, I shook my head. 'I have not, Uncle.'

He seemed pleased at my response. 'Plucky,' he muttered. 'Brave too.' Then, 'Shall we try again?'

Truth was I was frightened. That terror of falling beneath the water, of it closing all around, over my head, filling my nose and mouth, of my lungs being deprived of air, slowly filling with water. It is a horrid feeling. But I knew he would admire me more if I persevered. And so I did. My teeth were chattering both from fear and from the cold so I bit my lips to prevent them from exposing my cowardice.

However, after a further half-hour, he smiled. 'Come, Cicely,' he said. 'Enough for today. You have shown courage and have done well. Soon you shall be able to swim.' And, as we returned to the carriage to change, he added, almost to himself, 'One day it might truly save your life.'

It did not save his. I learned by the foulest and cruellest of means that swimming could not have saved him, that he was mortally wounded by hitting his head on a rock before he touched the water. I was almost sixteen when this happened.

How did I find out this grisly detail? you wonder. Effrontery. That is how. Sheer brazen flagrant parading of my uncle's death. Publication of the very tiniest detail. That man had the audacity to publish a record of my poor uncle's death combined with a torrent – yes – I use that word deliberately – a torrent of spurious tales and opinions as to my uncle's character. Words like *evil* and *king-devil*, endowing him with a criminal strain. A matter of opinion, I say, for cannot black appear white and white black in distorted vision? Cannot left look right from a reverse angle? I say my uncle was brilliant. Good and evil is irrelevant. He taught society that cold planning combined with a genius of a brain could achieve much. The snake-doctor writes his stories with a mixture of admiration and disgust but no understanding whatsoever. He did not know the man as I did. And I have had to keep silent and smile while I have heard my dearest uncle both insulted and complimented. Called *the greatest schemer, filled with devilry* and possessing a *controlling brain* while he, the arch-enemy, grudgingly but truthfully, tells us that my uncle James could have made or marred the destiny of nations. Tributes indeed, but the reader's opinions might well be distorted by the tone of these backhanded compliments. It is not Uncle James's intelligence that is under question, or his wealth, which I have good reason to believe remains unsurpassed, and which will, eventually, all come to me. No, it is certainly not his intelligence, but his morals that are under the microscope. I ask you then to adjudicate. Was this the act of an evil man, to teach a child to swim in the belief that one day she might need this skill? Truth is it was he, the king-enemy, who spoke the truest tribute to my uncle when he described his stooge as *foul-mouthed doctor* and sympathized with my Uncle James as *slandered professor.*

How true.

I have been denied the right to defend him publicly as I would like so it is the scribblings of this 'foul-mouthed doctor' that reach the public consciousness. Nor have I yet the opportunity to put the record straight to those who are deliberately misled as to my uncle's motives. Do they not realize it was all an intellectual exercise? To him, nothing but entertainment, a way of avoiding boredom and removing unwanted obstacles? But to defend him would be to expose myself and Uncle James taught me, not only to swim, but also the virtue of caution. 'Your greatest asset, Cicely,' he said one day shortly before his terrible death, 'is your anonymity. Nobody knows of your existence.'

My father too, though much less forcefully, has warned me of the same. 'You are safer, Cicely,' he said, following events with concern, 'to remain as you are.'

I nodded my acquiescence, understanding the advice.

But, in quiet and private moments, I still savour great pride in my uncle. Even the king-enemy described him as a Napoleon of crime, a genius, a philosopher, an abstract thinker possessing a brain of the first order. He acknowledged that Uncle James was the spider in the centre of a web that had a thousand radiations. A thousand, mark you. True. I subscribe to that. Even that king of smug devils has paid tribute to his intellect. 'My intellectual equal,' he called him, even as he cast his net around him. This mesh of which, I have to tell you, with some mirth, that my uncle had no trouble swimming through.

Initially.

Intellectual equal? An insult. How could he not realize my uncle's brain surpassed his one thousand times?

But there is one phrase he used which rankles. *Heredity of a most diabolical kind.* Was my uncle simply a result of genetics? Where does this leave his family? I wonder. My father? Myself?

And the word 'diabolical'? I think not. For, as I have pointed out, it depends on your point of view who is devil and who deity.

My second and third swimming lessons were more successful, though I still had not the confidence to swim right across the lake, which I knew was Uncle James's ambition. I lacked the skill or the strength and initially the confidence. But I persevered.

By the fifth lesson, I was swimming like a little fish. The crawl, the frog-like breaststroke, a backstroke, afloat, until my uncle slapped me on the back and I saw the pride glow from his deeply sunken eyes. Then I knew how I had pleased him.

On the eighth lesson, I finally succeeded in swimming right across the lake, my uncle by my side, urging me on, encouraging me and clapping when I reached the water's edge on the far side and then applauding me as I swam back. And myself? I thought I would burst with pride. I knew how I had pleased him. And I needed no more lessons in swimming. Something in my uncle seemed to relax then; lines of worry were erased from his face. 'One less thing to fret about,' he said, making a rare effort at jolliness.

When I was twelve years old, the relationship between us began to change. He no longer treated me as a child but more as an equal. He shared his secrets with me, began to school me in the complexities of business. He would ask my opinion and test me on mathematical equations. Discuss the solution to various problems.

His pride in my abilities made us closer than before and, for a time, his visits became more frequent as I grew older. When I was thirteen years old, he began to train me as though I was his

apprentice. 'Can you remember calculus?' he would bark and I
recited it.

'Pythagoras's theorem?'

'That too, Uncle,' I replied, confident in my memory.

His smile was rare and reward enough. Then, beetling
eyebrows meeting over deep eagle's eyes, 'Ah, but Cicely,' he
said. 'Do you *understand* them? Are you simply a parrot or do
you have a brain?'

And so I explained as though I was the teacher and he the
pupil. He watched me keenly for a moment then bent forward.
It was then, at that exact moment, that he took me further into
his confidence. 'One day, my child,' he said, 'you will understand
more than Pythagoras or Archimedes and you will have to make
your choice.' He then talked to me about the defeat of obstacles
whether mechanical or physical. He talked to me about ambition
and the cost to any who stood in the way of that. And I began to
have some insight into his life. I listened without judgment,
knowing that his talents brought him profit and a certain satisfaction, pitting his wits against many, but there was only one person
he considered worthy of his attentions. 'The man has his talents,'
he would say grudgingly. 'But he also has flaws, weaknesses to
which *I* am not prone. His brain,' he mused, 'is analytical but he
has a distorted allegiance to what *he* considers right and good.'

He watched me slyly. 'I have to warn you of this person,' he
said, 'and his sidekick, whose primary function, it would seem, is
to make my adversary appear more intelligent than he is.'

I listened and learned. He was silent for a moment before he
added softly, 'I may not always be here for you.'

I pretended I had not heard this unwelcome sentiment.

Even more softly, almost a whisper to himself, he mused, 'He
comes ever closer. I must protect you from him.'

Before I continue with my explanations, I must tell you that
from that day I met some of my uncle's associates: Colonel
Moran, who was unsure how to treat me and became embarrassed and awkward in my presence as well as alarmed that my
uncle was sharing so much confidence with me. Sometimes I
would hear him talk to my uncle. 'James, for goodness' sake. She

is just a child. Do not trust her with such knowledge.' And his glare at me contained hostility and something else. Something that appraised and frightened me. It was almost as though he perceived me as a rival? A rival? Ridiculous. I was a child. But, all the same, when I felt the chill of those cold blue eyes on me, I would clutch my uncle's hand tightly, wanting protection. And when Colonel Sebastian Moran looked down at me, as I clutched my uncle's hand, to my surprise, behind the ice I saw something else – fear. One day, I thought, there might well be conflict. And if I did not have my uncle to protect me would the Colonel still fear me? Or should I fear him? I wondered at this and, like a man flexing his muscles, I tested my own mental strength and found it equal to his.

Uncle James stuck up for me. 'A child indeed, Sebastian. Twelve years old by the year but with the intelligence of an adult. Surpassing many – no most – adults.' His face clouded and I knew he would like to have been able to substitute *most* for *all*. But his mathematical brain forced him to commit to facts and so even then he had to acknowledge the presence of the other.

'Why,' he continued playfully, 'this is a woman of awesome intelligence still in a child's body.' And he would parade me, like a dancing dog, to add up columns of figures or remember some complex cipher. He would show my talents off like a clown taught to catch biscuits in his mouth. And he would have a look of pride when I proved him right time and time again and the words he whispered in my ear made me glow. 'Well done, Cicely, my dear.'

And, once, I even met Porlock, the traitor, who trailed pathetically behind them, the jackal feeding off the lion's leavings, the remora cleaning the parasites from the skin of the shark. A lesser being in all ways and, it proved, a traitorous one.

The weak link in the chain who will meet his maker sooner than he thinks. *Wait for me, Porlock. I will find you.*

So back to the tragedy and its aftermath.

I knew Uncle James was a man who had enemies, a man who was frequently misunderstood. He had told me as such. Sometimes, he would not visit for weeks and I would become anxious and fret, worrying that these enemies were moving closer. 'Where is Uncle James?' I would demand of my father and he would pretend at first not to hear me, but busy himself around the station, reluctant to give me an answer. I believe that my father was, in fact, jealous of the relationship between myself and his brother. Perhaps, if not jealous then wary. It fretted him and made him jumpy and nervous. He was suspicious of all strangers, which could make life difficult, as his job as a station-master brought him into contact with the general public. He pondered my question as to where his brother was and when he had thought of an answer (for this is what I believe he did, made it all up), he would feed me some far-fetched tale, 'He is lecturing in Germany', or 'researching into some new astronomical phenomenon'. After Uncle James had left the university over a misunderstanding, my father would say he was, 'away on Army exercises', as he was subsequently an Army coach. Even, once or twice, when my father could think of no more convincing argument, he would come up with, 'taking himself a holiday'. Said gruffly in the knowledge that I was aware it was a lie. But I did not pursue the truth.

Uncle James was, of course, an academic, a man who had written books and such men do make enemies, but these jealous rivals (as I initially supposed them to be) seemed to annoy him greatly.

He asked me one day just before my fifteenth birthday what I thought of him being called a criminal.

I thought carefully before I made reply. Slipped my hand in his and looked up trustingly. 'By whom are you called this?' And when he did not provide an answer, I continued. 'It depends on your point of view,' I said coolly. 'Crime is simply disagreeing with rules set by a government. Perhaps there are times when those rules should be—' again I chose my word with great care '—ignored.'

He looked utterly thrilled at this. 'It depends on your point of view,' he repeated, smiling. 'Rules should be ignored.' Then, bright-eyed, 'Cicely, we need to work. The time has come.'

It began as a game – almost a board game – though I was

perfectly aware that it was, in fact, a test. He drew plans of a building. Doorway, windows, access front and back. A burglar alarm and a safe. He looked at me sideways, his face curious and alight. 'With what do you associate a safe?'

'With money, Uncle.'

'And so they protect it.'

I dropped my eyes back over the diagram and saw at once what detail he had filled in. 'But,' I began and his eyes now were aflame.

'That is true. So the test is, my dearest child, how do you gain access to the building without attracting attention? And then how do you extract the money from the safe?' He held up one long bony index finger. 'Not you, my dear,' he said quickly. 'I would not risk you. This is a theoretical problem. We employ others to carry out the deed. Others less important. We are the conductor of the orchestra, they the second fiddles. And we take steps to ensure that should events go awry they are not aware of our identity. This is an important detail, Cicely. You see, my dear, this is a game of no risk. For remember, even with the best of planning things can go wrong. Events can become subject to the rule of chance, which is no rule at all but the sad tendency of events to entangle themselves and introduce entropy, chaos and what less scientific brains might call bad luck. A policeman wandering tardily on a beat when he should have been long gone. A nosey neighbour, a barking dog. An obstruction. The risks are endless. No. We are, you and I, simply the brains behind it. That is our role. We have the ideas and the means to think of a way through the maze. We can evaluate possibilities; work out risk potential. They cannot. They are simple henchmen. The foot soldiers in our game.'

Another eagle's glance. 'And, tell me, Cicely, what if you should doubt the loyalty of one of these – erm – henchmen?'

I simply looked at him. Words were quite unnecessary. Our looks exchanged a thousand of them, flowing in a river of silent conversation. All the dark deeds and punishment meted out to traitors, the cruelty that was sometimes necessary to discipline. We understood one another.

I hardened my eyes and my mouth and uttered one word: 'Dispensable.'

He smiled his agreement, nodding that large head like a wise old mandarin. His hand twitched as though he would have patted me on the head. But he remembered himself and desisted, straightening his shoulders and moving back.

Then he returned to the question and the diagram. 'And so?'

I looked down and immediately saw the weak points. The burglar alarm on the outside of the building was a simple hammer attached to a bell. A piece of leather inserted before the door was opened would muffle the sound sufficiently. I relayed this fact to Uncle James and his mouth curved with pleasure. 'That,' he said, 'was too simple a test.' His gaze returned to the diagram and his finger moved to point out the second obstacle he had drawn. 'And the safe?'

'A simple matter of a stethoscope, Uncle. The turn of a wheel and the recognition of clicks as the cogs fall into place.'

He looked even more pleased. 'We shall have to increase the difficulty, my dear. That was too easy.'

And so he did. He gave me tests of people protecting themselves in moated houses, of others who surrounded themselves with bodyguards, of traitors who appeared to have vanished into thin air. Of lost identities, of inconvenient corpses, of murders made to look like accidents, and other deaths rearranged to mimic suicide. He gave me names of folk suitable for each job, both men and women, dedicated to carrying out his solutions to problems.

We enjoyed planning our ventures together, sparring as worthy partners as we exchanged ideas and searched for solutions to the most difficult of problems. No problem, I thought one day, with the conceit and confidence of the young, was insurmountable once we had *both* set our brains to tease it out.

And the spark that kept me alight? His approval initially followed by his admiration, never expressed by other than a light hand on my shoulder, a glow of pride in his eyes and a rare smile.

The problems he set grew ever more challenging. From access to difficult sites to people who protected themselves with locks and chains. But there is no lock that cannot be picked, with patience, a steady hand and a finely tuned ear. And so we sat with our lists of minions and their skills, with plans of buildings, with obstacles to be removed and we matched talent to chore. Then, shortly before my sixteenth birthday, I saw my uncle for the last time. This time he seemed agitated. Troubled – deep in his soul. 'My enemies close in on me,' he said, speaking quickly. 'Time is short and I must leave you, but only for a little while.' He then confided in me, telling me a secret. One he had kept from me until this time.

I never saw him again. My father remained stubbornly quiet on the matter however many times I pestered him and my mother simply looked blank at my questions, paling and stuttering out the fact that she did not know – anything.

Imagine then my horror to learn of his murder at the hands of *that one* of his enemies. And for the events to be told as a story, a tale perhaps, to be related to children to frighten them if they failed to behave. Presented as a little light entertainment to be enjoyed by people over their morning toast and marmalade. A small narrative to be gasped and gossiped over at the club. Cheap entertainment for the masses.

I read the detail presented in so cavalier a fashion with mounting fury. The decoying of the doctor, the finding of the Alpine-stock. Small details that hammered home my determination to exact revenge. I read on. The two lines of footprints – none to return, the torn brambles and ferns, the letter he had allowed his adversary to write, with the manners of the perfect gentleman he was. And then I too peered over the brink at the terrible falls and saw the white foam I had first seen on the lake. I heard the roar of water in my ears and knew I would never see my uncle again.

Initially, I had only one consolation: that his arch-enemy, spawn of the very devil, had died alongside him.

And then Colonel Moran came to the station to pay his respects, but he seemed distracted.

'What is it?' I asked.

'I am uneasy,' was his reply. 'I am not so sure the adversary is so easy to destroy.'

And so it proved.

It took time, but the stooge could not resist crowing at a later date, relating another version.

A most graphic account of my uncle's death sourced by the eyewitness, the arch-enemy my uncle had needed to destroy. '. . . *he, with a horrible scream, kicked madly for a few seconds and clawed the air with both his hands. But, for all his efforts, he could not get his balance and over he went. With my face over the brink, I saw him fall for a long way. And then he struck a rock, bounced off, and splashed into the water.*'

I read the account again, so carelessly presented for the entertainment, perhaps reassurance, of the masses and the cold fury spread through me, from my toes to my head, as though I had drunk hemlock. I put my hands over my face to block out light. Not dead then, after all?

Like Christ himself is the arch-enemy to be resurrected? I read of two of my uncle's henchmen to be dragged before the courts. Colonel Sebastian Moran and 'Porlock', the traitor. Paraded in front of the public. By the arch-enemy's hand.

I made my vow. Resurrected only to be destroyed – next time for ever.

So the moment has now come for me to let you into the secret my uncle confided in me.

I shall relate it exactly how it was told to me.

It was a little before my sixteenth birthday and we were sitting in the station waiting room, a room we had taken over as a base for our operations. Simply putting the 'Waiting Room Closed' sign over the door and drawing the blind was an easy way to deter the public.

'Cicely,' he said in a soft and gentle voice. 'I think the time is right for me to tell you a secret.'

I was instantly alerted. 'If you wish, Uncle.'

He sighed. 'You are a week short of sixteen, Cicely, old enough now to know what I could not tell you before. I could not have told this to a child.' He drew in a deep breath and looked disturbed. 'It involves a lady of whom I was very fond. The only lady whom I have ever considered worthy of my affection. We were – intimate.'

I wondered why he was telling me this but listened.

'It became evident that there would be issue.'

I held my breath.

He looked away from me. 'My brother, a poverty-struck stationmaster, and his wife, in poor health and unable to provide him with the child he so longed for. I knew my lifestyle was not conducive or safe for a child unable to protect itself. Merely to share the child's parenthood would have signed the same child's death warrant.' He fixed me with his eyes. 'You understand what I am saying?'

I did not answer. Nor did I breathe as he continued.

'And so a bargain was struck that suited us both. But, looking at you, dear Cicely, I see there is more of me in you than I had thought. You have not grown up the daughter of a stationmaster or of a reckless society beauty. You are pure me. You have my intelligence and caution. You have my almost intuitive sense of approaching danger. You have skill and bravery. A method of planning even I can admire. You are a true child of your father. I mean not the father you believe to be yours but your blood father.' He then whispered the secret in my ear.

And I will share with you that same secret, *dear reader*.

I whisper it very softly into your ear so others shall not learn of it. For with that knowledge would come, riding on the wings, triumphant as a Valkyrie swooping down on a dead warrior, danger. For my uncle had many enemies, some of whom will meet me one day. One in particular I already have in my sights. And his little stooge, the scribbler. I shall take my revenge. But I have one great advantage. Neither the king-devil nor his back-scratcher knows of my existence.

For I am Moriarty's daughter.

Author's note:

As anyone knows who is a fan of the Sherlock Holmes stories there are discrepancies in the facts we know about Professor Moriarty. In his first appearance in 'The Final Problem', Moriarty is merely referred to as Professor Moriarty. No forename is mentioned. Watson does, however, refer to the name of another family member when he writes of 'the recent letters in which Colonel James Moriarty defends the memory of his brother'.

In 'The Adventure of the Empty House', Holmes refers to Moriarty as Professor James Moriarty. This is the only time Moriarty is given a first name and, oddly, it is the same as that of his purported brother.

In *The Valley of Fear* (written after the preceding two stories, but set earlier), Holmes says of Professor Moriarty: 'He is unmarried. His younger brother is a stationmaster in the west of England.'

So I had a quandary. He has a brother called James; he is himself called James.

His brother is a colonel; his brother is a stationmaster. I had to make my choice. I have stuck with the name James and the occupation of his brother as stationmaster.

The Malady of the Mind Doctor

Howard Halstead

8 October 1886

My Dear Dr Watson,

I write to you in a state of perplexity – my days remaining on this earth will be few if this confounded confusion cannot be mastered. You see, dear fellow, I am accused of a hateful, abominable crime, one that suspends belief in the very virtue of mankind.

I have been boxed into this dark predicament. Although I have pleaded my innocence, my cries have not been heard amongst the clamour of the words "evidence" and "fact". Justice, usually of fair complexion and even countenance, has resolutely turned her back on me.

I can barely dare to write these words, but I must steel myself to face the truth of them: I now reside in a prison cell and face the gallows, having been found guilty of murder.

I have met you only once, sir, during the aftermath of the Royal Society's Special Lecture this June past. Although I am but a young man, you showed interest in my plans to set up a practice specializing in the treatment of nervous and brain disorders. I now know you by reputation to be a man willing to pursue truth even in the darkest corner. I can think of nothing else but to lean upon the kindness and good sense of yourself, and on the intelligence and curiosity of your dear friend, Mr Sherlock Holmes.

All I can offer you in terms of evidence are the pages of my sporadic diary, which reveal the episode as it unfolded. Along with this letter, the diary has been entrusted to Mr Richard Kennington for conveyance directly to your hands. I can trust no other man to perform this duty.

Read the pages carefully, sir, for I feel that the truth of my misadventure can be found amongst the scribbled lines, but I implore you to read them quickly. The apparatus of my death is already prepared.

Yours in trepidation,

Dr Trevelyan Blake

15 June 1886

What an evening this has been – though I am of scientific mind, it is an evening that proves beyond all doubt that the earth revolves with divine purpose.

It began as so many others have done since I returned from France: in an impoverishment not just of the pocket, but of the soul. I was sitting in this damnable, airless boarding room in Woolwich, counting coins enough for the train to town so that I could attend the Royal Society lecture, but not enough additionally to treat myself to a meal.

I decided against the lecture. What could Ernst Hechter say on the subject of neurology that I had not already learned from the lips of Jean-Martin Charcot, the most enlightened neurologist in Europe? What could Hechter divest on the topic of the ailing mind that I had not dissected, reconstituted and dissected again with my good friend Sigmund as we spent those months under Charcot's tutelage? And yet, even as my stomach made its displeasure known through a rumble, I carried those coins with me not to the Swan Inn for one of Mrs Webster's infamous pies, but to the railway station.

The lecture proved to be as dull as I had feared. Hechter may understand something of the malady of the mind, and he may realise that mental trauma can have a physical incarnation, but it was clear from his opening remarks that he has no understanding that such trauma may be eased by a cure of the mind, and not of the body.

As Hechter bored on in his heavily accented English, I divined that the only malady that this man was ever likely to cure was insomnia. I apologized to my stomach for my error of judgement, regretted the absence of the dubious pie, and let my mind wander. How I remember parting with Sigmund in Paris and our last words: a mutual vow to study and practise psychopathology. Although neither of us was yet to reach thirty, we agreed to stride forth separately and change all perception of the illnesses of the mind and their cure.

Even as I stood upon the railway concourse, shaking Sigmund's hand, I had to push away the fear that I would never be in a financial position to set up a private practice. Those months with Charcot in Paris had all but exhausted the last of my long-deceased father's bequest.

On returning to London, I threw myself upon the mercy of my guardian, Lord Kennington. I had promised never to return to his house or see his daughter again so I waited outside his club, White's, and, as he was a man of regular habits, his carriage turned up at the expected hour. It had been more than a year since my aberration, but my guardian's hatred for me remained as intense as ever. He had not forgiven me. He was clearly ill and weak, but his eyes were full of fierce hatred and he refused to speak one word to me. It was the last time I would ever see him. He would be dead within the week.

As Hechter droned on to his stupefied audience, I admit that I was overwhelmed by despair. A miserable room in Woolwich. A rumbling stomach. No prospect of setting up my practice. No possibility of redemption with the departed Lord Kennington. And no Eleanor. No, no chance of Eleanor.

I admit that it was underhand of me, but after the lecture, I followed some of the crowd into the reception held in Dr Hechter's honour, even though the price of my ticket only covered admission to the lecture. I desperately hoped there would be some form of victuals, but there was only a rather aggressive red wine that turned my stomach to acid and soon made me light-headed.

A kind gentleman named Dr John Watson fell into conversation with me. Although a retired army man, he seemed to be a keen student of the mind and, to my surprise, was a little familiar with Brentano's work and even von Hartmann's *The Psychology of the Unconscious*. He claimed, though, that he had come across no greater practitioner of a form of psychological deduction than the esteemed detective, Sherlock Holmes.

I was so relieved to find a fellow traveller, and somewhat heady from the wine, that I unleashed some of my tale of woe upon the good doctor. He knew of Lord Kennington's great wealth and had heard of his art collection, so he commiserated with me on being cut adrift by such a gentleman. I did not elucidate on the reasons for my fall from grace. He applauded my wish to begin my own private practice specializing in resolving illnesses, not least insomnia, that are a physical incarnation of a mental perturbation.

I think the wine may have helped me become surprisingly fluent on the subject. I noticed that nearby, in a poorly lit corner of the room, a gentleman with a large, drooping moustache and a tall, older fellow appeared to be listening intently. This made me giddier still as I perceived from the interest of this sample of the esteemed company that we were on the cusp of a new era of medicine and that I could become a torch bearer for the new age of reason. Foolish and arrogant, I know, but I felt so buoyant in that moment.

An hour later, I made to leave the Royal Society's premises – having suddenly become aware that I had been battering poor Dr Watson's ears for too long and that I was teetering on the precipice of being shamefully inebriated. Immediately as I stepped outside, I was approached by the attentive man with the drooping moustache. For the life of me I could not make out his name even after I asked him to repeat it. He was somewhat unusual in his bearing, and somewhat startling in his proposition.

The fellow had heard me tell Dr Watson of my desire to set up a practice and of my shameful pecuniary problems. He said he knew of a suitable property available for a limited time at a vastly reduced rent. Thus it was that at ten-thirty this evening, I was

standing alone at the gateway to a goods yard in Mayfair, awaiting a property agent.

The agent turned out to be a cheeky young chap in a tight-
fitting suit with the peculiar adornment of a pale grey bowler
hat that appeared to be too small for his head. It was strange
business to conduct at that time of night, but the young man
seemed eager to conclude the matter. The property itself was
hardly salubrious – the office and occasional bedroom of the
owner of a set of now defunct warehouses situated in the yard
– but it had potential. I ignored all reservations I had about the
agent's attire and his chirpy manner, and, within two minutes, I
found myself shaking his hand, thereby agreeing three months'
rental for what he assured me was less than a third of the
market rate.

As the agent whistled down the street towards Berkeley
Square, I remained standing in the yard, open-mouthed and
giddy at the twist of fortune.

I now had premises comprising a furnished office and a
bedroom. I had the means with which to begin my life's work and
fulfil my destiny. And I was less than fifty yards away from my
former home, namely Kennington House, the current abode of
Lady Eleanor Kennington.

21 June 1886

Monday: The day that marks the beginning of the rest of my life.

Even though I say it myself, after all my efforts, the main room
is clean and presentable. If it was not situated amongst the abandoned warehouse buildings, the new premises of Dr Trevelyan
Blake might be something to behold. My advertisement, the sole
one that I can presently afford, appeared in the evening newspaper on Friday:

Treatment for insomnia, hysteria and uneasiness of the mind.
Private and confidential consultations.
Dr Blake M.D., Barrel Yard, Bruton Place, Mayfair.

I hope the troubled ladies of Mayfair will take advantage of the situational convenience. And I pray that Eleanor, dear sweet Eleanor, saw the advertisement and flushed with pride that I was making my own way.

I sat down at the desk at precisely nine of the clock and waited. The dark cloud that had threatened my days since my return from France had lifted, Woolwich was no more, and I would never have to run the gauntlet of eating one of Mrs Webster's gristle pies again. I was too excited to sit still. I found myself twiddling the pocket watch that my father had bequeathed me. Then I stood up and looked through the grime of the window. People passed along Bruton Street, but none of them bore the appearance of the young ladies whom I thought were most likely to become my patients. Not one person even threatened to turn into the yard to make an appointment with the new doctor.

I sat down and fell to despair once more. I was a fool to think that even one soul in London would seek reparation in this chamber. I resigned myself to sitting in the room, utterly alone and festering amongst my dwindling hopes, for each day of the three months of my tenure. Yet I could not help but jump to my feet and look through the window again, like a restaurateur standing desperately at the doorway to his failing concern.

Suddenly there was a knock on the door. I jolted with surprise. I had seen no one turn into the yard. Perhaps my subconscious had conjured the noise. I, more than anyone, know what tricks it can play. But no – there was the knock again, impatient and insistent.

I collected myself, raising myself to my full height in the hope that I would impress the troubled young woman of my over-active imagination with the authority of my bearing. I opened the door and found myself looking up into the steady, deep-set eyes of my very first patient.

"Professor Moriarty."

I wondered momentarily if I had met the man before. His tall, slim stature, his thin face and those sunken eyes seemed vaguely familiar to me, but his name was not, and surely I would have remembered his voice. He had a very precise, solemn but forceful manner of speech. He strode past me into the room and set out his terms before I even had the chance to speak.

"I will meet you here at precisely this time for one hour, once a week, but you must assure me of absolute confidentiality, you hear?"

I nodded. He was more fearsome than any of the esteemed professors I had encountered in my education.

He sat down on the armchair and I took my position behind the desk in an attempt to assert some level of authority. "What ails you, Professor?"

He looked at me steadily, his eyes piercing me. I felt like the little orphan boy I once was, mother dead in childbirth and father taken when I was ten, standing alone and knock-kneed in terror before the cruel vastness of the world. That was until Lord Kennington, God rest his soul, swept me up and fulfilled a promise to care for his close friend's son. He had known enough hardship of his own – his own wife dead from a fever shortly after Eleanor's birth. Eleanor was his only child, his favoured jewel, but he treated me as he would a son.

Professor Moriarty's eyes seemed to soften slightly and he looked away, focusing on the bare wall. "I cannot sleep."

"At all?"

"Not beyond two hours."

I started to note the details of the case upon the foolscap. "For how long has the situation been endured?"

"Several years."

I perceived the weariness behind those alert eyes. "And you have taken draughts?"

"Ha!" he exclaimed. "Do I look like a fool? Sleeping draughts are nothing but a veil that obfuscates the clarity of the mind. They dull the body to alleviate the symptom, but the cause is not of the body's making. The cause lies in the dark folds of the mind. Do you agree with me, Doctor?"

"Yes, entirely."

"Good. Then let us begin." He clasped his hands together,

leaned forward and pierced me with his stare once more. "Let us enter the darkness."

A slight smile played upon his thin lips.

25 June 1886

I stood outside Eleanor's house again tonight, just to see if I could glimpse her through a window. Fortune did not favour me, but my imagination is so vivid that I could conjure her visage – every tiny feature from her elegant nose to the tiny mole that sits on her cheek immediately beneath her pupil, the shape of her ears, the curve of her eyelashes . . .

When did love come upon me so? For years I thought of her as I would a little sister. We shared stories and secrets, and giggled at the peculiarities of her father. I went out into the world to study at Oxford and Edinburgh, but I never found her ilk. I remember with unsullied clarity the day I returned home, having finished my training at the hospital in Edinburgh just in time to celebrate Eleanor's twenty-first birthday. Lord Kennington was so pleased with my progress that he shook my hand and agreed to fund my prospective studies with Charcot so that I would not have to draw upon the last of my father's money.

Amongst the commotion of the birthday celebrations, I found a moment to walk alone with Eleanor along the Upper Gallery of Kennington House. We stood in front of the painting of the windmill, just as we had stood together so many times whilst growing up. It is not as large, grand or famous as so many of Lord Kennington's paintings – the van Eyck, the Memling, the Bosch or even the Greuze. It is a small, eighteenth-century work by an unknown Dutch artist, but the image of a farmhand and a maid standing with joyful expressions beneath the sails of the windmill had always entranced us so.

I do not know how it happened. I made an uncontrollable leap into impropriety and suddenly my lips were upon hers. She did not resist. I swore my love for her, took her into my arms and kissed her again.

I felt the strike of Lord Kennington's cane across my shoulders and turned to see the deep hatred in his eyes. I knew from that moment on that the world would never be the same. I was banished from the house.

Soon a letter arrived from Eleanor's only cousin, Richard, who had long been a familiar presence in Kennington House. For such a brusque man, he took care to deliver the blow with some kindness. Eleanor had instructed him to implore me to douse my desire and, to save her from shame, to promise never to meet her again. My heart was broken, but I made that promise and I have kept it ever since.

Tonight, when I stood on that pavement in Berkeley Square, I wondered if she was looking at that windmill, thinking of me.

28 June 1886

Professor Moriarty is a conundrum. He decreed that we should delve into the darkness of the mind, but it has become clear that for him the mind is an intellectual and not an emotional property. To cure his insomnia I must seek out the root of the disturbance, to unearth some event from the past that first triggered the imbalance. Yet he resists memory. I attempt to make him reveal episodes of darkness and guilt, but in return he elucidates a theory that guilt can only come from regret and he has none. He talks of Malthus, the English scholar, and says that darkness must necessarily exist. For fear that the Earth cannot cope with the load of mankind, the population is naturally repressed, being kept equal to the means of subsistence by misery and vice. Therefore, he said in his cold, sober voice, how can one feel guilty about committing a crime?

I despair. I see only one way forward to recover the dark, troubled memories that sit at the heart of his condition: hypnosis. Only then will I uncover the truth of the man.

Richard Kennington has responded to my letter informing him of my new practice. My dear cousin, as I call him even though we are not related by blood, has continued to be my one strand of communication since Lord Kennington and Eleanor turned their backs on me. It was he who informed me of the death of Lord Kennington, and that no provision for either of us had been made in the will: the entire fortune was left to Eleanor. I had expected as much, but Richard, as the only other living Kennington, felt due some level of fortune. In truth, the good Lord had long been appalled by his sometimes foolhardy gambling.

The words in Richard's latest letter conveyed a new unhappiness to my own troubled soul. Eleanor is to marry a marquess of whom I know nothing at all. A cold wave swept through me and I had to steady myself as I read the missive. Her extraordinary wealth had made inevitable marriage to some esteemed yet impoverished aristocrat, but before I read those words there was just a sliver of a chance that one day . . . What a miserable fool I am!

29 June 1886

I am ashamed to say that I have been standing in the dark on Berkeley Square again, staring up at the lit windows like a desperate voyeur.

When I returned home, a plump fellow was standing in the yard. It was clear that he was in a state of high agitation, tapping his cane upon the ground, fiddling with the brim of his hat and checking his pocket watch, all within the few seconds it took to notice me walking towards him.

"Are you the good doctor?" he said in a peculiar, high-pitched voice.

"Dr Trevelyan Blake. Is there some sort of emergency?"

"Yes. No. Well, yes there is."

"Where is the emergency?"

"It's here, Doctor, standing before you."

Within a minute, he was sitting wedged into the armchair of my room, his long, ginger mutton chops quivering with agitation, his belly testing the buttons of his colourful striped waistcoat and his top hat squashed down on his collar-length, virulent orange hair.

"May I take your hat, Mr . . . ?"

"Goodness me, no." He touched the brim again. "One never knows what might fall from above." He laughed nervously throughout the sentence. "Smithington Smythe." He proffered his card.

"How can I help you, Mr Smythe?"

"Ah yes, yes." He started searching the pockets of his waistcoat and jacket in a flurry of commotion and finally produced a small cutting from a newspaper. "It says here that you offer treatment for uneasiness of the mind. Private and confidential. Yes, yes?"

I offered affirmation. He then stuttered and sweated his way through an explanation of his ailment, intermittingly singing snippets of what appeared to be that irrepressible ditty "The Flowers that Bloom in the Spring" as he did so. I abhor *The Mikado* but a man should not be condemned solely upon his taste in music.

"'Uneasiness of the mind.' That's exactly what my wife says I have. I have a young grandchild, a beautiful little girl, and there's so much danger, Doctor – rogues and vagabonds, carriages in the street, runaway horses, sharp knives at the dining table, rivers to drown in, uneven paving stones to trip over, masonry falling from the sky. The world is full of danger, Doctor. My wife says I am imagining it all and upsetting everybody, not least my little grandchild, who has picked up my agitation and screams every time she sees me. Please, Doctor, I beg you to help me to stop imagining all this evil."

He then made a strange request that he would come to me in the later evening at ten of the clock every Tuesday. He was indisposed at a more suitable time due to his important business in the shipping industry and his wish to spend the early evenings with his family. In exchange, he would offer me treble my fee, as long as I felt that I really could cure him.

I gave him my assurance that I could and he seemed much cheered. And, what is more, I truly believe that I can help him. As he left, he seemed much taller than I had realized on first impression: such is the power of the mind over the physical being, he had seemed to grow inches upon my assurance.

A second patient then. I will have enough to cover my weekly rent and to eat well. If a third patient emerges, perhaps I will even be able to purchase a picture to adorn these bare walls.

5 July 1886

It has been a momentous morning, one that will be forever seared into my consciousness. I have broken through the barrier – indeed, I have smashed it to smithereens – but the land behind that barrier proved to be dark and terrible. I wish I had never glimpsed its horrors.

Already aware of the work of the great Mesmer, I became a devotee of John Baird's researches into hypnotism while I undertook my medical learning in Edinburgh. Then, in Paris, Sigmund and I discussed hypnotism at great length and I became the master of self-hypnotism. I felt sure that I could use hypnosis to help any patient recover the occluded memories of events that had caused a disturbance of the mind.

With his resolute refusal to discuss his darker memories, I had decided that Professor Moriarty should be the beneficiary of my first foray into the hypnotism of a patient. Yet, as I fingered my gold pocket watch and studied his severe, angular face, his high-domed forehead and stony countenance, I faltered. Never in my life had I encountered such a fiercely intelligent and obdurate gentleman, one who was hardly going to allow himself to be put under another's spell.

However, to my surprise, he leaned forward and said, with that curious small smirk upon his almost lipless mouth, "Stop playing, boy, and do whatever it is you feel you must do."

I arranged proceedings so that we were sitting opposite each other and I carefully followed Baird's process. I held the pocket watch a fixed distance from the professor and asked him to stare intently at it. Five minutes of complete stillness and silence passed, but there was no change in the professor's demeanour. He stared fixedly, barely blinking, but the light of keen, conscious intelligence never left his deep-set eyes.

I was about to give up and return the pocket watch to my waistcoat when I noticed there was some delicate shift in his stare. I now seemed to be looking into the eyes not of a wise and cynical old man, but of an innocent boy.

I trod carefully at first, asking him to describe the world of his childhood in minute detail. In a sober, even voice, with his gaze still fixed upon the watch, he described his mother's bedroom and his father's study with a devotion to detail that I believe is beyond fully conscious memory. Then I asked him to describe some event that took place in his father's study, and that is when the darkness began.

The young Moriarty had allowed Indian ink to stain some linen and his father summoned him to the study, but, under questioning, Moriarty blamed his brother. Thereupon, while Moriarty watched, his protesting brother's bare legs were beaten with a cane, stroke after stroke after stroke, his father laughing manically all the while. It was only when blood ran freely down the back of the boy's welted thighs and calves that the punishment ceased.

There then, I thought, we have arrived at the likely root of the insomnia so quickly. Guilt, that emotion of which the professor is so dismissive, has disturbed his mind to the point that his body is in revolt and will not allow sleep, for the terrible occurrence no doubt haunts his dreams.

I was ready to coax the professor back into the present, but first I thought I would try to invoke a more recent memory to see if I could understand the depth of the professor's predicament. I asked him to describe his own study, which again he did in detail, and to picture himself seated at the desk. Was there anything that had taken place in that room that filled him with unease?

The professor uttered a short, dry, staccato laugh that seemed out of keeping with his induced state, but he continued in his solemn voice. The toneless delivery of the words soon proved an ill match for the horrors they described. With no more bidding, the esteemed professor conjured images of such vileness that my stomach turns to think of them. A specialist in astronomy, he described a universe of dark intrigue in which he was the sun and his criminal subordinates and "soldiers" were the stars, some linked into constellations, others orbiting alone upon his governance. He portrayed himself issuing command after command from the desk, arranging for burglary, deception, forgery and worse – murder and assassination! Politicians, lordly gentlemen and gentlewomen, shopkeepers and beggars: no one was immune from the evil effect of his communications, not even children. The river of stories was shoaled with the corpses of the innocent.

I was dumbfounded and a-trembling. At first I thought about running to the nearest constable. But it was then, in a moment of clarity, that I deduced that his tales were not true. As if this professor could possibly be running a network of the most damnable of criminals! No, the problems lay in the theories of Mesmer and Baird, and now I believed not one word of their supposed scientific reasoning. The hypnotized state was not a gateway to memory and truth – no! It was a mere portal to the vilest of imaginings that in the conscious world we can suppress and control, thank goodness. My ridiculous games had merely forced the venerable professor unwittingly to unleash a terrible fiction that had nothing to do with reality.

The professor had finally fallen silent and I saw that the keen intelligence had returned to his eyes once more.

"Remember, Dr Blake, that you promised complete confidentiality."

And, with that, he swept from the room, humming "Three Little Maids from School", which was somewhat incongruous to my state of confusion. Everyone in this city seems to be humming those insufferable Gilbert and Sullivan ditties.

It has been a sobering day. My understanding of hypnosis and recovered memory is in tatters, and I have no semblance of an idea how to proceed with the professor's treatment.

At least tomorrow I can look forward to the rather simpler case of Mr Smithington Smythe.

6 July 1886

It was nearly midnight, just half of an hour ago, when my door was nearly taken from its hinges with the banging. I had only just retired to bed, but had immediately fallen into a deep sleep and awoke in a state of high confusion. I stumbled my way out of the bedroom, into the consultation room and towards the noise. The door was shuddering with each determined blow.

"Who is it?" I shouted, trying to control my hands as I lit a candle.

"It is the Metropolitan Police. Open the door."

My thoughts immediately turned to Professor Moriarty. Was it possible that his words were not a fiction and the police were now investigating his manifold crimes?

If only that were so.

When I opened the door, I was looking up at a tall, portly man in a peaked cap who was accompanied by a uniformed officer.

"Are you Dr Trevelyan Blake?"

"Indeed."

"I am Inspector Bradstreet of Scotland Yard. There has been a vicious knife attack, doctor, not fifty yards from here."

"I will get dressed and come immediately."

"That won't be necessary, Doctor. The victim is beyond all help and the police doctor is at the scene."

"Then why have you awoken me?"

"I believe you know the victim, Doctor. Lady Eleanor Kennington."

I felt the candle drop from my fingers and the world went black.

A few minutes later, which was as soon as I could gather my senses, I said that I must go to Eleanor and made to leave immediately, even though I was in a nightshirt and my feet were still bare.

The inspector barred my way with a strong arm.

"It is not a sight you would like to see, sir. The dear lady has been cut . . ."

"Disembowelled," added the constable.

". . . in the manner of a medical man. You are a medical man, are you not, Doctor?"

"Of course I am. What are you saying?"

"Nothing at all."

Over the next ten minutes there ensued the most awful

conversation I have ever been forced to endure. No doubt armed with gossip from one of the Kennington servants, the inspector intimated that he knew all about my fall from favour with the deceased Lord Kennington and Eleanor's rejection of me.

"You are well acquainted with Lady Eleanor Kennington's house in Berkeley Square, and you are familiar with the precious artworks in the Upper Gallery, five of which have been cut from their frames. And you are also well acquainted with Lady Kennington's habits, are you not?"

"Well, yes. All that is true," I said, while still trembling at the thought of my poor, pure Eleanor's mutilated body.

"So you would have known that, as usual, the lady would be alone, reading in the library at about thirty minutes past ten this evening, exactly the time the dear lady was murdered."

"What on earth are you saying, man?"

"Nothing. Nothing at all." The inspector paused. "But where were you, Doctor, between ten and eleven this evening?"

I stared at the inspector in disbelief. "I was here."

"Alone, I dare say?" The man had a gleam in his eye.

"No, Inspector. I was in the company of Mr Smithington Smythe, a very respectable man of some importance, for the entire hour." By now I was in a state of anger. I ripped open a desk drawer and handed Mr Smythe's card to the inspector. Even in my torment at the news of Eleanor's death, I felt some satisfaction at seeing the gleam leave his eye. He looked thoroughly disappointed and turned to leave.

"Rest assured we will speak to Mr Smythe." The inspector stuck out his huge chest and stood in an imposing manner in the doorway. "You will not leave the city in a hurry now, will you, Doctor?"

And, with that, the policemen left me to myself, and to the fullness of my deep and terrible grief.

8 October 1886

I write this in the shadow of the noose. My dear cousin Richard has brought me a pen, ink and paper, and the warder has allowed me to write what may be the last entry to be appended to my diary, as well as a letter to Dr Watson. Richard has been a friend to the last. He has been the only person to visit me in gaol. When I told him of my final, desperate plan to attract the attention of Sherlock Holmes, he at first said it was futile and told me to resign myself to my fate, but once he knew of my determination he took it upon himself to pursue the matter. He has managed to extract the diary from my few possessions still held at Barrel Yard, and he will take those pages, along with this final entry and the letter, to Dr Watson.

And so I must return to the events of three months past.

The end, when it came, came swiftly. In the early hours of the morning after the murder of dear Eleanor, I went to Berkeley Square. I wanted to grasp some final part of her, to say goodbye to her, to make her awful, sudden absence more comprehensible. An officer of the law guarded the doorway to the house and so I turned away and wandered the streets for some hours, twisting and turning, not knowing to where I was going until my feet took it upon themselves to bring me back to my rooms. I fell upon my bed and wept once more.

There was another knock on the door. I was tear-stained and somewhat dishevelled but I was beyond such care. There, standing before me once more, was Inspector Bradstreet of Scotland Yard, this time accompanied by two constables.

The inspector pushed me back into the room.

"Doctor Blake, I put it to you that you have been seen staring up at Lady Eleanor Kennington's house on an almost nightly basis."

"I . . ."

"I put it to you that Lord Kennington cut you out of his will, and that Lady Kennington refused your advances."

All this was true, but I protested. His assemblage of the facts was skewed and inappropriate.

"I put it to you that you murdered Lady Eleanor and stole from her five paintings."

I was seared and discombobulated by his accusation but I stood my ground and retorted, using his own ridiculous language.

"And I put it to you, sir, that I can prove it was not me. Mr Smithington Smythe . . ."

"Mr Smithington Smythe! The address on the card you handed to me was for Wilson's funeral parlour in Clapham."

My knees weakened.

"No one has ever heard of this Smythe. There has been no sight or sound of him in either Mayfair or Clapham, and his name is not recorded in any ledger. He simply does not exist. Between quarter past and half past ten of the clock yesterday evening, you were not in these rooms, sir, sitting with Mr Smithington Smythe. You were stealing through the gardens of Kennington House to prise open a window that you knew would give access to the library. You then strangled and stabbed . . ."

"Disembowelled!"

". . . Lady Eleanor Kennington and stole the pictures from the Upper Gallery."

By then I had collapsed to my knees.

"Search the premises, Constables."

Within a minute, one of the constables had returned from the bedroom. "This was under the bed, sir."

Held outward, taut between his hands, was the small Dutch painting of the windmill that Eleanor and I had stood before so many times, back in the days when the world was wonderful and so full of promise. I looked on, dumbfounded and defenceless, caught in a web beyond my comprehension.

I have pleaded my innocence every day since. I have even broken my vow of confidentiality and talked of Professor Moriarty's mysterious universe of crime, but I am looked upon as one would a madman.

Not one soul believes a single word I say.

Obsession

Russel D. McLean

"You may call me 'Professor'."

He sits perfectly at ease, loose limbs remaining in control at all times. His high-domed forehead seems designed to keep his dark, and admittedly thinning, hair from creeping forward. There is a faint odour of hair pomade. He is clearly a man of intellect. Listen to the way he speaks. His skin is pale and his eyes are sunk into his forehead, giving him the gaunt appearance of an undertaker. But that is not his profession. Not unless he extracts a generous price from the families of those interred by his deceptively delicate-looking hands. He is wealthy. It is clear from his clothes and his demeanour. And the fact that he has paid for my time and expertise.

"Professor," I say, letting the name roll around my tongue.

He sits forward. "I would prefer," he says, with a hint of threat, "that we not deal in real names."

I sit back in my chair. Notebook open and pencil at the ready. The new leather squeaks as I adjust my weight. I look at the clock above the mantelpiece. My wife is waiting for me at home. This impromptu session will take no more than an hour.

The Professor says, "I do not require you to take notes."

"Professor," I say, "It is important that—"

"—there must be no record," he says. "You are already being rewarded handsomely for your services."

I try not to bristle at his tone. There is something patronising there. A disregard that I find personally insulting.

"You look uncomfortable," he says.

"No."

"Many people are uncomfortable in my presence. I have always had that effect on others. Even as a child."

I nod, and put away my notes. This "Professor" will be here for one, maybe two sessions at most. He is, like so many of the richer clients who seek my audience, merely seeking an outlet for his boredom. As the new medicine of psychiatry extends beyond the asylum, many of my colleagues fear it is destined to become merely another way for the privileged to relieve their boredom.

"Tell me," I say, "about your childhood."

The Professor is, in a purely mental sense, elusive as a butterfly that has not been sufficiently exposed to cyanide. He mentions his parents only briefly and dismissively, before implying that he has a brother who is a colonel in Her Majesty's armed forces. Beyond that he does not go into great detail. His blood relatives are merely facilitators of his existence. He does not speak to them and has not done so since he graduated from university education.

"My family became merely a means to an end," he tells me. "I was educated. I was never at a loss for money. I could buy and sell friends easily. But such friends . . . I found they tired easily. I do, however, find their lives and their habits fascinating in the way an entomologist finds the rituals of ants to be of great interest."

"You see other people as ants?"

He keeps quiet. Expecting me to answer the question for him. But that is not how the game is played. He has to understand the rules.

I say, "You have a superior intellect to most men?"

"I have published volumes on binomial theories in mathematics that shook the established order. And more still on the movements of the asteroids and the nature of the heavens."

"To acclaim?"

Again, he says nothing.

"But this is not enough for you? You were not recognised for your—"

"Recognition has nothing to do with it!" A sudden, unex-pected flash of anger. He sits forward. Voice close to cracking. There is a madness in his eyes that he had hidden before. His body stiffens as though bitten by a venomous snake. "Recognition is for those obsessed with the opinions of other people. A man of my intellect . . . There is no one whose approval I seek!"

"No one?"

He hesitates. Considers his response. Our most honest reac-tions, so I and others have come to believe, arise when we do not consider them. Instinct teaches us about ourselves. But men like the Professor – in need of control – suppress these automatic reactions, viewing them as weakness.

"Of late, I have experienced an itch," the Professor says. "Initially, little more than a minor irritation. But over months and even years, it has become something I can no longer ignore." He leans forward in his chair, brings me into his confidence. "There is no man who so controls his life as I do. Who is aware of, and able to control, every detail. No man surprises me or unsettles my plans. Except one. An individual who threatens to undermine my hard-fought discipline. We have never met and yet he thwarts me at every turn, threatens to cause a lifetime's achievements to crumble and float away on the wind as though they were mere dust."

"Who is this man?" I ask.

He takes a breath. This, I sense, may be the most honest thing he has said since entering the room. "He calls himself London's greatest – and only – private consulting detective. The itch that threatens to consume me at the expense of all other things is named Sherlock Holmes."

Sherlock Holmes.

Everyone knows the name. Over the last few years, he has emerged as a unique and quite brilliant eccentric in our coun-try's consciousness. Any man would rightly be able to quote you his address at 221b Baker Street, perhaps even name some of the many spectacular crimes that he has thwarted. He is a marvel of the modern age and, in the minds of many of my colleagues, the pinnacle of man's intellectual evolution.

And he is my Professor's nemesis.

"Tell me why this man vexes you."

"Your profession," the Professor says, "is little more than . . . quackery."

"Then why are you here?"

He sits back in his chair. Regards me for a moment. His eyes are intense. They seem to be constantly searching for something. I sense that they will never be able to find it.

"It was . . . suggested to me. You studied, alongside Kraepelin, I believe. A fine mind. I trust that some of his genius may have rubbed off on you. Certainly, you have a reputation for assisting members of the gentry in coming to terms with their . . . hidden desires and personal problems. You are more than merely a carer for the lunatics locked within this asylum of yours. You have even offered assistance in exceptional criminal cases. Not unlike the detective, I suppose. But you retired from that work." He smiles. "After the Ripper. But, fear not, I have read your notes and theories. Your work there was not without some results."

My work on the Ripper case had been conducted on the understanding that my notes and theories would remain unattributed. The only copies remain with Inspector Abberline. My name appears nowhere on any official documents.

"The killer remains at large."

"Perhaps," the Professor says, and smiles. I notice his canines. They are sharp. I think of a wolf on the prowl. I try not to think of the man known as the Ripper. "What I require, my dear Alienist, is such assistance as you may offer the habitual opiate user or the man overcome by desires he knows to be wrong. I fear that the great detective may have needled his way inside my mind. That I have developed a sickness. One that affects every action I undertake. I would be rid of this. You have helped others to overcome their worst instincts. To hide certain unpleasant symptoms of the mind. Some mere habitual quirks, and others . . . well . . . I have reviewed your roster of your private patients—"

"No! That is impossible."

"Nothing is impossible. Even the improbable. I have seen the files, have no doubt. And their names are as impressive as their problems are varied."

"No," I say. "You cannot—"

"I can and I have. I am one of the most remarkable and resilient minds you will ever meet. And you would do well to remember that."

"Then what do you want of me?"

"Your assistance. And your insight. No more. I am not asking for your subservience or obedience. I am asking you to . . . help . . . me overcome this obsession. Help me to see that this Sherlock Holmes is, as all other men, beneath me in intellect and capability. Help me to forget him."

He does not meet my eyes once during this speech. And, when he says the word "help", it comes out weak and reluctant. A word that sounds unnatural slipping between his bloodless lips, no matter how many times he may force it.

Our session runs late. I lose track of the ticking of the clock that hangs over the mantelpiece. It is, however, my last appointment of the day. The only person waiting for me is my wife. And, when I explain to her my reasons, she will understand.

As the Professor leaves, I see there is a man waiting for him outside. By his bearing, I judge him to be military. Is this the briefly mentioned brother, James? But when my client refers to him as "Sebastian", I dismiss the theory. During our session, he let slip only this one insubstantial sliver of personally identifiable information. I do not know if he did this on purpose or if his apparently infallible mind slipped for just a moment. But it fuels my own obsession to understand this strange and dangerous man, despite the fact my instincts scream at me to run into a dark hole and hide.

My wife is waiting for me when I return. She has been up since before I left, working in our shared library. She writes papers on the peculiarities of the human mind and, sometimes, I publish them under my name. We have discussed her submitting for a place of study, but the institutions we approach have been wary of a woman interested in psychology. Such is the way of the world. Perhaps one day, things shall change. Perhaps even in my lifetime.

"Where have you been?" She looks up from her desk and smiles at me.

"I am sorry. There was . . . I have a new patient."

"Yes?"

"I find him . . . interesting."

"Yes?"

I see the Professor once a week for the next three. At night, I return home and dictate from memory. My wife takes down dictation and overnight, as I rest, she writes up her thoughts and theories as the state of the Professor's mind.

In the third week, I do not speak of him on my return.

"Something is troubling you?"

"I have made a terrible mistake. In treating this man."

"Why?"

I try to answer, but the words stick in my throat.

"Talk to me."

I clear my throat, walk away to get a glass of water. When I return, Emily looks at me. Her eyes are wide. She has dark eyes, and in the wrong light they appear almost black. But in them, there is intelligence and compassion. I drink from my glass and say, "I feel as though I have made a deal with the devil. No, I am certain that I have."

Our theory – we treated it almost as a game, something light to indulge our curiosity – has become that the man was highly intelligent, and yet also delusional. He may or may not know Sherlock Holmes. He certainly claims that they have never met in person. I had believed at first that the Professor was an amateur detective himself and found the existence of Holmes to be a threat. But the truth is stranger than that.

The truth chills my soul.

"How can you hate a man you have never met?"

The Professor wags a finger. "A good question. You are full of good questions. No answers. But that is the nature of your profession. You rely on your patients to do the heavy lifting. It would not do for you to supply answers. To cow them with your intellect."

I shrug. I have begun to feel more comfortable in his presence. "It is healthier for the patient to come to their own—"

"I have had men killed for asking bad questions," he says. Quietly.

I almost laugh. It's there. In my chest. Bubbling up to the surface, ready to break the tension. But he's serious. Deadly serious. Looking at me now with those blue eyes, capturing me, letting me know that he will only tolerate me for so long before he snaps.

"You have?"

"I have had men killed," he says, as though correcting himself. "This doesn't surprise you, does it?"

"I had my suspicions that your activities were not entirely legal."

He smiles at that. "You thought that I was a detective. That my enmity regarding Mister Sherlock Holmes was simple professional jealousy. I can read you, my dear Alienist. Perhaps better than you can read me."

"You are a man who endeavours to be the best in his field."

"In any field. And I am," he says. "I am the greatest villain of this age. A criminal mind such as this world has never known. More than a killer, like Jack the Ripper, more than a thief. I control such men. I direct them. There is not a deviant act that occurs within this city that I do not have a hand in."

"Does that include . . . ?"

"The Ripper is something else entirely, I admit. Even God may occasionally miss the beat of a sparrow's wings. By acknowledging my fallibility, I am able to better prepare for the future."

The comparison to God goes unremarked. My wife and I have already written on his extreme egotism; a need to feel as though he is at the centre of all things. His self-perception is that of a spider at the centre of a web, reaching out and controlling all things in his domain with a simple flick of his limbs.

"That is why I am at conflict with the detective, despite our never having met," he says. "We are flip sides of the same coin, I fear. He is the only one in this godforsaken world who may match my own intellect. And yet he chooses to ally himself with tradition and order."

"And you?"

"Oh, do not be so blasé as to believe I chose evil," he says. He shakes his head, and his expression is the same as if he were talking to a child. "If I chose anything, I chose chaos. And for good reason. The great detective would prefer the world to remain entirely as it is: static and dull and uninteresting. He would have made a fine academic in that sense. Tell me, have you read the work of Charles Darwin?"

"I have."

"And?"

"He makes many interesting points about the evolution of life on this planet."

"Interesting points? You read and you do not understand. Darwin talks of a world that is in constant flux. Animals change and adapt to circumstance. Those that fail to do so, die. Evolution arises through change. I believe we may only discover our potential by introducing the unpredictable."

"In other words, you are an agent of natural order?"

He nods. "To a degree, then, you understand?" He does not wait for a response. "The old Empire is rotting. There is a new world order coming, and I intend to be at its centre. Its architect. But, everywhere I turn, I am thwarted. Holmes. Always Holmes. The Great Detective. The hero of the ailing British Empire. You read the papers?"

"Yes."

"How did his infernal biographer describe the case? Ah, the Red-Headed League . . ."

"One of yours?"

"One of mine. Almost all of them, you see. And now, not content with standing in my way, Holmes has discovered me. He intends to bring me into the light."

"But, then, I still don't understand. For what do you require my services?"

"In order to understand the great detective I need to

understand myself. Your reputation is beyond reproach. And deserved."

"Indeed?"

"Oh, yes, indeed. And now, I fear, you have become my co-conspirator. You had the chance, you realise, to turn me away?"

"I would never turn away any man in need. Whether seeking a cure for some mental affliction or simply attempting to understand his own mind."

"No, that's not it. You were intrigued by the puzzle I represented, by the very fact that you knew from the off I was not everything I appeared to be. You are a man of curiosity."

"And I know what curiosity did to the cat."

He grins. The wolf-teeth appear. I try not to shrink back.

"No," he says. "Curiosity is a trait to be encouraged." He leans forward. "Informing on one's own patients, however . . ."

"He threatened you?"

"He said he knew of the notes we had taken. He told me that I was to burn them all."

"And?"

"What choice do I have?"

She laughs. "What choice? What choice?" She stands, comes over and wraps her arms around me. I fall into her, breathe in the scent of her recently bathed hair. "The choice, husband, is to go to the police. The choice is not to submit to his bullying!"

I pull back and look at her. She does not understand.

"No," a voice says, from just behind the door where I entered. "There is no choice."

The man named Sebastian sets a light to our papers. We watch as he does so, powerless. He throws them on to the fire with detached efficiency. I think back to when the Professor told me that I was not to write down any of our conversations. I should have listened, then.

When he is done, Sebastian says, "Pack your bags."

"Why?"

"The Professor requires your services. He has one more task for you. The reward will be handsome." He speaks in short, declarative sentences. He is the Professor's blunt instrument, used when a scalpel is insufficient.

Emily grabs at my coat as I stand. I shake her off. I have no choice. I made this deal with the devil. I am now his plaything.

I say, "I require nothing more than the clothes on my back."

Sebastian laughs. "Your choice," he says. And then, mockingly, "Alienist."

The carriage rattles as we pass across the border to Switzerland. I attempt to pass the time by reading the newspapers, but am unable to focus on the stories at hand. Sebastian is no longer with me. He departed at Newhaven, after a young gentleman passed him a note on the platform. Judging by the expression on his face as he left me, it was not good news.

Two men enter my carriage. One of them is tall and gaunt, younger by some years than his companion. His forehead reminds me somewhat of the Professor's, and he has that same coldness to him. His friend is older, more portly, and, like Sebastian, has the bearing of a military man. But he has not allowed soldiering to rob him of his humanity. He smiles when his friend leaves, and takes a seat opposite me. "That man," he says, "can never sit still."

"Not a happy traveller?"

"Not happy at rest." He smiles. "Where are you travelling to?"

"Meirengen," I say.

"Oh? Business or pleasure?"

"Business. I have a patient there waiting for me."

"A doctor?"

"In a sense."

He nods. "I am a medical doctor, myself."

"The mind," I say. "I am an Alienist by training. I run an asylum within the confines of London. And a private practice for those who need lesser assistance."

"We, too, are headed for Meirengen."

There is silence between us for a while.

"Your business there?" I finally ask, for want of anything better to do. The rolling countryside has finally lost its appeal.

"My companion's business," the man says. "I choose to accompany him, however."

"A man should have friends," I say.

"Yes," the man says. "Without friends, who are we?"

Sebastian gave me a letter as we made our way to the station. Over the course of my journey to Switzerland, I periodically read and reread the Professor's missive, searching for some meaning that I might have missed.

> *My dear Alienist,*
> *As you advised, I attempted to talk to the Great Detective himself. We met at his rooms in Baker Street. I fear, however, that he is unwilling to reach a compromise between us, forcing me to take more drastic measures. I fear that even these may not be enough, however. He and I are on course for a reckoning.*
> *Over the last month, your work has proved invaluable. Self-knowledge, I believe, is the route to perfection. I have gained an understanding of myself and my priorities. I have quieted my ego. And yet still I cannot rid myself of this need to destroy the Great Detective, to see him utterly quashed. Not only that, but I am consumed by the desire to have him admit his inferiority; to force him to bow down to a superior intellect.*
> *You have provided a steadying hand. And now, as our confrontation approaches, I would have your counsel one last time before our encounter.*

On our approach to the station, I read the letter one more time. As I fold it to put away in my breast pocket, the door to the carriage opens and my new-found friend's companion bursts in. "We are nearly there!" he says. "Come, Watson, there is much to prepare!"

The doctor, who has been sleeping for maybe an hour, wakes quickly, and looks at me as he shrugs his coat about his shoulders. "He was never one for subtlety," he remarks of his companion. "A pleasure to meet you." He extends his hand. Silently, I take it and we shake before parting. "Maybe we shall meet again in Meirengen."

"Perhaps," I say. But it is all I am capable of. As they leave the cabin, my throat seizes up. For I realise now that my travelling companion was the estimable Doctor Watson and that his friend was none other than the great detective himself: Sherlock Holmes.

The Professor waits for me in private rooms, under an assumed name.

With little preamble after being granted access, I set myself up in a corner of the room. I sit down and say to him, "Tell me of your intentions."

"I want to kill him," he says. "Throttle him with my bare hands. Choke the life from him." As he speaks, his body tenses. His hands grip like talons. His skin becomes pale and his eyes manic.

I say, "You hate him."

"He is an annoyance."

"Don't downplay your feelings," I say. "You hate the man. You hate anyone you see as a challenge, as an obstacle, as an equal."

"I have no—"

"Don't lie to me!" Suddenly bold, I realise that I have nothing left to lose. He can kill me if he wants, but I will not be restrained by fear. "Don't lie to yourself! You are afraid of this man and you hate what you are afraid of!"

There is silence. He stands and looks at me. The silence becomes a physical presence in the room, crushing and choking. Have I made a mistake?

"Afraid?" he says. "Yes, yes. Maybe you're right. The idea that there is someone in this world who is my equal? Oh, when you believe yourself unique, the prospect is terrifying."

I allow myself finally to breathe.

"When you return to England," he says, "there will be money waiting for you. A sum to more than compensate you for your assistance. You will not hear from me again."

"You think yourself cured?"

"Oh, I don't know about that. But it is better to cut one's ties than become dependent, don't you think?"

But there is something else, too. Something unsaid.

I stand and offer my hand.

He smiles and accepts the gesture. "Do not mistake this for friendship," he says.

I leave without another word.

The following morning, I am preparing for my departure when I come across a commotion in the lobby of my hotel. I stop one of the stewards and say, "What is happening?"

"You are English?"

"British. Yes."

"Then . . ." He hesitates for a moment. "You have not heard?"

"Heard what?"

"The detective. The great detective. Sherlock Holmes. He is dead."

I gather the story through rumour and report. Make sense of what I can. But what I know is this: the great detective confronted his nemesis, and together they plunged into the waters at the Reichenbach Falls.

I send a telegram to my wife: "I am delayed by a few days, but I will be home." I say no more than this. In the space of a telegram, it is impossible to convey my feelings about the death of the Professor whose name, I have learned at long last, was Moriarty.

That afternoon, I return to my room. It is my last night before I board the first of several trains that will take me home.

There is a knock at the door as I open my case and prepare to fold my clothes. When I answer, I see my friend from the train. He says, "When I heard there was an Alienist here, I hoped it would be you." He extends his hand. "My name is Doctor John Watson. I believe that you may be able to offer some assistance to those overcome by traumatic events." He talks with the restrained air of one desperate to keep a lid on some strong emotion.

I merely nod at his greeting. And feel strangely responsible for his current state of mind.

He says, "My friend, the one who was with me on the train—"

"Mr Sherlock Holmes?"

"Yes."

"By all accounts, one of the finest minds the world has ever known."

"And a dear friend."

I invite him to take a seat beneath the windowsill. He does so. I find some water and pass it to him. He sips. The room is silent. From somewhere outside comes the sound of birds, chirruping almost joyously as though unaware of the clouds that myself and Watson can see.

"You, too, seem touched by sorrow."

I smile, but it feels unconvincing. "My patient," I say. "He also died yesterday."

"I am sorry. I suppose in the excitement over a figure such as Holmes, the deaths of others whose names are not known to the public may appear to be lessened."

I say nothing. I lean against the writing desk.

"How did he die? Your patient?"

"Obsession," I say. "There is no other thing to say. I feel as though there was something I missed. But he was so guarded. In the end, I fear that the obsession he could not admit to was what led to his demise."

"Holmes was much the same. Obsessive. The exclusion of all else. In that way, your patient and my friend, I suppose they were alike."

I allow Watson to talk. The more he talks about Holmes, the more the great detective becomes the Professor in my mind, both men mirror images. As the Professor had remarked, himself.

The immovable object and the unstoppable force.

There are tears on my cheeks. My eyes burn gently.

I wipe the tears away with a subtle gesture. Wonder at their cause, briefly.

Watson, in his own grief, does not notice.

The Box

Steve Cavanagh

This document, a personal memoir of Sir H. F. Dickens K.C., is heretofore sealed before me, and deposited in the archives of the Inner Temple, London, this Fourteenth Day of April 1916. I shall not break the seal, or suffer others to break it, until at least one hundred years have passed from the date hereof.

Sworn on this date, by Thomas Clay, Keeper of Manuscripts, The Inner Temple Library, in the City and environs of Westminster.

If you are reading this poor account, which is drafted in the full knowledge of its total inferiority in every material respect, in comparison to the work of my father, the late Charles Dickens, you should bear in mind that in all likelihood I am quite assuredly dead and literary criticism is the very least of my concerns. As I sit in my study of late, my career and middle age firmly behind me, I have been increasingly possessed of the notion to record my part in the most ordinary, and yet extraordinary, legal case of my career. By now you may have deduced that my name is Henry Fielding Dickens, King's Counsel and Common Serjeant, retired, and that whilst a practising counsel I was well known for my involvement in a brace of sensational murder trials conducted in that most august theatre, the Old Bailey.

The case I refer to is not one of murder, or treason, or any remotely sensational crime. Instead, the minor criminal act in this case could hardly have been more pedestrian in its nature or execution. It concerned a box. And I have for nearly forty years kept my silence about me with regard to the true nature of this offence. For if it were not for the intervention of fate, I shudder to behold the blight it may have left upon the very foundations of the British Empire.

I can hold my pen still no longer.

On the twenty-ninth of January in the year 1894, I stood before the prisoner, in his cell at the Old Bailey. His appearance was that of a despicable, young wight. Only a fortnight before had I met him, at Police Court; his trousers pressed, and a clean handkerchief in his breast pocket. A bright chain, which had once led to a gold watch, flirted about his stomach from the pocket of his waistcoat. Hardly a gentleman. Even then, his moustaches were matted with dirt, his shoes encrusted with mud and his shirt a stained casualty of his labours and circumstance.

"My name is Mr Dickens," I said.

The prisoner, at that time, lay down on the wet, black floor of his cell and said, "I have no coin for a brief. My apologies, sir, for I cannot pay you."

I regarded him as one would regard a rather foolish, but otherwise good-natured child.

"Mr Ruthnick, you need not concern yourself with the trivialities of payment. My brief fee, and that of my instructing solicitor, have been paid in full by your Italian benefactor," I said.

Whatever remained of his shoe leather shuffled and slicked across the slime coating the stone floor as he rose, staggered, and gathered his body beneath his skitting feet. A countenance of bemused delight appeared behind his dirt-ridden moustaches.

"Sir? A benefactor?"

"Come, come. Don't tell me your wits have deserted you completely. Sir Kenneth Horatio Rochesmolles, of Turin, lately returned from his properties in Piedmont, discovered your arrest and charge and immediately instructed my friend Mr Deery, of Deery, Nook and Bond, Solicitors, to have your downfall professionally attended."

My gallows humour failed to find favour with the prisoner.

"Downfall? You mean you cannot help me?"

"Forgive me, Mr Ruthnick. My attempts to lighten even the

darkest of predicaments serves as an endless source of embarrassment for Mrs Dickens. No, I shall not oversee your downfall. I rather fancy that I can see a way to your emancipation."

A flush of crimson fought to emerge through the layers of grime that besmirched his youthful cheek.

"I remember your appearance at the Police Court, and Mr Deery recalled my remarking upon your case at the time and sought out my services."

"Dear heavens, thank you, sir. Thank you . . . and my thanks to Sir Kenneth and to God Almighty," he said, in a tone of welcome surprise.

"Mr Ruthnick, God, his ways and mysteries, have yet to penetrate the Central Criminal Court. However, between Mr Deery and myself, we may be able to conjure a miracle. Let's hope for your sake that we can. You understand the charges that you face?"

"Not entirely, sir."

"I suspected as much. You are studying fine art at the Royal College?"

"I am, sir, and it is my fervent dream to return to my studies, if I am permitted. And, if that be the case, I shall explain to the Dean that I no longer wish to attend upon our esteemed visitors."

"Ah, now we come to the rub of it. It was your accompaniment of a visitor to the college that led to your incarceration, was it not?"

"Indeed, sir. And it may be the ruin of me."

The poor fellow sank to his knees, as if the very memory of those recent events were a great weight in his mind. Or perhaps his conscience? I recalled my meeting with Mr Deery, following my perusal of the brief in this case, and my recommending to him that he return the retainer to Sir Kenneth, as the defence of Mr Ruthnick was a lost cause.

"Mr Dickens, may I say that I arrived at an identical conclusion. That is, until I reread our letter of instruction from Sir Kenneth, and his particular, and rather unusual suggestion with regard to the defence of the prisoner."

And with that, Mr Deery, who always seemed to have the relevant document within ready distance of his counsel's nose, produced the letter from one of his many paper-filled pockets and handed it to me. It was made in a strong, male hand. The correspondence identified the author as Sir Kenneth, born of English and Italian descent. He confirmed that he felt a great affinity with the arts and made several large donations to the college annually. The Dean had made him aware of young Mr Ruthnick's plight, and he enclosed a cheque, drawn from his account in the Bank of England in the sum of £50 for the defence of Mr Ruthnick. The final paragraph was most curious.

> *"You may find, Mr Deery, that having taken instructions from Albert Ruthnick you are none the wiser as to a possible defence. The complainant, Mr Loffler, is known to me. Or at least his character is known to me. You may find that his prosecutorial energy will dissipate at once, if your counsel were to enquire as to the true nature and value of the items at the heart of this matter."*

"What do you make of it, Mr Dickens?" said Mr Deery.

"I think it dangerous, Mr Deery, for any counsel to ask a question in open court if he does not already know the answer. However, it has the singular effect of making an otherwise dreary case most interesting. We shall see, Mr Deery. We shall see . . ."

Court number three at the Old Bailey had almost exhausted its list. The presiding judge, his Honour, Judge Campbell, had at four o'clock sent a man of twenty-three years of age to Pentonville Prison, where he was to serve five years and submit to punishments under the Garrotters Act. Under this particular legislative provision the young man would receive up to fifty lashes in the presence of the press to aid his rehabilitation. His crime was the burglary of a ham from a private dwelling house. Judge Campbell filled his pipe whilst the convict was brought to the cells kicking and screaming.

"Now, case number twenty-six, the matter of Albert Ruthnick, may I have your appearances, gentlemen?" said the judge.

"If it please, Your Honour, I appear for the prosecution," said Mr Roderick – a rather tall and cold brother at the Bar, who often smelled vaguely of fish. It was his wont, following his securing a sentence of death, for Mr Roderick to ply his fishing rod to the Thames in the vain hope of securing a reluctant salmon for his table. Mr Roderick stood with a straight back, his head tilted towards the judge, who in turn sat on an elevated bench far above the ordinary misdealings of his fellow Londoners. Beside the judge a single candle fluttered a devilish glow upon his features, framed by his dull, full-length judicial wig. If one had not been familiar with the judge, one could be forgiven for regarding him as a rather jovial soul. His plump cheek, wide smile and clear blue eyes were a perfect mask with which to conceal his delight in inflicting cruelty on those prisoners who were unfortunate enough to appear before him.

"Your Honour, I appear for the prisoner," I said and, as I stood to announce my appearance, I caught the familiar odour of the Bailey: sweat, excrement and ink. Once that smell is in your nostrils, it is difficult to pass from one's memory. The prisoner, Mr Ruthnick, appeared in the dock to my right – his whole body aquiver as he regarded the jury for the first time. The jury were seated to my left; twelve men of property whom, according to the clerk's recollection, had yet to acquit a single prisoner that day. It is my unfortunate view that Judge Campbell's court often seated hard juries. Or more accurately, Judge Campbell had a way of leading the jury along his particularly harsh path.

Mr Deery sat behind me, ready to take a careful note of the evidence.

The clerk of the court stood and addressed the prisoner.

"Albert Ruthnick, you have pleaded 'not guilty' to the charges on the indictment, namely that you, on the sixteenth day of January this year of our Lord 1894, did commit Forgery in the construction and use of a letter, and that you did utter such untruths in pursuit of said forgery and attempted to procure property to which you had no lawful claim. Are you ready for your trial?"

Gripped in a paroxysm of fear, it was all that Mr Ruthnick could do to look in my direction. I nodded.

"I . . . I am," he said.

"Forgery and utterances," growled the judge, and made his disapproval apparent to the jury with the wobble of his jowls as his great head shook in contempt for the prisoner.

"Call your witnesses, Mr Roderick," he said.

At this prompt, a man of perhaps forty years of age, wearing a tweed suit, stood up in the public stalls at the rear of the court and made his way through those bloodthirsty members of the public who regularly attended the Bailey for their entertainment. Of course, not all of those gathered in the stalls were there for blood. A good deal of them attended simply for the warmth of the hearth and temporary respite from the snow.

The man in tweed made his way towards the witness box as Mr Roderick announced, "I call the Dock Constable, John Robinson."

At this announcement, the man in tweed arrested his trajectory, took a few paces backwards and sat in the front row of the stalls. In his place, a large man in police uniform stepped forward. I rather guessed the eager gentleman in tweed was Mr Hugo Loffler, the complainant, whose haste to resolve the formality of the prisoner's conviction struck me as rather more than the usual nerves of the stomach that afflict those who appear in court.

The Dock Constable took his oath, stated his name as John Robinson and bowed to the judge.

"Constable Robinson, you were on duty at Saint Katherine's Docks on the night of the sixteenth?" asked Mr Roderick.

"That is true."

"And, in relation to the matter before the court, what did you observe?"

"I had completed my rounds, and was making my way to the station house when I heard two men arguing on Saint Katherine's Way. As I approached them, I saw the complainant, Mr Loffler, and the prisoner in conversation."

"What was the nature of the conversation?" said the prosecutor.

"They were exchanging high words, Your Honour. I could tell by their pitch and manner that violence was imminent."

"Were you able to discern the nature of their dispute?" asked Mr Roderick.

"Indeed. At the time, the complainant, Mr Loffler, held a wooden box in his arms. I heard him say, 'You tried to steal my box.' At these words, I intervened, announced my station and presence and enquired if Mr Loffler required assistance?"

"And what was his reply?"

"He accused the prisoner of attempting to procure his box with a forged letter, but that was of no matter as the box had been recovered."

"And did the prisoner answer this charge?" asked Mr Roderick.

"He said that he had been handed the letter by a tall, thin man in a black coat, on the steps of the Royal College. He was unable to name this mysterious gentleman. Nor could he describe his face. He stated that the fellow's features were in shadow. However, he assured me that the man in the black coat knew of Mr Loffler, and that this man gave the prisoner a letter written by Mr Loffler, which authorised the prisoner to attend at the restaurant of Mr Triebel in Saint Katherine's Way, collect Mr Loffler's box and return it to the college."

"Did the complainant confirm the accuracy of this account?" said Mr Roderick.

"Indeed he did not, Your Honour. Mr Loffler said that he had never written any such instruction and accused the prisoner of forging the letter in order to obtain his property under false pretences."

A generous grumble erupted from the judge. It was well timed and several of the gentlemen of the jury nodded and answered the judge with disapproving grumbles of their own.

"What was your response, Constable?" asked the prosecutor.

"I ascertained the names and addresses of both men, and informed the prisoner that he was to accompany me to the station. I asked Mr Loffler to join me there, where he was to make a complaint."

"And were you able to obtain the forged letter?"

"I was indeed, sir. The prisoner had it on him, said he would need the letter if he were seen walking through the streets, box in hand, by a constable, and might have need of it to lend legitimacy to his endeavours. I have the letter here, shall I read it to you?"

"Please do."

"I am busy with my work presently. Please give my box to the bearer of this note, who shall ensure its safe return to me. Hugo Loffler."

"Thank you, Constable," said the prosecutor, taking his seat.

As the constable removed himself from the witness box, I heard murmurs from the jury as they spoke in unfriendly tones and pointed at the prisoner. Mr Ruthnick's future appeared quite bleak at this moment.

"Call your next wit—" said the judge, before I interrupted.

"My apologies, Your Honour, I would like to ask a few questions," I said.

A well-practised look of judicial astonishment appeared on Judge Campbell's generously proportioned face.

"If you must," he said.

With some degree of apathy, the constable returned to the witness box.

"Constable, you subsequently discovered that Mr Loffler and the prisoner had met before the events of that evening had taken place?" I said.

"Yes, I believe that Mr Loffler is a German painter, and visitor to the Royal College. I understand that the prisoner was tasked by the Dean to attend to Mr Loffler during his visit."

"That is so. Now, the prisoner, at the very first opportunity, told you that he had been instructed to retrieve Mr Loffler's box from a restaurant in Saint Katherine's Way and return it to the college. He told you that he received this instruction from a tall, thin man in a black coat. Tell me, what efforts did you make to find this tall, thin man in black?"

The Dock Constable appeared as if he had been struck, his head slipped back on his shoulders and his mouth popped open. His appearance was not unlike one of Mr Roderick's stupefied salmon.

"Well, er . . . none, sir."

"None?" I said, with an inflated air of incredulity.

"It was plainly a lie, sir. Mr Loffler told me that he had given no such instruction to any man. According to Mr Loffler's account, the man in black did not exist."

"And you believed him?" I said, inviting a common response from constables of the law.

"He gave me his word as a gentleman," was the reply. The precise answer that I had intended to solicit.

"Constable, come now, under English Law gentlemen are treated no differently from any other man. Waif, stray, baron and beggar are equal under the eyes of this jury, bound as they are to uphold the common law of England," I said, with a dramatic flourish.

I could see the twelve men of the jury positively beaming with the weighty responsibility of equality. It is a shame that they needed reminding of it at all, even through the prism of patriotism. Judge Campbell stifled a groan and gave me a most foul look. He knew I was attempting to wrestle the jury from his control, and he didn't care for it.

"So, Constable Robinson, you carried out no investigation to verify the prisoner's contemporaneous and consistent explanation?"

The good peeler shied a little, and said, "No. I did not. I had no cause to doubt Mr Loffler's word at that time."

"*At that time.* A most excellent choice of words. Constable, if you were, at this time, to begin to doubt the word of Mr Loffler, you admit that the case against the prisoner must fail?"

"That is a matter for the jury," said Judge Campbell.

"Of course, my apologies, Your Honour. Constable Robinson, your evidence was that when you met Mr Loffler and the prisoner in Saint Katherine's Way, Mr Loffler did not at first seek your professional assistance?"

"I'm not sure I understand the question, Mr Dickens," said the witness.

"Ah, well let me put it this way – according to Mr Loffler, the prisoner had attempted to steal his property in a devious, calculated and premeditated manner. Forgery is a serious offence is it not?"

"Indeed it is," conceded the witness.

"And yet, Mr Loffler, a gentleman as you say, did not insist on your arresting this vile criminal?"

"No, he appeared satisfied that the box had been recovered."

"And when you arrested Mr Ruthnick, and took him to the station, did you or your colleagues have need to press Mr Loffler for a formal complaint against the prisoner?"

He cleared his throat and said, "Now that you mention it, sir, Your Honour, my fellow officer did have to encourage Mr Loffler to make a written statement of complaint."

I chanced a quick look at the complainant. He shifted in his seat, and pulled at his collar. It is possible that I may have been mistaken, but at that time I formed the distinct impression that Mr Loffler was considering whether to make a charge for the door.

My moment's pause had given the judge an opportunity to grasp for the jury's mind once more.

"Gentlemen of the jury, giving evidence can be a daunting prospect. It is natural for one to have qualms before one commits to becoming a prosecution witness. May I remind you, gentlemen, Mr Loffler is not the person on trial here," said the judge.

"Your Honour, this case rests on the credibility of the complainant. He is not on trial, but I am at liberty to test the strength of his evidence," I said.

"Why of course, Mr Dickens, but see that it goes no further than that," said Judge Campbell.

I returned my labours to the Dock Constable in the witness box.

"You were present at the Police Court?" I said.

"Indeed I was present."

"Mr Loffler's statement of complaint at that hearing estimated the value of this box and its contents at approximately ten pounds."

"Correct," said Constable Robinson, with a knowing smile.

The box, preserved as a police exhibit, had been produced at Police Court and had also found its way on to the prosecution table at this hearing. I had been at Police Court when this case had been mentioned and I recalled the sheer audacity of the complainant's inflated valuation for what appeared to me to be no more than a battered, dented and stained pine box. My suspicion at that time was that the complainant would shortly make a monetary claim for this egregious overvaluation from Lloyd's of London, and pocket a healthy profit from the damage to his property, which he would no doubt claim had occurred during his struggle with the prisoner.

My theory, sound at that time, was to be proved quite wrong.

"Constable, the box in question is in court?"

Instead of answering, he pointed to the miserable item, around the same size and shape as a suitcase, which sat upon the prosecution's desk.

The jury were not impressed with the valuation, their faces registering their doubt.

"Thank you, Constable, nothing further."

It had taken the prosecutor, Mr Roderick, a short break and a good deal of persuasion to convince Mr Loffler to give evidence. I heard as much in the weeks following the case. However he managed it, Mr Roderick called Mr Hugo Loffler to the witness box and led him through his evidence in a brief and comprehensive manner.

Mr Loffler confirmed that he had been invited to lecture at the Royal College as a guest of the Dean. He had not long been in London, a mere month or two, and wanted to partake of the sights. The Dean had suggested that Mr Ruthnick should be the visitor's guide, and so for two days the prisoner had carried Mr Loffler's box as they traversed the great city.

On the afternoon of the sixteenth of January, Mr Loffler had asked to see Saint Katherine's Docks, and sample the beer from the local brewery. Apparently, he did not care for English ale and had heard that the beer from this brewery was akin to that of his Germanic homeland.

"When did the prisoner make his interest in your box known?" asked the prosecutor.

"When we left the tavern briefly, to walk out upon the dock to watch the police," said Mr Loffler, in a soft German accent.

"You mentioned the police, what were the police doing?"

"They were searching the vessels. Perhaps twenty constables. I had observed their arrival from the tavern window, and I wished to see their operations first-hand. The following day, I learned the constables were searching for the notes stolen from the Wisbech and Lincolnshire Bank."

The robbery had been front-page news for weeks. A gang of armed villains had broken into the bank during the late hours of Christmas Eve and made off with many hundreds of five-pound notes. The Metropolitan Police had yet to make an arrest and suspected that a criminal network was attempting to smuggle the notes abroad.

Mr Loffler continued. "I suggested to the prisoner that as there were few people in the tavern, my box would be safe remaining at our table whilst we went outside. At that moment, the prisoner said that he would carry the box outside with us, as he was fearful of thieves."

"And did you take the box with you when you ventured to the dock?"

"No. I had been sketching in the tavern. I took my paper and charcoal with me. I fancied that I might want to sketch the scene. My box remained at the table, under the watch of the innkeeper."

"And after you and the prisoner had viewed the police operation, what happened next?"

"I informed the prisoner that I cared to quarter in the area. We returned to the inn where the prisoner carried my box to the hotel of Mr Triebel. I told the prisoner that I should take a walk on my own, and that his services were not required for the remainder of that day."

"I see, and did you venture out that day?" asked the prosecutor.

"Correct. I dined first then left the hotel for an evening stroll. When I returned after a few hours, the hotel manager informed me that I had just missed my companion, Mr Ruthnick, who had taken delivery of my box in accordance with my instruction. I explained that I had given no instruction and enquired in what direction the villain had departed. I then gave chase."

"You chased after the prisoner?"

"Correct, Mr Triebel informed me that the prisoner had left only a few minutes before my arrival. I knew that he could not move swiftly with my box and I caught up with him quickly. I apprehended the thief with my property in his possession."

All was silent in the room, save for the soft rustling of paper as Mr Roderick produced the alleged forged letter and handed it to his witness.

"Mr Loffler, is this your handwriting, or your signature?"

"No, it is not."

"Thank you, nothing further, Your Honour."

Even as I rose, pulling my robes about me and ensuring that my wig had not slipped to a jaunty angle, I could see Mr Loffler's complexion transform into pale water. His fingernails still carried the remains of dark paint and would not keep still. Each digit beat an anxious, erratic rhythm on the mahogany rail surrounding the witness box.

"Mr Loffler, it was Constable Robinson's evidence that when he apprehended the prisoner you were somewhat reluctant to make a formal complaint. Is that a fair assessment?"

"No, no, no, my good fellow. I wish to see evildoers punished, of course, that is my duty as a citizen."

"So the constable is lying?"

"He is merely mistaken," he said.

"When you discovered the prisoner had made off with your box from your hotel, under false pretences, you did not ask Mr Triebel to alert a constable, is that correct?"

The anxious percussion of Mr Loffler's fingertips began beating to a higher tempo.

"I . . . I did not wish to inconvenience my host."

The jury were transfixed by Mr Loffler's curious worriment. Even Judge Campbell's ample visage had taken interest in the complainant's palpable distress.

I took it upon myself to test his resolve and identify the source of this solicitude. So I turned, quite slowly, and set my eyes upon the box. It was clearly an artist's portable easel. Once opened at the hinge, it would allow one to sit with the box on one's knees, have ready access to paint and materials and a secure, properly angled canvas from which to work. Such items were neither expensive nor uncommon. The dents, scrapes and paint stains on this box were evidence of its heavy use and history of travel.

"Your box, Mr Loffler, seems to be in a rather sorry state, does it not?"

At the word "box" the complainant's eyes widened. "It has been in my possession for some time."

"It is hardly worth ten pounds?" I said.

"Your Honour, I object to my friend's question," said Mr Roderick. "The value of this item does not address the matter of its illegal procurement by the prisoner."

"My question, Your Honour, may prove relevant should the jury find against my client. The value of the property is something Your Honour will no doubt bear in mind in relation to the issue of penalty."

"I'll allow the question," said the judge, who no doubt had begun to question the hefty valuation placed upon the item by Mr Loffler.

"It was a mere guess, Your Honour. If Mr Dickens is of the view that my box is worth less than this amount, so be it."

A pair of fat eyebrows shot beneath Judge Campbell's wig in astonishment.

"You conceded to my view very quickly, Mr Loffler. Perhaps I do you a disservice. Whilst the box itself may be estimated at a lesser amount, the contents could be worth considerably more, could they not?"

"No! Forgive me, I . . . I merely . . . Mr Dickens, the box is of little value," pleaded the complainant.

"I would like to view the contents of this exhibit, Your Honour. This witness has reneged on his earlier evidence, and the court cannot be convinced of his credibility on this issue. The court should observe the full contents of this exhibit."

A cry from the witness box was quickly silenced by the judge, who called forth Mr Roderick, box in hand, so that a judicial eye could pass over the disputed exhibit.

As the judge opened the box, the witness hung his head.

I watched the judge remove pots of paint, charcoal, paper, canvas and a host of brushes as he searched. I suspected he would discover beneath the artistic paraphernalia, at least one large five-pound note from the Wisbech and Lincolnshire Bank. I was sure of it. I did not believe Mr Loffler's visit to the docks, and his keen curiosity regarding the police search were in the least coincidental. This man was a courier for the bank robbers.

The judge threw up his hands, almost as if something within the complainant's box were lethal, and may strike at him at any moment.

I could tell, by the white dot of foam at the corner of his lips, that Judge Campbell was not best pleased with his discovery. He produced the offending item from the box and held it aloft.

A piece of paper. White.

But not a five-pound note.

Instead, he held a single page.

He flung it from the bench with all his might and it careened through the air to land on my bench. I saw then what had so enraged the unlearned judge. And I recalled the evidence of Mr Loffler.

Whist the prisoner and Mr Loffler had sampled the pseudo-Germanic beer in the Docks tavern, Mr Loffler had taken up his charcoal and drawn a sketch of the clientele. In the foreground was a serving girl bent over a table to retrieve a half-empty plate. And while Mr Loffler had sketched her serving frock, he had taken care to ensure that the frock was transparent. And his heavy scrawls left little to the imagination concerning the shapely form that inhabited the dress.

"Filth! Depravity!" screamed Judge Campbell. "Never have I seen such levels of debauched indecency represented on the page. Mr Loffler, you are no artist. You are a base pornographer. Your work, and the devilish tools you employ to manufacture these indecent images, are entirely worthless in this court. Case dismissed. The prisoner is free to leave the court. And Mr Loffler, you are very lucky not to find yourself in irons. The audacity!"

"All . . . all rise," said the clerk, stifling a chuckle as the judge gained his feet and departed.

The relief set upon Mr Ruthnick's face proved a perfect carnival reflection of the complainant's expression, which was pure, red shame.

I gathered my papers and glanced again at the sketch. It seemed to me, although erotic to the point of criminal indecency, not unskilled work. The table that the serving girl leant over had been perfectly drawn and delicately shaded. The patrons surrounding her had been well captured – indeed the fellow beside her who sat at the table was very well drawn indeed. He would've been a tall man, considering the length of his legs. And certainly an individual not ruled by his appetite, judging by his thin arms, legs and the half-full plate of food that was being taken away. His face was perhaps not too well realised. A high forehead, angular features, but one side of his face appeared in strange shadow. When I examined the remainder of the sketch, one could clearly delineate the angle of light that the artist had controlled, but the darkness on one side of this man's face was incongruous to the angle of daylight from the window. I surmised that it was not shadow, but perhaps a birthmark or an injury carried home from a military campaign.

I passed the sketch back to the constable, but not before I saw Mr Ruthnick point at the sketch as he descended from the dock. According to Mr Ruthnick, the tall, thin man in charcoal bore a striking resemblance to the fellow that had given to him the note and the instruction to retrieve the box.

I heard little more from Mr Ruthnick, post acquittal. He had returned to his studies, as he'd hoped, and went on to become a minor watercolour artist.

From memory, it was May when Mr Deery approached me in the Library. In fact, at the very desk I sit at now.

He gave me a letter, marked for my attention. And left without another word.

I still have that letter. Although its contents I can recite easily.

Dear Mr Dickens,

Congratulations on your triumph. I wish to apologise for not being entirely forthcoming with you during my initial correspondence. I do so now upon your word that this letter be destroyed as soon as it is read and that you maintain your silence.

I have heard from my contacts that Mr Ruthnick is prospering, and is engaged to be married. This is good news.

In relation to Mr Loffler, he was not prosecuted, even though I understand the judge pressed the prosecutor to do so. No, Mr Loffler had had quite enough of London, and required the funds to sail back to the continent sooner than he had envisaged. I acquired the sketch for a small stipend.

Although it is customary in these situations not to thank one who has performed a service for one's country, I make an exception in this case. Even though Mr Loffler was quite embarrassed to have his erotic visions, which he himself realised in charcoal, so publicly revealed – he has also unwittingly served his British hosts well. The tall, thin gentleman in the sketch was at one time believed to be dead. Resurrection is not so uncommon these days. He had taken up a position at that table in order to survey the full disarray of the police investigation, first hand. He must have realised that Mr Loffler recorded his image, and sought to retrieve it. He could not do so by force, that day, because he did not wish to draw attention to himself. Suffice to say, the sketch of this man is extremely valuable to a number of international police agencies. Already, it has proved useful in detecting his cohorts who so brazenly robbed the Wisbech and Lincolnshire Bank.

My thanks to you again, Mr Dickens.

Yours faithfully,

K. H. Rochesmolles

When I had finished reading that letter for the first time, all those years ago, I did something quite extraordinary. Even now, I cannot explain why I did it. Or how. It simply happened. I could not hold my hand still that day.

I took up my pen and ink and did this.

Yours faithfully,
~~*K. H. Rochesmolles*~~
s h e r l o c k h o l m e s

Jacques the Giant Slayer
A Steampunk Retelling of an Old Tale

Vanessa de Sade

Rosie

Rosie stands in the semi-dark, London fog licking at her face like a rambunctious dog who's been out running on the fens all day and brings the cold and earthy smell of the outdoors into your warm with him. Only two more girls to go and then it would be her turn. And the girl ahead of her had the advantage of huge breasts, though Rosie has heard her trying to conceal a cough as they stand waiting to be assessed.

But the queue moves quickly and a curvaceous blonde two ahead is refused and Rosie's buxom neighbour mounts the podium in a rustle of petticoats and unfastens her blouse, her famous bosoms like ripe tropical melons in the window of Fortnum & Mason's, blue-white in the moonlight with nipples like blobs of black cherry conserve on perfectly turned-out milk puddings. *They have to take her*, Rosie thinks, but the woman in black whispers something to the doctor and shakes her head, and the voluptuary stalks angrily off, back to the streets, fastening her clothing as she goes.

And then Rosie hears her name called. Feels her feet taking her up the two steps and depositing her in front of the selection panel, her own breathing loud in her ears. Then there is the doctor, fat and moustachioed, his ample belly protruding from his open white coat, careless stethoscope around his fat neck and a bulge in his pants. *Obviously a man who enjoys his work*, Rosie thinks wryly to calm herself, meeting the cold blue eyes of the woman in the black rocketeer's uniform with an unblinking stare. *She is German*, Rosie thinks, taking in the flaxen Aryan-blonde hair, as her cold fingers fumble with buttons and she bares her small breasts for them, distracting herself by imagining the woman as Brünnhilde, complete with horned helmet and triumphant Wagnerian score.

The rocketeer nods approvingly as her eyes rake Rosie's little nubs, the pale nipples perky with the cold. "How old are you, child?"

"Fifteen," Rosie lies, subtracting four years.

"And you are pure? Do not lie, child, we will check!"

But Rosie nods and swallows uncomfortably. Telling the truth this time, and hoping that she possesses a commodity that they can trade in.

The woman looks quizzically at the doctor and Rosie sees him nod. "Is good," she says crisply, meeting Rosie's gaze with her ice-blue eyes, storybook Snow Queen and Wicked Witch all rolled into one. "Go, take your seat . . ."

The big sky-barnacled airship sits like a mist-enshrouded grey whale in the dock, bobbing agitatedly against its moorings as Rosie gingerly mounts the gangplank, the creaking of the ropes like the cry of a great behemoth. She has heard many tales of these mighty Prussian Zeppelins, how they sweep unseen across the night skies like silent raptors, their immense engines muted as they swoop along the Thames, skiffing the towers and turrets of bridges, until the propellers engage and they head out across the sea for France, their luxurious cabins filled with rich men in search of debauchery in the lanes of Paris.

Tonight, though, long shadows dance in the chiaroscuro tones of this great liner of the sky, and the echoing staterooms are empty save for the chatter of girls who sit in regimented rows before the low-slung onyx tables with their gold filigree fittings, the chandeliers muted and the walls with their great panels of black marble giving the whole place a charnel-house look when bereft of their customary orchestra and glittering crystal illuminations.

"Here, sit with me," a freckled little redhead with rosy cheeks and multitudes of ringlets chirps, making room on the plush upholstered banquette for Rosie to join her. "They say we're to be taken to Paris and will dine in a café at the very top of the Eiffel Tower, is that not thrilling!"

"Yes indeed." Rosie nods, seating herself and giving the other's hand a squeeze. "But I do not think that there are cafés at the top of the tower. Though I'm sure that we can climb it and see all the lights of Paris spread out at our feet," she adds hastily, seeing the disappointment in her companion's eyes.

"I'm Mora," the redhead says agreeably in her soft Irish lilt, recovering swiftly. "But now that I'm here I think I'm going to be Antoinette. It's more French, don't you think?"

"Absolutely," Rosie agrees, settling down on the soft black velvet, as the big engines start to thrum and the huge ship casts its moorings and begins to rise majestically into the air.

Jacques

"Oh for God's sake, Jacques," Herriman laments, slapping a beefy hand to his wet, florid face, his rage making his big toad's eyes bulge even more than usual. "The first decent case we've had in months and you spend the whole retainer on . . . on . . . *THIS!*"

Jacques looks back at him irritatedly but tries to remain placid. He has worked for Herriman for two years now and is used to his histrionic tirades and, frankly, outdated methods of detection, which he now mentally lists to distract himself as his employer rants and raves. Fallacy One. The non-recognition of fingerprints as valuable evidence. Fallacy Two. The refusal to *ever* pay for forensic analysis at crime scenes. Fallacy Three. The fat man's insistence that all a good detective ever needs is a magnifying glass—

"Jacques! Are you listening to me, Jacques?" Herriman demands loudly, poking him in the chest and breaking his young assistant's train of thought. "Because, really, this time you've really gone too far. Five hundred credits of my money for this . . . *THING!*"

Jacques shakes his head in exasperation. "I'm telling you, Boss, this is no bag of magic beans," he explains. "This is an investment that is going to pay dividends. We *know* that they're using Zeppelins to transport the girls out of the country. And the only way we're going to find out where they're taking them is to follow one, way up into the sky."

"And you're going to go 'way up into the sky' on *that!*" Herriman snorts, almost hopping with rage as he indicates the small second-hand telecopter that Jacques has just purchased at the monthly robotics market, its two dented brass ulithium cylinders patched with scrap steel panels and missing rivets along its seams, the front propeller chipped and cracked. "In which case I hope you've left me a few coppers to advertise for a new bloody assistant, laddie, because I'm damned well going to need one when you nosedive straight into the Thames on that piece of scrap iron. *And* you can pay for your funeral out of your own damn pocket!"

He pauses momentarily for breath as behind them the chipped sign advertising "Discreet Investigations" creaks softly in a sudden breeze, and Jacques quickly shields his eyes and looks up into the night sky, trying to detect the grey hulk of a titanic sky whale against the pitch-blackness of the curfew dark. "There!" he whispers, pointing at what looks like a bank of fog creeping furtively across the starless sky above them. "There, there they go, another shipment heading for Paris or worse!"

Herriman starts to say something, but Jacques silences him by yanking on the cord of the oil-stained copper engine and the propeller coughs and then stirs sluggishly into life.

"Well, it's now or never," Jacques breathes, with a confidence he doesn't feel, as he dons his goggles and prepares to strap himself on to the exposed-to-the-elements pilot's seat.

"Nay, don't do it, lad," Herriman suddenly says, laying a fatherly hand on the boy's arm. "Don't go up into the air and out over the black, black sea in that old thing. It's too dangerous. Just stay here and we'll pretend that we've looked all over London for the girls. Tell their parents that they're gone, let them accept it and move on with their lives."

"We've *talked* about this, Boss," Jacques yells over the roar of the engine, as the worn propeller blades gain momentum and the little ship tugs at its mooring like an eager terrier desperate to be let off the leash. "If we take people's money then we *have* to do what they've asked. And, anyway, you know as well as I do that this is the big one. There's a giant behind these abductions, you mark my words, and we're just the men to bring him toppling down. Now cast me off, or I'll lose him in this fog!"

"Ah, Jacques the giant slayer," Herriman mutters, shaking his head ruefully, but the straining guy lines are already taut as wire and the whine of the labouring engine has become a scream, so, defeated, he unhooks the rope and sends Jacques speeding off into the black maw of the thickest fog of the decade.

Rosie

Mora is still chattering away excitedly about Parisian ice-cream shops and new hats with wax cherries on the brims, *like a little pet chipmunk unaware that it's about to be python food*, Rosie thinks as she tries to shut her out and scan the skies through the row of brass-riveted portholes, desperately trying to find a landmark to orientate herself.

"We went straight down the Thames," she whispers to no one in particular, consulting the tiny compass embedded in the heel of her boot. "But we've not crossed the Channel at the right angle for Paris. I think we're heading for Switzerland."

Jacques

He can barely feel his own face or his hands on the tiller, and his eyelids are frozen open even under the protection of the thick greenish bottle-glass goggles, but he holds grimly on, the image of that row of daguerreotypes spread across Herriman's desk like a winning hand of cards burned into his memory as he brings each lost girl's face to mind. They were all ordinary lasses, daughters of factory workers and manual labourers, not the sort of people who would have sway with the police or have the means to hire their own team, but pooling their meagre credits had led them to Herriman's door, the cheapest – and probably worst – private detective in all of Shoreditch, oftentimes more crooked than the people he supposedly investigated but basically decent at the core of his fat and lazy heart. Jacques saw to that.

And tonight they were going to crack open the case of the century, the trafficking of girls across Europe by Zeppelin for heaven knew what purpose other than the obvious. Though it was funny that none of them ever came back, alive or dead . . .

But the fog banks were diminishing now and the air was thin, almost too thin. Jacques was finding it difficult to breathe as red blood-spots began to appear before his eyes, and, no trained rocketeer, he would probably have fallen from his seat and tumbled head first into the abyss had he not been well strapped in and his hands frozen to the controls as the huge ship ahead of him nosed its way cautiously into a giant loading bay in the side of a mountain, the dull gunmetal of the doors bereft of any identification save for two words that spoke greater volumes to the young sleuth than any sizable treatise or tome:

Moriarty Corporation

Rosie

They were all clustered like indigo-blue limpets around the portholes by now, a chattering, giggling gaggle of humanity, like schoolgirls on a trip to the seaside. *And they're all so young*, Rosie mused, watching her companions carefully as the big airship manoeuvred itself into the dock below a turreted gothic hotel, which sat like a lone sentinel atop a snow-capped peak, sheer rock faces leading to glacial ravines on all the sides, the only way up or down a rickety funicular that clung perilously to the side of the mountain like a seaside automation.

The woman in black had appeared again, as if by magic or

some stage wizardry whereupon the Queen of the Night would be hoisted through trapdoors to a fanfare of magnesium flares and emerge triumphant to confront an amazed Tamino. Her hair was dishevelled and she wore aviator's goggles carelessly around her neck. Her face seemed flushed with little red spots on her otherwise pallid cheeks, her ice eyes sparkling with their own private aurora, as she segregated the chattering girls into two groups, little Mora being led off at the head of a large and noisy bunch all twittering about baked ice-cream desserts and boxes of bonbons dusted with gold.

"Mora, no," Rosie tried to cry out as her new friend was led away by quiet men in agonisingly familiar grey uniforms, but the black rocketeer silenced her with a frozen stare which would have planted ice splinters into the hearts of lesser mortals and even momentarily subdued our heroine. She watched powerlessly as the girls were led chattering into a subterranean chamber cut deep in the rock below the soft and welcoming lights of the Swiss hotel above.

Jacques

He was still frozen, but the heat from the Zeppelin's enormous turbine engines blasted him like a hot-air drying machine, and he began to gradually feel his numb limbs become sensate, as he dragged the little telecopter into a shady inglenook and watched aghast as a group of about twenty girls were led out by men in the familiar slate-grey uniforms of the Moriarty Corporation militia, the most savage mercenaries in all of Europe. And, though he tried to follow, a heavy copper-reinforced contagion barrier slid up noiselessly from within a high archway hewn from the rock and then slammed shut again as the last of the girls, like some Hamelin brood, vanished from sight and into the depths of the unassailable mountain.

Unsure of how to proceed, he paused, only to hear voices and see a second group emerge from the big grey airship, a blonde rocketeer he recognised as Hilda Braun of the Prussian Luftwaffe leading a party of four quieter young women up some steep stone stairs and into the bowels of the luxurious hotel above.

And at the front of the group walked Rosie!

Rosie. With her indomitable spirit and quick mind, her soft grey eyes flashing with rage at Herriman when she had burst into their office demanding their assistance with the disappearance of her father. Her long grey dress neat but with discreet darns at the cuffs and a patch at the hem, a thick band of mourner's crêpe knotted at her coat sleeve like a man would wear. And Herriman had given her short shrift. Spotted an illegitimate daughter with scant income, living on handouts from some toff now bored with paying for the results of an eighteen-year-old indiscretion and conveniently vanishing. He'd seen the same story a hundred times before, he'd later told Jacques. The man disappeared and left the mistress and her brat bereft. Plus, he added with a knowing man-to-man wink to his assistant, no money to pay for the almost-sure-to-be-fruitless investigation that they wanted him to carry out.

"My heart bleeds for you, my dear," he had said to Rosie with an obsequious smile that grey February morning when the soft mist floated down the river like a funeral cortège. "But, in my experience, when a man such as your father disappears then the likelihood of him ever being found is practically nil, and who's then to pay my fee, little Rosie, or ensure that my poor children see a meagre chop of mutton for their evening meal."

And, though Jacques had run after her and tried to call her back, she had tossed her curls dismissively at him, tarring him with Herriman's brush, and haughtily announced that, as they were unwilling to assist, she would find her father herself and "make a damn sight better job of it than you two buffoons!"

And that had been nine long months ago, and yet he still could not get the vision of her out of his head, and now here she was, being herded with a gaggle of trafficked girls in a mountain retreat run by the Moriarty Corporation right bang in the middle of nowhere and without recourse to any form of assistance whatsoever.

Except him, of course.

Rosie

The black-clad rocketeer led them up a series of shabby staircases and concealed servants' passageways, the metal segs of their leather boots clattering like horseshoes on the worn stone slabs, before they emerged into a darkened hallway on the upper floor of the hotel where the carpets were so thick underfoot that they were all suddenly muted, as if they had never existed.

A golden harp stood by the door, its faded frame reverberating to an old Rhineland melody, though no player plucked at its strings, and the high red-flock-covered walls, hung with rich impasto oils of naked girls, gleamed voluptuously in the soft light of pink-glass-shaded electric lamps.

Oh hell, it's a robot bar, Rosie whispered to herself, looking at the neat row of white-jacketed waiters behind the rich ox-blood and black lacquered counter, their waxen faces locked in a rictus grin of servility as hidden hydraulics powered the shiny alloy arms beneath their jackets in an obscene parody of human movement, the silver cocktail shakers in their hands gyrating like burlesque dancers in the mellow ruby-coloured light.

This means that whatever takes place in here will not be witnessed by the waiting staff, Rosie thought quickly, as the woman in black closed the room doors behind them. *But we've been permitted to enter, so does that mean we're not expected to leave?*

Jacques

He had scaled the winding stairways silently behind the girls, creeping into the warm womb-like glow of the plush robot saloon before the rocketeer barred the tall double doors and encased everyone inside the hermetically sealed chamber with an embalmer's fluid grace. And, unlike the outer halls with their clattering black marble floors, the cavernous dimly lit room was carpeted with soft Aubusson rugs that muffled his movements, giving him a welcome stealth, as he hugged the wall and stood like a statue-performer in a dark niche opposite a wall of panoramic windows, which gazed out at the splendour of a frozen Alpine night.

There were four men ostensibly lounging in leather armchairs in the room, though Jacques could detect a keen coiled-spring tension to their spines. The air around them was redolent with the scent of their ignored Cuban cigars, which even now smouldered in the chromium ashtrays, lazy trails of scented smoke spiralling loosely into the warm shadows above them. Three he did not recognise, erect and moustachioed military types identified by their uniforms as high-ranking Prussians, but the fourth was a face he knew only too well from the stacks of dog-eared daguerreotypes in Herriman's many filing cabinets back in Shoreditch.

Moriarty.

Rosie

She was aware of his presence, his spoor, even before she saw him across that dimly lit room and her blood ran cold. Though she had long suspected that he was the brains behind this operation, it was still a jolt to finally see him here, in the flesh, as it were, and not in the grainy line engravings she had saved so laboriously from the pages of the *Police Gazette*. And yet his cruel eyes seemed oddly fascinating under the heavy cadaverous brows, his face a death mask in alabaster, as he surveyed the girls brought before him as a tame hawk surveys the mice it will decimate for its master's amusement.

Jacques

And yet it doesn't fit at all, Jacques thought to himself, as he watched the haughty rocketeer parade the four girls for the men's inspection. *Pimping is a small-time racket, even when performed on a national scale. Why would the Napoleon of Crime even bother with it, let alone personally inspect the merchandise? And why just semi-pubescent girls from the East End? And why did none of them ever surface in the frequent police raids on the brothels of Paris or Berlin?*

And, as if in answer, the Professor began to speak in a low measured voice, as though he addressed an audience of imbeciles who required every nuance of his meaning explained.

"Gentlemen," he began, ignoring the girls and the black-booted rocketeer. "Gentlemen, may I demonstrate my ultimate fighting machines, who will be ready to obtain the European victory you so hunger for in but two short months' time. No patriotism-driven country lads easily scattered by a machine gun's fury or money-driven mercenaries easily bought by a rival's superior gold, these highly advanced soldiers of the future are undefeatable and completely incorruptible—"

"But, Professor, these are mere girls!" one of the generals interrupted with a derisive laugh, and would have said more had not Moriarty silenced him with a look that spoke volumes.

"Indeed," he replied, his hawk's eyes like steel ball bearings. "But observe tonight the miracle that is even now being performed upon hundreds upon hundreds of new infantrymen in our robotics workshops here in the catacombs so far below us. Commander?"

The rocketeer nodded, clicked her heels and pulled one of the girls roughly to the front of the assembled males. She ripped open the girl's bodice in a shower of black buttons like some Grand Guignol lecher, the girl's little breasts white and vulnerable in this strangely inhospitable room, with its row of grinning robots mixing drinks for non-existent guests and a pale bloodless moon illuminating the snow-capped peaks of the mountain ranges beyond the thick plate glass of the tall windows on the north face of the bar.

"Convert her," Moriarty said quietly, and, before Jacques' horrified eyes, the rocketeer swiftly produced a small rapier-like piece of platinum with a tropical scarab of iridescent electrodes at its head and plunged it straight into the heart of the girl, who immediately fell limp at her feet like a marionette whose strings have been unexpectedly and maliciously cut.

Again the generals protested, called out that this was mere murder, not warfare, until the Professor clapped his hands and the "dead" girl arose, her eyes now as white as Iona pebbles, her face expressionless.

"Now, gentlemen," he said in his same emotionless tone, though now finally permitting something resembling a satisfied smile to transform the lower half his austere features, though his steely eyes remained cold. "Allow me to demonstrate. Commander. Open a window if you please. Soldier, advance, to the window, excellent, at ease. Now . . . jump!"

And, without hesitation, the girl plunged out and was lost in the blackness of the frozen ravine below.

Rosie

"Our robotics scientists have carried out endless experiments on paupers of all ages and sexes, and have found that girls at the peak of adolescent desire but yet still physically pure respond best to the chemicals we coat our control stakes with," Moriarty was explaining to the dumbfounded generals who stood gaping like fish in a fairground hawker's array of coloured bowls, their minds already reeling with the possibilities of an army of expend-ables who would obey their every command without question and walk unhesitatingly through hails of bullets to achieve their appointed prize.

And, as if watching the scene in the jerking staccato motion of a promenade mutoscope machine, she saw herself rise suddenly like a meteor and send the rocketeer flying to the floor with a resounding blow. Saw, to her amazement, the earnest boy who had partnered that awful Shoreditch detective jump out of the shadows like a fairground apparition and grab the brass handles that operated the room's fire-break shields, an iron- and asbestos-curtain thundering down from the roof and isolating them from the moustachioed soldiers and the recumbent rocketeer.

Jacques

And he had thought that she would fall to the floor in relief, but instead she looked desperately all about her like a mad thing, her whole body shaking with fury like a cat who had pounced on the acid-yellow family canary but has had its prey rescued at the last moment by some interfering human and now howls its displeasure.

And, then, suddenly, her demeanour completely changed and she became wild-eyed and almost delirious, jumping the upturned armchairs like an Olympic hurdler and making a grab for a supine figure that even now was trying to slide like some dark thing and seek the shelter of the shadows and safety.

"Oh no, not so easily, my man," he heard her shout. Saw something like a glint of blue-hued metal flash in her hand as she palmed the cosh so carefully concealed up her sleeve and struck the figure, quickly grabbing it by the scruff of its thin neck and dragging it over to the open window.

"Rosie, no!" he shouted, recognising the Professor, as she dumped him unceremoniously on the open window frame, the bitter mountain wind ruffling the man's elegant frock coat and making him look like a bedraggled crow as he teetered between life and death on the narrow precipice that was the windowsill.

And, even as he rushed to try and intercede, he heard a low rumble and realised that Moriarty, like one of his automaton soldiers, had no fear and smiled unrepentantly at the girl as she towered over him, blood from the gash in his forehead trickling lazily down his sallow cheek.

"So, so, young miss." He almost smiled. "Who of yours have I so wronged that you slay me with such vehemence. What sainted mother have I corrupted, what virtuous sister defiled?"

And Rosie shook her head slowly, as her neat little hand stretched out and began to apply pressure, pushing his scarecrow's body slowly out over the abyss with a steely deliberation that knew her prey would eventually find its fulcrum point and topple headlong into the glacier far below.

"Neither, sir," she says now with a steady voice though her whole body shakes with emotion. "I slay you for my father, Sherlock Holmes. *This is for Reichenbach, Moriarty!*"

And, to this day, Jacques is still sure that he heard the Professor laugh hysterically as he tumbled flailing into the dark gorge of that freezing night . . .

Rosenlaui

Conrad Williams

I was stillborn, after a fashion.

Unable to speak, unable to move other than this blinking of the eyes. I was told my paralysis was due to a cerebrovascular disease passed on to me by my mother. I come from poor genetic stock, you see. My mother was descended from a bloodline that barely deserved the name: it was diluted red juice, she always said. It was rusty tap water. Her grandparents had died in their forties; her parents had done the same. Her husband came from a family who seemed to suffer heart attacks for fun; he died when I was but a child.

My mind, at least, flourished while the flesh surrounding it withered. I did well at school, having been forced, from a very early age (thanks to my ever patient and guilt-ridden mother), into developing a means to communicate. This I managed via an alphabet-based system connected to the frequency of blinks I managed with either eye, a practice that consumed many hours of painstaking trial and error.

Though my sight is keen, I often suffer from a number of optically related problems: double vision, flashes, headaches and so forth. I cannot cough, spit or swallow with any degree of success. I do not eat solid food. I'm unable to control my emotions and find myself oscillating between bouts of laughter-induced hysteria and racking sobs. I am blessed to be in the bosom of a family that loves me dearly, and they have sacrificed a great deal to make me comfortable, to ensure a future, of sorts, for me. A great deal of money has been spent to adapt a room at my mother's hotel (she and her brothers, Pascal and Tobias, have run the Schilthorn since the 1870s) so that it is comfortable for me. A special, raised bed – very heavy, so I am told – needed to be built on site. Ramps had to be added to the hotel infrastructure so that my wheelchair – itself of a bespoke design – could be more easily pushed around the grounds. My gratitude knows no bounds. But for my mother's love and devotion to me, and the support and protection afforded to me by my uncles, I might well have been abandoned, destined to live a miserable life in the cold, cruel poorhouses in Bern or Lausanne.

Nevertheless, I wished I had died in childbirth. I did not want to live. As soon as I was able, I begged my mother to help me go to sleep for ever, to end my suffering. But she refused; she was horrified. It was a sign from God, she told me. If I had been meant to die, it would have happened in the womb. She begged me to put such thoughts out of my head – she was convinced that the mind, if focused on one particular subject for long enough, could achieve its ambition – scared rigid that I would be delivered straight to hell should I be granted my heart's desire.

My mother's paraenesis went unheard, I'm ashamed to say. Lying in bed or sitting immobile in my fortress chair were causing my muscles to atrophy. I once heard the doctor telling my mother that the heart might not escape the same fate. Though it was beating, and strong because of that, it was having to work extra hard to serve my failing body. The doctor suspected my heart might eventually be affected by the malaise of the flesh and either stop working so effectively, or stop working altogether.

I lay awake at night imagining my heart in my chest, perhaps deciding if it was time to give up. But such thoughts did not panic me. I knew death would be a release. I knew it was every parent's concern that they might outlive their offspring, but I couldn't imagine what life would be like once my mother was gone. I could only envisage misery, and the interminable, wretched pursuit of her to the grave.

Some nights, when my misery seemed to know no lower limit, and I felt stretched and on the brink of dissolution, like a drip of molten wax, I thought of my heart – imagined it in the prison of my ribcage – beating more and more slowly, until it trembled and stopped. I willed it to happen. I wanted it more than anything else. I would wake the next morning, feeling cheated by God, and convinced He wanted me to live so that He could be entertained by my travails.

It was after this episode that I began to really turn my focus inwards. I began to study my feelings and I realised that although I was an intelligent young man – given the limitations of my affliction – I was retarded in terms of experiencing the full gamut of emotions. I have already mentioned that I shifted between extremes, albeit without any discernible external stimuli to trigger it. My emotions were chaos. In short, I did not understand them. I could not interpret them. Like me, my feelings were inert, broken, paralysed. I had learned to "talk", but there was no colour to my words. How could you develop a personality, how could you convey wit or spirit or character if you had never lived? My reaction to every situation was the same: dumb passivity. I could not engage unless I was engaged. I could initiate no kind of contact.

I thought more deeply. I thought of the broad issues of life; the crucial signifiers. I thought of death dispassionately, with a strange kind of curiosity. I thought of love with a greater sense of mystification. Mother, every day, before she turned in, would ruffle my hair, kiss my cheek and say, "I love you." I never reciprocated. I didn't know what it meant. I didn't know then how important for her it would have been had I signed the words *I love you too*.

In my room, I watched, incessantly, the bend of the larch trees under stiff north-westerly breezes. I could stare for hours at the trees, and the sun and shade flickering across the mountains behind them, and the clouds. I was jealous, and fascinated by, any kind of movement; my eye was fast upon it, wherever it might originate. These momentary distractions apart, I felt doomed. To die in my father's footsteps, relatively young from heart disease, meant that I was yet to spend over two more decades upon this Earth. Little was I to know how much my world would be changed over the course of a few days . . .

Who could have known that the events of those coming days would create ripples to be felt across the world? I can't help feelings that the reason for the ripples – the stone cast at the centre of it all – was me. If it weren't for me, then the dreadful business at Reichenbach would not have happened . . . could not have happened. I saved one man and sent another to his death – or at least that's what it looked like to me at the time. Everyone believed they both died that day, the light and the shade. The virtuous and the diabolical.

And so the strangers came to our village. This is no great shock, of course. I live in an agreeable part of the world, a beautiful place with fresh air and attractive scenery (we have mountains and meadows, alpine flowers and goats, a spectacular waterfall and, in the shape of Rosenlaui, a glacier of awe-inspiring note); we receive many visitors eager to partake of its rejuvenating qualities. I spend a great deal of my time in the small lobby of the hotel, people-watching. I suppose you could say I was attuned to the small fluctuations that occur in the general current of humanity which drifted through our hotel. Such as that created by the two fellows who arrived on the 3 May. I was drawn to them instantly. One was tall and rangy, the kind of fellow you know is aware of everything and everyone in a room without ostentatious scrutiny; his companion was somewhat shorter, more rotund, and reminded me of the pictures of walruses I had seen on the walls of the library in Zurich. He wore a perplexed expression that struck me as likely to be a permanent fixture. I watched them talk to my mother for a while, and she made little flip-flop gestures with her hands, a gesture I had seen many times before; it meant there were no rooms vacant. The shorter man's face lost its perplexity to a thunderstruck mien but the taller man – immaculate in his Inverness cape – smiled congenially and bent to ask my mother a question. She pointed through the window in the direction of Innertkirchen and the men bowed slightly and readied themselves to leave. Just then, the taller man espied me and tapped his companion on the shoulder. The perplexed look returned, but he remained where he was standing. The taller man approached me, that convivial smile countered somewhat by the greedy curiosity in his eyes.

"Sherlock Holmes," he said, in a rich, sonorous voice, "at your service. Forgive me, but I couldn't help noticing your predicament. You are a C4 quadriplegic, are you not?"

I was taken aback, not only by his direct and pinpoint diagnosis – my mother would have never volunteered such intimate information – but that he had approached me at all. Though I spent a lot of time in the lobby only my family engaged me in conversation. This was, I persuaded myself, because I was unable to enjoy any interaction – brief or otherwise – with people who were unaware of the method of "speech" I employed. But more likely it was because people didn't understand what they saw, and they feared me.

I decided to have some fun with Herr Holmes.

YOU WILL EXCUSE ME IF I DO NOT GET UP.

"Of course, young fellow," he replied, instantly. "It's heartening to see a man with a complete spinal injury who has retained a sense of humour."

He told me he admired my "silent, sombre observation" of the lobby and that he sensed in me a kindred spirit, a man enthused and intrigued by the human condition. He only regretted the fact that he would be unable to stay at our hotel.

"I wonder if you might do me the enormous courtesy of a favour, for which I would pay you the princely sum of thirty francs."

I was stunned by his apparently instant deciphering of my code; doubly so now that such a promise of money had entered our conversation.

HOW CAN I HELP?

"I've noticed you are a keen observer, and you have probably picked up on a number of physical traits and behavioural peccadilloes displayed by your hotel guests. My colleague, for example, Dr Watson. No doubt you've been struck by his seemingly perpetual aspect of befuddlement?"

I couldn't smile, but Mr Holmes detected humour in me; reflected it perhaps, in the twinkling of his eye.

"I'd like you to keep watch for a man who is . . . shall we say . . . looking for me. This man is very much like me, though it pains me to say so – he is tall, quite thin and has a bookish air; he is after all a quite brilliant professor of mathematics. His name is Moriarty, but he might well be travelling under a different moniker. Boole, perhaps, or Wild, or Newcomb. Perhaps even Zucco or Atwill. But no matter which pseudonym he hides behind, you will know this if you see him: there is something of the devil in his make-up. He moves as if hell is at his heels."

HOW WILL I GET WORD TO YOU?

I had known him but five minutes and already I felt compelled to help him. There was something urgent about him, something infectious. His curiosity, I aver: I wanted to know more about him. Where he was from, where he was going, why he was so far away from his native country.

"We will be taking rooms at the Englischer Hof," he said. "I shall endeavour to send someone to receive reports from you every evening."

And, with that, he stood up, thanked me, and placed thirty francs in my jacket pocket. He rejoined his companion – whose air of consternation deepened – and then they left, Mr Holmes turning to touch his hat and smile my way.

I never saw him again.

I ate my supper – a thin broth pumped down my throat (I have never tasted food) – on the veranda overlooking the peaks of the Wetterhorn and the Eiger and the Rosenlaui Glacier. I loved to watch the sun sink over the white crags, darkening and deepening the green alpine meadows. Away to the south, I could see thunderclouds forming, clenching into fists that would batter our village within the next twenty-four hours or so. It was a regular occurrence in these parts, and one I looked forward to immensely. My mother hated these attacks of low pressure, but they afforded me the closest proximity to understanding what it meant to be alive. I could almost believe that I felt the sensation of skin tingling under that bracing net of wet electricity. Part of me imagined – invited, even – the catastrophic visitation of one of those blue forks upon my body. I imagined the fire and heat coursing through my veins, effulgent, reinforcing. The lightning would either reduce me to a cinder or serve the miracle cure. Either possibility was eminently preferable to this endless, silent stasis.

Mother removed the feeding apparatus from my throat and withdrew. She knew I sometimes liked to take a nap upon receiving nourishment. Sometimes she asked if I would like her to read aloud, but she tended to shy away from the suggestion these days: my tastes are dark, and hers are not. She did not like to read *Frankenstein* to me, or *The Strange Case of Dr Jekyll and Mr Hyde*, which she recited only recently, and that with evident distaste colouring her narrative. She accused me of wanting her to read stories that would serve only to remind her of my plight, and I must admit that I received a certain amount of grim pleasure from watching her squirm.

The air this evening was warm and sweet, but the potential in that burgeoning storm could already be felt in the fingers of wind tousling my hair. Gradually, I succumbed, my eyelids becoming heavier. I saw him then, on the cusp of a dream, so that I could not be sure that he was real, or some shade conjured by somnolence. There was no question who this man was, though I was mired in torpor. He moved rapidly, a thin, tall man, his shoulders hunched by years of academic study. He resembled Holmes, to a point. But there was something predatory in his gait. There was something hungry about it.

I watched him keenly, anxiety flooding my mind. When would Mr Holmes send his emissary to query me? Why was he so keen to know the whereabouts of this man, unless he signified a very grave threat? I could believe it. I saw the beast in him. I saw—

The figure had stopped abruptly, as if someone had called his name. Or – the paranoid whisperer at my shoulder insisted – as if he had *read your mind*. His face, at this distance, seemed like a pale, inverted teardrop; I could see that the frontal lobes of his head were massive, could almost see within, the diabolical machinations of his brain, churning like some confounded engine. His eyes were a furious, black area of shadow, like the

cross-hatchings in a sketch by Hogarth. Did I feel the first frisson, then, of . . . well . . . what? Fear? Is this what fear felt like?
A spike in the gut, in the vitals, the incipient juice of me? Some
feeling that was no slave to the destroyed nerves in my body.
Something primal and basic, born of the will to stay alive.

I thought then that the will in me to die might very well be
countered by this ancient instinct in the flesh to survive.

He was coming towards me. I considered bluffing, pretending
I was asleep, but I just knew he would be the type of person to
see instantly through such a charade. When he reached the
wheelchair, he did not ask my name. Instead, he took hold of the
handles, disengaged the brake, and began wheeling me down
the path in the direction of the meadow.

Uncle Tobias, the previous summer, had grafted the thick tyres
from a wheelbarrow on to the chair, so that he was able to push
me across the unforgiving terrain, broaden my horizons, and give
me a different view of the world. Moriarty – for it must be he –
took advantage of that customisation now, putting distance
between us and the hotel. Again, I felt the unwinding of what
must be fear in the pit of my stomach, like a nest of adders coiling
against and around each other. Night was coming on; already the
sun had descended beyond the mountains, limning their edges
with golden fire. The blue of the sky was thickening. In the east,
stars were beginning to make themselves known. He pushed me
hard and fast, and I bounced in my seat like a bag of sticks, threatening to spill to the floor at every bump or swerve. We travelled
for what seemed like hours. At one point, I lost my blanket, and
the cold leapt at me like a wildcat, turning my hands blue. The
water from my eyes began to freeze on my cheeks, stiffening
them. For once, I was grateful that I could not feel pain.

Did I fall asleep at one point? Or was I plunged into senseless-
ness by the cold? Whatever it was, I emerged into calm. The sky
was fully dark now, and the stars in all their countless billions
seemed to be howling against their icy backdrop. I could make
out the shape of the mountains where they blocked those
pinpoints of light, but nothing else. He had taken me to the
tongue of the glacier and left me here to perish. He had—

"I spoke with your mother," he said. He was somewhere behind me. "As *he* did. Oh, she was most forthcoming. It is amazing, sometimes, the wag of the tongue when confronted with the spectre of appalling consequence."

I have never felt so trapped within my own body. I wanted to scream and snarl and rage at him. I wanted to tear his face from his skull and send it to the hungry winds like a scrap from a standard born by a defeated army. IF YOU HAVE DONE SOMETHING TO MY MOTHER – I signed, impotently.

"I know where Mr Holmes resides, and that lapdog of his, Watson. He is not much longer for this world, and, by God, I am ready to depart it too, should it come to that.

"Your mother spoke eloquently about you, young man," he said. "She told me you spent a lot of time together, talking of life and death and all points in between. She said you were hell-bent upon ending your life, and would have done so by now if you were able to lift a finger against yourself. She told me that you didn't even know what life was about. You had no frame of reference. You could not feel, yet you believed life was about nothing but feeling.'

I thought I heard the compress of snow underfoot. The ruffle of clothing in wind. I caught a glimpse of him, a shadow, wraithlike, at my shoulder. And for a moment I thought I could smell him too. He smelled of books and leather and, as in me, I smelled in him the sickly sweet redolence of death. Whereas I was inviting it, he was admitting it, he was cosying up to it within the folds of his heavy coat.

"Your mother talked of you as a child. They would bring you here, to the glacier, determined that the cold, fresh air would be beneficial. Of course, it wasn't, but she kept bringing you. In blind hope. In stubborn belief. You became agitated, and she saw that as a good thing; she thought you were stirring from this pitiful state, this curse of being locked within yourself. She thought you might suddenly stand up, rejuvenated by the magic of frigidity, and be miraculously cured. But I suspect it was because you were distressed. You were brought to a place that seemed only to mirror your condition. The cold, cruel, still mass of ice. The suffocation of life beneath it. The smothering. The glacier mocked you. It, after all, enjoyed some minute advance. The incremental creep through the mountains. More movement than you could ever dream of.

"I could leave you here," he said. "Nobody would think to check this location. You would be dead within the hour, of exposure. But I am no monster, despite what *he* says."

I felt the charge of his gloved fists upon the handles once more. We turned away from the great mound of the glacier, pale under the night as if it were blessed with its own light source. "I ask you . . . no, sir, I warn you not to involve yourself in this affair. My issue with Mr Holmes is a private one. He has put you in jeopardy to serve himself, which goes to show you, I think, that the true nature of monsters is not such a subject given to black and white hues."

I think the cold was getting to me, though I could not feel it. I was no longer shivering, and I was drowsy, as if injected with sedatives. I had read somewhere that once you stop shivering then the body is not far away from serious hypothermia, and that tiredness is a sign. But again it looked as if I would be cheated of death; Professor Moriarty was playing with me. When we got back within view of the hotel, I could see frantic movement in the grounds. Staff and guests were roving around with lanterns. I heard my name being called above the clamour of the wind.

"You can be a glacier," he told me. "Or you can be a waterfall. It is your choice, though you might not think it so."

I heard the snap of something behind me, and a rustling. He didn't say anything else. I smelled smoke, and a golden glow built, casting my shadow before me. I heard a cry: "There! Over there! Look. Fire!" And then many figures were dashing across the meadow towards me. Moriarty was long gone by the time they reached me. I was swaddled in blankets and my mother's scent was here, though I could not yet see her. She was crying. I heard her crying all the way back, and it followed me down into sleep.

When I awakened, a man was sitting opposite me, peering at me as if I were an arresting specimen in a museum. He said: "I was sent by Mr Holmes. He said you might have a message for me."

MY JACKET POCKET.

The man stood up and reached for my jacket. He withdrew an envelope. It was the money Holmes had paid me to be his watchman.

"No message?"

I did not reply. I waited until he had left. I fell into a sleep so deep it was like sinking into the cold fathoms of a lake.

Word began to trickle through the following afternoon, like the first thaw waters of spring from the crags, that Sherlock Holmes and his nemesis, Moriarty, were dead. Evidence of a struggle had been found at Reichenbach at midday, and a few artefacts belonging to the eminent detective. I had seen the falls once, when I was very young, and I had been cowed by its power and fury. If you were driven underground by that torrent of water, you would never surface again. But it had excited me too. That movement. That ceaseless thrashing energy.

I saw Dr Watson, bereft, exhausted, being ushered with his suitcase to the train station where he would begin his journey back to London. I wanted to offer him some crumb of comfort, but others more able than I were doing that job already, and so much better. After he had gone – I watched the puffs of steam from the locomotive dissipate like my own thought bubbles in the boiling Meiringen sky – Mother suggested I take to my bed for a rest. My fingers and toes exhibited signs of frostbite, and she thought it would be injurious to my good health to remain outdoors, but I was firm. I WISH TO SIT ON THE BALCONY. I would not be diverted. After a while, she gave up trying to change my mind and left me alone. I'm sure she was thinking that I might be abducted once more, but Moriarty was gone, and Tobias had replaced the rugged wheels on my chair with the original castors. I was unlikely to be making any more unscheduled trips again.

The storm hit Meiringen an hour later, leaden cloud bringing artificial night to the village. I watched the skin on my arms pucker, the hairs rise as if in supplication to the power swelling in the sky. This time I felt it, an echo of the fear I had known in Moriarty's presence, as if he dragged its trickery around with him like a humour or a scent. Lightning flashed and the thunder it created was instantaneous. Rain dropped as if shocked out of the clouds by the sound; heavy, brutal, pummelling rain. I had never felt so alive and, for a moment, I was grateful that I could never utter the name of the person who had triggered that in me. Fear was survival. Fear was life. I could feel. I could FEEL.

In the hiatus after a second lightning flash, I saw something different in the scenery imprinted upon the darkness behind my eyes. A figure was standing still to my left beneath the awning of the bakery a little way up the road from the hotel. The flash of lightning. A refreshed scene in acid white: the figure now closer. There was something wrong with its physique.

Flash. Everything remained the same: the great mass of the mountains, the reach of the trees, the wet template of buildings known to me as intimately as the pattern of freckles on the back of my hand. And this figure. Closer yet. Bent over and buckled like a child's model shaped from clay.

I tasted his name upon my tongue though I could not utter it. So much like some play upon the Latin phrase reminding us that we have to die.

Flash. A step nearer. Now I could see his face. The prominent lobes of his forehead split and bloodied. The cliff of his face blackened by bruises. An arm broken so badly it resembled a flesh scythe curling up around his back. Bone was visible in the soaked swags of his exposed skin, as if he were carrying some strange bag of splintered antlers with him, to ward off bad luck.

He looked at me with those massive gaping shadows deep in his face. In the next window of light, he had raised his good hand and let it fall haltingly, like a child's representation of rain or, perhaps, the deluge of a waterfall.

When the lightning returned again, he was gone.

The Protégé

Kate Ellis

Spring 1911

'I am a man of science. But I do appreciate art.'

The speaker was an elderly man. His face was long and thin, topped with sparse grey hair and there was a sharpness, a watch-fulness in his eyes that suggested great intelligence.

The young man he addressed looked sideways at him. He wore a puzzled frown as though he had not quite understood what the other had said.

But the older man continued. 'I think this work is particularly interesting. The look on the interrogator's face. The innocence of the child. He has no idea what is happening and why the strange man is asking these questions but, in his naivety, he will likely tell the truth in an unwitting act of betrayal. The only thing he knows, even at his tender age, is fear. See how his sister weeps. She recognises the danger.'

A small smile played on the speaker's thin lips as he turned his head to see his companion's reaction. But he saw nothing. The shabby young man with the greasy dark hair was staring blankly at the large canvas, lost in the scene.

'*And When Did You Last See Your Father?* It is a strange title, don't you think?'

The young man turned his eyes on the speaker. 'Please. My English is not good.'

A flicker of recognition passed across the older man's face. 'I detect a German accent. You are German, *mein Herr.*'

The answer was a vigorous shake of the head. '*Nein*. I am Austrian.'

'How long have you been in Liverpool?' The older man spoke in German, fluent and faultless as a native.

'For four months only,' the young man replied in his own tongue. He was in his early twenties and he fidgeted nervously with the sleeve of his threadbare jacket. His body was thin and gangling and he looked as if he was in need of a good meal. A controllable creature, the old man thought. He'd met his kind before: desperate for approval; desperate to belong.

'You are an artist, I think,' the old man said, noting the tense, paint-stained fingers.

The young man's small eyes brightened at the question. 'Yes, I am a very fine artist. But there are many who do not appreciate true talent. So many ignorant men who follow only the latest fashion.'

'I know precisely what you mean. My gifts too have long been underestimated.' The old man's lips twitched upwards in a bitter smile.

After a short silence he turned his attention once more to the painting hanging before them on the gallery wall. The picture of the small boy in the costume of a seventeenth-century Royalist being questioned by a Parliamentarian soldier with a cunning gentleness calculated to extract the Judas betrayal from the guileless babe. 'Could you paint something like this?'

The young man nodded eagerly. 'Yes. I think so.'

There was a pause while the older man studied his companion more closely. What he saw obviously pleased him because he came straight to the point. 'If I supply the materials, could you produce a replica of Yeames's masterpiece? A close approximation good enough to fool the casual observer?'

He saw pride in the young Austrian's expression and a visible straightening of his slouched spine. 'I would enjoy the challenge.' He suddenly frowned. 'But I have nowhere to work on such a large canvas. My accommodation is cramped and . . .'

'Do not worry. I have a large house where you can work. The only thing I ask is that you say nothing of the matter to anyone. Is that agreed?'

The young man nodded eagerly. 'Agreed. I hope you will not think me impertinent, but why do you wish for this copy?'

The older man smiled, showing his small, yellow teeth. 'That is none of your concern. I will pay you well and you will ask no questions.'

'You will pay?'

The older man saw the greed in the other man's eyes. Or maybe a desperation that had grown from poverty and rejection. He named a sum and saw the light of avarice flicker brightly.

'I will meet you in front of this gallery tomorrow morning at nine o'clock. Do not be late.'

'I will be punctual, *mein Herr*.' He hesitated. 'I will need to make sketches. I cannot copy this from memory.'

'That has already been taken care of.' The old man turned to leave.

'I do not know your name.'

'Names are not necessary. Until tomorrow.' He marched out of the gallery at a speed that belied his apparent age, leaving the younger man staring at the painting.

The young man arrived on the flight of steps in front of the Walker Art Gallery ten minutes before the appointed time. He wished to be punctual. Besides, he'd been eager to escape his brother's claustrophobic flat, away from his sister-in-law's hostile glances, the baby's screams, and the smell of damp and stale cooking.

He watched the traffic on William Brown Street; horse-drawn trams and carriages mingling with the noisy new-fangled motor-cars of the wealthier classes. At nine on the dot, a small black carriage pulled by two black horses drew up at the bottom of the steps. The coachman's black muffler was pulled up to his nose, protecting his nostrils from the thin spring mist drifting in from the river and masking the wearer's features. The carriage door opened to reveal the old man, who leaned forward and beckoned the young man in.

For a moment, he hesitated on the steps. He had no idea where he would be taken or what would happen when he reached his destination. But since he'd been refused entry to the Viennese Academy of Fine Arts he'd lived through desperate times, existing on the streets and taking any menial work that was on offer. This strange old man, judging by his well-cut coat, his silk hat and his talk of a large house, was clearly rich. If he didn't seize this opportunity, there might never be another.

With the boldness of a man who has nothing to lose, he climbed up into the carriage and took his seat opposite the man he hoped would become his benefactor. The old man did not smile or acknowledge him in any way. Instead, he knocked on the roof of the carriage with his ebony walking cane and sat back to gaze out of the window. As soon as they were out of the bustling centre of the town, he pulled down the blinds on both sides, making it impossible to see out, but still said nothing.

'Is it far?' the young man asked, breaking the uncomfortable silence.

'It is some way from the centre of the town, but do not fear, my driver will return you to the art gallery when you are finished for the day.'

He fell silent again. The drawn blinds had made it dark in the carriage, but the young man was aware of the other's cold stare, as though he were trying to penetrate his mind. Or his soul. He was relieved when the coach eventually slowed to a halt. The old man waited, sitting perfectly still until the coachman climbed down and opened the door. He alighted first then the young man followed, blinking in the daylight and taking in his surroundings.

It was a large, gracious house built of the local red sandstone with a gravel drive that swept up to an impressive portico before trailing away through a dark avenue of thick rhododendrons. From the birdsong in the air, they might have been in the countryside. However, from the length of the journey, the young man calculated that they were probably in some wealthy suburb amongst the opulent homes of those who had made their fortunes from the ships he'd seen on the river. It was a private place, not overlooked. All sorts of evil could go on in such a place.

The old man led him into a hallway with an elaborately tiled floor and a grand mahogany staircase. The young man stared at the paintings on the walls as he walked in and recognised a Gainsborough and a Reynolds along with some works by the Pre-Raphaelite brotherhood. A Turner seascape hung in pride of place at the foot of the staircase, but there was no time to stop and admire the master's brushwork. He was hurried up the stairs and along the landing and, when they came to a door at the end of a passage, the old man reached out, turned the handle and the door swung open to reveal a fully equipped studio. Spring light streamed in at the large windows on to a set of preliminary sketches set on easels around the room and a large canvas bearing faint charcoal outlines. He could see faint numbers between the lines and, on a far wall, hung a large sheet of paper with myriad dabs of colour, all with numbers printed neatly beside them. On a separate easel stood what the young man recognised as a photographic image of the painting he'd been commissioned to copy.

'I took the photograph myself,' the old man said, with a hint of pride. 'I told the attendant that I was a visiting art professor from Berne. I have spent some time in Switzerland so it was an easy matter to assume the manner of speech. And I am a professor, although not of art, alas.'

This was the most forthcoming the man had been and the young man wondered if he would reveal more about himself as time went on. But then he began to bark instructions, as if he was afraid he'd given too much away and wished to restore the distance between them. He said that the colours on the wall were the exact shades the artist Yeames had used in his painting and that they corresponded to the numbers on the canvas. The artist was to observe the photographic image as he worked. This was to be a facsimile that would fool the world, but not necessarily an expert.

'Who did the preliminary sketches and the outline?' the young man asked when the professor had finished speaking. 'They're very good. Very accurate.'

The professor's face clouded and he pressed his thin lips together. 'Somebody who was alive but is now dead. Somebody who asked too many questions.'

The young man knew the words were a warning and he suddenly felt afraid. He was longing to ask why the professor had chosen this particular painting but he knew he had to tread carefully.

'It is time to get to work,' the professor said. 'My man will bring you luncheon at midday and you will be returned to the gallery at four o'clock.'

With that, he left the room and, when the door shut, the young man heard the hollow click of a key turning in the lock.

He was a prisoner.

The work proceeded well, but his attempts to communicate with the taciturn man who brought his lunch had failed. The man was huge, with a hairless scalp, tattooed arms and a face that bore the scars of many dockland fights. The only sound he emitted was a low grunt and when he half opened his mouth he appeared to have no tongue. This wasn't the sort of servant he would have expected a man of the professor's obvious learning to employ. He wondered if the professor was providing work for an unfortunate out of charity. But somehow he thought this unlikely.

He worked on, barely aware of the hours passing, until the light at the windows was beginning to fade. By the time the studio door was unlocked and opened, he had filled one corner of the canvas with colour, but he knew the task would take several weeks. He was glad his brother never showed any curiosity about where he went. He and his wife, Bridget, were just glad to get him out of the flat.

He did not see the professor again that day and, when the man with no tongue led him out to the carriage, he realised that he had been the faceless coachman who had driven him there that morning. He had seen no other servants and he thought it unlikely that a single man could maintain the house in such a pristine state. But he knew better than to ask too many questions.

When he followed the creature through the house, he seized the opportunity to study the paintings on the walls. All of them were of high quality and many extremely valuable. Any man who held such treasures in a private collection would have to be very rich indeed. When he boarded the carriage, the coachman pulled down the blinds before he took his seat behind the horses. However, the passenger couldn't resist lifting a corner of the nearest blind and peeping out. The drive leading to the house was long and, just before a little sandstone lodge came into view, he spotted a gap in the rhododendron bushes. Through the wide parting in the glossy leaves, he could see a clearing and a dark patch of freshly dug soil in the centre of the undergrowth. A patch the size of a grave.

The routine was the same each day and the canvas was taking shape. Without the preliminary drawings, the task would have been considerably harder and the artist found himself admiring the work of his predecessor – and wondering why he hadn't finished what he had started so well. However, he had learned to keep his curiosity to himself. The professor didn't welcome inquisitive minds.

Two weeks after the work was started, the artist was surprised to hear the key turn in the lock soon after he'd arrived in the morning. He looked up from his work and saw the professor standing in the doorway, arms behind his back, his skinny frame blocking out the light.

'I wish to ascertain your progress,' he said in perfect German, before striding across the room to examine the canvas. At first it was hard to read his expression, but after a while his features became animated.

'See what power the soldier conducting the interrogation has over the helpless child, like a cat torturing a small creature for its pleasure. And the soldier with his arm around the crying sister. How easily he could take out a dagger and finish her pathetic life. See the women cowering in the corner. Feel their terror at what the child is about to reveal. And why do they wish to know the whereabouts of the father? Imagine what they will do to him when they find him. This picture is a study in cruelty, do you not think? A masterpiece.'

'Do you think my efforts match the original?' the artist asked nervously.

'It will suit my purpose. You have done well.'

'It is almost finished. When will I be paid?'

'When you exchange it for the genuine Yeames in the gallery. You will receive your payment when the original is hanging upon my dining-room wall. Cruelty is so good for the digestion, do you not agree?'

The young man looked at the professor and felt a thrill of realisation. He was right. Cruelty was invigorating. Power over the weak endowed the strong with energy, with life. He himself had been powerless once, but he would never return to that state again. There was another way.

'How will I exchange it for the original?'

'It is not difficult to gain access to the gallery. I have detailed plans of the building . . . and the death of a night watchman will be a small price to pay for my pleasure.' The professor looked his companion in the eye. 'Several young artists have accepted my commissions, but you are the first in whom I recognise something of myself.'

'What happened to the others? Where are they?'

The professor smiled. 'Their mortal remains are in the grounds. But where their souls are depends on whether you believe all that nonsense about heaven and hell. I myself believe they have been returned to nature, providing nutrition for the earth.'

'What about me?'

Unexpectedly, the professor put a bony arm around the young man's shoulder. 'I am an old man and I need young blood. I think I shall make you my protégé.'

'You live alone?'

The professor thought for a few moments. 'My associate, Colonel Moran, lived with me for a while but since his unfortunate death I have become lonely.' He withdrew his arm quickly. 'You remind me so much of myself when I was young.' He sighed. 'You live with your brother, you say?'

'And my sister-in-law and their baby. I came to Liverpool to make a new start.'

'And so you shall.' He took out his pocket watch. 'The picture will be finished very soon, will it not?'

The young man nodded eagerly. 'Two days at the most. And then . . . ?'

'We shall see.'

The young Austrian had not been told how the precise replica of the frame surrounding the original painting had been obtained. Nor did he know how the professor had gained such detailed knowledge of the workings of the Walker Art Gallery. And he knew better than to ask. The professor had methods known only to himself; methods that even his protégé was unaware of.

He delighted in the thought of being the professor's protégé; perhaps eventually taking over his grand house and his art collection when the inevitable happened to the old man. From now on, life would be good. He would no longer be mocked as a useless idler by his brother, Alois, and be forced to live with him, his nagging Irish wife and their screaming baby in their meagre flat. He would show them his true worth. They would soon see what he was capable of.

He hoped the professor would invite him to come and live with him; treat him as a surrogate son. Perhaps, the young artist thought, he was waiting to see how he performed on the night the paintings were exchanged. If he did well, he was sure he would receive his just reward.

The appointed date for the operation soon arrived. That night the young man did not return to his brother's flat in Upper Stanhope Street. Instead, he was shown to a lavishly decorated chamber with silk wallpaper and rich silk hangings around the bed. A fine linen nightshirt had been laid out for him. This was the night everything would change and the riches of the world would be his.

But first there was work to do. The carriage was too small to accommodate the finished forgery so they travelled in a horse-drawn van, sitting up beside the driver, wrapped up against the April chill. The artist knew better than to ask how such a vehicle had been obtained. The professor seemed to have the ability to conjure anything he needed. Such power.

They set off at midnight and the young man was able to note

the route they took. Out of the drive and past a fine church, then through prosperous suburban streets and past parkland before driving down the wide boulevard that led ultimately to the centre of Liverpool. He recognised the grand houses of Toxteth and the poor side streets that had become so familiar during his stay in the town. When they reached William Brown Street they drove round to the rear of the art gallery. There was a door at the back and the professor had somehow obtained the key. He felt excitement course through his body and realised how much he desired the professor's power. He longed to be feared like those soldiers in the painting. He wanted the respect he'd never had.

The professor kept watch while he helped the driver lift the canvas out of the van. Adrenaline made his burden light as they carried it into the building. He had memorised the plan the professor had shown him and he knew where the night watchman would be stationed. It would be up to him to deal with this obstacle to their success because the professor wanted no witnesses. The watchman would have to be eliminated and, for the first time, the artist would hold the power of life and death over another human being. The prospect thrilled him more than he'd expected.

They moved silently, the professor leading the way with a flashlight, and, in the corner of the room where the painting was displayed, they found the night watchman snoozing in a chair, emitting regular soft snores. So far they'd made no noise, but the young man knew that it would be impossible to make the exchange without waking him. The professor switched off his flashlight, but in the light of the full moon trickling in through the gallery skylight, the artist could see that his victim was a small man in late middle age, who wore an ill-fitting dark uniform and a peaked cap. A harmless man. An insignificant man. The professor gave the signal. It was time.

He took the man by surprise, creeping up beside him and clamping a cloth over his nose and mouth. It was important not to leave a mark on his body. The man struggled for a while, but he was unfit and lacked the strength of youth. The artist clung on with determination until the thrashing limbs stilled. Then, with the help of the coachman, he arranged the body carefully so that it would appear that the man had died suddenly in his sleep. Hopefully, the museum authorities would assume a weak heart; a small tragedy or, more likely, an inconvenience.

When it was done, he started to work with the help of the driver, while the professor held the flashlight. It was going well until the artist dropped his end of the forged canvas. It hit the floor with a loud crash and the three men froze, listening for running footsteps. But they heard nothing so they continued until the exchange had been made and it was impossible to tell in the flashlight's beam that the picture that now hung there in pride of place wasn't the original. After the painting had been carried down the stairs into the waiting van, the professor entrusted his protégé with the task of ensuring all trace of their presence had gone and the doors were locked behind them.

As they travelled back in silence, the young man felt an unaccustomed glow of strength within him. He had ended the life of another human being. He was no longer a nonentity, a failed artist. He was the professor's protégé and heir to the kingdoms of the earth. He had become as a god.

He was too excited to talk during the journey – until the van stopped and he saw that he was outside his brother's flat.

'It is best if you stay here tonight,' the professor said. 'To avoid suspicion.'

'I did well, yes?'

'You made a mistake. You let the painting drop. It could have been damaged and we might have been heard. It could have ruined the entire operation.'

'But we succeeded.'

The professor said nothing.

'When will I be paid?'

There was a long silence. 'We will talk of that tomorrow. You must leave us and say nothing of this.'

The protégé didn't argue. He climbed down meekly, wondering whether his brother and sister-in-law would notice a change

in him. But when he let himself in, he found they were asleep.
Perhaps it was for the best.

The next morning, he waited on the art gallery steps as usual to
be picked up. But the professor's carriage didn't appear. After
what had happened the previous night he felt a flash of anger. He
was the protégé, the heir. He had killed a man to aid the professor's project and it was wrong that he should be treated in such a
manner. He waited in vain for another half-hour before taking
the omnibus out to the suburbs. He now knew where the professor lived. And he was going to collect his dues.

After an omnibus journey and a lengthy walk, the protégé
arrived at the lodge and, for the first time that day, he felt nervous. When he passed the clearing between the bushes at the side
of the drive, he couldn't resist investigating, and he found that
the oblong of disturbed earth he'd thought he'd seen hadn't been
a product of his imagination. He wondered whether it might be
the last resting place of the previous artist. Had that man too
regarded himself as the professor's protégé? And had he failed in
some way that merited the punishment of death? He tried to
banish these thoughts as he continued towards the house.

When he arrived at the portico there was no sign of life and all
he could hear was birdsong. He took a deep breath and tugged
the bell pull beside the front door. It was a full minute before the
door opened to reveal a plump woman in black. By her appearance and manner he guessed she was a housekeeper but he'd
never seen her before.

'I look for Herr Professor,' he said.

The woman shook her head. 'Professor Moriarty has gone.
He's packed up and left.' Realising he was a foreigner, she spoke
slowly and clearly. 'The van came for all his paintings this morning. He's paid his rent for another month, but he said he has
urgent business in America. He's sailing at noon.'

'With his paintings?'

She looked at him as if he was a particularly stupid child
and he longed to take her by the throat and strangle the life
out of her.

'Of course, dear. That's what he does for a living. He's an art dealer.'

The news hit him like a physical blow. He had been tricked. He would receive no payment for what he had done unless he could find the professor before noon. That sense of power he'd experienced was slowly draining away. But he was determined that it would soon return. He had killed. He was not a man to cross.

He retraced his steps and ran all the way to the nearest tram stop. If he could get to the docks, he would tackle Moriarty and make him pay him what he owed. He was hurt by the thought that the professor hadn't planned to take him to America as his protégé. But he would make the man change his mind or he would have his revenge. The young lion would challenge the ageing master of the pride.

The artist spotted the professor walking on the quayside and called out. Moriarty swung round. He was dressed in his usual immaculate black with his tall silk hat and ebony cane. He looked like a large and predatory spider.

He stood his ground as the younger man approached, his face an expressionless mask.

The artist stopped a few feet away. 'You said you'd pay me.' The words sounded more desperate and pleading than he'd intended.

'We cannot discuss the matter here,' the professor hissed, grasping the young man's elbow and leading him to a quiet corner of the dock, well away from the bustle of passengers and goods being loaded on to the huge ship.

'Where's the painting? Is it on the ship?'

'It is in a place of safety with the other works I have acquired over the years.'

'Where?'

Moriarty smiled and said nothing.

'Tell me.'

'Why on earth should I do that, little man? It is none of your concern. Just be thankful I saw something in you that made me spare your life. Your predecessor wasn't so fortunate.'

'Answer my question. Where are the paintings?'

Moriarty tilted his head to one side, an amused smile on his lips. 'They might be in England. Or I might have sent them to France. Or maybe Belgium. But one thing is sure, a nonentity like you could never amass such a collection. Now leave me. I have important business to attend to.'

The young man saw the contempt on the professor's face. The contempt and distaste one might reserve for a particularly repellent insect. He felt fury rising inside him and his self-control began to slip away. All those hopes, all that power that had been dangled before him was vanishing now like mist on the river. Without thinking, he reached out his arm, gave the older man a mighty shove and watched as he staggered on the dockside cobbles before losing his balance and tumbling with a high-pitched scream into the grey water.

For a few seconds, he stood there frozen with horror. Then he suddenly became aware of shouts and running feet and he knew he had to escape before he was seen. He yielded to the temptation to take a last look at the old man struggling in the water, surfacing to take a desperate breath then sinking beneath the surface.

Once the old man was dead, the artist thought as he hurried away, someone would be able to take his place.

He arrived at his brother's flat at one o'clock after running all the way from the dock.

'Where's Alois?' He bent double, gasping for breath and only just managed to get the question out.

His sister-in-law looked at him suspiciously. 'At work. Why? What's happened?'

'I'm leaving.'

'I wish you'd learn to speak English properly. You've been here since November. It's sheer laziness, that's what it is.'

The young man regarded the woman with hatred. Maybe he should kill her and experience that thrill of god-like power again. But he knew that would be foolish. Once her body was discovered and they found that he'd fled, it would trigger a manhunt. And his plans didn't include submitting to the hangman's noose.

He put his face close to hers. 'I am going to Germany. Munchen.'

'The sooner the better,' she spat. 'I'm fed up with you. I just hope you work harder in Germany than you have done here. I've never known such a useless layabout.'

He felt his fists clench. One day he would show this woman his terrifying strength. 'This time it's going to be different. I'm going to paint . . . and I'm going to collect art. Great art. I'm going to be important. People are going to listen to me. Point at me and say what a great man I am.'

Bridget Hitler shook her head. 'You're deluded, Adolph. Like your brother says, you'll come to a bad end. Now get out of this house. I never want to hear your name again.'

Author's note:

It is widely believed that Adolph Hitler spent five months in Liverpool in 1910–11, living with his brother, Alois, and sister-in-law, Bridget, in their Toxteth flat. The house where he was said to have lived was destroyed by bombing during World War II.

And When Did You Last See Your Father is one of the most popular paintings in the Walker Art Gallery – and can be seen there to this day.

A Scandal in Arabia

Claude Lalumière

To the Professor he is always the Detective. In dreams, in thought, or in conversation, he seldom refers to him under any other name. In the Professor's mind, he eclipses and predominates the whole of his profession. It is not that he feels any emotion akin to affection for the Detective. All emotions, and that one particularly, are abhorrent to his cold, precise and mathematical mind. The Professor knows himself to be the most perfect calculating machine in the history of the world; no one would ever mistake him for a caring human being. He never speaks of the softer passions, save with a jibe and a sneer. Such emotions are quantifiable variables to be measured by the objective observer – elements in the equations that predict and manipulate the movements and actions of individuals and populations. For the trained mathematician to admit such intrusions into his own delicate and finely tuned psyche would be to introduce distracting factors that might throw a doubt upon all his calculations. Yet there has ever been but one significant opponent to him, and that opponent was the Detective, of dubious and questionable motives.

This morning, as the orange light of the Middle Eastern sun hits the glass windows of the Professor's Dubai penthouse, his thoughts are again of the Detective. For the past decade, now that his centuries of calculations have elevated him beyond any stature he had imagined when he first stepped on to the path of crime and corruption, every night he has dreamed of his illustrious opponent. In these dreams, the two of them spar like they used to, the Detective meticulously untangling every strand of the Professor's web of conspiracy. In these dreams, the Detective is relentlessly victorious and the Professor is inevitably undone and humiliated.

The Professor believes that the Detective is dead, has been dead for nearly a century, and yet a doubt lingers. The Professor does not like chaotic variables to mar the precise beauty of his equations, is dissatisfied at having to rely on ambiguous opinion, even his own, rather than proven and quantifiable data.

The Detective retired on 7 July 1902. By that time, the Professor and the Detective had been duelling, at times publicly but most often secretly, for two decades. The Professor's agents kept watch over the Detective during his retirement, but he never showed any signs of interfering with the Professor's designs. Indeed, the Detective, in those elder years, seemed to lose any interest in meddling with the criminal world. Emboldened, the Professor embarked on what was, at that time, his most ambitious plot yet. Even the British government, who had pulled the Detective out of retirement to aid in the War Effort, did not know what only the Detective had correctly deduced: that the Great War was set into motion by the Professor to further his long-term plans.

The Detective's belated interference prevented the First World War from achieving its full potential – the Professor's equations had not accounted for the Detective's involvement – but the Professor nevertheless profited from its outcome, albeit not as richly as he had initially calculated.

After the Great War, the Professor lost track of the Detective. Indeed, the historical record was altered in such a deliberate and methodical way by the Detective's older brother – a shadowy puppet-master operating behind the scenes of the British government – that the world now regards the Detective as a fictional character created by a failed physician with a credulous penchant for spiritualists and fairies.

All in all, the Professor and the Detective matched wits for a mere three decades! That brief period, now more than a century in the past, outshines any other in the Professor's long life.

Enough! The Professor chides himself for indulging in such nostalgia.

Teenage twins from India – brother and sister – stand naked at their station in his private spa, to minister to his morning needs. Afterwards, there is a full day awaiting him: following breakfast, a teleconference is scheduled with his worldwide network of operatives; after lunch, he has a full slate of brief meetings with financiers and politicians from all over the globe; after dinner, he will read the day's reports; for the rest of the evening, he will pore through the near-infinite datastreams now available to him thanks to the surveillance society he has manipulated into being; finally, at midnight, synthesizing everything he has learned in the last twenty-four hours, he will revise all his equations and send off fresh instructions to his agents.

But now: the twins. For the body must not be neglected.

The Professor, contrary to what the Detective's biographer has reported, is not British, although he pretended to be for many years, adopting an Irish name and fabricating an entire life story, calculated to maximize the efficiency and impact of his persona. The Detective eventually saw through the deception, but, as far as the Professor knows (with a probability of 97.86 per cent), never shared the truth with his biographer, or with anybody else; the Detective must have feared (with a probability of 98.34 per cent) being taken for a madman should he try to convince anyone of the truth behind the Professor.

The Professor was born in Shiraz, one of the greatest cities in Persia, in what would now be called the thirteenth century. As a young boy, the Professor already displayed an uncanny aptitude for mathematics. His father, an Arab who had travelled north in his youth and settled in Persia, was a religious scholar employed at the court of Abu Bakr ibn Saad. The ruler took a liking to the young boy and delighted in his mathematical acuity. By grace of Abu Bakr's patronage, the boy received the best education Persia could provide – and at the time Persia was the most learned of all the world's nations.

The boy excelled in academics, easily impressing his teachers when mathematics was the subject or deceiving them when philosophy, especially ethics, was the theme at hand.

From an early age, the boy perceived the world differently than those around him. Every moment, every interaction, every thought, every action – everything – expressed itself in his mind as a mathematical equation. Any outcome could be reached if the correct equation could be articulated, solved and applied.

In his mind, the equations grew in complexity and scope, but the reality they described could not be achieved in a single life-time. According to his calculations, he would not witness the results of his equations in the mere decades of life he could reasonably expect his body to endure.

That, too, he knew could be solved with the application of the proper equation.

All those gullible fools who thought the Fountain of Youth was a place waiting for any idiot to stumble on to! Eternal life was, like everything else, a mathematical equation. Once the Professor decided to apply his formidable mind to the problem, it was only a matter of three years, two months, four days, two hours, fifty-six minutes and thirteen seconds to resolve the mathematical formula that gave him complete control over his body and its processes.

In different times and eras, it is more advantageous to look a specific age – young, middle-aged, elderly; the mathematical formula that grants him immortality allows for such variables. In England, in the nineteenth and twentieth centuries, it suited his purposes best to exude the gravitas of a man of late middle age with paling skin and greying hair, and so that was the age and appearance he selected when, first, he adopted the persona of the Napoleon of Crime, in those glorious years when the Detective's keen intellect posed the most serious challenge to his superiority he had yet encountered, and second during the Cold War, when he (using as a codename the same initial that had brought him such notoriety as the Detective's greatest enemy) headed the Secret Intelligence Service, deploying it and its posse of spies and assassins not to the advantage of the United Kingdom and its allies, as everyone was so easily duped into believing he was doing, but to serve his own agenda.

Now, with the nation of his birth so close – a few kilometres away across the Persian Gulf – he once more resembles a healthy young man in his late twenties, his tan skin and dark hair restored to their natural luxuriance.

No! Why is his mind turning so easily to nostalgia and sentimentality? In anger at himself, he rips his white shirt while attempting to pull it on. In such rare moments, when the Professor's emotions – how he loathes succumbing to these trivial distractions – make him lose control, the speed with which his head oscillates from side to side in a menacingly reptilian fashion increases, as if he were about to strike his prey and spew deadly venom.

The Professor regains control of himself as he pulls a fresh shirt from his wardrobe and finishes dressing. The oscillation of his head abates somewhat, so that the inattentive observer might not be able to pinpoint exactly what it is about the Professor's demeanour that is so disquieting.

No, the reason he has once again adopted the appearance of a young man of Middle Eastern origins has nothing to do with nostalgia for his long-ago youth. What rubbish! No, it is a practical and calculated move: in this era, youth is valued over maturity, and in this time and place an Arabic mien smooths his path to dominance and influence.

Fully dressed, he inspects himself in the mirror and notices a splotch of dried blood on his cheek. He returns to the spa adjoining his bedroom, careful to avoid the corpses of the Indian twins, and walks to the sink to carefully wash the stain off his face.

Before exiting his private rooms, he leaves a note for the maid service: tomorrow, he would enjoy the ministrations of three young she-males from Thailand.

The Professor makes his way to his office for this morning's work. There is a world to dominate. His mind teems with merciless equations.

The Professor is distracted, scarcely able to pay attention or to retain any of the information presented to him. His operatives, beholden to him as they may be, are idiots, unable to parse what is important from what is trivial. The morning teleconference ends, and the Professor cannot bring to mind any fresh data to feed into his equations.

While eating his lunch, he decides to eschew the usual format for the afternoon meetings with financiers and politicians. There will be no string of confidential tête-à-têtes; instead, he issues an order that all of the day's supplicants convene together in the conference room.

Half an hour later, 156 of the cowardly and opportunistic toadies he has positioned as figureheads in the spheres of finance and politics are crammed nervously in a room that is designed to hold no more than sixty comfortably. None of them dare crowd the Professor, and so he is naturally bestowed the wide berth that allows prey to feel a modicum of false security around an alpha-predator.

For three hours, he allows them to chirp at him, but again his mind retains nothing.

In the entire world he can count on the fingers of his two hands those few financiers and politicians who are not his vassals. Those who serve him, each and every one of them, have profited greatly from his patronage, and yet there is not an ounce of loyalty in any of them. All they understand is fear and profit. Today, they annoy him more than usual.

He lets their sycophantic blather fade into background noise, and he abandons himself to the equations of world domination that cascade through his mind. He pauses on one equation – one with no discernible profit but rather imbued with petty vindictiveness. Before being aware of having made a conscious decision, he articulates the practical application of that equation.

The assemblage falls immediately silent at the sound of his voice – everyone here is justifiably afraid of offending the Professor in any way.

Not a single one of these men and women can understand the implications of the instructions they have received. If they obey his will – and they shall; they always do; they always must – it will mean the ruin of 58 to 63 per cent of those present, and that of 27 to 31 per cent of their colleagues around the world.

No matter; they are all of them interchangeable puppets: those currently in positions of power; their supposed opponents ostensibly championing other political, economic, or moral paradigms; those waiting in the wings; the defenders of the status quo; the terrorist militias; the progressives; the conservatives; the socialists; the capitalists; the industrialists; the civic crusaders; the revolutionaries; the charities; the religious institutions . . . Worldwide, 93.72 per cent of those who toil in the halls of economic, political, and social power obey the unyielding influence of the Professor's equations.

A wave of self-loathing washes over the Professor. He has acted with impulsive emotion, not from the cold and objective perspective of the perfect mathematician he knows himself to be.

Unable to stand their presence a second longer, he dismisses his loathsome congregation.

He sits alone for another hour, realigning the precision of his intellect by focusing on the equations most in need of his attention.

The Professor skips dinner. He shuts himself in his study to parse through the current state and equilibrium of his equations before reading the reports that have accrued throughout the day.

But, within minutes, comfortably nestled in his armchair, he drifts off to sleep, to once more do battle with the Detective.

Emerging from his accidental nap, the Professor's heart beats wildly with excitement. In his latest dream, the Detective was especially cunning and relentless; his adversary had only one string left to pull and the whole of the Professor's empire would have come crashing down, dismantled beyond repair. At the last minute, the Professor applied an unexpected equation into the fray, and the Detective's carefully constructed body of evidence and countermeasures untangled, humiliating the Detective, leaving him disgraced, his reputation and authority forever tarnished.

Never before has the Detective been defeated in the Professor's dreams. What has changed? The Professor delves into the mental universe of his equations, scrutinizing every element, variable, algorithm and solution.

Re-examining his earlier equation, the one with which he seemed to succumb to his annoyance with his sycophantic puppets, he understands now that it was the correct and timely move in his complex game of domination. It reassures him that, even on those rare occasions when emotion seizes him, his mind will nevertheless act on the correct equations, ignoring these irksome distractions that sometimes flutter on the surface of his consciousness.

Every once in a while – the equations reveal that the intervals must appear chaotic although they follow a complex algorithm – the masses need to be placated with a scapegoat, a sacrifice, a deception. The larger the bloodletting, the more the public is appeased and fooled into thinking the world has turned in their favour, that justice has been served.

The coming financial and political upheaval will restore common people's belief that they wield some control over their collective destiny. In truth, the equations of world domination are unfurling according to the Professor's designs. Time now to dive into the datastreams.

In the last two decades, the Professor's equations have grown exponentially in both complexity and accuracy. The information society that he calculated into existence has yielded, as per the model based on his equations, a surveillance society that collects so much data that only the Professor's exquisitely trained mind can synthesize it.

The Professor wields every string of the surveillance society like a master puppeteer. It is a world of his own making, a world in his own image. He rules it. He dominates it. And no one – not even the Detective, even if he were, improbably, still alive – will ever wrest it from him.

That night, for the first time in a decade, following his unprecedented nap-time victory, the Professor does not dream of the Detective. Does not dream of the Detective defeating him. The Detective is again absent the next night . . . And the next . . .

A pyramid, reflects the Professor during a trip to Egypt, is the perfect mathematical expression of the perfect human society. A construct of concentric rungs, each superior tier smaller than the inferior yet dominating the lower and larger tier, until the top rung is reached, and that rung has only one component. The ruler. The pharaoh. The alpha. The Professor.

The Professor is in Cairo to oversee a crucial play in his game of world domination. His personal attention is not strictly required, but without his presence there is a 17.3 per cent probability that the move will fail. Factoring his on-hand intervention, that probability falls to 0.002 per cent.

The three arms dealers, the four bankers, the seven foreign diplomats, the one representative of the Egyptian government, the two environmental activists, the six revolutionary militia commanders, the three insurance brokers, the five industrialists, the two civil rights advocates, and the three religious figures do not meet each other. The Professor handles every discrete aspect of the negotiations, and it all goes smoothly, exactly according to the Professor's calculations. Having now met all the actors in this particular action, the Professor recalculates that, even without his presence in Cairo, the likelihood of this venture's success would really have been 99.12 per cent.

World domination is so ridiculously effortless. All that is needed is to apply meticulously the proper equations and act on them without mercy or hesitation.

It has now been one year since the Detective has been banished from his dreams. The Professor is as all-powerful in dream as he is in reality. The world responds to his every whim as if it were a limb directly attached to his perfectly calibrated brain. The world is his, and there is no one, not a single person on the entire planet, with even the slightest potential to pose any serious, or even minor, challenge to his hegemony.

On the night of the anniversary of his conquest of the Detective of his dreams, the Professor falls into slumber with perfect serenity and confidence.

. . . Only to be once again visited by the Detective, who all this time has been secretly plotting against the Professor. The Professor's worldwide empire collapses. His operatives and vassals turn against him. All of his schemes are revealed. His web of influence is ripped apart. The Detective is ruthlessly victorious, the Professor utterly ruined and destroyed.

The Professor wakes before dawn, his entire body covered in sweat. It takes him a moment to realize that his body feels different, uncomfortable.

He rushes to a mirror and gazes upon the naked body of an ashen old man. He once more resembles the persona he adopted against the Detective in the late 1800s. But older – more decrepit, more defeated.

The Professor cancels all of his appointments for the day. He spends the next few hours recalibrating the formula that keeps him alive, the legendary Fountain of Youth. He lets himself appear a few years older than he has recently done – late thirties rather than late twenties. Neither young, nor old. Eternal.

That settled, he dives into the datastreams to lose himself in the ceaseless flow of information at his disposal, but after thirty minutes he disengages in disgust.

There is no real information in the datastreams. Everything is as he has calculated and put into motion. There are no surprises. There is no chaos. There is no opponent. The grip of his will upon the world is as precise as it is unshakeable.

That night, he again dreams of absolute destruction at the hands of the Detective.

For the first time since his childhood eight hundred years ago, the Professor's mind is in disarray. His own equations are subtly beyond his grasp. The datastreams are incomprehensible gibberish. When faced with the prospect of issuing instructions to the network of subordinates who sustain his empire, he is dumbfounded.

How long can he afford to ignore his life's work? How long before entropy sets in, unhinging the precision of the equations at the foundation of his world order?

His mind refuses to supply the mathematical solution to these questions.

*   *   *

The Detective continues to haunt the Professor's sleep. Every night, in dreams, the Detective relentlessly pursues, outwits and conquers the Professor.

Every minute of every day, the Professor feels his body ageing and decaying. He can no longer recall the mathematical formula that gives him control over the ageing process.

The Professor goes through the motions of his daily routine. The teleconferences with his operatives. The meetings with politicians and financiers. Reading the reports. He must maintain appearances. He must appear in control.

If any of his agents and vassals wonder at his prolonged silence, at the absence of fresh directives, they do not voice their apprehension. But the Professor feels that the balance of power is shifting. At least some of them are intuiting his current weakness, perhaps even planning a coup.

Despite the Professor's neglect, his empire runs along smoothly, wealth and power trickling inexorably upward, poverty and oppression spreading in concentric circles of dominance. The world is still the world of his creation. His vassals are still getting wealthier and more powerful every passing day. Nevertheless, the Professor expects that unless he soon regains his mathematical acuity someone or some faction will attempt to usurp his position. If the potential traitors hesitate, it is because they fear that upsetting the status quo might disrupt the system that grants them the riches and privileges they crave with such greed and desperation.

But the lust for power cannot be underestimated. The most predatory among his entourage must be able to smell his weakness. The instinct to pounce can only be ignored for so long. Someone will act. And soon.

The Professor wakes from yet another dream defeat at the hands of the Detective knowing that the time has come. The air in the tower is supercharged. As the day progresses, everyone is oh so careful to appear subservient. The tension mounts with each passing second, and it can only be relieved with a bloodletting.

But who will die? Who shall be the sacrifice? The Professor or the usurpers?

The sun sets, and still no overt move has been made against him.

In his office, he pretends to log in to the datastreams. He has been unable to sift through the information for weeks, but still, should he be surveyed, he makes a show of interfacing with the flow of information. He must maintain the illusion of control, of power.

But he ignores the digital babble and focuses on his immediate environment. His caution is rewarded: they are here, in this room. There are three of them. They no doubt believe they are being stealthy.

It is not by chance, or even by mathematics alone, that the Professor has survived eight centuries.

It takes him two and half seconds to disarm and kill the two most dangerous ones, the ones who moved with a modicum of skill and confidence – the latter assailant managed to nick the Professor's cheek, drawing blood – and another half-second to disarm the weakling among the trio, the leader.

The two he killed were not conspirators, but merely hired assassins. He has never seen them before; their trim, taut bodies betray their obvious training. The one left alive is a plump but merciless bank executive from Belgium. The professional assassins had wielded knives; the cowardly banker had held a gun that he did not even know how to grip properly.

The Professor spends the rest of the night torturing his would-be usurper. He finds out the names of all those who supported his move against the Professor. Even though every piece of information has been squeezed out of the banker, the Professor ministers his cruel attentions on his prisoner until sunrise. The Professor has not slept, but he feels refreshed, more rested than he has in a long while.

He convenes an emergency meeting in the reception hall. Attendance is mandatory for all those currently in the tower: financiers, politicians, operatives, staff, slaves – everyone. Within twenty minutes, there are 764 people gathered in the hall. The Professor keys in the code that locks all doors in the building.

Emerging from behind the stage curtain, the Professor drags the bloodied and bruised banker, so as to let the repugnant creature be seen by the gathered congregation. Holding up the semi-conscious man in front of him, the Professor crushes his neck with his bare hands and then flings the corpse aside.

He waits one full minute. There is scarcely a breath to be heard in the entire room. They all wait on his word.

The Professor's head oscillates from side to side in a menacingly reptilian fashion. He starts naming names, his cold, merciless gaze falling one by one on those he lists. After having pronounced thirty-seven names, he falls silent. For a full minute, the only movement in the room is the oscillation of his head. Then he utters two words: "Kill them."

The assemblage sets upon the designated victims. Upon the conspirators.

The blood is lovely. The atavistic savagery is sublime. The unquestioning obeisance is perfect.

As the congregation sacrifices the unworthy to the altar of the Professor's dominance, his mind is unshackled; it once more teems with the equations that are his lifeblood.

There were seventy-one other conspirators who were not present on site. The Professor had them dispatched with the application of one efficient formula – a slight shift in the markets that targeted them and them alone. Within four days, they were all destitute and under investigation by whichever force polices financial crimes in their respective countries. Within fifteen days, they had all either taken their own lives or been assassinated in such a way as to mimic suicide.

The Professor has not dreamed of the Detective since his victory over the conspiracy that sought to topple him. But he knows that the spectre of his opponent is waiting to pounce the moment his mind once more grows idle. The Professor cannot risk being so enfeebled again.

The random chance that gave birth to the Detective is no longer possible. The Professor's control over the world is now too absolute to allow for the nurturing of such a mind as his one true opponent's.

That must change, and yet it must also not change.

Working on the problem for two hours every evening, it takes the Professor seventeen days to calculate the exact variables to feed into a new equation. It will take three generations from this moment, but a new opponent shall rise. And from then on twice every century a new adversary will be born, each time from a random location, from random circumstances, driven by different motivations, with a different set of skills with which to spar with the Professor.

That will do, yes; that will do. Life is long, and the Professor must face fresh challenges – even if he must manufacture them himself – lest his mind and psyche stagnate and wither.

The Professor steps out on to his private rooftop terrace, facing inland, and, with a cold sneer, breathes in the brisk night air of Dubai, of the world. Of his world. His head oscillates in that distinctly inhuman manner that distinguishes him as the ultimate predator. Below him, the sands of Arabia stretch far away in time and distance.

The Mystery of the Missing Child

Christine Poulson

'Where do you suppose Mrs Hudson goes on a Thursday evening, Watson?'

'I have no idea, Holmes.'

'And why is she so reluctant to tell us? She has so far evaded my tactful enquiries.'

In Mrs Hudson's absence, Maisie, our little skivvy, brought up the tea. Holmes poured it out and winced at the sight of the straw-coloured liquid.

'That is one half of the mystery,' he said. 'The other is why the wretched girl can never learn to let the water boil.'

Holmes was not in the best of humours. He had not had a case for some weeks. He was restless and bored and, if this state of things were to continue, I feared recourse to stimulants stronger than tea. But I need not have worried. The case that was about to begin did not perhaps see him at his best, but it was a case full of interest, and one that went a long way towards explaining his enmity for Professor Moriarty.

It was a dismal day in late November in the year 1890 and dusk was drawing in. I was standing by the window, watching the lamplighter make his way down Baker Street, when a hansom cab drew up and the cabbie gestured with his whip to our door.

'Unless I am much mistaken, Holmes,' I remarked, 'a new client is in prospect.'

A minute or two later, the skivvy showed a lady into our

drawing room. She was wearing a half-mourning costume of lavender and mauve, and couldn't, I judged, be more than thirty. Hers was a delicate face with arched eyebrows, but what struck me first as a medical man was her extreme pallor. She took a few faltering steps into the room, and I was just in time to reach her before she fainted. Between us, Holmes and I lowered her on to a couch. Her hands were ice-cold. Holmes chafed them while I had recourse to the sal volatile.

She was soon sufficiently revived to sit up on the couch. I placed a glass of brandy close at hand.

She was composing herself to speak, when Holmes raised a hand. 'Let me guess the reason for your visit. Though one need scarcely be a detective to perceive that you have recently arrived in England from Italy, that before your marriage to a wealthy man you were accustomed to work for your living, that you are devoted to the memory of your late husband, and that you are desperately worried about your child.'

A glance at the lady's face told me that Holmes as usual had hit the nail on the head.

'But, how?' she stammered.

Holmes smiled and picked up one of her hands. 'Brown hands on a cold November day tell their own story. You have come from the south of France or Italy. It has been unseasonably cold in the south of France, so Italy it is. You were not born to money, in spite of those fine garnets you are wearing; otherwise, you would be accustomed to protect your hands from the sun. And for a lady such as yourself to be so afflicted, there must be a husband or a child in the case. And as you are a widow – one who still wears her husband's signet ring on a gold chain around her neck—'

She managed a shaky laugh. 'You are quite right, Mr Holmes. Before I married Harry, I was a governess and I have never managed to accustom myself to wearing gloves in warm weather. And, alas, it is all too true that I am at my wits' end to know what has happened to my darling boy!'

She took a sip from the glass of brandy.

'You must know, Mr Holmes, that though my dear late

husband, Harold Armstrong, was somewhat older than myself, we were the most united of couples and three years ago there was not a happier woman in the world than myself. Little Arthur was two and our baby daughter had just been born. Despite Harry's wealth, he came from humble origins. His own efforts and his brilliance as an engineer were responsible for his founding the engineering company of Armstrong and Morley. His sudden illness and death two years ago was a grievous blow. Still, I have my children to live for, and Harry has left me a wealthy woman, Mr Holmes. Our children shall never know want.

'That brings me to the present. My little girl is delicate and I decided to spend the winter in Italy for the sake of her health. Two weeks ago, there was an attempt to snatch my son from our garden. It was foiled by the quick thinking of his nurse, Mrs Shaughnessy, and the ferocity of our guard dog. Kidnapping is not uncommon in that part of the world. Fearful of another attempt, but unable to move my little Alicia, who was suffering from a low fever, I made a plan to get Arthur to England and out of harm's way. Mrs Shaughnessy left secretly at night and travelled incognito with Arthur as her own child. I was to follow on as soon as Alicia could safely travel. Mrs Shaughnessy sent me a telegram on arrival to let me know that she had arrived safely and was at the Midland Grand Hotel at St Pancras.

'Alicia was by then much improved. We set off for England and arrived back in England only today. And then—'

She seemed on the point of breaking down again, but, after a sip of brandy, she composed herself and went on. 'We arrived at the hotel this morning to find that Mrs Shaughnessy and Arthur were not there. The staff at the hotel had seen nothing of them since the day before yesterday, when they left the hotel in a cab. Of course we informed the police. When I explained about the earlier attempt to kidnap Arthur, they sent someone from Scotland Yard. But it is clear to me, Mr Holmes, that they have no clue as to what has happened or where my son is. I have read accounts of your successes and I had the idea of coming to see you. Rufus was not so sure, but—'

'And who is Rufus?' Holmes asked.

'My stepson, Mr Holmes. My husband's son from his first marriage. Rufus is twenty and has been a great support to me. He is waiting at the hotel in case there is a ransom demand.'

'Who is in charge of the case?'

'Inspector Lestrade. He too is waiting at the hotel.'

'I know Lestrade,' Holmes replied. 'A good man in his way, but somewhat lacking in imagination. I think our first move will be to return with you to the hotel.'

'Then you will take the case, Mr Holmes? Oh, thank you, thank you.' Hope shone in her eyes.

'I will do my best, dear lady,' Holmes said gently. 'I cannot say more.'

I have mentioned before that Holmes was a stranger to the tender passions, but a situation like this, involving a devoted wife and mother, was just the kind to draw out all that was chivalrous in his austere nature.

I had heard of the Midland Grand Hotel as one of the most luxurious hotels in London. We stepped out of a raw, drizzly November evening into an atmosphere of warmth and bright lights and deference. A magnificent sweeping staircase led up to an opulent apartment, the ceiling of which was lavishly decorated with gold leaf. A young man was lounging by a blazing fire, and sprang to his feet as we entered. Lestrade was there too, standing by the window, looking out of place with his heavy boots and worn overcoat.

Mrs Armstrong looked at them with an appeal on her face. Both men shook their heads and her face fell.

She introduced the young man as her stepson, Mr Rufus Armstrong. He was a little too well dressed for my taste, but then I am old-fashioned and do not care to see men wearing diamond cufflinks.

'I'm not sorry to see you, Mr Holmes,' Lestrade said.

'I am glad that Scotland Yard is taking the case seriously.'

'Oh, yes,' Lestrade said grimly, 'when an heir to a fortune, and a child at that, goes missing, we take it seriously all right. Any little assistance you care to give us will be welcome, Mr Holmes.'

There was a sardonic twist to Holmes's lips, but he refrained from comment. He turned to Mrs Armstrong. 'Mrs Shaughnessy would scarcely have foiled the earlier attempt if she had been in the pay of the kidnappers. She is, I take it, beyond suspicion?'

'Oh yes, Mr Holmes, she has been with us since Arthur was born and she is devoted to him. She would defend him with her life, I am sure of that.'

At that moment there was a knock on the door. Lestrade answered it and I glimpsed a constable outside. They conferred in low voices.

When Lestrade turned to us, he looked grave. 'The body of a woman was found in the Regent's Canal this afternoon.'

Mrs Armstrong gasped and her hand flew to her bosom.

'Of course, it may not be Mrs Shaughnessy,' he continued, 'but if someone who knew her could come to the mortuary . . .'

Mrs Armstrong was about to speak, but her stepson stepped forward. 'I can accompany the Inspector, Mother,' he said, the name sounding incongruous on his lips, for there can have been no more than ten years between them.

Holmes nodded his approval. 'We also will accompany you, Lestrade.'

Leaving Mrs Armstrong in the care of her maid, we departed.

I felt a sense of foreboding as we passed through the wrought-iron gates of the mortuary. A wind had got up and the bare branches of the surrounding trees swayed and rustled. If it was chilly outside, it was bitter within, as the cold struck from the tiled walls. I am not a fanciful man, but on that chill November evening it was like entering the very gates of death.

We were shown into a room by a gaunt attendant, himself of a cadaverous appearance. On a marble slab, the body of a woman lay covered with a sheet. Fearing how Mr Armstrong might react, I positioned myself at his elbow. When the attendant drew back the sheet, we saw the face of a woman of about forty, framed with a mass of dark red hair. It was a strong face, full of character, even in death.

Mr Armstrong nodded. 'That is Mrs Shaughnessy. But whatever can have become of Arthur?'

He was very pale, but otherwise remarkably composed. Lestrade and Holmes exchanged glances and I guessed what was in their minds. Who knew what further secrets might be concealed in the murky waters of the canal?

'We'll do our best to find out, Mr Armstrong,' Lestrade said. 'Come with me. I'll arrange for a constable to accompany you back to the hotel.'

'With your permission, Lestrade, Watson and I will linger a little longer,' Holmes said.

When the two men had left the room, Holmes and I examined the body. One side of the face was badly bruised. I picked up her hand. It was icy cold and the fingernails were broken. All down her arms were clusters of small bruises.

'Mrs Shaughnessy struggled with her attacker,' I concluded.

'She has certainly been subjected to some rough treatment,' Holmes agreed. 'She may have marked her assailant. Where are her clothes?' he asked the attendant.

'Over here, Mr Holmes.' On a table in the corner of the room, lay a pile of sodden garments, neatly folded, but stinking of the canal.

'Something curious, Mr Holmes,' the attendant went on. He showed us a small oilskin packet. 'This was in her bodice, next to her skin, like.'

'Have you opened it?' Holmes asked.

'I was waiting for the Inspector.'

Lestrade returned at that moment and we opened the packet. It contained a piece of pink and white ribbon, about three or four inches long.

Holmes examined it. 'Not new, by any means. Cut straight across at one end, and diagonally at the other end, with a notch or zigzag in it. What do you make of it, Lestrade?'

'Oh, some lover's token, I expect. I can't see much significance in that, Mr Holmes.'

'Well, well, you may be right. You won't mind if I take possession of it?'

Lestrade waved his consent. 'The way I see it, is this: the gang snatched the child and the nurse tried to prevent it. They killed her – probably didn't mean to – and dumped her body in the canal. So now it's a hanging offence. Question is, do they still mean to demand a ransom, or have they panicked and got rid of the child?'

Holmes nodded his agreement. 'You'll have the canal dragged?'

'As soon as it gets light. In the meantime, I'll return to the hotel in case a ransom note is received.'

'I can be better employed in Baker Street,' Holmes said, 'but, Watson – it may be as well for the lady to have a doctor on hand. Perhaps you'd consent to spend the night at the hotel.'

'By all means, Holmes.'

I advised Lestrade to say nothing to Mrs Armstrong about dragging the canal, I gave her a mild sedative to help her sleep, then I myself retired to the sofa in the drawing room of the suite. For an old campaigner like myself, this was no hardship. I soon was fast asleep, and no doubt snoring into the bargain.

I was awoken by someone shaking my shoulder and opened my eyes to see Mrs Armstrong gazing down at me.

'Dr. Watson! It's Rufus! He's gone.'

I struggled up on to an elbow. 'Gone? Gone where?'

Lestrade was behind her. He cleared his throat. 'The facts appear to be these, Dr Watson. The constable, who escorted Mr Armstrong to the hotel, says that a message was waiting for him at the desk. Mr Armstrong broke the news of Mrs Shaughnessy's death to Mrs Armstrong, and then when Dr Watson arrived, he retired to his own quarters. But his valet found this morning that his bed has not been slept in and he is nowhere to be found.'

Mrs Armstrong wrung her hands. 'Oh, Dr Watson, I am so afraid that he has gone out to look for Arthur and has met with some harm.'

Even in my sleep-befuddled state, one thing was clear. 'We had better send for Holmes,' I said.

'No need,' said a familiar voice from the door.

It was extraordinary, the way that the atmosphere of that room changed on an instant. Mrs Armstrong became calmer. An expression of relief, quickly masked, flitted across Lestrade's face.

Mrs Armstrong went to Holmes. He took her hand between both of his and led her to a chair.

He turned to Lestrade. 'I'm assuming that you have not found the note that was left at the desk.'

'We have not,' Lestrade said. 'Either he burned it, or more likely took it with him when he went out.'

'You have no idea where he may have gone, Mrs Armstrong?' Holmes asked.

Tears were welling up in her eyes. 'I cannot understand it, Mr Holmes. Rufus scarcely knows the city. Do you think he heard from the kidnappers and went to confront them? Oh, surely he would never be so foolish as to go without saying a word!'

'You are quite certain he knows no one in London?' Holmes persisted.

'No one! Though, but no, surely . . .'

'You've thought of someone?'

'Harry was keen that Rufus should go into the firm, but Rufus has struggled a little with his schooling. So we engaged a mathematics tutor for him, a man eminent in his field, who lived with us for a while. Rufus liked him – and I think he lives in London.'

'His name?'

'Moriarty. Professor James Moriarty.'

Moriarty! The man Holmes had described to me as the Napoleon of crime, the spider at the centre of a Europe-wide web of crime and corruption. His was the last name I – or Holmes, I warrant – had expected to hear. If Holmes was as taken aback as I was, he didn't let it show.

'When was this, Mrs Armstrong?'

'It must have been around four years ago. He stayed with us for six months. But I think he and Rufus have kept in touch. He lives in Kew, I believe.'

Holmes was silent for some moments and, when he spoke, it appeared to be at a tangent.

'What were the terms of your husband's will as regards his children, Mrs Armstrong?'

She stared at him. 'Rufus and Arthur will inherit the company when they come of age. For Rufus that will be next year. Arthur's share is kept in trust until he reaches his majority. I and my daughter are provided for separately.'

'And should one son predecease the other before reaching their majority?'

'The survivor will inherit everything. But, Mr Holmes, you can't think . . . why, Rufus is devoted to little Arthur. He thinks the world of him.'

Holmes was saved from replying to this by the appearance of a nanny who told Mrs Armstrong that her daughter was upset and asking for her. Mrs Armstrong left the room and Holmes turned a grave face to Lestrade and myself.

'This puts a very different complexion on matters.'

'You think Mr Armstrong is implicated in the kidnapping, Mr Holmes?' Lestrade asked.

'I am certain of it. As it happens, I know the address of Moriarty's house in Kew, though I doubt that we will find the beast in its lair.'

So it proved. Moriarty's housekeeper could tell us only that her master had left the previous evening and had told her he would be away for some undefined period. No, he hadn't told her where he was going, but it was her belief that he'd gone abroad. He could be gone days, he could be gone weeks. There was no knowing. Holmes had expected no less, yet it was still a disappointment,

We returned to Baker Street to find a message from Lestrade. The canal had been dragged but nothing had been found. Mr Armstrong had not returned to the hotel. In short, there was no news.

Holmes flung himself into a chair by the fire. 'So we are no further forward.'

'While there is life, there is hope,' I remarked, pouring out the tea that Mrs Hudson had brought up.

'But is there life, Watson, that is the question? It is true that Moriarty would not lightly dispose of so valuable a commodity as this child. But in that case why has no ransom note been received – and what has happened to Rufus Armstrong?'

Holmes reached for his pipe and stuffed it with shag. He sighed and stared gloomily into the fire, frustrated by our lack of progress. I handed him his tea and a copy of *The Times*. It was his habit to peruse the personal columns every day and I hoped it might prove a temporary distraction. Though he took it up with a show of reluctance, he was soon engrossed.

I leaned back in my chair and closed my eyes. For a while there was no sound but the crackling of the fire and the rustling of the pages of the newspaper, and I had almost dozed off, when an exclamation from Holmes jerked my eyes open.

'Good God, Holmes, what is it?'

'There is to be a sale tomorrow in Paris of eighteenth-century French paintings and drawings, containing a number of works by Jean-Baptiste Greuze, Moriarty's favourite painter. Strange that a man as cold-hearted as Moriarty should be drawn to paintings that some – myself included – regard as sentimental, even mawkish, but so it is. It is an obsession with him, his one weak spot. He will be there tomorrow, not a doubt about it. Make a long arm for the Bradshaw, Watson, and look up the times of the boat train, there's a good fellow.'

A Channel crossing at night in November is not something I recommend and I was heartily relieved to reach Calais. As we came ashore, a change seemed to come over Holmes. I myself am unmistakably an Englishman abroad, but it was not so with Holmes. I had not realized that his French was so fluent. 'Why, Holmes,' I declared, 'you could almost pass as a Frenchman.'

He smiled, but said nothing.

We reached Paris and took a cab straight to the saleroom on the Faubourg Saint Honoré.

The auction had not yet begun and a small crowd, mostly male, was engaged in viewing paintings set up on easels and portfolios of drawings.

Holmes nudged me and pointed. 'What did I tell you? There he is!'

Moriarty was very much as Holmes had once described him to me: a thin face, grey hair swept back from a high, domed forehead. There was a strange contrast between his ascetic appearance, every inch the unworldly academic, and the voluptuous picture at which he was gazing. It was not one I should have cared to view in the company of a lady.

Moriarty was too engrossed to notice us approaching, until Holmes remarked, 'That is a very fine Fragonard, is it not? Do you intend to bid?'

It must have been a shock to see us there, but to give him this due, Moriarty showed no sign of surprise. He merely remarked, 'Good afternoon, Mr Holmes. And this, I assume, is your confederate, Dr Watson. As for the painting, alas, it is far beyond my modest purse – and not entirely to my taste either.'

'Modest purse! Are you not the owner of a painting by Greuze worth well over a million francs?'

'A gift from a friend, Mr Holmes. A gift from a wealthy friend in gratitude for services rendered.'

There was a pedantic precision about his speech that made my flesh creep.

'You have a number of wealthy friends, have you not?' Holmes enquired. 'Among them Rufus Armstrong, who would be even wealthier were it not for the trifling obstacle of a younger brother?'

Moriarty moved on to the next picture. This one, I saw from the signature, was by Greuze. It showed a little girl playing with a kitten and was not much more to my taste than the last.

'I will pay you the compliment of frankness, Mr Holmes. I do not have the child, nor do I know where he is. If I did, I would be only too happy to hand him over in exchange for an appropriate reward.'

Only a warning look from Holmes prevented me from seizing him and thrashing him there and then.

'Rufus Armstrong is also missing,' Holmes remarked.

'Ah, Rufus. A hot-headed young man, and arrogant into the bargain.'

'Do you know what has happened to him?'

'Perhaps some accident has befallen him, Mr Holmes.' Moriarty leaned forward to examine the picture more closely. 'The streets of London have become so dangerous, have they not? Now look at the whiskers of that kitten: the handling of the paint just there: superlative, is it not?' Perhaps the sentimental picture had touched his stony heart, for I saw that his eyes were moist. 'If the streets of London can be dangerous for a young man, they are desperately so for a lost child. I hope the police are doing their utmost to find little Arthur. And now the auction is about to begin, so our interesting little chat must end. Good day to you both.'

The cabbie was waiting for us and Holmes instructed him to go to the nearest telegraph office.

'Now that we know what happened,' he said, 'I had better send a telegram to Lestrade.'

I was taken aback. 'What did happen?' I enquired.

'Why, did you not hear what Moriarty said?' Holmes spoke with a touch of asperity. 'Is it not evident that Moriarty, blackguard that he is, corrupted this young man while acting as his tutor and they hatched a plot to snatch the child? The nurse put up more of a fight than Moriarty's thugs anticipated and the child managed to get away. Moriarty and Armstrong fell out over the failure of the plot and Armstrong, as one would expect, came off the worst.'

'So you really think Moriarty doesn't have Arthur?'

'You must understand how his mind works. It is merely a matter of business with him. If he had the child, he would have demanded a ransom long before now. As it is, he has wasted no time in cutting his losses.'

'But if Arthur managed to run away, where is he?'

'Where indeed, Watson? Lestrade must step up the search. And it is time to get the Baker Street Irregulars on the case.'

Holmes spoke briskly, but I could tell that he was troubled. Arthur had been missing for three days now. He had disappeared into the maw of London. If he had fallen into the hands of the underworld – well, it did not bear thinking of.

'Can Moriarty not be brought to book for his part in this?' I asked.

'If, as I strongly suspect, Rufus Armstrong is out of the way, Moriarty will escape justice – on this occasion. It was the poet Longfellow who wrote, "Though the mills of God grind slowly, yet they grind exceeding small". Moriarty will get his just deserts. I shall see to that.'

We arrived at the telegraph office and Holmes disappeared inside.

He soon returned.

'What now?' I asked.

Holmes took out his pocket watch. 'We have a few hours before our train departs. I wonder, Watson . . .' His voice trailed off and I looked at him in surprise. It was not like Holmes to sound uncertain. 'There is someone I should like you to meet . . . of course, she might not be at home, but . . . yes,' he decided. He leaned out and gave the driver an address in the Place des Vosges. He flung himself back in his corner and closed his eyes, leaving me to wonder whom this mysterious 'she' might be.

Holmes and a woman, a Frenchwoman at that! I remembered his impeccable French and wondered even more. Surely this could not be a romantic attachment, an old flame, perhaps even an ex-mistress? Unthinkable! And yet I *was* thinking it. What else could account for Holmes's diffidence?

After a while, we left behind the broad boulevards with their brilliant lights and plunged into a dark maze of little streets lined by workshops. We emerged in the Place des Vosges. In the gathering twilight, mist drifted between the linden trees and the fine old sixteenth-century facades.

We got out of the cab and Holmes rang the bell.

The door was answered by an elderly maid, whose face lit up at the sight of Holmes. The next moment, an elegant woman rushed past her and with an exclamation of '*mon cher* Sherlock!' threw herself into Holmes's arms. He returned her embrace, while I stood gaping.

After a few moments, he pulled away and turned to me,

laughing. 'Let me introduce you. Tante Yvette, this is my great friend, Dr Watson. Watson, this is Madame Pujol, my aunt.'

I saw now that her trim figure and modish dress had deceived me as to her age. Even so, she scarcely looked old enough to be his aunt. Later, I discovered that she was his mother's younger sister. They were the nieces of the French artist, Horace Vernet, whom Holmes had once mentioned as an ancestor.

'Ah, *le grand* Watson! *Quel plaisir!* One has heard so much.' She held out a slender hand laden with rings.

There was only one thing to be done. I took her hand, bent over it and kissed it. '*Enchanté*, Madame.'

She laughed and spoke in a torrent of French, of which I made out only the world '*galant*'.

'I thought you two would hit it off,' Holmes remarked dryly. 'But stick to English, *tante* Yvette, if you want Watson to be flattered by your compliments.'

In no time at all, we were seated round a dining table, drinking the kind of soup that is made only by a French cook.

Over the meal, Holmes told his aunt about the case. He spoke to her as an equal, omitting nothing, and explaining his chain of reasoning. She listened intently, her eyes never leaving his face, nodding approval now and then at some step he had taken. You would not at first have thought they were related, but the resemblance was there, not only in the keen intelligence that shone from her clear grey eyes, but also in the curl of her lip at the mention of Greuze.

At one point, the beaming maid took away the soup plates and brought in a dish of lamb cutlets and a bottle of good claret.

When Holmes had finished his story, Madame Pujol sat back and considered. Holmes tucked into his cutlets.

At last, 'You have missed something, Sherlock,' she said in her accented English.

Holmes looked up from his plate. 'What have you spotted?'

'The nurse took the boat train and arrived at Victoria, did she not? There are many good hotels near Victoria. Why then did she book into the Grand Midland Hotel? It is on the other side of London. No woman travelling alone with a child would choose to prolong so arduous a journey without an excellent reason. Sherlock, I have told you before, you do not take the female point of view sufficiently into account.'

A thought occurred to me. 'You don't think the nurse had something to do with Arthur's disappearance?'

She smiled at me. 'No, no. Sherlock is right there, I am sure. She gave her life for that child. All the same, "*Cherchez la femme.*" That is my advice. There is more to be discovered about that nurse and the circumstances of her disappearance.'

'There is no one on whose intelligence and intuition I put more reliance, not even Mycroft,' Holmes told me as we drove to *la Gare du Nord*.

Indeed, his first act on reaching Victoria after another wretched night crossing was to take a cab for the Grand Midland Hotel and question the manager. He learned that on the evening of her disappearance Mrs Shaughnessy had asked for a cab to be brought to the servants' entrance. Clearly she had desired to leave the hotel unseen.

So began three days of the most intense frustration. Lestrade's men questioned local cab drivers with no result. Holmes instructed the Baker Street Irregulars to find out if Mrs Shaughnessy had been seen in the streets around St Pancras. They found a chestnut seller who had seen someone fitting her description walking up Judd Street, only a few minutes from the hotel. She had been alone.

'My theory is this,' Holmes told Mrs Armstrong. 'Mrs Shaughnessy feared there would be another attempt to snatch Arthur. She took him to a place where she thought that he would be safe, somewhere close at hand, for I believe she was walking back to the hotel when Moriarty's men accosted her and tried to find out where the child was.'

Mrs Shaughnessy's own relatives all lived in Ireland, but she had worked for a family in London for some years. This seemed to open up some possibilities, until Holmes discovered that the family was in America so she could not have lodged Arthur with them. But there the trail went cold.

Mrs Armstrong grew thinner, and the shadows beneath her eyes became more pronounced. She was supported only by the need to care for her little girl. It grieved me to see her and I know that Holmes felt keenly his failure to relieve her anguish.

On the morning of the fourth day, we had a late breakfast. Holmes was turning over his notes on the case, trying to find some chink in the darkness that had gathered around us.

He thrust the papers to one side. 'It's no good, Watson. There's nothing.'

I caught sight of the ribbon that had been wrapped up in oilcloth and concealed in the bosom of the nurse.

'We never did get to the bottom of that ribbon,' I remarked, as Mrs Hudson came into the room with a tray of dishes.

'We probably never shall, since Mrs Armstrong could throw no light on it.'

In his usual meticulous way, Holmes had also consulted a local haberdasher, but had learned nothing of interest. Cheap ribbons exactly like it could be purchased in any number of places.

He examined it. 'Still, it is curious, the way this end has been cut in a jagged line. Lestrade may be right, some kind of lover's token—'

Behind me I heard a gasp, followed immediately by a great crash.

I looked round to see kedgeree all over the carpet and Mrs Hudson standing with her hand to her heart.

'What on earth is the matter?' I cried.

Holmes was on his feet. There was an eager light in his eyes. 'You don't mean to say that you know the meaning of that ribbon, Mrs Hudson?'

She nodded. 'I believe I do, Mr Holmes.'

We took Mrs Hudson with us and collected Mrs Armstrong from the hotel. Very soon we were drawing up outside a plain Georgian building off Brunswick Square. We asked to see Mr Brown, the warden, and were shown into an office with walls lined with ledgers.

A man of about fifty with keen eyes and mutton-chop whiskers rose from behind a desk.

'How can I help you, ladies and gentlemen?' he enquired.

'I think you will recognize this,' Holmes said. He laid the piece of ribbon on the desk.

Brown frowned. 'Can you tell me how you came by this?'

'It was concealed on the body of Mrs Shaughnessy.'

'The body!' He was visibly shocked.

'You didn't know that Mrs Shaughnessy was dead? It was in the newspapers.'

He shook his head. 'I am a busy man, Mr Holmes, with many souls in my care. I rarely read the newspapers. Is this lady . . . ?' He gestured to Mrs Armstrong.

'Yes, this is his mother.'

Brown turned and took down a large and ancient ledger. He laid it open on the desk. As he turned over the pages, I saw other scraps of ribbon attached with rusty pins. What a tale of heart-break and loss each one could have told! Near the back was a ribbon of the same design as the one we had brought with us. Brown fitted them together. They were an exact match.

'The hospital discontinued this system in favour of a written receipt long ago,' he said, 'but in this instance it seemed wise to revert to it. Follow me.'

He led us down a long corridor and opened a door into a large room full of wooden tables and benches at which children were seated at a meal of bread and cheese. They were all boys, aged from about five up to around ten, all dressed alike in brown serge. Some of them looked up as we came in, but most were engrossed in their food.

A pleasant homely-looking woman came towards us.

'Would you get Thomas Paine for us?' Mr Brown asked. 'Mrs Shaughnessy thought it best not to use his real name,' he added.

'Mama!' It was a cry to wring the heart. A small boy started up from a table in the middle of the room.

'Arthur! My Arthur!' Mrs Armstrong took a few steps forward and her arms opened. Arthur came hurtling towards her and, the next moment, his arms were round her knees and she was press-ing him to her.

I am not ashamed to confess that there was a lump in my throat. Holmes was strangely silent, too.

It was left to Mrs Hudson to ask Mr Brown how was it that Mrs Shaughnessy had thought to bring the little boy to the Foundling Hospital.

'She and my wife were old friends,' Mr Brown explained, 'girls together in Ireland. She had reason to fear that Arthur was in imminent danger and we promised to take care of him and to surrender him only to the bearer of the token. We fully expected that she would return in a couple of days.'

'A brilliant idea,' Holmes admitted, 'to hide him among paupers. It is the last place anyone would think of looking for the heir to a fortune. That nurse was a woman of genius.'

Holmes declined his fee, Mrs Armstrong insisted, and they compromised on a substantial donation to the Foundling Hospital and a handsome present for Mrs Hudson.

Holmes told her about it later that day when she brought up the tea tray.

'That will be ample for a new gown and a bonnet or two, eh, Mrs Hudson?'

'Indeed, Mr Holmes. Mrs Armstrong has been most generous.'

Holmes was too busy cross-referencing his index to the most infamous criminals in Europe to see the twinkle in her eye.

'And what will you really be spending your little windfall on?' I asked.

'I've been going to the penny lectures at Morley College on Thursday evenings, Dr Watson.'

I had heard of this new venture. The lectures were given by some of the most eminent scientists and philosophers of the day and were open to the public. I had sometimes thought of going myself.

Mrs Hudson went on. 'Now I can afford to do an extension course in German at the University of London so that I can read Mr Marx's *Das Kapital* in the original.'

It is one of the very few times that I've seen Holmes lost for words.

After Mrs Hudson had left the room, we were both silent for a few moments.

Holmes sighed. 'My aunt is right. I fail to take the female point of view sufficiently into account. But I ask you, Watson, how can one ever get the measure of them? It is a hopeless task.'

For me, one question still remained. I followed Mrs Hudson down to the kitchen and asked how she had come to think of the Foundling Hospital.

'Oh, no, Dr Watson, you can't think that I . . . ' She sighed. 'Though if I had, I wouldn't have been the first poor girl newly arrived in London . . . but no, when I was first in service, I knew a parlour maid . . . I went with her when she took her baby to the Foundling Hospital. She was one of the lucky ones. She married a good man, who let her go and get her baby back.'

One final note must be added. I fear that Holmes's conjectures about the fate of Rufus Armstrong were correct. When he left the Grand Midland Hotel that night, it was as if he'd vanished off the face of the earth. He has not been seen from that day to this. Arthur inherited the whole business when he came of age and has proved worthy of his distinguished father.

Author's note:

The Foundling Hospital was established by philanthropic sea captain, Thomas Coram, in 1739. Residential provision ceased in 1954, but it continues its work for young people as the Thomas Coram Foundation. The Foundling Museum in Bloomsbury tells the story of the Hospital, the first UK children's charity.

The Case of the Choleric Cotton Broker

Martin Edwards

"My collection of M's is a fine one"
Sherlock Holmes, *The Empty House*

The Diogenes and the Tankerville clubs occupy premises a mere
seventy yards apart, yet concealed behind their doors are worlds
as divergent as Mayfair and Madagascar. The sound of a raised
voice in the silent sanctuary of the Diogenes would startle a
listener as much as a volley of gunfire. By way of contrast, the
bustle and argument indigenous to the Tankerville calls to mind
Charing Cross Station at six o'clock on a Friday evening. When,
one chilly April afternoon in 1889, a sturdily built visitor to the
Tankerville proclaimed in loud and forceful tones his disdain for
Colonel Sebastian Moran, nobody paid the slightest attention,
except for myself and Professor Moriarty.

"How dare you, sir!" the man thundered. "Place this city out of
bounds to me, would you? I never heard of such impertinence!"

The other three men were unaware that their conversation
had an interested witness. This was as well. My life would have
been in the gravest peril had they known that I was eavesdrop-
ping. I had taken up my station, in a tall, high-backed, and thankfully capacious William and Mary armchair, some twenty minutes
before Moran ushered his guests into the Reading Room. This is
the smallest and least frequented of the public areas in the
Tankerville. Members seeking to take advantage of the facilities

offered by that institution have more pressing concerns than literature, although the club library caters generously for those with recondite tastes. My chair was separated from the three confederates by an untenanted chess table, and a small desk at which an elderly member who, having discarded his ear trumpet, was poring over an exotic calfskin-bound book, privately published in Marseilles. Occasionally, he emitted peculiar yelps of pleasure at the more extravagant illustrations.

Intelligence had reached me indicating that Moran had summoned a senior associate to an urgent meeting at the Tankerville. The agenda was unknown, but believed to be of the utmost gravity. I deemed it essential that we should learn something of whatever fresh devilry was contemplated by the Professor's henchman. Of my two most trusted lieutenants, however, one was recovering from his injuries after being set upon by a gang of Moriarty's thugs in the Old Kent Road, while the other's face was already familiar to Moran from a previous skirmish in Berlin. With the utmost reluctance, I concluded there was no choice but to take the exceptional step of involving myself directly in the matter.

The organisation that I shall, for the purpose of this narrative, identify simply as the Office had procured the recruitment of two of its agents to the staff of the Tankerville. One man, T, who served as a porter, had made sure that I was furnished with a forged membership card, while his colleague, J, supplied an occasional glass of brandy in the capacity of waiter. The Reading Room was reputed to be Moran's favourite haunt, and the location where he liked to issue instructions to his acolytes. What we had failed to anticipate was that the Professor would also attend the meeting. Nothing could more clearly confirm the seriousness of their business, since despite the intimacy of their relations, it was unheard of for Moriarty and the Colonel to be seen in public together.

"How I amuse myself in private is none of your business." The man's accent suggested a curious mixture of influences. Having made a small study of the subject, I concluded that he was a native of Liverpool (the south of the city, rather than the north, in my opinion) but one who had travelled far and wide. I even detected a faint twang redolent of old Virginia. "And that, sir, is an end of the matter."

Prior to my arrival, J had effected subtle adjustments to the positioning of the furniture, so that I was able, by craning my neck, to benefit from a view of much of the room in an ornately framed mirror without myself being observed. In the reflection, I saw Moran take a single pace towards his guest. Advancing years had not diminished the Colonel's formidable physical presence, and he resembled a ferocious tiger – of the kind he had bagged so many times in India – about to pounce. Any ordinary man would have quailed at the malevolence in those penetrating blue eyes, but his companions were no ordinary men.

Moriarty did no more than allow his eyelids to flicker, yet it was enough to halt the Colonel in his tracks. When he spoke, the Professor's voice was clear, yet pitched low enough for it to be difficult for me to hear.

"Gentlemen, please. Such a display of rancour is unseemly. You must appreciate, my dear fellow, that the Colonel is simply anxious for your own well-being."

"You . . . authorised this command?" The man appeared taken aback. He thrust a hand into the pocket of his jacket, drawing out a small pillbox. With *legerdemain* of a kind born only of long practice, he extracted two tablets, and swallowed them whole.

"Indeed, my dear fellow. I count myself not merely as a colleague, but a friend. I am motivated solely by a desire to ensure that you come to no harm. So far, you have enjoyed considerable good fortune, but I fear that will not last for ever. Better quit the game now, while you remain ahead of the pack."

An expression of uncertainty disrupted the other man's well-fed features. I diagnosed a swaggering and aggressive personality, to which any hint of doubt was inimical. Yet the way in which he tugged at his heavy moustache suggested indecision. His sudden change of mood was easy to comprehend, for the silky menace lurking behind Moriarty's suave protestations of good-will was a thousand times more alarming than a crude threat of violence. I did not wonder that he phrased his reply with a humility conspicuously absent from his contemptuous riposte to Colonel Moran.

"You will appreciate, Professor, that I have not the slightest wish to incur your displeasure. The goodwill that subsists between—"

"Enough!" Moriarty lifted his right hand, and gave a smile cold enough to freeze flesh. "We shall say no more on the subject. I believe that your train departs from Euston in thirty minutes. Let us summon a cab without delay, so that you are sure to arrive at the station in time."

Before the man could speak, Moran interjected. "After all, you would not wish to be too long absent from the company of that beautiful young belle of yours. Eh?"

The provocation in his jeering tone was unmistakable, and the other man appeared to fight a battle within himself before responding. When at last he spoke, caution prevailed, but evidently it had been a close-run thing.

"Very well, gentlemen. I shall take my leave of you. Professor, I shall reflect on what you have said. I owe you no less."

With a crisp bow, he took his leave. Once the door had closed behind him, Moran turned to the Professor.

"Dangerous."

Moriarty inclined his head. "Such is the nature of a loose cannon."

"Pity. These past two years, he has made himself damned useful."

The Professor gave a gentle sigh. "You will recall my mentioning after my first conversation with him that his proclivities would render him unstable in due course."

"Yes, I must admit that you were right. As usual." The note of admiration struck me as genuine, not grudging. "How fortunate that we have prepared for all eventualities."

"Good fortune has nothing to do with it, Colonel. Planning and preparation, therein lies the secret of sustained success in any field of human endeavour. The nursemaid is aware of what is required?"

"Our people in the north country assure me of her reliability."

"Excellent. And the staff at Flatman's?"

"They are ready to provide evidence of impropriety, should the police display their customary ineptitude in following up clues helpfully laid before them by the nursemaid. I have every confidence that the path we have constructed will lead to the gallows."

Moriarty permitted himself a thin smile. "Do not be so sure, Colonel. The machine of justice in this country is as susceptible to malfunction as the most antiquated equipment in the humblest factory. Happily, that is of little consequence. What matters is that our activities continue to flourish without risk of compromise."

The Colonel clicked his heels. "You may be assured of that."

With this, they departed the Reading Room, leaving me to muse on their cryptic conversation for another half-hour, until a loud and echoing squeal of delight from the aged student of exotica finally drove me to seek refuge in the infinitely more congenial environment of the Diogenes Club.

I took time to reflect on what I had learned at the Tankerville. During the course of my life, I have been accused of a medley of vices, but nobody has yet sought to characterise me as that dullest of oafs, the man of action. Haste on the part of the authorities, a stubborn insistence on being seen to be doing anything rather than nothing explains much that is wrong with our world. Hence my insistence on ensuring that my work is conducted out of sight from the public I serve. I exclude my brother from criticism in this regard; a man in business as a consulting detective cannot afford complete anonymity. Nevertheless, his celebrity gave me cause for concern in relation to Professor Moriarty. It seemed to me that it was merely a question of time before the two men's paths crossed, with consequences that I found myself reluctant to contemplate. I saw it as my duty to make sure that my brother remained unaware of the full extent of the Professor's nefarious activities until I was left with no choice but to reveal how much I knew. Even then, I would need to insist that he refrained from divulging matters of detail to his chronicler. One kingdom, two distinguished lives, and at least a dozen pristine reputations depended upon our discretion.

The man from the north country intrigued me. We had for some time been aware that Moriarty's web stretched across the continents, but we had struggled to identify the individuals who supervised his criminal affairs outside the United Kingdom. In particular, neither the American authorities nor the energetic men of the late Mr Pinkerton's Agency had been able to identify Moriarty's representative in the United States. Plainly, a man of business whose legitimate commercial interests stretched across the Atlantic would prove an invaluable asset to the Professor, and I suspected that I had been in the presence of just such an individual. I found, as usual, that an hour or two of gentle slumber followed by a first class Chateaubriand proved unmatched in facilitating the deductive process, and by the time I was joined for a postprandial port by the Home Secretary's right-hand man, I was ready to disclose my conclusions.

"A riddle and a half!" W exclaimed, once I had recounted *verbatim* the discussion that I had overheard. "A nurse, a hotel, the gallows . . . what do you make of such disjointed fragments?"

I savoured my drink. The importance of the day's events justified a certain indulgence, and I had chosen the vintage of 1834, and that colossus of ports, Kopka's Quinta de Roriz.

"Let us begin, my dear W, with Moran's subordinate. What do we know of him?"

"Very little," my companion responded grimly. "We need to redouble our efforts to trace his identity."

"The task may be easier than you suppose. The timbre of his voice is unusual and suggestive. A Liverpudlian of the mercantile class, whose domestic or work commitments have led him to spend significant periods of time in London and the east coast of North America in recent years. One infers from the exquisite tailoring of his suit – to say nothing of the satin waistcoat with ivory buttons – that he enjoys considerable wealth. His choleric demeanour, however, is unlikely to be the product of a background of privilege. Those born to wealth are educated from an early age to conceal their tempers behind a cloak of good manners."

Sir W snorted. A hereditary baronet, he may have detected an ironic thrust, notwithstanding my beatific smile, but I was unrepentant. My endeavours earlier in the day entitled me to mix business with a little personal amusement.

"I surmise that his travels are attributable to business rather than pleasure, and that he has enjoyed success in his chosen line. Given that the Liverpool Cotton Association dominates commerce within his native city, the assumption that he is a merchant or broker in cotton is reasonable if not beyond argument. Consider. If, through Moran, our friend Moriarty secured the loyalty of such a man, his ability to conduct covert operations in the United States would be greatly enhanced. A successful broker with interests in, say, Virginia would have unimpeachable reasons for coming and going across the Atlantic. I suspect that his usefulness would by no means be confined to delivering secret messages to American crooks. He might himself direct operations in accordance with the Professor's plans for spreading criminality across the civilised world."

"Damnable!" my companion exclaimed. "But why would such a man – an entrepreneur – put himself at Moriarty's disposal?"

"I was intrigued by the fact that his complexion is pasty, with hints of grey and yellow. One would expect such a choleric fellow to be red-cheeked. Evidently, he enjoys indifferent health, and I speculate that the faint tinge of yellow may be attributable to a bout of malaria in the past. The disease is not uncommon in the cotton fields of Virginia. His readiness to swallow pills suggests to me that, however genuine the maladies that he has suffered, he is also something of a hypochondriac. The conclusion, as I am sure you will concur, is plain."

W stirred in his chair. "I cannot claim that it is obvious to me."

"The man is a drug fiend, depend upon it. The pastiness of his cheeks is due, I suspect, to an overfondness for arsenic. Some medical men recommend it for the treatment of malaria. Quinine is more effective, but less appealing to those with unconventional instincts. The peasants of Styria take arsenic as a means of freshening the complexion, but our friend is more likely, in my opinion, to favour arsenic because of its aphrodisiac qualities."

"I say!"

I raised a hand to still W's protests. "Deplorable, perhaps, but we must take the world as we find it, rather than as we would wish it to be. Believe me, even a man with the finest mind and purest heart may resort to desperate remedies in moments of acute stress, and, although this fellow is no fool, I doubt there is much in his life that is pure."

"You think this arsenic habit has weakened his moral fibre?"

"He may have been blessed with little enough moral fibre to start with," I replied. "I caught sight of a betting slip protruding from one of his pockets. It had been crumpled, perhaps in disgust. A man with a fondness for the racetrack will often display other weaknesses of character and, although his attire was at first glance immaculate, my eyesight was keen enough to detect a faint shadow of crimson on his collar, no doubt the legacy of an amorous liaison earlier in the day."

"My dear fellow!"

"Even an affluent businessman may find such pastimes expensive. A desire to supplement his finances may cause him to consort with rogues. And scoundrels come in no more sophisticated guise than Colonel Moran and Professor Moriarty."

"Very well, I am persuaded. You said that in the conversation between those gentlemen, mention was made of a nursemaid and Flatman's. Have you formed a view as to their significance – if any?"

"Flatman's Hotel is to be found in Henrietta Street. It happens to be frequented by members of the cotton-broking fraternity, but may no doubt prove a suitable venue for intrigue, as well as discussions about trade over tea and crumpets. The vague outlines of a plot are taking shape in my mind, but they are nothing more at present than shadows in mist. The data available to me is inadequate, and precisely what fate Moriarty intends for his Liverpudlian aide, I cannot be sure."

"You believe the man's life is at risk?"

"Unquestionably."

"We must do something to save him!" W cried. "This wretched

villain may prove a source of vital information about the activities of Moran and Moriarty. If only . . ."

I shook my head. "You will be disappointed, I fear. The fact that the Professor has taken the extraordinary step of breaking cover illustrates the strength of his determination to resolve whatever difficulty he faces. I have never known a human being who was his equal in both callousness and ingenuity. When Moriarty described the man as a loose cannon, he sounded uncannily like a judge passing sentence after donning his black cap."

In the days that followed my foray to the Tankerville Club, fresh information dribbled out, like drips from a leaky tap. Within three weeks, it had formed a murky puddle. The man from Liverpool was indeed a cotton broker, James Maybrick by name, and his business interests took him regularly both to London and to Norfolk, Virginia. While crossing the ocean some eight years earlier, he had been introduced to a comely fellow passenger twenty-three years his junior. The girl was called Florence Chandler, and her late father had once been the mayor of Mobile, Alabama. The relationship prospered, possibly due to an attraction of opposites, and the couple married in Piccadilly in July 1881 before settling in Aigburth, on the outskirts of Liverpool. Their home, Battlecrease House, stood across the road from Liverpool Cricket Club, of which Maybrick was a member, and his wife a lady subscriber. He was known to have more than one mistress, and rumour had it that one woman had borne him no fewer than five children. Florence was now the mother to a young boy and girl, but she too was not lacking in admirers. James Maybrick's younger brother Edwin was among them, and so was a man called Brierley, another cotton broker who was a member of the cricket club. While the parents were otherwise engaged, the children were cared for at Battlecrease House by a woman named Alice Yapp. Her previous situation had been at Birkdale, near Southport, and, unusually, she had been engaged by James Maybrick rather than by his wife. I did not doubt that Alice Yapp was the nurse-maid of whose reliability Colonel Moran had spoken.

Each new titbit that came my way deepened my anxiety. The fog in my mind was clearing, and the criminal design that was emerging was nightmarish in its cunning. Moriarty and the Colonel were, if I was right, contriving to commit a murder that could never be laid at their door.

Soon my worst fears were realised, as news came that James Maybrick was dead. The police worked swiftly, and arrested his wife three days later. She was subsequently charged and, at the inquest, a coroner's jury returned a verdict – by a majority of thirteen to one – that Florence Maybrick had administered poison to her husband. It was tantamount to a verdict that she was a murderess.

The trial was held in the magnificent neo-classical surroundings of St George's Hall in Liverpool, but although I arranged for my subordinate P to hold a watching brief on behalf of the Office, I did not attend personally. This was not entirely as a result of my distaste for travel. Any contribution of mine must be made far from the glare of scrutiny by the press and, in any event, someone in this dreadful business needed to have the luxury of being allowed to think, rather than feeling compelled to run hither and thither to no particular purpose. The police had been extremely active, and so had the family, led by the deceased's brother Michael, well known as a composer of popular music, and a man determined to establish that his sister-in-law was a cold-blooded killer.

I found myself, to my surprise and regret, unable to rule out the possibility that she was guilty. It was impossible for her to deny that the marriage was unhappy, and not merely because of her husband's many peccadilloes. Beyond question, she was an adulteress. Rumours were swirling around Liverpool like Mersey waters during a thunderstorm, and some said that Edwin Maybrick, youngest of the brothers, and the junior partner in James's business, shared more with the dead man than a blood tie and a business interest. He admitted his closeness to Florence Maybrick, but insisted that theirs was a platonic relationship, and whatever suspicion attached to him, no evidence came to light to gainsay his word.

Alfred Brierley, by contrast, could not plausibly deny his misconduct with the wife of his friend. It appeared that, as recently as March, he and Florence Maybrick had shared a two-room suite in Flatman's Hotel, reserved by her in the names of "Mr and Mrs Thomas Maybrick of Manchester". The feebleness of that particular subterfuge was not her only error. An improperly affectionate letter she had written to Brierley had been discovered shortly before James's demise. She had unwisely given it to Alice Yapp to post, and the nursemaid – claiming that it had become damp after being dropped "in the wet" by the Maybrick's young daughter – had opened it. Shocked by its contents, she had reported them to Edwin, who in turn informed Michael. The noose was being placed around the young woman's slender neck even before her husband drew his last breath.

While P supplied regular instalments of news about witness testimony, I wrestled with the problem. One could readily conceive half a dozen credible solutions to "the Maybrick Mystery", as the newspapers called it, and many more that were fanciful but not wholly beyond the bounds of possibility. James Maybrick may have died accidentally, after taking an overdose of arsenic, and suicide was not out of the question; he was a long-suffering hypochondriac, he may have tired of the ceaseless battle against ill health. If murder it was, he might have been the victim of someone other than his wife who happened to bear him a grudge. Among members of the household, Nurse Yapp herself was rumoured to have attracted her employer's attention, and this might explain her fiancé's recent decision to end their relationship. Edwin was not lacking in motive. And then . . . but no, speculation is the enemy of rational deduction. I reminded myself to concentrate my energies on analysis of the facts, and nothing else.

By 8 August, although I had failed to reach a definitive conclusion on the mass of contradictory information before me, members of the jury were sent out to consider their verdict. Upon their return, they announced that Florence Maybrick was guilty as charged. Old Stephen, the judge, whose mind appeared

– not least to P – to be failing, displayed an unholy relish in passing sentence of death.

"My dear fellow, what on earth is to be done?" W demanded, as we sipped sherry in the Diogenes Club.

"What would you have me do?" I yawned in a vain attempt to mask my discomfiture.

"These are dark days. If it were not bad enough for us to lose a first-class man . . ."

I said nothing. The body of J had been fished out of the Thames at Wapping thirty-six hours earlier. Marks found on his body established incontrovertibly that he had endured such excruciating torture that death must have come as a welcome release.

". . . now we have to address the consequences of this infernal murder trial! The whole case represents a stain upon our glorious system of justice. I can tell you that the Prime Minister is deeply concerned about the prospect of continued unrest after those dreadful scenes in Liverpool. Have you read the newspapers?"

I inclined my head. "The same mob that howled for a hanging a short time ago jostled and elbowed the woman Yapp as she left court after the verdict. Journalists who were baying for Mrs Maybrick's blood now fulminate against the verdict. To read the editorials, one would presume the woman is a saint, and the dead man a lecherous ogre of whom the world is well rid."

"The latter point, at least, is well made. In comparison to her husband, Mrs Maybrick is as pure as driven snow."

"But she is a woman, and he was a man. Therein lies the critical distinction. The verdict is tantamount to execution for adultery. We may never be able to determine the precise truth of her husband's fate, but I am certain that Moriarty had a hand in it. Thanks to the bigoted summation of a decrepit old man teetering on the brink of insanity, however, a woman faces the long walk to the gallows. I hear that the prison governor has already had the scaffold built. It is utterly monstrous."

"My dear fellow," W said, "I have seldom seen you so roused."

I realised that I had raised my voice. An elderly club member seated at the far end of the room had raised bushy eyebrows, and an expression of concern crinkled his leathery features. Such expenditure of energy and emotion was quite alien to me. Slumping back in my chair, I felt overcome momentarily by the weight of frustration and dismay.

"I ask you one question, my friend. In England, the country each of us loves and serves, how can such injustice be tolerated?"

"Most unfortunate, I concur." W gave a helpless shrug. "But we do not have a court of appeal."

Three Sundays must, by law, elapse between sentencing in a capital case and execution. Whilst I ruminated, the conviction of Mrs Maybrick was denounced on both sides of the Atlantic. Fourteen days after the verdict, I was ready to take the short stroll to Whitehall, where the Home Secretary had consented to see me.

Sir Henry's tenure in office had coincided with a sequence of regrettable scandals, most notably his refusal to prevent the hanging of the Jewish umbrella stick salesman Lipski, and the failure of Scotland Yard to apprehend the maniac responsible for the Whitechapel murders. Now he was besieged by protests and petitions concerning the fate of a young belle from Alabama. A barrister by profession, he had previously struck me as shrewd but aloof. This evening, I glimpsed the real man behind the face he presented to the public: weary, bewildered, and tormented by conscience.

After a brief exchange of pleasantries over a glass of the most splendid Amontillado, we turned to the matter in hand. "I understand that Her Majesty is not unsympathetic to the plight of the convicted woman."

Matthews bowed. "It has been conveyed to me by the Palace that she will accept my recommendation. But to overturn the unanimous verdict of a jury without further evidence of the most compelling nature . . . I tell you candidly, it would amount to much more than a confession of weakness on my part. It would launch a Whitehead at the ship of state. Yes, sir, the admission that our courts are unjustly is more damaging than any torpedo's blast."

"You regard capital punishment as morally repugnant, do you not?" I said quietly.

The Home Secretary sat up with a start. His cheeks were a becoming shade of pink. "What in great Heaven prompts you to say such a thing?"

"I am aware of your deeply held Catholic faith, and – forgive me – my observations of your pallor and nervous mannerisms at the time you allowed Lipski to die, following a trial tainted by prejudice, make me certain that the case caused you unusual distress. You held fast to the belief that a man in your position must do the right thing, but secretly you feared it was not right, but morally wrong."

The heat from the coal fire was intense. Sir Henry mopped his brow. He was not the first decent man to have been brought low by the cares of high political office, and he would not be the last.

"My duty is to administer the law without fear or favour. I could no longer with honour remain in office if . . ."

I drained my glass with a wistful pang. It was as fine a sherry as I had tasted in a twelvemonth. "We can agree – can we not? – that the glory of the English law lies in its inherent pragmatism. Moreover, the secret of our island race's survival and prosperity is due to our gift for compromise. Very well. A solution is within our grasp."

"What do you propose?"

"You may advise Her Majesty to respite the sentence of death, and commute it to penal servitude for life."

"No legal ground exists upon which . . ."

"Pshaw! Let us invent one that preserves the dignity of the court, as well as the wretched woman's life. The evidence, one might say, leads to the conclusion that she administered arsenic to her husband, but there remains a reasonable doubt that it caused his death."

"But that amounts to convicting her of a crime of which she was not charged. It is ridiculous! I never heard of anything quite so abhorrent to a logical mind."

"I heartily concur, but for many years I have made the point to my brother – you have met him yourself, have you not? – that for all its virtues, logic is apt to be overvalued. We must confront the world as it is, and a little untidiness is a small price to pay for a life. I surmise that, in due course, the sanction will be further ameliorated, and it would not surprise me in the least if she were to be freed within the next fifteen years."

"Nevertheless, that is a very long time."

"True, my dear sir, but we must keep in mind that she may be guilty."

One week later, Mrs Maybrick remained incarcerated in Walton Prison for the foreseeable future, but the scaffold erected for her had been dismantled, and, although her supporters continued to press for a pardon, the storm around the Home Secretary had abated. *The Times* had gone so far as to commend his decision, saying "It makes things comfortable all round . . ."

I meant to render Sir Henry one further service, and I was aided in my task when a messenger arrived at the Diogenes Club, bringing me an unsigned card inviting me to participate in a game of chess at the Tankerville.

Moriarty had read my mind, as I had endeavoured to read his.

"An elegant solution," the Professor said, as he contemplated options for safeguarding his king.

"The British do not lack imagination," I replied. "To characterise us as stolid and lacking in the power of creative thought does us a great disservice."

"It is a mongrel race," the Professor remarked. "Your grandmother's brother was Vernet, the French artist, was he not?"

"You are well informed." I inhaled deeply. The aroma of cigar smoke in the Reading Room was far from unpleasant. "Would you be so good as to satisfy my curiosity on one or two little points?"

"That was our shared purpose in meeting, was it not?"

Each of us had taken sensible precautions as regards our attendance at the Tankerville. Agents from the Office were stationed at every exit of the building, while Moriarty's associates had gathered in the bar. I was, however, confident that this encounter would not end in bloodshed. Our respective organisations had too much to lose.

"I take it that J sought to play a double game?"

Moriarty nodded. "He approached the Colonel shortly after your previous appearance within these unhallowed precincts. His claim that he wanted to be on the winning side was plausible, and he gave an account of your visit here as an earnest of his bona fides. Such a fellow might have proved useful, but alas! A cursory check on his rooms by one of our ruffians who has a way with a jemmy revealed that the man kept a private journal, and had been so incautious as to make a detailed note of his conversation with the Colonel. No creature on earth is so vile as the blackmailer, as no doubt you will agree. It was sensible to give the fellow his quietus before he made some threat in response to our failing to meet his financial aspirations."

I nodded. "And Mrs Maybrick?"

"The woman Yapp insists that she administered the fatal dose, as Moran had instructed her to do. She occupied Maybrick's bed more often than his wife over the course of his final months, and had every opportunity to do our bidding. And yet, for all her dogged protestations of guilt, I cannot help wondering . . ."

With a sigh, I moved my remaining bishop one square back. "Such is the difficulty when a man provides so many disparate persons with cause to put him to death."

Moriarty's thin smile indicated that he had anticipated my move, and was gratified by it. He consolidated his excellent position by shifting forward his rook. His triumph was barely suppressed. Mate in five moves.

"You understand our own embarrassment?"

"Most certainly. For a criminal gang to discover in its midst the most notorious murderer of modern times might seem in some quarters almost a cause for pride. In practical terms, I suspect you found it deeply worrying."

"Quite so. I am reluctant to withhold admiration from Maybrick, to the extent that the crimes in Whitechapel have escaped detection, but it was abundantly clear that his good fortune would not persist for much longer. Drugs enslaved him – I am tempted to say that the arsenic-eating was the least of my concerns – and his libidinous appetite seemed incapable of satiation."

"Five women dead, butchered in such a manner as to signify an increasing depravity and lust for blood."

"The emotive terms are yours, not mine. The harlots themselves were of no consequence." He caught my frown of disapproval, and dismissed it with a gesture of his claw-like hand. "My people maintain premises in five cities of this kingdom which offer a menu rich and varied enough to satisfy the most extravagant tastes. That was not enough for Maybrick. He failed to acknowledge that our success depends upon management and control. The risk that he might be unmasked at any moment was intolerable. Barring him from London was no more than a stopgap measure. Soon he would have embarked upon a fresh murder spree on Merseyside. Consider our dilemma. You run an organisation yourself, and will readily understand the need to pinpoint any weak link, and then eliminate it."

I advanced my queen's knight, and saw from the sparkle in my opponent's eyes that he regarded the heroic sacrifice as an act of desperation. "You may be assured that is precisely why I arranged to grant J the opportunity to encounter Colonel Moran in person."

Moriarty clapped his hands. "Bravo! You may lack the skill of a Staunton or a Paul Morphy, but in your chosen field, you are nonpareil."

His rook seized my knight. Pursing my lips, I said, "You flatter me, Professor. For me, it is an honour to place my services at the disposal of Her Majesty."

His grunt was laden with contempt. I moved my bishop again. "Check."

I studied with interest the emotions washing over that devilish face. Shock, anger, despair. His intellect enabled him to calculate his options within a matter of moments. With a stifled curse, he knocked over his king.

"Another game?" he muttered. "You must allow me the opportunity to . . . take my revenge."

I rose, but did not extend my hand. "Some other time, perhaps."

A cold hatred flared in those cruel eyes. For just an instant, it made me tremble, but then I exulted, for I had won more than a game of chess.

"Until the next time, Mr . . ."

I raised my hand. "No names, please. In my organisation, we trade solely in initials. Please call me simply . . . M."

The Last of his Kind

Barbara Nadel

'Who is there?'

The grainy darkness behind the piano shivered. A face, pale, thin, no longer young, looked at the old man in the tattered dressing gown and said, 'It is only me.'

Ancient lungs sighed in relief and the old man put his pistol back in his pocket. 'How did you get in?' he said. 'I am told that my brave young soldiers from Macedonia are preventing anyone from entering my palace. They fear there may be elements who wish to do me harm.'

A tall, spare man walked out of the darkness and stood with the old man in the vast pool of light cast by the ceiling chandelier.

'Isn't electricity marvellous?' he said.

The old man, his face drawn down by a nose that resembled both a beak and a knife, sniffed.

'You still think it's dangerous?' the younger man said. There was a mocking tone in his voice.

It wasn't lost on the old man. 'Keep a civil tongue when you speak to me,' he said.

The man tilted his head, signalling his understanding. 'I apologise unreservedly, Your Majesty.'

'My Kizlar Agasi is just outside . . .'

'No. No he isn't. You know I do think your chief eunuch may have gone, sire.' He drew a thin finger across his own neck. 'Bit concerned for his head. Can't get the staff these days, can you?'

The spare man located a heavily gilded chair and sat down.

The old man, Abdulhamid II, Sultan of Sultans and Caliph of the Ottoman Empire, Shadow of God on Earth, widened his night-black eyes. In thirty-three years, no one had ever sat down before he did. But his guest wasn't just anyone and he knew it.

'What are you doing here, Professor?' he said. 'Do you have information I can use?'

The Professor examined his fingernails. 'You know, sire, they have electricity at my hotel, the Pera Palas. Electric lights, even an electric elevator to take guests and their luggage to their rooms. It's very modern, very innovative. Built by a Frenchman. Surprised you allowed it at the time, given your fears . . .'

'Get to the point, Moriarty.' The old sultan sat. The room, though vast, was stuffed with heavy, dark furniture. The largest item, a desk covered with notebooks both open and closed, filled at least a quarter of the chamber. Every so often it would draw the sultan's gaze. 'If you are here, then you either want something from me or you come with an offer. What is it?'

'What is what?'

Outside in the darkness in the grounds of the sultan's palace of Yildiz, the sounds of animals, their hunger sharpened by the desertion of their keepers, made noises halfway between howls of pain and the last gasps of the dying. Amongst the monkeys, parakeets, giraffes and gazelles, roamed lions and leopards and other creatures Moriarty had only half spotted as he'd ascended the hill leading up to the sultan's quarters.

'Your purpose,' the old man said. 'Now that things are . . . as they are . . . What can you want with me?'

Moriarty smiled. 'Ah, so you do know the truth, sire,' he said. 'I wondered whether your fears, and there are so many of those, would let that in.'

'There have always been people who have sought my death. You, Moriarty, will know that better than most.'

Professor James Moriarty said nothing. The sultan lit a cigarette.

'I know the precise date and time you first came to me,' the sultan said. 'It was the twenty-third of May 1878. Three days after my people attempted to take my throne and give it to my insane brother. At five p.m., exactly, my doctor ushered you into my presence and said, "Here, Your Majesty, is a man who can cure all your nightmares."'

'Ah, dear Dr Mavroyeni.' Moriarty smiled. 'What a *good* man he was.'

The sultan's eyes expressed pain. 'Yes.'

'I met him in Paris in 1876,' Moriarty said. 'Place called Montmartre. Holidaying, it turned out, amongst the bohemian artists' colony that continues to thrive there. His French was so good, I thought he was a native.'

'And you befriended him.'

'I rather liked him. A fellow man of science. But when I found out he was personal physician to Your Imperial Majesty he became, I must confess, irresistible to me.'

'You saw a business opportunity.'

'I identified a method whereby I might serve your empire, sire.'

Abdulhamid rose with difficulty and walked over to his desk. He picked up a leather-bound notebook and turned to the first page. He read. '"City of Kayseri. There is a carpet seller in the bazaar, a man with an Armenian mother and a father who is lame. He organises secretive meetings late at night at the back of his shop. Other men of poor appearance attend. What is discussed can only, sadly, be treasonous. I beg the pardon and the pity of Your Majesty for bringing this to your attention. Your humble slave", etc.'

'Plots are like fungus, sire, they thrive in the dark.'

'Moriarty, your organisation has been bringing me information about my enemies for over thirty years,' the sultan said. 'You have served me well.'

'A network of agents was needed that far exceeded even my calculations,' Moriarty said. 'It is the same, I fear, sire, in all the great empires of Europe. The French opened the door to revolution and . . .'

'And we all speak the language of revolution now, don't we?'

'Many people speak French . . .'

'Including you and I and those who like to see themselves as the elite. It enables them to understand these Gallic ideas that resulted in an emperor losing his head.'

'Sire, it is a long way from reading a book to . . .'

'Is it?' The sultan put the notebook down. 'You know, Moriarty, these journals from your agents across my empire have consumed my waking hours. Descriptions of illiterate Druze tribesmen in Palestine, hungry for my death, sellers of yogurt passing messages to Armenian agents in the streets of my capital city. Poor people.'

'In some cases, yes, sire.'

'In all.'

The sultan sat behind his desk. 'I ask again, Moriarty, what do you want here? I know you cannot have gained entry to my palace without the collusion of my "loyal troops" from Macedonia. The ones who can speak and read French and on whom your agents have always been silent. Fortunately for me, other contacts I have cultivated over the years have not been so reticent in that regard.'

'My agents have only ever reported what they have heard, sire.'

'And I have paid you, and them, well for it.'

'Indeed.'

'Indeed. And yet . . .' A small, manicured fist came down quickly and suddenly on the top of the desk. 'Here we are, Moriarty, in the eye of a revolution against my rule. And you didn't see it coming. Or did you? I have done everything for my people! I have given them the Constitution they apparently craved, I have made a powerful ally of the German emperor, built a railway to the Holy Cities of Mecca and Medina. I even allowed my poor mad brother to live out his insane life at my expense in spite of the fact that these Macedonian revolutionaries wanted to replace me with that drooling fool. My people are children. I am their loving father. It is not a carpet seller from Kayseri that will come to hang me tomorrow and end the House of Osman forever, but an educated, French-speaking army officer. You, Moriarty, I would venture, have deceived me. The game is not "afoot" as your nemesis Sherlock Holmes once said, but it is up.'

Moriarty sat. His pale face didn't move. Then he smiled. 'You have me there, sire.'

'You find it amusing that you have failed me? That your so-called "professionalism" should be called to account? Do you not even have the urge to defend yourself?'

'Against what?'

The old man looked down at his desk, at the bell that should call his chief eunuch to his side. Could Moriarty be right that he had fled? There was only one way to find out, which he resisted.

'I am still absolute monarch of my empire.'

'A Colonel Rustem Bey opened the gates for me,' Moriarty said. 'Blond, French-speaking, charming man. He'd ridden all the way from Macedonia to be here. Tomorrow he'll probably stand beside that lovely lake you had dug out in your park and wonder what a man who claims to be the Shadow of God on Earth was doing hiding himself away in a fantasy world. When did you last leave this palace, Abdulhamid? I don't just mean to attend the mosque at the bottom of the hill, I mean leave the complex completely?'

Had Moriarty's use of his name passed the sultan by?

Thin, arthritic fingers steepled underneath his chin. 'So now we come to be candid with one another, do we, James?'

'It's why I'm here.'

'To tell me that you have tricked me?' He shook his head. 'Maybe you did. Maybe you have come to gloat over my inevitable demise. I know it's almost here. But it, and you, are no surprise. Do you honestly think I never knew that the baker from Diyabakir, the imam from Adana and all the other little people you brought to my attention were innocent? Of course they were. Or rather what they said was said in ignorance and without malice. But power, Moriarty, as you know, has to be demonstrated. Often. It has never given me pleasure to sign an order to put a man to death, but I know that in order to remain in control and do what is best for one's people, it is essential. My empire responds to the sword. These young officers with all their dreams about equality and democracy will learn. They call themselves the Young Turks.' He laughed. 'What does that even mean? This empire is named after my family. We are Ottomans. They will learn. When they have hung me from their gallows and my people have risen up against them and they have killed them in their thousands, they will learn.'

'Maybe.' Moriarty smiled. 'But at the moment they have history on their side. In fact that's been the case for some time.'

The sultan put one cigarette out and then lit another.

Moriarty took his own cigarettes out of his pocket and held his case up for the old man to see. 'May I?'

'Of course.'

'Thank you.' Moriarty lit a black Sobranie. 'In all my journeys around your empire, sire, I have learned many things. I have learned that the Armenians want their own country, that the Jews desire only to be left alone and that there are more diverse and bizarre sects and societies in eastern Anatolia than there are jewels in the Austro-Hungarian emperor's crown. But what these groups all have in common, and I include Turkic Muslims too, is their desire for a life that does not begin in filth and hunger and ends the same way. Your people, Abdulhamid, want exactly what the poor all over Europe want. They want education, money, electricity . . .'

'They only have need of God!'

'I'm not talking about what they need, but what they want,' Moriarty said. 'Oh, they will fight for you and your religion but what sort of chance do you think they will have against foreigners with flying machines? I take it, sire, you know that man can now fly?'

'I do. But he should not. It is against God.'

'And if your empire goes to war with a country like France, which has flying machines, it will have to train men to go against God if it is to stand any chance of winning. Your time is over, sire, it has been for a very long time.'

'During which you have made a lot of money out of me.'

'Because, if you recall, sire, you begged me to help you rid your empire of dissent,' Moriarty said. 'You didn't want another incident involving your imprisoned brother. And with my help you didn't get one. When did Murad die?'

'Five years ago.'

Moriarty leaned forward in his chair and whispered, 'I'd be prepared to bet you know the day, the hour . . .'

The sultan didn't reply. His older brother, Murad V, had been a thorn in his side all his life. Older and some felt more rightfully due the title of sultan, Murad had been declared insane within weeks of ascending to the throne. Abdulhamid had been put in his place. But, deranged as Murad was, the sultan had never stopped thinking about him and neither had many of his people. Now all that remained were his younger brothers. Also old men, they had lived their entire lives in states of terror. Of him.

'I knew all along that to kill dissent entirely is impossible,' Moriarty said.

'I beg to differ.'

'Which was why my organisation was such an easy sell to you,' Moriarty said. 'You wanted the impossible. And I gave you that illusion for thirty years. But, as I'm sure you must have realised, my very presence here now tells you that I was always looking for the tide to turn. Anachronisms have no future.'

'So now you work for these "Young Turks"?'

'No and yes. I have helped them in the past. I plan to again.'

'You have betrayed me.'

Moriarty put his cigarette out. He shook his head. 'Your Majesty is one of the most intelligent men I have ever met,' he said. 'But, sire, your fears for your own life have always held you back. When I met you, you shook. Do you remember? Mavroyeni had to hold your hand. Then, in the years that followed, I watched every charlatan – astrologer, dervish – whatever they chose to call themselves, exploit those fears and manipulate you to their own advantage. I knew you couldn't last. I am amazed you are still here now.'

'You underestimate my family's influence over the religious life of the empire.'

'No, I don't think so. I know your Muslim subjects will still fight for Islam. But will they still fight for you? You underestimate what they know, Abdulhamid. Talk to any man in the Grand

Bazaar about you and he will tell you lurid tales of cafés built on the side of your lake where you try to convince yourself you are not the only customer, of gardeners shot by you because you mistook them for assassins. And most scandalously and stomach-churningly of all, of the little girl you had tied in a sack and thrown into the Bosphorus. Wasn't that barbarous custom something your ancestors did away with? I thought so.'

The already grey face of the sultan became white.

'And that too was when I knew for certain that I had to find another horse to back,' Moriarty said.

'That child betrayed me,' the sultan said, 'with my own son!'

'Prince Selim, your eldest. Where is he now?'

The sultan lit a new cigarette from the dying ash of his last one. 'Away.'

'Since 1898. Mmm. Some backwater of the empire. That must be hard. You know it was in 1898 that I really began to notice these young officers from your Macedonian province. The boys from Salonika. Speaking French, using the word "democracy" . . . Trouble was they didn't hate you. They saw you as a poor, isolated creature, desperately reaching out to your people but surrounded by those who sought to undermine you, and them. And that was partly true. But I also knew another you. The one that would sacrifice anything and anyone for his own miserable life.'

The sultan's face flushed. 'You are a traitor, Moriarty. What more is there to say? Get to your point.'

'My point? My point is, sire, I knew that those nice young officers would defeat you one day. I could also see a lot of business opportunities in a relationship with them for myself.' He smiled. 'I saw the future. I just had to help it along. And so I paid your Kizlar Agasi, your chief eunuch, a lot of money.'

'To do what?'

'To tell you about how that lovely little blonde girl your sister had given you for your birthday was having sex with Prince Selim.'

The sultan turned away. 'You're lying. My Kizlar Agasi would never betray me.'

'Well why don't you ring your little bell and summon him so that he can answer you?' Moriarty said.

The sultan looked at the bell; a present from his one-time friend, the Emperor of Germany, it was cast in gold. He remembered the day it had been given to him. He had almost felt as if he had a real companion. But the kaiser had better things to do than visit an old man in a hillside fortress these days. He, it was said, was preparing for war. Abdulhamid locked eyes with Moriarty and rang the bell. The professor sat back in his chair and knitted his fingers underneath his chin. Like the sultan himself, he could have, when he wanted it, infinite patience.

Fifteen minutes of silence, save the ticking of a grandfather clock, passed.

The sultan was the first to blink.

'So shall we say that your Kizlar Agasi is not and was never to be trusted?' Moriarty said.

The sultan didn't reply.

'Well, I will, he was and is not,' Moriarty continued. 'I knew this, I exploited this and found that, given the right incentive, he was a very willing confederate. I came here tonight, sire, to tell you that Prince Selim's protests of innocence were entirely truthful. He did not sleep with that girl, nor was she pregnant with his child when your not so loyal chief eunuch put her in a sack and threw her into the Bosphorus. She'd only slept with you.'

The sultan did not move. He didn't appear to breathe.

'She was pregnant . . .'

'I'm not a fool! You don't have to spell it out!'

'But what a story, eh?' Moriarty said. 'Doing the rounds of every bazaar from here to Jerusalem. Didn't have to be true. But it was and so it travelled much more quickly and easily than it would have done if I'd just made it up. What do you think all these Cleaners of the Imperial Nargile Pipes and Court Dwarves actually do? You smoke cigarettes and you don't find dwarves amusing. They're bored, they gossip.'

While he'd been talking, Moriarty hadn't noticed the sultan take that pistol out of his pocket again.

Then he did.

'Ah . . .'

'You killed my child,' the sultan said.

'In utero.' Moriarty nodded.

'I have no doubt that your Colonel Rustem Bey is within earshot,' the sultan said. 'But why should I care? They will kill me tomorrow. You have finally miscalculated, Moriarty.'

'You think so?'

It wasn't easy to look down the barrel of a gun held by a man who had never been known to miss. But it was hardly the first time Moriarty had faced his own death.

He took one deep breath and said, 'Actually no, sire.'

'No?'

'No, Colonel Rustem Bey is with his men outside the palace. They won't enter Yildiz in the hours of darkness. Would you? With all the strange sounds and peculiar movements around the park of your starving animals? No, they will come in the morning. But they won't kill you.'

'You expect me to believe that? Why not?'

'I don't really know,' Moriarty said. 'Considering you suspended your empire's constitution for over three decades, killed thousands of your own people and tried to use religion to further your own ends, I can't rightly work it out. You'd get no mercy from me.'

'I've had no mercy from you.'

'But these Macedonian boys are quite civilised. They won't stay like that of course. Power will corrupt them,' Moriarty said. 'I've high hopes for them. But they won't kill you. They just can't bring themselves to do it – yet. They may live to regret that. But it's their choice. Unless, of course, you kill me now. Then they won't have a choice. You know it's eerily silent down with those fresh-faced, earnest democrats outside this palace. They can hear a twig snap. They do hear them when your tiger goes in search of a monkey to eat.'

'You're lying.'

'Am I?' Moriarty shrugged. 'Pull the trigger and see what happens. I won't stop you.'

'Are you armed?'

'Looking for a gunfight, sire? Of course I'm armed. I would have to be insane to walk through your park with your zoo on the move without a gun. But, if I shot you, I'd just make you stronger. I'd undermine the Macedonians and harm my own business. I'm counting on your own good sense to preserve my life. Because I know that at the end of everything all you care about is yourself. Religion? Your throne? Even your children don't matter, do they? Only you matter and that's why you won't kill me.'

'My life will be nothing without my throne.'

'Then shoot me and let them hang you. You know there is a doctor in Vienna called Freud who has this idea that all of our obsessions, our character traits and our foibles are developed in childhood. How one turns out will depend upon what one experiences as a child. Makes me wonder what happened to you, Abdulhamid? What kind of childhood does a royal Ottoman prince have?'

'That is not your concern, or this man Freud's.'

'I bet your father favoured your brother, Murad,' Moriarty said. 'His firstborn son. Gregarious, open and jolly as a young man as I recall. The constitutionalists had high hopes for him.'

'He was a madman.'

'He was an alcoholic, which was unfortunate. But if you'd stopped his endless supply of champagne and brandy he would have got better. Ah, your gentle father, Sultan Abdulmecid, must have loved such a boy . . .'

'Shut up.' It was said coldly. It was a tone Moriarty knew of old could only be interpreted as the sultan at his most dangerous. He looked at the floor.

Through a small gap at the bottom of the heavy brocade curtains at the sultan's window, he saw that the sky outside was beginning to lighten. Soon the Macedonians would come. Armed with a fatwa signed by the highest religious authority in the empire, the Sheikh ul Islam, four Ottoman gentlemen, none of them Muslims, would depose this sultan and send him into exile. He would be replaced by his brother, Reshad, who was a pleasant, weak man in Moriarty's experience. Perfect for a monarch required to be little more than a puppet. The Young Turks were already beginning to think like autocrats in some respects, which was excellent. Autocrats always paid more for information. They were always more worried than most.

Moriarty stood. 'Well, much as I'd like to stay, I really do have to go,' he said. 'I know there's thousands, probably millions of Ottoman *lire* in this palace and you do owe me money. But what's the point, eh?'

'I owe you nothing, Moriarty.'

'I'd beg to differ, sire,' he said. 'Had you read between the lines of the reports my agents sent you right at the start, it would have been apparent what was happening in your empire. And, in the end, you did see the truth. I mean why would a very religious imam from Adana want you dead? And yet you executed him and thousands like him so that you could rule by fear. You put these Young Turks where they are today and, if I'm right and Germany goes to war with Russia, they will fight alongside the kaiser and I will make a lot of money out of that.'

The sultan aimed. 'You are the devil, Moriarty!'

Moriarty smiled and then turned his back on God's Shadow on Earth and began to walk towards the door.

'I think you'll find I'm *a* devil, Abdulhamid,' he said. 'There are a lot of us about these days.'

He put his hand on the doorknob and turned it. Out of the corner of his eye, he could see that the sultan's pistol was still aimed at his head.

He said, 'You know, I will be sorry to see you go, Your Majesty. Your brother Reshad is weak and, although you won't be the last of your line, you are the last of your kind. For the moment, your empire doesn't need a divinely appointed autocrat. You time is done.'

He opened the door.

'You imply a time may come when the Ottomans need an autocrat again?'

'Maybe.' Moriarty shrugged. 'One must never say never about anything, sire. And while there are men like me about, men like you may be supplied to regimes who need, shall we say, a firm hand. It's all about betting, you see. On the right horse, at the right time. Quite a science that.'

He walked through the door and pulled it shut behind him.

With a turn of speed he could not normally achieve, the sultan sprang from his chair and ran after him. But, when he opened the door on to the corridor outside, Moriarty had already gone. As had any sign of his chief eunuch. There weren't even any guards.

Abdulhamid II, Sultan of Sultans and Caliph of the Ottoman Empire, Shadow of God on Earth, last of his kind, was entirely alone for the first time in his life. He put his pistol down on top of all those works of fiction sent from Moriarty's agents across his vast empire and he waited, alone, for the dawn.

Author's note:

Abdulhamid II was the last autocratic sultan of the Ottoman Empire. Paranoid and fearful, he operated the largest network of spies in history. He was indeed deposed on 27 April 1909 and was sent into exile. The tale about the harem girl and Abdulhamid's son is a commonly heard story. This story is simply a take on this monarch's last night as Sultan of Sultans.

A Problem of Numbers

David N. Smith and Violet Addison

The world was full of victims.

The old man who had just left the bank was a prime example. He had neither the physical strength to put up a fight nor the speed to make an escape. He was easy prey. The high street always had a police presence, but this fool was heading off into the alleyways, far from their protective influence. If he had just withdrawn any money then, after a handful of punches and kicks, those paper notes would shortly become the property of Irving Beck.

Following the old man, Irving kept his cap pulled low and stayed in the shadows, so that any onlookers would not recognise him. He kept his distance for a few minutes, studying his target, waiting until they were far enough from the high street that he could strike.

The man had a large, distinctive high-domed forehead, a receding hairline and sharp, angular features. Irving had seen him before, coming and going from the university. It was James Moriarty, a professor of mathematics, who was frequently spoken of in high regard in almost all circles of society; even those at the very bottom of the social strata to which Irving had always belonged. Regardless of the professor's reputation as a man of intellect, Moriarty carried himself with an undeniable air of confidence and intelligence, which rather begged the question: why was he doing something so thoroughly foolish?

Irving slowed his step, keeping his distance, his instincts screaming at him that there was something wrong with the whole scenario. However, he could not just let such easy prey walk off when his pockets could be lined with money, could he? What was there to be scared of?

Nothing frightened Irving Beck. The professor may be tall, but Irving was taller. Having spent a decade toiling in the brickyards, mines and ironworks, he had developed broad shoulders and thick forearms, which intimidated most men. He had triumphed in many bar-room brawls, even fought in a few semi-professional bare-knuckle boxing tournaments, so taking down a wiry academic should have posed little concern to a man like him.

"You are not going to disappoint me, are you?" Professor Moriarty had stopped in the middle of the alleyway, with his back to Irving, still presenting the easiest target that could be imagined. One punch to the back of the head and the man would be down for a considerable amount of time. "Come on. I had the highest expectations for you."

Irving came to an abrupt halt.

Professor Moriarty spun on his heel to face him, spreading his arms in a defenceless way, moving with a surprising agility for a man of his age. How old was he? There were perhaps not quite as many lines around his eyes as Irving had first imagined.

"What are you waiting for, Irving Beck?"

While he recognised the professor, as he was something of a local name, there was absolutely no chance that a man of his standing should ever have heard of the name Irving Beck.

He could not risk an assault now.

"I'm just passing on my way home, sir." Irving resumed his walk, pulling on the rim of his cap in deference as he strode past the professor, keen to put as much distance between himself and these strange events as possible. "Didn't mean to spook you, sir."

"Oh, splendid," the professor called after him. "An explanation, an apology, and you called me sir, acknowledging my natural superiority. You are evidently an honourable, honest and humble man. Although, saying 'sir' the second time was a little too much, it made it sound like an act."

Irving kept walking.

"Your stratagem contained numerous flaws," the professor

continued. "Primarily, there is an unnecessarily high risk of the crime being witnessed, plus an uncertainty over whether I even withdrew any money. Great risk, for potentially no reward? That is bad mathematics by anybody's calculation."

Irving was disconcerted by the professor's confidence. Despite having deliberately followed the professor into the unpopulated alleys, he was suddenly very keen to be surrounded by people again. He felt suspicious that rather than having orchestrated events himself, he had in fact blindly walked into a scenario contrived by the professor.

There was a dark-haired woman ahead, leaning against the wall. She was a common streetwalker, her young face covered in an unattractively large amount of white powder and black eyeliner, her skirt already hitched vulgarly above her knee.

Under normal circumstances, he may have stopped to talk to her, but for now Irving was just grateful that someone else was present. The feeling did not last long.

"The professor ain't done talkin' yet, love." She stepped out to block his path, while toying with a small knife, bringing him once again to an abrupt halt. "You're bein' rude."

Even armed with the knife, Irving imagined he could over-power her. Most people did not have the courage to use weapons; if she hesitated for a moment he would be able to disarm her and knock her down. There was, however, always the chance that she was comfortable using the knife – the way she spun it playfully around her fingers certainly implied she had some experience using the weapon. He was also unsure just how far the old man was behind him – if Moriarty intervened at the same time, then things would almost certainly end badly for Irving.

"Still calculating the odds, Mister Beck?" Professor Moriarty stepped up behind him, having been a lot closer than Irving expected, speaking directly into his left ear. "Very wise. It always comes down to the numbers in the end. I do assure you, the best thing you can do is listen to me."

Irving turned to face the man.

He was momentarily tempted to thump the professor in the

face, but a gentle touch from the streetwalker, directly between his shoulder blades, reminded him that such ideas might end very badly for him.

Moriarty smiled. "Separately, you could easily overpower either me or this young woman, but together we are more than a match for you. As Aristotle observed, the whole is greater than the sum of its parts. We can always do more if we organise and co-operate."

"What do you want with me?" Irving asked, by now certain that this was no accidental meeting.

"I am recruiting, Mister Beck."

"I can't see me working in any university, Mister Moriarty."

"Mathematics is but one of the fields I work in," the professor replied. "I have also been known to operate in other fields some-what more outside the modern moral code."

"Crime," translated the streetwalker helpfully.

"My normal associates are otherwise engaged, so I find myself in need of individuals who can recognise an opportunity and pursue it, like you did outside the bank. I need men who are prepared to risk their lives, who have no qualms about liberating wealth from others, but who are able to think on their feet and adapt their plans as necessary. Again, I believe you are such a man. Are you?"

Irving considered his options.

Life had rarely given him many opportunities, except the ones he had taken by brute force, but he had little to lose by playing along with this man's plans for now.

He nodded. "If there's money, I'm always interested in taking it."

"Excellent," Moriarty replied. "You see, I said, it always comes down to the numbers. Be on the nine a.m. train if you wish to pursue this most auspicious opportunity, Mister Beck. I shall explain all once the full team is assembled."

Moriarty spun on his heel and marched off down the alleyway, disappearing with remarkable speed.

"I do apologise for the knife," the streetwalker added, walking past him, swinging her hips provocatively, while slipping the weapon into her sleeve. "But you do get the most unsavoury sorts down these back alleys."

Irving boarded the locomotive and worked his way through the carriages. He found Moriarty sat in a first-class cabin, with one eye on his pocket watch and the other on the compartment door.

The professor beckoned him in.

There were two other members of the team already seated around the table.

One of them was the dark-haired streetwalker, who sat in the corner with her feet pulled up on to the seat, her chin placed just above her knees. She gave Irving a small smile as he sat down at the far end of the table, gazing at him through her dark eyelashes. The final member of the team was a burly middle-aged sailor, in a smart blue uniform, with a great grey moustache that ran all the way around his face and into his sideburns.

"Nine o'clock." Moriarty clicked his pocket watch closed and then tucked it into the pocket of his waistcoat. A moment later, with a great hiss of the steam, the locomotive began to pull out of the station.

"Lady and gentlemen, this is our target." Moriarty dropped a photograph on the table, which showed a black and white image of a three-masted steamship. "This is the RMS *Heroic*."

"I don't see no lady here," growled the sailor sourly, ignoring the photograph and glaring at the streetwalker.

"Oh, love," she replied, "I can be anything you want, if the price is right."

Moriarty leaned over and grabbed the sailor by the ear.

"Given the crimes we are about to commit, I suggest you give up any delusion of having any moral high ground. As I hope we are all aware, such scales are meaningless, they are just a way to keep the rabble powerless."

He let go of the man's ear and tapped his long index finger against the hull of the ship, refocusing their attention on the photograph.

"On the ship there will be two passengers of note," Moriarty continued, passing out two envelopes – one to the streetwalker and the other to Irving. "They are both wealthy individuals relocating to the United States, so they are taking every valuable they own, every pound note of it, with them. The safes in the staterooms will be loaded with riches you cannot imagine."

"You want us to break into these safes?" enquired the streetwalker.

"No." Moriarty shook his head. "They have four tumblers, with ten digits apiece, which is over ten thousand combinations. As ever, the numbers win."

"Or, we could blow a hole in the side," Irving suggested. He had a little experience with explosives.

"Crude," Moriarty replied, shaking his head. "The best way of getting away with any crime is to make sure nobody even knows it has been committed."

Irving frowned. "Then how do we get into the safes?"

"Our victims will open them themselves." Moriarty smiled. "This vessel is about to have an accident. It will sink shortly after leaving the harbour. Even when the ship is sinking, despite all logic and reason, these two individuals will risk their lives and go back for the contents of their safe. They value wealth above all else. However, once they are on the lifeboats, they will eventually trade those riches for mere handfuls of food and water, which we will be carrying. Having been defrauded of every penny they own, they will still be thanking us for saving their lives."

The streetwalker laughed, delighted by the Machiavellian beauty of the scheme.

"What about the passengers and crew?" she interjected. "I do not mind risking my life, but I'm hesitant about committing mass murder."

"There will only be a small number of passengers on-board, so there will be adequate lifeboats on hand for all," he said, trying to assuage any remaining moral doubts. "The rest of the passengers are not due to board the ship until it reaches Liverpool, for the onward trip to New York, which are two stops that this ship will no longer be making."

"What about the captain?" Irving asked, curious to see the

professor's response. "It is traditional for a captain to go down with his ship."

The sailor glared at him.

"Oh, I'll be fine," he replied gruffly, tapping the four gold rings around the cuff of his uniform jacket, which denoted his rank as captain.

Irving shrugged.

Moriarty tapped a finger against the two envelopes on the table.

"Inside, you will find a boarding ticket for the RMS *Heroic*, a plan of the ship, a photograph of your target, plus details about them and of what I expect to be in their safe. Befriend them. Stay close to them. Make sure they end up at the lifeboat indicated on the plan, with the contents of their safe, but do not take anything from them, unless they give it to you of their own free will. Let's not give anyone a crime to investigate."

Irving carefully opened the envelope and let the contents fall into his hands.

The photograph showed a tall man, in a military uniform, with noticeably thick upper arms and large fists. Amongst the paperwork was the name "Major-General Fitzwilliam".

The streetwalker opened her envelope and plucked out what appeared to be a photograph of an elderly woman.

"What if they don't want to trade away their wealth?" Irving asked.

Moriarty smiled.

"Then they will starve, dehydrate and die, as the victims of an unfortunate shipwreck. And we take their money anyway."

The RMS *Heroic* was waiting in the dockyard.

To Irving, she looked invincible. He could easily see how such a giant could conquer the worst storms, but was equally aware that she was no match for Moriarty's cold intellect. He would be able to sink her with no more than a tiny hole.

Irving made his way up the gangway on to the deck. He was wearing a new suit, provided by Moriarty to help him fit in with upper-class passengers. He felt uncomfortable in its stiffly starched collar. His discomfort was not shared by the captain, who had boarded the ship shortly before him and was already ordering around members of the crew.

The streetwalker was the next one up the gangway. She had somehow transformed her appearance during only a handful of minutes locked in a public lavatory. She had changed her dress, removed and redone her make-up, restyled her hair so that it was now fashionably braided around the crown of her head. The streetwalker was gone, replaced by a lady, who was gliding elegantly along deck with a parasol in her hand.

"Oh, where shall we begin?" She pouted, her alleyway accent replaced by a more sophisticated drawl. "A stroll around the deck perhaps?"

"I would suggest the cargo hold," advised Moriarty, as he climbed aboard. "They are loading their lives aboard this vessel, but these are people of money, so they will want to supervise proceedings. They would not be capable of entrusting such an important task to people they regard as their inferiors. Become acquainted with them, a meagre measure of familiarity now will make them more inclined to trust you later."

Having given his instruction, Moriarty moved off towards the rear of the ship.

"A cargo hold is no place for a lady alone." The dark-haired woman smiled, offering Irving her arm. "Perhaps you would be kind enough to escort me, sir?"

"And what should I call you?"

"I, sir, am Miss Emma Bennett, and you would be?"

"Irving Beck."

"No, sir. That is not the name written on your ticket."

Irving glanced at the piece of paper in his hand, which bore a different name entirely.

"Isaac Brewer," he replied, noting that Moriarty had kept his initials the same, so that the name was easier for Irving to remember. Despite all the flattery, the man clearly did not place much trust in Irving's intellectual abilities. He was here because of his physical strength, in case things went wrong. It had never been said, but Irving knew it was true. "Tell me your real name."

"You overstep yourself, sir."

"Yes, I do." Irving nodded, opening a door for her. "Frequently."

"He made my pseudonym from the names of two characters devised by Jane Austen; evidently he thinks I have a romantic nature." She smiled, as she stepped inside the ship and folded away her parasol. "Or perhaps it is just a cruel joke, because of my former employment, one he thinks I will not get. Either way, he is wrong."

Much of her statement confused Irving, he had never had much time for books, but his best guess was that she was referring to works of literature of which he was unaware.

"I doubt the professor is ever wrong about anything." Irving shrugged, covering his ignorance. "Given your knowledge, it is an easy name to remember. I imagine he chose it to make things simpler for you."

The woman glanced at him, raising a curious eyebrow, surprised by his observation.

"Everything is certainly planned to the smallest detail, but I'm not sure I can trust him and, on a doomed ship I would be a fool not to trust someone, so I will trust you," she replied, curtseying slightly. "I'm Nora Crogan."

Irving bowed slightly, feeling uncomfortable faking such social formality, given their previous meeting and criminal intentions.

"Come on." Nora grinned. "Let's find our victims."

The hold was unlike anything Irving had seen in his life. It was two storeys high and ran almost two-thirds the length of the ship. There were piles of packing crates, suitcases, numerous wagons, industrial-sized freight pallets and even livestock. Irving let out a low whistle, surprised at just how much had been crammed into the cargo compartment.

"Where's yours?" Nora's accent had shifted back to that of the back alleys of the city.

Irving nodded to the rear of the hold, to where he could see a man in an old-fashioned, bright scarlet military tunic shouting at the men loading his belongings.

"Let's go and introduce ourselves, shall we?" Nora picked up the hem of her skirt and stalked forward. As they approached, she gently fell back into character, letting go of her skirt, straightening her back and raising her chin. Her voice gushed with feigned excitement. "Good afternoon, sir! Are you heading for a new life in the United States too? It certainly looks that way. It is the most exciting enterprise, is it not?"

Major-General Fitzwilliam was not a pleasant man. He met their enquiries with short, blunt answers, evidently more interested in his cargo than making new acquaintances.

"What an absolute arse," Nora summarised succinctly once they had moved away. "And imagine how much worse he'd have been if we'd been the real us?"

Irving shrugged; he was not particularly bothered by how people treated him, especially when he was planning to take every single pound they owned.

"Is your target here too?" he asked, glancing around the shadowy hold.

Nora nodded. "Over there. The heiress Estelle Lloyd-Trefusis. Her husband was one of the largest landowners in the south-west, before he died in mysterious circumstances."

"I can't see her."

"Over by the pigs, looking terrified."

Irving moved his gaze over to the livestock pens and smirked at the sight of a well-dressed woman, her nose pinched between her thumb and forefinger, frantically shouting orders at her farmhands. She was so agitated that she lost her footing, overbalanced and ended up trapped amongst the squirming pigs. She screamed.

Irving laughed. "She's in her element."

"I'll handle this one. You laughing won't help us." Nora patted him on the arm and then gestured with her thumb, pointing behind him. "Besides, it looks like the boss wants you."

Moriarty had appeared on the walkway above them. He stood there silently, looking out across the hold. Irving, not wanting to draw any attention to them, slowly climbed the steps up to him, until they stood side by side.

"Do you know why they own all these possessions, while you

own so little, Irving?" the professor asked, while making sure his pocket watch was fully wound.

"They earned it in some clever way, I guess." Irving shrugged. He had never been one to question his status in life. There did not seem much point, given there was so little that he could do to change it.

"They earned it?" Moriarty raised his eyebrows and scoffed. "Not the farmhands who tend to those pigs, or the young soldiers that the Major-General sent to their deaths?"

Irving shrugged again.

"The likes of you must have Karl Marx spinning in his grave." Moriarty shook his head sadly. "Economics is just another branch of mathematics. I see the equations to which you are blind. Where you see only chaos, I can see intellects manipulating the values. It truly is the perfect crime. None of you can even see the riches that have been taken from you."

"What can we do about it?" Irving shrugged.

"We can take it back."

"You see yourself like a Robin Hood then? You steal from the rich, give to the poor?"

Moriarty laughed. "What a fantastical notion. An honourable crime." The smile faded from his face. "No, I don't steal from the poor, because the poor have nothing worth stealing. Why pick a pocket, when you can empty a safe? Why rob a craftsman of his tools, when you take his valuable skills and enslave him for a pittance of pay? The only way to have any power in this world is to take it from those who have it. To not be enslaved by dictates of others. That is what I do."

Irving nodded. He had no qualms about stealing from the people here. He had no qualms stealing from anyone. He needed to make sure he had clothes on his back, food in his stomach and a dry place to sleep; those were his priorities. As long as Moriarty offered him those, who was he to question his motivations or instructions?

"Go and have dinner, Irving. Then catch a little rest in your cabin if you can." Moriarty clicked his pocket watch closed. "You have exactly nine hours. The explosive charge is in place, the captain will be detonating it at ten minutes after midnight. Nobody will ever guess what started the fire in the engine room. Let Emma know. Be ready."

Moriarty turned on his heel and left via the door to the deck.

Irving stared at the sprawling contents of the hull. It really was a shame that such riches were going to go straight to the bottom of the ocean. He felt especially sorry for the pigs. They would drown. Nobody would care.

Irving was sitting on the edge of his berth, waiting for the inevitable explosion. He envied Moriarty his pocket watch, the man was undoubtedly calmly counting down the seconds, but Irving had no way to measure the time. Pocket watches were expensive. He had not slept. All he could do was anxiously wait for the explosion, never knowing exactly how close they were to the moment of detonation.

Would he even know it when he heard it?

He had his answer a moment later. There was a short, sharp bang, followed by the scream of tortured, twisting, juddering metal. A vibration ran through the walls and flooring, shaking the room. A moment later, there was the sound of doors opening, followed by voices in the hallway outside, as worried passengers left their staterooms. Irving rose to his feet and opened his door, to find Major-General Fitzwilliam and a host of other passengers standing outside, discussing the noise. As a noticeable burning odour slowly filled the air, their faces paled. The major-general muttered the one word that no sane person on a ship ever wanted to hear.

"Fire."

An alarm bell began ringing.

Taking charge, Major-General Fitzwilliam marched off down the hallway in search of the captain, so Irving followed. He did not want to let his target out of his sight. The agitated man rudely pushed past Nora and the heiress, to be confronted by the captain coming the other way.

"We have a fire in the engine room," the captain announced, pointing along the hallway. "I need you to make your way to the lifeboats! Now!"

Panic-stricken gasps rippled along the hallway.

The illusion of polite society dissolved in a moment, as people began fleeing, not paying any attention as to whether they were stepping on their companions. Major-General Fitzwilliam stormed back down the hallway, but, just as Moriarty had predicted, he hesitated by the door of his stateroom and then made his way back inside. The heiress, shrieking in fear, flew back into her room and slammed the door.

Irving glanced at Nora, who at some point in the last few hours had acquired a large oilskin coat and a sailor's canvas knapsack, which she was carrying over one shoulder.

"Given the situation, is there anything in the world you would go back for?" he enquired.

"My daughter," she replied, without hesitation. "Everything I do, I do for her. My respectable family disowned me when I had her out of wedlock, left me to fend for myself on the streets the only way I could; so my daughter is the only thing in the world that I would risk dying for. You?"

The frank answer took Irving by surprise, so much so that his own answer had turned sour in his mouth.

"No," he muttered. "There is nothing I would go back for."

He had never understood before quite how little he had. He did not even own the clothes he was wearing. He had nothing.

Irving leaned into Major-General Fitzwilliam's cabin, to check on the man's progress. The major-general had quickly pulled on his uniform's scarlet jacket, and was now down on his hands and knees, dialling numbers into the lock of his safe. He slammed his fist against the metal door in frustration, evidently having made an error in his haste. Irving had no idea how long it would take for the ship to sink, but he knew this was no time for delays. The hallway was rapidly filling with smoke.

"Help me, man!" the major-general cried frantically, not questioning why Irving was lingering in his doorway. "Get me that bag!"

He pointed to a leather satchel that had been discarded by his berth, which Irving dutifully fetched, as the soldier finally managed to get the safe open. Inside were stacks of white paper notes. It was more money than Irving had ever seen in his life. The major-general quickly rammed the money into the bag, along with various other deeds and bonds, most of which were beyond Irving's understanding.

He also saw a military revolver go into the bag.

He would have to make sure that the weapon somehow parted company from the man, as otherwise events could quickly spiral beyond even Moriarty's control.

"You must tell nobody how much I am carrying! Understand me?" the major-general barked at him as he made his way out into the smoke-filled hallway, momentarily moving in the wrong direction. "The world is full of thieves and villains these days."

"This way!" Irving grabbed him by the elbow, guiding him back towards the lifeboat. The man almost certainly now owed Irving his life, but he did not stop to express any gratitude. He barrelled down the hallway, running for the door to the deck.

Glancing back down the hallway, Irving could see the heiress, still stuffing a handbag with necklaces and other pieces of jewellery. Nora fought to shepherd the distraught woman out on to the deck, but she eventually had to abandon all manners and brutally shove the woman outside. Irving followed them out, pulling the door shut on the smoke-filled hallway.

The nearest lifeboat was crammed full of frightened people.

Smoke was blossoming out of almost every vent in the rear of ship.

Irving leaned against the railing, trying to find a way to board the already packed boat.

Moriarty was crouched at the end of the vessel, helping the heiress aboard, taking a moment to reassure the frightened woman and guide her to a seat. He produced a cork lifejacket, which he helped her into, then fastened around her. She was so taken in by his duplicitous charm that she hugged him for a moment and kissed him on the cheek, complete unaware that she was pouring her gratitude on to the man whose ruthlessness was responsible for her plight.

Nora was already on-board, seated beside the heiress, pulling on her own cork lifejacket.

"This is all the passengers from the first class," Moriarty shouted above the noise of panicking passengers and alarm bell. "How much longer should we wait?"

He threw the question at the major-general as if it were a dagger. He was an adept manipulator; he knew there was only one answer a frightened, selfish man would give.

"Let's go now! Many more and we will overload the boat."

Moriarty spun to face the deck, his finger pointing directly at Irving. "You there! Operate that winch! " Moriarty ordered. "Lower us into the sea!"

Irving glanced at the winch, which controlled the ropes at the prow and stern of the little craft. Was he to be left behind on the sinking ship? He did not put it beyond Moriarty. It would save paying him later. Nonetheless, he found himself obeying the order, turning to the winch and spooling out the rope. He had been complicit in these events, so the least he could do was make sure these people survived. The little boat hit the dark ocean, with a splash that sent a small wave crashing over its own side, eliciting surprised screams from all on-board, except Moriarty.

"Come on, man!" Moriarty shouted. "Get aboard."

Irving did not hesitate. There was so much smoke billowing out of the ship that he had nowhere else to go. He clambered over the railing, hanging on to the rope, and attempted to climb downwards. He lost his grip and fell.

The cold water consumed him, closing over his head, sucking him down.

He flailed blindly in the dark for a moment, unable to breathe, unsure which way was up and which was down. Was this how he was going to die?

It turned out he did still own something that he did not want to lose: his life.

He broke through the surface of the water. He heard Nora yelling at him. He saw Moriarty's hands reaching out towards him. Before he could draw a breath, a wave closed over him, pushing him down. He had never felt so cold in his entire life.

He gave one last kick, but was not strong enough to reach the surface again.

Moriarty's fingers wrapped around his wrist.

Irving gasped for air.

The star-scattered night was gone, replaced by the pure blue of a daytime sky. The world spun around him, tilted over and then spun back around the other way. His stomach heaved, so he scrambled up on to his knees and vomited over the side of the boat.

His wet clothes had been removed, replaced by the warm blankets, an action that would almost certainly have stopped him dying of hypothermia. He briefly wondered to whom he owed thanks, until he realised that Nora was sat beside him.

"It's nothin' I ain't seen before," she whispered, winking at him, pushing his clothes back into his hands.

Irving took hold of the ruined shirt and suit, which had been dried in the sun, and put them back on. Somehow, now they were crumpled and damaged, he felt more at home in them.

"Perhaps now he is awake again, you would like to ask his opinion too!" Major-General Fitzwilliam's angry shout smashed against Irving's already throbbing head.

"Oh, I shall," Moriarty replied from his seat at the back of the boat. "What is your name, my good man?"

Irving blinked. "Isaac Brewer," he replied.

It was a simple question, but not asked for simple reasons. With one enquiry, Moriarty had been able to determine secretly whether Irving was in control of his wits. By answering with his correct pseudonym, he would have proven to Moriarty that he was sufficiently recovered to participate in whatever game he intended to play.

"This young lady is hoarding fresh water and food." The major-general scowled at Nora. "And despite being trapped together for the best part of a day, she refuses to share."

"I expect him to pay its worth," Nora corrected. "Not a difficult concept for an honourable soldier, is it?"

"That's extortion!"

"You've got money, a bag full." Irving laughed, deliberately belittling the man.

Major-General Fitzwilliam's face reddened, his fist balled, his anger and fury rising to the surface. It was at that moment that Irving remembered he also had a revolver in the bag.

"This is a perfect example of Alfred Marshall's theory of supply and demand, sir," Moriarty explained slowly, patronising the angry man, trying to break his resolve. "She has the only supply, we need the water, so the price is high. It's simple mathematics. You cannot argue with whatever price she names."

"I should just take it from her."

"I would stop you," Irving replied. It was a dangerous response. A few punches he could handle, but a bullet was quite another matter.

"And how will you pay?" the major-general taunted Irving.

"His is free, sir," Nora interjected. "His reward for having offered to defend me from you, if required."

"Have a pity, woman." The major-general seethed. "I have just lost everything I own!"

"And yet you still have more than I have ever had," Irving replied, unable to quash the idea that Moriarty had seeded; that people like Fitzwilliam had somehow been cheating him since the very moment of his birth in ways he did not even understand. "Perhaps we should all step off this boat as equals."

The major-general snorted his derision. "We are not equals. I am an officer and a gentleman, from one of the most respected families in all of England. What are you?"

"An orphan, with little education." Irving stood up and advanced on the man, until they stood nose to nose in the centre of the boat, barely a handspan separating them. It was a short enough distance that Irving could throw a punch, long before the soldier had retrieved the revolver from his bag. "Does that make me less than you? We all need water."

The heiress coughed, delicately attempting to defuse the argument.

"I shall pay my share. I need the water," she said, shattering the tension. Her cotton-gloved hands pulled gold chains and bracelets from her handbag. "Provided it covers a supply for my farmhands and the staff from the ship."

"Noble sentiments," Nora replied, taking a bottle of water from her knapsack and handing it over to the heiress, in exchange for the bag of riches. "Naturally, it shall."

"Fool!" the major-general exploded, his envious eyes fixed on the bottle. "Now you have lost everything!"

"Now I have nothing," the heiress replied glumly. "Save for my life. But for that I shall be eternally grateful."

"Come, sir." Moriarty leaned forwards, a flicker of impatience crossing his face. "This is but a microcosm of the real world. Embrace the misfortune of circumstances with good grace, pay the lady what she is due."

"I shall."

There was no intonation of acceptance in the soldier, just resolve and anger, as he turned and picked up his satchel. Irving had been in enough disagreements to know when a person had reached their breaking point and was reaching for a weapon. The major-general's hand plunged into the bag of pound notes, but pulled out the revolver.

Irving grabbed his arm, turning it out to sea, as the shot exploded out of the barrel. The shot passed harmlessly into the waves. He punched the soldier in the side of the head, knocking him down.

Moriarty moved quickly, pulling the gun from the man's hands. He looked at it for a moment, appearing disgusted, before throwing the weapon out into the ocean, making it disappear from the world for ever.

Moriarty rounded on the officer, grabbing him by his uniform's lapels.

"I have never witnessed something so abhorrent!" Moriarty seethed, physically shaking the already befuddled man. "To threaten and extort what you want from an innocent person, it is contemptible. You are no gentleman! You are no better than a criminal!"

The words sounded genuinely heartfelt, but they were laced with so much hypocrisy that Irving was surprised Moriarty could even say them. Nora coughed politely, precisely imitating the sound the heiress had made earlier.

"Let us finish out transaction, sir. Pay me for the water, or die of thirst." Nora smiled. "Your choice. See if anyone else here cares."

Moriarty let go of the soldier, letting him fall to the deck.

The major-general glanced around the little boat. He was suddenly adrift in a sea of horrified faces. He was outnumbered nineteen to one. He threw the bag of money at Nora. One or two of the white paper notes took flight, fluttering out into the ocean.

Nobody chased after them.

Irving was woken by a kiss.

He was lying in a warm bed, in a luxurious seafront hotel, with Nora's naked body partly coiled around him. Given the amount of times he had woken up in an alleyway, cold and alone, things were definitely looking up.

A distant clock tower tolled the time, while Nora nuzzled in his ear.

"We're supposed to be meeting Moriarty for breakfast in an hour," she whispered.

"An hour?" he responded, turning to meet her lips. "Best not waste that time then."

An hour later they had dressed, and made their way downstairs to find Moriarty sitting by the window reading the newspaper. The front page was filled with photographs of RMS *Heroic*, the newspapers were still obsessed with stories of the passengers, all of whom had survived the disaster. Even the captain, who had stayed with ship until the end, had apparently been pulled from the sea, having managed to cling to wooden wreckage that had drifted towards shore. He had been given an award for his bravery.

Their own lifeboat had made its way to shore shortly after the money had exchanged hands. To many passengers, it appeared to be a miracle, but once Irving had found out that Moriarty had been in charge of the little boat's navigation, it suddenly seemed a lot less miraculous.

"I took the liberty of ordering you breakfast," the professor informed them, folding up his newspaper as they sat down opposite him. "I do hate to ruin a good meal with business, so let us conclude our dealings before it arrives, shall we? Give me the money and jewellery."

Irving and Nora had discussed this trade at great length the previous night. They could have taken the money and run, however they would have then spent the rest of their lives living in fear of his retribution. They did not want Moriarty as an enemy; they doubted such people lived for long.

Instead, they had discussed how much they should ask to be paid for their participation. Nora had eventually persuaded Irving to simply see what Moriarty offered. He had so far proven to be a generous employer, having covered the costs of their tickets, clothes and hotel rooms. These were costs he would need to recoup.

Nora handed over a satchel, containing both the money and jewellery, which Moriarty checked with a glance and placed on to the seat beside him.

"You have removed nothing for yourselves?" he asked.

"No, sir." Irving shook his head. "We leave the subject of pay to you."

Moriarty nodded. "I offer you a quarter of our takings, or the opportunity to continue in my employ. Would you prefer to continue working for me?"

Both offers took them both by surprise.

The money would enable them to live well for many years, but the chance to continue working for him could lead to infinitely more.

They were granted a moment to consider the offer due to the arrival of a serving girl, who delivered three fried breakfasts to their table, causing them to suspend their discussion until she had moved on.

"It has been a profitable partnership, so far," Nora replied, although oddly her eyes were focused on her plate rather than Moriarty. It was unlike her to appear so humble. "Would our quarter also include the value of the ship and cargo?"

Moriarty laughed. "I have one hundred and five witnesses, including her captain, who will all testify that the RMS *Heroic* is at the bottom of the ocean."

"One hundred and four," Nora pressed. "All I saw was a lot of smoke. And I can't help but notice that the RMS *Moriarty*, docked outside, looks remarkably similar to the vessel in question, save for a little paint and the name on the side."

"I underestimated you, Miss Crogan."

"'Appens a lot, sir." She smiled, using her knife to cut the bacon on her plate. "I'm assumin' we're eatin' the livestock?"

Irving looked down, becoming properly aware of the sausages and bacon that he had piled on to the end of his fork.

"I waste nothing," Moriarty told him. "But branded pigs are difficult to sell whole."

Irving stared at the fork, raised it into his mouth, then chewed and swallowed the mouthful of flesh.

"My offer does not include any of the value from the ship or cargo," Moriarty clarified. "You did not assist in their acquisition."

"Well, I reckon we might accept the job offer then," Irving replied, once his mouth was clear, glancing at Nora for her approval. They had both agreed that they would make the decision together.

"Yes, we shall," Nora agreed.

"Of course, you will." Moriarty nodded. "What other choice could you make? I shall organise rooms and money in London for you. I have plans there."

As he sat at the table, finishing his breakfast, Irving Beck glanced at Nora Crogan and James Moriarty and realised that he had been mistaken in his previous beliefs. The world was not full of victims. The world was full of conniving thieves and villains, who were sophisticated and organised, constantly pursuing a chance to progress in the world, unconcerned about how they affected anyone else.

He could be one them, or he would be nothing at all.

The Fulham Strangler

Keith Moray

London, 1888

Life had been extinguished in an instant. A single sharp blow with a wooden cube, an executioner's block, and whatever sentience a spider might have was either obliterated or immediately sent into a higher plane to join the creatures who had lived before it and trapped millions of assorted insects in their webs. It was the penalty it paid for having the temerity to walk over the desk where the experiment was being conducted.

At other times, Professor James Moriarty might have given the creature's life and that of its ancestry some academic thought. A mathematical genius, whom some said rivalled the great Fibonacci himself, Moriarty had written a treatise on the binomial theorem at the age of twenty-one, a book on *The Dynamics of an Asteroid* and numerous academic papers on subjects as diverse as the invention of zero and the limits of growth of the human brain. His mind revelled in both pure and applied mathematics and sought distractions in abstruse problems such as the population explosion of spiders. Yet on this bleak, smoggy day in London, when other more mundane problems demanded his attention, he was less inclined towards frivolous pursuits.

He wiped the mangled arachnid body from the bottom of the die, one of the three pairs of dice that he had been experimenting with, and immediately cast the dice on the desk.

'Two and five and three. Ten again!'

He added the total to the row of figures he had been

recording, each entry precisely made in his scholarly hand. Had anyone been looking in on his study, that is precisely what they would have seen. A scholarly gentleman with pince-nez spectacles resting on an aquiline nose. An aesthetic man with a Shakespearean brow, receding black hair swept back and piercing, unemotional eyes. His posture was slightly stooped, presumably from years of bookish study. Indeed, the impression of a man of learning would have been entirely correct, for Professor James Moriarty had previously held the chair of mathematics at Durham University for several years, before his contretemps with the university senate that saw his departure for London, a spell of private tutoring of prospective Army candidates while he established and built his somewhat unique business empire.

There was a tap on the door that evoked a curt call to enter from the professor. The oak door opened and an elderly manservant with neutral, almost transparent hair entered. He was carrying a silver tray upon which were a glass of claret and an envelope.

'Are your dice calculations going well, Professor?'

Moriarty eyed the servant dispassionately. As he did so his head oscillated slightly from side to side in a manner evocative of a reptile sizing up its prey. It was a look that the man knew well, but which never failed to produce a disagreeable shiver of discomfort at the base of his spine.

'They are, Joshua. Entirely as Galileo predicted, with three dice the total of ten will show up more often than the total of nine. Totally predictable, of course, since there are two hundred and sixteen possible combinations with three dice. Of these, there are twenty-seven combinations that form a total of ten and twenty-five that form a total of nine.' He sat back and sneered. 'Unbelievable that the Duke of Tuscany paid the greatest scientist of his day to solve such a minor problem.'

Joshua, a family servant since the professor's childhood, who had seen to his master's personal needs since then, placed the glass of claret on the desk and laid the envelope in front of him. 'And does this mathematical curio alter the instructions that are given to your gaming house managers, Professor?'

'Not a whit, Joshua! Not one whit. They will still use the Fulhams and the tappers as usual to give the houses an edge. And they will be backed up by the enforcers if anyone is inadvertently caught in the act. The usual disposal methods are to be used.'

He sat back and sipped his wine, his eye falling momentarily upon the blank area on the wall where, until so recently, his prized painting *La Jeune Fille à l'Agneau*, by Jean-Baptiste Greuze, had resided. Losing it only a few days before had been partly responsible for his present state of irritability, manifested in the ruthlessness with which he was prepared to dispense death to spider or any creature who dared to cross his path, and the reason why he had sought to distract his mind with dice problems. He found that when he wanted to develop a plan his mind worked best when it had several things to think about.

'So, tell me, has O'Donohue received the consignment?'

'He has, Professor. He said that it will be ready for you whenever you are ready.'

Idly, Professor Moriarty reached for the envelope, neatly labelled with his name, but without postage or other markings. 'How did this message come?'

'The usual courier.'

The professor opened it and drew out the note from within. It was written in code, which, as the inventor, he could read as if he were merely reading in one of the dozen languages in which he was fluent.

Joshua noticed the pinpoints of colour develop on his cheeks, a sure sign of anger, which could have any of a dozen consequences for someone.

'They dare send me this!' he said after a moment, his voice calm, but with a steely edge that was apparent to Joshua.

'Is it ill tidings, Professor?'

'For someone, Joshua. For anyone who thinks that I am someone that can be given instructions like a hireling.'

Sherlock Holmes had not bothered to remove his old grey dressing gown all day. Indeed, it had been his companion over most of the preceding three days, ever since he had solved the case of the missing cavalryman, to much acclaim from the journalists of the *Telegraph* and the *Daily Chronicle*, to say nothing of the gratitude passed on from Her Majesty, Queen Victoria's inner circle, via a runner from Downing Street. Yet all this meant little to the great detective, who made no secret of the fact that he selected his cases for the sheer intellectual challenge they presented rather than for any promised honour or fiscal reward.

In the absence of a suitable case or conundrum to occupy his mind, he was wont to lapse into a fit of melancholy, which he assuaged either by playing his Stradivarius, or by using a seven per cent solution of cocaine or by smoking copious quantities of tobacco.

It was the latter that he had opted for on this occasion, thanks mainly to a promise he had made to his friend and chronicler, Dr John Watson, before he had departed to visit his ailing uncle in Norfolk. The violin lay unused in its case.

Food interested him not one whit, despite his housekeeper, Mrs Hudson's attempts to coax his appetite with all manner of little snacks. Her entreaties to open a window to let in fresh air fell on deaf ears as he studied the spiders that he had allowed free rein to weave their silvery gossamer webs in the darkest corner of his rooms. Their behaviour intrigued him for they were among the most efficient of nature's killing machines, as he had witnessed at first hand in the case of the Patagonian Ambassador.

His mood had not been helped when he surfaced that afternoon after taking a nap in his bedroom to find that Mrs Hudson had taken the opportunity to air his room and to remove all of the cobwebs and their architects with duster, dustpan and brush.

The arrival of a telegram came at the right moment, when the bookcase with the dummy book in which he kept his syringe and secret supply of cocaine started to tempt him.

He tore it open with his thumb and read:

Mr Holmes. Would value your opinion about Fulham murder. Strangulation. Will call at 7 p.m.

Inspector Alistair Munro

With an exultant cry, he skewered the telegram to his mantel-piece with a stab of his jackknife, his usual method of filing documents of interest. A thin smile crossed his lips and almost immediately he felt his mood had lightened.

At a couple of minutes before seven o'clock, Holmes heard the sound of a Hansom cab pull up on the wet cobbles outside his 221b Baker Street residence. True to his word, Inspector Alistair Munro rang the bell at exactly seven o'clock and, moments later, upon being admitted by Mrs Hudson, his footsteps could be heard bounding up the stairs. Holmes opened the door to his robust rap.

Alistair Munro was a good-humoured man of the same height as Holmes, albeit of slightly broader build. He had sandy-coloured hair and moustache in keeping with his Highland ancestry and an accent to match. He removed his customary bowler and Ulster as he came into the room. He tossed them on to a free chair, while Holmes busied himself with the whisky decanter and the gasogene.

'Warm yourself by the fire, Munro. You have had a busy evening, I see. You mentioned a murder in Fulham, yet I perceive that in the hours since you sent the telegram you have been across the river in Putney in order to search for clues as to the reason that the pawnbroker was murdered.'

'How the devil did you know that, Mr Holmes?' the inspector asked incredulously, sitting forward to gratefully receive his whisky and soda.

'A simple matter. In the band of your bowler hat you have a seven-penny omnibus ticket, which is the second-class fare from Scotland Yard to the stop on the south side of Putney Bridge. Your telegram talked about the Fulham murder, which you will note already has a whole paragraph in this evening's edition of the *Daily Chronicle*. Yet the *Chronicle* article talks about the murder of a Putney pawnbroker. Ergo, you had already been at the murder scene in Fulham then returned to Scotland Yard to report to your senior before heading across the river by omnibus. I presume that you chose that method of travel rather than using an official vehicle in order to be incognito as you investigated the pawnbroker's shop and home in Putney. Having done so, you travelled here by Hansom.'

'Exactly so, Mr Holmes,' Munro replied, waving his hand in refusal of the cigar box which Holmes held out to him. 'You forget I don't smoke,' he added with a half-grin.

'On the contrary, Munro, I keep hoping that you will one day turn to tobacco. It is a great aid to the detective mind.' He shut the box and tossed it on the floor by the fire. 'Now, pray tell, why exactly should the murder of a pawnbroker in Putney be of interest to me.'

'Because, Mr Holmes, the pawnbroker is none other than Liam O'Donohue, Professor Moriarty's quartermaster.'

Holmes had picked up his cherry-wood pipe, but at mention of Moriarty's name his jaw muscles tightened. 'Then give me the facts, Munro.'

Munro took a sip of his whisky then laid the glass on the side table. 'Very well, Mr Holmes. This morning one of the local constables was on his beat on Dawes Road in Fulham when a woman rushed into the street screaming murder. He recognised her as one of the cleaners at the Fusilier's Club, a so-called gentlemen's club. I say 'so-called', because it is nothing more than a gaming house and bordello. Men go there to gamble with cards, dice, playing all manner of games with rules of their own devising. That is, it is a place full of professional cheats and rogues. There is a bar where they can drink or they can enjoy the company of ladies of the night in an upstairs lounge, or, after negotiation, in one of the many boudoirs.'

'Is the Fusilier's Club one of Professor Moriarty's establishments?'

'No sir, it is independent. It belongs to an American consortium as far as I have been able to ascertain. It is run by Jack Lonsdale, a manager who oversees the gaming and by Mrs Dixie Heaton, the madame.'

'And O'Donohue, was he a member?'

'He was. That was why it was such a shock to the cleaning woman. She knew him. She opened one of the downstairs rooms and found him lying splayed out on the floor, dead as a doornail. He'd been strangled.'

'What with? A garrotte of some kind?'

Munro shook his head and took another sip of whisky. 'Bare hands, Mr Holmes. Or rather, it looks like one hand. There were bruises on his throat, you see. The constable was a competent fellow, he didn't disturb the scene of the crime, but locked the door and reported to the Fulham Road station. The inspector there knew of O'Donohue's connection with Professor Moriarty, so he sent word for me at Scotland Yard, knowing that I deal with anything to do with him. I went straight there and examined the scene and questioned everyone in the club before going back to the Yard to report to my superintendent.'

'You are presumably confident that the murderer was no longer there, but I perceive that you have no real clue as to who the murderer is.'

'Exactly, Mr Holmes. My worry, and the superintendent's worry too, is that this could spark off a gang war. Apart from Moriarty's criminal empire, there are lots of other gangs that would love to take over some of his activities. There are Chinese tongs in Limehouse, Italians in Clerkenwell and . . .'

'I am possibly even more aware of many of the lesser gangs of London than you, Munro,' Holmes said with a dismissive wave of his hand. 'Yet I must agree, if someone has been foolish enough to execute one of Moriarty's gang, especially a high-up member such as O'Donohue seems to have been, then they can surely expect repercussions.'

He picked up coal tongs and lifted a glowing cinder from the fire to light his cherry-wood pipe. 'And then you went to Putney to check his shop and his living quarters.'

'I did, but I found nothing that could help me. Yet although I know he is Moriarty's quartermaster, I don't know exactly where he keeps his warehouses. I have men scouring the wharfs in both directions from Putney Bridge.'

Holmes smoked in silence for a few moments then abruptly stood up. 'Then let us go. It is time to view the body.'

Munro drained his glass and stood with alacrity. 'That is just what I was hoping you'd say, sir. I instructed the Hansom driver to wait. We will go straight to the mortuary at Fulham, where I had the body taken.'

The body of Liam O'Donohue lay covered by a blanket atop a slab in the green-tiled mortuary.

'I delayed the post-mortem examination until you had inspected the body,' Munro explained, as the mortuary attendant, a bucolic-looking constable by the name of Grimes, removed the blanket.

Holmes immediately began his examination by scrutinising the man's head and neck. He was a short, stocky man of about five and a half feet in height, with a spade beard and a bald head. His eyes had been closed, but his mouth was slightly open, the jaw muscles fixed in rigor mortis. About the eyes were telltale petechial haemorrhages, so often found in cases of strangulation and asphyxiation.

'As you say, the bruising is consistent with strangulation with a single hand. The left hand, in fact.'

He whipped out a magnifying glass from a pocket of his coat and inspected the bruising, before turning his attention firstly to the torso, then to the hands.

'The hands are soft, but they have seen physical work in the past. They are now kept clean and the nails are well groomed. Note also the curious signet ring with the symbol of what seems to be a pentagram.'

'I had noticed that, Mr Holmes. Do you think it is significant?'

'Possibly,' the detective replied, non-committally. He bent over the open mouth and sniffed. 'Curious and curiouser.'

From another pocket, he drew out a pair of fine forceps. Then over his shoulder: 'Bring the lamp closer, please, Constable Grimes.'

Inspector Munro and PC Grimes looked over his shoulder as, by the lamplight, Holmes prised open the lower jaw and inserted the forceps into the mouth and deep into the throat. Then slowly he started tugging something.

Gradually, he pulled out a bundle of jute.

'Good grief!' exclaimed Munro. 'The swine killed him with that. I can see it now. He had him by the throat and shoved that piece of sacking to block his windpipe.'

'What sort of devil would do that?' asked the constable in disgust.

'It is not just sacking, Munro,' Holmes said, laying the jute bundle on the slab. 'There is something inside.'

He unwound it to reveal three pairs of wooden dice.

'The plot thickens, Munro,' he said, as he swept up the dice and the jute bundle. 'I think we have seen enough for now. With your permission we shall take this to Baker Street for further examination and some experimentation.'

Upon arriving back at his Baker Street rooms, Sherlock Holmes had Mrs Hudson rouse Billy the pageboy and sent him off on an errand.

Then, with his cherry-wood pipe lit to his satisfaction, he lay the jute bundle on the table between himself and Munro. 'Now, for a bit of experimentation. What do you make of these, Munro?'

Munro prodded them. 'Well, I never!' he exclaimed. 'Just looking at them they seem perfectly normal, but this pair have four, five and six on three faces, and the same repeated on the other sides. And this pair have only the numbers one, two and three.'

'Quite correct,' said Holmes, with a wry smile. 'The higher ones are called "high despatchers" and the lower ones are "low despatchers".'

He picked up the remaining pair and tossed them. They came up one and six. Instantly, he scooped them up and tossed them again with the same result.

'And these are Fulhams, meaning they are loaded. They will always come up as a total of seven. Fulham was renowned as the part of London where dice-sharpers lived and plied their trade in Elizabethan times. But it seems that the trade has now moved south of the river to Putney.'

'So it begins to look as though whoever killed him was making a point. He had been caught cheating at dice,' Munro conjectured.

'Now for some chemistry,' Holmes said, rising with the piece of jute and crossing to the table in the corner of the room, which was littered with retorts, test tubes and assorted chemistry paraphernalia. He lay his pipe down in an ashtray and pointed at the window. 'Chemical analysis is incompatible with smoking,' he said, with a humourless laugh. 'It would be as well to have fresh air, if you wouldn't mind opening the window, Munro.'

He sat at his chemical table and arranged several bottles of solutions and reagents in readiness.

'First, we need to snip a piece of the jute off and soak it in a test tube with ether for a short while. Then we shall apply the Greiss test.'

Munro watched with interest as he shook the test tube for several minutes.

'Observe as I then decant this liquid into these two conical flasks. Into the first I am going to pour a test tube of sodium hydroxide. You see that it remains clear. Now, as I add this Greiss reagent, if the liquid turns pink it will tell us that there are nitrites present in the liquid.'

He poured several drops into the flask and grunted in satisfaction as the liquid immediately turned pink.

'And now, if I simply pour the reagent into the second flask without the alkali – nothing happens. That makes it absolutely clear, don't you agree, Munro?'

The inspector shook his head. 'I have absolutely no idea what you are talking about, Mr Holmes.'

'No? Then I would recommend that you devote some time to the study of chemistry, you will find it invaluable in the pursuit of criminals. I have just shown that the jute cloth was used recently as a wrapping for nitroglycerine. In other words it had at some stage a stick of dynamite in it.'

Inspector Munro's mouth opened and closed as he struggled to find words for the thoughts that tumbled through his mind. Just as he was about to speak the bell rang downstairs and moments later they heard a rush of many feet upon the stairs.

'Ah, Billy has returned with the help we need.'

'What help, Mr Holmes?' Munro asked in some confusion.

'Enter!' Holmes boomed out as the footsteps reached the landing atop the stairs.

The door opened and a group of a dozen dirty and ragged urchins were led in by Billy the page. With a wink to the urchins and a bow to Holmes he left.

To Munro's surprise some of the street urchins were barefooted and all of them looked in need of a square meal.

'Inspector Munro, you see before you the unofficial force – my Baker Street irregulars.'

One of the boys was taller and older than the rest and was clearly the leader.

'Wiggins, have no fear of the Inspector here. He is one of Scotland Yard's best. I have an errand for you all. I need you to find me a man. You are to locate him only, not attempt any communication, for he is dangerous. As soon as you find him, and I have no doubt that you will find him somewhere in the gaming houses of Fulham, although I doubt if that is where he lives, you are to report to me. There is the usual scale of pay and a guinea to the one who finds him.'

'But Mr Holmes, we have no idea what he looks like,' Munro protested.

'Oh we know something that distinguishes him, Munro,' Holmes returned.

Then to the urchins:

'You are looking for a tall, powerful man, of six foot two in height. He is American and a fervent gambler with a quick temper, ready to use his fists. He wears a signet ring on the fifth finger of his left hand and he smokes large Cuban cigars, which he habitually holds between the fourth and fifth fingers of that hand. Now off you go. Report to me any time of the day or night.'

Once they had gone Munro was quick to ask for an explanation.

'It is simple, Munro. He is a tall man who could easily hold O'Donohue down with one hand, keeping out of reach of the Irishman's flailing hands. That and the size of the hand give us his height. He stuffed the bundle with the crooked dice and the sacking into his throat. I trust that you noticed the bruises on the throat of the dead man?'

'Of course, it was a left hand.'

'But did you miss the imprint of a ring on the bruise made by the fifth finger? Not only that, but smelling the throat the over-powering smell of Cuban cigars was evident between those fingers. This man is a continuous cigar smoker.'

'But why an American?'

'The Fulham dice, Munro. They are loaded to always show up a seven. If you were familiar with the game of craps, which is highly popular in America, not only in their saloons, but in the alleys and back streets of towns and cities from coast to coast, then you would know that a seven can both win a game and at other times lose it. A dexterous dice-sharper can substitute a pair of dice at an instant. This man was playing with O'Donohue and that means that O'Donohue was used to playing craps with him. He probably regularly cheated him.'

'So, this American discovered that he had been duped, prob-ably over many games and literally stuffed the dice down his throat. I see.'

'But do you see, Munro? I bring your attention back to the ring. To the rings they were both wearing on the fifth fingers of their left hands. I would be very surprised if our American does not have exactly the same design on his ring.'

'A pentagram? You mean there could be something to do with the satanic arts?'

'Perhaps, but I think not. However, I do think that they were both members of a secret organisation.'

'You mean Moriarty's gang?'

'No, to my knowledge, Moriarty is neither particularly reli-gious nor superstitious. I think that they are both members of an anarchist group, entirely independent of Professor Moriarty.'

'Anarchists? With what aim?'

'Total disruption of society. One thing I think is likely, the dyna-mite was part of a consignment, which suggests that they planned to steal from Moriarty. Or rather, O'Donohue was planning to help the American steal the consignment, but the American decided to silence O'Donohue. They may have been gambling companions, but silencing the professor's quartermaster could be a way of completely covering his tracks. This all implies that this man has a hot temper and he is totally ruthless.'

Munro stroked his moustache pensively. 'So what now, Mr Holmes?'

'I think it is time for you to retire to your home. It is late, but, for me, I have thinking to do. It is quite a three-pipe problem and I would like now to be on my own. There is no more to be done this evening.'

Professor Moriarty was wakened at five o'clock in the morning by Joshua.

'My apologies, Professor. I thought it best to tell you straight away that young Decker, our urchin who runs with Sherlock Holmes's irregulars is here. He and his fellows have been given a task by that meddlesome Holmes. It concerns the O'Donohue murder.'

The professor slid out of bed and donned the dressing gown that his elderly manservant held in readiness for him. 'So it looks as if the great detective is somehow on the case. Have our people discovered anything yet?'

'They are checking out Rossetti's gang. It all points to them, according to Jack Lonsdale at the Fusilier's Club.' He sighed, then: 'But I am afraid that the dynamite consignment has gone. Does that mean you will be moving against Rossetti?'

'Not until I am ready. In the meanwhile I will listen to what young Decker has to say and I will give him instructions. Bring him to my study.'

Inspector Munro received the telegram from Sherlock Holmes in the early afternoon.

> Munro, bring six men in plain clothes all wearing black to St Barnabus Church, Bethnal Green. Meet me on Roman Road at 3 p.m.
> S.H.

A thick fog had fallen when Munro and his men met Sherlock Holmes in the cemetery of St Barnabus Church.

'You see, Munro,' said Holmes. 'The window in the shape of a pentagram! Why the architect chose it has always been a mystery, but this is the reason for the pentagram on the rings of O'Donohue and the American. I am sure that you will find that this church was built with foreign money.'

'We will find out in due course, Mr Holmes. But did your irregulars track your American here?'

'They did, as I had every confidence that they would. He is Irish-American and he happens to be the vicar, the Reverend Elliot Sanderson, from Chicago. He is taking a service this afternoon at three thirty, which is going to be attended by the Prime Minister Lord Salisbury and almost all of his cabinet. You remember that Collingwood, the MP for Stepney, died suddenly last week.'

'Shall we go in now?'

'No, I am going inside alone. Give me five minutes then come in, prepared to make your arrest.'

Sherlock Holmes entered the church alone and Munro and his men waited anxiously, alert to move quickly.

After almost exactly four minutes, there came the sound of two shots from inside the church. Munro and his men rushed in to find Sherlock Holmes half collapsed on the front pew clutching his left arm, a heavy revolver still clenched in his right hand.

On the floor, sprawled out, was the body of a clergyman. He too had a smoking gun in his right hand, but whereas Holmes was merely wounded, the vicar was dead with a bullet hole between his eyes and a rapidly enlarging pool of blood about his head. His vestments were already soaked crimson.

Upon his outstretched left hand a signet ring with a pentagram symbol was plainly visible.

'You will find dynamite with concealed wires leading to one of H. Julius Smith's diabolically clever dynamo blasting machines behind the pulpit. I disabled the plunger and disconnected the wires, much to the Reverend Elliot Sanderson's displeasure.'

'You shouldn't have tackled him alone, Mr Holmes,' Munro remonstrated.

'One man could slip in and have a chance of upsetting his

scheme. Had a flock of police officers, albeit disguised as mourners, then I fear the outcome could have been worse. I think the Reverend of the Pentagram Society intended to martyr himself when he murdered the prime minister and the cabinet and everyone else who attended the funeral. As it was, he chose to play dice one last time when he accosted me.'

He smiled as he raised his revolver. 'As you can see, I play with loaded dice, too.'

Then the great detective fainted.

Two days later, Sherlock Holmes was the talk of London and beyond. The conspiracy to murder the prime minister and his government by the anarchist group known as the Pentagram Society, a title given them by the sleuth himself, had fired the public imagination.

After hospital treatment of the flesh wound to his left arm, Holmes had returned to Baker Street where he had been inundated with telegrams and letters from well-wishers, a visit from Lord Salisbury himself and talk of a knighthood.

All of this Holmes greeted with his usual private disdain and with his public display of modesty. Yet he was pleased to see Inspector Munro when he dropped in.

'Ah, Alistair – I trust that on this occasion you will not object to my use of your Christian name; it seems apt after our handling of this unholy affair by the anarchist Pentagram Society.'

'Of course, Mr Holmes, that is perfectly in order. But, if you don't mind, I will still use your title. That too seems only right, although I heard that it may soon be Sir Sherlock Holmes.'

Holmes adjusted the sling that he was wearing over his old grey dressing gown and laughed. 'As you wish, Alistair. Yet I am sure that after this coup you yourself will soon be advancing in rank at Scotland Yard. Will you take a brandy?'

'I'd prefer a whisky and soda if you don't mind, Mr Holmes.'

'Of course. And I shall join you. Make yourself comfortable by the fire while I pour them. It may take me a moment longer to operate the gasogene with one hand.'

'Will you be getting Dr Watson to chronicle this case, sir?'

'In due course, after a period of time to let it slip somewhat from the public mind.'

'What will you call it, Mr Holmes?'

'I thought "The Case of the Crooked Dice" or perhaps "The Case of the Fulham Strangler".'

He turned and handed Munro a glass then picked up his own. 'Shall we drink to our success, Munro?'

'Oh, I think so. It has been a glittering success, a lesson in detection.'

'Kind of you to say so, my good fellow. It will, I think, display the art of deduction to perfection.'

Munro gave a short laugh and then the smile faded from his face. 'Or rather it could show the art of deception.'

His eyes suddenly seemed sharper, unblinking and his head oscillated right and left in a manner reminiscent of a reptile.

'My God, can it be you?' Holmes gasped, dropping his whisky and soda and darting his right hand inside his sling to come out again with his revolver. 'But, as you can see, Moriarty – I never take chances.'

In answer, Professor Moriarty merely smiled and took a sip of his drink. 'Put it down, Holmes. It is full of blanks. I exchanged the bullets after you fainted and we packed you off to hospital. That's better, now let us talk frankly.'

'What have you done with Munro?'

Moriarty smiled. 'There is no other person by that name that you need concern yourself about. Effectively, I am Alistair Munro, as I have been for two years. You pride yourself on your ability to disguise yourself, as the world knows from your egotistical tales, which Dr Watson publishes on your behalf. I too have several personae that I use, which require certain disguises. They are of various people in authority whose position is such that they can come and go as they please, so I can show up as them when it is convenient for me to do so. Munro has been my particular hobby, fostering a disciple-like relationship with you as I built his career. And, as this case demonstrates, he has been very useful.'

'In what way useful, Professor?' Holmes asked, regaining his composure. 'Why would following me aid you?'

'Because I didn't follow you, Holmes, I guided you at every step. From the elimination of O'Donohue, one of my men whose incompetence necessitated his removal from my service.'

'You killed him?'

'I eliminated him. Then I used his death as a means to eliminate Sanderson.'

'Why would you want to eliminate an anarchist and his group?'

Moriarty laughed. 'Actually, a bit of anarchy is very good for business. You can see that, can't you? A headless state means total confusion. When the authorities are preoccupied it is perfect for my organisation and others like mine. You have seen how anarchy has worked for my colleagues in the Balkans and across Europe.'

He sipped his drink again. 'But this had nothing to do with anarchists. And there is no such organisation as the Pentagram Society. Elliot Sanderson, on the other hand, was perfectly real. He was a fanatic, but he was not an anarchist. He was an Irish nationalist, an American Irish nationalist, of course. His organisation and I do substantial business from time to time and they requested that I aid him in blowing up Salisbury and his government. They supplied the money to obtain explosives and together we removed Collingwood the MP for Stepney so that his funeral could be performed at St Barnabus Church.'

Holmes stared at him in disgust. 'What about the rings, the dice, the jute with the dynamite?'

'Oh, those were all real. I planted each and every one of them and you made the deductions that I knew you would. I anticipated the Griess test that you would do to conclude that dynamite was involved. As for the dice, well, I have been making a study of them, you see. All manner of crooked dice are used in my establishments, but I have been considering dice probabilities and looking at the American games of chance. I hoped that you would make the link with the game of craps. It was a test for you.

'And the rings, well, that was a simple matter of obtaining a duplicate of Sanderson's ring. It was given to him by the Church actually, not by a secret society. O'Donohue never wore one. I simply put it on his finger after he was eliminated and his body prepared with the little bundle down his throat. I congratulate you, since you followed that all up rather well. Of course, you didn't realise that you were on a false trail being manipulated by me.

'Which brings me to our irregulars. Would you be surprised if I told you that the urchin you rewarded with a guinea is called Alfie Decker. He has been very useful to me these last two years.'

Holmes picked up the whisky glass he had dropped and placed it beside the revolver. 'But what was the purpose of this incredibly elaborate ruse?'

'Partly to get rid of Sanderson without showing his organisation that I had anything to do with it. Sherlock Holmes would be the person responsible. Which may mean that they will have plans to seek revenge later, but that is an occupational hazard you are already well aware of, of course.'

Holmes stiffened in his chair. 'You will hang for this, Moriarty. You are putting your neck in the noose with every little piece of information you give me.'

'I think not, Holmes. You see, it is almost certainly you that will hang. After all of the information that Inspector Munro has been accumulating on you these past two years. So often you have gone beyond your remit as a detective, and you have taken it upon yourself to be judge and executioner as well. He has details of these cases. He has proof, eyewitnesses, physical evidence of all the crimes you have aided and abetted and committed yourself.'

The professor's head oscillated again and his unblinking eyes seemed to enlarge, reptilian fashion, as if he was going in for the kill.

'He has bank details of all of the stolen money, lost money and money defrauded from clients. And he has bank clerks who will swear that you had made those deposits in person. You see, you are quite a distinctive fellow. It was a challenge to emulate you, I admit, but as you yourself have seen these two years, I am fairly proficient at disguise and in sustaining a role.'

Holmes sneered. 'All done with mathematical precision, I see. What is to stop me from tackling you here and now, eliminating you, as you would say?'

'Firstly, with that arm you would be no match, I assure you. Secondly, if anything happens to me, the dossier falls into the hands of several journalists, who are in my employ already, as well as copies going straight to Scotland Yard. More than that, though,' he said, draining his whisky, 'at any time, Inspector Munro could be found dead, murdered, by Sherlock Holmes. Oh, I can arrange that quite easily. A body of the right height and weight can easily be found. How he was murdered would not matter much: a knife in the back, a slit throat or a bullet to the brain. His face would be eaten away by concentrated sulphuric acid, just like the supplies that you have on your chemistry table, which are supplied to you by Benson & Son of Tottenham Court Road. Together with the evidence that Munro had against you, it would be a certainty that you would be convicted and ignominiously executed for his murder. You have undoubted motive, as anyone can see.'

Holmes picked up his pipe and thumbed the bowl. 'So when do you propose that this is going to happen?'

'Oh, it will only happen if you choose it,' Moriarty said, with an innocent smile. 'If you decide to be sensible and back off, you are free to enjoy your consulting detective practice, accumulate more adulation and feed that enormous ego of yours. One step in my direction, however, or any interference with my organisation and you will be headed for prison and assuredly to the gallows. London is a large city, Holmes. You can ply your trade, just don't come near my fishing pool.'

He stood and pointed to the violin case propped up against the wall below the bullet-pocked holes that spelled out V.R. for Victoria Regina.

'By the way, you will not of course be able to play your prized Stradivarius for some time because of that wound. I do hope that you will be happy with the fiddle that I swapped for it. I purchased it at a market on the Old Kent Road for 1/6d. Consider it a reply to your removal of my painting *La Jeune Fille à l'Agneau*, by Jean-Baptiste Greuze. I had meant to tell you that there is one thing you need to be aware of. No matter how good your disguise, a man who continuously smokes the strongest, most foul-smelling of tobaccos as you do will always leave an odoriferous trail that is quite offensive and distinctive to those of us who do not partake of the habit.'

The bell rang downstairs.

'Ah, I imagine that is Dr Watson, returning from looking after his uncle, to come and congratulate you on your latest success and get the background for his next tale to peddle to *The Strand*. I will take my leave.'

Moments later, Dr Watson opened the door and came in, travelling bag in hand.

'Holmes! I've been reading the . . .'

He stopped, dropped his bag and held out his hand. 'Munro! Congratulations to you, too, old man. Your country owes you both a great debt.'

'Thank you, Doctor,' replied Inspector Munro. 'I'm afraid that I can't stop, though. I have to get back to Scotland Yard.'

'No, we mustn't keep him,' added Sherlock Holmes. 'Watson, I know that you will be eager to know all about this trivial business that Munro and I have had the pleasure to work on together. We were just debating what title you would give it.'

'I think we have come to an understanding, though, haven't we, Mr Holmes?'

'Indeed, Munro. Indeed. We'll leave it up to the good doctor here.'

The Adventure of The Lost Theorem

Julie Novakova

Prague, the Austro-Hungarian Empire, 187–

A gunshot resonated through the narrow alley. In the quiet streets of the Old Town long after midnight, no other sound would be more shocking and out of place.

If any of the inhabitants of the old houses opened their window and looked out, they would see a young man running fast through the streets. He was wearing no hat or overcoat, though it was freezing and the pavement was covered in snow. If the accidental observer saw lamplight illuminate his face, they'd wonder if they hadn't seen a ghost: so pale and thin had it seemed.

Had they been at the Franz Joseph railway station three days ago, they would have met him under very different circumstances and probably wouldn't have remembered the encounter. They would see a rather thin, tall young man in an impeccable if somewhat boring clothing, with a simple yet elegant ebony walking cane. He had one of these unexceptional, hard-to-recall faces. Except for the eyes. A more astute observer would surely notice the slightly sunken grey eyes and their piercing stare. They would pigeonhole him as a high clerk or a man of learning – and in this they wouldn't be wrong, as he'd been a mathematics professor at a small yet renowned English university.

What casual observers wouldn't see was the blade concealed in the man's cane, the small derringer resting between two shirts in his case and the Sheffield switchblade in his coat's pocket. Those who would have seen any of these items probably wouldn't be inclined to tell others about them, if only for the impracticality of conversing if you're dead.

The man's name was James Moriarty and, at this moment, his main concern would be avoiding this impracticality himself.

There was a quiet knock on the door. "Do you wish any refreshments, sir? Today's newspapers?"

Moriarty shook his head and the salesman left for another train car, searching for other compartments with lights on to offer his goods.

The sun hadn't risen yet but James was up habitually early. A lot of his business tended to go on in the wee small hours of the morning, if not in the middle of the night. Luckily, he never felt the need for much sleep. Sleeping only kept you from more *thinking* – and thinking was what James Moriarty valued most of all.

He reached into his jacket's inner pocket for a small folded piece of paper. This had been the reason he was sitting in a train going to Prague after all.

> *Dear Professor Moriarty,*
>
>   *I am writing you because it has recently found a way to my ears that Herr Robert Zimmermann in Prague uncovered information implying the existence of a certain Bernard Bolzano's manuscript, previously thought to have been destroyed. The work in question is said to concern a rather unusual approach to the binomial theorem. I believe this to be of interest to you, sir.*
>
>   *Your sincere friend*

Little could be derived from the letter. It had been sent from Prague and written in the plainest black ink on a plain paper, put in a completely plain envelope. The handwriting had apparently been altered, though if he were to secure a sample of a suspected author's usual handwriting, he would surely recognize it. Otherwise, he had nothing except for one important fact. That someone had been very careful. Moriarty, in fact, expected that the letter had not been written by its real author, merely transcribed by someone else.

As for the self-described identity of the author: James Moriarty had no friends and did not believe in benefactors. Everyone followed their own agendas in the end. The secret of gaining power over others lay in knowing exactly what theirs were.

Now someone thought he'd known his agenda. Moriarty would gladly let them think that.

As soon as he found a decent hotel and checked the exit routes from his room, James Moriarty went to introduce himself to the Prague academic society.

After his university's small town and London, Prague was a pleasant change. It was a smallish city by a Londoner's standards but impressive nonetheless, much more interesting than the town he'd been living in these days. Under the city's famous thousand spires, he walked toward the mathematics wing of the Faculty of Philosophy of the Charles-Ferdinand University. To get to Zimmermann's office, he used an alias from a colleague from Edinburgh, certain that no one would know the Scot personally here, and a story remarkably close to the truth – that he heard the professor had been compiling Bernard Bolzano's work and he's interested in it. He had sent Zimmermann the note about his arrival yesterday, apologizing for such a quick notice. One day was still passable for an eccentric professor and not long enough for Zimmermann to start making serious enquiries, should it come to that.

Moriarty had developed a custom of not forming assumptions before having acquired the facts, but the first encounter with the renowned scholar surpassed his expectation nevertheless.

First glance into his office: a disorderly mess everywhere. Books lay open on the floor, table and spare chairs. A mug of what presumably had once been tea fulfilled the role of a paperweight. The papers beneath – full of sweeping handwriting not remotely resembling the anonymous friend's letter – looked an incarnation of chaos.

Robert Zimmermann himself was a tall, broad-shouldered man with a mane of dark hair greying at the temples, clad in what may have been fashionable here at least a decade ago. He spoke in fairly good English, albeit with a strong Teutonic accent: "Ah, Professor Galbraith, is it so? I received your note! I've heard a lot about you!"

I doubt it, Moriarty thought. Aloud he said: "And I've heard a lot about your work, Professor Zimmermann. Your accomplishments in both philosophy and mathematics are astounding and your work on uncovering Herr Bolzano's manuscripts is commendable. I have been studying his *Grössenlehre* because some of my own work centers on the binomial theorem that he mentions there, albeit briefly, not having published possible other manuscripts on it . . ."

That much was true. But he had always taken an unusual approach to problems, unlike the real Galbraith or the present Herr Zimmermann. Their intellect, however impressive for most people, had been limited, short-sighted. Bernard Bolzano defied this stereotype, even though in matters of philosophy Moriarty disagreed with him without having to apply himself too much.

"Um, I cannot say I recall this particular area of your work," Zimmermann began.

Moriarty just smiled indulgently and went on describing his alias's fictional study while they drank tea – not what they would call tea in England, though. He took care to notice Herr Professor's expression throughout the whole time and tweak the story accordingly. He saw that he had captured Zimmermann's interest.

So very little is needed to beguile someone. Add a dash of appeal to their pride, a spoonful of shared interests, two slices of engaging questions . . .

". . . but if I could see the original work, it would be such an honor for me—"

His version of Professor Galbraith was excited by the mere thought. Unfortunately, before Zimmermann could answer – and Moriarty was certain he would offer him to go through the documents – a knock on the door interrupted them.

"Come in," Zimmermann said in German.

A young woman entered: a nondescript dark blonde in a nondescript greyish dress. Moriarty would presume her likely to be a secretary, but her manner suggested otherwise. Before he could read her more thoroughly, she spoke: "Oh, I'm sorry, Robert. I didn't realize you had a visitor."

"Don't apologize, I announced my arrival rather late," Moriarty said in deliberately badly-accented German.

Zimmermann recalled his manners. "Professor, this is my sister Eva. Eva, meet Professor Galbraith. He traveled here all the way from Edinburgh to learn more about my work on classifying my late mentor's legacy."

"Pleased to meet you," Eva chirped.

"Likewise." He produced another one of his wide repertoire of carefully practiced smiles: crafted for young ladies in polite society, garden variety.

She blushed a little. He looked down for a second, then his smile widened. He might need to get closer to the Zimmermanns later. Eva could be useful for that.

Her gaze lingered a second too long on him before turning to her brother. "I came because Josephine took ill and cannot go with us to the opera the day after tomorrow. I wasn't sure when you'd be home and was nearby anyway, so . . ."

Late nights at the office, with this detestable tea and philosophical papers? Or does something else keep Herr Zimmermann?

"Thank you, dear. I'm sure I'll think of someone else—" The professor suddenly looked at Moriarty. "Would you like to visit the opera with us? It would be my pleasure to show you our city's culture as well as its intellectual enticements. They're having *Faust*, it's a truly good work, if you haven't seen it yet. I would prefer to take you to Mozart, as is traditional, but we could always do that later if you're staying in Prague for some time."

Eva's eyes shined. "Oh, Herr Galbraith, you must come!"

Moriarty waged quickly. He would miss an opportunity for a certain mission he'd been planning; on the other hand, it would do no harm to get to know the Zimmermanns better.

"It would be my honor." He nodded.

* * *

His move may have earned him even more trust from Robert Zimmermann than the previous academic discussion. Practically without any encouragement, he offered Moriarty to come the next day and look through every piece of Bernard Bolzano's unpublished manuscripts, provided he would discuss his findings with him without delay.

The filing of the documents was nearly as chaotic as Zimmermann's office. Moriarty detested disorderliness. Just finding some sort of system in the papers took him a while. He could consider himself lucky he was a fast and observant reader with a keen memory.

But in the end, there was *nothing*. After two whole days of careful shifting through the fragments and unpublished manuscripts from dawn to well after dusk, not a thing even remotely resembling what he had hoped for. He found many indications that the presumed work had existed – most likely the information his unknown benefactor had mentioned. Yet nothing at all pointed at its fate now!

James Moriarty had been an ice-cold man for most of the time: rational, calculating, self-controlled. But, occasionally, he gave in to his temper. And when he did, he was capable of showing more fury than one would think imaginable.

Such a moment *almost* came now. But Moriarty would take the anger and melt it down to cold determination to *find out*: whether the manuscript in question had really existed, who was playing games with him and why.

Emotion was not the enemy of reason; one just had to learn to work with it properly.

He would go to the opera with the Zimmermanns tonight and apply himself to learn more about them. Had the professor been hiding something, playing some game? Or had he been what he seemed: the harmless little philosopher, unable to comprehend the true impact of his long-dead tutor's works?

I feel like a chess piece on somebody else's board, he thought derisively. He *would* find a way to look at the game as a whole. *Then we shall see who wins.*

* * *

What do mathematics and crime have in common?

A more fitting question would be what they *don't*.

Hard work, self-control and a brilliant mind are necessary assets in both, should you be successful. Most people couldn't even understand a simple derivative of a function. Most attempted crimes failed. Not spectacularly, not even a little bit interestingly, because there was nothing spectacular or interesting about them. They were as dull, small-minded and stupid as a child's tantrum. Not thought through at all.

But that much could be said about many professional fields. No, there was more to this.

Others wouldn't understand the unique connection, pondered Moriarty as he changed into evening dress. *They wouldn't see how beautiful it is.*

The beauty lay in the slow revelation of the puzzle and the process of its solution; the careful evaluations of all components of the equation; solving one piece after another . . . It was a rigorous task, demanding patience and care. In applied mathematics, he would typically start with a problem, account for its variables and determine the outcome. Sometimes the work concerned numerous variables difficult to estimate, like his current work at the university. He had recently started working on a new task concerning the dynamics of an asteroid.

In crime, the procedure was a little different. He would start with the desired outcome and then determine the values of variables needed for it. They were much more complex to account for but it was feasible if he picked the problem carefully. He loved the process of thinking it all through, moving the invisible pieces on his imagined board. There it was – a passion stronger than for pure mathematics, stronger than anything else the world could offer.

Usually, he was the one to determine the parameters of the equation to his needs. Then, though with certain degrees of freedom, the result was the one he'd anticipated.

Not so now. He was a variable in someone else's equation, a state he very much despised.

Patience, now. I'll be playing their game a little while longer

*and then, when I deem it most useful, my variable shall become
truly unpredictable. Then I'll make it my equation.*

He could learn a lot from it. And the sweet, sweet reward
awaiting him if he succeeded . . .

In criminal enterprises, one could learn a lot from mathematics, even where hardly anyone would expect it. The binomial
theorem, while interesting, was becoming a child's exercise.
Even its applications in combinatorics and various distribution
functions, the principal points of Moriarty's earlier academic
work, were about as surprising for a professional as the statement that the sun rises in the morning and sets in the evening for
any layman.

So why try so hard to get one's hands on a work presumably
concerning the theorem? Moreover, work a few decades old and
in all likelihood outdated?

One would need a unique kind of imagination to see the possible implications. Such as James Moriarty undoubtedly possessed.

The signs scattered through Bolzano's documents suggested
the existence of an ambitious extension of the good old binomial
theorem, such that would make complicated and hardly attain-
able operations like accounting for all crime in a big city at least
feasible if not easy or reliable. But the specifics . . . Moriarty
longed to see the theorem more than anything else.

*I wonder if Bolzano saw this implication too and therefore
hid this particular manuscript of his. He surely wouldn't
destroy his own work, but hiding it would explain the rumors
and indications and yet the absence of the document itself,*
Moriarty mused. *It would become him. He seems to have been
a very* . . . honest *man.*

Honesty. It usually made for a good variable. It tended to be
quite predictable.

A hired carriage, already bearing Zimmermann and his sister,
stopped in front of the hotel just on time. The professor seemed
a little distracted, while his sister gave "Herr Galbraith" her full
attention. She had exchanged her previous dull dress for a blue
evening gown, which suited her very well. Clad in it, she seemed

a different woman. Even the wittiness of her conversation on the way to the theater managed to surprise Moriarty.

Sweet yet sophisticated perfume. Expertly applied face paint. Her behavior and movements – all balanced on the edge of appropriate and enticing. Hmm.

If he needed to get even closer to the siblings, he would know the way. For now, he always replied politely and laughed at her jokes, but made no sign of an advance whatsoever. Her brother didn't seem to notice a thing. Moriarty felt a little relief when the opera finally started.

The performers were good and practiced, but mostly unremarkable. Only one of the chorus girls, almost still a child, caught the attention of his ear. He skimmed through the program to see her name. *Hmm, Adler. Let's hope to see more of her in theaters in the future.*

The opera itself was good albeit not at all innovative. The Faustian legend seemed an infinitely deep well of inspiration for multitudes of artists. Their efforts amused Moriarty greatly. They were like crows picking at an especially fat corpse. But he had to admit the legend had had a certain appeal. Revealing the mysteries of nature and history – that was an admirable undertaking. So what if there had been a bit of devilish help? Moriarty fully approved of that; he only detested the awful moralistic ending.

He shot a brief glance to the Zimmermanns. The professor looked as if he'd rather be somewhere else. In contrast, Eva seemed fully absorbed in the play. Her eyes gleamed as she stared at the singers.

Moriarty could imagine the music broken down to its frequencies and individual tunes, translated into equations; but the passion onstage and in the auditorium was something he understood from observation only. His passion lay far elsewhere.

When the final applause died down, Eva exclaimed: "Wasn't it exciting?"

"A true masterpiece," Moriarty agreed, with an awed expression. Though he felt that should he act like this much longer, his face muscles would start to twitch.

Eva gave him a long look, too long to be comfortable. He was already preparing some innocent reply when Zimmermann spoke. "Allow us to invite you for a glass of wine, Professor Galbraith. I'm sure you're thirsty after the long performance."

"Please forgive me but I won't accompany you. I still have some work to do tonight."

"If we get a carriage, we can at least take you to your hotel," Zimmermann offered.

"You're very kind, but I think I'll walk. It is not too cold tonight and it's the perfect opportunity to see the beautiful city at night."

Eva looked disappointed that they would part already but said nothing.

The night truly was quite mild, given that it was late winter. At first, Moriarty considered going on a previously planned mission, despite his not ideal appearance. But, as he walked through the city as it was growing quiet, he soon noticed a strange presence behind him.

Am I being trailed?

He stopped in the middle of a bridge, seemingly looking at the panorama of the Prague Castle, only just noticeable in the dark but still magnificent. Actually he threw a sideways glance towards where he suspected his pursuer to be.

There: a shadow of a statue, and a part of it just a shade deeper than the rest. Now he was sure he was being followed.

He hadn't taken his gun to the opera, only his walking cane with a blade inside. Perfectly sufficient, provided his opponent would not have a gun.

Should he confront the pursuer? He could gain much information from it – but he'd also give some away. No, he had better wait. He would give whomever was following him an innocent story to tell: how the man walked from the opera house back to the hotel and did not emerge until morning.

And so it would seem to any unsuspecting observer.

A shadowy figure emerged from the hotel kitchen's window into an empty street plunged in darkness. When faint moonlight finally fell upon it, it revealed a gruff man in worker's clothes and a shabby hat, which concealed most of his face. What could be glimpsed were a short unkempt beard and a large nose.

The figure walked swiftly through the city, like someone who knew every inch of it, and stopped before an old house in Mala Strana.

The face turned upwards. Moonlight reflected briefly from its bright piercing eyes.

Moriarty concluded that his surroundings really were deserted, and started working on the house door's lock. It took his skilled hands only a couple of minutes to open it. He slipped inside and closed the door quietly.

The rooms he was interested in were on the third floor. A small office had resided here for many years now; he'd checked on it before he decided on this small escapade.

The lock on the office's door was even more ridiculous than the one downstairs. He entered and saw that Professor Bolzano's old home had become a place of dereliction and decay. The office that occupied it now cared not for the crumbling plaster, creaking floor or draught coming from the old windows. No wonder, judging from the state of their own affairs: the desks and cabinets seemed about as tidy as Herr Zimmermann's room at the university.

It was unlikely that the manuscript would remain hidden here, but he had nowhere else to start. He would check every loose brick, every plank in the floor, if he must.

He spent a few demanding hours turning the office upside down – and found nothing.

Despite telling himself that it was to be expected, that he only had to eliminate the most obvious possibility, James Moriarty felt the rage coming to him once again.

He looked around the room. He was certainly in no mood to tidy up after himself.

At least it may teach them to organize their work in some sort of system – even if only they would understand it, better than nothing.

Then it struck him. *A system. A code.*

Was it possible that he had missed something in Bolzano's documents? Was he looking too superficially?

The prospect of going through the disordered pile again did not attract him, but hard work often bore fruit . . . He would try tomorrow.

But tonight he'd try to make use of other sources as well.

"Professor Galbraith! You look a little tired today. I hope you slept well."

"I slept quite soundly, thank you. It must still be the travel," Moriarty answered smoothly. He poured himself a cup of what they dared to call tea here.

In truth, he'd slept barely two hours. His excursion into the Prague criminal underworld, however, brought forth at least some results. There was a recent shift of status quo, some other player had entered the game and seized it firmly. The new king remained unseen, pulling the strings through his minions. His actions had made quite a splash, as the previously rival worlds of German and Czech criminals merged in some areas. What he'd heard that night truly left him wondering. Czech and Germans working together for a common goal. Efficiently, even, from what he'd learned. So moving. Had Moriarty been more inclined to displays of emotion, he might have shed some tears. Maybe state officials should consider building criminal enterprises as a way to bring together the ever-quarreling nations.

As it happened, he was not inclined to displays of emotion. Therefore, he only frowned slightly and noted the fact for later use.

It surprised Moriarty that there hadn't even been any rumors about the new king's identity. Was it possible that this mysterious figure had been the one to lure him here? But then he'd need to have access to Bolzano's documents and at least a partial understanding of them . . .

Anyone from Zimmermann's university department or with access to it could have gotten to the manuscripts. And Moriarty had a suspicion that Zimmermann, being as lax as he was, may have taken the precious papers home as well. His servants could have seen them too.

But who would find the signs he had spotted as well, and recognize their meaning?

He returned to going through the manuscripts, remembering where the spotted indications had been and trying to make more sense of them. When Zimmermann asked him to lunch, he politely declined.

He was left alone in the office.

Going towards Zimmermann's despicable desk, Moriarty produced a set of small lock picks from his pocket. Chaotic as he may have been, Zimmermann didn't leave most correspondence lying around, but, Moriarty noticed, put it in a desk drawer.

Click. The drawer opened readily.

He flipped through the correspondence. After a few letters, he understood why the otherwise reckless Zimmermann had paid attention to locking the drawer. He and a certain Josephine would undoubtedly find it most humiliating if their exchanges were made public. That would also explain his distractedness at the opera.

But petty human concerns like this were of no interest to Moriarty. He focused on the academic correspondence, notes from colleagues – and there was no match for the writing from his note, even taking deliberate alterations into account.

He closed the drawer and looked at the desk again. *Could something have been left here?* Ah, that pile: a few newer notices from colleagues, a note from sister, letters from Brünn and Vienna . . .

He almost failed to notice the approaching quiet steps. A second before the door opened, he put the pile back as it was and made a leap into the other room.

Just in time.

Eva Zimmermann entered, bearing a small basket. She stopped when she saw him through the open door between the rooms. "Oh, I didn't want to interrupt your work, Professor Galbraith. I thought you were lunching with my brother. I . . . I brought him a snack for the afternoon."

"Waiting for the moment he wouldn't be here." He nodded calmly.

A panicky expression flickered through her face. "Well, I . . . I meant to . . ."

He got up and walked slowly to her. "Just tell me the truth."

She gave him a hopeless glance. He noticed she was wearing perfume and her day dress and jewelry were unusually ostentatious.

"H-Herr Galbraith, I d-don't . . ." she stuttered.

"You thought you would find me here alone, didn't you?"

"Yes," she admitted, her gaze firmly fixed on her toes.

"Well, I find this kind of attention very flattering from a beautiful and respectable young lady like you, but think of what others would say if they heard. You are a remarkable woman, Fräulein Zimmermann. Don't let pointless rumor ruin your life. You deserve better."

Now she was blushing to the roots of her hair. "Thank you, Herr Galbraith," she managed. "That – that's very wise of you. If you'll excuse me now."

She almost ran through the door.

Moriarty allowed himself a little chuckle and went back to work.

In spite of skipping lunch, he felt more energized than before. Absorbed in his search, he didn't notice Zimmermann returning from lunch.

"Did anything happen while I was away?"

"Nothing at all," Moriarty murmured, not taking his eyes off the old texts. Thus he spent the next hour, and the next . . .

. . . *the theorem in reference . . . praying my work brings peace and understanding but so uncertain about this . . . pure mathematics, yet what others may do . . . if one prays to God, true and pure, where the Lord can see him, then he may know . . .*

He stopped and almost broke into laughter. "I'm famished," he said to the surprised professor. "Are you going to dinner?"

"Ahem, I'm very sorry, I have other plans for the evening though I could—"

"Do not worry, Professor. I will see you tomorrow!"

Or not, if I'm right, he added to himself.

Moriarty's steps resonated in the empty church. It was long closed by now; however, he had means to enter places. He walked to the first carved bench, then knelt down as if to pray.

Where the Lord can see him . . .

There was a large statue of the Christ gazing down at his lambs. Moriarty moved a little to the right – yes, here. The statue seemed to stare right at him at this spot.

He began to fumble around the bench, hoping it hadn't been replaced in several decades.

At the beginning of the century, Bernard Bolzano worked as a preacher at the St Salvator's Church by the Clementinum. He'd been there for nearly fifteen years and remained a very pious man throughout his whole life. Where else would he turn to when hiding a work he considered dangerous in the hands of someone not as devout as himself?

Moriarty's fingers found a strange shape under one of the carved ornaments, something that didn't quite belong. He palpated it, pulled and pushed and, after a couple of minutes, it finally gave in. A small leather sheath fell out into his awaiting palms.

Yes! He hid it here, this is it . . .

Once safely outside, he couldn't resist opening the sheath and unwrapping the frail paper. There it was, before his own eyes: the lost theorem!

He had already packed, all that was left to do was to take his belongings and catch the late night train to Berlin, from where he would continue to England.

He took a little detour and then returned to his hotel. The door didn't look as if it had been tampered with. It should be safe to retrieve his possessions. He unlocked the door, entered the dark room—

The door suddenly closed behind him and the light went on. "Stay where you are. Hands up and turn around slowly."

He obeyed, and saw Eva Zimmermann, clad in a dark grey practical dress and aiming a Webley pocket revolver at him. "You don't look surprised to see me."

"That's because I'm not."

She smiled coldly. "What gave me away?"

"A simple mistake, truly. You left a note in your handwriting lying on your brother's desk. It was most likely that someone close to your brother – or he himself – had sent me the note that had brought me here. Why would I fail to check on you, so deep in the circle of suspects? Just because you're a woman? I never underestimate anyone based on superficial characteristics. But it surprises me you didn't use someone else to write the letter."

"This is my doing only. Who else would understand the importance of it? I cannot let anyone think I'm entertaining myself with useless pursuits. I worked hard to attain my current position."

"So why risk it for an old document?"

"An old document?" she exclaimed. "I would never have expected to hear these words from *you*. Don't you see its significance? Oh . . . I see. You just wanted to see my reaction, didn't you? Good. Now hand it over."

"I don't have it on me. I hid it in the lining of my suitcase just after I found it earlier. I have to tear it again. If you'd allow me to use my knife . . ."

"Good try. First, give me your coat, slowly . . . And you may do what you propose – *without any blades*." Still holding the gun firmly and pointing it at him without ever wavering, she fumbled in her purse with her other hand and then threw him some small nail clippers. "These should suffice. And hands where I can see them."

While she was searching his coat, finding he hadn't been lying about not having the manuscript on him, he began to work on the tough lining. It was slow going with the clippers. While he was working at it, he spoke: "You are the new king of the local underworld, aren't you? Let me pay you my proper respects. But how have you come to it? And why Bolzano?"

"My brother is not a bad philosopher but he's a hopeless mathematician. He doesn't understand most of his mentor's legacy and cares not for classifying and publishing it. He kept it at home for a while. I used to read it, work through the theorems . . . It was I who helped him with homework and essays when I was still a child and he a student; who *taught* him so much – and what for? Though I loved the brain-work, I was expected to stay home and devote my time to searching for a prospective husband! I would have loved to become a mathematician, yet you cannot do that covertly if you want to succeed in the academic world. So I found myself another hobby."

"I understand you saw the importance of the lost manuscript for your . . . hobby as well as your original passion, but what made you think I would retrieve it?"

"Get on with it," she said harshly, observing his efforts with her nail clippers with dissatisfaction. "And don't pretend you're just a mathematics professor. Your reputation precedes you, Moriarty. Or have you not gained much of your current standing by . . . let's say, very unofficial ways? It may have started as a means to pursue your academic career, but it has become much more since then, has it not? You and I seem to have a lot in common."

The lining was almost done now. "So that's why you pretended to take a different kind of interest in me? Not just to observe my work, but to get closer to the fellow mathematical criminal, is it so? And may I just say, you need to work on that yet. You were overacting. It was all too obvious." He shook his head. "You really overdid it today at your brother's office. You went there to check on my work – whether I had found it already, yes? The excuse itself was believable, but your behavior . . . I don't think any lady outside romantic novels would act that way."

The lady in question sneered in a very un-ladylike way. "Remind me to act properly ambivalently the next time. Oh, wait – you won't be there for any *next time*."

He stopped, hands just above the torn lining. "Are you going to dispose of me? I cannot quite believe you've lured me here all the way from England just for one manuscript and then to kill me. That doesn't make sense if you add the benefits, risks and costs."

"If you only found the manuscript and learned nothing more, you would return home freely. You must admit you've brought this fate upon yourself."

"But still – I could be a useful asset for your expansion abroad. If you had so high a regard of me and my ability to find the document, why stop with that?"

Eva produced a sad little smile. "We both know the rules of this game. Or, rather, their lack. Sooner or later, one of us would betray the other. Knowing this, we'd both be compelled to be the first to do so. Our collaboration would be brief and unfruitful, if I'm anticipating this right. Well – give me the paper. Let's not prolong this any more."

Moriarty opened the lining. There was nothing inside.

Eva's cheeks reddened with anger. "Fine! Should I shoot you in the knee first for you to suffer?"

"If I tell you where it is, you'll kill me. If I refuse to do so, you'll kill me as well, if more slowly and painfully. It seems that if I cared about my well-being in my final moments, I should give you the document. But that would be in case I haven't anticipated the possibility of this outcome and taken some precautions."

Given my note got delivered and he would come at this hour . . .

Her eyes narrowed. "What do you mean?"

Moriarty risked a glance at his pocket watch. "We should be—"

A knock on the door interrupted his sentence.

"—expecting company," he finished. "Come in!"

Robert Zimmermann entered and froze just by the door. "Eva?! What's going on?"

The gun in her hand must have truly shocked him. Moriarty allowed himself a dash of relief that his assumption based on the facts known about them, namely that Herr Zimmermann knew nothing of his sister's enterprises, had proven correct.

"*Auf Wiedersehen,*" he mumbled as he made a run for the door. *Or better not.*

She did not shoot; one step and he was behind her brother and then outside the room. He could hear shouts and a hollow thud from there while he was running hard through the corridor and downstairs. An instant later, he heard her running after him. He only gained an opportunity to escape and a very small advance, but he would have to calculate with that.

He burst out of the door. All contingency plans, all calculations of his precise mind suddenly seemed out of reach. He just ran.

A gunshot barked behind him, loud and shocking in the quiet night.

Moriarty urged himself to run faster. He had to, for himself and the work as well . . .

He had thoroughly familiarized himself with the map of Prague, but now he found himself uncertain where he was heading.

Another shot resonated through the empty street. He ran harder, almost out of breath now. She was a more capable pursuer than he'd anticipated . . .

Ah, I know it here! There's the way to the riverbank . . .

He made a quick turn.

Faster now, faster . . .

The black water opened before him. On the very edge of the river, Moriarty turned around and ran quickly forward.

Eva Zimmermann was right there, he could almost glimpse her finger closing on the trigger, and then he dodged, less than a second before it was too late . . .

A shriek cut through the night a fraction before the loud splash.

Moriarty staggered back to the riverbank but could see nothing on the black surface.

Could she swim? Did she resurface somewhere?

He couldn't see. He couldn't see . . .

Two days later, sitting safely on a train approaching London, James Moriarty was reading the newest issue of *Prager Tagblatt*, a certain valuable manuscript safely tucked inside his jacket's inner pocket, and a faint smile flickering across his lips. A capable observer would nevertheless notice traces of sadness in his expression.

The very night of the unfortunate pursuit, he retrieved the manuscript from the cache near the railway station where he'd hidden it, and caught the first westbound train. He changed his startling unkempt appearance in Leipzig, and traveled further still to the British Isles without any incidents. In Hamburg, he managed to find and purchase a copy of *Prager Tagblatt*, and found some news of interest. The disappearance of a young lady and a strange attack on her brother, who claimed to have lost all memory of it, made quite a splash in Prague society. The sudden confusion in the criminal community was less apparent but noticeable from the news if one knew what to look for.

He had a lot to think about. Especially Eva Zimmermann. He had to admire the woman, even though she had tried to kill him. *No other woman had ever tried before . . . I wonder if she survived. Shall we meet again in that case?*

She had built a truly remarkable little empire, albeit a short-lived one. He always thought that if he attempted something like that, he'd wait until he had more experience and money – yet her example refuted these concerns.

But Eva Zimmermann did not wrap herself in enough shadows to remain at a safe distance. He should consider it a cautionary tale – not the usual moralistic kind, but a practical one. The fact that she'd heard about him also disturbed him greatly. He should be even more careful from now on. Who knew who else might have got some idea concerning him . . .

I should remain truly unseen, my hands clean and reputation impeccable. But if I engage in any kind of criminal activity, I'm still taking the risk of exposure. How can I avoid that? It's not like I could advise others in crime and stay clean myself . . .

He froze.

That's true, there is perhaps no specialized criminal adviser in the world . . . An empty niche.

Safe and profitable. Ideal for my equations.

Consulting criminal.

The corners of his mouth twitched in an amused smile.

Yes; this sounds good.

The Last Professor Moriarty Story

Andrew Lane

It seems to me, as I look back over the landscape of my life, that the impression I will leave behind is that I have spent most of it chronicling the exploits and adventures of someone else – my close friend Sherlock Holmes. I do not regret this for one moment, but it does seem passing strange to me that my time as an Army doctor in Afghanistan and elsewhere, my ill-advised period of medical practice in San Francisco, my years of service as a general practitioner in London and my many and varied marriages have faded into the shadows, while the image of me sitting in a smoke-filled room on the first floor of a house in Baker Street listening to Sherlock Holmes expound on the differences between various species of grasshopper, or playing his violin with such beauty or such crassness that I was reduced either way to tears, is chiselled into the granite of history. Perhaps it is always the way that we are remembered – *if* we are remembered – for something other than we believe should be the case.

I find that my thoughts are consumed more and more with mortality these days. Gone are the times when I could spring to action, revolver in hand, in support of my friend while he was investigating some bizarre case. My arthritis precludes me springing anywhere these days. Holmes does not move as quickly as he used to either, and his tall frame is stooped now as he moves around our shared living room, but his mind is as sharp as ever.

We left Baker Street behind some years ago. London had

changed for the worse, what with the gradual replacement of horse-drawn carriages by motorised vehicles and the legacy of the bombing raids carried out by the kaiser's infernal rigid dirigibles during the war that has been described by others as 'Great', although I feel it was anything but. I am unsure now which of those two innovations eventually caused us to leave, but after a period apart, I was invited by Holmes to join him in his Sussex cottage, where I could spend my time cataloguing some of his (I do not dare say 'our') past cases that, for various reasons, had gone unrecorded at the time. Mrs Hudson had long since retired to live with her sister in Liverpool, and it is a local lady, Mrs Turner, who now looks after our needs. Sometimes, while staring at the pile of paper beside my typewriter, I do think about writing my own life story, setting down some of the adventures that I have had without Holmes by my side, but the desire soon fades away. I know full well that my place on this Earth is to record for posterity the life of Sherlock Holmes. He provokes an interest in people across the world that I do not.

Holmes, by now, is acting more in a consulting role than as a detective in his own right – partly for those members of the police who still remember him and partly for those secretive areas of government that his brother Mycroft had set up and left behind on his death. We also find that more and more academics from our great universities are seeking him out, not for assistance in solving a mystery, but to interview him about the criminals and crimes of that era, long gone now, that has been given the designation 'Victorian'.

One visitor did, however, cause some disruption in our lives – a visitor connected to a past that we thought was firmly behind us.

It began with the newspaper that was delivered to our cottage one summer's morning. Mrs Turner brought it in with our breakfast. The sun was shining and, looking out through the window into the garden, I could see Holmes's bees forming a cloud around their hive as they left and arrived. Holmes had recently been conducting an experiment whereby he planted different varieties of plants in flowerbeds at set distances from the house, then covered certain ones up, to see whether the bees had any preference and what the effect was on the pollen they collected. For myself, I was firmly in favour of the honey produced after they had visited his lavender flowers. A spoonful of that honey mixed in with a warm glass of whisky was, I found, a tonic for most ailments – and I say that as a medical man.

Holmes turned immediately to the personal advertisements, as was his wont. His bushy eyebrows twitched as he scanned through the small print, gaining some insight into the lives and the foibles of the people who had placed them. Once or twice he frowned, as if his sensitive antennae had picked up on an anomaly therein.

Having read through the personal advertisements, Holmes then turned to the 'Births, Deaths and Marriages' announcements – a section that fascinated him more and more as the years passed. Suddenly, I heard a '*Hah!*' from where he sat. I glanced over to see his face mobilised by an expression of excitement that I had not seen for some time.

'We shall be receiving a visitor,' he said. 'Please tell Mrs Turner to prepare a light lunch.'

'There is something in the newspaper that you will be consulted over?' I asked, an old but familiar tingle running through me. 'A crime of some kind – insoluble and baffling?'

'Alas, there are no decent criminals any more,' Holmes replied. 'The crimes I see reported in the papers every day are bereft of creativity and audacity. Violence has replaced intellect as a means of gaining financial advantage. The war has brutalised the criminal classes as it has brutalised society as a whole.'

'What then?' I asked.

'Professor Moriarty has died,' he said simply.

I felt a strange mixture of relief and bereavement well up within me. Professor Moriarty had been such a part of our lives for so long that I had assumed he and Holmes would either live forever or die simultaneously. The world had, of course, been told once before that they had died together – many years ago, at the Reichenbach Falls in Switzerland. It had taken fully four years for Holmes's survival to be revealed to me and to the world.

Professor Moriarty's survival had taken a little longer to come to light, but since then Holmes had seen his hand in numerous crimes, both here in England and abroad, and had confounded his plans on several occasions. For a variety of reasons I had not publicly chronicled their clashes after the Reichenbach Falls incident, although I have kept copious notes, which I have been gradually expanding into publishable form for posterity. The professor had, however, been notable by his absence from crime for several years, and my assumption was that he had gone into semi-retirement in the same way that Holmes had done. To find out now that he had died was strangely like hearing that some venerable elder statesman or dignitary had passed on.

'Where has he been?' I asked. 'What has he been doing?'

'The good professor was living out his old age quietly in the Malvern Hills under an assumed name,' he said. 'He has provided some consultancy to the next generation of criminals, as I have to the next generation of detectives, but he has devoted most of his remaining time to compiling a *vade mecum* of crime, a comprehensive guide to the planning, preparation and execution of a variety of carefully thought out, nefarious and illegal activities. Blueprints for the perfect crimes, if you like.'

'And how did he die?'

'According to the obituary in the newspaper, he – or, rather, his alter ego – suffered a fall while walking in the hills. He never regained consciousness.'

I had not been an associate of my friend for so many years without picking up a few tricks of my own. 'And you fear that there will be some fight to obtain this document of his before it is destroyed or lost.' I paused for a moment, thinking. 'Ah – more likely, you believe that you will be consulted by the police or the government in the hope that you can *find* this document before anybody else does.'

'You have hit the nail solidly upon the head,' Holmes said. 'The document itself is likely to be of very little use to anybody – as I indicated earlier, today's criminals have replaced intelligence and finesse with explosives and guns. However, as an addendum to his *magnum opus* the late professor has spent his twilight years gathering together material that could be used to blackmail not only the current crop of politicians, diplomats and industrialists, but also men who are still at Oxford or Cambridge and who have been marked for great things in the future.' He snorted. 'It is typical, sadly, of our society that mistakes made in youth can come back to haunt us in adulthood. It is typical of Professor Moriarty that he can store up this compromising material for many years on the assumption that it will eventually prove useful.'

'And *this* is the object you think will be attractive to other criminals?' I asked.

'Indeed.' He paused momentarily. 'I have had an agent in Greater Malvern for some years now, keeping an eye on the professor. He has instructions in the eventuality of the professor's death to gain access to the cottage quickly and search for both documents: the *vade mecum* and the repository of blackmail material.'

'Then the problem is solved, surely!' I exclaimed. 'You have the professor's material, and so all that remains is for us to have a decent lunch with whoever the police or the government send to ask for your assistance.' A thought struck me. 'I shall retrieve a bottle of Beaune from the cellar, I think.'

'Not so fast, old friend,' Holmes said. 'The Professor had lost none of his cunning over the years. I anticipate that he will have secured the material somewhere else – possibly even abroad. My agent will not find it, although one should never fail to conduct the obvious activities for fear of missing something.'

I opened my mouth to make a further observation, but Holmes held up his hand to stop me.

'I know exactly what you are going to say. You are about to tell me that if the professor's material is hidden somewhere then it is beyond the reach of other criminals anyway, and so our job is done for us. I wish that were true. No, I suspect that Moriarty has left clues that would enable a worthy successor to find what he has left as his legacy. The clues will be hard enough that no common criminal can follow them, but not too hard to deter everyone who might try. A fine line to walk, in fact. Now – no more! I have work to do before our visitor arrives!'

Holmes was, as always, correct. At midday precisely there was a knock on the door. Moments later, Mrs Turner showed a young man in a suit in to see us.

'Arthur Chidlow, from the Home Office,' he said, looking from Holmes to me and back. 'Gentlemen, I am frankly honoured and awed to meet you.'

'Please, let us set aside the needless compliments,' Holmes said, although I knew that he was pleased at the fact that his reputation was still as strong as it ever was. 'You are here to ask for my assistance in securing the effects of the late and unlamented Professor James Moriarty.'

Chidlow smiled, and shook his head admiringly. 'News travels fast,' he said. 'As we should, given the circumstances. Do you have any thoughts as to how we should proceed?'

Holmes indicated the newspaper, where it lay on the table beside him. 'The answer is in there,' he said.

Chidlow frowned. 'I read the newspaper on the train,' he said. 'Apart from the bare notification of the death of the professor's other identity, I saw nothing.'

'You saw,' Holmes chided, 'but you did not *notice*. Permit me to draw your attention to the announcements of "Births, Deaths and Marriages".' He glanced at me. 'Watson, perhaps you could do the honours. What do you see there, apart from the particular item that I have circled – the one that announces the death of the professor under his assumed name?'

I picked up the paper and glanced at the page in question while Mrs Turner poured tea for Arthur Chidlow. Something did strike me, as I perused the announcements, and I went back to check to make sure.

'Two items in particular catch my eye,' I said. 'They do not appear to be connected, but they are both in bold, and in the same font – a font that is not used anywhere else on the page.'

'Indeed,' Holmes said. 'Be so kind as to read the first item out.'

'"In memoriam: Maria Jostmery," I read. '"Of Dutch parentage on both sides".' I hesitated. 'Odd phraseology, I grant you, but I do not discern any hidden message.'

'Neither do I,' Chidlow said. 'It seems innocuous enough.'

'I would draw your attention,' Holmes said, 'to the fact that "Dutch parentage on both sides" could indicate that the unfortunate Maria Jostmery is double Dutch. "Double dutch" also means "nonsense", of course, and if we rearrange the letters of her name to make more sense then we get "James Moriarty".'

Arthur Chidlow hit his forehead with the heel of his hand. 'How stupid of me!' he cried.

I felt much the same way, but I hid it better. 'All that we have there is the professor's name,' I pointed out. 'That tells us nothing.'

'Look at the second entry in the same emboldened font. Read it out, please.'

I did so: '"Re: Tim and Sam Mirnlic. Rearranged funeral service at St Alkmund's Chapel, Wimbledon: Tues, nine o'clock prompt."' I glanced at Holmes. 'The name is unusual, probably Eastern European, and the use of abbreviated Christian names is regrettably casual, but that is a sign of the times, I fear. I presume, however, that we are not dealing with the deaths of two brothers of foreign extraction here?'

Chidlow had been scribbling notes on the back of his hand. 'It's another anagram,' he said. ' "Re: Tim and Sam Mirnilc" can be *rearranged*, as the announcement suggests, into the words "criminal mastermind".'

Holmes laughed. 'A jibe directed at me, I suggest,' he said. 'The late professor knew that I would be keeping an eye out, and I have certainly described him in those terms often enough. Interesting that he had taken it so much to heart. He must have had his own agents ready and waiting to submit these items upon his death.' He glanced at Chidlow, and then at me. 'If we want to know more then I suggest we attend St Alkmund's Chapel in Wimbledon tomorrow morning for the funeral service of Timothy and Samuel Mirnilc.'

After lunch, and a closer examination of the newspaper to little effect, Arthur Chidlow left for London, with an agreement that we would meet outside the indicated chapel at a quarter to nine the next day. Later that afternoon, a telegram arrived for Holmes from his agent in Greater Malvern, confirming that there had been nothing of interest in the professor's cottage. Holmes spent the rest of the day tending to his bees, while I read and reread the newspaper, looking in vain for more hidden messages.

Holmes and I caught the milk train to London before sunrise the next day, and at the appointed time we were at the chapel: a small church of grey stone located in the middle of a row of grey houses. Arthur Chidlow was already waiting for us, wrapped up in an overcoat and in a state of some agitation.

'I have seen a large number of men enter the chapel,' he said. 'Several I recognised as being members of the various criminal gangs that currently vie for control of London and the Home Counties.'

'No Eastern European relatives then?' I asked facetiously. 'At least this isn't a real funeral service.'

'To my certain knowledge,' he went on as if I had said nothing, 'there are representatives of the Yiddishers, the Hoxton Mob, the Bessarabian Tigers, the King's Cross Gang and the Watney Streeters in there – it's like a villains' League of Nations! What's going on?'

'I suspect we are here for a cross between the criminal version of the reading of Professor Moriarty's will and a treasure hunt,' Holmes said darkly. 'Everyone in there wants Professor Moriarty's list of current and future blackmail targets, and possibly his guide to conducting criminal operations as well. The only question is: what will the professor be asking them to do for it, from beyond the grave?'

'Most of them sent their bodyguards or followers in to search the place first,' Chidlow continued. 'I presume they wanted to make sure that the professor did not intend settling some old scores from beyond the grave by means of a well-placed bomb.'

'That is not the professor's style,' Holmes said. 'I think they are projecting their own blunt methods upon him.'

'Forgive me,' I said, 'but if you recognise them, can't you just arrest them and save yourself a lot of trouble?'

Chidlow shrugged. 'I wish I could, Doctor. I may know who they are and what they have done, but I have no real evidence. No court of law would believe me.'

'Exactly the problem I have had with Professor Moriarty all these years,' Holmes pointed out.

We entered into the chapel. It was small, with barely ten rows of pews. At the front, in the midst of the area set out for the choir, was a table. On the table was a wind-up gramophone player.

The pews were nearly filled with a ragtag selection of humanity's worst representatives. Some were well dressed and some not so much, but they all bore marks of violence such as scars, flattened noses and cauliflower ears. One man, of Maltese extraction I believe, had twin letter 'H's carved into his cheeks. I wasn't sure if that was a mark of belonging to some gang or the sign that he had displeased someone with a sharp knife.

Everybody turned to look at us as we entered, but nobody seemed willing to dispute our reasons for being there. We slid into three spaces at the end of a pew. I found myself sitting next to an elderly man with a wizened face and a mane of white hair. His head projected from his old-fashioned wing collar like that of a tortoise from its shell. He glanced briefly at me and nodded, then looked away. I couldn't help but wonder which criminal fraternity he was associated with. Perhaps he had just wandered in to warm his old bones.

I checked my watch. It was very nearly nine o'clock, and a flurry of excitement ran through the cold, draughty chapel as a man walked in from the vestry towards the record player. He was holding a shellac phonograph of the same kind that Holmes used to listen to music. The man was nondescript – in his early forties, perhaps – and expressionless. He wore spectacles with round, smoked lenses. Without looking at his audience, he bent over, placed the phonograph on the gramophone player, lifted the stylus and placed it at the beginning of the disc, and then wound the gramophone up and started it going.

A crackling sound filled the chapel. We listened expectantly and, after a few moments, a voice started to speak. It was rough and distorted, but I recognised it as the ash-dry voice of Professor James Moriarty.

'I predict that there will be a reasonably large audience for this, my final declaration,' he said. 'I will not bore you with any preamble, any list of my accomplishments or any attempt to have the final word in the various verbal disputes I have entered into over the years. That will gain me nothing now, and you would not be here if you were not already familiar with my history. As I do not believe in Heaven, Hell or a Deity of any kind, I can only assume that my consciousness, my genius and all my memories have now dissipated into the random motion of atoms and molecules. All that I leave behind is this recording, my various published works of a mathematical or scientific nature, and the unpublished manuscript of my philosophical and practical dissertation on crime, with descriptions of practical examples.' He paused momentarily, leaving a silence broken only by crackles and pops from the phonograph. I had never credited Professor Moriarty with a sense of humour, but he did seem to be pausing for effect. 'It is the latter,' he went on, 'for which I presume you are all here.'

'I cannot help,' Holmes whispered, 'admire a man who refuses to drop a participle, even in death.'

'Money is of no use to me now,' the professor's voice continued, 'yet I do not wish to just give my life's work away to the first person who can get to it and fight the rest of you off. My observations over the past few years depress me: there is little intelligence and even less creativity in English crime now. From the continent has come a flood of clumsy protection schemes and drug rackets, whilst from America has come inter-gang warfare conducted by means of machine guns and "concrete boots". I confess to wishing that someone with even a fraction of my wit could weld all of this rough material together and hew it into the kind of organisation that could control crime across entire continents. The problem, of course, is that most criminals these days have a one-track mind – excessive violence is the only solution. Solving this mystery will require more than a single-track approach.'

'A frightening thought,' Chidlow murmured.

'If you are worthy, then this recording is all you will need in order to find my manuscript. I mean that literally – you need consider nothing else in this chapel but the phonograph you see revolving in front of you. My agent, who is standing before you, knows absolutely nothing. His sole instructions have been to be here at a certain time, to play this recording as many times as you require and to take it away and smash it when you have exhausted its possibilities. If you try to take the recording away with you then he is instructed to smash it anyway. I cannot wish you good luck, for luck is nothing but mathematical probabilities resolving themselves in a favourable manner. Nevertheless, I do hope that at least one of you can solve the mystery and prove to me that my work will go on.'

The professor's voice fell silent, leaving only clicks and pops behind as the stylus circled endlessly in its final groove. A murmur filled the chapel as the various criminals and gang members discussed what they had heard.

The man with the carved 'H's in his cheeks stood up. 'Play it again,' he ordered in a gruff, accented voice.

The man staffing beside the gramophone nodded. He lifted the stylus from the phonograph and moved it back to the beginning.

We sat there, silent, as the professor's voice echoed around the chapel again, repeating everything he had said previously. Some in the audience – perhaps I should say 'congregation' – made notes, while others strained to hear if there was anything in the background, any other noises that might give the location of Moriarty's baleful manuscript away. Holmes leaned back against the pew, eyes closed, his fingers moving as if he was conducting an orchestra.

A man whom I took to be of Italian extraction, based on the width of his lapels, stood up and walked to the front of the chapel. 'Let me see that thing,' he said, pointing to the disc.

Another man – swarthy and unshaven – stood up and said: 'If you try to touch that, I'll cut you – I swear I will.'

The Italian turned and stared at him. 'Sit down,' he said quietly, 'or I'll slice your throat open and pull your tongue through the hole like a necktie.'

The swarthy man sat down, muttering, and the Italian man held out his hand. Moriarty's agent took the phonograph from the gramophone and handed it across. The Italian examined it carefully, turning it over and over in his hands.

'No label,' he said eventually.

'What about the other side?' someone called from the back of the pews. 'Play that!'

The Italian held the disc up so that everyone could see it. The reverse side was smooth. 'Nothing there,' he said. 'It's single-sided.'

'Again!' an East End thug said. He looked as if he would be more at home in a boxing ring than in a chapel. 'Play the damned thing again, and louder this time!'

In all, we listened to the professor's voice say the exact same things fourteen more times. By the end of the final recital I could have repeated his speech word for word, with all the gaps intact.

Some of the criminals had left after a few replays. Judging by their expressions they were disappointed and angry that Moriarty's final secret had not been revealed in a more obvious manner. Others huddled together in small groups, comparing notes and attempting to descry whatever hidden clues Moriarty had left behind – if, indeed, this entire performance hadn't been a charade intended as a final insult from a dead master criminal. All the while, Moriarty's agent had moved to one side when it became obvious that nobody wanted to hear the recording a sixteenth time. The table, the phonograph and the gramophone he had left behind. A small group of criminals had gathered around it and were examining the record, turning it over in their hands and looking for some hidden message. Others were arguing with Moriarty's agent, trying to get him to talk, but he kept shaking his head, saying nothing.

The elderly man beside me had listened to each reply, head thrust forward and eyes closed. Eventually, he too shook his head, made a 'Tch!' sound, stood up and pushed past the three of us. When he got to the aisle he turned and shook his fist at the gramophone player, his lips moving silently. He shuffled out.

There were barely half of the original attendees present by then. Holmes gestured to me and to Chidlow that we should join him at the back of the chapel. When he got there, in the relative shadows, he turned to us. 'What do you think?' he asked.

'I am at a loss,' Chidlow said. His expression was grim. 'I am hoping that you, Mr Holmes, have managed to spot something that I have not.'

'Watson?' Holmes asked, turning to me.

'Assuming that the Italian gentleman is correct, and that the phonograph has no label affixed to it, then the only thing I can think is that there is something scratched into the shellac itself.' I nodded towards the front of the chapel. 'I suspect, however, that the gentlemen up there have been examining it for exactly that.'

'And such a clumsy means of hiding information would be beneath the professor's dignity,' Holmes pointed out. 'This is his final problem. He will not have made it easy for his putative successor.'

'Does nothing occur to you, Mr Holmes?' Chidlow asked despondently. 'I cannot help thinking that one of the criminals who has already left has picked up on a clue that has passed the rest of us by.'

Holmes stared at him from beneath his bushy eyebrows. 'I seriously doubt,' he growled, 'that any of these people has spotted a clue that has evaded my attention.'

'Then you have spotted no clues yourself?' he pressed.

Holmes looked away. 'There are some indicative factors,' he muttered. 'But nothing definitive. Let us take our own look at the gramophone and the phonograph. Perhaps we may see something that the others have missed.'

Holmes led the way to the front of the chapel. There were eleven men still there, standing around and looking uncertain. One or two were talking together, but most of them appeared to have decided that they would operate alone.

Holmes went straight to the gramophone. As he approached it, Moriarty's agent took a step forward. He watched to make sure that Holmes didn't try to remove the disc. I noticed a bulge beneath his jacket: he was armed, and presumably willing to use force to ensure that the professor's instructions were followed to the letter. His face was as expressionless as ever, and his eyes were invisible behind his shaded lenses.

Holmes picked up the phonograph and checked it minutely. 'No label, as we were told,' he murmured, 'no recording on the other side, and no extra information scratched into the material. I am beginning to think – hello, what's this?'

'Something of interest?' Chidlow pressed, moving closer. Several other men from the congregation moved closer to listen.

'Ah, it is nothing,' Holmes said dismissively, and handed the phonograph back to Moriarty's agent. The criminals moved away again, disappointed.

'What if,' I suggested in a whisper, a thought having struck me, 'the clicks and pops on the recording that we were meant to assume were caused by scratches were actually some kind of introduced code!'

'That's it!' Chidlow said excitedly.

'Alas, no.' Holmes shook his head. 'Your suggestion is plausible, but it had already occurred to me. During the fifteen repeats of the message, I timed the occurrence of the apparently extraneous sounds using my heartbeat as a guide. I discerned no regular pattern – they occurred randomly, as far as I could tell.' He smiled slightly. 'I did detect something else, however, which I will tell you about in a moment.'

Chidlow frowned. 'What about the gramophone itself? Is there something about it that might provide a clue?'

Holmes shook his head. 'Moriarty himself clearly said: *"this recording is all you will need in order to find my manuscript. I mean that literally – you need consider nothing else in this chapel but the phonograph you see revolving in front of you"*. I think, under the circumstances, we have to take the professor at his word.'

We stood there silently for a while, as the last few criminals drifted away. Eventually, we were alone in the chapel with the gramophone, the phonograph, the table and Moriarty's agent. He looked at us, his face still impassive, then nodded towards the gramophone – enquiring, I suppose, whether we needed it any more. Holmes shook his head, and the man busied himself with slipping the phonograph into a cardboard sleeve, then lifting it and the gramophone off the table and carrying them away.

'We can talk now,' Holmes said. 'Everyone else has left – either disappointed that the professor wasn't being any clearer or because they think they have detected his hidden message and are currently following whatever clues they think they spotted and everyone else missed.' He paused, smiling. 'I can guarantee that none of them have spotted the real clue.'

Chidlow stared at Holmes with something close to awe in his eyes. 'You *did* hear something! What was it?'

'Did you remark upon the fact that the professor made reference to this very place?' Holmes asked.

Chidlow frowned. 'I believe he did mention it. You used the phrase just now.'

'He said,' I recalled, ' *"you need consider nothing else in this chapel but the phonograph you see revolving in front of you"*.'

'No, he said "church", not "chapel",' Chidlow corrected me.

'I am fairly sure he said "chapel",' I countered.

'In fact,' Holmes interrupted, 'he said both.'

Chidlow and I stared at one another. 'How is that possible?' the Home Office man asked.

'I memorised the entire recitation the first time it was played,' Holmes replied. 'Moriarty clearly said "chapel" then. On the subsequent fifteen repeats, he said "chapel" eight times and "church" seven times.'

'But . . .' My brain was turning over and over in confusion. 'But there was only one recording!'

'Not so,' Holmes explained triumphantly. 'The phonograph contains not *one* spiral groove into which the professor's words have been encoded by means of vibration, but two, each running alongside the other. Whether the stylus falls into the first groove or the second one when Moriarty's man places it on the shellac is up to chance. Each groove contains the same message with one crucial difference – in one he uses the word "chapel" and in the other he uses the word "church".'

'He told us,' I whispered. 'He actually *told* us. He said: "*Solving this mystery will require more than a single-track approach*". He was right! We needed both tracks!'

Chidlow nodded thoughtfully. 'That has to be significant,' he mused. 'Chapel and church – but what could it mean? Is his manuscript here, in the building – close by for us to find?'

'Certainly not,' Holmes said. 'Take those two words and ignore the rest of the message. "Chapel" and "church". Ignore the common letters – this gives us the apparently meaningless "apel" and "urch". Now remember Moriarty's fondness for anagrams, as demonstrated in yesterday's newspaper. Swap around the initial vowels and we get "uple" and "arch". Rearrange "uple" and we get "Lupe", which is an administrative region in the centre of France.' He smiled. 'Being of French descent on my mother's side, I recognised it instantly. I would suggest that if you travel to the small region of Lupe you will find a decorative arch, commemorating the Great War perhaps, or as the entrance to some public building. Professor Moriarty's legacy will be there, buried at the base of the arch like the treasure at the end of a rainbow!'

'Incredible!' Chidlow breathed. 'Mister Holmes, you are a marvel – a true marvel. I must arrange travel immediately. Are you gentlemen happy to make your own way home if I leave you here? Be assured, you have provided your government with a great service.'

'You must go, of course,' Holmes said, patting the Home Office man on the shoulder. 'Send us a telegram when you have found the professor's manuscript, and the list of potential blackmail subjects.'

'I will!' he called back over his shoulder as he sprinted down the aisle.

I shook my head. 'Holmes, you continue to amaze me, even now.'

He smiled. 'There will be no telegram,' he said, as we heard the door at the front of the chapel slam.

'You don't think he will find the manuscript?'

'Oh, I am quite sure he will find it. The problem is that his name isn't Arthur Chidlow, and he does not work for the Home Office.' He cocked his head to one side and raised his voice. 'Does he, Professor?'

The Professor's agent stepped out of the shadows. The smoked glass of his round spectacles made his eyes look like two dark holes in his face. He reached up and removed them. Underneath, his eyes were a watery and faded blue, and they seemed to have dark rings all the way around them. Abruptly, he pulled the hair from his head, revealing it to be a wig covering a bald, liver-spotted pate. He reached behind his head with both hands and pulled forwards. His entire *face* seemed to sag as he peeled it off. Underneath were the lined features and querulous expression of a man I had seen several times before in my life. Professor James Moriarty.

I could feel my heart beating rapidly in my chest, and the stone floor of the chapel seemed to lurch under my feet. I took several deep breaths to calm myself down. At my age, shock is something that should be avoided whenever possible.

'His true name is Jon Paulson,' Moriarty said in the same dry-as-dust voice that I had recently heard on the phonograph. He placed the wig and the mask – made from some kind of gutta-percha, I suspected – on the table where the gramophone had been. 'He is, perhaps, the closest I have to a rival in the criminal fraternity. Unlike his rivals, he is a clear thinker, able to plan and execute the most complex of operations. There are numerous fake paintings hanging in galleries around the world in place of those he has stolen, and I would also recommend that the Bank of England checks all of the gold bars in its vaults for purity. Some of them are merely lead covered with a thin gold film. I presume it was his shoelaces that gave him away?'

'That,' Holmes said calmly, as if discussing the weather, 'and the knot in his tie.'

Moriarty gazed at Holmes in curiosity. 'What gave me away, Mister Holmes?'

'Your neck seemed older than your face,' Holmes replied. 'That, and the slight but noticeable extra muscular development of your neck muscles due to that habitual nervous tic you have exhibited for so long.'

Moriarty nodded. 'It is now under control, thanks to recent developments in pharmaceutical products. I should have worn a neck prosthesis, as well as the mask.' He smiled thinly. 'Ironic, is it not, that you have spent so many years made up to resemble various older people, whereas it is left to me to disguise myself as someone younger?'

My brain was slow to catch up with the apparently casual conversation that the two of them were having. 'So Arthur Chidlow *wasn't* Arthur Chidlow at all, but a career criminal named Jon Paulson?' I shook my head. 'And he retained Holmes's services to help solve the final mystery of your legacy, which turned out not to be your legacy at all? But why go through this elaborate charade?'

'Mister Holmes?' Moriarty murmured, raising an eyebrow.

'The professor was simply eliminating his closest competition.' He raised his own bushy eyebrow at the professor. 'What will he find, Professor?'

'A bomb, I presume?' I muttered.

Moriarty shook his head. 'I abhor the kind of casual violence that the criminals such as the ones gathered here today exhibit. No, the manuscript is there, as promised. The problem that Mr Paulson will find is that the crimes so meticulously described have several major flaws in them. If he tries to replicate them then he will fail, catastrophically and embarrassingly.'

'If he is as intelligent as you say, he may spot the flaws,' I pointed out.

'That would be a distinct possibility if the pages of the manuscript had not been coated with a chemical that I have distilled from ergot fungus. It will render him . . . highly suggestible and subject to strange hallucinations. He will believe what he reads without question.' He smiled – a stricture of the mouth that had no humour in it, and made him look momentarily like a venomous snake. 'If he does try to "adjust" my instructions whilst under the influence of the ergot derivative then I will be intrigued to see how close to surrealism crime can get.'

'And the blackmail information,' Holmes asked. 'Completely false, I presume?'

'Indeed. It should prove most entertaining if he tries to make use of it.'

I glanced from Holmes to Moriarty and then back again. 'Surely,' I started, 'we should . . .'

'We should *what*?' Holmes asked. 'Stop one criminal from rushing off to find a fake manuscript left as a trick by another criminal? Why is that something we should concern ourselves with? Arrest either of these criminals for breaking a law? Which laws have either of them broken to our knowledge? Somehow raise concerns that the professor here has faked his own death? The newspaper announcement was not a legal notification and, besides, it mentioned a name belonging to no real human being, as far as we know.' He laughed abruptly. 'Well played, Professor. Well played indeed.'

'Believe it or not, your praise means a great deal to me, Mister Holmes. Thank you.' His head moved slowly left and right: a nervous habit now, I presume, rather than an actual physical problem. 'You and I are living fossils, Mister Holmes, like the horseshoe crab. The world has evolved around us, leaving us behind, stranded on the beach of time. I have spent the last few years regretting this, and I have decided – reluctantly – to do something about it. I am coming out of retirement, Mister Holmes. Thanks to the pharmaceutical industry I expect I have a good few years left in me, as have you. I give you fair warning that I am planning something that will rock this nation to its very foundations. Stop me if you dare, Mister Holmes. Stop me if you *can*.'

Holmes gazed at the professor for a long moment, then turned to me. He seemed to be standing straighter, and his face, although still lined and old, was alive with fierce intelligence.

'Professor,' he said firmly, 'it will be my pleasure.'

Quid Pro Quo

Ashley R. Lister

December 1867

"You summoned me, Professor Moriarty?"

Moriarty glanced up from his paperwork and shook his head. His features were sharp and angular. He was youthful, barely out of his twenties, but his hair was already the grey of a pending thunderstorm. He could have appeared austere and menacing if not for the brightness of his genial smile. The flash of his teeth shone with obvious good humour and kind, inoffensive mirth.

"Professor?" Moriarty laughed. "Goodness, no. I'm likely the Moriarty you're looking for. It's not a common name around these parts. But I'm not a professor. I'm only a humble reader. I haven't been offered the chair yet."

He encouraged his visitor to enter the room and motioned for him to sit on the other side of his cluttered desk. There was still snow dusting the shoulders of the visitor's woollen jacket. His uncapped head glistened with melting snowflakes, which perspired down his brow and over his cheeks.

"Please," Moriarty insisted. "Make yourself comfortable. The weather is very festive today, isn't it?"

"Thank you, Professor."

Like many of the academic offices in the university, Moriarty's quarters were cramped to the point of claustrophobia. The shelved walls were overflowing with books. The desk was littered with pens, pencils, correspondence, papers, opened and unopened tomes, and piles and piles of marked and unmarked assignments. A copy of that month's *Lancet* lay open on the page with Lister's article about the benefits of his "antiseptic surgical method". Beside that was a copy of that morning's *Times*, head-lined with the words CLERKENWELL OUTRAGE.

Moriarty tapped the largest bundle of papers on his desk and said, "Unless my treatise on the binomial theory meets with unprecedented success, I'm likely to remain a humble reader here for a long while."

His guest, settling into the discomfort of the office's only other seat, said nothing.

Moriarty found a black leather-bound notebook on his desk and began to leaf through the bright-white pages. The size and shape of the book suggested it might be a diary or a jour-nal. Lettered in gold on the front were the words *"quid pro quo"*. Chasing his finger down one neatly written journal entry, Moriarty's lips moved as he read through his day's scheduled appointments. Eventually, he looked up from the book with a grin.

"It's Gordon, isn't it?"

Gordon nodded.

"Thank you for taking the time to come up here, Gordon. I understand you have a lot of important assignments to complete before the university closes for the Christmas holidays so it's very much appreciated."

"Why did you want to see me?"

"Good," Moriarty laughed. "You're direct. I like that. It suggests a focused mind."

Gordon said nothing. He waited expectantly.

Moriarty picked up the leather-bound notebook and waved it importantly in the air as though it explained everything. "Professor Bell asked me to read through one of your papers. He believes you've been cheating."

The light in the office was good. It was lit by a large window to the east and the morning sun washed the room with stark wintery warmth. Snow on the sills and ledges added to the brightness, making every detail in Moriarty's quarters superbly lit.

The sunlight illuminated Gordon's face.

After Moriarty mentioned the accusation of cheating, Gordon's pale cheeks blushed with the faintest hint of pink. His lips remained closed. His mouth was an inscrutable line, neither smiling nor frowning. Purposefully, he said nothing.

"This is a serious allegation," Moriarty went on. His tone was etched with concern. "You're in your final year, Gordon. It has to be said, your results on the whole have been unremarkable so far. But, up to this point, they've always been deemed honest. This accusation could prove ruinous for you."

Gordon remained silent and motionless.

Moriarty watched the young man intently.

"You'll note that I said 'the accusation could prove ruinous'," he went on. "With a scandal like this the accusation doesn't have to be true. Accusations alone are often enough to devastate a fledgling career." He pointed at the newspaper headline: CLERK-ENWELL OUTRAGE – a dozen dead, one hundred injured. "If they're left unchecked, accusations can have that sort of impact," he said darkly.

Gordon met his gaze. His lips didn't move.

"What do you have to say for yourself, Gordon?"

Gordon straightened in his chair. He rolled his broad shoulders and squared his jaw. "I don't suppose it matters what I have to say for myself," he began carefully. "If Professor Bell asked you to read through my paper, the only thing that matters is what you think. Do you think I've been cheating?"

Moriarty laughed again. It was a cheery sound and his tone seemed genuine.

"I wouldn't want to play cards with you, Gordon," he decided. "I'd wager you've won a fair share of bluffs in your day, haven't you?"

Gordon didn't answer.

The silence that stretched between them bordered on being interminable.

Moriarty reached for pen, ink and paper. He placed them on the blotter and began to write a missive. As he wrote in a fussily neat hand, he read the words aloud.

"Dear Professor Bell," he began.

Gordon's eyes narrowed.

"At your request I have carefully examined the academic paper you suspected of being plagiarised."

Moriarty glanced up from the note and studied his visitor.

Gordon tapped his shoe lightly on the floor. He could have been trying to dislodge snow from the tread, Moriarty thought. But, from the student's posture, it seemed obvious that the toe of his boot was now pointing towards the office door. Even if Gordon was unaware of the fact, Moriarty thought, the young man appeared to be planning an escape route.

"I can understand why you had suspicions about this piece." Moriarty continued to read the words aloud as he wrote them. "After having read some of the other works you feared had been copied, I also noted that there were some strong similarities in their structure, lexical choice and derivative conclusions."

Gordon's lips had tightened to a puckered scowl.

Wrinkles of concentration creased his otherwise smooth brow.

His hands were curled into fists.

Despite what he'd said before, Moriarty suspected, if Gordon really was a poker player, he should be well advised to limit his gambling to low stakes games. The blush was now more than a faint suggestion of pink. It was difficult to tell where the melting snow ended and Gordon's nervous perspiration began.

"However," Moriarty continued.

He paused long enough to write the word.

"I am comfortable confirming that, in my opinion, this is all original work. The student appears to have worked hard on this paper. His efforts, whilst wholly conventional and lacking in imagination, are all his own endeavours. I trust his labours will be acknowledged appropriately without further recourse to unfounded accusation."

Moriarty added his signature to the letter. Gordon watched him fold it three times and seal it with wax before sitting back in his chair.

"Why did you do that?"

"You really are very direct," Moriarty mused. "I do admire that quality. It shows a discipline of thought that so many lack." He pointed at the open *Lancet* article on his desk and said, "That's the same level of disciplined thought as Doctor Lister has shown in using carbolic acid to treat infection during surgical procedures. If only more of us could be like that great man."

"Why have you just declared me innocent of plagiarism?"

Moriarty closed his journal. His fingers drummed on the gold-lettered words: *quid pro quo*. Eventually, he picked up the book and the letter and started out of the door. "Follow me, Gordon," he called over his shoulder. "Let's see if Professor Bell is in his office."

He didn't bother looking back to see if Gordon obeyed the instruction. He turned a sharp right out of his doorway and headed along an ancient Yorkshire stone corridor that led towards the courtyard. Readers and professors alike were dressed in a uniform of cap, gown and hood at all times. Moriarty's robes flowed behind him like black waves of night. He marched through the halls that led to the courtyard with a brisk pace that made Gordon stumble to keep by his side. His boot heels clipped loudly against the stone floors of the university's hallowed corridors.

Passing students and lecturers nodded curt greetings to Moriarty.

The occasional student stopped to doff a cap.

Moriarty acknowledged each address with a polite smile and a word of greeting. He had the charming ability of remembering faces and calling people by their names and titles. It was no wonder, Gordon thought, that the man was so popular in the university's halls.

"You haven't answered my question," Gordon reminded him. He kept his voice lowered to a hush. "Why have you told Professor Bell that I'm innocent?"

Moriarty opened his mouth as though he was about to reply.

"Sir?"

Before Moriarty could speak a red-headed youth stepped in front of him, stopping him abruptly. His whey-coloured complexion was lost beneath a murk of rusty freckles. His clothes had the pristine cut and starch of a privileged third year. Over one shoulder he carried a boxy leather bag. Clinking noises came from within the bag. Gordon recognised the sound as the musical tones of full glass bottles kissing together.

For an instant Gordon thought he could see a menacing glower on Moriarty's features. Unlike the honest smile and full joviality of the man's usual disposition, this was an expression that seemed appropriate for the narrow face and the iron-grey hair. This expression was a flicker of feral ferocity that could have belonged to a very violent man. If the expression had rested for an instant longer, Gordon would have stepped between the pair to prevent the younger man from suffering injury. Moriarty was raising his arm and looked set to smash the whey-faced youth to the floor.

"Sir," the redhead youth repeated earnestly. "I was just coming up to find you. Indeed, this is fortuitous."

"Hunt," Moriarty beamed. He brought his arm down and clapped Hunt warmly on the shoulder.

Whatever suggestion of menace Gordon had thought was in Moriarty's expression now seemed to have disappeared. The idea that it might ever have been there struck Gordon as damning evidence for the poor quality of his imagination.

"I thought you'd have left by now," Moriarty told Hunt. "Don't tell me you want to do another year's Latin?"

Hunt laughed with inordinate enthusiasm. He clutched Moriarty's hand and pumped it enthusiastically up and down. Glancing slyly at Gordon, he said, "Do you know this fine gentleman is the only reason I was able to continue my studies?"

Gordon raised an eyebrow, encouraging him to continue.

"I had the most miserable first year," Hunt explained. "My interest in economics was failing. I didn't feel as though I'd made any friends at the university. But Professor Moriarty here—"

"I'm not a professor," Moriarty cautioned him. "I'm only a humble reader. I haven't been offered the chair yet."

The interruption seemed to surprise Hunt. "Haven't you submitted your treatise on the binomial theory?"

"Yes, but Professor Phillips remains the incumbent in the

mathematics chair. And, unless my treatise meets with unprecedented success before the board of governors, I'm likely to
remain a humble reader here for a long while."

Hunt laughed again. This time the mirth sounded like genuine
merriment rather than the forced laughter of a sycophant. "I
think the board of governors will have to offer you a chair when
they see your treatise. It's the work of a genius."

Moriarty lowered his gaze and looked abashed. "You're too
kind, Hunt. I'm sure I'd feel a lot more comfortable about such
a situation if you were on the board of governors."

Hunt shook his head apologetically. "The only person I know
on the board is Williamson's father and you know that Williamson
and I don't see eye to eye." Hunt paused and added, "Of course
you know about that. You were the one who intervened when
Williamson demanded I face him in a duel."

As Gordon watched, Moriarty tightened his hold on the
leather-bound volume. His thumb ran along the gold-printed
lettering on the cover. He seemed to be tracing the shape of each
letter in the three Latin words: *quid pro quo.*

"Headstrong Williamson," Moriarty remembered. "He really
did fancy himself as the romantic hero of some *Boys of England*
narrative, didn't he?"

Hunt laughed.

"And," Moriarty went on, "now you mention it, I do believe
you're correct. Williamson's father is on the board of governors,
isn't he?"

Hunt nodded.

"Williamson's father did seem relieved that I'd been able to
talk his son out of facing you with pistols at dawn," Moriarty
remembered.

Gordon watched the pair. The three of them stood in tableau
for a moment before Hunt finally spoke.

"I just wanted to thank you again," he said. From the bag he
was carrying he produced a bottle of whisky. Gordon could see
the words *Ballantine's Finest* printed on the label as Hunt passed
the bottle to Moriarty. "It's a token of my gratitude, sir."

"Whisky?" Moriarty seemed curious.

"Just a small token," Hunt assured him. "And if there's ever anything else you need from me in the future . . ."

He left the open promise of eternal obligation unspoken.

It hung between them like a physical presence.

Moriarty smiled and graciously accepted the gift. "Thank you, Hunt," he said solemnly. "It's been a pleasure having you in my lectures." He lifted the whisky and added, "I'll make sure to toast your name when I open this bottle."

Hunt grinned. His teeth were crooked but his smile was easy to like.

Moriarty stepped past him and continued on his way to the courtyard. Over his shoulder he called back, "Hunt, please congratulate your father on his promotion to governorship of the Bank of England." As he said the words, like a curious involuntary action, his hand squeezed on the book. His thumb rubbed across the lettering: *quid pro quo.*

"How did you help him with the bullies?"

Moriarty shook his head. "It was nothing really. Hunt is prone to bullying. I suspect it's with him being red-headed. Many people assume a red-headed man has Irish blood in his veins and there's always been a lot of anti-Irish sentiment brewing in this country." He frowned and said, "I suspect it will get worse after the Clerkenwell outrage last night."

Gordon nodded agreement. He'd read that morning's *Times* before visiting Moriarty. The explosion at the Clerkenwell detention centre appeared to have been an ill-conceived catastrophe. Fenian activists had botched an attempt to help one of their comrades escape incarceration. Twelve innocents were dead. More than a hundred had been injured.

"Is Hunt Irish?"

"No," Moriarty admitted. "There's no Gaelic in his lineage. But that didn't stop a gang of students from making his existence a misery because they thought he looked Irish."

"How did you intervene?"

Moriarty paused and turned to face Gordon. His thumb stroked the gold letters on the book again. "We came to an amicable agreement about the situation," he said carefully.

"Some of those involved in the bullying come from prominent families. You know Gladstone's children come here, don't you?"

Gordon nodded. He was aware that the leader of the opposition's children patronised the university. Cohorts over the previous years had included European royalty, the sons of celebrated military heroes and the children of industrial tycoons. Gordon considered himself fortunate that his parents had invested so much into his education so he could study alongside the future leaders of the country.

"A lot of prominent families send their children here," he agreed.

Moriarty nodded.

"Hunt's family didn't want to pursue the incidence of bullying. They were aware that things could reflect badly on Hunt if he was perceived weak enough to be a victim of bullying. The families of the bullies were equally relieved to learn that the matter was being resolved without becoming public knowledge. The whole situation was resolved amicably."

Gordon digested this quietly for a moment. Hunt and his family were now indebted to Moriarty. The eminent families of a gang of bullies were equally beholden to him. Was there anyone in the university who didn't owe this kind man some small favour? Was there anyone in the universe who wasn't in his debt?

"How do they pay you back?"

Moriarty blushed. He turned and started back towards the courtyard. "We all find a way to pay our debts, Gordon."

Gordon wanted to pursue the matter, but Moriarty had reached the courtyard and was striding purposefully towards Professor Bell's offices.

The lawns were covered in a thin veil of white. The slates of the building roofs were frosted with snow. The air was cold enough to make each exhalation plume softly. Moriarty seemed embarrassed by the question of repayment and Gordon was trying to think of a way to retract the question. Before Gordon could find the right way to put his thoughts into words they were again interrupted.

A tall, broad man approached. He walked with the gait of a

military gentleman. A stick in his right hand clipped softly through the snow as an accompaniment to every other step. Moriarty slowed as the man neared and, when they were close enough, the pair clasped hands with the ferocity of lifelong friends.

"Sebastian Moran," Moriarty called cheerfully. "It's so good to see you."

"Likewise, Professor."

Moriarty laughed the epithet away. "I'm not a professor yet. I'm only a humble reader. I haven't been offered the chair yet."

"Haven't you submitted your treatise on the binomial theory?"

"It's been submitted," Moriarty assured Moran. "I'm waiting for feedback from the board of governors. And even then, there's the issue of Professor Phillips."

Moran sighed. "Did you see the Fenians botched their escape plans last night?"

"I read the piece in *The Times*." Moriarty shook his head sadly. "Some people say the city is in the grip of an organised criminal mastermind but this seems to have been a very disorganised affair."

"Informers had notified authorities," Moran told him. "But the authorities didn't heed those warnings."

"It's almost as though they were given help," Moriarty mused. He stared wistfully across the courtyard. He seemed unmindful of the light snow falling about him. "It's almost as if some mastermind, acting in the interests of the Irish Republican Brotherhood, called in favours and asked figures in authority to turn a blind eye to any of the warnings they received." His thumb rubbed across the gold lettering on his leather-bound volume: *quid pro quo*. His smile looked to have frozen in the chill morning air. "It's almost as though someone went to all that trouble. And still the Fenians botched everything."

Moran cleared his throat.

Moriarty frowned and studied Moran with a peevish glare.

Moran nodded at Gordon. "I'm sure this student doesn't want to hear about your speculation on last night's bombing," Moran said pointedly.

"A good point," Moriarty agreed. "Perhaps we should meet for lunch this afternoon and share our speculation on the Irish problem then?"

"A splendid idea," Moran agreed. He hefted up the walking stick he'd been carrying and passed it to Moriarty. "Before we part I must show you this device. A German colleague engineered it for me."

"A walking stick?" Moriarty smiled. "Do we really need German engineers for such devices?"

Moran took the stick from Moriarty, placed the handle against his shoulder as though he was wielding a rifle, and then aimed into the distance.

A sprinkling of snow continued to fall from the sky.

To Gordon's mind, unless Moran was the world's most exceptional marksman, whatever he was pointing the stick at, the target was fully obscured by the weather.

"Moran?" Moriarty asked doubtfully.

There was a hiss of air.

Gordon thought he saw some small missile explode from the pointed end of the walking stick. But it all happened so fast he couldn't be entirely sure. More interesting than Moran's hissing walking stick was the distant sound of shattering glass across the courtyard. The noise was followed by a shrill whisper of wind. It made a sound like a heartfelt cry of dismay.

"Fascinating." Moriarty sounded genuinely impressed. "I can imagine we'll find plenty of future uses for such an ingenious creation when we're having lunch."

Moran agreed. He bade them both a good afternoon and allowed Moriarty and Gordon to continue walking towards Professor Bell's quarters.

"What was that device?" Gordon asked when Moran was out of earshot.

Moriarty shrugged. "I have no idea," he admitted. "I suspect Moran will tell me all about it over lunch."

A light wind blew through the settled snow, dislodging a small flurry of flakes across their route. Moriarty's black gown and mortar board were both white with icy residue and Gordon thought the man looked like some saintly figure from the days of the Bible. Hurrying behind him, desperate to escape the frosty elements, Gordon bundled himself tight in his woollen jacket and kept his head down until they had entered the building on the opposite side of the courtyard.

Moriarty shrugged the snow from his cape with a roll of his shoulders. Gordon tramped up and down to dislodge snow from his boots and shake it from his head. They hadn't started on the stairwell up to Bell's quarters when an elderly man approached them.

"Professor Moriarty," he began. "May I have a word?"

"Chancellor White." Moriarty's smile remained polite. "Of all the people I need to remind, surely you know I'm not a professor yet." He said the words with easy cheer. "I'm only a humble reader. I haven't been offered the chair yet."

Chancellor White shook his head. "I've just come from a meeting with the board of governors. We've been reading through your treatise on the binomial theory. The governors would like to offer you a chair in mathematics, *Professor* Moriarty." He stressed the title, took Moriarty's hand and squeezed it in his own. "Congratulations," White muttered. "And, please remember, I'm still in your debt."

Moriarty seemed briefly puzzled.

"Without your intervention my daughter would have been locked away in a sanatorium. If you ever need any favour from me, any favour at all, please rest assured I'll do whatever is in my power to—"

"I might just take you up on that offer one day," Moriarty broke in genially.

He continued shaking the elderly man's hand.

He held the leather-bound journal in his other hand. His thumb continually stroked the gold letters: *quid pro quo*.

"I should also tell you," the chancellor went on, "that your appointment to the chair is timely."

"Timely?"

"The chair was previously held by Professor Phillips. Not ten minutes ago he collapsed in his study."

"Good grief," Moriarty gasped. "Collapsed?"

Chancellor White nodded. "His office window is broken and it's almost as though someone shot him."

"Who on earth would want to shoot an incumbent professor in the chair of mathematics?" Moriarty asked.

White shrugged. "Maybe one day there'll be a great detective who can solve such mysteries," he admitted. "But, until such a person comes along, the likes of you and I shall have to muddle along in ignorance, oblivious to the causes of such matters."

He shook Moriarty's hand for a second time, acknowledged Gordon with a curt nod, and then left them to make their way up the stairs to Professor Bell's quarters.

They paused outside the room.

"I'll give this to you now," Moriarty told Gordon, handing him the letter. "And I'll leave you to talk with Professor Bell. If I'm going to make that meeting with Moran I'll need to get back to my quarters and change."

Gordon shook Moriarty's hand and held it a moment longer than necessary.

"How fortunate you're a good man, Professor Moriarty," he mused.

"How so?"

"It just occurred to me, because so many people are in your debt, you could one day wield a lot of power. If you were not an honest man – if you were a dishonest man – the empire of your control would be a formidable one."

Moriarty considered this for a moment. "What an interesting thought."

"At the moment," Gordon went on, "people are in your debt because of your kindness. But, if you chose to blackmail any of those individuals with your knowledge of their circumstances or indiscretions, you could control the same web of corruption as the criminal mastermind you speculated about earlier."

Moriarty nodded. "Indeed," he said. "I can see how that would work." His easy smile flashed briefly and he added, "It's fortunate that I'm honest."

Gordon shook his hand. "Thank you for saving me from the accusations of plagiarism," he said earnestly. "I'm now another who is in your debt. I have desires to work in the constabulary and an accusation of dishonesty would have posed a serious threat to such a career ambition."

"The constabulary?" Moriarty sounded surprised. "I had no idea."

He paused and considered Gordon expectantly. "And, in future years, should I ever need the intervention of a police officer would I be able to call on you?"

"Of course," Gordon promised.

"Very well then." Moriarty smiled. "I shall bid you farewell now and look forward to meeting you in the future, Officer Gordon."

Gordon shook his head. "You have me wrong, Professor Moriarty," he apologised. "Gordon is my first name. My surname is Lestrade."

The Jamesian Conundrum

Jan Edwards

After the disastrous events at the Reichenbach Falls, I had returned to London a wretched man. My grief at the loss of my dear friend Sherlock Holmes was immeasurable and, at that time, in my mind, intolerable. That his sacrifice also saw the end of Professor Moriarty was small recompense. It was only the love and support of my darling wife, Mary, that enabled me to carry on with the everyday duties of my medical practice; and, at times, with the very act of breathing.

Indeed it was Mary who suggested I write an account of that fateful day, to refute the version of events reported by the professor's brother, one Colonel James Moriarty. It was a splendid show of generosity on her part given the manner in which Holmes had treated both her, and my leaving Baker Street. His had been a mercurial mind of immense range and ability, ever questing after new facts and investigating anomalies. Yet his inability to accept change in real terms was one of his greater quirks among many.

My recounting emerged in the press as 'The Final Problem', and, as Mary had intimated, the writing of it had indeed been a cathartic process. The reception of it by the public at large was also quite gratifying.

Imagine my chagrin then, to receive a note some days later, from Holmes's brother, Mycroft, asking that I visit him at my earliest convenience to discuss my 'ill-advised publication of the facts'.

'It's all perfectly correct, Mycroft,' I told him. 'Nothing is written there that cannot be verified.'

Mycroft shifted his bulk, the better to gaze at me from the depths of a vast wing-back chair in the Strangers' room of the Diogenes. He examined me minutely, as a toad might a fly that it considered consuming, and so complete was that image that when he finally opened his mouth to speak I very nearly started back to avoid the curled, sticky tongue I felt sure was about to envelope me.

'Facts, my dear boy, are exactly the problem,' he said. 'It is patently obvious that you gave a true account. The whole of London is talking about it.' He puffed ruminatively on his cigar, softening his jowly features in a haze of blue-grey fumes. 'By and large that would not be a problem, except that Professor James Moriarty was not the only person to use that name.'

'Colonel Moriarty?' I said. 'My recounting was in answer to his abominable attack on Sherlock's memory. Also a James I believe?'

'Some parents lack imagination, or else the elder was not expected to live.' Mycroft laughed, a bubbling chuckle from deep in that cavernous chest. 'No. I doubt that man is any keener to confront you directly than he would Sherlock. He is not a fighting man despite his rank. But you know the form. Eldest gets the title, the rest have politics, soldiery or the Church. There is . . . a younger brother.' Mycroft took a sip from the brandy balloon at his side, savouring the gold-brown liquor for a moment before continuing. 'In point of fact there are – were four brothers, but one seemed to have passed on some years ago. I am referring to the youngest, also James, though he calls himself Jacob.'

'He took the cloth?'

'No . . . The youngest of the clan is a humble stationmaster, would you believe, near the family home in the West Country.'

'And what is he to do with all this?'

'He is a wild card. Sent down from Oxford. Cashiered from the Dragoons. Bad lot all round. Disinherited in theory, though as his sainted father died before he arrived home from India who's to say? The will is a matter of court record. The estate specifically excluded him from benefitting in any way but his siblings appear to have supported him nevertheless. Hence the railway appointment.'

'In some isolated spot away from polite society?'

Mycroft snorted quietly. 'I think the location has far more to do with its convenient links with . . . illicit sea-trading?'

I nodded. Tales of smuggling in that county were as old as the land itself. 'You feel this Jacob Moriarty is liable to do me ill?'

'I have reliable information that not only is he liable to cause you considerable harm but has plans afoot to do so.' Mycroft leaned forward, the leather creaking beneath him, as loud as unoiled hinges in the quiet of the Diogenes. 'My advice to you, Doctor Watson, is to take a little trip. I am told Scotland is quite lovely at this time of year. I believe your mother had connections there?'

'How did you know . . .'

'I know you have gone to some pains to hide that link, which is good. Few people know of it. Go. Find your roots. Take your good lady wife, and allow us to deal with James Moriarty the younger.'

'I have never walked away . . .'

'I am not asking you to walk away, my dear chap. I am strongly advising you to run. I will contact you when we have the situation under control.'

'But how on earth . . .'

Mycroft only smiled, before sealing his lips around his cigar and obscuring himself from my gaze behind fresh tobacco fog; a familial gesture that I knew too well. Argument would be futile.

That was not to say that I would do as bidden. Hiding like a child was not in my nature. I am a fair pugilist, perhaps not in Holmes's class, but can make a good fist when required of me, and I was certainly the better marksman with pistol and rifle alike. Yet I had responsibilities. Mary should not be placed at risk, of course. I also had a thriving practice and patients who needed my expertise, or at very least a suitable stand-in to care for it all. It was this duty that delayed my departure. My damnable sense of duty and obligation.

So it was three days later that we, my Mary and I, were on our way to Euston Station to catch the sleeper train to Carlisle and thence on to my ancient family home. Accidents are not uncommon, and I had indeed requested the cabbie to hurry, as time was short. The first we knew of it were the shouts of the driver before that terrible impact.

It was a dream. A nightmare. Vague images of darkness and fire . . . sleet and rain had only added to the chaos of shouting men and screaming horses . . . and the sergeant major calling for stretcher bearers in the heat of the Afghan plains. Pain in my shoulder and leg and dizzying effects of blood loss . . . the cries of injured men, no, singular: a man, little more than a boy, or perhaps a woman. I was trying to crawl free, pulling myself across the wreckage, and gunfire . . . a gunshot . . .

I woke in a hospital bed – screaming – for my Mary. My poor darling. Gone. Dead. I knew that before I opened my eyes, because I remembered, even in my dreams.

Massive bruising and minor lacerations. All minor really. Only the wound to my head had been enough to render me unconcious. A severe blow, the young doctor told me. I knew otherwise. I had treated enough of them in my army medical corps days to know them.

I knew who was the cause. Witnesses told later that a dray had pulled across the street and shed a rim. Nobody could explain why the dray had no team attached, or who it had belonged to. I knew.

Mycroft had moved me to a private sanatorium after the accident and, to those who asked, I had died with my dear wife. Mycroft explained in great detail that there was an operation in progress to mop up the residue of Moriarty's empire and that by the time I was recovered it would all be over. I did not bandy words with him. I had ideas of my own.

It was a month or more before I was able to slip away from my jailors. Protectors, Mycroft insisted. But I saw it otherwise. I left the sanatorium at the dead of night and was on the early train to St Ives before the nurses' first rounds.

As always in such moments the question I had begun by asking myself was 'What would Holmes do?' The answer would always be to examine the facts and deduce. And since I was unlikely to gain any help from Mycroft I had to rely on my own wits.

It took just a few enquiries at Waterloo to ascertain where James 'Jacob' Moriarty plied his trade. Lellantrock had once been a thriving village, but had become little more than a halt on an isolated section of the Cornish north coast. It had grown up around two tin mines, which had, I was told, ceased to be some twenty years before.

Not wanting to alert my quarry, I alighted at the next station and found lodgings at a local inn before hiring a horse to ride the coast paths. I had thought to pass myself off as a hiker, thinking that would have been the kind of ruse Holmes might have perpetrated, but my old injuries gathered in the Afghan campaigns would never allow me to hike the distances required. Horseback was the safer option, travelling the lesser byways. Not as a doctor but as a student of local customs and antiquity. Such persons asking questions and taking notes would, I reasoned, barely register in local minds. The preservation of the memory of arcadia was a near obsession in some quarters. As Holmes once said to me, 'One can hardly move for historians in any country tavern you care to enter.'

So, clad in country tweeds and riding one of the local moorland ponies, I trotted into the village, pausing first at the post office.

'Because in the country there is nothing like a postmistress and the publican for knowing all there is to know,' Holmes had maintained. And, as ever, he was correct. Under the guise of gathering additional information for the Ordnance Survey, I asked casual questions about the village and its byways and, as currency for my visit, asked for a book of postage stamps.

'The railway station is used still?' I asked. 'Now that the mine is closed there can't be a great deal of use for it.'

'I often think that myself,' the postmistress said. She was a handsome woman of middle years, her dark hair, paling at the temples, pulled into a nest chignon and fastened with plain silver combs. Her dress was of the immaculate kind that you would expect of an educated woman. High-necked dress in a plain dark green with just a hint of cream lace around the neck and cuffs. An educated woman, yes, but one all too eager to chatter on about her neighbours and neighbourhood. 'The village is half the size it was. But then there's some folks always get what they want.'

'Local squire is not fond of industry?'

The postmistress glanced each way, though I was sure she knew the room was devoid of all others but the two of us. 'The old squire turned the mines into a good living. He was a devil, but he worked hard. His son's a different kind of demon. Never seen up at Lellantrock House. He's always away up in Lund'n with his sciency ways. But funny you should mention the railway.' Another quick glance to right and left before she leaned across the counter and said in muted tones, 'It's that one down there. He's the one as says what's what.'

'Really?' I feigned surprise that would have made Holmes proud. 'Who would that be, Mrs . . .'

'Saxby. Gertrude Saxby, sir. And I means smugglers.'

'Smugglers? Here?'

She leaned back to stare at me, a probing stare that saw all there was. 'Not local are you?' she said at last. 'Down from Lund'n yourself?'

'Well . . . yes. That is where our offices are.'

Mrs Saxby nodded. 'You'd be excused for not knowing. This coast's got a long tradition for the Gentlemen. Mostly local, and mostly brandy and stuff. Harmless really. My uncle George wasn't past bringing the odd barrel ashore. But him down that railway! He's not like any of the Gentlemen I ever met.' She sniffed, derision in every nerve. 'But then he's a bad'n. Educated man, but a bad'n. Too much learning's not always a good thing for some. Meaning no offence, sir.'

'None taken.' I leaned towards her a little. 'So this chap is a bit of a villain is he?'

She flushed around her neck and her gaze flickered towards the door. I noted the muscles in her jaw tightened as what I was certain was her natural tendency to gossip fought with . . . fear? 'Doesn't do to gainsay,' she murmured. 'Not with Jake being the squire's kin.'

'I never divulge my sources, especially a good woman such as yourself,' I added. 'But smuggling? It all sounds very exciting.' I smiled. 'You should not tempt me with such snippets, ma'am.'

She blushed once more, her plump cheeks cherry red and I felt a little guilty at my deception. 'Well, sir, I can't say as I know much. 'Tis common talk all those Moriarty boys are a bad lot. Their poor mother would be mortified. Alice, my own mother's cousin, nursed her ladyship at the end.'

'Ladyship? I was led to believe the gentry here were not titled.'

'Her ladyship was the last one. James Moriarty the elder was an engineer. He turned a dying estate around, but it didn't make life easier for all of us.' She leaned close, so that stray hairs escaping her cap brushed my forehead. 'Folk've gone missing, sir. Local lads. Half a dozen at least.' She scowled. 'My cousin Mave's boy, George, just last year. Vanished. Told his mother he was going across to Redruth for a few days' work, carting, and never came home. Good lad, always looked after Mave after her Percy was lost at sea.'

'Singular,' I said. 'For a family man to vanish.' I smiled at her. 'You said "them". Do I take it this Jake has an accomplice?'

'Off and on. Mostly off. He's not so liable to taunt the Excise when the squire's up in the house. He's back home from foreign parts. My aunt, Alice, got called back there to nurse him like she did his mother before him. Mortal ill I heard, though I've not seen Alice for a month at least.'

'Is that so?' I looked, my heart pounded, a miasma descended across my senses as I digested the import of her words. I moistened my lips and looked down, searching my watch pocket for a coin or two as a ruse to hide my shock. Had I heard correctly? That Moriarty lived? When my dearest friend had perished? I had come to avenge my wife; convinced that Moriarty the younger was responsible. But this changed all things. I could not doubt that if Professor Moriarty lived then it would be he who had ordered my assassination, and that of my wife. The fuzz of anger subsided and I forced myself to smile lightly and listen to what else the woman had to say.

'Yes, indeed,' the postmistress was saying. 'Nothing much goes on in these parts that doesn't get talked of by someone. And I tell you that . . .'

A cart rumbled past the shopfront, heading up hill, and slowed as it drew level. From the dark of the shop interior, it was easy to see the outside quite clearly and I watched as the man seated next to the driver stared at my horse tied to the post outside and then towards the post office. His massive head, held low between his shoulders as though his thin neck struggled to support it, swung towards me. He was a thin man, though in no way puny, more rangy like a wolfhound, and with something of the wolf in his gaunt features. I was reminded with a jolt of the time I had seen a face very like that. He clutched a shotgun across his knees, which he caressed thoughtfully as he peered towards the shopfront.

I doubted they could see much of the dimly lit interior but nevertheless the postmistress stopped short at the sight of him. Her face had turned such an ashen white that as a medical man I was concerned for her.

'Miss? Are you feeling well?'

'What? Oh. Yes . . . My goodness look at the time. There's last post to sort. I can't stand chatting all day. That is a shilling for your stamps. If there's nothin' else you'll be wanting, sir?'

'That fellow seemed very interested in my livery horse. Who was he?'

'Mr Moriarty, sir. That was Jacob Moriarty.' Her face was devoid now of all its animation of the previous moments, guarded and wary. Yet she was a good woman at heart because, with a glance to the window to be sure the cart had moved on, added, 'He does not welcome incomers or visitors. If you are a wise man, and I think you are, then leave here. Now.' She leaned across the counter to touch my arm. 'Please, sir. Go back to where you came from and hope that evil young pup does not choose to hunt today.' She turned away and hurried into the next room. The conversation was plainly at an end.

Yet I had heard enough. Jacob Moriarty was every bit as much a villain as his brother, if on a lesser scale. That the lawful squire of this backwater estate was none other than the professor himself, and that the arch-enemy of my closest friend; perhaps even the nemesis in its truest sense as the cause of his demise. That the greatest villain of all time was living still. I felt inordinately proud of gaining that information with relatively little effort. Though I could not help feeling these were facts that the elder of the Holmeses could have furnished me with in far shorter order. I did not imagine Mycroft was not very aware of the professor's survival, and it explained his insistence that I go into hiding until the threat had been overcome.

Mycroft was quite certain that Moriarty – one or both, or perhaps all three, because I could not ignore the existence of the military Moriarty – were planning to do me harm. To kill me, in fact. I could not deny that I had helped Holmes in his various skirmishes with Moriarty so perhaps some kind of revenge was to be expected. Be it a trained brigade or a pack of brigands, in times of conflict one took sides and one fought and hoped that you had might and right on your side. But I knew a deal of good men who had perished in various conflicts and any assertion that right was might could not be relied upon.

There was a great deal to consider. My first instinct was to fly to Mary's tender embrace; except that Mary's arms were no longer embracing, or tender. She was gone, and it seemed to me that running was not the answer in any event. If Moriarty wanted to find me then he would, and the postmistress had been quite sure about his imminent mortality. My answer lay in dealing with him whilst he was still vulnerable. How that could be done I had yet to ascertain, but I was suddenly resolved to do what I must. I am a medical man first and foremost, but also a military one. Running went against everything I had been brought up to.

I stepped out into the quiet village high street and collected the horse, taking the time it took to adjust the girth and mount up to look in either direction. The cart that had silenced the inestimable Mrs Saxby so effectively was jolting out of sight amongst the trees lining the road leading up to the cliff top and Lellantrock House. My first step would seem to be to test the lay of the land; spy out the enemy's lair. I turned the gelding towards the hill and tailed the cart at a discreet distance.

Lellantrock had possession of an idyllic spot, perched on a high, wooded hilltop, overlooking the glittering blue sea, yet its builders seemed not to have taken account of that beauty. Even from a distance it was a grim square building constructed from local grey stone. There were no vines to soften its starkness. Tall dark windows of the kind popular at the start of the century marched around its three floors in a symmetrical pattern. Behind it lay a series of low single-storey buildings in similar style, giving the overall effect of building blocks abandoned there by some giant child. This was a fortress, and was by no means quiet in the absence of its 'squire'.

I pushed my mount at an easy pace along a well-worn path that led around the estate. The main house was surrounded by a stone wall, which I estimated to be some six to eight feet high, and the gate through which the cart had gone was manned by no fewer than three men. They seemed at ease, but I was aware of how carefully they watched me as I walked the bay gelding up the steep incline towards the cliff top. I tipped my hat to them and called out a polite greeting. Two of them replied with curt nods and tugged caps.

The third man was none other than Jacob Moriarty. He stared at me with narrowed eyes and then melted away into the court-yard beyond the archway. I am sufficiently vain to consider myself possessed of a pleasing face. Perhaps not a truly hand-some man, and not as memorable as Holmes had been, but suffi-cient to be easily remembered. I had no doubt a description of myself and my mount would be with Moriarty residing within in very short order.

I pushed the horse on a little faster. It was foolish of me to come here. Had I been identified then I was in immediate danger. There was no way I could have known of the professor's survival, but I should have anticipated that some of his hench-men would be loyal to the estate.

Holmes would not have been so headstrong. He would have come here, of that I had no doubt, but he would have had a plan. Perhaps with one of his cunning disguises to conceal his identity. Or else hiring one of his seemingly endless associates to scout the territory for him. What he would not have done was parade himself past the main gate like some Soho streetwalker.

I kicked my horse into a trot and moved out of sight of the gates. There was little cover along the cliff path beyond a few stands of scrubby gorse and hawthorn and I kept moving until I came to the tall, square fortress-like mine building, which stood almost a quarter of a mile from the walled house and garden. I dismounted and secured the gelding by a convenient trough in the shaded side of the stone building. As the horse drank, I sat back on the remnants of a cart and considered my options.

The mine was abandoned, and seemed to have been for some time. The wheel that should have topped the station was already gone and the windows stood dark and glassless. I tried the only door and found it locked, which was curious in a place so obviously ill kempt. I peered through the nearest window. The inside was stacked with boxes, barrels and chests, all far newer than the abandonment of the building would allow. Not hard to imagine what was in the array and easier still to link it all from the post-mistress's gossip to Jacob Moriarty.

I stepped back to peer around the side of the sheds towards the house visible across the rabbit-cropped sward. There, in that stately array, was the man I found in the darkest portion of my heart to hate with an implacable depth of feeling I had not thought myself capable of. A hatred that doubtless bordered on insanity in that moment.

The weight of my service revolver, which I always kept close when travelling wilder places, pressed heavily on me as a reminder of my soldierly past.

Presumably the reputation of the family, and the fact that it was broad summer daylight, lulled them into believing themselves safe from intruders. I am certain no sane person would have attempted entry, but in the event it was simplicity itself even taking in my own derisory health.

Once inside, I made my way to the house in short order through a neglected garden and ramshackle collection of recently constructed outhouses. It must have been an impressive manor at some point but had been let go. Sad, in some respects, but to my advantage when it gave me a great deal of cover to approach the house itself.

I slipped across a small walled terrace and in through an open window. Still no sign of any guards or staff, though I could hear voices coming from the service quarters raised in ribald laughter. Plainly not a house run on traditional lines, because no butler or housekeeper of my acquaintance would have allowed such laxity. But once again this was only to my advantage.

Once inside, however, I was at a slight loss. I crammed myself into a dark alcove, praying I would not be discovered, and stood for some minutes weighing up my situation and wondering if I should retreat.

Above stairs was eerily quiet with none of the noise I had heard earlier permeating into the main house. Like the gardens, the house was shabby, and as clean as one might anticipate. The carpets were unswept and the walls stained above the lamp sconces. No electricity or even gas in this ancient place, just oil lamps and candles like any commoner's cottage. I was surprised, therefore, to hear the tinkling of a telephone. A tall figure strode across the hall to where the instrument sat. It was Jacob. His end of the conversation was abrupt and the call short and unwelcome from the way the younger Moriarty slammed the handset back into its cradle.

He turned back the way he had come, shouting 'Cole! Get my horse. We have a cargo!' He paused. 'Mrs Dench? Mrs Dench!'

'Yes Mr Jacob, sir?' A portly woman of mature years bustled along the hallway. She was dressed in the traditional blue dress and white apron and cap of a nurse and I smiled. This, I reasoned, must be the postmistress's missing Aunt Alice.

'I must be out for a few hours.' He glanced up the stairs and swore vehemently – and I saw the poor woman flinch. 'I will be back as soon as I may. I trust you to keep things on an even keel.' He swept away, leaving the woman visibly shaken. Once he had gone, she hurried up the staircase, and to the end of the landing. She entered a large bedchamber, and I was close behind.

Inside the room was dark and fetid. The curtains were drawn

and a fire lit despite the warmth of the day. It smelled strongly of bodily functions, of sweat and urine and worse. And there, in the depths of a huge four-poster bed, lay the man that I had dreamed of facing ever since my return from the Reichenbach Falls.

As I stared at Professor James Moriarty so Mrs Dench was staring at me.

'Who are you?' she demanded.

'A doctor,' I replied. 'How is the patient?'

'Close to the end, sir. The infection of the lungs is too deep.'

I nodded, approaching the bed as calmly as I was able, though my blood raced noisily in my ears. 'Fever?'

'Up and down, sir. Mostly up. And his pulse is weaker by the hour.'

I nodded and smiled. 'Thank you, Nurse. Would you be so good as to fetch me some soap and water?'

'Sir.' She inclined her head and withdrew.

Only when she had left the room did I approach the bedside.

The man was little more than a skeleton: eyes sunken deep into hooded brows as dark as bruises; yellowed skin, taut across his face, dampened with fever. He lay prone in a welter of snowy-white pillows, his cracked lips moving slightly with silent words as he raised his head.

He was a pathetic wreck of a man yet those eyes blazed with every particle of that vast intellect which had made him infamous still very much intact. This was the man who had driven Holmes into fleeing across to the Continent, and the man who had taken the dive into those violent waters of Reichenbach. The man, I had no doubt in that moment, who had ordered the carriage accident and who had ordered me shot – executed.

The eyes opened slowly, pale blue eyes that were surprisingly sharp for one deep in the grip of ague. Eyes that focused on me and crinkled in amusement. 'Ahh . . . my—' he struggled to draw a noisy breath '—good . . . Doctor . . . finally.' He laughed . . . wheezed . . . coughed, and laughed again. His frail shoulders shook with the effort and his eyes watered, but through the tears those gimlet eyes never left mine.

Blood hammered at the back of my eyes in a red rage, which

fogged my thoughts. I don't recall picking up the pillow. I have no recollection of holding it between both hands and pressing it firmly across the arrogant face of the most evil man I had ever encountered.

His hands brushed at mine, too feeble to grip my wrists or push me away. His legs moved, knees raising the coverlet by just a few inches and back again. His hands fell away to flop across the cover, twitching feebly for a second or two longer before even that slight resistance had ceased.

I raised the pillow to stare at that face. Those eyes were wide and staring. Looking at me and yet not. I did not need to feel for a pulse to know he was dead. And at my hands – I who had sworn an oath to protect all life. To treat. To heal.

There was a slight scuffing from across the room and I turned rapidly, the pillow dropping from my nerveless fingers, to see Alice Dench in the doorway, watching me with a shrewd gaze.

She advanced, setting the jug of hot water on the washstand before asking, 'How is the patient, Doctor?'

Her expression held the paucity of emotion employed by all our profession. Had she seen what I had done? I had no way of knowing. Indeed I hardly believed it myself.

'Gone,' I whispered.

'I thought as much.' She pulled the cords from the drapes around the bed and sat in the bentwood chair at the dresser. 'I suggest you render me unable to raise an alarm. Doctor Watson, isn't it?'

'How do . . .'

She motioned to the door and held a finger to her lips. 'Young Mr Jacob has been studying your likeness, and your good lady wife's for many a month. Ever since Mr James here was brought home,' she murmured. 'He holds you to be a part of Mr James's illness. He already knows you are here in Cornwall. He said as much not half an hour since. And now? He will kill those dear to you. That is what Jacob does.' She sighed, her hand going to her throat. 'Leave, quickly. Save her.'

I closed my eyes and shuddered. 'I should stand judged for what I . . .'

She touched her lips lightly once again. 'You only hastened what the Good Lord and our own medical man had predicted. He had days at most. And the world will not miss him. Praise God their dear mama did not live to see what her boys have become. I would not be here, but for her memory.' She blanched at a strident voice from the main hall. 'Go, Doctor. Go back the way you came. But . . .' She held up the cords. 'Bind me. That way at least I may survive.'

I hesitated, for the smallest of moments. Guilt was far harder to overcome than she might wish. But I thought of Mary and her awful fate and knew I could not fail her memory now. I took the silk rope and sat her in the chair, and bound her hands behind her. I raised the fine scarf she had around her neck to gag her mouth, noting the scars that it revealed, and was only able to wonder what dire circumstance had led to them. I gave a final tug at the ropes to see that they were loose enough not to cause pain but sufficient to appear real.

I gave one last lingering look at the cooling body on the bed and hardened my resolve.

I crossed to the window balcony and looked out. The ivy covering the wall was as neglected as the rest of the garden and thick enough to take my weight. It went against all I held sacred to leave a woman in peril, and to leave a crime of my doing unacknowledged. But Mary . . . The garden on this side seemed empty still and I swung myself out on to the green ladder to swarm ground-wards with all speed that my old injuries allowed.

I ran for the wall, very much aware of the furore breaking out in the house behind me and scaled it in good order. Another time I might have been proud of that, but all I saw was open space to where my horse was secured.

The garden was full of noise: voices and gunshots and yammering of dogs. No time to plan. Just to run. I set off across the grass, keeping to what small cover there was, until I reached the mine, the noises of pursuit loud in my ears. I skittered into the yard. My horse was there, exactly where I had left it, but not as I had left it.

The poor creature lay in a pool of its own blood. Its throat had been slit and belly slashed. Death would have been rapid at least. My pity for the animal was short-lived as I was forced to take stock of my own situation. My human and canine pursuant alike were closing fast. Perhaps a half-minute behind. The mill's door was firmly secured still, and the windows barred so there was no chance of seeking refuge within the building itself, and thus the mineshafts that lay beneath.

I ran through the yard and out into the cliff path beyond. The trackway lay open to left and right for some distance. Too far for a wounded old soldier to even consider sprinting. And even had I been as lithe of limb as I had been before my war service, I could never have outrun the dogs.

I scurried to the edge of the cliff, looked down and swallowed hard. The tide was in, with white-foamed waves surging against the rock face. Time slowed, lending added grace to the wheeling gulls over the sea, and gazelle-like spring to dogs and men who closed in from the landward side. At the head of the pack was Jacob Moriarty, his face impassive and implacable. I had seen that face before on old comrades charging into battle. The very visage of death.

Another glance towards the water and the foaming waves, with no way of knowing what obstacles lay beneath. Yet even as I made the decision to jump I was hit amidships by a flying mass of solid muscle. I felt myself topple, arms flailing, felt the wind in my hair, my ears, felt the impact with the water hard as iron . . . and then I hit the water, which felt every bit as solid as the ground above, knocking the breath from me as a hammer blow. Waves wrapped themselves around me as the current sucked me down and the light faded. I wondered in that moment if this was what Holmes had felt in his final moments at the falls.

Then I felt myself being pulled upwards. I kicked hard to propel myself through the water, and found myself being hauled none too gently into the bottom of a lobster-fisher's skiff. I made to sit up and was kicked soundly by a sea-booted foot.

'Stay down,' a voice growled. 'We'll be landed soon enough.'

I did as I was bid, curling low in the bottom boards amongst the spare pots and ropes and debris. My lungs ached, as did a dozen abrasions and bruises that I dared not investigate. I was chilled through to the bone despite the sun, but I was alive. Against all odds, I had survived the drop. 'I thank you, sire.' My voice was hoarse and I found myself coughing up saltwater, retching frothy bile into the bilge.

The fisherman watched me with no comment or emotion and only when I lay back exhausted did he make comment. 'I've to take you along the coast,' he said. 'The gent from Lund'n has an agent waitin'.'

'What gent . . .'

The man looked down to me and tapped his nose. 'Not fer me to say. So don't you ask.'

'But who?'

'A friend. I was set to watch fer you. An' just's well. You'd be fish bait, else. Quite a tumble you took.'

'I was pushed . . .'

'Argh, you were'n all. Big dog it were. Gorn now.' He said no more, hand to the tiller and gaze fixed on the shore. He seemed of a kind, familiar and yet not. I was fairly sure we had not met, and equally sure I would never see him again once we reached the small harbour. I stepped ashore to find a package awaiting me.

My own valise with a change of clothes and money, and a single sheet of paper with a few curt sentences written upon it:

"A foolish move that was wholly expected. I will be waiting for you at Baker Street. Go there and await my further word. I have news that will be of great interest to you. M.H."

I did not think to argue. Indeed I doubt that I could have, had my life depended on it. Instead, I lay in the gently rocking embrace of my rescuer's chariot, gazing up at the sky and contemplated what the 'other' Holmes might have in store.

The Caribbean Treaty Affair

Jill Braden

There is no question that the Diogenes Club is superior to all other gentlemen's clubs in London. While the younger Mr Holmes may refer to my fellow members, including his own brother, as the most unsociable and unclubbable men in town, he also rightfully praises it for comfortable chairs, the selection of periodicals and, most importantly, its silence. While a member might clear his throat in outrage at some bit of nonsense in the afternoon papers, he wouldn't grip the pages and give them an irate snap as Colonel Moran does now to his magazine as he sits in my chambers.

Will he not be still? We are celebrating, after all. When this evening's business is complete, he will have sufficient funds to fritter away on his habits, and I will possess an item I have coveted since I donned my professorial robes.

Nothing can go wrong. So, why does a centipede of ire crawl up my spine, each spiky leg plucking at a nerve? Every contingency has been planned for, but the details of the intricate plan set into motion this night nip at the heels of my contentment. It's excruciating to place fate in the hands of others, but if my instructions are carried out precisely, they cannot fail. They will not fail!

It is early April, and the air still bears a chill that seeps around the windows into my lodgings. Too much warmth lures a man into a mental torpor, so I welcome the tendrils of cold occasionally caressing my neck above the collar of my dressing gown.

Years of hunting in the wilds of India and Africa have inured Moran to harsh conditions and he is comfortable enough in his sporting tweeds. Yet I had the girl put on more coal and turn up the gas as this promises to be a long night.

His foot bounces in irritating jerks. The gaslight shines on the leaf of a rare flowering shrub clinging to his boot. There are only three Nepalese rhododendrons in London, and two of them are at Kew. Moran doesn't strike me as a horticulturalist. He has been loitering outside a certain Georgian monstrosity despite being told to stay away. The match to light the flame of my temper has been struck.

Moran fidgets then slaps the page with the back of his hand like a knight brandishing his gauntlet. "Here he goes again. 'The Adventure of the Gloria Scott'."

"*The Strand*? You've only suffered from your own folly in purchasing it." Rattling my own page, I turn a shoulder to him. If I'd watched his foot bounce in that uneven rhythm much longer, I would have fetched my walking stick and beaten it into stillness.

"You read the agony columns."

There was simply no equating the two. He reads a popular periodical for entertainment. I read the agony columns because in our line of work it was important to understand the thinking process – if you can call it that! – of the ordinary Londoner. Long ago, I'd assumed I was raised by kindly, if slow-witted, aberrations and that I'd find my peers in the wider world. Sadly, I was mistaken. If Darwin had studied the population of this great city rather than finches, he never would have surmised that "fittest" described those who survived.

Moran leaps to his feet and paces past our chairs. The clutter that is so fashionable now in sitting rooms is esthetically displeasing to me. I detest flounces. My books share shelf space with specimens collected through the years and some oblique mementoes of my most stimulating capers, but there are no figurines of shepherdesses and country lads on my mantel.

With decisive steps, Moran strides to the windows, pulls aside the curtains with two fingers, and watches the street. My lodgings are in the city. Mansions sit but a few minutes' walk away, but so does a rookery. Hackneys, hansoms and country squires in town for the season alike stable their horses across the street at Hocking's. The pageant of life passing on the street below presents every level of society. It is nothing remarkable to either of us. When you consult with criminals, you necessarily mix out of your own set. It's helpful to live where the comings and goings of others arouse no curiosity from one's neighbors.

After lowering the curtains, he takes a turn around the small room. My fingers tap against my knee. His walk ends at the mantel, which he lounges against. A semblance of calm is restored.

He laughs like a barking seal. It is an unexpected noise. My eyebrow rises but he chooses this moment to scrape the sole of his boot on the andiron. Before reluctantly closing the almanac in hand, I place a copy of the latest publication from Lloyd's between the pages as one does to press a spring flower and hope that my train of thought will be similarly preserved. In truth, Moran doesn't interrupt me. I've read the same chart of expected ship arrivals several times but cannot tell you what words were contained within it.

It is good that the sun has already set. Many people will not venture out again for the evening. In a city of two and a half million people, there's always the random chance of someone seeing something, though. No. I can calculate the odds in my mind. It is a simple enough exercise. Most people don't understand what they see. Tonight's adventure will not attract attention. Even if one of those millions should happen to witness a wealthy young man in evening attire hurrying back to his chambers in a certain Ministry building, they won't realize what they're seeing. And even if doubt does niggle at their brain and keep them awake tonight, by morning they will either have forgotten, or it will be too late. No one will even be sure that a crime was committed. Nothing will be missing, and everything will be exactly where it should be – precisely where it was earlier in the day. The importance of that was made quite clear to our client. This affair, as precisely planned as watch works, will conclude without a trace of evidence. Of this, I am reasonably certain. Then why do I feel the need to take up the pacing that Moran has so recently abandoned?

With his hand on the mantel, Moran stares down at the fire. His shoulders hunch around his thoughts. "What would be the look on Holmes's face if I ever wrote up your exploits?"

Moran authored two volumes recounting his hunting adventures that were a trifle too grandiose for my taste, but they excited an interest among the general public. He and Doctor Watson share that vice. It must be a malady army men suffer from. If the urge to write about me ever overtook him, I would be sorry to lose such a marksman.

"No doubt his bulldog Watson would bring it to his attention," I say quietly.

Overwrought by his thoughts, he flings an arm out to point an accusing finger at his magazine. "That isn't even a new case. He's so desperate to keep Holmes in the public eye that he writes of a mystery many years past. Only old generals need to relive their glory days."

"Hmm."

It isn't a remark designed to encourage further conversation. Moran isn't the sort of man who talks, which is why we are comfortable in each other's presence. Speaking, even more than pacing, gives away his state of mind. Mine also roils. Every detail is correct. The plan will succeed. We should be celebrating. Or, if he's superstitious about such things, we should at least be quietly content.

Nothing will go wrong.

"Every detail," he grumbles. "Are you sure?"

Tension worries my shoulders. "Meticulously checked."

"There were many."

He's right. I hadn't put together such a detailed lay in several years. I'd sat in my favorite chair at the Diogenes Club, where the silence – which I could not replicate in my own lodgings – and the general air of intellectual fortitude made it possible to break down the plan into its most basic components. Those, I'd assigned to various players. Chimney sweeps, a diplomat, maids, bankers – the sheer breadth of it had at first appalled me, but it excited me also, as few challenges could. Moran had asked me if I'd gone mad when I'd shared my vision with him.

Months, it took us to piece together. At times, success at even the small things had hinged on uncaring fate and we'd held our breaths until it was done. While we'd kept as much secret as we could, necessity made us risk exposure on two occasions. Even though the danger was long past, the memory of those nights still gnawed at my stomach. Most of the talent we'd hired were happy to do their part and take their coin no matter how trivial the pull seemed to be. Then there where those who could not stop asking why, who sensed there must be more to it. Those unfortunates found themselves at the fatal end of Moran's barkers.

All totaled, it took a small fortune to put it together, and it will take a larger fortune to profit in the exchanges from the information gleaned from this night's work. Some crimes are purely the privilege of wealthy men.

Moran lunges for the umbrella stand near the door to grab his gun. I clutch my chair as I listen intently, expecting to hear a stealthy footstep on the landing.

"Maybe I should just go have a look. To make sure," he says.

It takes a few moments for me to realize he wasn't reacting to a threat but rather his own impatience. A few more ticks of the clock pass before I am able to relax. "I've told you, we must take pains to distance ourselves. A web strand was plucked several years ago over the Netherland-Sumatra Company affair. It has not stopped reverberating since. Holmes will insist on poking around it. He doesn't see it, but he senses it's there. We must be discreet and not attract his interest."

A long intake of breath betrays some worry on his account. "Does Watson exaggerate his abilities?"

"From all accounts, no. The elder brother is his superior in every way, but the younger has an annoying habit of acting on what he sees rather than letting it float past him. London is a river of crime. Only a madman casts a net to pluck out the one that glints enough to catch his eye then calls himself a dam."

He casts a dubious glance at me before regaining his chair. He perches on the edge, knees wide apart, hands clasped between

them tightly. We both glance at the clock. The minutes drag their
heels in passing.

"What was your first consultation?"

I know he doesn't care to hear my reminiscences, but we both
need the distraction, so I settle back and prepare to indulge him.

"In 1852, my *Treatise Upon Binomial Theorem* was published
to some acclaim. On the strength of it, Durham University
offered me a post, and, in 1854, at the age of twenty-three, I
arrived there. It was a tedious position. Few true scholars graced
my lectures. Instead, I suffered the presence of young men more
interested in obtaining a university bearing than knowledge."

"I met enough of that kind in India. No stomach for soldiering,
but they liked their uniforms."

I nod. "At the break, I found myself at loose ends. A fellow
professor kindly lent me his copy of Laplace's *Traité de Mécanique
Céleste*. Mathematics had been my sole focus since I was in the
nursery, but, in reading it, I became absorbed. Since then, a
sudden urge to plumb the depths of a subject heretofore
unknown to me has gripped quite often—" I gesture to my
collection of bottled oddities "—but at the time it was a new and
exciting prospect to be driven by a seemingly unquenchable
thirst for knowledge I'd not cared about only the day before. It
was terrible and wonderful at the same time. I read every book I
could find. Most were utter balderdash written by men who had
the funds to build an observatory but not the stamina to sit night
after night in them, or the mental discipline such work requires.

"Finally, I resolved that I had to observe the phenomena
described for myself so that I would know the real scientists from
the gentleman hobbyists. The university observatory wasn't
available to satisfy idle curiosity, so I offered my services as a
computer to Albert Marth, who had just been appointed to the
position of lead observer."

Moran's brow furrows deeply. Those ridges are as familiar to
me as my own countenance, although they usually only appear as
he readies his aim. "Computer?"

"The language of astronomy is mathematics. Precision is key.
Someone must check each formula and calculate each answer."

"You were a clerk, like Uriah Heep."

Moran has an unfortunate habit of trying my patience. No wonder so many men he served with tried to kill him. He should have known better than to poke and pry at me at such a time. I have need of him though, so I ignore his jests. "Unlike his predecessors, Ellis and Rümker, Marth focused on asteroids," I continue. "After a year of transcribing his notes, I was allowed to make my own observations in the waning hour of darkness, which led eventually to my writing *The Dynamics of an Asteroid.*"

Moran lights a match. The flame bends to the end of his cigar until the tobacco glows like a coal. He shakes out the match and tosses it into the grate.

"It's cold work, but you'd find searching the heavens for bodies similar to hunting game," I say.

"I've slept on the ground and looked at the night sky many times. The stars are useful to navigate by, but I've never been inspired to stay awake just to watch them. There's no life to them." He exhales a harsh cloud of smoke. I swear the blend he prefers is part gunpowder. "So what crime did you commit? Did you turn the telescope on Marth's window? Or did you teach the Earth to go around the sun?"

We exchange wry smiles.

A glance at the clock warns me that there are still several hours to while away. There's no need to rush through my tale, so I play the host and refill our glasses, start my pipe and sink back into the depths of my chair before continuing.

"As I said, it was cold work through a long night. We talked the entire time in an effort to stay awake. There's only so much talk of pure science one can indulge in before the secular world creeps into the conversation, however, so—"

"You gossiped."

The man is addicted to danger. Or he believes he has a sense of humor. Neither one is congenial to my person. As usual, I ignore him and continue my memoir.

"A sensational crime had been committed that was much in the papers. As with the search for undiscovered celestial objects, it presented an interesting puzzle."

He sighs and crosses his legs.

"A gold shipment bound for the Crimea disappeared from bound safes in a locked train car seemingly while the train was in motion. It was estimated to be worth over twelve thousand pounds."

Although he sucks on his cigar contemplatively, the darting of his eyes betrays his interest. When tonight's work is done, he can expect to see five thousand pounds for his efforts. He has no interest in numbers, but even he knows that twelve is a great deal more. The Great Gold Robbery was – to use the language of the criminal class – a ream flash pull.

"Did you have a hand in it?" he asks.

"No."

"I thought you would tell me about the first time you consulted."

"This is better. It's why I saw the need for my services. May I continue with my story?"

He removes his cigar from his mouth and gestures for me to go on. The flippancy of it does not make me feel more kindly toward him.

"Every three months or so, the payroll for the troops in the Crimea was sent from London to France and from there was shipped to the Black Sea where those fools Cardigan and Raglan were playing at command."

Moran makes a noise that might be commentary on military commanders *in toto,* or on those two in particular. While the particulars have never interested me, he had been obliged to leave the army several years before we met. Having seen what comprises perfectly acceptable behavior by officers, I can only deduce that he either seduced someone's wife or a commander took offense at his being Irish.

"The safes were checked at the station, and reputable men swore they were filled with gold. They were closed and secured by locked iron bands. Each safe required two keys to open. This was before Alfred Nobel gave us dynamite. Nowadays, any brute with a stick or two may blow a safe into pieces, but back then, you had to have the keys, and keys, as you are well aware, are small things easily concealed.

"The car was then closed and secured – yet another key – and the train left the station. When the safes finally arrived in Boulogne, the boxes of gold were removed from them and weighed. There was a discrepancy. The boxes were opened and found to contain lead shot of nearly equal weight to the gold that had been taken. A switch had occurred, but where, and when? The French were our allies, but just barely. The scandal was an international incident, with both sides pointing fingers across the Channel and accusing the other of being in league with the thieves.

"As you can imagine, the pressure to find the gold was intense. The police both in France and here in England arrested everyone but could pin it on none. The professional police forces then were fairly new and employed few men capable of a real investigation, but they managed to eliminate the boat that brought the shipment across the Channel and Folkestone Station as the sites where the crime was committed. Likewise, because of the matching weights, the trip from the boat to Paris to Boulogne was assumed secure. As I said, there was no question that the gold was on the train when it left London. The only remaining explanation then, no matter how extraordinary, was that the burglary must have occurred whilst the train was in motion between London and Folkestone.

"These were no ordinary criminals."

He leans across the small table between our chairs. I've seen that shine to his eyes before when he's keen on a scent. "Did you solve the case after spying reddish dirt on the conductor's sleeve?"

"I never left Durham. All this running about town and poking about the scene of the crime is very energetic and looks good on the pages of *The Strand*, but it's unnecessary. Everything I needed to know was in the papers, or easily deduced. I said as much to my colleagues. They scoffed, so I challenged them to place wagers. However, as the months passed and the right people still had not been arrested, well, I went to the police—"

"You!"

"Here is where I find myself in agreement with Mr Holmes.

The detectives of Scotland Yard are at best an unimaginative lot. How he works with that buffoon, Lestrade . . . Bah! I gave them the solution, but they ignored it."

He smiles around his cigar. "Until."

It gives me great satisfaction to remember it.

"Men like you and I understand the value of silence, Moran."

"Many a man has gone in the stir for the crime of talking."

"There have been crimes more spectacular—"

"Vamberry," he muttered.

The compliment was acknowledged with a slight nod. "And many have been more lucrative than Pierce and Agar's caper. What set this crime apart was that Agar bragged about it in court. He laid out the entire scheme from start to finish in amazing detail. They matched, in essence, what I'd predicted two years before."

I'd read the papers avidly. Each edition had carried new revelations to the readers, but they'd only confirmed what I'd already deduced. It was so obvious that to this day I am amazed that anyone could be mystified. But it also informed me that, as a whole, people are easy duped into thinking something is difficult when it is, in fact, quite simple. From their narrow brows and sloping foreheads, one must surmise that most people in London are descendants of some other strain of humanoids than myself and the Holmes brothers.

"You said the rozzers ignored you." Moran taps his cigar against the table. An inch of downy ash drops into the Persian rug at our feet. "You were finally able to collect on your wagers though."

Naturally, that is the part that interests him most. His evenings are spent at the card tables. The idea of refusing to honor a gambling debt offends his deepest-held sensibilities. Cheating at cards, however, does not. Several men have died for saying as much aloud, so I turn back to my story.

"Some of my colleagues had conveniently forgotten their bets. I lost my temper. It caused a small scandal and my post was no longer secure. I collected what I could, which was still considerable, and moved to London. Eventually, I extracted my due from each of those scoundrels at Durham. Not only in coin, but in reputation. I cast my web and waited for an opportunity to pluck at their strands. One after the next has been ruined by their own folly."

"I'm glad to hear it."

Moran isn't in my employ merely because he's the best shot in the Empire. He's the kind of man accustomed to, and not fazed by, certain demands of our line of business. A man of good moral character would have been useless to me.

"While there had been some unfortunate incidences that began to cloud my academic career, I'll admit I'd never lent my prodigious mental abilities to those exploits. They were merely . . ."

I wave away what I cannot explain in words. Sometimes I had taken things I did not need and hadn't even desired simply because I could get away with taking them. Regret wasn't a word that came to mind, but I was ashamed of my lack of discipline.

"I was what I've come to despise the most, a lazy criminal. In reading the details of that daring escapade, clarity struck me. It was fascinating, a treatise on how to commit a crime of exquisite detail and complication, not unlike the working of the celestial plane, or the working of a watch. A thing of beauty."

Moran puffs on his cigar. "They got caught. There's nothing beautiful about that."

I smile. "Yes, they did. That was the most instructive part."

"How so?"

"Do you know what gave them away? Greed. If Pierce had only paid Agar's woman the amount he'd promised from the haul, she never would have gone to the authorities and talked. He would have lost half, but better that than lose it all."

"What sort of stupid thief goes to a beak and cries about not getting her cut?" He tosses down his copy of *The Strand* and walks over it as if it offends him. He returns to the window and peers out of it.

"That's why I insist on silence. The man who utters my name knows he'll die for it."

Now there seems to be no corner unturned in our conversation. We let it cool, then die.

My thoughts stay on Agar's Judy as the quiet curtains over our shoulders. I hadn't thought about her for years. What had she hoped to accomplish by complaining to the prison warden, of all people? Appealing to the law for her share of the take from a robbery gained her nothing. Yet, in more than one of Holmes's cases, thieves have stolen from maharajas, but there was never any cry to return the proceeds to those victims. Rather, the heirs of the thieves have been shown time and again to be the rightful owners of the ill-gotten gains. So why shouldn't she have expected the same treatment?

I suppose that the difference was that the victim was an English bank this time and not some foreigner. Steal a shilling, and your reputation is forever ruined. Steal a hundred thousand pounds, and even the Bank of England will roll over and show you its belly. Or perhaps the social rank of the heir was of the utmost importance when deciding these things. Holmes, it seemed, was a better judge of what exactly defined justice than was I. My aim was to avoid the law, not to dance about its niceties like a swain at a ball.

Thoughts left unchecked tend to wander. Mine plunge into the abyss I've avoided while reminiscing about the Great Gold Robbery. Tonight, a certain gentleman of no discernible talent but excellent connections is at the house of Countess R—, where he is enjoying a musical evening. Will be, that is, until a letter is placed in his hands. After he reads it, I envision him questioning the men who had given it to him. I've trained them to convey a sense of urgency and reinforce the need for secrecy. My guess is that he will assume he can handle the situation and will follow my men without another thought. Perhaps he'll cast a glance at his intended before he slips out. I've heard that she plays beautifully. Her fingers, it is said, are perfect for the demands of Liszt's melodies. She would make a fine pickpocket.

Moran consults his pocket watch. Similarly, I check the one on the mantel and found the hour far later than I expected. We should have heard by now.

Moran shares my nagging thought: "What if they decided not to share the information with us?"

That centipede has renewed his climb up my back, and the chill settling on my spine is not from the drafty window. This time when Moran strides to the door, I do not try to stop him. He takes his gun and scope.

It seems the very air around me vibrates. Strands have been plucked in pizzicato. My imagination creeps cautiously down them and hopes to be met by news traveling in the other direction. The mute chiming of the quarter-hour and echo of passing footsteps on the street grates on my nerves.

Normally, I am not a man of action, but the growing fury at the unknown will not allow me to meditate in stillness. What has gone wrong? Nothing could have. Scenarios rising in my mind are quickly rejected. Nothing could have gone wrong.

Finally, it is too much. After telling the landlord's boy to hail a cab, I remove two firearms from my desk and prepare them for action. While not possessing nearly Moran's skill, I am a fair shot.

As I reach for my cloak, I hear hurried footsteps on the stair and know Moran has returned. It is a great relief to me, as I know that he must bear good news and an explanation. He and I can laugh at our folly and shake hands, knowing the night's work is done.

Yet, something in the rhythm of his step pricks at my brain.

He flings open my door. Our gazes meet, and I know even before he says, "They had him in the coach, then he decided to act the hero. There was a fight and he escaped. Two shots were fired—"

"You saw this?"

"Collier and Black told me." Moran pulls off his gloves and slaps them against his open palm. "Thankfully, one of the shots wounded him. I followed the trail."

"In the dark?"

"That's what you pay me for, isn't it?" He makes a face. "While not fatal, the wound was enough to slow his steps."

"Not fatal?"

He holds up a hand to stop my questions. Very well. He can tell it in his own time.

"I followed him to Baker Street."

My knees weaken. I grip the back of my chair.

"One shot spun him around. I grabbed the key and the letter." Moran shows me the envelope he has taken from our quarry. A corner has been ripped away. "He lurched back from me. I ducked into an alleyway when I heard people running toward us. By the time I realized it was our men, he'd already managed to draw Holmes and Watson's attention. He collapsed at their door before he could speak and passed away at their feet. I made sure of it." Moran grabs my cloak and shoves it at me. "But I have the key. There's still time, if we hurry."

Moran's offer seems a balm for my bitter disappointment, yet I know it for what it is. At this moment, I know how Eve felt when the serpent offered her the apple. I shake my head and return to my seat before the fire.

Doctor Watson glanced up at Sherlock Holmes and shook his head before turning to the dead stranger at their feet. The gas lamps in the foyer cast Holmes's shadow over the corpse and into the street, where it joined with the night.

"Did he say anything?" Holmes's laconic tone indicated little interest in the answer. He hadn't moved when they'd heard the urgent knocking, or when Mrs Hudson had screamed. He'd only come down the stairs when it seemed Mrs Hudson would remain in their rooms demanding he do something about the bleeding man at her front stoop, as she was certain her famous tenant was the cause of this latest outrage.

Watson shook his head again. "He groaned. A last death rattle and nothing more."

Like a heron stalking the reeds at the edge of a pond, Holmes's head suddenly tilted. In an instant, he was down on one knee with the dead man's hand clasped in his. He forced the fist open. A scrap of paper fluttered to the step. Holmes held it up to the light and squinted at it then secured it in the pocket of his mouse-colored dressing gown.

Holmes sniffed the man's face and lapels. He rose and swiftly circled the body. After regarding the boots for a long moment, his nostrils narrowed as he inhaled sharply.

"There isn't a moment to lose. We'll send the boy to fetch the constable. Hail a cab. And bring your pistol."

"Holmes!"

"I'll spare you the obvious clues that tell me who this man is. We can talk about that in the cab. But I will explain our rush, because I know the abandonment of this still-warm corpse disturbs you."

"At times, you're as cold as an insect."

"It does no good to hover over him now, Watson, but we can be of service elsewhere. A secret treaty between our government and that of the United States concerning the Caribbean and the southern Americas is currently being negotiated. Certain members of our government have been known to use their knowledge of similar negotiations to take advantageous positions in bonds and currencies before the news is made public. This young man's uncle made his fortune with such information, and I'm sure we'll find a copy of the uncle's instructions to his bank in the deceased's office. He was probably planning to emulate his uncle's financial success. If we do not hurry, the person who did this—" he gestured to the body at his feet "—will find that letter and use it to his own gain. We must stop him."

Holmes turned on his heel and bounded up the stairs.

Watson wearily came to his feet. Holmes was right. Nothing could be done for the young man lying at their doorstep. He pulled his handkerchief from his pocket, unfurled it, and drew the square of silk gently over the corpse's face.

The Copenhagen Compound

Thomas S. Roche

It was late night in Copenhagen, far from the centre of town. In the city's disreputable district, I sought the parlour of "Madame Satine".

I am not the type prone to seek out such a business in the Danish capital or any other city. It had not pleased me to voice such a transparent request to Jens, the concierge at the Hotel Aalborg. The man did show discretion. But what doubt could there be about somewhere called Madame Satine's?

It was also not to my taste to walk the streets of a red-light district so long after dark. Such an hour had long since ceased to be part of my regular workday. One awful moment at Reichenbach Falls ten years earlier had seen to that. A decade's abstinence from such adventures, and I found myself greeting every sound, every breeze, every footstep with concern.

Still more concerning was the mysterious manner in which Mycroft's letter had been written. Delivered by government courier, it had said only that he required my services in Copenhagen, and the manner of my inquiry to Aalborg's concierge. Oblique at the best of times, Mycroft had here been both direct and obtuse. My attempts to contact Mycroft's associates in London proved fruitless; he was "on holiday", I was told. The thought of the famously sedentary Mycroft Holmes taking a holiday in Copenhagen was perplexing enough. I saw no way to verify that the note was from him.

Could this be a trap? Were Moriarty's survivors extant? Would they seek revenge on me? Was I walking into a trap?

I felt a deep pang of absence, not for the first time. Sherlock Holmes would have deduced whether it had come from Mycroft or the Devil himself. In a certain mood, he might conflate the two, certainly; brothers are brothers. But Sherlock Holmes would have found any clue I had missed – and that thought, frankly, terrified me, for reasons I thought unrelated to Copenhagen.

Holmes was well versed in the art of handwriting analysis. He had taught me that a man's writing can prove sufficient to indict him for his crimes.

What of mine, then? What of this tale? Were Holmes alive, could he indict me for my crimes at Bethlehem Hospital? Would he detect what I had done, one year earlier, pressing the plunger into my wife's arm?

I arrived. *Madame Satine's.* There was no sign, but the door knocker could not be mistaken for anything other than what it was: the face of a gargoyle, with one claw-tipped human finger vertically across its lips. "Madame Satine will keep all your secrets," it said. I was glad of that, at least; of those, I had few, but just one was enough to have broken me.

I knocked. Above the gargoyle was a Judas gate. The panel opened. Out glared a pair of suspicious sky-blue eyes, crow's feet quite visible. It was a man.

"*Ja? Hvad vil du have?*"

The Danes can be said to be jarringly informal when at their best. Even so, this was hardly the kind of reception I expected from such a place.

"*Taler du Engelsk?*" I asked.

"Yes, yes, what is it?"

"Madame Satine's?"

"Name!" the man said bluntly.

"Ormond Sacker," I told him.

The Judas gate closed; the oak door opened. The man did not say "Come in," but I did.

Inside was a sparsely furnished entryway. The man who admitted me seemed ancient; he wore a long blond beard like some caricature of a Nordic warrior of old. He did not look at me, nor did he speak. He merely motioned me into a corridor draped with tapestries and lit with a long row of flickering gas lamps. The floor was thick with rugs. The point of the furnishings was obvious; even the sound of my own footsteps was swallowed up by the cocoon of rich fabric. The silence seemed oppressive. I heard no music, no clink of glasses from beyond the heavy door at the end of the corridor.

I deduced that I had just stumbled into Europe's grimmest brothel.

The bearded man did not bid me farewell. He merely opened the door, pointed me through sternly, and pushed past me to return to his post.

What lay beyond that door surprised me. It was not a house of ill repute, but a club as one might see in London. It was not empty of patrons, as the absolute silence might have suggested. In fact, it was quite packed with men, mostly blond-haired and blue-eyed – more than a score of them. They were seated in armchairs, mostly engrossed in books and periodicals. Some merely glared at their drinks, pale lips tight.

No word was spoken. No sound was made. In fact, the silence was so complete that my gasp of surprise drew considerable notice.

A dozen or more of the club's patrons glared at me warningly. They seemed ready to come to blows should my *faux pas* be repeated.

But I could not be faulted for my outcry, for two things had struck me at once. First was the realization that this could be none other than some Copenhagen branch of the Diogenes Club.

Second was the fact that one of those armchairs was occupied by none other than Mycroft Holmes.

I felt a sense of relief. This was not a trap. And it was good to see a familiar face in a foreign capital.

I started towards Mycroft with hand outstretched. He had not yet looked up to see me. As I approached, I realized the man sitting next to him was a familiar figure, but I could not place him. My pace abated, I stared at the stranger in growing discomfort.

The stranger scrawled furiously in a journal, his hands awkwardly close together. Faint scratching could be heard from his pencil, but he drew no glares of reproach from the club's other members, as I had. I moved close enough to read the man's notebook and realized that his wrists were cuffed.

He was scrawling equations.

Anger flared. His name came to my lips unbidden.

I cried, "Moriarty!"

There was an audible rustling, as men shifted in their seats. Volley after volley of tight-lipped and wide-eyed glares were hurled in my direction. The members were furious. This was an outrage!

But no one could be more furious or outraged than I, for I know this was Professor James Moriarty. I had only glimpsed him once, from a distance, but I had witnessed that image many times more in my mind's eye.

I reached into the pocket of my greatcoat, my hand closing on my revolver. But I did not draw it. Moriarty was handcuffed. Was he Mycroft's prisoner?

Moriarty looked up at me with saturnine defiance. Mycroft looked up and seemed unsurprised to see me. He did not even look at Moriarty.

Mycroft raised one finger at me, insisting that I wait.

I did so, staring in frank disbelief.

Mycroft went on reading, completing the page he was on and continuing into the next. I could see he was near the end of a chapter.

Moriarty went back to his calculations, scrawling furiously.

While I stood waiting, a club attendant approached me and held out a small slip of paper. He frowned at me apologetically. I took the ticket. On it was scrawled: "Ormond Sacks: 1 demerit." I crumpled it in my hand and threw it angrily on the floor. More glares followed.

Mycroft at last finished his chapter, replaced his bookmark with great care, and set the volume on the table. Its spine said: *Principles of Bee-Keeping*.

Mycroft stood and gestured first at me, then at Moriarty. He pointed insistently down a nearby corridor.

Mycroft was followed by Moriarty. I followed him. I did not relish the thought of that villain behind me ... even in handcuffs.

The room to which Mycroft led me was Copenhagen's version of the Strangers' Room, known as the one place in the Diogenes Club where conversation is permitted – or, at least, *not forbidden*. The room was furnished with Spartan flavour – to discourage its use, I suspected. We sat in hard-backed chairs.

Moriarty said, "It's a pleasure to finally meet you, Dr Watson."

"Go to the Devil!" I sputtered.

Moriarty, apparently, knew better than to extend me his hand. He shrugged and sat down at the table.

"Good to see you, Watson." Mycroft did extend his hand, but I would not shake it. Instead, I pointed at Moriarty.

"To the Devil!" I said.

"Yes, yes, in good time, Watson, of that I've no doubt. But for now, things are afoot that require us to engage the professor. Have a seat, Watson."

"I won't sit with that ... that ... explain yourself, Mycroft! That man should hang!"

"And he would have, already – or suffered an even less pleasant fate – if he had not alerted us to something that requires us to employ him."

"Us? What is that supposed to mean, Mycroft . . . Bethlehem?"

"The Crown," Mycroft said drily. "But it's good of you to bring that up. Have a seat."

"Your employer?" I sputtered. "What branch of Bedlam, exactly?"

"It is fortuitous that you bring up Bethlehem Hospital, Watson. We shall talk about that. But, first, take a seat. Professor Moriarty is unarmed, I assure you. He knows no arcane and invented martial arts, unlike my late brother."

I reddened. "How dare you! I wrote that as a way to ..." I realized I did not know the answer. "My readers refused to believe he was dead." I gestured wildly at the professor. "I saw you fall, Moriarty! You, *and* Sherlock Holmes! Both of you. How did *you* escape?"

"Irrelevant!" Mycroft said. "There's time for that later. If you would, Professor, please relate your crimes to Dr Watson."

Moriarty's eyes narrowed. He seemed haunted . . . almost human. Much to my chagrin, I realized that I had invented a man in my own mind, drawn from the few grandiose claims that Sherlock Holmes had made before his death. I knew nothing of the man himself.

Moriarty began: "What do you know about rocketry, Dr Watson?"

"Little," I said. "Nothing. I saw a few in Afghanistan. That was quite some time ago."

"You are aware that some believe man will one day use rockets to explore the heavens?"

"I think we have our hands quite full here," I said, glaring at Mycroft, "if men like you are to go free."

Moriarty ignored me. "For some time, rocketry was limited by its reliance on solid fuels. A Russian mathematician named Tsiolkovsky proposed a model by which a new high-density *liquid* fuel could be used, in combination with the de Laval nozzle used in steam engines, to propel a rocket faster than the speed of sound!"

"Impossible!" I said.

"Improbable, perhaps, on the face of it . . . but it pains me to tell you that not only is it possible, however unlikely – *it has been done*!"

"By you?"

Moriarty waved his hand dismissively. "My contribution, I'll grant, was significant. The mathematical calculations required are complex, to say the least. After your friend destroyed my means of financial support—"

"Criminal!" I hissed. "An empire of thieves and killers!"

"—I was left with no choice but to seek out employment. I was approached by an agent of a foreign government—"

"Which government?" I demanded.

"One that does not yet exist," Mycroft said. "Or no government at all, if you prefer."

"Anarchists?"

"That is our deduction," said Mycroft.

"He called himself Von Szabovich," said Moriarty. "I believe that was a bit of an inside joke. He claimed, at various times, to be of German, Russian and Austrian origin, but his speech hinted at none of those. From our few meetings, I deduced the man's accent to be fabricated, and his mother tongue to be English."

"In fact," said Mycroft, "his name is MacQuaid. He is known to us. He is an American chemist of Irish descent, educated at the finest schools there – or he *was* an American. He was expelled for his terrorist activities. That was after the Boston Fenians expelled him with extensive prejudice. The Irish want nothing to do with him, but he bears the Crown significant ill will."

"That is putting it mildly," said Moriarty. "This Von Szabovich shared with me designs for a liquid-fuelled rocket-ship intended to ferry up to twelve passengers at greater speed than even the fastest locomotive. He engaged me in performing necessary calculations for construction, fuel consumption, and navigation between Hamburg and London. I was sceptical, but, as I mentioned, I was in some dire financial straits. Once I saw his design, I realized it was possible to make his design work."

I said: "Travel by air? Twelve passengers? Impossible."

"As I said, improbable," Moriarty replied. "And, yes, impossible. The original specifications called for twelve passengers. My calculations established that Von Szabovich's design would carry only two."

"Even that . . ."

"Once I deduced that the design was feasible, even for only two passengers, I became something close to a partner. In return," Moriarty said, speaking now with some difficulty, "I sought Von Szabovich's help as a chemical engineer to utilize the formula for a certain . . . *compound* . . . that had been designed by associates of mine in years past, but never manufactured . . . and most certainly never tested. They had no stomach for its proposed effects."

I felt a great weight come upon me. My hand found its way into my coat. I gripped the butt of my pistol.

"What sort of compound, Professor?"

I shall never forget the look on his face. It was some amalgam, I believe, of self-satisfaction and guilt.

I stood up. "What compound, Moriarty? Tell me!" I had guessed an answer, but I doubted its probability. All else was impossible, however. Who else could do such a thing?

"What did you create, Moriarty?" My pistol was in my hand.

Mycroft was out of his chair before I could aim. I had never seen Mycroft move quickly before. Now, he was so swift his movements blurred.

Mycroft's arm seized mine in an arcane embrace; I felt a great pain in my elbow. With a sweep of one enormous leg, he struck the backs of my knees. I collapsed into a kneeling position. The pistol discharged once, into the ceiling, before Mycroft seized it from me. I was deafened.

Moriarty stared, unperturbed.

Mycroft said: "He killed your wife, Watson, naturally."

Now on all fours, I trembled.

Mycroft bent down and patted me soothingly. "Justice in due time," Mycroft said. "For now, the Crown has business with both of you. There's a boat waiting. Make haste!"

Staring at Moriarty in dismay, I said: "You are the Devil!"

Moriarty glanced at Mycroft. "Me or him?"

"You!" I said. "Both of you!"

Moriarty said mildly, "If it improves matters, Watson . . . I was trying to kill you."

In 1805, the Royal Navy bombarded Copenhagen and seized neutral Denmark's shipping fleet to aid Britain against Napoleon. Now, in that same harbour, there waited for us a modest steam trawler called the *Jannike*.

It was some trouble getting there, given that Copenhagen's version of the Diogenes Club was in quite an uproar – its first ever of such magnitude. In such an establishment, discharging a firearm was an act for which there was no precedent and no official rule. It took even Mycroft some effort to extract us from the resultant tumult. This was achieved only once I had been formally banned from re-entry for life.

When we finally made our escape, there came with us three younger men of the club, who turned out to be in Mycroft's employ. Their names, as Mycroft informed me, were Adams, Baker and Cowell. We did not greet each other. We did not shake hands. The men remained true to the club's tenets even outside its walls; so did the crew of the *Jannike*. This was to my own taste, given my bilious spirit.

The ease and discretion with which the *Jannike* handled its passengers told me that they were almost certainly smugglers of one form or another. This would not otherwise have concerned me, but the night's events had shaken my faith in Mycroft's reason. Until tonight, I had always trusted Mycroft to deal with trustworthy scoundrels.

Sherlock Holmes's assertion that Mycroft was more than he appeared seemed far more credible now after tonight's events. My old friend had claimed that, at times, Mycroft *is* the British government. If that was true, there was far more than just culpability for Mary's death at stake.

Mycroft retained my pistol, despite my many requests for its return. Perhaps he was wise. I watched Moriarty's every move with simmering fury.

The *Jannike* weighed anchor.

I sat in the hold, glaring, thinking of tragedies passed.

Mary had taken a year to die. It was not the last year that a husband would wish for.

By the end, the diagnosis would remain acute encephalitis of unknown but presumably infectious origin. The contagion in question had never been identified.

Onset had been rapid and catastrophic. My wife had become violent, assaulting me and harming herself. She rushed into the street and assaulted passers-by, screaming. Later, she attacked the staff at Bethlehem. She was restrained. The mouth I had kissed for a lifetime became that of a monster.

After three days, she recovered from her first period of violent agitation and came to her senses. She wept for a time, in remorse and fear. We spoke. For twenty-three hours, she remained rational.

Then change came again. Her condition worsened over the course of an hour. She grew still more agitated. Her second attack was more violent than the first. Sedation provided no relief. The most powerful opiates had no effect on the patient's arousal. Only physical restraint kept my wife from destroying herself – and harming or killing her tenders at Bethlehem in the process.

That was the first week.

For a year, her oscillations varied. She passed through periods of bestial disposition, ranging from one hour to one week, only to return briefly to periods of lucidity. In the former, she would take no normal food, only meat, freshly killed but uncooked.

With the return to lucidity, she expressed revulsion at what she had become . . . and fear of her condition's return.

And return it did, always.

My heart broke each time.

After my wife's first few fluctuations between madness and sanity, some of her spells began to retain aspects of the latter while she was clearly possessed of the former. She screamed obscenities. Progression was unpredictable. She retained enough mental capacity to hurl vicious personal insults and abuse at me. She screamed secrets shared between husband and wife, in the unkindest terms. She abused my colleagues and her keepers.

Infectious diseases were never my specialty, but with such motivation, I sought out the best experts and learned very quickly. I could not deduce a possible agent. No form of encephalitis evinced variations of this style or magnitude. The prodromal phase of rabies had been known, in very rare cases, to last more than one year before death, but had it been rabies, such acute variations between madness and lucidity were inexplicable. In any event, there had been no bite, no reasonable indication of rabies transmission.

Priests were called in. All fled in horror.

Her attacks persisted month after month. Her periods of lucidity grew rarer, but clearer. In some ways, this was far worse. During her returns to sanity, she began to accept what she could anticipate. She rejected it.

"James," she had choked through the variegated mess of foam, spit and blood that her mouth had become. "Don't hold out hope where none exists. Leave me to heaven, James. Do this for me. End it before I return again?"

Those were her last words. She lapsed into madness again.

Years of discretion in matters of medical tragedy, I found melting away, as if they'd never happened. I was a boy again, weeping over a woman I knew and yet did not know. With her heart, Mary had loved me, yet her mind was no longer her own. I knew she was right.

I honoured her request. I broke my most sacred vow.

My many years adjunct to the practice of professional detection had given me practical skills in the matter of poisons that proved undetectable to all but the most aggressively deductive mind. That made it easy.

I knew the compound to use. Reader, do not expect me to relate it here; should it fall to you to perform such a crime, you will find it a great mercy that you do not know the way. My footsteps will not lead you.

How would Sherlock Holmes solve such a murder? Would he detect the compound, deduce my crime, unmask the villain? And would he indict me? Would he, then, also indict Hippocrates – for the madness that was medicine in such cases?

If Mary persists in the Beyond, cured and at last, again, well – if she has been left to Heaven – perhaps she and my friend Sherlock Holmes now share deductions incomprehensible to the living.

For that, I envy her.

In the Spartan hold of the *Jannike*, I had returned to my own form of lucidity. I retained a bestial disposition simmering under the surface.

"What's our destination, Holmes?" I demanded, feeling a pang of regret upon calling him that.

"A tiny island," said Mycroft. "It's known as Æbelø." His pronunciation was markedly exotic. "It is uninhabited except for a medical facility."

"And why is our friend still alive?"

"Watson, do not be sarcastic. It does not suit you. I assure you, Professor Moriarty is not my friend. He is alive because he knows MacQuaid's liquid rocket-ship design. He can disable it."

"Possibly," said Moriarty. "As I keep telling you, Holmes, mathematics is not engineering."

"For the time being," said Mycroft, "I shall take what is within my grasp. The professor also knows the compound in question. If my reports from Æbelø are accurate . . . we shall find ourselves in need of him."

"How can we trust him with either, Mycroft? How do we know he won't—"

"*We* trust him, Watson. Not *you*. *We. The Crown* trusts him, and only so far as we must. I ask you to trust me that Professor Moriarty is a changed man."

"Why would I ever do that?" I asked.

"Because, my dear man, *I am Mycroft Holmes*," he said with great pomp. "What I need you to do, Watson, is to examine Æbelø's patients and tell me if their condition appears . . . *familiar*." Mycroft's face took on a dark aspect. "By the way, Watson, I *am* very sorry for your loss."

Ignoring Mycroft's belated condolences, I turned my attention to Moriarty.

"How did you do it?" I demanded. "Did she ingest it? What was the compound? Where did you get it?"

Moriarty was distracted, furiously scrawling equations in his notebook.

"These are very good questions, Watson, but you must forgive me if I am not wholly forthcoming. At this time, details are all that keeps me alive. I will say these things, Watson. The compound is at present unnamed. I obtained the formula from an Austrian chemist named Hoelscher. The substance is inhaled or ingested, but more effective if inhaled. Atomized in an envelope, it likely passes unnoticed. I sent it to you in a letter; your wife, as it seems, opens your mail – or *did*. It persists in water, but flame will destroy it. The syndrome it causes is incurable."

I felt a dizzying sense of relief. Moriarty read my face too quickly.

His manner changed quickly. He said to me with surprising warmth: "I speak the truth, Watson. There is no cure. I am sorry for killing your wife, but it was an accident. What is very important is that you need not blame yourself for ending her suffering."

"What are you suggesting?" I snapped. Then, I remembered to whom I was speaking: the Devil. I sighed. "How did you know?"

"Watson . . . you, of all people?" Moriarty shook his head. "It was quite elementary, my dear man. I *deduced* it."

Inside, I boiled. Moriarty's warmth was gone; he showed no sympathy. That brief flicker of human compassion was gone from his face. Mine was hot with anger.

I demanded: "What is the compound?"

"As I said, it has not, at present, been given a name. What you must know is that it affects the emotional cortex of the human brain. In the dose your wife received – unfortunately, and again, my apologies – it reduces emotional inhibition to the point where the victim's cognitive faculties become quite irrelevant. In short, it increases emotion, decreases rational thought. At the weaponized dose, socially learned inhibitions are obliterated, until the—"

The professor's throat seemed to close. He clutched his chest. He started trembling. He convulsed. He doubled over.

"Mycroft!" I cried. "What is going on?"

Mycroft said, "Let the man speak, Watson."

Moriarty remained doubled over, shaking and weeping. Medical instinct told me to intervene, or at least to examine the patient. Instead, I held tight to the crate on which I sat. I watched.

When Professor Moriarty finally straightened, he stared at me with glassy eyes and wet cheeks.

His voice trembled as he said: "Sorry, I'm sorry, Watson. I'm so sorry. It seems I was . . . in the . . . compound's manufacture, I . . . mine was a low dose, but . . . I can't control myself . . ." He started shaking his head violently, tears scattering. "I won't do violence, Watson. You needn't worry about me any more. I've tried; believe me, I've tried. Sometimes I can't even think. I try, but I grow overwhelmed. I received only the smallest exposure, but . . . Watson, I'm sorry!"

"Go to hell," I told him.

Moriarty doubled over again and began to weep.

Mycroft clapped me on the back. "As I said, Watson, let the man speak. Tell me, is that not a pleasure to see?"

At Æbelø, the *Jannike* moored alongside a rickety old pier. We disembarked. A Gideon lorry waited for us. We piled in the back and it whisked us through the night at terrifying speed and bone-rattling intensity. In my younger days, I would have found such a ride distasteful at best. Now, it was excruciating. How poor Mycroft survived it, I'll never know. He had surprised me several times tonight, but by then he looked quite worse for wear.

The facility we approached bore a wrenchingly familiar aspect: one that hovered between prison and hospital.

It was both.

Mycroft introduced me to one Dr Østergaard, who spoke excellent English. Østergaard explained that he was in charge of the *"Sektion til Særlige Patienter"* – "Section for Special Patients" – in Ward 6.

It was a madhouse, in every connotation.

Beds were crammed as close together as possible. Each patient was cuffed at four points – wrists and ankles. They strained against their cuffs, rabid. Teeth snapped and bit. Some had been forced to wear muzzles. Even those made an unholy noise, through structures insufficient to cope with their bestial howling. Now and then, peals of human laughter would echo through the torrent of animal noises. From the depths of Ward 6, I heard screamed obscenities. Some metal frames had been reinforced with extra struts; Østergaard explained that this was because patients exhibited exceptional strength, as had Mary.

"Disease progression is rapid," said Østergaard. "From a patient's first presentation with dizziness to the condition you see here takes only a few days. After that, further progression can take months. Periods of lucidity are followed by severe instances of disorientation. Our best diagnosis is encephalitis of unknown infectious origin. Until last month, we had seen only five cases in the entire country. We could not implicate an infectious agent, or any connection between the patients. Then, this month – well, here they are. All from Vigelsø Island, yet we can find no vector of transmission—"

While I observed, one man seemed to experience a lucid period, recovering just enough mental facility to beg for—

I could not hear it again. I plugged my ears. I fled.

Grimly, I confirmed to Mycroft that the patients in Ward 6 were the victims of Moriarty's nameless compound.

The professor was again doubled over, weeping. He trembled uncontrollably, bleating apologies. He'd been sick several times. So had I, in the washroom just outside Ward 6. I did not share that fact with either of them.

"Vigelsø," Mycroft said. "It isn't far from here. *Bloodhound* is already en route. A gunboat," he added, seeing my quizzical look. "But it falls to me to get Moriarty there. He can reset or disable the navigation system. Sorry, Watson, but you're coming along."

I nodded at Moriarty, who was still weeping. "Can he do it if he's in that state?"

"How should I know, old man? You're the physician. You're the world expert, Watson. Even Østergaard's still playing catch-up. What's the prognosis?"

I said, "Professor?"

"They were just numbers!" he howled. "Facts, figures . . . It was a high dose, Watson! You understand that, yes? I only wished to kill you! How you escaped exposure, I don't . . ."

He descended again into paroxysms of grief.

Tears flowed: Moriarty's and mine.

I had not escaped exposure at all, I deduced. Months of attending to Mary's care . . .

I squelched my emotions. I turned to Mycroft and said: "We must hope our dear professor has one of his spells of lucidity soon."

We returned to the *Jannike* and set out for the island of Vigelsø.

Some time after we left Æbelø, Moriarty recovered his composure. He stared ahead blankly. He approached catatonia.

But when I addressed him directly, he responded.

He grew stone-faced.

"I withdraw my apology," said Moriarty. "The last several hours are foggy to me. Whatever I said, disregard it. I was not in my right mind."

Mycroft and I shared a look of surprise.

Moriarty began weeping again.

Dawn broke the horizon just as we came within sight of the small island's barren coast. The lightening sky showed the outline of a lighthouse. Offshore, *Bloodhound* could be seen, her great ten-inch gun still pouring smoke.

My eyes were red. My head throbbed. I felt a great weight in my chest.

Moriarty sprawled on the deck of the *Jannike*, catatonic again.

Mycroft held out my revolver. "Can I trust you with this, Watson?"

I took the pistol and held it as we approached shore.

On the shore, there was fighting. *Bloodhound* had landed troops, who advanced on what appeared to be a lighthouse. In the dim light, I saw flashes. Riflemen atop the lighthouse were firing back at the advancing troops.

Atop the lighthouse, glass shattered. Shards of it glittered in the dawn's building rays. Fragments of stone and long strips of metal peeled away from the top of the tower.

Mycroft stepped over the sprawled professor and ran for the pilot-house, waving and gesturing. The *Jannike* picked up speed – near, now, to running aground.

Rifle shots ricocheted as the *Jannike* reached the pier near the lighthouse. It was too close for self-preservation, but even so, we were too late. Smoke and flame poured from the base of the lighthouse.

Our troops fell back, repelled by the blast. *Bloodhound* fired. The boom of its great gun was lost in the snarl from the rocket-ship. The shell went wide, detonating on the beach.

The roar of the firing rocket engines drowned out all speech and all sound, also. Beneath the ruins of what had been the light room atop the tower, the silver tip of the rocket-ship could be seen. It was a conical spearhead, polished and featureless but for a single hatch near the top. The rocket-ship trembled with the force of its firing engines.

It was, I admit, quite a wondrous sight. It might have been a vision of the future. Ten years hence, twenty, with passenger service from Hamburg to London in one hour. One hour hence: London as Bedlam.

Twin futures held me enthralled, and would not let go – even when Moriarty came up behind me.

He felled me with a spanner, while I gaped at impending doom or salvation – or both at once. His blow laid me out on the deck and, when Mycroft hauled me to my knees at the railing, my vision swam.

I no longer saw futures: just two Moriartys, swimming before me, scaling two ladders outside of two lighthouses. He neared the top as they resolved into one. Mycroft had field glasses. The professor was blackened, parts of his clothing alight. The spanner he'd hit me with – I presume – was tucked into the rear of his belt.

He reached the railing and leapt atop the great silver rocket. He withdrew the spanner and fitted it into what looked like a hatch. The flames at the base grew more intense.

The hatch came open. Moriarty dove inside the nose of the vessel just as the rocket-ship started to rise. The walls of the lighthouse gave way. Silver fins became visible at the base as the great silver body rose into the air.

Its speed increased. Day had come. *Bloodhound* fired again, but the rocket-ship had ascended to the point where the ten-inch gun could not reach it.

The vessel rose into the air at an increasing pace. The silver ship became lost in the flames of its engines . . . and then, all heaven was engulfed in sun-fire.

I covered my eyes. Mycroft pushed me down. Shrapnel rained down around the *Jannike*, striking the water with great force. The remains of one great silver fin ripped through the trawler's front railing and hit the water so close to us that I felt the spray and the steam hissing around it.

Under its skin, the rocket-ship possessed a metal skeleton. It fell on the shattered remains of the lighthouse. More shrapnel followed.

Numbly, I said: "Moriarty said flame would destroy the compound. Was he telling the truth?"

Mycroft shrugged. He reached into his coat and took out a handkerchief.

"Trust, Watson, is the luxury of the mad and the desperate. For the time being, you and I are neither. Let's get out of here." Nodding at the ball of smoke overhead, Mycroft added: "Rest in peace, Moriarty."

"Rest in peace," I repeated grimly. "To both our dead."

Jannike reversed her engines and rounded the spit.

We made for open water.

The Shape of the Skull

Anoushka Havinden

This story pains me to tell. I beg the forgiveness of your compassionate understanding, reader, as I suffer the recently refreshed regret of long-buried weakness.

Some might say that the need to unburden myself is a purely selfish act. But as I heard the reports from Europe of the final fall of that man whose name has haunted me, the memories floated up unbidden. There is always the hope that this may stand as a cautionary tale to those callow enough to be at risk of repeating the many mistakes that I made. And so, let me begin:

As a newly appointed tutor, freshly wax-whiskered and thrilled with the task charged to me – that of educating the privileged boys of the High School Of ****** [*Editor: Name redacted to protect the reputation of this august institution*], I had not an inkling of the potential of the human mind. I'd a head stuffed brimful of theories that I found very pleasing, yet I could not have conceived of either the depths of the mind's depravity or the heights of its genius. Needless to say, Moriarty was to teach me plenty on both accounts.

My first glimpse of the child may have been the true beginning of my own education. He stood at the head of the steps, on the first day of term, as his father's carriage drove away. Around us were scenes of the most heart-rending misery – boys fighting tears, mothers with pink spots high on their cheeks, nurses bad-tempered and blustery, cases and bags all in disarray while everyone got on with the grim task of separating charges from guardians with the minimum amount of emotional drama.

I was there at the conclusion that my earnest, if naive, philosophy had brought me to: that I should use my own gifts to further the well-being of others. I believed, with all my righteous scholar's heart, that I could and should be the helpmeet and adviser of these unformed charges, as troubled or as slow or undeveloped as they may be. To shape young minds! To pass on the knowledge of the ages!

As you can tell, I was inexperienced. In any case, I was struck immediately by the singular appearance of this one. Moriarty, his high forehead smooth and domed, stood with eyes fixed on the gate. It seemed he'd been deposited by a faceless driver, who left without ceremony or farewell. The boy's appearance was, from the first, unsettling. His soft hair was a shade of mud that has settled at the bottom of a pond. His bone structure was as fine as a bird's, his cheekbones sharp and proud, his eyes deep set and also startlingly pale. He had the face of an old man, as yet unlined. That high forehead suggested, to one with an interest in the art of phrenology, a mind that was practically outgrowing the skull's cavity – I itched at once to consult the china head in my study, to measure and compare it with that of the child in front of me. Which areas were so enlarged, and what effect would it have on the character?

And it seemed to me, though I could not have known, that what was rushing through his head was not the usual piteous ache of longing for his family or the trepidation of the rest of the boys, little snarling and hollow-eyed wretches as they were. I felt, as he turned to survey his new situation, more a rapid and shrewd calculation, as if he were counting many things at once. His eyes seemed to take in everything with the same flickering dark stare, as small and slippery as the beads of an abacus. The fine, carved whinstone of the building, its gargoyles, the slight deterioration of the window fixtures, the good cloth of the drapes, the quality of the carriages leaving through the gate. Looking around, as he was, I saw as if through a camera lens, the boys and women broiling on the steps, each a tiny storm of hungers and sorrows and fears. And, at the top of the steps, the head, like a walrus in his grey coat with his impressive whiskers, as immovable as a rock amidst the storming sea.

Moriarty seemed to catalogue all of this, somehow, with his quick and narrow gaze. A pencil, the end sharpened to an arrow's point, twitched in his fingers, and I noted the book protruding from his pocket. Was he truly taking notes? My eyes widened in surprise, and it was then his met mine.

I am ashamed to admit that I could not hold that gaze. I was, it was to be supposed, his superior, in age, social station and position. Yet I felt as if I were myself counted, and found lacking. As though he were noting and ticking through my secret weaknesses: my own unease at this, my first job, my uncertainty of how to inspire fear and respect, as it seemed the housemaster wished that we should. Deep down, could he divine the uncomfortable struggles between my desperate Romantic's heart and my brain's suspicion that the clockwork universe did not perhaps share my beloved morals? And then, he showed me his teeth. It was not a smile. The points of his incisors shewed, as if a warning.

Would that I had heeded it, reader!

Instead, alas, I felt the lurch of righteous pity. I divined that I was in the presence of a child perhaps disturbed, but surely in want of sustenance – emotional and literary, moral and intellectual salvation! What hunger he must have for a loving guide! What enormous need of help! Inevitably, this sparked the fire of my foolhardy ambition. The resolve to nourish this woeful-looking brat was born in me in that moment, and I believe he saw it happen. Certainly, he took full advantage of the weakness he seemed to have registered within me. In any case, our fates were joined that day – me, the redeemer, he the *enfant terrible* in need of generous and charitable guidance.

The first term was enough to prove my initial suspicions of his disturbed nature accurate. In order to achieve the position he apparently desired – that of ruler of the school, albeit in a manner both invisible and free of responsibility – Moriarty had presumably calculated that his first task was to sow fear, disruption and discord among children, staff and tutors alike. At the time, no one would have credited a child his age with such a depth and detail of vision. But now, looking back at the dark catalogue of his adult life, I can only concur with that learned Austrian who has asserted that the damaged child will unfailingly become the malevolent man, and exorcise his demons in ever worsening manner.

In the first few weeks of September, the school was beset with problems that had not – I was assured, by various white-faced and weeping serving maids – ever darkened the building before in its long and glorious history. The cook, an able and godly woman, left in a cloud of hysteria after the entire sixth form were poisoned by rice pudding. The head's secretary, a loyal servant of excellent standing, lost his wits entirely after mysteriously failing in duties he'd carried out for twenty years. After an unpleasant scene in the common room, he was sent swiftly and discreetly to a retirement home and never returned. The boys, meanwhile, fought relentlessly. Money was stolen, personal treasures disappeared, accusations blizzarded through dormitories, only for the various items to reappear, insolently, on the nightstand of some rival boy. Gossip proliferated. Gangs formed and battled, on the stairs, in the gymnasium at midnight, on the sports field.

A detached observer might have perhaps noticed that throughout all of this, Moriarty remained unaffected, an island of preternatural calm. Perhaps the merest curl of a smile was caught in that thin mouth of his, like the hook at the end of a fishing line. He was, somehow, nobody's fag. The butt of nobody's cruel jokes – although the boys that year seemed close to a pack of frightened feral dogs, and blood drawn, punches thrown, almost nightly. This, in a beloved palace of learning, dedicated to the highest arts of humanity! I had planned to study the Greek plays that first term, but decided immediately to concentrate on less inflammatory works.

Anyway, Moriarty. He spent much of his time in his room. How he came to have his own 'room' is itself unexplained. The boys, especially the first years, were confined to the coldest, most miserable barracks on the upper floors. Yet Moriarty, due to vague murmurs about his health and a queer determination on the part of the housekeeper who oversaw the dormitories, found himself installed in a quite comfortable little cabin on the first floor. It overlooked the stairs, being in truth a glorified closet, and, from there, he could survey the comings and goings of almost everyone in the school.

He had soon taken his measure of the staff and established a network of allies and lackeys who fed him steadily with information, gossip and any other useful thing that he decided he required.

There were never any overt signs to identify Moriarty as the artist behind all the chaos, although a thoughtful observer might have considered the utter absence of involvement telling in itself. Thus, the head found himself in a most untenable position – tortured by suspicions he could not voice without making accusation, bound by a moral and financial debt to the boy's family, and caught between his own wish to suppress any burgeoning trouble and the need to root out the demon at the heart of the multifarious plots and schemes.

'This school,' he said one night, while clutching a glass of whisky that I expect was not his first of the evening, and peering hard at the dying embers in the fireplace, 'has been my life. The damn thing may be the end of me, too.'

As Christmas approached, it certainly seemed the institution was in jeopardy. Three boys left, after some hysterical scenes involving parents, newspapers and, if I recall, a nest of rats. A small fire broke out in the library, after which Moriarty was – rather than being implicated and interviewed – somehow excused from his English lessons.

But once he had the place running to his liking, things seemed to settle. Although, in retrospect, it was the uneasy tension of a prison with malcontent inhabitants awaiting the next disaster, rather than the true peace of a contented community of fellows dedicated to self-improvement.

Over the next few terms, he and the head came to a place of

watchful, antagonistic stalemate. Moriarty showed no interest in the arts, and, privately, I was relieved, although curiosity occasionally tormented me – what damage had been done to the boy's soul to have him act this way? Was it possession by a demonic force? Blood circulation, a disease of the brain? If he were feeble-minded, we were past the days of beating or bleeding the idiocy out of him. Besides, he seemed unnaturally intelligent. On occasion, after reading on the Phenomena of Soul and Mind, I mused on the causes of cruelty within one so young.

But, for the most part, I merely gave my lessons. They utterly lacked the fervour of my initial resolve, for I had learned the safety of sinking into the shadows. The boys adapted, as children do, and apart from one or two who were removed or begged to leave, carried on with their education as best they could.

Inevitably, Moriarty grew bored. Though he wanted for nothing – keeping a store of fine port, sugared almonds and cigars in his little closet, and a small army of boys to do his bidding, shine his shoes, write his letters home, and read the paper to him – he found himself outgrowing his role as secret oligarch soon enough. It was then that he took to mathematics, with an astonishing ease – apparently the one discipline for which he would not prefer to enlist another child to carry out the curriculum on his behalf. Within a month, his mathematics tutor was petitioning the head to have him apply to a school on the Continent known for its mathematical prowess. Whether that was out of a genuine belief in the boy's ability, or whether the poor man, who had developed various nervous tics and smelled frequently of sour alcohol, merely wished to relieve himself of the boy's presence, I cannot say. In any case, Moriarty refused to consider moving.

Now, he was the ex officio maths genius of the school, and still waging a half-secret war against order and institution. When he at last pushed his luck to the limit and beyond, calling his maths tutor 'a buffoon', mocking him openly in class and questioning his reasoning, qualifications and ability, the head had no choice – in the face of threatened resignation of the tutor – but to suspend the boy from all maths classes. This would likely not have bothered a boy like Moriarty, who truth be told was far ahead of any teaching on the subject that could have been offered him in our school. Unfortunately for all of us, though, his suspension coincided with another event. The combination resulted in a most calamitous series of events.

It happened that the school was bequeathed by a wealthy and grateful benefactor – an alumnus who had gone on to great things within the service of science – a rare treasure of incredible preciousness and value. A ceremony was planned with all the pomp and fanfare that the head could muster. Perhaps in an effort to turn around the flagging reputation of the school, which had lately started to suffer a drop in applications, he determined to make a great fuss of the occasion. The entire body of staff and pupils, as well as some local dignitaries, including the mayor and a few learned professors from the university, were invited to an announcement, whereby the treasure would be presented to the school and a prize competition launched.

The day was to be held in the school's grand but chilly ballroom. Situated at the heart of the school, it was a windowless hall with ornate plasterwork and grandiose Corinthian pillars lining the walls. A small stage stood at one end, and the room was kept locked due to the presence of a glass cabinet of trophies. The gift was to be displayed in the centre – a new velvet-lined plinth having been made especially for it.

What was the priceless object? No one knew, but the alumnus had insisted on stringent security. Nobody was to be admitted to the hall alone. Cleaners would attend in pairs, overseen by a tutor. The entire preparation was shrouded in secrecy, and a new and impressive cast-iron lock was fitted to the door; guaranteed pick proof, we were assured. The night watchman-cum-caretaker borrowed a fearsome dog, named somewhat unimaginatively Cerberus, which slavered and growled appropriately and was installed at the man's office by the front door to ward off thieves – though whether these were shadowy criminals from outside, or inhabitants of the school itself was not quite spelled out.

Some weeks before the ceremony, I was handed a note written

in Moriarty's cramped, but precise handwriting. It begged for my intercession, for he had lately felt he had some concerns related to sinfulness, and believed I was understanding in these matters. Every hair on the nape of my neck stood on end, reader, and I felt a dryness in my mouth. Nobody was associated with the boy without a measure of unease or, in the case of smaller boys, outright fear.

I attended his room as requested, feeling that if there was the smallest chance this was really a boy in need, as implied in the short but apparently sincere note, it was my godly duty to attend. I admit, also, that one small part was curious to speak with this little demon alone and gauge for myself if he was, as his chemistry tutor claimed, truly evil.

He had made his cubbyhole into a miniature office. Spartan, but furnished, I noticed, with a decanter, two glasses, and a shelf of books whose spines looked to have been well worn. Wearing a smoking jacket and a slightly shabby pair of shoes, he stood at the makeshift desk and met me with an expression I will not forget. As ever, he seemed to count and calculate as he briefly looked me up and down. Those eyes! At twelve years old, they retained a child's clarity, but twisted with the brooding and bitterness you might see in an old man's. How bizarre, to see such an expression on such a young face.

'I appreciate your coming, sir,' he said, his voice thin and high as a reed. 'I had feared I would be left alone again—' he nodded at the corner of his room, where I noticed a boxed-in section of wall '—to listen to the music of the pipes.' I frowned. Was he truly turned lunatic? 'They call all night,' he continued, 'bringing me noises I could swear were human.'

'I regret you are not making sense,' I said, shortly, for my patience was wearing thin. There was a high-pitched, insistent buzz weaving around my head. Before I could pinpoint the source, Moriarty stepped forward, snapped his fingers, and held them in front of me, with a flourish. I looked down, somewhat taken aback to see the lifeless body of a housefly pinched between his thumb and fingers.

'My apologies. I am not making myself clear?' he said, and

quirked a thin, snakish brow. 'Would it be more understandable if I were to specify that the sounds I hear on a Thursday night were not so much speech as the calls produced most usually when a young woman is—' he frowned, pursed his lips '—how should I put it? Entertaining a friend?' He dropped the body of the fly upon the floor and casually ground it into the boards with the tip of his shoe.

Now he locked his eyes on mine, and I felt the poison of his intent shoot through my veins. For, as this is a full confession, reader, I am bound to admit that I had recently made the close acquaintance of one of the chambermaids, finding myself quite smitten with her, and we occasionally enjoyed each other's company in the confines of her attic room. Most often on a Thursday night.

Moriarty reached out and removed a small section of timber from a panel in the wall, behind which were revealed around half a dozen pipes. He tapped one with a fingernail and I heard it ring and echo. 'These pipes—' he smiled '—with the aid of a small listening glass, are my great entertainment.

'Oh!' cried Moriarty, rolling his eyes. I swear he mimicked the exact pitch of Esther's voice. It was repulsive to me, to hear her voice in his mouth. He closed his eyes and took on a pained expression. Now his voice was deeper and more guttural.

'Oh, sweet love of God,' and I heard my own silly, feverish words echoed back at me, spilling from this precocious, vindictive ventriloquist.

I felt myself blush, to my fury, and despite my peaceable nature could have easily wrung the wretch's scrawny neck. But, of course, I restrained myself, and stood in his room and allowed him to lay out his terms.

I was to find out every possible detail of the prize, including, crucially, its dimensions. I was to note security arrangements and timings. I was to report back to him with everything I could find, on pain of his revealing my sorry dalliance with Esther and ruining both my own career and her reputation.

While he laid out his instructions – quietly, fluently and without hesitation – I fixed my eyes on his desk and read the titles of the leather-bound books stacked there. I was surprised to see some science books, including *Notes on the inhalation of sulphuric ether* and *The Jubilee of Anaesthetic Midwifery*. A curious choice, for a young man, I thought. Clearly he read my mind, for he paused in his monologue to say: 'My sainted mother, sir, left the world as I entered it. I have since kept a fascination for the reason of these things.' I was surprised again, for I'd thought him incapable of any sort of filial feeling. Perhaps this was the root of his problems?

'Do not pity me,' he said sharply. 'Rather, listen closely to my request. And do not think to hold back anything,' came his child's fluting voice. 'Remember, sir, the walls bring me news of your every word and action.' With that, he produced a laugh so twisted and strange it thoroughly turned my stomach, and if I never heard it again it would be too soon. Still, it echoes in my ears and makes me shudder.

I was wracked with guilt and fear of being uncovered. Nevertheless, I set to acting as his spy. I revealed, through gradual and careful interrogation of the head's assistant, liberally bribed with a bottle of good French brandy, that a tournament would be held, and the prize was no less than a pallasite meteorite – a chunk from the 1783 Great Meteor! These stony-iron lumps were so rare that their worth was several hundreds of pounds – a fine prize indeed. A beautiful heart-shaped rock, the size of a small hen's egg, studded with olivine crystals, by all accounts.

'Best of all, though, the meteorite is accompanied by a bursary for Oxford University!' said the head's new assistant, in a stammering stage-whisper.

'And all can enter?' I asked, refilling the man's glass. We sat in the staff common room, hunched over our drinks and our furtive conversation.

'Any boy with a perfect attendance record in Mathematics is eligible,' he recited. I watched the bob of his Adam's apple as the secretary swallowed, and I turned the news over in my head.

It was clear that Moriarty had heard rumours to this effect, hence his sudden intense curiosity. His family, while of reputable standing, were hardly equipped to pay for a top-class degree from the best university. To realise a chance like this would surely be his greatest, most wildly ambitious dream. Yet, I realised, with a jolt, he was disqualified. Since the mathematics tutor had blankly refused to tutor him – privately, the other tutors murmured that the boy had outshone him already and he was humiliated – claiming that the boy disrupted his class and refused to show proper respect for his betters, he could not have any hope of entering the maths tournament or of winning this unimaginably generous prize.

With a sensation like cold water slowly spiralling into my gut, I realised that this situation was unlikely to have a happy outcome. I went on to quiz the secretary, as casually as I could, as to the story about Moriarty's mother. He confirmed that yes, she had died in childbirth. Now, my dread swirled with the most intense pity. For no matter how sinful, he was undeniably also half an orphan, who had lacked the tender ministrations of a woman's soft heart. No doubt this loss had torn through his developing emotional brain, leaving an insatiable hunger for power and gain in its wake. I imagined, picturing my own sweet mother's face, the lack of her, and ached for the piteous child.

I resolved to give Moriarty solace and comfort, and perhaps provide guidance in how he might make reparation with the head to allow his entry into the competition. But, on visiting him, he betrayed no hint of emotion, and I was dismissed with a curt nod.

'This must be sorely disappointing news,' I said, hanging back at the door.

He eyed me curiously. 'Disappointing?' He smiled that eerie grin. 'I am hardly surprised to hear the Head create such a condition. It merely confirms how he is disposed to me.'

'To you?'

'Clearly he wishes to crush me. It makes things interesting, at least.'

I left with a cold sense of dread puddling in my guts.

On the day, Moriarty was far prompter than usual. The crowd of boys that filled the body of the ballroom parted mutely for him, and he strode to the front as if he were one of the visiting luminaries, rather than a slightly shabby, unprepossessing pubescent with greasy hair and a stooped posture. Behind him scuttled a small, runny-nosed child who had attached himself to Moriarty and acted as his tiny butler, carrying out errands and attending to his schoolmate's minor requirements.

I watched Moriarty during the ceremony. His gaze never wavered from the meteorite – as it was revealed by the alumnus's manservant, to general awed murmurs, as the Head addressed it and detailed its origin, and as it was placed reverently within the glass case that stood at the head of the ballroom.

While the head described in detail how the boys should apply themselves for the chance to win both their name inscribed on the plinth below this prized lump of rock and the opportunity to fly to Oxford, I saw Moriarty burn as pale and furious as a whale-oil lamp. His eyes flickered with hatred and his mouth, reader, was as a line drawn and underscored with the blackest charcoal.

'Of course,' said the head, and I believe I saw the sheen of triumph in his eyes, 'any boy who has not a perfect attendance record for the lessons of Mister °°°°° [*Editor, name redacted, again, to protect the parties concerned*] shall not be eligible to apply for the prize, or for the scholarship. Thus we shall be sure it will be awarded to a pupil both virtuous and steady in his diligent studentship.

'Perhaps this will serve to teach a lesson greater than any other – that our highest purpose must be not to further our own interests but to serve the benefit of all. He who fails to learn this lesson should find himself awarded not a dunce's cap, but a far worse fate. He shall be cast out, despised and undoubtedly, ultimately, he shall fail both as a student and as a human being.'

The atmosphere in the room seemed to drop a couple of degrees. I knew Moriarty must be not only defeated, but humiliated.

As everyone filed out, his head turned away and I caught his eye. For once, I felt the chill of the bereft void of his heart. This was the look I was used to seeing on the faces of boys left abandoned, alone and scared. This was the expression that I had seen lacking on the day his father's carriage had pulled away. Yet it was not his family he mourned for, but a life he could never have, that he'd seen paraded in front of him like a piece of glittering, unearthly mineral. I sensed again the unimaginable losses he'd suffered, and my heart ached.

I went to bed with a mixture of dread, sorrow and unspecified agitation that was only exacerbated by the lack of the company of Esther, the young chambermaid I'd recently averred not to see again. I tossed in my cold sheets that night, and yearned for her kinds words and soft touch.

That night, the security guard was posted outside the locked ballroom door. The dog was installed at the front office, certain to wake at the slightest twitch. We retired to bed, pretending that the foreboding hanging over the place was of our imagination only. Around dawn, I believe, I fell into a dark and dreamless sleep.

The next morning, the guard was sprawled on his back on the floor, apparently unconscious. He did not come round when slapped, or when shouted at, but only a half-hour later when cold water was thrown at his face. He remained groggy and could barely speak. The door, of course, was lying open, the treasure gone. The dog, while conscious, had not made a glimmer of noise and the front door remained locked and apparently untampered with.

The head immediately ordered the school to be locked and searched. While he did not say so explicitly, Moriarty's room was bound to be subject to the most rigorous search of all. I was witness to it, for the head rounded up two of us younger tutors to do the dirty work under his supervision. On my knees, I hunted for loose boards, checked every possible cranny within that small room. We turned the mattress, pulled every book from the shelf, removed the panel to check behind the pipes. Throughout, Moriarty stood unmoving, a wry smile twisting his mouth, and at last the headmaster, shaking his head, ordered his case to be opened.

'I doubt anyone would be so damn stupid as to put such a thing in their suitcase, but let us check to be sure we have done a thorough job.'

As the suitcase was pulled from under his bed, however, I saw in Moriarty's hands the tiniest shake, as if he had stopped himself from moving forward. I watched with my breath held, both wanting and not wanting the irregular, curious brightly studded surface of the meteorite to appear.

Inside: folded clothes; a writing case; a bound Bible – and, lying atop all this, a large, wax-faced doll. The head lifted her with a mixed expression, part disgust, part suppressed hilarity. The doll had a wistful expression on her foxed, worn face, arched brows, a rosebud mouth and hair in ringlets. The forehead seemed curiously shaped, and I thought I saw in its protuberance an echo of Moriarty's own strangely domed brow. The head, still apparently lost for words, lifted the doll's skirts as if he imagined he might find the meteorite hidden beneath them.

'Moriarty?' the head barked, shaking the limp cloth body of the wretched doll at his pupil's face. Moriarty, meanwhile, looked for once almost on the verge of tears. Was this the real boy, underneath all his scheming and plots? Were we seeing him at last, stripped of his shell and as vulnerable as any frightened child? Two high spots on his cheeks echoed the pink of the doll's own cheeks, though his colour was, against that pallor of his, unworldly, like that of a fever victim. I thought I saw in his eyes genuine turmoil at that moment.

'I . . . I cannot sleep without her,' he whispered at last, and I believe I have never felt so utterly wrong and terrible in my whole career since. 'Please do not take her from me. Please.' The boy looked close to tears, his pale blue eyes shining wretchedly. 'She was . . . my mother's.'

The head, meanwhile, was shaking his head, and examining the doll with utter bemusement.

'Sir,' I interrupted, blurting out the words before I'd had a chance to think, 'I beg you to consider the difficulty a child faces in a strange house with the lack of a mother to send him comforting letters or keepsakes. The loneliness would be intolerable. He may well find some small measure of emotional solace in the figure of such a toy.'

The head looked at me curiously.

'Even were a child in need of stern guidance, even were he in danger of growing from a delinquent boy into a sinful adult, surely a doll could do no harm? Is the offer of childish solace not more likely to appease a troubled youth's mind than provoke it?'

The head glared at me. Then at Moriarty, who was breathing heavily. At last, he shrugged. I fancy he may have discovered that usually dormant part of himself that genuinely cared for the well-being of children, and wished them to be if not happy, then at least quietly stoic.

'God have mercy on you,' he muttered at last, and flung the doll back in the case, before nodding to us that our hunt was finished in this room.

I nodded as I passed Moriarty, and he stood chin fixed ahead, showing not the slightest sign of gratitude. I fancied there may have been, though, deep in his murky eyes, a flicker that may have been the burning of a tiny coal of human warmth.

The hunt continued – oh, we turned the place upside down. In the chemistry laboratory, beakers and bottles were left strewn on the benches, and the chemistry tutor subsequently deduced that bleach and acetone and a puddle of melted ice had been mixed and made into chloroform – the method of knocking the poor guard unconscious. The head spat and fumed and came as near to cursing as his Calvinist upbringing would allow. A vein pulsed on his head and I saw in wonder that it seemed to bulge, as if his very brain were swelled with fury.

But, other than that, there was no trace of a break-in, or of the prized rock.

Could I help Moriarty overcome the terrible darkness that threatened to overwhelm his heart? Would he lash out at anyone who tried to offer him a way to heal the wounds of his brain's sickness? Had he taken the meteorite, and where was it?

We were never to find out. The next morning, Moriarty sent a message to his father and, within two days, the carriage came for him. He looked small, but almost dignified as he stood at the top of the steps, waiting out his last few moments. Alone among the staff and his fellow pupils, I joined him there, feeling it my duty not to let him leave without some sort of goodbye.

'The world can be a lonely place,' I said. 'Especially for someone with gifts who does not yet know how to use them.'

'Really?' he said, adjusting his gloves. 'Perhaps you have mistaken gifts for afflictions. Sir.'

'Do you feel yourself afflicted?'

'I have no need of your concern, sir.'

'Then whose concern do you seek, Moriarty?'

He fixed me with his mud-dark eyes. 'Concern, sir? I only seek freedom.'

'From accusation?'

'From the predictable,' he said, 'and from the tedious interferences of moral guardians whose own private lives do not bear close scrutiny.' He smirked at me, as if mocking all I'd tried to do for him, and I felt my scalp prickle again with anger and shame.

Here was his carriage, coming through the gates with the same blank-faced driver whipping the horse dully. Moriarty descended the steps.

'No matter how hard you try,' were his parting words, tossed over his shoulder, 'you can't see inside people's heads.'

And, with that, he disappeared into the dark chamber of his father's coach and was gone. I looked up to see the head, watching through the common room window, his jaw working furiously as if he were chewing a tough piece of gristle.

At last he muttered, turned on his heel and marched back into his study. Thus I believe the head liked to think he had won the war, even if he'd lost every battle waged between them and had still to placate a furious patron.

The scandal was hastily buried and the school buckled down to a quieter – and perhaps a duller – routine. Having abruptly cut off my nascent relationship with Esther, I spent much of my time from then on in my room, reading, and considering wistfully the quality of a woman's bare skin in the most hidden parts. I had not the courage to make reparation between us, to try to explain my sudden betrayal without revealing more than I thought I could bear, and so I lost her.

I heard reports now and then – Moriarty went to a smaller university, and at length went on to make his infamous reputation worldwide. I remained at the school for four years or so, before taking a post in a quieter provincial school, and am happy to say I never came across the likes of the boy again.

It was only last autumn, having heard of Moriarty's fatal accident at the Reichenbach Falls, I found the memories of that dreadful time burst free as if from behind a dam. I called an old colleague, the chemistry tutor at the school, and from his enquiries discovered the whereabouts of the long-forgotten Esther and contacted her. She is now a ladies' maid, not far from the school itself, and I paid her a visit.

Although I am now, of course, a man fairly on the brink of the winter of his own life, I found myself still trembling when I stood outside the house where she is engaged. She answered the door and my heart tripped just as it had when I'd first seen her, walking briskly and sweetly down the corridor outside the ballroom at the school.

Though her hair is paler and her skin has lost the shine and pink of a young woman, she is yet as beautiful, if not more so. We fell immediately into talk of the old place, the characters of the tutors and – inevitably – of the boy who had, even if indirectly, caused our separation.

'Oh, it was an awful time,' she said, her attention falling to the fire, which burned low and fitful in the grate. She prodded it distractedly, not meeting my gaze. 'All that scandal, and – not seeing you. I just wanted to pack up and leave.'

'I am most terribly sorry, Esther,' I say, faltering over my words. I hold my hat in my lap and find I'm worrying the brim as if it were a string of rosary beads. 'I felt that I could not—'

'I know,' she says, reaching out to lay a hand on mine. 'It couldn't be helped. We weren't destined to be together. I cried myself to sleep for a month, you know,' she said, a wry smile on her face.

'Oh, Esther.'

'Well, I was a girl, wasn't I, Ernest? Just a daft lass, really. Worst of it was I'd lost my doll, even, imagine that!'

'You'd what? I beg your pardon?' The hair on my neck rose again, as if a cold breeze had swept into the room straight from the past.

'I'd a dolly. I told you, I was just a girl. It was my mam's, and she'd left it to me before she died. Violet, I called it. She had brown eyes and ringlets and little leather boots. I took her everywhere. Silly, probably, but I loved her. And then she disappeared, just at the time all the troubles broke out. And . . . What is it, Ernest? You've gone so still?'

'Did you find it?' I managed to grate the words out.

'Yes, actually, I did. A week or so after I lost her. But she was beyond repair. She was lying face down out in the playing fields, just destroyed.' Her voice was bitter, even now, as she described it. 'All those beautiful ringlets, just muddy tails, and her head . . . Oh, it was like a gruesome thing, Ernest, I know it sounds ridiculous, but you know how one gets attached to things sometimes, and her head was all caved in . . . She was wax, you see, and it was like someone had dug a hole in the back of her head, it was all burst. Like the skull was bashed open with a poker or something. Just unnecessary. Those boys.'

She dug angrily at the fire, which spat sparks at her and refused to glow any brighter. I found myself unable to speak. I remembered Moriarty's face, his wretched look as we searched his room. The infinitesimal glow in his eyes as I left him, like little fragments of crystal buried in his head, and the doll flung on the mattress, where the head had left her. And realised that I had, indeed, reader, been most gravely mistaken, after all.

A Function of Probability

Mike Chinn

The professor turned the visitor card over and over between his thin fingers. It was of common enough stock and cheaply printed: each of the letters *a* in the plain typeface was faintly smudged. Square-edged, no attempt at ostentation. Quite unremarkable. Except—

Moriarty placed the card against a wooden rule from his writing desk, nodding his satisfaction at the dimensions thus revealed. He allowed himself a thin smile; as suspected: the card – and the visitor still awaiting his pleasure beyond the study door – were so much more than both pretended to be. The professor took up the card again, using it to point at Hawes, who was silently awaiting his master's command.

"Show him in."

"Yes, sir." The college porter bobbed his head and disappeared through the study's only door. Moriarty reached for his desk lamp, angling the shade so that the greatest measure of its light fell upon the chair opposite. Settling against the tall back of his own chair he steepled his fingers. A moment later, Hawes reappeared, leading the intriguing visitor. He was tall, pale of complexion and eye; his hair a nondescript shade that tended towards neither blond nor brown. His beard was of a reddish hue, and cut in the imperial style. He was dressed in a simple grey suit, a hat of matching colour held in his left hand whilst a black stick dangled languidly from his right. In all, the figure aspired to the same degree of outward unremarkableness as his card; the professor was not fooled for one instant. Indeed, he felt mildly irritated that this sallow man considered him so easily foxed.

For his part, the visitor quickly surveyed the simple study with colourless eyes. He looked less than impressed by the surroundings – perhaps expecting something more lavish. His pale gaze paused briefly on the painting of a coquettish young woman, resting negligently on the floor to Moriarty's right; his smooth brow puckered for the shortest time before continuing the careless scrutiny.

Moriarty waved towards the opposite chair, indicating the man might sit. He did so, blinking in the light cast by the angled lamp. He handed both stick and hat to Hawes, who left once more without needing to be bidden.

"Mr Leonard Eastman?" Moriarty repeated the name printed on the card.

The man inclined his head in acknowledgement. "Professor Moriarty. I am delighted to at last make your acquaintance." There was the faintest trace of an accent.

It was the professor's turn to nod. "I was unaware you had wished to make it, Mr Eastman. Your name is not familiar to me; are you associated with the field of astronomy?"

The man shook his head. "Not at all, Professor—"

"Banking, then?"

Again the visitor shook his head.

Moriarty fought to bury his faint smile: for all his irritation with the man's facile deceits he was enjoying the game. "So. In what way might a simple professor of mathematics be of help to you, sir?"

The man hesitated, considering his next words. Moriarty leaned forward, careful not to enter the deflected pool of lamplight. "Whilst you debate what answer you will give, might I remark that I do not appreciate lies – or deceptions of any kind. Especially ones as transparent as this." He raised the visitor's card before tearing it in two, allowing the halves to fall on to his desktop. "Shall we begin again, Your Grace?"

The tall man flinched in his chair, face projecting his

uncontrolled feelings. It was clear that, in his daily routine, he was unused to being challenged; his will questioned. Small wonder his attempts at deceit were so easily pierced. After a moment, he composed himself, straightening his still immaculate suit coat.

"You think you know me, then?"

"I flatter myself that I am one of the few men in Europe who might. You are The Most Noble Leofric, Duke of Granat-Östermann and Baron von Reichschliesser. You have many titles, but, alas, no land. What little money you do have is either wasted in self-indulgent attempts at political intrigue or lost at the gaming tables. You aspire to being a major piece on the chessboard of Germanic ambition, but are still nothing more than a pawn. You dream of an expanded German Empire – one to rival that of both Britain and Russia. One that may rule both across Europe, and abroad." Moriarty settled back, enjoying the spectacle as the colourless face opposite him grew increasingly florid and sullen. "And more, despite your name, your rank, your infantile meddling, you remain a nobody in your homeland; less so abroad."

Duke Leofric drew himself up. "Herr Doctor Professor, I did not come here for you to—"

Moriarty raised a hand. "Professor is sufficient. In England we do not aspire to more than one title at a time."

The duke frowned and attempted to speak; Moriarty continued regardless, having no wish to endure whatever self-serving excuses the man might invoke.

"Your Grace, you came here under the most ludicrous of disguises – one a child might penetrate in moments. Little wonder your feeble attempts to influence Imperial German affairs remain frustrated: you have no imagination. No flair. To be frank, you have insulted me."

"Herr Professor—"

"No, Your Grace – I will hear no more." Moriarty dismissed the duke with an impatient flap of his hand. "I neither know nor care why you thought to seek me out. I permitted this charade merely so that I might express my opinion to your overindulged face. If the word 'no' had been applied more rigorously years ago, I fancy you would be a better man today. Good day."

"Professor—!"

"Good day, sir!"

The study door swung open and Hawes stood framed between the door jambs, the duke's hat and stick held ready for retrieval. Duke Leofric glanced first towards him then at Moriarty, who was fastidiously placing the torn halves of the visitor card into a waste bin.

"Professor, you accuse me of having no imagination. Of lacking flair. Perhaps this is true, but before you eject me may I just say one thing: the ensured death of Kaiser Wilhelm . . ."

Moriarty replaced the bin on the floor and dusted at his hands. He glanced once at Hawes and the man vanished from the study as silently as he had entered. The professor heard the faintest click as the door was prudently locked.

He gazed deep into Leofric's eyes; the duke remained ignorant of the intense scrutiny. "Despite four assassination attempts, I think the emperor enjoys excellent health . . ."

"Indeed. Obstinately so. But I believe you to be in a position which may alter that."

"I?"

"I am not the only man in this room who plays at charades." The duke leaned forward, his face earnest. "We are neither of us who we claim to be. If I have insulted you, then I apologise unreservedly; please do not compound the error by seeking to offend my own intelligence – as wanting as you believe it to be."

Moriarty settled against his chair. He templed his fingers and touched them against the smile he could no longer contain. "You prefer plain speaking, then? No more guises?"

"It will be refreshing." The duke took a silver cigarette case from within his coat, offering one to Moriarty. The professor refused, but did not go so far as to forbid Leofric himself from smoking – much as he detested the stale smell of tobacco in his study. After lighting his cigarette, the duke appeared to relax: he settled into his chair, holding his smoke between thumb and forefinger. Its fragrance told Moriarty that the cigarette was of Balkan origin.

"The emperor is ninety years old," the professor said. "It must surely be a matter of time before nature will take its course."

"Wilhelm clings to life tenaciously. His son, Friedrich Wilhelm Nikolaus Karl, is seriously unwell and not expected to last out the year."

"I believed the emperor well loved by the German people."

The duke waved an impatient hand. "He is, but at heart he is still a Prussian. More, he has liberal tendencies, and poor advisers."

"You speak of von Bismarck?"

"The chancellor has long demonstrated that he pursues policies of his own; it is no secret that he and the kaiser disagree on many subjects. But every time Wilhelm tries to rein him in, von Bismarck threatens to resign and His Imperial Majesty capitulates. They are like children arguing over a rattle!" Leofric took a long pull on his cigarette. "And there is his wife, of course . . ."

"Of course." Moriarty thought carefully before again speaking. "If the Emperor were to outlive his son before dying – of whatever cause – the natural successor would be Friedrich Wilhelm Viktor Albrecht von Preussen. A man noted neither for a cool head, nor his tolerance for Chancellor von Bismarck's policies – despite both men initially being close." He rested his hands in his lap. "Such a man might not be content to allow Germany to rest on its laurels; or be persuaded to be less content."

"You have it!" The duke sat forward again, his cigarette wielded as a fencing foil. "With the kaiser's grandson at its head, the Fatherland will step free of von Bismarck's overbearing shadow and pursue its manifest destiny."

"Indeed? And why should I – a loyal servant of Her Majesty and the Empire – embrace such a scheme? I see little gain for Britain, and no small risk to it."

The duke made an expansive gesture. "Is the prince not also the oldest grandson of your queen?"

"The bitterest rivals are most often to be found within the embrace of close family. Blood is no shield."

"You are a cynic, Herr Professor . . ."

"I am a realist, Your Grace. But let us be clear." He took a thin ledger from a desk drawer, dipped a pen into ink and began to write slowly and carefully upon a fresh page. "You are proposing that the kaiser should meet a premature end?"

"Indeed." The duke drew an ashtray closer, stubbing out his spent cigarette.

"Indeed." Moriarty recharged his pen. "And you are of the belief that I should be able, in some ways, to effect this?"

Leofric's beard was twitched by a crooked smile. "I thought we spoke plainly, Herr Professor. You pride yourself on being one of the few outside my homeland who might recognise me; I pride myself in having an information network as extensive as your own. Perhaps greater. I recognise you, Moriarty; I know you."

"Indeed." The professor wrote a further line before rotating the ledger and sliding it towards the duke. The written page was caught in the full glow of the lamp. "Read carefully what I have transcribed. If you are in agreement as to the figures, kindly sign here and we shall consider – how may I say it? – that your account has been opened."

The duke glanced at the book and then up at Moriarty's shadowed face. "You will put this in writing?"

"You say you know me. Then you will know that I am a careful man. I commit to no cause until I am sure of it. And I will trust no man who is not willing to put a name to his own enterprise."

The duke paused a while longer, reluctant. Eventually, however, Leofric took up the pen and signed his name with a flourish. Moriarty slid the ledger back towards himself, casting his eyes over the signature before slamming the book closed.

"We understand one another, Your Grace. And as gentlemen, we need not say another word upon the subject." He reached a thin hand across the desk; after a moment, the duke took it. They shook solemnly.

"When may I expect to hear from you?" asked Leofric, standing.

"You may not. The event of which we speak cannot pass unnoticed: it will feature in every newspaper within the civilised world. Then you may wish for another audience, and, at such a time, we will discuss the termination of the account."

Leofric bowed with a click of his heels. Hawes appeared once more with hat and stick as though he had heard every word spoken in the study. The duke took them and, with another curt bow, left Moriarty and the porter alone. Hawes closed the door on the duke's back.

"An interesting coincidence, sir."

Moriarty blinked slowly; clearly the porter's thoughts ran along similar lines to his own. "Coincidence is but a function of probability, Hawes, not the workings of some supernatural agency."

"Indeed not, sir. But it chimes closely with your plans."

Moriarty turned the lampshade back to its regular position, partially releasing his face from its shadowy seclusion. "The voyage to Germany already booked for next week, you mean. Indeed, it is quite fortuitous." Prior to their unification under the kaiser, the Germanic states had been little more than serfdoms ground under the boot of police oppression. Crime had been easy to uproot and crush. The burgeoning empire was, however, fresh-tilled soil for one with the right seed. A united country meant united criminality; the professor had long been planning an incursion into that nursery and cultivating his own peculiar vineyard.

"Two birds with one stone, eh?" Hawes took up the portrait of the young woman from the floor.

The professor grunted. "I have never considered it prudent to involve myself too directly with my contracts. From the lowest stews of London to the mandarins of government itself, I have agents at every level; agents upon whom I may call to act precisely as they are directed. But after last year's Buckingham Palace humiliation, I wonder if I should not, on occasion, take upon myself direct leadership; especially when the prize is inordinate, the odds great."

"And the colonel?"

"Moran has much ground to recover before I again entrust him with a major enterprise." Moriarty allowed himself a dry chuckle. "Advise him of my imminent absence. He will recognise the opportunity to be once more reckoned an asset. And if he does not, well— Give him every assistance."

"You know that I will, sir."

"Indeed." Moriarty glanced at the painting clutched in the porter's hands. It was unfortunate that he must lose it, but the moment it became clear that ridiculous detective from London had recently gained access to his chambers, the item's fate was irrevocable. It had been sheer hubris to hang the portrait in plain sight: any man with the slightest eye for art would know a Jean-Baptiste Greuze to be far beyond the plain income of a university professor. It was a rare error; one soon to be corrected – and never repeated.

Moriarty sat with his untouched coffee pushed aside, carefully rechecking the column of figures in his notebook. It was a fine, cold day and outside the small *kaffeehaus* the *Unter den Linden* was sparsely populated. The professor was the shop's only customer. He glanced up, eyes focused on something far beyond the window. To his right towered the Brandenburg Gate, but he was blind to its triumphalism.

The shop's door tinkled open, allowing in a breath of late winter air. Moriarty ignored the rotund, heavily swathed figure that entered, apparently oblivious to his presence even as he came to stand at the professor's table.

"A refreshing day." The stranger spoke German in a dialect that suggested Vienna rather than Berlin. He removed his tall hat. "But not one for enjoying the boulevard, I think. The leaves of the Tilia are still little more than buds."

Moriarty took his gaze away from whatever he had been seeing, focusing instead upon the newcomer. The man's round face was red from the breeze, framed by unfashionably long brown hair and a magnificent handlebar moustache. His black overcoat sported a thick astrakhan collar. He unbuttoned the coat, all the better to enjoy the *kaffeehaus*'s warmth.

"It is certainly not a day to be abroad on frivolous matters," replied Moriarty, his German flawless.

"And the *Kaiserreich* is not the regime to encourage frivolity."

Moriarty closed his notebook, resting a hand upon its black cover. With his pencil he gestured for the newcomer to sit. "Thank you for coming, Herr Eisenerz."

"It is my pleasure, Herr Schiffersohn." He summoned the waiter with a snap of fingers, ordering coffee, schnapps and a slice of chocolate cake. Drawing a large humidor from his coat he offered a cigar to Moriarty, who declined with a brief shake of the head. Once his smoke was lit to his satisfaction, Eisenerz asked: "So, what may I do for you?"

"You have the reputation of being, shall we say... a facilitator."

Eisenerz smiled broadly and spoke around a vast plume of fragrant smoke. "I have contacts, if such is your meaning. It is true that I am able to—" he drew on his cigar "—ease introductions."

"Such was my understanding." Moriarty recalled to mind an image of the column of numbers in his notebook. "My particular requirement is not an introduction, as such."

"Ask away." Eisenerz's order arrived. The segment of cake looked, to Moriarty's eye, to encompass at least a forty-degree angle. "Ask away," he repeated, feeding a generous forkful into his mouth. His eyes wrinkled in delight.

"I require entrance into the *Berliner Stadtschloss*."

Eisenerz swallowed his morsel and washed it down with coffee. "My dear fellow, you may enter the *Stadtschloss* whenever you wish." He took up his schnapps and drained the glass in one swallow, immediately signalling for another. He dabbed at his moustache, grin broadening. "But if I understand you, you will not wish to do so under normal circumstances."

"Your understanding is faultless, Herr Eisenerz."

The large man took another mouthful of rich gateau; Moriarty was content to let him play his game: he could be patient. "If you had come a little later in the year, this request would be so much easier. The *Stadtschloss* has been the Hohenzollern winter home for generations, and the kaiser is, in many respects, a man of tradition." Eisenerz enjoyed another forkful. "Although with security understandably heightened it is still conceivable that a window may be accidentally left ajar or an open lock overlooked.

I am certain that in such a place the staff are overworked and under-appreciated. Mistakes are inevitable."

"It is only human." Moriarty opened his notebook at a fresh page and quickly wrote down a figure. Carefully he tore the page free and slid it across the table with a fingertip. Eisenerz glanced down, seeming to take little interest in what was inscribed there.

"That is inordinately generous, Herr Schiffersohn." He raised his coffee cup and some of the dark liquid splashed across the sheet, masking the numbers. "Ah. Clumsy of me."

Moriarty stifled a smirk, screwing up the wet paper and dropping it into the saucer of his own, now cold, coffee.

Eisenerz's second schnapps was delivered; this time the large man took his time, sipping thoughtfully. "I will not presume to ask why you need this done, Herr Schiffersohn, but I confess to being intrigued."

Moriarty relaxed against his chair. "There is an item I wish to procure."

Eisenerz devoured the last morsel of chocolate cake and drained his coffee. "That is no more than I expected."

For more than a decade, Moriarty had assiduously created a variety of aliases across the continent: names and reputations, costumes ready for him to don should the occasion arise. Let the vainglorious detective in London have his music hall disguises to complement the abductive reasoning upon which he so heavily relied. It was the price of the fame against which he so unconvincingly protested. The strongest disguise was anonymity. Just as in England Professor James Moriarty was a well-respected, if dull, professor of mathematics, in Germany Heinrich Schiffersohn was a less reputable but equally renowned collector of the strange and obtuse; a man for whom nothing might stand in the way of his desires. Already the European newspapers had reported the disappearances of eight priceless and outlandish *objets d'art*. All blamed on the mysterious Schiffersohn, and all equally fictitious. The professor had no intention of wasting time and resources on genuine thefts when a suitably outrageous lie would suffice.

"The kaiser has come into the possession of a certain . . . item. His claim upon it is questionable. If the true owners became aware of this, the repercussions would echo across the globe. I intend to relieve His Imperial Majesty of the burden."

Eisenerz smiled again. "And he can hardly report the theft of such a piece. I congratulate you: a masterly design."

"Thank you." Moriarty noted that the man had failed to question how the fictitious Schiffersohn had been able to learn of this nonsensical item when the supposed owners had not.

"But can you not wait until the kaiser is no longer in residence? It would be prudent."

"He takes it with him at all times. I must relieve him of it personally, as it were."

Eisenerz's eyes grew as round as his face. "Audacious. Then I wish you luck, for I believe you will need it."

Moriarty's lips twitched in a brief smile. "I am not an advocate of luck or chance, only probability and logic. All which is beautiful and noble is the result of reason and calculation." On a fresh slip of notepaper he wrote an address. "This is the hotel at which I am staying." He handed the page across. "The staff may be trusted. Once all of the arrangements are made, send word."

Eisenerz slipped the note into an overcoat pocket. He stood, taking up his hat and making a crisp bow. "A pleasure conducting business with you, Herr Schiffersohn." Buttoning his coat as he went, Eisenerz left the *kaffeehaus*.

"And you, sir." Moriarty turned back to the page on which stood the column of figures. He crossed out the first number, delighted that he had predicted it so accurately.

Although the hour was late, the household had not fully retired. Moriarty expected no less. As he strolled through the lowly quarters of the *Stadtschloss* – those dim and ignored corridors frequented only by the servants – he would occasionally pass a member of the night staff, hurrying by on some errand. He was rarely acknowledged, never challenged, perceived as just another dusty retainer going about his own business. The palace staff was numerous, frequently rotated with those from other state buildings; an unfamiliar face would not be unusual. Indeed he had been at greater risk of discovery beyond the building: both the *Unter den Linden* and *Schlossplatz* were still frequented by two-wheeled *droshkies* and pedestrians enjoying the cold night air.

It had taken Eisenerz a fortnight to report back, during which time Moriarty had surveyed the *Stadtschloss* and its environs at all hours and weathers, filling his notebook with figures, observations and timings. By the time the awaited message had been delivered, the professor was confident he knew the palace's routine better even than the highest-placed member of the emperor's household. A disaffected Serb agreed to leave a door unbolted, one far away from the streets and their attendant lighting. The man cared nothing for reasons – Germans were no better than Austro-Hungarians in his eyes, and deserving any ill that might befall them – only for the banknotes Eisenerz had pressed into his hand. It was a prudent and fortuitous choice: if chance should play a hidden trump, or the professor's calculations contain an unlikely error, the Serb would be a convenient and logical scapegoat.

Moriarty briefly consulted a map of the building, assuring himself of his position within its walls. He had to admit to a *frisson* of a kind he had not experienced since his formative years. Was this, he wondered, why that detective so frequently took what to the professor appeared to be foolish risks? Was he addicted to the excitement? The danger? Not for the first time, Moriarty regretted he had not himself attended to the disastrous Buckingham Palace contract: not only would his presence have likely ensured its success, he may even have enjoyed the hunt.

The moment passed; he waved the thought away with an irritable flick of his hand and pocketed the map, lest another passing servant wonder why he should need it.

The Emperor's rooms were on the floor directly above him. Normal access was through a well-guarded corridor, but the palace had its own undisclosed, tangential world. Hidden from view within the palace's very walls, a secret to the general staff, through which the most trusted servants might come and go, quietly and unhampered, almost invisible to their masters

Moriarty checked his watch: timing was of paramount importance. Wilhelm had been in poor health for many days; confined
to his chambers and tended by his personal physician, the
emperor's person was checked with Prussian efficiency every
hour. The next observation was forty-three minutes away.
Enough time, the professor calculated, to enter the rooms via
the secret access and guarantee the eventual succession of
Wilhelm II.

He paced silently along the corridor; a map of the palace's
hidden ways unrolling in his mind. There was only one physical
plan detailing the concealed world: that of the architect Andreas
Schlüter, who had overseen the reconstruction of the palace
during the previous century. A plan the German authorities
misguidedly believed safely hidden in a Nuremburg bank vault.
The panel he sought was simple and unadorned, placed unob-
trusively amidst a gallery of Hohenzollern portraiture. Even
though he was actively seeking it, Moriarty passed by and walked
on a further ten feet before realising his error. Retracing his
steps, he made a thorough search of the spot where his mental
diagram told him the hidden entrance must be. Marvelling at the
artistry with which the panel was disguised, Moriarty eventually
located the catch – placed high above a length of moulding,
beyond where it might be accidentally triggered – and depressed
it. The panel swung open no more than an inch, and with
commendable silence. Checking that the corridor remained
empty of observers, the professor stepped through the portal,
easing it shut behind him.

He lit a candle and surveyed his new surroundings. The space
inside the walls was no wider than a yard, roughly plastered, the
floor muffled by faded strips of carpeting; all immaculately clean.
Those who knew of and used this maze had no intention of arriving at their destination covered in dust or shreds of cobweb – no
matter how private or unheeded. Moriarty forged ahead. There
would be narrow steps leading up to the next floor, and from his
eidetic map he knew it was a mere dozen feet away, in the darkness beyond the candlelight.

The steps loomed out of the blackness: half the width of the

passage, constructed of smoothly rendered brick so that even the
heaviest tread would be muffled. Moriarty ascended, admitting
to himself that now his goal was but scant feet away he was experiencing a further quiver of anticipation.

The steps ended at what appeared to be a blank wall. Raising
his candle, Moriarty made out the outline of another disguised
panel; one that, should Schlüter's plans be accurate, must lead
directly into the chambers where Wilhelm slumbered in blithe
ignorance. There was a dark spot on the smooth panel at eye
level. Moriarty leaned forward: it was a lens set into the panel, no
bigger than his smallest fingernail. Pressing an eye to it, the
professor saw a distorted view of the chamber beyond. A single
candle flickered from a dresser in the furthest reach of the room,
next to a wide doorway, casting a thin, uncertain light. Other
than a figure bundled upon an opulent bed, the room appeared
to be empty of human occupants.

Moriarty snuffed his candle and left it upon the top step
rather than risk even the smallest trace of dripped wax in the
room beyond. After carefully easing the panel open, he stepped
into the dim room and engaged in a second, more thorough
visual search. The four-post bed had a single occupant; the
walls were partly clad in a wood that looked black in the poor
light, the rest papered by what Moriarty was surprised to recognise as either a William Morris design or a clever copy. The bed
and windows were hung with drapes of a matching pattern. He
found it repugnant.

A swift glance at his watch told him there were twenty-eight
minutes remaining. He removed a tiny paper bundle from a coat
pocket, silently approaching the bed across a thick carpet. The
emperor lay on his back, breathing slowly and with the faintest
rattle. In the candlelight, his face, neat moustache and bristling
side-whiskers were all a matching sallow shade. From the paper
bundle, Moriarty removed a needle, careful not to graze himself
on the sharp tip. Kneeling at the bedside he took the emperor's
left hand and slid it across the covers. The old man hitched a
breath and the professor froze, not moving until the German's
breathing returned to its steady, soft rattle. Fitting a jeweller's

loupe to his left eye, Moriarty leaned close to the hand, bringing the needle up to a fingernail. Gently, knowing a sudden, sharp prick might awaken the old man and all would be undone, he slid the needle under the nail, breaking the skin with a gentle scratch. Wilhelm coughed, but the professor held the hand steady. He allowed ten seconds to pass before removing the inoculating needle and packing it once more in the paper. There was a faint red mark under the nail where no one would think to look. The emperor was ill; if he should take a more serious turn and ultimately die, even the most suspicious of doctors could see nothing unusual in that.

Moriarty stood, once again consulting his watch: there were eighteen minutes before the emperor would next be checked. He gazed at the sleeping man, awarding him a brief bow. "*In Frieden ruhen, Herr Kaiser.*" Then he left through the secret Morris-patterned panel.

Hawes opened the study door and stood aside, allowing Moriarty entrance. "Welcome back, sir. I read in the newspapers that your journey was fruitful." The porter tactfully failed to enquire why the professor had not returned immediately: it was almost three months since the passing of Emperor Wilhelm.

Moriarty responded with a skeletal smile, placing a valise upon his writing desk. Hawes assisted with the removal of his overcoat, cradling it across an arm. "And that German gentleman has visited, sir. Five times."

Moriarty removed his notebook and ledger from his bag, placing both on the desk. "And I fancy he will be shortly dropping by a sixth time: his hired informants will have already passed on the news of my return to England."

"Of course, sir. Will there be anything else?"

"You need only show in His Grace when he arrives." Moriarty looked at his watch. "I anticipate his arrival within the half-hour."

"Very good, sir." The porter closed the study door softly behind him.

Moriarty breathed in the air of his venerable study. It was

good to be home. The sun blazed through his window, lighting the room even as the rays left his writing desk in shadow. The only change was the painting hanging above his chair, replacing the Greuze: a bucolic scene of cloying sentimentality that he loathed instantly. It was perfect. He sat, opening both notebook and ledger. Taking up a pen, he began copying figures from the notebook into the larger volume, totalling them, and comparing it to the original figure he had presented for the duke's approval. The numbers were gratifyingly close.

He leaned back in his chair, content now to await Duke Leofric's arrival.

Moriarty had many reasons for remaining so long in Berlin. He had wished to observe the fruits of his deed at close quarters, and it had been necessary to enact certain precautions. After the successful completion of the contract, he considered it unwise to quit the country whilst the health of anyone who might later bear witness against him continued in a robust manner. He did not imagine Eisenerz to be such a fool that he could not solve the equation, and his respective share within it. And even though Moriarty did not consider the Serb to be any form of threat, the man had swiftly deleted himself from the balance: killed in a drunken brawl with two Austrians.

Eisenerz's eradication was neither so casual nor straightforward, for he was by nature and experience discreet and circumspect. Nevertheless, for all his caution, Eisenerz died under the wheels of a runaway dray on the Königgrätzer Strasse, less than four hours before the kaiser drew his final breath. Moriarty had arranged for an anonymous wreath to be laid during the man's funeral; after all, in the days before his accident, Eisenerz had arranged introductions between Heinrich Schiffersohn and many of the more ambitious businessmen from German society. Moriarty saw it as a gesture of heartfelt thanks.

As expected, even though terminally ill, Wilhelm's son had been invested as the Emperor Friedrich III; and equally expected, as Moriarty sat in his study awaiting Duke Leofric, it was clear that Friedrich was only days away from joining his father. Even though it had been no more complex than the simplest subtraction, the professor still felt pride in his achievement. That he was present added a certain piquancy to the affair.

There was a knock on his door. "The Duke Leofric is here, sir," announced Hawes.

Moriarty glanced up, frowning. He had been lost in rêverie; most regrettable. "Show him in," he said, closing both books and piling them neatly on his right. Leofric swept into the study, an air of brash confidence roiling in his wake. He dropped his hat on to the desk and sat without an invitation, one hand resting on his walking stick. Moriarty lay back in his chair, retreating into the dimness behind the sunlight streaming through his window.

"The news from Germany seems to agree with you, Your Grace."

Leofric's pale face spread in a wide grin. "And why should it not? Soon we shall have another kaiser – a fresher, more invigorated one. Through which the Fatherland may finally realise its destiny."

"Is there anything more ephemeral than political certainty?" Moriarty tapped the leather binding of his ledger. "You have come to settle your account?"

Leofric withdrew one his infernal cigarettes and lit it. He crossed his legs and relaxed against the chair. "Not at all, Herr Professor. I think I do not owe you so much as a farthing."

"Indeed? And by what route did you reach this conclusion?"

"You were engaged to despatch the late kaiser to his eternal reward, but he died of natural causes. It is in all of the newspapers."

Moriarty tapped his fingertips together. "Ah, then I must have misunderstood Your Grace. I did not realise that His Imperial Majesty's death was to be a sensational and obvious murder."

A little of the duke's élan dissolved in the wash of the professor's chill demeanour. "Is this how your reputation was gained, Professor? By the taking of credit for the inevitable?"

"I admit to usually working through intermediaries, but I will only claim the dues that are rightfully mine." He tapped the ledger again, a little harder. "I would advise Your Grace to settle this particular debt, and with alacrity. At our first meeting you said that you knew me; if that claim was – as I trust – not simply the boast of a spoiled prince then you also know I will not be gainsaid. It is a dangerous practice."

"No." Leofric extinguished his cigarette and stood, taking up his hat. "I shall not pay, *mein herr*, for I do not believe you have satisfactorily completed the contract. You will not pursue the debt; in this the courts are closed to you. So I will bid you *auf wiedersehen*." He opened the study door, not waiting for the vigilant Hawes.

Moriarty stood slowly, straightening his coat. He crossed to the open study door, signalling the astonished porter standing beyond with the briefest shake of his head, and closed it. Retracing his steps, he opened the study window and left it ajar by six inches before sitting himself behind his desk once more. He slid the ledger towards him, opening it at the page listing the calculations for the duke's contract. Beyond the window, he heard a woman's abrupt screech, the horrified cries of men and the screams of an injured horse. Ten seconds later, Hawes opened the study door and peered through.

"I'm afraid there's been a bit of an accident, sir. It appears that German gentleman stepped out in front of a speeding cab . . ."

Moriarty opened his notebook to the line of figures he had jotted down whilst returning across the Channel. He swiftly compared them with the ledger's numbers, nodding to himself as he mentally reconciled both columns. Taking up a fresh pen, the professor dipped it in ink and carefully inscribed three red words across the ledger page: PAID IN FULL.

The Perfect Crime

G. H. Finn

Sunday, 8 August 1937

While the spires of Oxford may not have been dreaming, they did seem to slumber lazily as they basked in the sunshine. Edwin Fitzackerly, sticky and rather hot about the face as he pedalled his bicycle toward the university, was firmly wishing he hadn't habitually followed his mother's parting advice to always wear a vest, but it was too late to worry about that now. He was already perilously close to missing his appointment and undergraduates did not keep senior lecturers waiting – at least, not if they hoped one day to become faculty members themselves. Steering his bicycle one-handed, Edwin glanced at his watch. He grimaced and muttered, "I'm late!", feeling more than a little like the White Rabbit in *Alice's Adventures in Wonderland*. Then he couldn't help but smile, as it struck him this was remarkably apt considering he was currently on his way to examine some effects of the late Charles Dodgson, better known as Lewis Carroll, author of the "Alice" books.

It tended to annoy Edwin that among the general public Lewis Carroll was often regarded as merely a writer of whimsical nonsense for children. At least in the cloisters of Oxford University, Charles Dodgson – who had died in 1898, almost forty years previously – was still respected and admired for his consummate skills as both a mathematician and a logician. As a child in his nursery, Edwin had been very fond of Alice's adventures but as a young man he also had developed a love for

Dodgson's works on logic. Edwin considered himself very lucky to have been asked to write a biographical article about a man he regarded as something of a hero, even if it was only for his college's student newspaper. It was perhaps even more fortunate that one of the more doddering of the elderly Masters at the college had by chance remarked that he possessed a jumble of Dodgson's old effects and papers, stored for posterity but for many years forgotten, mouldering away in his attic. Apparently these papers included some private correspondence with another professor of mathematics, but Edwin's informant could remember no further details.

To his great delight, Edwin had been given permission to come and sort through these relics of Dodgson to decide for himself if any might be helpful in writing his article. While he knew that in all likelihood he would find nothing more exciting than a ledger of household accounts, secretly he hoped he might stumble across some unpublished mathematical theorem, or perhaps even the manuscript of a third Alice adventure!

Arriving at his destination several minutes later than the firmly stipulated two o'clock (and amidst a steady stream of perspiration), Edwin was unsure whether to be worried or relieved that his octogenarian benefactor had not bothered to wait for his arrival. Placed under the brass knocker of the front door was a sheet of paper bearing the words "Punctuality is the politeness of kings. Louis XVIII", beneath which was written "I see no reason why your lateness should be the cause of my own. You are welcome to use my house to conduct your researches in my absence. It being the Sabbath, my servants have been granted a day of rest thus you must be prepared to fend for yourself. The chest is in the drawing room. Let yourself in and try not to make too much mess." The note was signed with an entirely indecipherable flourish that seemed to have more in common with a hieroglyph than a signature.

A short while later, Edwin was seated at a table, steadily unpacking the contents of a battered leather trunk that had been recovered from the bottom of a large tea chest. He had begun by carefully removing one item at a time and attempting

to devise some system for cataloguing his finds, but he quickly
gave up on this idea. He realised he first had to work out what it
was he was trying to examine. There were a few books, which he
stacked neatly at one end of the table. There were also many
sepia-tinted photographs, most probably taken by Dodgson
himself, which Edwin placed carefully in a pile of their own.
There were batches of handwritten notes, which Edwin was
sure would warrant closer attention but which for now he began
to assemble into a heap in front of him. And then there were
letters, private correspondence, mostly between Dodgson and
someone who might have been a colleague of his – judging by a
quick glance, it was indeed some professor of mathematics – but
whether one who had taught at Oxford or elsewhere Edwin
could not judge. The letters bore no address and for the most
part were signed simply "M."

Finally, there was a most singular item. At the bottom of the
case, Edwin found a heavy, clear glass bottle. Curious, thought
Edwin, for while the bottle held no liquid, on careful inspection
it had been most thoroughly stoppered, and sealed both with
lead foil and wax. More and more curious, thought Edwin, who
had had the bitter lessons of accepted grammar beaten into him
while at prep school. Looking through the glass, inside the bottle,
Edwin could very easily see a sealed paper envelope, inscribed
with the simple instruction "Read Me".

Not being at all sure what to make of the mystery bottle,
Edwin stood it on the table and stroked his chin. While, unsurprisingly, the items arranged before him did not seem overly
likely to conceal a hitherto unknown novel about the amazing
Alice, they still might contain many deep insights into Dodgson's
life and works. But there really was only one way to be sure
whether any of them may have any use at all. And so Edwin
resolved to work his way through his finds, one by one. He was
tempted to start with the photographs, as he felt they could
perhaps be examined more swiftly than the various writings,
but Edwin rejected the notion on the grounds that they were
also less likely to shed any light on either Dodgson's mathematical research or his literary endeavours. At first glance, the

notes seemed rather unclear, if not decidedly cryptic. They would require quite some time to study properly. Nodding to himself, Edwin resolved to begin by reading the letters from Professor M.

While Edwin was not always the most organised of men, he was reasonably diligent and methodical. He began by sorting the professor's letters into date order. Then, with the earliest first, he began to read. It quickly became apparent that Charles Dodgson and the professor must have held each other in high regard, either academically or intellectually, and it seemed they may perhaps have been good friends, for in the course of the correspondence, M. had suggested Dodgson might like to play a game of logic and deduction with him. The professor would pose a problem, the solution to which, if Dodgson were to solve it, would lead Dodgson to the location of the next clue.

What a jolly old fellow, thought Edwin. I wish more professors were like him. In Edwin's own experience, most members of the university staff not only did not possess a sense of humour, they vehemently objected to their students doing anything that might be considered enjoyable under any circumstances.

Reading further, it was obvious Dodgson must have accepted this amusing challenge, for the next few letters each contained complex riddles, mathematical puzzles, codes, cyphers and perplexing problems of the most baffling nature. How Dodgson had unriddled these mysteries remained unknown. Unless . . . thought Edwin, perhaps the handwritten notes might shed some light on this? But regardless of the methods he had employed, clearly Dodgson had indeed solved M.'s enigmas – and Edwin suspected he would have thoroughly enjoyed the process of doing so. He also wondered whether the professor had been pleased to have his conundrums picked apart so easily, or whether M. would have felt annoyed that an intellect existed to rival his own? Judging by the letters, the professor certainly was something of a genius when it came to plotting out cunning mental tricks and traps. At times his writing suggested a hint of intellectual arrogance. Yet it seemed Dodgson had always been able to best M. in this game of wits.

At last, Edwin began to read the last of the letters from the mysterious Professor M.

In it, M. congratulated Dodgson on how well he had played their game thus far, and then, rather than immediately present another puzzle, Professor M. began to expound upon a somewhat disturbing subject. At least, it would have been unsettling were it not so obviously a joke. It had to have been a light-hearted addition to the game. Surely it must . . .

At that moment, Edwin was distracted by a pencilled addition to the inked writing of the letter. The professor's habitual "M." had been circled on this particular sheet, a line drawn from it, and in the margins, in what looked very much like Dodgson's handwriting, was a question mark and the comment "Why does M. never sign his name?" This meant very little to Edwin, although for some reason he had a nagging feeling that maybe he should know the identity of Professor M . . . Then again, Oxford was always awash with so many doctors and professors, it probably wasn't of any particular significance.

M. had introduced a new topic into this last letter. It would have been scandalous if it were not framed purely as an exercise in logic. The professor had begun by asking a question.

"Have you given any consideration to the problem of how one might commit the perfect crime? From the standpoint of the logician, it is a most interesting subject upon which to formulate an analysis."

While Edwin would admit that, from an entirely abstract perspective, the question was harmless enough and might be interesting to idly speculate upon, nevertheless there was something about the change in the tone of the writing that subtly disturbed him. The professor continued, expanding on his theme and offering a few hints as to his thoughts on how a "perfect crime" might be constructed – from a purely logical and hypothetical standpoint, of course. As ethically questionable as the subject may have been, Edwin did find M.'s suggestions compelling – but there was a far more startling revelation to come. Having once introduced the subject, within a few paragraphs the professor went on to state that he had, theoretically, devised a method for committing such a "perfect" crime, but then he stopped short of explaining the details of his theorem. There was a trace of sardonic mockery in M.'s writing as he all but boasted of this artfully crafted master plan, constructed upon simple logical premises yet which he also described more than a little challengingly as being "an unsolvable enigma".

Edwin frowned and again wondered where he had heard of a Professor M. before. He shook his head and returned to read the closing paragraph of the letter:

"Would you like to know the details of my perfect crime? Would you really? The question in my mind remains, are you worthy to know this secret? I propose a final round to our game of logic and deduction. If you solve my greatest riddle (and with this you will either sink or swim) then you will be led to a message in a bottle – you will most certainly recognise this if you are clever enough to find it. In my final letter I shall withhold no secrets, rather I will lay all information before you, demonstrating exactly how a man might commit a perfect crime and yet despite this I most decidedly assure you, the crime is of such a nature that even with evidence fully provided it will never be solved. Here is your puzzle."

The rest of the sheet of paper had been torn off, but Edwin was not overly interested to know what the professor's last riddle may have been. Whatever it was, it was perfectly obvious that Dodgson had solved it – the proof was standing on the table before him. Edwin sat, staring at the strange sealed bottle with its enigmatic envelope nestling inside it.

And then another mystery occurred to Edwin. Having deduced the solution to M.'s final puzzle, why then had Charles Dodgson not opened the bottle?

The young man frowned and stared at the letter. All he could see was "Read Me".

And then he decided that he would.

Somewhat hesitantly, he broke the scarlet wax seal around the top of the bottle, removed the cork and vainly attempted to reach the envelope inside. A strange but not altogether unpleasant fragrance emanated from the bottle, filling his nostrils and almost making him sneeze. It had a heavy note of perfume. Absent-mindedly, he wondered if the letter inside the bottle had been written by a lady, for surely a gentleman would not have scented his writing materials in such a fashion? Unless perhaps he was a foreigner? Edwin was sure there were plenty of European professors with a surname beginning with "M" . . . Maybe a Professor Medici or a Professor Machiavelli or some-such? A hint of the Orient had seemed to suggest itself amid the pungent miasma that assailed his nose. A Professor Ming or perhaps a Professor Manchu? It seemed unlikely . . . After a few moments spent in a fruitless attempt to reach the envelope by alternately inserting a finger into the neck of the bottle and then, abandoning this approach, turning the bottle upside down and shaking it, he eventually decided that the simplest course of action would be to break the bottle. He reached for a heavy candlestick that had been conveniently left upon the table. Remembering that he had been instructed to avoid making a mess, he first carefully wrapped the bottle in a fold of the table-cloth then struck it sharply with the base of the candlestick. Nothing happened, but a second harder blow produced a satis-fying splintered cracking sound. Cautiously, Edwin placed the open top of the tea chest under the table, unfolded the table-cloth from around the bottle and let the combination of broken glass and sealed envelope fall into the otherwise empty tea chest. Then he reached carefully inside and retrieved the enve-lope, which he found was held shut by a blob of black sealing wax bearing the imprint of a skull, with the word "memento" and a larger ornate "M" embossed beneath.

Edwin's curiosity could not be suppressed any longer. He swiftly broke the seal, opened the envelope and removed a sheet of paper from within. Once again his nose was assaulted by a pungent aroma. He felt sure he could detect the scents of sandal-wood, attar of roses, cinnamon, frankincense, patchouli, musk, and beneath these, some acrid cloying after-scent that he could not put a name to.

He began to read.

The paper bore a single word as its heading –"Martyrio".

Edwin had no difficulty in recognising this as a Latin term for "testimony", in particular that of a martyr about to be put to death. He considered absent-mindedly that the term was perhaps grammatically incorrect when used in this way, but he gave it no further thought and began reading.

"To Whomsoever is reading these words,

"Logic, that sweet sibling of mathematics, has long been an interest of mine. My fascination for the subject is due not only to its stimulation of the cerebral processes, but also to logic's purity of form and its – oh so useful – practical application to the problems of the manifest world. As with mathematics, logic is pure in that it is entirely free from petty human illusions such as fashion, compassion, sentiment or morality. Rather it rests upon the application of laws greater than those found in either church or courtroom, laws that are rooted in intellect and science rather than in foolish faith or the judgement of twelve good mental weaklings on a jury.

"Moreover, logic can – as I shall demonstrate – be bent to serve the will and purpose of its master, regardless of whether such a purpose be deemed 'moral' or 'immoral' by the lesser intelligences of the general populace. To this end let me present to you a conundrum that has vexed me for some years: 'How might one commit a perfect crime?'

"I suggest you make yourself comfortable and read on, as through the medium of this letter, I intend to show you.

"Before applying logic to solve this problem, let us first define and agree some terms and parameters.

i) For a crime to be perfect, it must be a crime recognised in law, or by some other self-inflating and objectively irrelevant authority such as religion – preferably it will be deemed a crime both by Church and state. For our purposes here, a crime is not a crime unless it be near universally accepted as such.

ii) The crime must have a manifest reality and the crime must actually occur – I therefore preclude from this discussion petty 'crimes' which have no tangible basis in the physical world (such as verbal blasphemy, treason or slander) and also any 'crime' which may be deemed to take place only in the heart and mind of the individual or in any other way to lack a concrete nature.

iii) For a crime to be 'perfect', it must be unsolved and must remain effectively unsolvable.

"It has been argued that 'a perfect crime' would be one that is undetected and undetectable. This I refute. Such a crime would certainly be agreeable, and fit with the concept of a 'perfect crime', were it not that it would be scientifically unverifiable. If a man claps his hands in an effort to frighten away lions, this we may consider to be logical. If no lions appear, logically the method may be a sound one. But should the man claim that his clapping drives away lions from his home in London, we should scoff at him and his method, rightly pointing out that an absence of lions does not prove that his clapping has driven them away. So too a man claiming to have developed a methodology for committing a perfect crime cannot simply state that he has done so and offer the lack of the detection of his crimes as proof of their perfection, otherwise he would run the risk of being considered either a simpleton or a lying fool.

"I therefore add further conditions to my definition of 'a perfect crime':

iv) At least one person besides the Master Criminal must be aware that the crime has been committed.

"This stipulation will help to ensure the scientific validity of the method. After all, one should hardly simply take the word of a self-proclaimed Mastermind of Crime as I, or rather they, may, of course, be lying. In a puzzle of logic, one must always be on one's guard against statements which may later prove to be false.

v) It would further be desirable that in addition to at least one person knowing of the commission of the crime (whether by directly witnessing it or by deduction), ideally there should be undeniable physical evidence of the crime – yet naturally, this evidence must be such that it cannot be used to prove the identity of the perpetrator of the perfect crime, or as I might immodestly refer to him, the Perfect Criminal.

"Whilst in theory many crimes might be suitable for the purpose of our little experiment, let us not trifle with inconsequentialities. Let us set the stakes of this game high. Let us assume that the perfect crime must be at the apex of all criminality. Let us choose for our crime nothing less than murder.

"How then may our Perfect Criminal commit a murder and yet remain unfettered by any undue fear of detection?

"Let us first make a few assumptions about our Mastermind.

"Let us assume that he is no ham-fisted bungler apt to leave behind a mass of readily understood clues to his crimes. Let us assume he is a man of high intelligence and diligence, possessed of no small measure of guile. Let us assume he is educated to the highest degree, well placed in society and canny enough to work for the most part through intermediaries and that thus he is able to still further reduce the already limited risk of detection.

"Should then our Master Criminal be afraid of being caught in the perpetration of a crime? Should he fear that he might leave some unfortuitous item behind at the scene of his activities, such as a misplaced monogrammed glove or a carelessly dropped calling card bearing his address? No, for he has a veritable army of lesser criminals to carry out his orders while he, like any prudent general, remains far from the field of conflict and concerns himself primarily with strategy.

"Should he fear the risk of betrayal by one of his deputies? Not if he is canny enough to ensure very few men know his true identity, and also to arrange that those slender few who could identify either his name or his face are themselves in far greater fear of him than ever they would fear a hangman's noose.

"If then our Master Criminal may justly feel himself safe from the risk of discovery by the victims of his crimes and if likewise he may understandably feel unendangered by the humdrum investigations of the denizens of Scotland Yard, who then *should* our Master Criminal guard himself against?

"In certain Chinese schools of thought, and likewise among the ancient Manichean philosophers, there exists a concept of a natural law of opposites. For there to be night, so then there must be day. For there to be darkness, so too there must be light. If there is such a person as a Master Criminal, so, inevitably, one day there must come a Master Detective.

"While our Master Criminal may justifiably fear no ordinary policeman, being himself of an extraordinary nature far beyond the reach of normal men, it would only be prudent for our Master Criminal to guard against the possibility of his discovery by an equally extraordinary detective, one who's wit and knowledge, training and temperament, skills and powers of reasoning are close to being a match for my own. Such a Master Detective might yet see through any obfuscating fog I employed to baffle lesser minds. If he were to apply his superior abilities unceasingly, forgo food and sleep until he'd solved a problem, then he might eliminate six impossible things before breakfast and thus be left with the truth – no matter how improbable it might seem that anyone could truly be a threat to one such as myself.

"That such a Master Detective shall one day arise, I regard almost as an inevitability. Indeed, I feel it is likely I have already become aware his presence, exploring and investigating the outer strands of my web. While I am not entirely certain, it is my belief that the existence of a Mastermind of Crime – though not as yet my actual identity – may already have been deduced by some hidden nemesis. Thus I have taken steps to attempt to identify who among the brightest minds of our time might be disguising himself and hiding amongst my shadows? Who is it that may one day threaten me? Yes, I write 'me', for the time for all pretences has now passed.

"I have, thus far, considered eighty-seven potential threats to my continued operation as a Criminal Mastermind – people who I reasoned might, under certain circumstances, prove themselves capable of becoming a danger to my anonymity, or indeed to my very existence. I reasoned early on that I could not easily have so many prominent individuals killed – for most are doctors, lawyers, clergymen, scientists, authors, petty nobles and the like. I could not simply have them *all* killed, at least not without causing far too great a public outcry and arousing suspicion and interest where as yet there is none. I therefore began to test each of my suspects to determine which of these eighty-seven might truly become a poisoned thorn in my side. I watched them. I studied them. I devised tests. I set puzzles. Those who failed to solve my riddles, I let go. Like a benevolent fisherman throwing back the small fry, I removed the barbs of my hook from the throats of those of lesser intellect, reasoning that if they failed to solve the problems I had presented them with, they certainly could not succeed in outwitting me in games that were played for higher stakes. I whittled down my eighty-seven to forty-three. I reduced forty-three to seventeen. From seventeen I subtracted a further eleven. At last I had half a dozen firm suspects, six Napoleons of Detection who might potentially one day face me in the field. To my great surprise, one was a female. The woman I decided to treat as a special case. The other five men I determined to test still further. Each of these five had passed all my earlier trials so I determined to send each one a puzzle so intricately complex that I could but barely solve it myself. Should anyone decrypt this problem I would know that individual could undoubtedly pose a threat to me. I arranged that the solving of the problem would lead ultimately to the discovery of the bottle containing this letter.

"When I began to write, I addressed you, my dear reader, with the phrase 'To Whomsoever is reading these words'. In truth, as I am writing this, I do not know which one of you has solved my most artful puzzle and claimed this letter as his prize. If no one has solved my greatest riddle, then I write these words to no one and I am at no risk at all. If you have opened the bottle and for some reason you have not immediately read these words then for reasons which will shortly become clear, I know I still am safe. Likewise, if by remote chance the hiding place of the bottle had been discovered accidentally and its letter has somehow fallen into unintended hands, again I need feel no concern and I am in no danger, as you will realise when you read further. But whoever you are, if you are now reading this, it is only fitting that I explain why I have no fear that you will use my words against me in any court of law.

"You may have wondered why I have set down this information in so rambling a manner? Why haven't I as yet got to the point? Why do I seem to procrastinate and delay, taking my time in telling you of my plans, drawing out the moment when I will reveal my secrets? Indeed, you may wonder why I have set down any information at all?

"Before I answer that, let me offer some further data. I am well known as a mathematician. My training in the sciences is however both wide and deep. I have no small knowledge of chemistry. There exist certain substances which are described as being *pyrophoric* – a term stemming from the Greek πυροφόρος, *pyrophoros*, meaning 'fire-bearing'. A chemical that is pyrophoric will ignite spontaneously when in air at normal room temperature. I have myself discovered that this reaction can be abated by storing the pyrophoric substance in an inert gas. No doubt others will also soon discover this and publish their findings. No matter. For now, however, I have kept my research and discovery a secret, for I have my own uses for this knowledge. The bottle that contained this letter was filled with such a gas. I trust that you did not imagine the gas was poisonous? I hope I did not give you any undue cause for concern on that account. I can assure you the gas was entirely harmless. Besides which, any poisonous gas would either be so strong as to have killed you instantly when you first opened the bottle or else would be so weak as to be easily dispersed in the air, thus becoming harmless. Now where was I?

"It was no particular difficulty for me to impregnate the paper upon which I have written these words with certain pyrophoric chemicals. It was a far greater task to mix them with a selection of other reagents in order to delay such a reaction so that the paper would not burn the moment it was exposed to air. Such chemicals can create quite an unpleasant smell so I took the precaution of disguising them with a liberal application of varied perfumes. By the time you have finished reading these words, the paper upon which they are written will almost certainly have begun to smoulder imperceptibly and then shortly afterwards will burst into flames, so I advise you to continue reading while you still have the opportunity. In case you are wondering, water will not stop the reaction, it may even hasten it. You have no way of preventing this paper from self-immolating within the next few minutes.

"You may now see why I feel confident that even though I present you with an explanation as to how I will perpetrate a Perfect Crime, I need have no fear of this evidence being used against me, for, within moments, it will no longer exist. By explaining all this in writing, I am presenting you with a full confession, but one that will shortly disappear before your eyes in an almost proverbial puff of smoke. My crime will have a witness, you yourself shall be that witness, but you will be quite unable to act upon your knowledge. I am *doubly* sure of this.

"I posed the question as to why I have written this letter in so protracted and circuitous a fashion? I will now answer that. I did so in order to increase the time it would take you to read my words. I wished to ensure ample time for the chemicals with which I have soaked and coated the paper you are now holding to do their work. I am sure that even if you read extremely quickly, by now their full absorption is utterly inevitable. I ensured that I coated the paper with a sufficient strength even to penetrate through cloth, in the highly unlikely event you are reading this whilst wearing gloves.

"As time draws irrevocably on, I feel I should however at last make a true confession. I have not as yet been entirely honest with you. Did you expect me to be? Did you think I would play this game by anyone's rules but my own? In tests of logic one must always consider the possibility that any given statement may be false. Even so, I have not lied to you.

"Or have I?

"I will admit that I have withheld some information up until this point.

"You may have noticed a rather unusual odour emanating

from the paper upon which my words are written, an unpleasant smell not fully hidden by the aromas of exotic scents that I applied to this letter. I told you that this was due to certain chemicals with which I had coated the paper. That was the truth.

"I implied that these chemicals were simply to delay the speed at which this letter will begin to combust. That was only partially true. *Some* of the chemicals I used were employed for this purpose. Others – well, there is no polite way of putting this and I'm afraid you may think me rather ill-mannered, – some of the other chemicals were employed solely for the purpose of poisoning you. This letter was thoroughly soaked in a mixture of some of the finest toxins that can be bought (or indeed, stolen). One I even isolated myself, from the bile ducts of the little known rodent *Rattus Gigantus Sumatranus*. But I digress, and, under the circumstances, that is rather rude and I hope you will forgive me for my lapse in manners.

"I have conducted rigorous tests of the poisons that have by now been thoroughly absorbed through your skin and are even at this moment coursing through your veins. I would estimate that at present you have probably already lost most motor-neural functions, that you cannot stand and are effectively suffering a numbing paralysis in all your limbs— No, don't try to get up, you will only fall and, besides which, it is quite pointless. Very soon this paralysis will spread to your heart and your lungs. Your pulse will slow and your breathing will become laboured. The toxins will not as yet have clouded your mind, which, being your greatest attribute, I have generously allowed you to retain as a functioning faculty for as long as possible, as I am sure such an enquiring soul as yourself will be interested to observe all the details of this experience.

"I feel that there is little more to write and, as you have such a short time left, I would not wish to waste it further.

"I bid you a fond farewell and hope that, in whatever moments remain to you, you will be assured that I remain your humble and obedient servant,

"Prof. Moriarty"

* * *

It was hard for Edwin to make out the name through the wisps of smoke spiralling up from the paper, which gently dropped from his now nerveless hands, falling on to the pile of letters arranged upon the table and swiftly setting them ablaze.

As Falls Reichenbach, So Falls Reichenbach Falls

Alvaro Zinos-Amaro

*So rapidly does the brain act that I believe I had thought this
all out before Professor Moriarty had reached the bottom of
the Reichenbach Fall.*

Sherlock Holmes, "The Final Problem"

The place is London, the time is October 1892, and the theme is
self-banishment.

Professor Moriarty is in his study, near an unlit fireplace,
captivated by the narcotic-like effects of the settling dusk.

In days past, before his accident, nightfall would have inspired
a subtle, appreciative smile in Moriarty, distilled from the recollection of his many years of nocturnal outings.

But that chapter of his life has ended. Ever since his accident
a year and a half ago, Moriarty has become a shadow of his
former self, a delicate organism stricken with an extreme sens-
ibility to the vicissitudes of life. As a result, he has elected to
sever all ties with his former associates – most of whom, in any
case, believe him deceased – and to live a housebound existence,
isolated from the world save for his wife's ministrations. Moriarty
once adored unpredictability and improvisation, the thrill of
rising to the occasion and surpassing it. His new cocoon is habit.
The slightest irregularity in his daily schedule disturbs him

greatly. He craves the dull routine of existence. He abhors mental exaltation. His mind, or what remains of it, appears to thrive on what others might term stagnation.

And so tonight's dusk should leave him indifferent, as happened yesterday, and the day before, and the day before that. But it does not. The darkness he currently beholds appears . . . alive in some way, directed towards him. Shadows swim over the walls of a deserted Albermarle Street, dimming the already diffuse light of the street lamps, sliding across door jambs, and finally reaching, tendril-like, into the professor's cavernous study.

Moriarty raises his arms, a gesture empty of effect. He is assailed by a wrenching sensation of vertigo deep within his breast. The Universe is spinning madly about him. The name of his wife forms on his thin lips, but before it can be born, he clamps his mouth shut, even as he keels over and falls to the floor. For if there is one thing of which he is certain, it is that he must face this – whatever *this* is – alone.

He twists on the carpet, feeling as though the ground is buckling beneath him.

Recourse to your ratiocination! he tells himself. This must be a sensory trick, an illusion, nothing more.

And so Moriarty stills his body, rubs his eyes and, with great effort, dispels the pitch black that seems to envelop his study, at first in swaths, then in receding flecks, until at last he has reclaimed the meager but sufficient illumination provided by his table lamp.

But the episode is not yet over.

Still splayed on the ground, as though an insect in wait of pins, Moriarty is assailed by a piercing cold and the sound of rushing water. Somehow, he thinks, the chill night air has transported itself into his body, cutting fine frozen rivulets in his lungs. His flesh is soaked in cold; he imagines himself cast into a vast, furious river, submerged in its icy currents.

Again, he summons the powers of his cognition. Again he defeats his foe.

By the time he rises and shuffles to the study's door, he is trembling, and cannot escape an accursed residue of bone-chilling damp. Fictive or not, it permeates his soul.

Moriarty coughs. Moments later, his wife appears beside him. She pauses to study the ghost of her husband, or rather the ghost of the ghost that her husband has of late become.

"Dear?" She need say nothing more; indeed, the monosyllabic question, cast against the severe repression of emotion evident in the professor's pallid features, proves superfluous. For Moriarty has sealed himself off from his wife, and his hermetic encasement cannot be breached, by her or any other living soul.

"I must take my leave of this place," Moriarty declaims. He studies his surroundings, as though aware of them for the first time in years.

His wife waits, eyes sullen but patient, for him to continue.

"Positively do not expect me by the return coach tomorrow," he says. "Do not even be alarmed if I tarry three or four days. But, at all events, look for me at supper on Friday evening."

She does not enquire as to the object of his impromptu journey.

That is a good thing, Moriarty muses, for even if she did, he would be unable to reply, ignorant as he is of this fact himself.

She fetches his drab greatcoat, a hat covered with an oilcloth, his top boots, and an umbrella. In the meantime, he prepares a small portmanteau.

Minutes later, upon reconvening outside Moriarty's study, the atmosphere between husband and wife is one neither of warm appreciation nor frigid alienation, merely the acceptance by both of a mysterious, unappealable fate.

Without another word, Moriarty leaves. In such an inauspicious manner commences his great journey.

His travails do not take the professor far. A scant seventeen minutes after his departure, on a street not far removed from his own, he sees a residence that is accepting tenants and, after a not inconsiderable withdrawal of cash from his portmanteau, he is welcomed at these new lodgings.

His body is at his journey's end, his mind merely at its beginning.

* * *

Moriarty does not understand the scope or implications of the project upon which he has launched himself. He can recognize, in a detached way, that his rash behavior starkly contradicts everything he has assessed to be true about his character since his accident; he has behaved impulsively, deviating from his most beloved schedule, utterly failing to plan ahead. He should feel anxiety and dread. He should be beset by the convulsions of the unknown.

But his recognition of these theoretical responses creates no actual preoccupation or burden within him. Feeling, on the contrary, leavened by his situation, he settles into his new bed with unaccustomed ease, and slips into a profound, blissful slumber.

The following morning Moriarty feels no temptation to turn his thoughts inward. He spends the day diverting himself with abstruse mathematical thoughts, and, when he retires that night, again finds sleep to be deep and unproblematic.

The following day takes a similar course, as does the next, and the next.

Friday arrives. Moriarty thinks of his wife, of the pain she will feel when he does not arrive for supper, the measures she will take to try to locate him. He is moved by her plight, but he cannot change his present heading.

On Saturday morning, Moriarty awakens to find himself unshackled. Friday represented a test, and he has passed. Now he can at last allow himself to understand what he is doing here.

Comprehension dawns throughout the day, but unlike the real aurora, delivers cold rather than heat in its wake. For Moriarty's purpose is now clear: he is to investigate the symptoms of the physical distress that he suffered on the night of his departure, to analyse them, banish them and then resume his life. Though his attack was physical, the underlying cause must surely be mental. If it were not, he could not have overcome the vertigo that had penetrated his chest, or dried himself from the illusory wetness that clung to him, by mere thought. And yet he had.

So he will stay in these lodgings, he resolves on Saturday evening, as long as he must in order to vanquish the disease.

The symptoms return, on and off.

That sound of rushing water, like a whisper inside Professor Morarity's mind; the viscerally unsettling queasiness of a man infinitely far from terra firma.

Every day Professor Moriarty beholds his home, though he makes sure that his perambulations are timed so as to miss Mrs Moriarty. Despite the precaution, once or twice he glimpses her either leaving or entering their domicile at 83 Albermarle Street, and he feels a stab of remorse at the sight of her forlorn countenance.

Days and weeks and months go by, and Moriarty, increment by increment, makes progress in the deconstruction of his *maladie imaginaire*.

An unsentimental examination of his symptoms – the severe vertigo, the sound of rushing water – has made it clear that he must focus his mental energies on the one memory he has until now most assiduously avoided. The memory of his accident at Reichenbach.

Accident. The word itself, he realizes now, is denial. What Moriarty really means is *struggle, fight, violence, fall*; the clash of an irresistible force with an immovable object.

What he really means is *crime*.

Attempted murder.

Near-death experience.

There. He can think these things now, without guilt or shame.

But then, why should he have censored himself in the first place? Moriarty wonders.

There is nothing wrong, after all, with murder. Everyone dies, and if some passengers on the inevitable train of doom are conveyed by Professor Moriarty's adroit hands to a compartment nearer the train's front, then, surely, that is no great tragedy. If examined closely, he is convinced that his life's actions have also regressed other passengers towards rear compartments. It would be as ill-advised to feel guilty over the former as it would to celebrate the latter. Life itself is but a splendid calculus, in which minute adjustments of one's position and velocity, expertly wielded, recompense the wise, while rendering the timorous their instruments.

Nevertheless, something haunts Professor Moriarty – and it haunts him severely – about his attempted murder of his great accuser, his implacable adversary, Sherlock Holmes.

Years pass. Moriarty continues to live mere streets from his former abode. He is never spotted, identified, or called upon. By now Moriarty's death has been reckoned with by his wife. His estate has been settled, his name dismissed from memory. His wife has adopted a mantle of autumnal widowhood without the expectation of ever lifting it from her bosom.

In short, a vast gap has opened up between Professor Moriarty and the world to which he once belonged.

And now something unexpected and terrifying arises within that chasm.

It happens on a Tuesday evening, shortly after supper. Moriarty takes all his meals in his room, and he has just fastidiously wiped his lips. He is preparing to settle into that mild postprandial stupor that often results from overindulgence, when he hears the familiar susurration of rushing water. But this time the sound is right behind him.

Startled, he turns.

In his room, the walls recede, the floorboards disappear and a tremendous abyss opens before him.

For an instant, Moriarty is standing on nothing.

And then he falls.

He tumbles head first into the abyss.

Rocks race before him and gray mist sprays his skin. The sound of rushing water that lured him into this precipitous dive moments ago intensifies a hundredfold: enormous, cascading waterfalls crash inches behind him.

Dear God! There is no mistaking this place, or what occurred here. It is happening all over again. He has just struggled with Holmes on the fall's brink; Holmes has attempted and failed to defend himself with baritsu; they have fallen together.

The world spins, and Moriarty clutches at the empty air, hoping to discover a foothold, an outgrowth of rock, anything.

Then he closes his eyes and thinks. *This must be a dream, an hallucination!* There is no physical dimension to his experience. It is a projection of his mind. And it is on those terms that he must combat it.

This thought has a peculiar effect. He is still falling, but more slowly than before.

He focuses his mind again. His velocity of descent decreases once again.

But is it really him that is slowing down – or the world?

The roar of the waterfall is muted, deepened, transformed. Its spray still cools his skin, but its particulate nature feels finer, less overwhelming.

Time, Professor Moriarty thinks. *I am slowing down my perception of time.*

With a few more moments of practice, he finds that he can bring himself almost to a halt. The more intensely he concentrates on the problem, the more time slows down, and the more time he has to keep perfecting his craft.

Finally, practically frozen in mid-fall, darkness descends upon him, and he thinks no more.

Moriarty wakes in pain. His room feels hot beyond reason, and so he opens the window.

Moments later, thirteen bumblebees swarm in, buzzing loudly.

He remains calm. The bees approach him, encircle him, then depart.

Raising a hand to his forehead, Moriarty determines that he is feverish.

Any life is made up of a single moment, Moriarty reflects. His is indubitably his fall at Reichenbach.

It comes to filter his every experience of the quotidian world, until barely a day goes by – an hour – that he is not transported back to that place, recreated by his mind with utter and bewitching fidelity.

Nineteen years have passed since Moriarty left his wife. He is not much changed in outward appearance. The frontal development of his head, if anything, has increased, and his eyes are perhaps more sunken than before. But he is recognizably the same man.

Today he wakes with an uncanny clarity of mind. His disease will soon be behind him, he intuits. The definitive remedy to his mental problem is at hand. Somewhere outside, a message is waiting for him, and he must simply locate and decipher it.

He sets about the task with diligence and alacrity. The sun shines with unaccustomed vigor, and the sky is unblemished by even the faintest cloud gossamer.

Moriarty walks briskly, but with no particular destination. He stops here and there, memorizing details of what he sees, searching for patterns.

Twenty-three minutes into his jaunt, he encounters a cluster of bees as bright as the sun. He counts eleven of them. They follow him for a full minute, without any apparent intention of provoking harm, and then disperse into the skies.

Thirty-seven minutes after leaving his lodging, he finds himself near a book-vendor's stall. As if in a trance, he ambulates towards it. Five minutes into his visual perusal of the titles on display, he locates a tattered copy of the second edition of Nathaniel Hawthorne's *Twice-Told Tales*, and, without knowing why, purchases it.

Sixty-one minutes into his walk, bees return, this time hundreds of them.

Moriarty contemplates them, placidly. As before, they pose no threat. They hover for a while then fly away.

Moriarty studies his notes. He shuffles the facts like cards.

The numbers must mean something.

His former address: 83 Albermarle Street.

He lives seventeen minutes away from that residence.

The time intervals between significant events during his recent constitutional: twenty-three, thirty-seven, five, sixty-one.

The number of bees during each encounter: thirteen, eleven, two hundred and twenty-seven.

Holmes's destiny is softer than Moriarty's. Water will break Holmes's fall, shattering his bones, and he will sink below the surface, evanescing from the world in quiet poetry.

Moriarty, however, will strike rock. His cranium will be split and a string of bloodied brains will be ejected forth from it as if from an air gun, and he will rebound from the rock and land twisted on solid ground, face caved in.

Moriarty doesn't know how he knows this, but he does.

Wake up! Wake up! He sees his skull-opened corpse staring up at the heavens, at himself.

No! Not real.

Just a dream.

Wake up.

Wake up.

Moriarty's eyesight has declined with age. Multiple times he tries to read the Hawthorne tome he purchased during his recent outing. But the words on the page appear blurry, indistinct.

He sighs and puts the book down.

Twenty years have now elapsed since Moriarty exiled himself from his former life.

His investigation is nearly at an end. His being tingles with the promise of impending revelation.

He thinks about Holmes. Moriarty remembers imagining, a long time ago, that Holmes might take up some solitary profession, like beekeeper. He might retire from the business of being a London consulting detective and move to the Sussex Downs. Is that where he is, then? Is that what he's doing?

Yes; the bees. Maybe Moriarty's adversary had found a way to teach them to follow his commands. Perhaps he instructed the bees to find Moriarty, to relay a message to him. If so, what was it?

Moriarty grows impatient in his room, suddenly feels caged. In a fit, he takes the Hawthorne book, which has so taunted him with its nebulous print during the last few days, and flings it at the wall. It falls open. Disbelieving his eyes, Moriarty finds that he can easily read the page on which it has landed, without even having to bend down.

Enraptured, he picks it up and reads, hungrily. The page marks the opening of a story called "Wakefield", composed by Hawthorne in 1836. The story tells of a man who walks out of his house one day, leaving his wife behind, moves into a building a few streets away, and then returns to her twenty years later, without explanation or purpose.

Moriarty recognizes himself at once in the tale's pages. Stunned, he places the book on his bed and staggers away from it, as though it were a living entity. *He, Professor Moriarty, is Wakefield.* But how could Hawthorne have foreseen—

No, he thinks. Hawthorne did not predict anything. Moriarty has been *enacting* the story, playing it out, drawing on it from some secret recess in his memory and patterning his life after it for some inscrutable reason.

Trembling, he reads it again.

This is how it ends, then? He simply walks back to 83 Albermarle Street and reunites with Mrs Moriarty?

Something is wrong. In the story, Wakefield suffers no mental malaise, no symptoms of previous trauma. But clearly Moriarty does, for it was those symptoms that instigated his separation in the first place.

My mind is the chief suspect in this investigation, Moriarty declares. *My mind has fastened on to a fiction and treated it as reality. The story of Wakefield.*

Wakefield. He repeats the name. He rolls it on his tongue. *Wakefield.*

Fiction as reality, he thinks.

A story, told as truth.

The breakthrough is imminent now. He is shaking like a man

in the throes of *delirium tremens*, his whole body heaving, contracting, quivering.

Delirium. Another key word, lodged into his brain. There for a reason.

Think, Moriarty! You are alone, attempting to unveil a great mystery. You are an outcast of the Universe. Like Wakefield.

His mind produces a scene: a long sweep of green water roaring forever down, and the thick flickering curtain of spray hissing forever upward. Forever.

Forever.

The Reichenbach Falls. He's there again. This is where it all begins, where it all ends.

The dreadful cauldron of swirling water and seething foam, hundreds of feet below.

How many feet? Eight hundred and nine. *Precisely.*

How does he know this?

He is skilled at mathematics. Mathematics is his playground. He remembers other numbers. Eighty-three, seventeen, twenty-three, thirty-seven, five, sixty-one, thirteen, eleven, two hundred and twenty-seven, eight hundred and nine. They are of prime significance. And then he thinks: *That's it! Primes!*

All the numbers are primes. Why?

Holmes would figure this out in an instant, he thinks. But he is superior to Holmes. *Superior.*

Holmes lives at 221B Baker Street. Two hundred and twenty-one is a pseudo-prime number.

Primes are superior to pseudo-primes; purer, the real thing.

And more: 83 Albermarle Street is not Moriarty's actual address. He has never lived there. He remembers now. He lived at 50 Albermarle Street! Why the change to eighty-three? Prime, yes, but there must be something more.

Eighty-three. Then he knows. A simple sliding over of the decimal place. *Eight point three.*

That is how long he will be in the air at Reichenbach before his collision. The math is simple. His mass, one hundred and twenty-eight pounds; the distance, eight hundred and nine feet; an air resistance of point one six pounds per foot; a gravity of nine point eight meters per second squared. Outcome: he will fall for eight point three seconds.

He is Wakefield because his mind has been asleep but knows that it must wake. In his dream life he lives at 83 Albermarle Street because he is better than Holmes, and because he will fall for eight point three seconds. In dreams, print is hard to read; thus the difficulty of seeing the writing in Hawthorne's book.

Until now.

He has been asleep.

Wake yourself! he commands.

Reality sunders, regroups.

He is falling.

This is the truth of his existence.

This is the reality.

He has never left Reichenbach.

Falling.

His brain has apprehended that he will die in seconds, when his head smashes against the rock below. And to give himself an escape, it has created an elaborate fantasy for him to flee into. It has resorted to Wakefield. It has spun an entire universe out of it, nestled his consciousness inside a place where real time is not felt. A year in his Wakefield cosmos is a fraction of a fraction of a fraction of a second of real time.

But the illusion was imperfect. It contained all the clues leading to its own unraveling. *Wakefield*, the man who must *wake*. The primes. The bees.

He has failed, then.

He is falling and he cannot stop.

Time is about to catch up with Professor Moriarty.

Moriarty plunges back inside the dream with whirlwind force. Twenty years spent in the fog makes its inhabitation comfortable and automatic, easy to re-enter at will.

Ah, yes. He is back in his rented room.

With quick, precise gestures Moriarty packs his scant belongings and leaves a brief note behind informing the owners that he will not be back. *And here is a gift, a small token of my apprecia-tion*, he adds, and places the note atop the Hawthorne volume.

Several times during his stroll back to 83 Albermarle Street Moriarty hears rushing water and is almost tempted back into that Other World. But each time he resists, forcing himself to think of classical compositions that will appeal to his mathematic-al mind – Bach's "Goldberg Variations" and "Canonical Variations", with their kaleidoscopic symmetries – and allow him to elude the danger.

He saunters about London without checking how long, for it is best to keep time periods undefined in his mind. Eventually, he makes his way to Benekey's pub, which serves a fine wine and provides private booths. Walking to his chosen booth down the main room, lined with dark wood alcoves, he passes a mirror and there sees a reflection of his cold, gray eyes, filled with inexor-able purpose. For a flicker of time the gray in his eyes reminds him of another grey, that of a mist. He pushes the image aside.

Sitting for a long time, drinking his wine, Moriarty asks himself: *How long can I keep this up?*

How long can he promote his self-hypnosis, continue to hold the gauze of this reality over his senses, so as to blind them to his predicament in the Other World?

Then his lips spread into a crafty smile. He must only keep it up for the rest of his natural dream-life, for when he dies inside this universe, it will matter not what happens to his body in the Other World. His consciousness will have expired.

Considering his current age, the period in question is unlikely to exceed ten, or perhaps fifteen, years.

With this insight, Moriarty's body relaxes. He feels his whole fate turning on a pivot.

To prevent this great dream from dissipating, he thinks. *That is my task, nothing more.*

His mind turns to mathematics once more. In his youth, he performed work on the binomial theorem. He has heard that the German mathematician George Cantor has made great advances in the understanding of infinity, as envisioned through set theory. If infinity can be so tamed, then there is ample hope for Moriarty.

The professor pays and departs Benekey's. As he wends his way back home, he realizes that to strengthen the constitution of his belief, he must take up reading in a voracious way. The clearer the print on the page, the more firmly entrenched he will be inside the dream. And so he stops en route to purchase several fine books and journals.

During the last stretch of his trip, he thinks of Holmes, and Holmes's attitude towards the retiring mathematical coach. He knows full well that Holmes's horror at his crimes was lost in his admiration at Moriarty's skills. He can think of no higher praise. In this place, Holmes too still lives. Perhaps one day Moriarty will pay him a visit.

But not today. Today he reunites with Mrs Moriarty and reclaims his life.

At last he arrives.

Pausing near the house, Moriarty discerns, through the parlor windows of the second floor, the red glow and the glimmer and fitful flash of a comfortable fire. He sighs in an anticipation of domestic contentment. Moriarty ascends the steps lightly, for, though twenty years have stiffened his legs since he came down them, his new convictions and determination more than compensate for the loss of vitality.

The door opens. As he passes in, in a parting glimpse of his visage we recognize his crafty, knowing smile, a smile that speaks of worlds within worlds to which only he is privy.

We will not follow Moriarty across the threshold. Suffice it to say that Moriarty has found his place, and his place is not ours.

The place is Reichenbach, the time is May 1891, and the theme is self-banishment.

A Certain Notoriety

David Stuart Davies

Planning for future security is essential in order to be successful in a criminal career.

Professor Moriarty

The lights in the theatre dimmed and the curtain rose. The set
was the drawing room of a London town house. The butler
entered. As he did so, Colonel Sebastian Moran, sitting in the
first row of the stalls, touched his companion's arm. 'That's the
fellow,' he whispered. He paused for a moment, allowing a gentle
smile to touch his lips. 'What do you think?'

At first his companion did not respond but stared with fascination at the man attired in the butler's livery, while the stage
gradually filled with other members of the cast and the drama
commenced for real. The actor was very tall, thin with a balding
high-domed head and moved with remarkable ease.

The butler's role was small but his manner and bearing were
impressive. After a few perfunctory lines, he made his way off
stage. On his exit, Moran's companion chuckled, the eyes
gleaming with pleasure. 'I think he will do very nicely. Very
nicely indeed.'

Alfred Coombs was enjoying a glass of stout in the communal
dressing room at the end of the show. He had sloughed off his
butler's outfit, swilled away the greasepaint and was dressed in
his own rather shabby civilian clothes ready to return to his lodgings. He was deliberately slow in effecting the metamorphosis

from Gerald the butler to Alfred Coombs the lowly actor, so that by the time the transformation was complete, the rest of the cast had gone, leaving him with the luxury of a peaceful dressing room and his bottle of stout. He loved this quiet time at the end of a performance. He felt he had the theatre all to himself. It allowed him to daydream of that time, not too distant he hoped, when he would have a dressing room of his own as befitting a principal player. There would be a dresser hanging up his costume, before bringing out his evening suit, which he would wear for a late supper at the Café de Paris or maybe the Ritz.

He took another swig of the rich dark ale, easing his mind into the fantasy. He had been long in the profession, never rising in the ranks, always below stairs as it were, but with Alfred Coombs hope sprang eternal. He really believed that one day he would take the starring role, be thrust centre stage into the limelight and accumulate all the glossy trimmings that went with being a star.

As he was contemplating this eventuality, almost a nightly ritual, there came a knock at the dressing room door. With a sigh of annoyance at having his rêverie disturbed, Alfred dragged his feet down from the make-up table and wandered to the door. On the threshold were two figures: a man and a woman. The man was a bluff-looking fellow with wiry blond hair, a heavy moustache and bright blue eyes, which shone out of a ruddy face. But it was the woman, standing behind him, who captured Coombs's attention. She was a striking figure, tall, dark-haired and pale-faced; beautiful in a cold and clinical fashion. Her dark eyes gazed upon him in a hypnotic manner that seemed to penetrate Alfred's tired brain as though gaining access to his very thoughts.

'Good evening, Mr Coombs,' said the man. 'We did enjoy your performance tonight.'

Alfred did not know how to react to this compliment. He had never received one for his acting abilities before and it crossed his mind that the comment was tinged with sarcasm and that he was being ridiculed.

'Indeed, you show great promise,' continued the man with enthusiasm. 'We were so impressed that we have a proposition, which we feel will enable you to demonstrate fully and indeed develop your thespian talents.'

'You are theatrical agents? Producers perhaps?' enquired Coombs, his heart skipping a beat.

The man smiled and cast an amused glance at his companion whose face remained immobile.

'Not exactly,' said the man.

'Then . . . then what is this all about?'

The woman moved forward, the rustle of her costume filling his ears.

'We are offering you a unique role, one that will bring you a certain notoriety and significant remuneration.' Her voice was low and mellifluous and Coombs, who was something of an expert on accents, thought he could trace a faint Irish lilt. The words 'significant remuneration' excited him.

'What is the role?'

The woman gave a hint of a smile for the first time. 'It is that of a certain mathematical professor. A creation of my own.'

Sherlock Holmes flopped down in a chair in Inspector Patterson's office in Scotland Yard. He sighed heavily.

'I reckon you could do with a brandy,' observed the inspector with a wink, withdrawing a bottle and two glasses from the bottom drawer of his desk.

'I'll take a nip, thank you, Patterson,' said Holmes wearily, 'but I don't think brandy will solve our problems.'

'You got nothing more out of Barney Southwell then?' said the policeman gloomily, passing over a glass of brandy.

Holmes shook his head. 'I reckon Southwell told me as much as he knew or was allowed to know.' He banged his fist down hard on the desk in frustration. 'This is happening now on a regular basis: a number of robberies in the city carried out by small-time professionals who individually would have neither the wit nor the foresight to organise these projects. They are mere puppets dangling on strings controlled by someone else. But they are part of a growing organisation, which in time I am convinced will, like rats in the sewers, overrun the city.'

'That's quite a dramatic claim.'

'I am not given to exaggeration, Inspector. My theory is based on fact and evidence. Someone is organising the itinerant malefactors of the city into some kind of criminal association, no doubt utilising the safety-in-numbers principle. It is a masterstroke. The work of a genius and it is my task to track him down.'

Violet Carmichael laughed. It was a full-blown demonstration of her amusement and not a ladylike tinkle or a repressed chuckle. 'It is all going brilliantly, Moran. The coffers are overflowing thanks to the success of our little mercenary exploits. This enterprise grows in importance. So much so that we have attracted the attention of no less a personage than Sherlock Holmes.'

'As you thought you would,' agreed Moran, lighting up a cigar.

'As I knew I would.' The eyes flashed arrogantly. 'Now we need to take things further. I believe it is time to set out the birdlime to catch our fine-feathered friend. Is Coombs here?'

Moran strode to the door, opened it and, leaning forward, made a beckoning gesture. Alfred Coombs entered. His appearance was much altered and he seemed somewhat nervous and apprehensive as he approached the large desk behind which sat his new mistress, his new employer, Violet Carmichael.

She gazed at him and gave a nod of approval to her companion. 'You have done an excellent job, Moran. The fellow looks every decrepit inch a mathematics professor. The shoulders slope nicely, features are pale and ascetic-looking. What about the voice? Come, sir. Give me a little dialogue.'

Coombs took a step forward and nodded gently, his head beginning to sway from side to side in a strange reptilian fashion. 'Mr Sherlock Holmes,' he said, in a voice that resembled a creaking door, 'you hope to beat me. I tell you, you will never beat me. I am your nemesis. I am your doom.'

Violet Carmichael clapped her hands together with pleasure. 'Excellent,' she said. 'Your transformation from Alfred Coombs into this . . . this creature is magnificent. I particularly like the movement of your head as though you were some venomous lizard seeking a fly.'

Coombs grinned. 'Just a little touch of my own,' he said. 'I thought it gave the fellow a certain kind of danger.'

'So it does. So it does. Well, Moran, I am more than ever convinced we are ready. Do you feel ready, Mr Coombs?'

'I do, ma'am.'

'Good. There is just one thing. You will no longer respond to the name Coombs. From this moment on you *are* Professor James Moriarty.'

'Of course I am.' The deep-set eyes glimmered brightly and the head shifted unnervingly from side to side.

Sherlock Holmes also had a great facility for disguise, although his friend Watson always secretly believed that he tended to overdo the theatrical touches. The characters that emerged from the detective's bedroom ready to go out on to the streets of the city were always to Watson's mind a little larger than life. He certainly thought so when Holmes presented himself as a rough labourer in readiness for his latest excursion. There was perhaps too much rouge around the cheeks and on the nose and was that amount of stomach padding really necessary? Certainly the straw-coloured wig could have been abandoned, but Holmes seemed particularly pleased with his transformation and even the good doctor had to admit that the creature before him looked nothing like Sherlock Holmes.

The detective's destination that evening was the Rat and Raven, a shabby public house in the east end of the city which was the bolthole of a certain Percy Snaggles, a nasty little nark who had been of great service to Holmes in the past.

It was about ten at night when the detective entered this squalid establishment. The heat and the smoke were the first thing that assailed him, followed by the frenzied, raucous rattle of conversation. There were deep-throated oaths mixed with high-pitched female laughter from gaudy tarts, who were either having a respite from their labours or attempting to pick up new trade. Holmes made his way to the bar and in a rough cockney voice, typical of the other inmates of this alehouse, ordered a glass of porter. While he waited for his drink, he cast his keen gaze around the room. It

did not take him long to spot Snaggles. He was slumped in a corner
with a one-eyed man, apparently playing a game of cards. Holmes
paid for his drink and, squeezing himself through the boozy throng
of clients, approached the nark. On seeing this strange-looking
cove bearing down on him, Snaggles pulled himself upright in his
chair, his eyes wide in apprehension.

'Need to talk,' said Holmes, maintaining his cockney accent,
while he made the secret sign with his hand that told Snaggles
who he really was. The nark's features quivered and he glanced
over at his companion. 'Half a mo, Wally, while I conduct a bit o'
business with this geezer here.'

The one-eyed man looked up from scrutinising his hand of
cards. 'You take your time 'cause when you get back I'm gonna
fleece you rotten.' He laughed, revealing a row of crooked, blackened teeth.

Holmes and Snaggles made their way through the crowd to
the door and into the comparative quiet of the street.

'His name is Moriarty. Professor Moriarty,' said Snaggles
breathlessly, his voice emerging as a harsh whisper. 'He's the one
who sets up the jobs for us, organises things. We're like members
of his army and woe betide us if we don't obey orders.' He made
a throat-slitting gesture.

'Have you seen this Moriarty?'

'Just the once. A funny-looking cove: very tall, large head, bent
shoulders and moves funny.'

'Moves funny?'

'He don't seem to be able to keep his head still. It keeps
wobbling about.' He demonstrated the movement.

'Where are his headquarters?'

Snaggles gave a brief grunting laugh. 'You must be joking. No
one knows. It's being a tight-close secret that makes him so
successful. But I tell you this: it ain't just robberies that he's into.
He has his fingers in many pies: blackmail, counterfeit dosh,
murder even. I can tell you that he's in charge of most of the
crime in London. He's a dangerous fellow, Mr Holmes. If I were
you I'd steer clear of him.'

* * *

Snaggles grinned nervously. 'So then I says: "He's a dangerous fellow, Mr Holmes. If I were you I'd steer clear of him."'

The man who had become Professor Moriarty nodded his head in appreciation. 'You have done well, Snaggles. You have no doubt whetted Mr Holmes's appetite for the game considerably – which was my intention.' He slid a small bag of coins across the desk towards Snaggles. 'A little reward for your efforts.'

'Thank you, Professor.'

'You may go now.'

'Yes, sir. Thank you, sir.' Snaggles retreated with haste from the room.

Moriarty cast a questioning glance at Moran who had been standing in the shadows.

'Yes,' Moran assured him.

Moriarty blew down the speaker tube on his desk. A voice responded.

'Cartwright,' said the professor, speaking into the tube. 'Make sure that Mr Snaggles does not leave the building alive. Retrieve the bag of coins from his person and return them to my office as soon as possible, there's a good fellow'.

'I am getting there. Slowly. But it is hard work, Patterson. Far harder than I anticipated.'

Sherlock Holmes slumped down in the swivel chair opposite the Scotland Yard man. He was dressed as a common workman, complete with copious side-whiskers and an earring dangling from his left lobe. His features were ruddy and lined and a clay pipe peeped out of the top pocket of his disreputable jacket. When he had entered Patterson's office, much to the distress of the young constable in the corridor, Patterson had not batted an eyelid. He was used to Holmes visiting him in a whole range of disguises. Indeed, since he had taken up the Moriarty case, Patterson had not seen the detective in his usual 'civilian' clothes.

'I tell you, this professor is the Napoleon of crime,' Holmes was saying. 'He commands the minor criminals in London like the Pied Piper. They dance to his tune all right. However I try, I can only get so close to him, but no closer. It is very frustrating.'

'That may be so,' said Patterson, 'but you have foiled many of his plans, upset his apple cart more than once in the last few months.'

'Yes, but that does not seem to stop him. He rolls on like the sea and I am a feeble Canute. However, I am getting ever closer to him. My dossier on this master criminal is growing by the day. Soon I believe there will be enough evidence in there to incriminate him and all his minions.'

'I will look forward to receiving it. I've never known you fail, Holmes. If anyone can bring this villain down, it is you.'

Sherlock Holmes pursed his lips. 'We shall see. I have it on good authority that he has a most ambitious bank job in the planning. If I can scupper that . . .'

Violet Carmichael held the photograph of Sherlock Holmes in her hand and gently ran her long forefinger down the front of the picture, her sharp nails leaving a faint line across the features of the detective. She was barely containing her anger. 'It is now time that he was stopped. Initially, I was amused by his arrogance, his brilliance. It entertained me to watch him grow in confidence and expertise and fall into our trap. But now he has become too dangerous. He is coming too close for comfort. My comfort. And the closer he comes, the more damaging intelligence he collects. The professor is the mask I have created to protect me. Holmes must never see beyond it. Fortunately, he has become obsessed by Moriarty as I hoped he would and so we must take advantage of this obsession and eliminate him.' With a deft movement she crumpled up the photograph and threw it down on her desk. 'It is time to have done with the man. Time for our little imposter to come into his own.'

As Alfred Coombs – the man who had become Professor Moriarty – climbed up the seventeen steps to Sherlock Holmes's sitting room at 221B Baker Street, he knew that he was about to give the performance of his life. His knees trembled as he reached the landing and his throat felt very dry. 'Come on, old boy,' he whispered in his normal voice, one that he had almost forgotten how to use.

He tapped on the door and entered the room. Sherlock Holmes rose from his chair, his hand rammed into his dressing gown pocket where, Moriarty deduced, he was clutching a revolver. So, the great detective was that scared. The thought amused and relaxed Moriarty.

'Certainly, Sherlock Holmes was rattled. He spoke with bravado, but an actor knows when another is acting,' observed Coombs, before lighting the Havana cigar he had just been given.

'Excellent.' Violet Carmichael smiled. 'I have arranged for a number of assassination attempts to be made on his life: sniper bullets, falling masonry – that sort of thing. None will be successful, of course. Such a death would only arouse suspicions with Scotland Yard. He will be dealt with later.'

'What then is the purpose of these attacks?'

'I need to prompt Mr Holmes to hand over his files to Patterson – who in turn will hand them over to me.'

'He is your spy at the Yard.'

'One of several.'

'In the meantime, what about me?'

Violet Carmichael gave Coombs a feline smile. 'You must prepare yourself for a journey.'

Watson gazed at his friend in the half-light of evening which filtered into his sitting room through the net curtains. The detective looked tired and ill but Watson observed that there was still that bright spark emanating from those fierce grey eyes.

'My case against Moriarty is complete, old fellow, and the villain knows it. The proof being that I have been attacked several times today and only narrowly missed losing my life.'

'Great heavens,' Watson cried, shocked and alarmed at this statement, which was uttered so casually.

'It is a very good omen. It shows that the master criminal is beginning to panic.'

'And that your life is in danger.'

'Always quick to making the obvious point, eh, Watson. Yes, indeed, London is too hot for me now. I have passed over the

relevant papers to Inspector Patterson of the Yard and, within a
few days, Moriarty and his gang will be rounded up. In the
meantime, it would be judicious, I think, to absent myself from
England for a while. A trip to Europe beckons and I was hoping
that you would be my travelling companion. Would you come to
the Continent with me? We could wander up the Valley of the
Rhone, through the Gemmi Pass into Switzerland and on, via
Interlaken, to Meiringen. And thence to Rosenlaui, not forgetting to make a stop at the magnificent Reichenbach Falls.

'Of course. Anything you say, Holmes.'

Holmes was now alone on the narrow path overlooking the
Reichenbach Falls. Watson had departed in haste to attend to a
sick English lady who was staying at the hotel in Meiringen. The
detective knew that the summons was a ruse to draw his only
companion away, leaving the field free for the appearance of his
arch-enemy, Professor James Moriarty. And, indeed, through the
mist of spray, there appeared a dark silhouette, which shim-
mered indistinctly at first then clearly materialised into the figure
of his arch-enemy.

The two men faced each other, the roar of the falls drumming
in their ears.

'At last, Mr Holmes.'

'At last, Professor Moriarty.'

Holmes prepared himself for what he believed would be a
hand-to-hand struggle to the death. Moriarty smiled, his head
slowly vacillating as he withdrew a revolver from the folds of
his coat.

'No one said we had to play fair.' The professor smiled, pointing the gun at Holmes.

This scene was being observed from a distance, higher up the
steep incline overlooking the falls. Colonel Sebastian Moran
adjusted the sights on his rifle and steadied his aim. As he saw
Moriarty raise the pistol and aim it at Holmes, in quick succession he fired twice. Two bullets whizzed through the damp air
towards their targets. Both figures below remained frozen like

dark statues for a moment as the bullets tore into them. Death took them swiftly and silently. In an instant they both toppled over into the deep chasm of the creaming, boiling waters of the Reichenbach Falls.

'Any attempts at recovering the bodies were absolutely hopeless and there, deep down in that dreadful cauldron of swirling water and seething foam, will lie for all time the most dangerous criminal and the foremost champion of the law of his generation.' Violet Carmichael put down the copy of *The Strand Magazine* and chuckled. 'Brilliant,' she exclaimed. 'Quite brilliant.'

Watson smiled. 'I thought you'd like it.'

'Indeed, I do.' Still smiling, she poured out two glasses of champagne. 'John, your help has been invaluable in this matter. I look forward to you being more involved in my affairs now that the field is clear of all obstructions. I shall always need a good man close to me whom I can trust implicitly.'

The good doctor smiled enigmatically and raised his glass of champagne.

Fade To Black

Michael Gregorio

I took the opportunity to drop in on Sherlock Holmes after visiting a patient in the vicinity of Baker Street. I rang the bell and Mrs Hudson opened the door some moments later. She seemed pleased to see me, asking after my wife with an inquisitive twinkle in her eyes. On hearing that Mary was well – and nothing more than well – she led me up to the first-floor suite of rooms which I had once shared with my eminent friend.

Holmes looked up from a letter that he was reading.

"The married man returns," he proclaimed in a measured, melodramatic drone, as if it were the title of some droll West End comedy. "And how, pray, is the dear sweet married lady?"

Had Holmes and Mrs Hudson had the same thing in mind? Did both of them suppose that was I bringing news of the first in a line of prospective Watson juniors?

"Mary is tip-top, thank you," I said with all the politeness I could muster, hastening to excuse myself for my extended absence from Baker Street. "Married life is so time-consuming, Holmes. Would you believe it? We have still not finished furnishing the house to Mary's . . . that is, to *our* satisfaction. And my practice keeps on growing, thanks to your endeavours and my more recent literary fame as your amanuensis. When a patient walks into the surgery these days, I am never sure if it is their own health, or the diseased workings of the criminal mind, which brings them there." I decided it was wise to take a strategic step back into the not-too-distant past. "Why, I sometimes regret the carefree days of my former bachelor state in your most stimulating company."

Holmes stared at me, raised his eyebrows, then said, "Tosh."

"Here's something that may interest you," he said, holding out the letter to me.

"It is written in French," I said, as I glanced at the letter.

"An accurate observation," Holmes remarked. "I'll sum it up for you. The French authorities are concerned about the increase in organised international crime, and the unhappy fact that the British police force seems to be doing nothing about it. Indeed, largely thanks to you, Watson, the French believe that Professor James Moriarty is behind it all."

"The elusive master-criminal—"

Our conversation was interrupted by a loud rat-a-tat at the front door downstairs.

Holmes glanced at the carriage clock on the mantelpiece. "My brother, Mycroft," he said. "His knock is the true representation of himself. He means to be gentle, but bulls in glass factories do far less damage. A matter of national importance, I would say, yet not so pressingly urgent. Some notion has engaged his mind, though he has still not decided whether to let the Minister in on the secret. And that, Watson, is where you and I come into it."

I began to protest. I was far too busy to take time off to chronicle another adventure of England's only private consulting detective, even if it did concern the Good of the Nation and the consulting detective's elder brother.

Footsteps sounded on the stairs, then a gentle tap on the sitting-room door was followed by the appearance of Mrs Hudson's face.

"An exotic gentleman to see you, sir," she announced.

Well, that *did* surprise me. Had Mrs Hudson never met the brother of the most famous private investigator in England? Apparently she had not, though I would have sworn in a court of law that she had, for she showed him into the sitting room without any further word of introduction.

I stared at Mycroft Holmes for some moments. Despite his unusual height and bulk, I might not have recognised him myself. Was he going to a fancy-costume ball? And if so, why was he dressed for it so early in the afternoon?

As Mrs Hudson left the room, the visitor threw off his unseasonable brown cloak, removed a high green fez from off the crown of his head, unhooked a bushy beard held with wire clips behind his ears, and lifted a black Bakelite pince-nez from off his large nose.

"*Voilà!*" he said, depositing the accoutrements on a chair. Then he sank down on the sofa at my side, his steel-grey eyes shifting from me to his brother. "I am being followed, Sherlock," he said.

"I am not surprised," said Holmes, "dressed up in that rig."

Though quite his younger brother's equal in every mental faculty – superior, perhaps, in his mastery of the global implications of diplomacy – Mycroft Holmes had a tendency towards a careless belief in his own schemes.

"It's been going on for a month. As you probably know," Mycroft said, then suddenly stopped and stared at me. "You read the newspapers, do you, Doctor Watson?"

"The *Telegraph*," I replied.

Mycroft smiled for some reason. "You will have noticed, then, that London is currently enjoying the patronage of some of the most bizarre specimens of the internationally rich. That is, in almost every case, *myself*. I never leave the house or Whitehall in the same clothes twice. This week alone, I have been a Yankee railroad millionaire, a Turkish vice-regent, a Serbian ambassador, the Emir of Bukhara, and much more besides—"

"Indeed," his brother interrupted him. "I have been following your adventures in the columns of *The Times*. *The Chimes* is good for high society gossip, if nothing else. The thing that troubles me, Mycroft, is why it took you so long to consult me on the subject."

As everyone who knew him closely was aware, Sherlock Holmes was a *maestro* of disguise. I have seen him play every imaginable role, from drunken clergyman to sober chimney sweep, and admit that I have been taken in on every single occasion.

A knock came at our door, and Mrs Hudson entered with a pot of tea. "I hope you're feeling better now, sir," she said to Mycroft. "You must have been uncomfortably hot in those unseasonable clothes."

Mycroft looked up at her in alarm. "Did you recognise me, ma'am?"

"It's the eyes, the nose, the mouth, sir. You can't make a pig's ear from a silk purse—"

"Thank you, Mrs Hudson." Holmes broke in upon this learned disquisition. "It is the opposite, I believe, despite the intended compliment. And yet, as you say, there are aspects of the human physiognomy that will always distinguish one individual from another, even one monozygotic twin from his identical fellow. Now, if you'd be so kind as to pour the tea."

Mrs Hudson did as she was asked, then left us alone.

"Darned woman," Mycroft said, breathing in deeply, then hissing out the words.

"She is correct, however, as Doctor Watson, Thomas Carlyle or Charles Darwin would inform you, Mycroft. *Genetikos.* There's no getting away from it. Each man is the sum of his constituent parts. That is the point of a disguise, by the way. You must appear to be what you are not by nature."

"What a strange world is this!" Mycroft laughed. "I came here with exactly the same thought in my head. I dressed to dissemble, as I was telling you, but how am I to know that the man, or men, who are watching me, are not equally cleverly disguised?"

"Cleverly?" Holmes remarked. "In your case, Mycroft, I would dispute the adverb. Your talents are vast, but hiding your true self is not one of them."

At this point I decided to intervene. When the brothers Holmes began to dispute about the niceties of any subject, the argument was likely to be examined in all its multifarious aspects. In a word, we might have been there for many hours.

"Why are you being followed?" I asked.

Mycroft looked left and right, as if there might have been someone else in the room.

"Foreign spies," he said quietly. "They are literally everywhere since the signing of the Convention of Constantinople last March. Unchecked maritime passage through the Suez Canal may be all well and good in peacetime, Watson, but *not* during war. I was strongly opposed to the agreement, I can tell you."

"Is a war about to erupt?" I asked in alarm.

Holmes stepped in before he could answer. "What have you to do with the Suez Canal?"

Mycroft examined the tea tray, as if there might be spies lurking behind the sugar bowl. "Hush-hush, dear boy. Don't ask, because I cannot tell. Of course, the only way to guarantee safe passage through the straits is to tighten up security. I have had a hundred thoughts about the best measures to be taken, then wondered whether a less conventional approach, such as yours, might help."

"Is there anything more conventional than logic?" Holmes fired back at him. "Forgive me, Mycroft, I know the crushing strain that working under the wheels of government occasions. You wish to identify some means of monitoring the passage of persons, as well as ships, through the Suez Canal. Very well, though there is, I believe, a more universal principle behind the specific case, with which I shall be happy to engage. I will need a couple of days. Shall we meet again towards the end of the week?"

"Thursday next?" Mycroft replied, and so it was agreed.

While Mycroft left the house in the guise of Sherlock Holmes, ten inches shorter without his towering fez, his large ears hidden beneath the flaps of an untied grey tweed deerstalker, his bulk constrained within a narrow-cut trench coat, his brother and I stepped into Baker Street but a short time afterwards.

We made a strange pair, I am sure, myself 'disguised' as the doctor that I am with a bowler hat on my head and a brown leather surgical bag in my hand, while the man who accompanied me wore a large black beard that was evidently false, a fez that added greatly to his height, a Bakelite pince-nez that kept slipping down his aquiline nose, and a winged cloak like a Eurasian nomad's tent, which might have accommodated a family of five.

True to his role – and aping Mycroft, I fear – Holmes ploughed forward through the crowd, scattering ladies and gentlemen left and right, trampling children, cocker spaniels and careless nursemaids beneath his feet with equal unconcern.

"The French authorities may well be right," said Holmes.

"England is too small to contain a criminal intelligence such as Professor Moriarty. What Mycroft says perplexes me, however. What possible interest could the Napoleon of crime have in the Suez Canal?"

"It is difficult to imagine," I said without thinking. "A narrow strait through which the greater part of the world's trade passes, carrying goods from India and South-east Asia to Britain and France. If a ship, or ships could be boarded and captured, just think of the contraband, the ransom."

"That may be it, Watson."

We headed north on Baker Street. "Where are we going?" I asked.

"A short way up the road," the Mad Mogul at my side replied.

At 55–56 Baker Street, we turned into the photographic studios of *Messrs Elliott & Fry, estab'd 1863*, and climbed the stairs to the first floor. The premises consisted of an ample waiting room fitted out with red leather chesterfields and large glass chandeliers, a swinging double door, which marked the entrance to the *Portrait Parlour*, another one marked *Strictly Staff Only*, while a third door bore a legend that caught my eye immediately: *Ladies Dressing Room*. Far wider than the other doors, it had been designed to accommodate the enormous crinolines and bustles that had been so fashionable only twenty or thirty years before.

A pert young woman stepped forward from behind a desk to greet us.

"I would like to arrange a sitting," said Holmes.

The young woman looked troubled. "Are you in town for long, sir?" she asked, glancing at his bizarre outfit, perhaps wondering whether he had arrived in Baker Street by camel or seated on a flying carpet, and might be returning to his country of origin by the same means of transport within the hour.

"I would like to do the thing as soon as possible," Holmes replied.

While the receptionist went to check her appointments book, then disappeared into the *Portrait Parlour*, we took the opportunity to look at a vast display of photographs of the Great and the Good that were hanging from the waiting-room walls.

"What's all this about, Holmes?" I asked. "I cannot imagine for an instant why you would wish to be photographed in that get-up."

"It's the perfect opportunity to test a principle, assist the French and help my brother," Holmes replied.

"Which principle?" I said.

I could see no sense in dressing up as someone else to have one's picture made.

"Lombroso's," he replied. "I was in Hatchards, Piccadilly, the other day, when I chanced upon the new, illustrated edition of his published treatise, *L'Uomo Delinquente*. Have you seen it? It posits the most ridiculous Positivistic theory about criminals. I quote: 'The brain and the intelligence are inversely proportional to the size and the weight of the stomach, muscles and bones.' Just think of Mycroft! He is the very opposite. He may be extra large, but his brain is unequalled in all the realm. Lombroso talks of atavism, as if the criminal were a throwback to primordial predatory instincts. Hm! Nothing could be so far removed from the man who published *The Dynamics of an Asteroid* in his youth, confounding the greatest minds in the field of pure mathematics . . ."

"You mean Professor Moriarty?"

"Who else?" said Holmes. "Lombroso has hit upon a method without considering the secret at the core of it. He illustrates his notions by reference to photographs of criminals he has examined. Well, Watson, let's see what Messrs Elliott and Fry will make of me. I have a corollary notion of my own – though Shakespeare beat me to it – that 'clothes maketh the man'. Dress up a murderer as a lord; he may be convincing, yet he remains a murderer. If we know him only as a lord in white ermine, there is no way of predicting what he may eventually do."

I knew of Cesare Lombroso, of course. Was there a doctor in the world who didn't?

"Just take a look at this one," Holmes remarked, examining a portrait of a chap whom I had never heard of. "Observe the undulating brow, the infantile quiff of hair, the squashed potato of his nose, and that walrus of a moustache lounging on his upper lip. Lombroso would have classed him as a lowly confidence trickster, I have no doubt."

I read a name beneath the portrait. "Arthur Conan Doyle, writer, it says here."

"Never heard of him," Holmes said as he moved on to the next one.

A man appeared very shortly and introduced himself to us as Mister John Joseph Elliott.

"I have a spare half-hour and can fit you in," he said. "The receptionist came in, announced your names as Mister Holmes and Doctor Watson. When I turned back to the camera, my client had disappeared down the backstairs, taking my slide-holder and a glass-plate negative with him."

"What was he like, this man who stole his own shadow?" Holmes enquired.

Mister Elliott smiled. "It is a mechanical process," he said. "Having seen so many individuals, I must admit, I have no memory for faces. Remember, too, that I see my sitters upside down through the lens of the camera."

With no more a-do, we followed the photographist into the Portrait Parlour.

Holmes sat for far more pictures than I could have imagined, all of them in the "vignette" style, that is, showing only the head and the neck.

Mister Elliott had seemed disappointed when Holmes announced his purpose "head, no shoulders", but he warmed to the task as the bearded potentate in the ridiculous pince-nez dictated precisely what he wanted. "Face front, eyes closed, eyes open. Left profile, chin up, chin down. The same sequence for the right profile. And, finally, the back of the head, which tells us more about a man than his dissembling face may wish to do."

Seven photographs in all, and Mister Elliott retreated to the processing room with his bundle of glass negatives safe inside their slide-holders.

"We'll need another set of seven," said Holmes, as the photographist withdrew.

I imagined that he wanted to have my portrait taken, too, and I knew that Mary would be delighted. I was wandering around the large studio, examining a variety of painted backdrops. Here, we were in the country by a lake with swans; there, we were in a book-lined library with a writing desk, a clock and chair. Curtains and pillars seemed to play a large part in photography. Vases, too, a shelf of them in ascending order, small to large, together with a selection of banisters and balustrades of wood and plaster, which the artist could call upon as he felt fit. Then, suddenly, I heard a voice behind me.

"Where is he?"

The photographist was staring at Sherlock Holmes, who was sitting in the posing chair where previously the Grand Mufti of Jerusalem had been seated.

"To whom are you referring?" Holmes returned with a smile, indicating the fine raiments of his brother's disguise, which he had deposited on a chaise-longue.

Mr Elliott looked from Holmes to the clothes, then back again.

"Come, come," said Holmes, "an experiment, forgive me. Now, if you would just repeat the sequence of poses exactly as before, we will waste no more of your time."

There were no plans for a photograph of me, though I managed to persuade Mister Elliott to take my likeness when Holmes had finished with him.

Ten minutes later, we left the studio, our enterprise complete. Holmes was now wearing only his knickerbocker suit, having donated Mycroft's fancy dress to Mr Elliott, observing that the cloak, fez, beard and pince-nez would serve more useful purpose there than anywhere else in London.

The photographist promised to have the proofs delivered on Thursday to 221b Baker Street.

Thursday came, and Thursday went.

The photographs had been delivered in a package that morning, but Mycroft did not present himself as the Sheik of Araby, Chief Sitting Bull, or any of the other ethnic costume transformations that an indulgent minister would allow him.

It was Mrs Hudson's half-day holiday, and Holmes was brewing tea on an enamelled Hungarian samovar, which some noble Magyar well-wisher had presented to him in remembrance of an investigation that had been successfully resolved.

"It is most unlike him," Holmes remarked.

As the clock struck five, he reached for the telephone and made a call to Whitehall 1212.

"Have any corpulent corpses in foreign national costumes been found today?" he asked.

The duty sergeant reported that nothing of the sort had been reported, Mister 'olmes, then he passed the call on to another Whitehall number, which cannot be mentioned here in the interests of national security.

Mycroft was not in his office.

"There's only one hope left," said Holmes, as he dialled another number. "The Diogenes Club."

The co-founder was, indeed, in his club, but another couple of minutes passed before he managed to reach the telephone in the hall from the billiards saloon.

"Mycroft," Holmes pronounced in a tone of reprimand, "your tea is almost stewed."

He listened for some moments, then said: "Very well, tomorrow, then."

He dropped the telephone back on its hook. "He had forgotten entirely, if you ask me, though he made some lame excuse about rampaging Ethiopian privateers. Would you care to play mother, Watson?"

By which he meant would I serve the tea.

I served, of course, though I was certainly not in a motherly frame of mind. I had taken off the whole afternoon by the mean expedient of tacking a note to the surgery door, saying *Called out to an emergency.* The majority of my private patients were valetudinarians, their health was not the true cause of their problems. What mattered more to me was the loss of the consultation fees, which would help me to pay for the nursery. Mary had told me just the day before: I was to be a father!

I had persuaded myself that I deserved a half-day holiday, just like Mrs Hudson. But I had been expecting to partake of a fascinating conversation regarding atavism, positivism, Lombroso and photography. The one thing missing was Mycroft Holmes.

"Just one cup of *chà* and one cigar," Holmes announced, "then you and I will examine the contents of that package on the table by the window."

"Our photographs?" I asked, as I handed him his cup, and watched with horror as he dropped five cubes of sugar into the queer-coloured liquid.

"The very same," he said, his eyes lighting up with amusement as I sipped my tea, then coughed and spluttered.

"Do you call this *tea*?" I said with disgust, and set my cup back on its saucer.

"It is called Woojeon," Holmes said, labouring carefully over the pronunciation. "Hand-picked before the monsoons began last April, it is the finest first-flush green tea produced in the hills of North Korea. The natives call it *chà*, which differentiates it from the Chinese pronunciation of the same word, *cha* . . ."

"It really is rotten," I protested. "Can't we have a decent cup of Rosie Lee?"

"It is part of my latest experiment," Holmes insisted. "I have been informed that there are four hundred and sixty-seven distinct varieties and blends of tea, and I intend to catalogue them all for forensic purposes. As you know, tea and tea leaves go together, but there are many other important characteristics that have never been adequately chronicled. How do the leaves dry at the bottom of an empty cup? What patterns do they form? How long does the distinctive aroma persist? Does the addition of one, two or more cubes of sugar alter the rate of desiccation? And so on," he said with a wave of his long, bony fingers. "I feel pretty full, I must admit. I have been drinking tea all day."

We smoked our cigars, and Holmes drank his cup of *chà*. "It is not to my taste either, Watson. But one must oftentimes suffer in the interests of science. Hand me the package, will you?"

I took the bulky envelope from off the table. It was inscribed with a florid "Elliott & Fry", and the flap had been closed with an adhesive rosette in the shape of an orange dandelion. "It's far heavier than I expected," I said as I handed it to him.

"They are cabinets," he said, laying the unopened package on the table, "larger than *cartes-de-visite*. I was thinking of using the imperial size at first, but the format is even larger, too expensive for the scheme I have in mind."

"Scheme?" I said.

To be frank, I had almost forgotten that there was a purpose behind our expedition to the photographic studio, and that it had something to do with the security of the Suez Canal.

"We were speaking of eyes, noses and mouths the other day, as you will recall . . ."

"And Mrs Hudson spoke of dressing up a pig as a silk purse—"

"I am sure she was speaking metaphorically," Holmes interjected. "And then we went to the photographic studio and had some studies made of the human physiognomy . . ."

"Your face, you mean?"

"Exactly, Watson. We have some of the most wonderful inventions of the nineteenth century at our disposal, yet we do not use them to the full. If I am correct, and I believe I am, we may have found an answer to Brother's conundrum. Do you, by any chance, have your passport about you?"

"I have it here," I said with a laugh. "I carry it in my medical bag out of habit, I suppose. One never knew at the start of a day in London whether we would end up sleeping in Ostend or Biarritz. You have such a habit of charging off . . ."

"May I see it?" Holmes asked. He held it up without opening it. "Is there any reason why I should not present myself at the customs in Alexandria or Aden, and claim that I am you?"

"None at all," I began to say, then I saw where he was leading. "But with a photograph affixed . . ."

"Indeed, a photograph, taken in a specific fashion to reveal what makes each man himself, would mean that only one man – the man portrayed in the photograph – could use the document."

"What use is that?" I asked. "If a man of unknown qualities were to present himself . . ."

"No man is of unknown qualities today, Watson. If a man is a spy, a government representative, or a known criminal, and if such people were systematically photographed in the manner that I hope to be able to demonstrate to you in a few moments, there would be little or no chance of his being able to get through the customs barriers without being recognised. If Lombroso were correct, and if there were a criminal type, an atavistic delinquent, the matter would be simpler, of course, but it hardly matters, thanks to another great invention of recent times."

"Which one?" I asked.

He paused, and waved the passport at me before he gave it back. "Ernest Hummel's telediagraph."

"That's new to me," I said.

"By copying the original photograph on to shellac foil, the picture can be sent one hundred or ten thousand miles by telegraph."

"I still don't see it," I said.

"More tea?" asked Holmes.

"No thank you," I replied smartly.

"Imagine that a man presents himself at the customs in Dover. If doubts were raised about his identity or intentions, his picture could be transmitted to London – Scotland Yard, let's say, New Scotland Yard as it will soon be – where a classified photographic Rolodex system of known faces could be kept. By referring to the most prominent facial features – the eyes, nose, mouth or ears – an identification could be made, and an order sent by telegraph to Ostend, Calais or Boulogne to have him arrested on arrival."

"I see," I said. "But where is the system in it?"

"It is a question of geometrics," Holmes replied. "Did you note how close the camera was to my face? Exactly thirty-seven inches. Four footsteps, plus one inch. And the lens?"

I shook my head.

"A Vöigtlander Rapid Rectilinear Portrait. Which means?"

"What does it mean?" I asked.

"If such a lens is used at such a distance, always and invariably, we can say that a triangle traced between the tips of the ears and the point of the nose will always correspond in that person, and no other. Equally, a triangle drawn between the centre of the pupils and the extreme point of the chin. Or between the corners of the mouth and the meeting of the eyebrows. 'Biometric' would be a suitable word for it, I believe . . ."

"Let's examine the photographs and see," I said, breaking in on his enthusiasm. I had understood what he intended about triangles, I think, but like Doubting Thomas I wished to stick my finger in the gaping hole and make certain.

Holmes picked up the package and broke the seal. Then he picked up a wooden ruler. "Do you have a pencil and paper?" he asked me, taking out one of the cabinet photographs.

I took out my silver propelling pencil and my pocket note-book. "What do I have to do?"

"Simply write down these measurements as I give them to you." He laid the portrait on the table, laid the ruler on the photograph and said: "Corner of eye to corner of eye, 285 milli-metres. Corner of eye to tip of the nose, 207 millimetres. We could take more measurements, using the lips or the chin, but these will do for the present purpose. Now, a profile," he said, taking out another of the photographs. "Point of brow to tip of nose, then the distances from those two extremities to the tip of the ear lobe. If we chose the left profile instead of the right, the measurements would differ significantly."

He gave me the distances, and I made a note of them.

"Why are you using the decimal system?" I asked.

"Surely you mean the metric system. It's the only useful thing to have survived from the French Revolution," he said. "I'm amazed it has not been universally adopted, allowing a fragmen-tation towards the infinitesimal with which the British inch cannot compete. Now, Watson, I want you to draw a T based on the longest measure in each case, then draw in the triangulation and cut them out – I have a pair of sharp scissors ready for the task. At that point, we may see whether our triangles accurately measure the distances in the other pictures in our sample."

"Ingenious," I murmured, as I cut along the lines, "though it makes a mess of my pocketbook."

At that point, laying out the portraits of Sherlock Holmes with

– and without – his false beard and pince-nez, we placed the frontal and profile triangles over the photographs.

"They match perfectly every time!" I congratulated Holmes.

"Wouldn't you care for a drop of tea to celebrate?" he said, turning to his samovar, while I examined the remaining portraits.

"Thank you, no," I said. "Now, where is my photograph, I wonder?"

Apart from the fourteen cabinet cards of Sherlock Holmes, the only other thing contained in the package was a black paper envelope of slightly smaller dimensions. We had paid no attention to it, believing it to be, I suppose, a receipt for the work done, a sum which Holmes had paid when the package had been delivered that morning by a boy from the Elliott & Fry studio.

Holmes was busy, loading his cup of loathsome Woojeon tea with six cubes of sugar. "The final test in the tea series for today," as he himself remarked.

I opened the black envelope, pulled out a flimsy sheet of paper.

"It's a photograph," I said, "but not mine. It must belong to someone else." I turned the picture over, and found a large letter M written in blue crayon on the back of it. "And what in heaven's name is this supposed to mean?"

Holmes put down his cup and came across to look. As he took the picture from my fingers, I noticed that the portrait was rapidly beginning to turn black.

"It hasn't been fixed," I said.

"On purpose," Holmes remarked, holding up a portrait of a man with a high-domed forehead and a thin nose. "Mister Elliott was busy in the Portrait Parlour when we arrived, do you remember? And then he complained that the sitter had made his escape down the backstairs when our names were announced by the receptionist."

"Escape?" I said. "Why would he wish to escape?"

"Can't you guess who he was? I have a score to settle with that man," said Sherlock Holmes.

"Which man?" I asked, perplexed.

"You've never seen Professor Moriarty, have you, Watson?"

"Moriarty?"

Holmes handed me the black sheet of paper. "The professor inherited tendencies of the most diabolical kind," he said. "Well, now we know that he has a diabolical sense of humour, too. He was probably following Mycroft. He may have known, or guessed, what my brother was up to. On the other hand, he could have been visiting the studio for some purpose known only to himself."

"A passport!" I cried. "Having a suitable picture made before it becomes law."

"He knows of Mycroft's plans, then."

"And the picture faded away before we had the chance to take his measurements."

"I'll catch him yet, I promise you," said Holmes.

He walked across to the grate and dropped the blackened sheet of paper on the smouldering coals. As the heat took hold of the paper and twisted it, a negative image appeared for a moment or two. A face? It was more like a skull than the semblance of any normal human being. White pinpoints of eyes set in two black cavities, sunken cheeks and sharp high cheek-bones, a thin nose, high-domed forehead, and a frightful smirk on his twisted white lips.

Then the paper turned black and exploded into flames.

"The ghost that haunts me," Holmes said, sitting down in a slump on the sofa.

What was he going to do now, I wondered, reach for his violin, or his cocaine and syringe?

"I think I'll have another cup of Woojeon," he said. "Are you sure you won't join me, Watson?"

The Skeleton of Contention

Rhys Hughes

The heroes of Chaud-Mellé find their costumes in locked boxes
in the shadows of walled-up markets or under floorboards in the
houses of invisible aunts. They sometimes digest food they have
not eaten and they can do other strange, troubling things.

Often they languish in prisons, misunderstood and despised,
where they pass the time fighting time itself, the dripping ceil-
ings and boot creakings that count it for them.

Costumes might be found even there.

The prisons of Chaud-Mellé are full of real men chained to
iron balls, iron men chained to pulsing globules of flesh washed
up on the shores of stagnant inner seas, and tiny men who have
painstakingly hollowed out rooms in their own black spheres and
dwell inside, peeping from frosted glass portholes and dreaming
that two imprisonments, like two negatives, can be combined
into one freedom.

But freedom is not always a positive.

Meanwhile, in the cinemas there are enough colours to balance
out the greys and glooms of the dark places, enough pure sighs
to cancel the groans of the unwashed spaces, and awe in abun-
dance to enhance the prodigious mystery of indigenous faces in
a city where not to be odd or dangerous is to be eccentric.
Cinemas are popular.

The audiences in this city that is also a mountain republic have an insatiable appetite for new films, the latest productions from France and Italy, the gaudier the better, the brighter the nicer, the thicker the palette the thinner the communal despair. They fill ten thousand seats every night, rowdy as bullfight spectators, lips pursed in mocking whistles, slamming folding chairs, stamping, bawling, slapping from their shoulders flakes of fake pale skin shaken from the trembling alabaster cherubs that cling to the ceiling like divinely warped geckos.

Now the safety curtain is lifted and the projector beam becomes a bridge of motes to the screen and the huge hush is more startling than the former hubbub as muscles relax and bodies slump deeper into ripped plush chairs and the first comprehensible images appear.

The cinemas are the only places in Chaud-Mellé where people achieve satisfaction while all pointing in the same direction.

Real living heroes are not welcome.

The Bone of Contention hoped to meet enough compatible people over the years to form a Skeleton of Contention that would clatter most challengingly over the bridges of the cobble-scaled city. Kindred spirits and sibling souls he sought with increasing fervour, almost to the point of forgetting to be what he was, an enigmatic hero.

The cobbles of the streets and alleyways were not placed there by human agency. A shower of small meteorites deposited them and the roads were later designed to follow the chance patterns. This neatly explains the pointless twists and turns.

The Bone wore a costume of black silk, a mask the colour of marrow and on his chest was stitched the symbol of a femur. He had difficulties climbing, jumping and swinging, but he played all types of xylophone with amazing dexterity, unfortunately.

His rancour at the injustices of urban life was extreme.

In his heart might be located bitterness, anger, love, loneliness, desire for unknown things that always seemed about to reveal their true characters, a fluctuation between the conviction he had wasted his youth and spent it superbly, deep frustration at the inadequacies of his own idealism; and these conflicting feelings might be easily seen as solid objects by an emotion lens, which is a device never yet invented by any scientist, mad or otherwise.

The Doctors of Progress were meeting this very night.

In the lowest room of the highest tower of the ancient university on the steepest hill below the moon, they gathered, cloaks limp without the arousing wind, spectacles shining.

"It seems a chemist in Stuttgart has refined the process further. More than a billion new colours are available!"

"This is good, but a billion is not a trillion; and in fact is as far from being so as a strudel is from being a knockwurst."

"How can we be sure that—"

"Only through further experimentation may we—"

Tempers were bubbling, boiling.

"Gentlemen!" The voice imposed itself like a wedge into the debate, propping open the gates of mouths.

They looked to see who had spoken.

Professor James Moriarty.

They knew him as you know him, as everyone knows him, and he was everything he ought to be, and more. The domed forehead shone but did not glisten, despite the overheated atmosphere that prevailed in a chamber where so many feared the scorn of their peers.

His cane rested against the table.

With only a single droplet of sweat to trickle down his nose and hang on the tip like a miniature vessel of molten glass, he leaned forward and the effect in the half-light was peculiar, as if perspective was wrong, as if he had learned to loom suddenly from a great distance.

Then he spoke and the movement of his lips appeared to lag slightly behind the utterance of the words, as if he was a character in a foreign film that had been badly dubbed. He said:

"The invention of new colours is doubtless a worthy pursuit in a world that has faded due to the erosions of war and its resultant shortages; and yes, the utilisation of these bright and uplifting pigments in various industries is a boon to civilisation and something for which we should be grateful. Textiles, photo-graphy, publishing, cosmetics, and many other sectors of commercial enterprise will continue to benefit enormously, but are we going to focus our minds on superficialities? We are above that."

He rested his arms on the oaken table and smiled.

There was an anguished pause.

One of the others present made bold to answer: "What are you proposing?"

"Something grand." And he made no grand gesture to accompany his words; and this lack of a gesture served as the gesture itself, in the same way that an absence may more acutely define a presence and the depiction of the space around an object outline that object with awful clarity. There was a snuffling behind him and he nodded.

The eyes of the notables peered in that direction.

"Was it necessary to—"

"I am sorry to say that it was." Moriarty was the only one who did not look back. "Because this city of yours is infested with heroes who are fools but inconvenient all the same; and although our chamber is difficult to enter without permission, it still takes only boldness and determination to bypass the other security measures and burst in upon us. One extra safeguard is not a bad thing. A last line of slobbering defence."

"He has the girth of a Cerberus!"

"Yes, he does, rather."

Yellow eyes shone weakly in the gloom and though they were a sickly hue, the beast itself was in robust health, a mass of blackness with the occasional gleam of tooth and sparkling chain of saliva, a drool consisting of prismatic pearls on a slimy cord that pooled at the front paws of the slavering bulk. Felt rather than seen or heard, the hound imposed its presence by increasing the pressure on the ambient shadows.

Moriarty had chained him to a bronze ring on the wall, which was the last reminder of days when Chaud-Mellé students rode horses to the college and stabled them in lecture theatres.

His existence was a magnetic anomaly in the room.

Attracting anxieties like iron filings.

"Most heroes who live here," ventured an old fellow, "have been put in jail. I assert that one can be *too* cautious and that some precautions are a graver danger than the thing they avert."

"I never saw a more malevolent beast," said another.

"Barely a dog at all but a—"

Moriarty replied crisply, "He is a black Šarplaninac, a breed from the mountains of Albania, but this is unimportant. What I wish to discuss with you is the subject of profits through science."

Only with glacial urgency did the attention of the attendees return to a contemplation of the business at hand, the plotting and planning of crimes to supplement their meagre academic salaries.

"I intend, gentlemen, to bend the fourth dimension to my will."

"Time travel!" came the communal gasp.

"Of a special kind, yes."

"But that is absurd and outrageous!"

Moriarty shrugged and his shrug demonstrated purer tedium than the widest yawn. It seemed to agree with the sentiment that had been expressed and yet despise it at the same time; and also to be weary of the contradiction. Everyone waited for him to speak but he was plainly in no rush. He drew the moment out by rubbing his jaw slowly.

Then he said, "Nonetheless, I have found a method."

"A time machine? Surely not!"

Now he rubbed the nape of his neck, eyes shut.

His other hand was busy tapping the tip of his walking cane against the wooden floorboards, a gentle rhythm.

"Gentlemen, you are not amateurs, you are not beguiled by fantasies, I will never be able to trick you with words. Of course I am *not* talking about using a time machine in order to enhance our prospects. It would be useless for such a purpose. In fact, I have one with me and it has never been of any benefit at all. Permit me to demonstrate."

He reached into his pocket and withdrew a thin silver spoon and a metal spring, then placed them on the table with an air of mock reverence and pushed the handle of the spoon into the spring so that the coils encircled it like the solidified orbits of agitated air molecules.

Then he stood straight and nodded benignly at nothing. "May I have your opinion, gentlemen?"

"*That* is a time machine?"

"Not exactly." He gazed sadly down at the conjoined objects. "But it might as well be, for it is no less effective than a real time machine and just as useful to us, which is to say, not at all."

The murmuring was subdued but deeply unhappy.

"You jest with us, but why?"

Moriarty sighed. "Very well. If I must explain everything, then I shall. Were our little gathering to agree to employ a time machine in the evolution of our plans, we would have to invent the device ourselves, for I am utterly convinced that one does not exist elsewhere."

He rocked on his heels and continued. "Pay attention now. Suppose a machine of this kind was actually developed. We rejoice at the belief we are free to create all sorts of havoc in the past, to manipulate events in previous ages in order to enhance our present prospects; but that assumption is a gross error; for the instant we attempt to propel the device against the flow of time our hopes fly apart. They disintegrate even as the body of the machine does, for its component parts have a personal history that is no less real than the history of the greater world in which they exist.

"Do you follow? The nuts and bolts, cogs and wires, all the elements that constitute the body and engine of the device only come into conjunction with each other at the instant when the contraption is created. Thus the time machine cannot be sent back to a time earlier than that, because the separate parts necessarily exist in different locations.

"So when a brave explorer mounts the vehicle and, gripping the lever resolutely in his hands with a faraway look in his eyes, shifts it into reverse, the vehicle must come to a halt at the precise time it was first completed. It cannot proceed any further backwards, because the parts that make it work will no longer be together but in the places they originally came from, the drawer of a junk room, the highest shelf of an electrician's garage, the cellar of an ironmonger's. They will be scattered.

"Thus to employ a time machine to travel a great distance backwards in time, for example, several centuries, we must construct the device and then *wait* for a length of time exactly equivalent to those centuries. Our maximum range into the past is only the moment when the machine was successfully completed. That is why this humble object on the table before you is, to all intents and purposes, a working time machine, for it is equally useless to us, equally incapable of taking us into the past."

With the air of a lecturer who has rushed through a lesson in order to go to lunch early, Moriarty spread his arms.

They were offended, humiliated.

"So much for the past!" huffed one guest. "What about the future? A time machine could be used to facilitate illegal deeds in coming weeks. To anticipate stock market fluctuations and—"

"The future? Gentlemen, the future is overdue."

There was a dull reverberation at the solid door that was the only entrance and exit from the chamber. It was an explosion but oddly muted, as if the entire force of the blast had gone into the body of the door and remained there. But the door swung open anyway.

The intruder lurched forward, regained balance.

His silk costume was so dark and so perfectly clean that it was plainly visible in the muddier gloom beyond the reach of the lamp above the table. The eyes behind the mask scanned the chamber, fixed on Moriarty, and the entire mask creased itself, powered by a hidden frown. "Here is the future," said Moriarty theatrically. "A little late."

The Bone of Contention took a determined step.

And the dog was on him.

The chain that held it to the bronze ring was long.

The lunge was horribly graceful.

Like a storm cloud pregnant with a violent downpour flinging itself at the mass of a granite mountain, the hound rushed through the air towards the disguised hero. The impact was like the smack of a hand on a fully satisfied grotesque belly but enormously magnified.

They went down together.

They rolled, snarled, grappled. Cloth tore, bone snapped.

Moriarty observed, carefully aloof.

Other spectators were more excitable, aghast.

"Your dog is losing!"

"Yes, he is, but I never bothered to name him, so let us not grow too sentimental at his impending demise."

The Bone of Contention was a hero and heroes have powers and skills and the holy blessing of contrivance. Bloodied and numbed, garb in disarray, rents of silk hanging down like thirsty mutant tongues, he staggered away from the canine corpse, slipping once in the gore smeared on the soles of his boots, accelerating towards the table.

Moriarty calmly watched and waited for the right moment. Then he lifted his cane and aimed it at the avenger.

A click as he pressed a button in the handle and a tranquilliser dart embedded itself in the chest of the hero, like a darning needle that misses its tangent, a rose thorn turned inwards into its own stem. The Bone collapsed, a ripped sack of flesh and adulterated blood.

"Help me lift him. Clear a space there! Now fetch the dog too. I am serious. It will take at least three or four of you."

Moriarty lay out the unconscious Bone almost tenderly on the surface of the table and applied scissors to the lopsided mask, cutting it off, setting at liberty a young troubled expression, the visage of a vigilante with more enthusiasm than strength, more strength than sense, more sense than luck. A few more snips and the face was fully free.

"Hurry with the hound! Every second counts."

His medical bag was open beside him, the array of instruments within the voluminous leather depths twinkling and gleaming like icicles in a cave. He selected the ones he required with due care, almost lovingly. Meanwhile, a quartet of the bespectacled professors struggled with the cooling burden near the damaged door, grumbling loudly as they attempted to drag it across the varnished floor. Relying on its own dripping ichor to grease the way, they were uncoordinated and inefficient.

"You are pulling the head while I pull the tail! Push the head or there will be no progress whatsoever tonight—"

"Pah! There is progress every second of every minute of every hour somewhere in the world. A chemical reaction here, a hypothesis there, the discovery of a distant star or new particle."

Arguing and wheezing, they finally manhandled the beast to the side of Moriarty, but they were quite unable to elevate it on to the table next to the prone Bone. "No matter, gentlemen. What you have achieved will suffice. I bid you sit and recuperate your energies."

They rested, heads in hands, until the satisfied murmuring of Moriarty proved too much of a temptation; and then they looked. Men who had sawn off the heads of birds for transplantation on to the necks of toads flinched in distaste, recoiled and even grimaced.

"You are blinding him. This it barbaric indeed!"

"No, my friends, I am performing an operation of extreme delicacy, a procedure that is far more of an art than a routine at the present moment and may remain so indefinitely. The eyes of the dog for the eyes of the man. An unprecedented exchange!"

"The purpose of this surgery?"

"It is, I hope, the method by which I will make time travel possible. It is likely that all will be made clear soon."

Two bodies with craters in their faces now troubled the chamber. The violator of human geometry wiped his hands quickly on a towel and returned to work. The eyes of the living man were cast negligently on to the table like peeled eggs, allowed to roll randomly.

The dead dog's eyes, in contrast, were treated with devotion, gently inserted into the gaping sockets of the patient and meticulously positioned. Moriarty even swallowed dryly during the task, not flustered but pushed to the limit of his abilities. Yet he was pleased.

"I am confident of success, gentlemen! Let us see!"

They winced at his last word.

He dipped into his bag for a flask of fluid, dampened a cloth with its contents, pressed the cloth hard over the mouth and nose of the Bone; and the shoreline susurrations of his lungs ceased.

The body jerked, kicked out, the heel of a boot catching Moriarty on his left hip quite by accident, without force.

"The antidote to the tranquilliser," he confirmed.

The Bone sat up, bending at the waist like an open book that wants to shut itself, to hide its words from reviewers.

Moriarty adroitly stood aside, moved far back.

The Bone contracted unusual muscles, propelled himself off the table on to his feet, tottered but did not tumble.

Then he blinked and reached out, gropingly, in awe.

"What is happening? You must tell us!"

Moriarty laughed out of the shadows. "The eyes of a dog are different from those of a man. A dog can only see in black and white. What does this mean? That dogs live permanently in a monochrome world, the same world depicted in old movies and newsreels!"

"We fail to comprehend—"

"The same world, gentlemen, shown nightly on cinema screens before the advent of colour films."

"The significance of this is beyond our—"

"Have you never wondered what a dog is doing when it interacts with things that are seemingly not there? You tell yourself it is mapping the world with its olfactory sense, sniffing traces of the intangible, and surely that is partly the case. But it is not the whole story."

Moriarty modulated his voice, projecting it in such a way that it was an echo without a source, confusing the Bone, who listened furiously but was unable to locate it. He added, "A dog can see into the past, into the old times, into the black-and-white world, into the era when motion pictures had just begun. That is real time travel!"

"You arranged all this for what purpose?"

"You are mostly elderly men. The modified hero before you can see into the days of your youth. Back then, you lacked the

wisdom, experience, resources and tenacity you have now. You
are all survivors, more durable than you like to pretend. Even I
could not be certain of defeating you all on my own. You have
learned many things over the long decades and those lessons
have become conditioned reflexes.

"But remember, my friends, that when you were callow youths
you had not yet honed your survival skills. You had weaknesses,
your defences were relatively frail, you were not yet survivors
because you had not lived enough years or endured sufficient
experiences to claim that distinction. So your younger selves are
easier to thwart than the tough shrivelled editions you have
become. The Bone sees you as you once were.

"And thus he can perceive your weak spots, the glaring chinks
in your armour, and take advantage of them. He can destroy you
with little trouble by concentrating on those weaknesses, target-
ing them, for now he exists in two worlds simultaneously, the
present and the past. Gentlemen, I must say farewell. I will be
leaving your city tonight."

The Bone had crouched, as if compressing the helix of his
soul, and now he suddenly uncoiled and hurled himself about
the chamber; and the bodies of broken experts and geniuses
bounced off the walls, were flung like rolled-up rugs into corners,
while one man watched the carnage with perfect equanimity, not
even twirling his cane.

And the unexpected defences of the victims were of no avail to
them, but they interested Moriarty. Hidden pistols and concealed
knives, phials of acid and hollow teeth containing poison gas.
Each defence was a product of the nature of the man they were
supposed to protect, a question of his taste, and the Bone could
foresee what they would be, whereas Moriarty could not. It was
educational and edifying for him.

Not quite ten minutes passed. The screams ceased.

The Bone had finished. He was tired but not exhausted. He
turned to confront the master, scanning his bulging and borrowed
eyes up and down the entire length of the nonchalant figure.
Then his body relaxed, the strips of his torn costume hanging
more limply than ever.

"I perceive that in *your* youth you were no less formidable than you are now. Discretion is still the better part of valour and so I have no intention of engaging with you. I have done enough."

"As I expected," said Moriarty.

"Just tell me why? Why did you betray those who wanted to work with you? Who wished to aid your crimes?"

Moriarty was affable but also philosophical. He smiled thinly, rubbed his chin and said, "In a place where there are so many heroes, more than all the jails can hold, the villains will necessarily be superior to those that are encountered elsewhere. In cities where the criminals are in the majority, the outnumbered heroes evolve into mighty beings. Here the opposite is true. I did not want competition I could not deal with. Villains here were improving all the time and would continue to improve until my own privileged position and status were under genuine threat."

The Bone bowed and clicked his heels and hastened out of the room with the panache of an incontinent ghost.

Moriarty packed away his surgical instruments, tucked his cane under his arm, strolled unhurriedly out of the building.

The night was full of people.

The cinemas were emptying. Posters for the latest colour films, some of them torn, rippled their garish spectra at him. But he walked past. Not far was the train station, a place where the platform, rails, guards, locomotives, soot and unbearable partings were still in black and white, anachronistic, a not yet erased segment of a panoramic past.

He secured a carriage to himself. The train crossed a bridge almost at the top of the city and he was able to peer down.

All was well in Chaud-Mellé.

The Fifth Browning

Jürgen Ehlers

By chance I heard that a Mammoth Book of Adventures of
Moriarty *was being planned, and so I asked the editor whether I
could contribute a few clarifying words about my dear grandfather, Professor James Moriarty. Not enough is widely known
about his work.*

*My grandfather was not a criminal in the true sense of the
word. No lesser man than Sherlock Holmes himself once said to
Dr Watson: "In calling Moriarty a criminal you are uttering
libel!" I will however not deny that my grandfather sometimes
did things that could be seen as unlawful in a different context.
He always kept an eye on the greater good. Or at least his own
good. But don't we all? The end justifies the means.*

*James Moriarty kept a detailed diary until shortly before his
death. My account is based on this diary. In my report, I would
also like to answer a few questions that those learned men
researching Sherlock Holmes have thus far not been able to
answer satisfactorily. These are:*

*1. The detailed circumstances of the meeting between Sherlock
Holmes and my grandfather in Meiringen in May 1891,*

*2. The events that took place in spring 1904, which led Sherlock
Holmes to retire from public life for an extended period and*

*3. The crisis of the summer of 1914, when Sherlock Holmes
tried one last time to sabotage my grandfather's work.*

These events are inextricably linked. In my grandfather's diary, they can be found under the heading of "The Case of the Five Brownings".

Meiringen, May 1891

When in spring 1891 I had Sherlock Holmes know that I would like to meet him, the great detective initially hesitated. His opinion of me was not great, and he suspected that I would, one way or another, double-cross him. His fear, however, was wholly unfounded. I am always honest if the circumstances allow it. In order to exercise discretion, I suggested a meeting abroad. Meiringen in Switzerland seemed suitable. This small town of three thousand citizens in the Bernese Oberland region is so insignificant that nobody would ever guess that decisions of world historic importance could be made here. No reporters would stray here. Meiringen had a train station, which simplified getting there.

We arrived separately. Holmes had difficulties getting rid of his loyal friend and companion Dr Watson, so he arrived two days after our agreed date at the Hotel du Sauvage on Bahnhofsstraße in Meiringen.

"What a lovely spring day," said Holmes when he joined me at my table on the terrace. "May I?"

"Please. A lovely spring, yes, but there are dark clouds on the horizon."

"Politically?" Holmes of course knew that as political adviser to the British government I was up to date on all current crises. "The Mahdi Uprising?"

I shook my head. The revolt in the Sudan was indeed dominating the headlines – Muslim fanatics had not only beaten the British troops but also invaded Ethiopia and killed the emperor – but that was unimportant.

"It's not about Africa," I said. "It's about Europe." I told Holmes what had happened. Kaiser Wilhelm II had been on the throne for three years now. He had sacked Bismarck and terminated the Reinsurance Treaty with Russia. This meant that the stable foreign policy of the German Reich was at an end.

"I know nothing about that," said Holmes.

He couldn't have known anything about it, as the Reinsurance Treaty was a secret treaty. Counter-measures were urgently necessary. Holmes said that that was my job as military adviser. I replied that my influence merely stretched to military-technical topics. And that in situations such as this, politicians also needed to be involved. My idea was to establish the necessary contacts via Holmes's brother Mycroft.

"So, you are thinking of reshuffling the War Office? And who should, in your opinion, get the top job?"

"Not Lansdowne in any case," I said. "We need to arm ourselves. And we need politicians who will see to that. Your chronicler, this Dr Doyle from Edinburgh, has repeatedly said that England should invest more in arms, and I agree."

Holmes smiled. Of course he knew that I had invested my considerable fortune into the arms industry.

"You surely won't begrudge me my enthusiasm, will you?" I said.

"Money is unimportant," he said. "But arms deals are always criminal. And I don't like to work with criminals. Do you know Basil Zaharoff?"

I nodded. I had hoped that Holmes would not touch upon this topic. But he was, as ever, too well informed.

"Who is this mysterious man? There is not a single photograph of him. Sometimes I ask myself whether he actually exists."

"He exists, Mr Holmes. He exists, and he sells weapons. And successfully so, I might add. The first functioning submarine that the Turkish Navy bought . . ."

"Yes, and people say he has screwed over Maxim, the inventor of the machine gun. Screwed him over good and proper."

Yes, that was true. "We bought him," I said.

"People say Zaharoff is responsible for Maxim's financial difficulties. They say sabotage . . ."

"Rumours," I claimed.

"Sometimes, I get the impression, Moriarty, that *you* are this mysterious man."

"If this were the case, our country should count itself lucky.

Zaharoff has guided us to some of the most powerful weapons currently under development."

"The submarine? The Nordenfelt-U-boat that Zaharoff sold to the Turks and Greeks?"

I nodded.

"So, you think Great Britain also needs such a submarine?"

"One? We need fifty U-boats!"

"Fifty? Do you know how much that costs? Thus far, the Bruce-Partington Plan is nothing but a plan, isn't it? And if we buy the submarines from Nordenfelt in Sweden . . ."

I tried my best not to show my surprise. Bruce-Partington! The construction plans for the submarine were top secret. Obviously Mycroft had got wind of the matter and told his brother all about it. But, in any case, it was out of the question to buy the submarines in Sweden.

"We'll go about it differently," I said. "We will buy Nordenfelt."

"We?"

"Vickers in Sheffield. Talk to your brother Mycroft about it. Convince him. I have already spoken to Tom Vickers. He thinks it's a great idea. And while you negotiate with the politicians, I will keep the competition at bay."

It took me some time to eliminate Holmes's qualms. In order to concentrate all our efforts on our joint aim, it was necessary for us to stop all our other pursuits. This would work best if we were both declared dead. So, we spread the rumour that Holmes and I had been killed in deadly tussle.

Watson was – as ever – easy to deceive. He really believed that we had both plunged to our deaths at the Reichenbach Falls, while in reality we had hidden in a rock crevice until the devastated doctor had disappeared. Thus, the British-German arms race began.

Kiel, July 1905

People who, like me, are financially dependent on a never-ending effort to keep the country's defences up, invariably also have to make contact with the other side. The opponent must always remain so strong that further investments in arms on our own side are absolutely necessary.

Sherlock Holmes, with whom I had worked seamlessly together until this point, did not approve of this method. He was satisfied that in 1904 John Fisher was made First Sea Lord, which entailed a comprehensive reform of the fleet. Finally, the construction of modern battleships and submarines was given full priority. Holmes believed we had reached our goal. He moved to Sussex to devote his life to beekeeping.

I, meanwhile, made contact with Admiral Alfred Von Tirpitz. He was responsible for realising the emperor's dream of a powerful German fleet. But in 1905, this was but a dream. I met the admiral in a harbour pub in Kiel, and he was pissed as a newt.

"This is the current situation," he slurred. "This is the situation: Germany has twenty-two battleships. Together, Great Britain and France have eighty. Germany is hopelessly outnumbered by all its potential opponents. The kaiser may dream of a powerful fleet, but he will never get one. Our place in the sun is gone. We need to end the arms race."

I had feared this much. My German opponent seemed totally defeated. He merely brightened up a little when I bought him another drink. I said: "Don't lose hope, Herr Admiral! Admittedly, it doesn't look too good at the moment. But what would you say, Herr Tirpitz, if we simply scrapped our current fleets and started all over?"

"From scratch?" I had aroused his interest. "How could that work?"

"Simple. Next year, we will launch the Dreadnought. A new type of battleship, which is sure to outperform all other vessels. All you can do is scrap the rest."

"Congratulations."

"Thank you. It is great to have such a ship. But it is, of course, just a single ship. And no one can keep Germany from building two ships of this type . . ."

"For that we would, first of all, need the plans."

"For the right sum of money, that could easily be arranged . . ."

*   *   *

Sherlock Holmes was furious. "You have betrayed our country!" he bellowed when I told him about it.

I shook my head. "Mr Holmes, you understand nothing of arms deals. We need a kind of balance of powers. The Germans need to believe that they can catch up. Our shipyards have a much greater capacity than the German ones. And to get a nice advantage right from the start, I have changed the construction plans slightly. The first new German ships will be significantly slower and not armed quite as well as the British Dreadnoughts."

What I failed to mention to Holmes, but which was of great significance to me, was: with Germany arming its navy, Great Britain was obliged to follow suit. Investing in arms remained lucrative for me. Investing on both sides, that is.

Sarajevo, 27 June 1914

In spring 1914, I travelled to Belgrade in my capacity as unofficial representative of the largest British arms manufacturer. Officially, I was there to supply the Serbian army with Maxim machine guns. In reality, it was about something else entirely. A group of Serbian nationalists had planned an assassination attempt on the Austrian heir to the throne, who was expected for a visit in Sarajevo at the end of June. Sarajevo was the capital of Bosnia. Bosnia belonged to Austro-Hungary. The plan was precarious. Apparently, there was a lack of guns.

Assassins without guns are, of course, ludicrous. In order not to endanger the project, I offered to provide the gentleman with suitable weapons. It was said that they would be three to four people. Just to be on the safe side, I promised to bring five pistols. Naturally, I knew that the connection between the assassins and the Serbian government was ideal to conjure up a larger conflict. If this came to light, a war was unavoidable, and – due to the existing treaty obligations – Russia, Germany, France and England would have to intervene.

On 26 June, I took the train to Sarajevo. The following day, after dusk had fallen, I made my way to our agreed-upon meeting point. I had visited the graveyard in advance, so I did not have to search for long to find the grave of Bogdan Žerajić. Žerajić had been a student who had tried to shoot the Austro-Hungarian Governor for Bosnia and Herzegovina four years previously. He had fired five shots and missed. With the last bullet, Žerajić had shot himself.

Now, the men who wanted to shoot the Archduke Franz Ferdinand of Austria the following day had met at this dubious hero's grave. They were seven men, most of them very young. Some of them probably still went to school. Princip, for example. They all had primitive bombs from Serbia, and they had three revolvers in total, which they had also brought along from Belgrade. They talked too much and too loudly, just like school-boys, who still had to convince themselves that their terrible plan might actually work.

I gave them four of my Browning pistols. The new model 1910, 9 mm, six shots. The fifth pistol was spare, so I kept that one for myself. I wanted to suggest that everyone fire a couple of shots to get used to the weapons, but it never came to that. All of a sudden, there was a shrill whistling sound. "A spy!" the lookout shouted.

"Where?"

"Over there!"

Several shots rang out. I disappeared discreetly. I was not keen on a night-time shootout with the police. If indeed it was the police. I was not too sure. Fact was that only the prospective assassins were firing their guns. And fact was, too, that every shot missed. The shadow the lookout had seen remained unharmed.

As I vaulted over the low wall at the rear end of the graveyard, someone cleared his throat quite close by. I plunged my hand into my jacket to draw my pistol, when I heard a familiar voice: "Come, come, Professor Moriarty, we wouldn't want to shoot one another now, would we?" It was Holmes.

An hour later, we sat together at the bar of our hotel. "To be honest, I did not expect to see you here in Sarajevo," I said.

"You should always expect me," replied Holmes.

"Did you tail me?" I had taken good care along the whole journey to ensure that nobody was following me. At least I had
thought I had.

"I did not tail you," said Holmes. "I saw you alight from a taxi
at Victoria Station in London, and I was curious to what your
plans were. I observed you for a moment and then drew my
conclusions. It was quite simple: you bought your ticket at the
station. That means that you are here neither on behalf of the
British government nor on behalf of Vickers. You bought a ticket
for Lüttich. And you are not someone who is interested in Gothic
cathedrals. Therefore I knew that Lüttich was not your final
destination. You wanted to travel on. For example to Herstal.
Herstal lies just five kilometres away from Lüttich. And Herstal
is home to the Fabrique Nationale d'Armes de Guerre."

"I admire your astuteness."

"As you are travelling with two large trunks, I knew that you
did not want to stay in Lüttich either. Your large pieces of luggage
indicated that you wanted to travel to a place where the neces-
sities of life are not always easily available. As you were not going
by boat, but by train, I knew you were travelling somewhere
inland. And as you are an expert on military equipment, the most
likely destination was a place with a need for military equipment.
The area with the greatest unrest on the continent is currently
the Balkan."

"But how did you know I would go to Sarajevo?"

"Again, simple. Your visit in Herstal had nothing to do with a
larger arms order. Such orders are usually submitted by post.
You bought weapons that can be easily stored in a travelling case.
That eliminates rifles. Which means you bought pistols. FN
produces one of the best pistols in the world, the Browning."

I confirmed that I had indeed bought Brownings.

"Now, the Balkan has seen a number of wars in recent times,
but it seems that the era of wars is currently taking a break.
However, the territories occupied by Austro-Hungary are in a
state of upheaval. Bosnia, for example. And at the heart of all the
unrest is, logically, the capital of Bosnia: Sarajevo."

"You followed me after all."

Holmes shook his head. "I travelled ahead. As I knew your destination, I took the shortest connection via Paris and waited here at the hotel for you. I was sure that you, too, are no friend of bedbugs and lice and that you would therefore stay at the best hotel in the city."

"Perfect deduction, as usual. But why are you here? Surely not to show off your superior wit?"

"I am here to remind you of our agreement. Our aim is to ensure stability. Peace. We both signed a contract. But what you are doing here will not bring peace. You are supporting terrorists, murderers. You are playing with fire, Moriarty. If the assassination attempt succeeds, there will be war."

"Yes, probably. But we are well armed, thanks to your and my relentless work. And if war does indeed come, we will win. Don't forget that. And a cleaner, better, stronger land will lie in the sunshine when the storm has cleared."

Holmes shook his head. "That is cynical. There could be thousands of deaths."

"Thousands? Hundreds of thousands, my dear Holmes! But the higher the number of victims, the greater the deterrent effect for the following generations. This will be the greatest war the world has seen, but at the same time this will be the last war ever. This is the war to end all wars."

It was clear that Sherlock Holmes did not believe me.

"You are a pessimist," I said.

Holmes threatened to sabotage the attack. But of course he had no chance. Me included, there were seven men who wanted to start a war. And just one man who wanted to stop it.

"What do you want to do?" I asked. "We have positioned six men in different places. Each one has a bomb and a gun."

"They are inexperienced men."

"That does not matter. If each of them fires their six shots, there are thirty-six bullets flying at the Archduke. And then there are the bombs. Don't you, too, dear Holmes, believe that even the most resistant Archduke will be finished after thirty-six shots and six bombs?"

Holmes shook his head. "You may have worked out the

dynamics of an asteroid, but you have no idea of the dynamics of an assassination attempt."

I hate to admit it, but Holmes was right. The first assassin did nothing. He simply let the motorcade pass. The second assassin threw his bomb wide. The third, fourth, fifth and sixth assassin did nothing at all when the Archduke passed them on his way to the town hall. The chance was lost. The peace remained intact. Most unfortunate.

After lunch, I sat in front of the delicatessen Moritz Schiller near the Latin Bridge, brooding over the morning's events. At the table next to mine sat Princip, drinking a cup of coffee. The failed assassin was lost in thought and did not recognise me. And then, something unexpected happened.

"They are coming," someone shouted.

I looked up. Indeed. The motorcade was returning from the town hall, and they were turning into our street. There was the archduke, there was his wife, and there was Holmes on the footboard of the car. I looked at Princip. He sat as if paralysed in his chair and stared at the archduke. And then the archduke's chauffeur stopped. The motorcade had taken a wrong turning and needed to go back. The car had to be turned and had halted right in front of us. Finally, Princip reacted. He suddenly sprang to his feet, tore his pistol from his pocket, ran towards the car and fired at close range. There was nothing Holmes could have done to stop him. But Princip had missed and hit the archduke's wife instead. Everybody jumped up. As did I. But, while most people just screamed and ran away or scrambled towards the dying woman, I simply stepped on to my chair, calmly drew my Browning and fired a shot over the heads of the crowd. My shot fell simultaneously with Princip's second shot. I hit, whereas Princip's bullet went wide. I pocketed my pistol again. No one had noticed me. I paid for my coffee and walked away unchallenged.

We don't know what happened then. Fact is that my grandfather travelled back to London via Paris the following day. Sherlock Holmes also returned to England. He was last seen alive on 2

August 1914, when he was able to arrest the German spy von Borck together with Watson. Shortly after that, the great detective must have died. After this date, James Moriarty was also never seen again. Maybe they killed each other during their last encounter in Sussex or Sheffield. Today, there are over 1,500 Moriartys in Great Britain, but none of them is a direct descendant of my grandfather.

But if Sherlock Holmes was right and my grandfather was indeed the mysterious Basil Zaharoff, of whom there is no photograph, then he must have survived the war. He did excellent business and was even made Grand-Officier de la Légion by the French president. He was also awarded an honorary doctorate from the University of Oxford and lived happily and in good health until his end on 27 November 1936.

As we all know, my grandfather's dream of a terrible war to end all wars did not come true. After this spectacular failure, my father thought it prudent to change our family name. So, don't be surprised when this article's author is not called Moriarty. Or indeed Zaharoff. Us Moriartys / Zaharoffs are everywhere, even if we sometimes go by a different name.

Of course we also moved to a different address. We always go where there is good business. For example, in Germany. Germany is the world's third largest arms exporter. So, if you are in need of tanks, submarines or helicopters, please do not hesitate to contact us. We would be happy to help you get the necessary export papers. If you want peace, you need to be strong. And you do want peace, don't you?

Translated by Ann-Kathrin Ehlers

The Modjeska Waltz

Rose Biggin

From the private papers of Irene Adler. Undated; from its tone, possibly intended for posthumous publication. It is in that hope, in any case, that we reproduce it here.

My first and most intriguing adventure with Professor Moriarty was – in more than one respect – an elaborate dance.

Shortly after the affair I note Dr Watson refers to as a 'scandal', although it had been nothing of the kind from my perspective, I found myself travelling the Continent. It was a pleasure to do so, and enabled me to put the unfortunate fire in my London lodgings far in the past. On the occasion the professor entered my awareness, I had dabbled in reprising my position at the Imperial Opera of Warsaw. Although I declared myself perfectly content with minor roles and chorus parts, I had been coaxed into accepting first a single solo aria, and then a full prima donna position. Indeed, by the time a grand tour took me back to London and Moriarty sought me out, it had become rather difficult to enter my dressing room for the sheer density of roses. Such is the life of a performer of my calibre.

It came to me via the usual routes for society gossip, tipping out of the opera boxes down to the 'merely players' on the stage below, the news that the King of B— was organising a ball for his son, to be held in the city; and it was perhaps due to my prominence as the Countess of *Figaro* that season that I was presented with a gilt-edged invitation. I make no claims on my vanity as an actress (or, indeed, as a dancer) as to why the professor called upon me. Neither did he wish to accompany me to the ball for the chance to dabble in society. He hinted towards the fact that he and I were the only two minds ever to best our mutual friend, and that *this* was the reason for seeking me out, and not attempting to gain entry to the ball another way. This did flatter me, I confess. But I have reason to believe, in the cold mist of dawn, that even this was only a front for obtaining an invitation.

I was in my dressing room shortly after a performance of Mimi, given to great acclaim, although *La Bohème* does not, artistically, stretch me. A boy brought me a visitor's card – and although I have thought at length upon it since, I cannot now remember why I chose to pay attention to this card in particular, as so many came my way. Perhaps it was the lack of embarrassing praise, confessions of love, poetic follies, amateur drawings. No, only a request to meet, the naming of a respectable tea house in a fashionable part of London quite far from the theatre, a table number (most intriguing!) and a time. And a coat of arms, which I did not at first recognise. I was curious – perhaps the first moves of the dance between us were being felt out, even then. I told the boy to return to the giver of the card with the news that I agreed to the meeting. After that I was preoccupied with rehearsals and fending off would-be paramours until the appointed date.

The tea house my mysterious companion had chosen was one known for its discretion. Young men hovered around the edges ready for any reason they might be needed, while remaining distant enough that the diners could maintain their privacy. I arrived approximately seven and a half minutes late (as is my wont) only to find the reserved table empty, but, as soon as I had announced my name to the maître d' and been seated by the window, a cream tea was set before me.

'I do apologise for the mistake,' I said, 'but I have not placed an order.' I did not wish to deprive the cream tea's true owners of their afternoon delicacy.

'No, 's definitely for this table, miss,' said the serving boy, as he placed the jam and milk down. 'Sir says you are welcome to start, miss.' Only a slight quiver to his hands betrayed his nervousness;

new to the role, perhaps. 'He said to say he'll b-be with you anon.' I recognised the stutter over a learnt line.

I thanked the boy – my companion's impudence was not his fault – and decided to pour my tea. A moment passed which I spent gazing out of the window, before a silver-topped cane passed by my place and, within another moment, a gentleman was sitting opposite me.

He wore a topcoat whose slight shabbiness belied its original expense, and when he removed it I noticed that his grey suit, as fine as it was, was fraying at the edges. The chain of a pocket watch glinted from his velvet waistcoat, and the silver-topped cane was placed gently down, against his chair, frequently toyed with and never out of his reach. The overall impression was of a man who rarely attended such a social event as afternoon tea, although he could afford to do much more.

'Do I have the pleasure of sitting opposite the great Irene Adler?' he cried. I nodded, and any nervous tension he was carrying disappeared to be replaced by an eager courtesy that belied his years. 'It is a pleasure to make your acquaintance at last. I do beg your pardon for my lateness; a measure to determine that I would not be surprised by . . . any unexpected guests.' As I was not fully acquainted with the professor's criminal reputation at this point, this struck me as only mildly eccentric – not justifiably cautious!

'And you are?'

'Oh! I do beg your pardon.' He stood and leaned over awkwardly to shake my hand across the table – thus compiling a baffling set of social inadequacies that marked him out as a professor more readily than the chalk marks on his lapel ever would. 'James Moriarty, at your service,' he said.

'And what brings you to request the pleasure of a cream tea in this particular establishment?' I said. 'It is beyond the salary of a poor actress. I imagine also that it is outside of the usual range of experience for a scholar.'

'I am attempting to establish a social life,' he said, and gave a nervous laugh that showed he recognised – and respected – my correct deduction of his profession. (Although it was, of course, only half correct.) He then contradicted his stated desire for sociability: 'Madam, I shall get straight to the point.

'I have a great interest in the musico-social event that has been recently announced in honour of the Prince of B——. An impudent whelp, by my reckoning, to require his father to throw a ball so that he might reveal himself before everyone like a society debutante.' He checked his annoyance, and continued. 'In any case, the event is to be hosted by George Frederick St Clare, the King of B——, one month from today. I do not need to outline these facts to you, of course, as from what I have seen of the society pages, you will be gracing the occasion yourself.'

I nodded. It was a novelty for a man to be so forthright about the extent of his prior research.

He continued: 'I have invited you here, then, if I may put it bluntly, to beg you to attend with me as your guest.'

This surprised me – I have rarely known such bluntness, and was not expecting such an assertion from a man who seemed to be all elbows, and visibly desperate to return to his inkwells, or his abacus, or some such environment, not a ball for the highest of society. (I still had the man in mind as a shuffling, shy academic at this point, I confess.)

'I wish to attend the ball, Miss Adler, because I wish to gain a closer inspection of a specific gift the society pages inform us the prince will be presenting to the Dowager Duchess of Croome.'

'A brooch,' I said, to show that I was as knowledgeable as he about this event, and did not need it explaining. 'We believe the prince and his father have designs on arranging a marriage to one of the duchess's many relatives. This gift is to sweeten the strength between the two families.'

I said *we believe* to make the professor assume that we were still talking about information gleaned from the society pages and the gossip of chorus girls, but I had heard this from a very close source and knew it to be the case.

'Indeed,' he said, and continued to outline his plan. 'I must be absolutely honest with you, Miss Adler. If the timing is right, and I am able, and, with your good assistance, I will be able to – I wish to obtain the brooch for myself. Merely to inspect it, nothing more. No damage shall be done to it, of course. It is priceless, et cetera. But it is vital that it is in my capable hands by the end of the ball. The trick, as I see it, will be to take it after it has been officially presented to the duchess. The crowd will have seen it go to what is presumed to be its rightful home; and then we get closer to it by means of strategic socialising – I leave this in your responsibility, as an actress – and remove it before we leave the ball.'

'Well,' I said, when he had finished. 'The plan you outline sounds foolish at best; criminal at worst.'

He merely nodded; clearly this much he already knew. So I continued.

'The chief problem, as I see it, sir, will be convincing the guests that you belong amongst their number. As respected as you may be in your field, this is a grand occasion. There will be few present who do not own, or lay claim to, at least two countries in the Commonwealth.'

He opened his mouth to interrupt, but I spoke over him. 'You are, no doubt, wondering how I myself achieved an invitation. Indeed, it is a question I have pondered. I believe it could be something to do with the desire of the host to add some culture to the affair; several singers, ballerinas, pianists – even a painter if the rumours I have heard are right – have been invited to attend. I fear I am primarily intended to be decorative.'

I did not mention the letters I owned from the prince, begging me to attend the party as the last chance he would have to his 'true fair *Rosalind*' before the machinations of political marriage took him. I had barely considered the letters myself, and intended to take up his invitation in order to enjoy myself.

'So you see, Professor, it is not merely a question of behaving appropriately to the occasion. It is a question of clearly *belonging*.'

'You will be allowed to bring a guest, as you have an invitation,' he said, as if I had never spoken. 'Surely nobody will question your choice.'

'Sir!' I said. 'As a gift to the prince, the king has commissioned the composition of a new dance. All guests will be dancing the

Modjeska Waltz. You could stumble once and give the game away.'

'What is the Modjeska Waltz?' he said.

'*Ah*,' I said. 'It is something that was not included in the society pages so as to weed out those who might attend without permission. It is a dance that the guests will know. I myself know enough of it to pass, but only because I am surrounded by chorus girls for my work at the opera. They are all experts in the newest society dances and take pride in a comprehensive knowledge of the newest fashions. I can only imagine who is teaching the other decorative attendees.'

'Most interesting,' he said (and it was truly as if he did not know), 'and the Modjeska Waltz will be a partner-changing dance, I suppose, in order to allow the illusion of social mingling without forcing the grander guests present to deign in actual conversation with the lower orders?'

I nodded, assuming that he regularly read the society pages as another point of professorial eccentricity.

'Fascinating. And who is Modjeska?' he asked.

'Oh, some snippet of an actress or a singer of some sort, that the prince feels pertinent to honour with a tune or two,' I said, and I sniffed to show that I had no interest in this matter.

'Very well,' said the Professor. 'In any case, you consider this to be a barrier to my entering the ball?'

'I do indeed'.

He thought for another moment. I was considering buttering a scone when he changed tack.

'You are aware of my thesis, *The Dynamics of an Asteroid*?' said Moriarty.

I gave him a look that said, *I am not*. I consider it irrelevant whether or not I really knew.

'It is my most renowned monograph,' said the professor, and I guessed that he was not as confident as his words suggested. It was a forced boast.

'Indeed,' I said. 'I suppose your other writing is concerned with too niche and obscure a subject to warrant a large audience.'

'It is composed of such pure mathematics that no man can

refute it!' he cried, knocking over his Earl Grey. A starched-apron'd whelp ran to the table to wipe the mess.

'I am sure,' I said, once the whelp had departed, 'that your thesis is highly renowned in the circles of those who speak, as you say, pure mathematics. However, my primary languages are those of the arts, Professor, and I cannot see why you wish to speak with me.'

Moriarty sighed, and commenced the story anew.

'Did you read in the newspapers last year, of the discovery of a fragment of asteroid in the Netherlands?'

'I cannot say it stuck in my mind, if I did,' I said. (And that was true; the latest scientific discoveries of the age were of some passing novelty interest, but of little use to me in any greater capacity.)

'Well, the news struck me with great force. For my experiments, it is vital that I have access to the stone.'

'It is for the Dowager Duchess of Croome,' I said, seeing now that his interest in the ball was nothing to do with the society pages. 'The prince has had the stone embedded in a brooch, which he will present to her at the ball.'

'It is *not* for the Duchess of Croome.' said Moriarty. I was put in mind of a child denied a sugar mouse.

'You seek to contradict royalty?' I said. 'Who – or what – do you suggest the stone is for?'

'It is for Mathematics!' he cried, and beat his fist upon the table so that the china rattled. I saw several whelps start at the sound and wonder if they would be required to mop up a further spillage.

Moriarty had, perhaps, even startled himself with his violence, and he spoke next with a more controlled voice. 'I need entrance to the ball,' he said. 'You are invited.'

'I am,' I said.

'I need entrance. I need to get close enough to the duchess to acquire the brooch. It is no use sending an agent in for this, I must do it myself.' I raised an eyebrow, and he explained: 'It is a matter of mathematics. I act in my professorial role; I do not propose to become a criminal.'

'You propose to steal.'

'It is the KING OF B— who has stolen!' he cried, and this time I feared for the teapot. 'Stolen a prime specimen from under the very eyes of Science! To reduce such a discovery of such importance to the modern age to a piece of . . . a piece of *costume jewellery* . . . !'

I let the jibe at costumes stand, and waited.

'I need to get to the ball, Miss Adler, and I need to remain there long enough to acquire the brooch. I need to appear to *belong* at the ball. Miss Adler, I need to know the Modjeska Waltz.'

I waited for more, but he sat back, sipped his refilled cup, and waited.

Finally, the penny-farthing dropped. 'Professor Moriarty,' I said, 'are you asking me for . . . *dancing lessons?*'

For the first time in this escapade – and, I wonder now, perhaps the only time – Moriarty seemed truly embarrassed. He pushed scone crumbs around his plate. 'Well,' he said, 'if that is what it will take to get me close enough to acquire the stone, then that is what it will take.'

I let him suffer as I pondered this.

'I must say, I do rather fancy the challenge,' I said. 'But first you must tell me, Professor. You claim to wish to accompany me to the dance in order to examine a brooch. Such a robbery would be tantamount to high treason; you do not seem to think I would quail at this. There is social danger, even if we are not caught in our designs, in our attending this event. There are better dancers than I, who would be able to instruct you in the Modjeska Waltz. And so I ask you, Professor Moriarty – why have you come to me?'

Now the embarrassment faded, and a sharp keenness flashed in the professor's eyes like a stolen jewel in the wrong place. 'We are of one mind, Miss Adler.' He said. 'Or rather, we have both bested the same mind. I can think of nobody I would rather trust with such an important mission of personal and professional pride.'

'I know who you are thinking of,' I said. 'This is a case, I take it, of "my enemy's enemy"?'

If I have a fault, it is that, when poetic justice requires it, I am also, sometimes, willing to put personal and professional pride above common sense. We shook hands and agreed on the date of the professor's first lesson.

'This is nonsense! Why ever do people do this for fun and frivolity?'

'That is not for us to question. Let us begin again, Professor. And do *try* not to move your lips as you count.'

We were using the stage of the Opera House, a space that suggested the dimensions of a ballroom dance floor well enough. The manager of the theatre owed me a favour, which I was intending to call upon if ever a paramour caught my attention enough to warrant a moment of privacy about the stage door; but I decided that this was a more exciting reason to call in my favour and take temporary ownership of the stage.

Moriarty stumbled through a passable imitation of the Modjeska Waltz – the complex patterning was simpler to his numerically inclined mind than the turns of the standard waltz and foxtrot. He placed his hands on his thighs, bending over slightly in a cruel parody of the gentlemanly bow with which the dance had begun, and breathed and wheezed out his hatred of the activity. I made no response to his complaining, and merely amused myself by making faces at the painted cherubim that decorated the opera boxes.

'So, ah, when,' he asked, between gulps of breath, 'we approach the duchess—'

'I have heard enough criminal machinations,' I said, and before he could take another gulp of air to protest my use of the word 'criminal': 'Let us run through the middle-turns twice more.' He made groans of protest, which I ignored. 'This is the part where the partners change, Professor! It is the most important part of all to get right.'

The professor grumbled his way through the rehearsal and, following that, he suffered regularly for two lessons per week until the date of the ball. I confess, I was surprised that he committed to the full programme. After the first lesson I felt sure he would refuse the scheme. I was starting to wonder if I had underestimated his desire to obtain the Duchess's brooch.

The ballroom was built to resemble a grand Orangery, or perhaps it *was* a grand Orangery once upon an era. Its glass-domed ceiling was open to the sky, and we were blessed with a clear canopy of stars. The great space was lit on all sides with candles and framed with gleaming wood, silk and silver. The musicians played a selection of pieces arranged for strings and bassoon. The waiters moved with brisk efficiency around the samovars and between the great teetering settings of sweetmeats and jellies in the shape of castles. And the guests themselves were the prize jewels. Filling the great hall – although not, yet, approaching the dance floor – were dukes and barons, countesses and princesses, and everywhere glinted tiaras and medals.

I suppose the more excitable kind of reporter might have called it 'glittering'.

We approached the ballroom and my name was announced at the door but the professor was not even asked his. I wonder now whether this was a deliberate move on his part, whether coins had changed hands at an earlier stage in order to bring about this cloak of anonymity. But I was occupied with making the necessary small talk with the other guests as I deposited my furs with a porter (including a minor peer who claimed he had once sent a bouquet to my dressing room, and received no thanks; this was most likely true), and then it was time to descend the stairs to the ballroom. I had no time to quiz the professor as to whether he had made any plans without informing me and, in any case, it was soon put out of my mind. The prince, I noticed, was deliberately avoiding my eye.

We had not been present long when the king had his crystal glass refilled with port, and he tapped on it with what looked like a golden letter opener.

'My fellow guests!' he cried, and the hubbub of high society quietened in deference and expectation.

'You are all most welcome,' said the king, and he barely

concealed a hiccup. I could tell he needed to drink no more port
this evening, and the ball had barely begun. 'We are gathered
here to celebrate the coming-of-age of my son and heir, Prince—'
and here he named his son, who I protect here with the same
anonymity the professor was currently enjoying by my side.
There were several names and titles, and the king named them
all. Finally, we were encouraged to applaud the existence of this
young man.

'Thank you, Father,' said the prince, and at his voice the king
sat down heavily, visibly confident in his son finishing the
required address. (Perhaps the prince had made deductions that
matched my own regarding the king's capacity to speak with vast
quantities of port and brandy wine inside him.)

'Thank you, everyone,' he said. 'I would like to thank you all
for attending tonight. I am truly honoured to have so many excellent friends.' I fought the temptation to snort. 'In honour of the
occasion, I have asked one of the nation's most skilled composers
to create a dance for us. Thank you.' And he made a gesture at
the conductor, and bowed for further applause. It was hardly a
triumph of oratory.

I was surprised, furthermore, that the prince had not
presented the Dowager Duchess of Croome with the brooch.
Professor Moriarty had been insistent that it would happen
before we took to the floor, so that he might examine it during
his twirl with the duchess. His puzzled frown suggested that we
had an accord of confusion.

The conductor gestured for silence and the first, gentle strings
of the new composition floated over our heads from the violas
and cellos. It would have been pleasant, had I not been with a
man plotting something akin to high treason in three-three time.

'That's the Modjeska Waltz,' said I. 'It is time, Professor, to
prove that you belong here.'

'You mean,' said he, 'it is time to prove that *we* belong here.'

'No,' said I. 'You seem to be forgetting that I was already
invited.'

'Ah! My mistake. You were always on the guest list, of course.'
If the strings had not been soaring at that very moment, I might

have thought more carefully about this remark. As it was, we had no time. We reached the floor, bowed and curtsied as required, and positioned ourselves ready to begin the dance.

The understanding reader will indulge me for a moment in a minor side note about the matter of ballroom dancing.

There are two roles in ballroom dance: he who leads, and she who follows. To he who leads, therefore, it follows that even the dance with the speediest and most frequent partner changes will flow as smoothly as if he were dancing alone. To she who follows, each partner brings a host of potential dangers, embarrassing errors and awkward collisions, each new body the host of an unknown collection of possible faults, idiosyncrasies, potential tumbles and physical suffering. For the most part, at the manner of event we were enjoying, the men were, of course, highly practised and considerate partners. But she who follows can never truly relax during such an occasion, as she never knows what her next partner will bring, and how she will need to adjust her own performance so that he who leads can continue to remain unaware of the challenges his dancing brings.

I mention all of this because, to whit, I wish it to be known, formally, dear reader, that I accomplished everything Professor Moriarty did, albeit I frequently found myself going backwards, and in a pair of stolen heels.

But I shall explain the latter in good time. Let us return to the ballroom.

We had successfully performed the first steps of the dance, and had made it beyond the first turn. Ballroom dances proceed in promenade, and I had made sure to begin in a position that gave us a long wall to travel down, to allow the good professor as much time as possible to get into the rhythm of things before we were forced to turn a corner. But eventually, the necessity of moving about a finite space could not be avoided, and the first *chaînés en dedans* approached us.

The professor's jaw was set firm, and there was fierce concentration in his eyes. Even the most casual onlooker would know that he was counting. I decided against reminding him of the need to smile, as I felt certain it wouldn't help his mood. We managed the corner thanks to my subtle steering – I dreaded to think how the professor would get on without a guide. He was in the arms of fate, as were his partners.

I had a momentary respite when the first change arrived. The professor positively had to be pushed away from me. I enjoyed the small talk of a friendly young man who claimed to be a writer and wit living in the city, who told me he had witnessed my Desdemona at the Royal and enjoyed it immensely.

Having not yet played Desdemona, I made do with giving him the ghost of a smile.

When Moriarty returned, he clutched my wrist as if it were the only thing keeping him on the floor.

'It is nonsense,' he said, already out of breath, 'to change on the three, when mathematically it is not at all expedient—' Mercifully, he was whisked away again. It took another minute or two of rapid changing of partners – I enjoyed the solid steps of a considerate brigadier and suffered through a clumsy duke with far too loose a shoulder line, and damp hands – until we were together once again for the next quarter-turn.

'I despise this,' said the professor.

'I am hardly having a debutante's delight,' I replied.

'Let us take the brooch now, and escape this infernal place.' The ordeal of dancing had made him anxious to commence the scheme and hasten our opportunity to leave. I sympathised, but it was far too soon, and I opened my mouth to protest. 'The duchess is ahead,' he said. 'Let us—'

'Professor!' I hissed, 'the prince has not yet presented—' But I was too late. After what followed, I feared I could never again spend time in polite society.

To describe the horror briefly: with the insistent strength of the professor pulling me along, we danced out into a glittering tailspin, rocketed past the four couples ahead of us and stumbled directly into the duchess as she danced with a dashing dragoon.

I heard a crack in my right foot, and braced myself for agonising pain. Fortunately – or perhaps unfortunately, given what happened after – it had come from my shoe, not my foot, and an examination revealed the heel had broken. I wanted to scream with frustration; damn the professor and his entire expedition!

The prince ran to the aid of the duchess and continued to studiously ignore me as he helped her walk to the edge of the dance floor. In response, the dragoon made a show of helping me arise and walk to safety. This was difficult, given the condition of my newly broken shoes, which I confess I allowed the dragoon to assume was a limp born of injury.

The biggest concern – and the focus of the rest of the guests – was directed at the professor himself. He had performed his out-of-control waltz so well the ballroom was humming with worries about the frailty of the man. Eventually, he had assured everyone of his health to their satisfaction, and he joined me. I was still sitting where the dragoon had placed me, having bid him adieu so he might jostle with the prince for care of the duchess. All the attention was focused on that end of the ballroom, while at the other, the professor approached the actress.

'I have it!' said Moriarty, hissing at me through great excitement. He took out the pocket watch from his waistcoat, and I saw the red glint of the ruby setting.

So the prince *had* presented the duchess with the brooch – at an earlier, private moment, before the ball began! I wondered, and the reader will forgive my vanity, whether this had something to do with my own presence.

'You have successfully committed a serious crime,' I said, 'but I fear we have greater problems. The stumble has damaged the heel of one of my shoes.'

'No matter!' he cried. 'Let us ask my good friend the porter whether he might find us any spares lying about the place.' And, before I could protest, I was being steered to this curious man's station, which through the whole evening had been maintained with military stillness and concentration by the door. They had a whispered conversation beyond my earshot, after which the porter swiftly disappeared.

(I have since wondered whether this mysterious porter fits descriptions I have heard of one Colonel Sebastian Moran.

Although the porter does roughly match what I know of this dastardly gentleman's description, I would not feel comfortable confirming this as fact. For one, surely such a figure as the colonel would be instantly recognisable to a great number of those present at the ball. Instead, I am afraid to say that the identity of the professor's wicked assistant still eludes me. I understand he has many helpers spread throughout his home city and beyond.)

The porter brought me a box he assured me contained a pair of replacement shoes, and said, 'The prince was keeping these for just such an emergency.' Then he winked at me! – after which he returned to his place by the door. I sighed, no longer able to contain my foreboding about the recent turn of events, and opened the box. The shoes beneath the crepe paper were very fine. They were shining with diamonds and decorated with a delicate filigree. Further inspection revealed the coat of arms on the sole – to my horror, I realised that these shoes belonged to none other than the Dowager Duchess of Croome!

I could not return the shoes without making it obvious to the whole ball that I knew the dowager duchess was keeping spare items of her wardrobe in the prince's stores.

Moriarty smiled and, for the first time, I felt I was able to see through the passionate mathematician and eccentric if harmless scholar. I saw an entirely different person lurking beneath. I felt I was looking into the eyes of the very devil.

'And now, my dear Miss Adler,' said the professor, 'perhaps one more dance, or we might take a turn about the samovar, and I propose we leave the evening. I have had quite enough of high society, and, I assume, so have you. Waiter! Champagne!'

The robbery was discovered shortly before the last dance of the evening, when the prince and duchess came together and presumably attempted a secret look at the brooch that bound them together. By that point the professor had already bid me adieu, and the porter had opened the door for him, bowing him through it. We had made some more small talk with the various guests, and taken a few turns around the ballroom, but we did not dance again. When the time came to escape the evening,

Moriarty was comfortable leaving me on my own, satisfied that putting me in a pair of stolen shoes would stop me from drawing any attention to myself. The duchess's outcry at the discovery of the stolen brooch had set the ballroom alight, and the prince (and the dragoon) called for their pistols. Soon the ball had dissipated into uproar and, if one listened carefully, one could already hear the newspapers preparing the story. *This* would not be limited to the society pages.

Moriarty had the reputation, among those who knew him as a criminal, of pulling off a stunning *coup de crime*. He had removed a priceless brooch from under the nose of the Prince of B—. (And the king, too, although he had been snoring in his chair since the welcome speeches.) News of the theft mingled in the air above the guests as they whispered and screamed, and shot up into the sky, spreading across London. Those listening out for tales of crime – perhaps in Baker Street, over the sound of their violin – would surely know instantly that Moriarty was responsible for such a terrible accomplishment.

But, I am happy to say, if I did contribute to the professor's already formidable reputation in this city, let it be known that I did, at least, remove some of the satisfaction in this particular case. I may have aided Moriarty the master criminal, but I scuppered Moriarty the mathematician.

Even as the uproar began, I was leaving the Orangery. In the grounds, before I hailed a hansom, I paused by the hedge maze and felt beneath my breast. I removed the brooch from an inner pocket of my coat. I had sewn the pocket in myself, and used it to store the trinkets of paramours I felt could afford to lose the weight. I looked at the stone. The professor had not noticed my taking it from his waistcoat pocket as he beckoned a waiter to pour champagne, with which he toasted our success. To store it in my skirts I only required a split-second loss of concentration from the good professor; I got it when he tipped the porter a salute, and a wink.

The asteroid fragment itself was not stunning to look at; it was grey and did not sparkle. One could hardly countenance that it had dropped on to our humble orb from the depths of space, only to be locked into a ruby-studded mount for a dowager duchess to aid the politicking of a sycophantic prince.

I ground the asteroid to dust beneath the heel of my stolen shoes, and hailed a cab to return me to London, and thence to continue my own travels.

To this day I could not say, looking back over my dance with Professor Moriarty moment by moment, who was leading, and who followed behind.

Moriarty's Luck

L.C. Tyler

The old Queen had been dead for over a year, but the weather was much the same. In Baker Street, the gas lamps were obscured in equal measure by the yellow mist that had rolled in off the Thames and the large white snowflakes that had been falling since teatime. A dozen cabs had rattled past, all fully occupied, at first to our resigned amusement but increasingly to our profound annoyance. We had a table waiting for us at Simpson's in the Strand at seven o'clock, but we were still no more than a few yards from our rooms.

Holmes took out his gold half-hunter and frowned. 'I think, Watson, that we should abandon any hope of transport in this weather and resign ourselves to walking to our destination. If we put our best foot forward, we shall still be at Simpson's on time.'

'Walk from Baker Street to the Strand in twenty-five minutes?' I exclaimed. 'It will take thirty-five at least.'

Holmes smiled for the first time since we had set out. 'Twenty-five and not a minute more. If we are not at our table by seven, Watson, then I shall be happy to pay the bill for both of us at the end of the evening.'

I shook my head doubtfully. 'If we are there by seven, which I do not think possible, then I shall of course pay.'

'It is in the nature of wagers, Watson, that there is some reciprocity of risk, though the "mug" bears most of it. I hope you have some cash with you.'

'Mug?' I enquired.

'A technical term,' said Holmes.

I patted the pockets of my ulster and felt my wallet's reassuring shape. 'Of course,' I said. 'And I give you my word, Holmes, as a former officer and as a gentleman, that I shall not deliberately lag behind.'

Holmes smiled again. 'As for the guarantee that you offer for your conduct, I think that arch-villain Colonel Moran could have claimed the same distinction. In this new century, His Majesty's commission is no assurance of gentlemanly behaviour.'

I was about to protest that the morals of the late Professor Moriarty's henchman could not be allowed to blacken the character of the entire British Army, or even of his own rather unfashionable regiment, but Holmes, giving no such assurances of his own, had already set off at a brisk pace. For some time we proceeded in silence. I was struggling a little to keep up and Holmes's eyes were fixed on some distant point. He seemed to be recalculating our arrival time as we passed each landmark. Though we walked no faster than I had feared we might, I had not counted on Holmes's detailed knowledge of the geography of London. Twice we took short cuts that had me baffled for a moment, until we emerged again into some familiar street. The race, it appeared, would be won by brainpower rather than leg muscle alone. But, no sooner had I become convinced that my friend had the better of me and that I would be paying for dinner, than Holmes came to a sudden and unannounced halt at the corner of Bentinck Street and Welbeck Street. He took out his watch again and studied it before replacing it in his waistcoat pocket.

'Excellent. We have four and a half minutes in hand, Watson. Time I think to have my shoes polished by this gentleman here.'

Holmes indicated an old man, crouched beside his paraphernalia of blacking tins and brushes, wrapped in an old brown overcoat and with a scarf wound round the lower part of his face. There was something about the decrepitude of the figure that invoked disgust but, in a mind as noble as Holmes's, pity too. He removed an overly generous half-crown from his pocket and held it between two fingers.

'This is for you, my man, if you can clean these boots to perfection in precisely four minutes,' he said.

The old bootblack looked up. Perhaps he had been dozing, in spite of the cold, because Holmes's voice had clearly startled him. But he set to work without a word, dabbing his cloth nimbly and expertly. When he had applied the blacking to one boot however he paused and observed: 'I see, Mr Holmes, that these boots formerly pinched, but that you have now worn them in satisfactorily.'

Holmes in his turn suddenly looked startled. The great detective was of course used to making deductions of this sort himself, but rarely had anyone returned the favour and analysed either his character or his footwear in this way. His reply was clipped and somewhat ungracious. 'I should like to know how you have come to that conclusion.'

The bootblack looked up, taking in both Holmes and myself with a long, slow stare. I noticed for the first time his bulbous forehead and piercing eyes.

'As a bootblack,' he said, 'I have acquired an extensive knowledge of shoes and boots of all sorts – ladies' and gents' alike. These are clearly expensive and well made but they are of a pattern that was fashionable three or four years ago. They are, however, like new. The heels, always the first part of a shoe to suffer, are still perfect. Why would you buy an expensive pair of boots and then not wear them? The answer is simple: that they were initially very uncomfortable. But you are wearing them now and you and your friend approached at some speed, proving that you now feel no discomfort at all – hence I must conclude that you have finally worn them in.'

I laughed and applauded this strange reversal of roles. I turned to Holmes expecting him also to congratulate the old man but he was scowling at him.

'You finally recognise me then?' sneered the bootblack.

'How could I not?'

'Who is this person, Holmes?' I asked.

'Someone you know well, but have never seen, except for a moment as his train sped past us at Canterbury,' said Holmes. 'Somebody neither of us ever expected to see again.'

'Professor Moriarty?' I said, in disbelief. 'But . . .'

The old man unwound his scarf and, for the first time, I found myself face to face with my friend's most implacable enemy. There was an old scar that ran from his temple to his jawline. 'You thought I was dead?' he asked.

'If you don't think it impolite of me, I had rather hoped so,' said Holmes. 'We struggled. I overcame you. I saw you fall . . .'

Moriarty shook his head. 'It is true that I slipped from that ledge above the Reichenbach Falls.'

'That was no slip,' I interjected. 'Holmes defeated you by using the ancient art of baritsu. Had he not, he would have perished at your hands.'

'Baritsu?' Moriarty sneered. 'Was that what he called that strange posturing and flailing of his arms? Was that why he uttered those shrill noises that he possibly imagined to be Japanese? The path was wet. I had been waiting there for some time. It is hardly surprising that I could not keep my footing. I simply stumbled and fell. But the pool below the waterfall is deep. Very deep. Quite improbably deep. I was temporarily stunned as I struck the water, but its coldness revived me. I rose to the surface, but swimming in that torrent was impossible. I was swept along by the current and dragged under again, this time striking my head against a rock. I do not know what happened next, but some minutes or hours or chapters later I found myself being pulled ashore by a Swiss peasant. He and his wife carried me home, more dead than alive – I mean figuratively rather than mathematically obviously because otherwise I would on balance have been dead.'

'That all sounds very unlikely,' I said.

'Not as unlikely as some of the explanations I have heard for Mr Holmes's survival,' said Moriarty.

'Fair comment,' said Holmes.

'Go on,' I said. I'd never been quite sure that baritsu really existed. I hoped that the rest of Holmes's account of his survival could be trusted.

'They nursed me,' Moriarty continued, 'for two months, until I had recovered – at least physically. In return they asked for nothing. Nothing at all. Their simple everyday kindness humbled me. When I left I tried to give them all I had with me – my money, my watch – but they refused to take anything. I went on my way determined to lead a better and nobler life. I returned to England to resume my academic career.'

'Then how do you find yourself here?'

Moriarty gave a bitter laugh. 'Publications,' he said. 'As a university head of department you have a great deal of administrative work that the university expects you to carry out. Then you have students to teach, however asinine and unteachable they may be. Finally, you must undertake research and publish in the leading journals. Most academics find that it is difficult to do all three, and very few of them also run a criminal empire spanning much of western Europe. Of course, it was the research that suffered – it always does. Each time I went to an interview I was faced with the question: "Professor Moriarty, I see that you haven't published since 1889. Why is that?"'

'Eighteen eighty-nine? Your famous paper on mathematics?' asked Holmes. 'What was it called again?'

'*Towards a post-modernist re-evaluation of the binomial theorem*,' said Moriarty with a sigh.

'Of course,' said Holmes. 'A masterpiece.'

'Your criminal activities counted against you,' I said. 'You could not have hoped for employment, even at one of the newer institutions.'

Moriarty laughed again. 'How little you know of our universities,' he said. 'All vice chancellors are obliged to maximise revenue from any legitimate source. There was one selection panel which, when I told them how I had extorted ten million marks from the government of Saxony, were completely lost in thought for five whole minutes. In the rejection letter that followed, they said that, if they had imagined for a moment that the trick would have worked twice, they would have had no hesitation in offering me a Chair.' His voice tailed off wistfully.

Holmes stood there, one boot covered in blacking, the half-crown still held between his fingers. 'But, you have now come to this . . .'

'Indeed. While you are able to buy the very best boots and

leave them in your wardrobe, I am obliged to wear a coat that scarcely keeps out the snow on a night such as this. The hovel in which I live has neither food nor coal in it. We have been obliged to burn the doors to keep warm. The landlord long ago sold the roof to some venture capitalists. Even the bare walls now form part of a toxic property bond. I share the bed with three others, none of whom are in any way to my liking. But I am trying to live honestly, as you can see.'

'And would be insulted by any suggestion of charity, no doubt,' I said.

'I didn't say *that*,' said Moriarty. 'I definitely didn't say *that*.' Though still kneeling, he had grasped Holmes by his coat. 'A guinea, sir? You'd never even miss it.'

'Holmes!' I exclaimed. 'This is the wretch who tried to murder you – and would have done had you not known . . . er . . . baritsu. He is the man who was, for years, at the heart of every major crime that was committed in London, and at least one in Saxony. You cannot possibly offer him a penny.'

Holmes said nothing. He was staring out into the falling snow.

Moriarty swung round and now held on to my ulster. 'Or you, Dr Watson? You must be making good money writing up Mr Holmes's cases – surely I deserve a small share of that for instigating the crimes that are making you rich?'

I muttered something about advances being rather less than the newspapers reported, while at the same time trying to pull myself away from him. His grasp was, however, vice-like on my overcoat.

'Watson! Do not strike the poor creature!' Holmes exclaimed.

I realised that I had raised my arm as if to do just that. I lowered it slowly and Moriarty released me, shuffling back on his knees until he was crouching before us like some beaten cur. He now lifted his own arms, as if to fend off whatever blow might fall. It was melodrama, but it was good melodrama.

'This,' said Holmes, 'is all that is left of what was once the Napoleon of crime. Look at him, Watson, and pity him. This is the man who wrote *Towards a post-feminist re-evaluation of the binomial theorem.*'

'*Post-modernist,*' said Moriarty.

'Whatever,' said Holmes. 'He has, or had, one of the greatest minds I have ever encountered. And now he kneels before us. We are lucky, Watson. We have looked death in the face – you in Afghanistan, I in many places – and lived to tell the tale. We shall eat well tonight and each have a soft bed to retire to afterwards. And this poor fellow . . .'

'We make our own luck,' I said.

'You think I deserve to be as I am, Dr Watson? Perhaps you are right. I could have been Lucasian Professor of Mathematics. All I had to do was publish regularly and not build up a vast criminal empire. I ask not for what I deserve, but for your charity.'

Holmes again toyed with the silver coin in his hand, but I was determined Moriarty should have nothing.

'Holmes,' I said. 'The wager!'

My friend looked at me. It was as if some spell had been broken. 'Of course,' he said. 'You are going to pay for dinner. We can still be at Simpson's by seven.'

'But only if we leave *now*,' I said.

I had, however, no need for further words. Holmes had already set off. I paused only to smile in what I hoped was an ironic manner at Moriarty before I hurried in the great detective's footsteps. We had gone some two hundred yards before I managed to catch up with him. He clearly thought there was still a chance of winning the bet.

'Your nature is far too forgiving,' I panted, as soon as I drew level with him.

'I saw merely an old man down on his luck,' said Holmes. 'He will have to sit there all night even to make half a crown whereas very shortly we shall be at Simpson's. Indeed, I calculate that we shall arrive at . . .' Holmes felt in his right-hand waistcoat pocket, then in his left. Then he stopped abruptly. 'I was sure that I had my watch with me . . .'

'Your gold half hunter? Of course, I saw it.'

'I was checking it just before we met Moriarty . . .'

We both turned and looked behind us. We could still just

make out the junction of Bentinck Street and Welbeck Street, but there was no sign of any bootblack, no sign of his tins of blacking. All we could see was the swirling mist.

I laughed. 'It would seem that the professor has taken advantage of your good nature in more ways than one,' I said, 'but never mind, I shall pay for dinner as some recompense.' I felt in the right pocket of my ulster and then in my left. 'Holmes,' I said, 'I was sure that I had my wallet earlier.'

But he was already searching for his own pocketbook, without success.

'I think we will have to forgo our dinner at Simpson's,' I said. 'That villain has left us without a penny.'

'Not quite,' said Holmes. 'We have one piece of luck ourselves. I still have this half-crown. It will not provide the dinner I intended, but if we take a right turn just ahead, we shall in due course come to the Alpha Inn, where we may obtain two pints of ale and some goose pie. The landlord is what you might describe as a diamond geezer. That is a consoling thought, is it not?'

'Indeed,' I said. 'And there is one more consoling thought: that while I shall most certainly continue to chronicle your remarkable cases, nobody will ever write another word about the exploits of Professor Moriarty.'

The Death of Moriarty

Peter Guttridge

The National Archives in Kew, London contain many secrets. Some are revealed in full through the diligence of researchers, others remain tantalisingly out of reach because a single clue is all that can be found. And then there are those that fall somewhere in-between – a short series of clues that stir the embers but aren't sufficient to take fire.

Take the 1891 Census of the population of the United Kingdom. No need to visit Kew to explore it; it's online. Type in the name 'James Moriarty'. There are just eighteen men and boys with that name in the entire population in that year. Their occupations, ages and places of birth are listed.

Labourers in field and factory; two soldiers (a sergeant and a private); young scholars and those too young for school. Seven born in Ireland, one in Scotland, nine in various English counties and one in London. In Highgate. Where in 1891 he also resides, though it is not evident if it is at the same address at which he was born. He stands out, too, because he is an educated man. A professor.

The census took place before the famous struggle in 1891 at the Reichenbach Falls that saw Professor James Moriarty and Sherlock Holmes plunge to their deaths. (Although the death of Sherlock Holmes was, of course, greatly exaggerated.)

Little is known about Moriarty but his rarefied work, *The Dynamics of an Asteroid*, is famous. Famous but unread because unobtainable. Even that behemoth of book-selling, Amazon, doesn't sell or resell *The Dynamics of an Asteroid*.

However, there are references galore on Google, all ultimately referring back to the single mention of it in Dr Watson's 'The Final Problem', his account of the 1891 death of Sherlock Holmes and Professor Moriarty.

Wade through the pages of references to it on Google and on the ninth page there is mention of a Conference on New Methods in Astrodynamics, held in January 2003 in Pasadena, California. A paper is available on PDF entitled *Geometric Mechanics and the Dynamics of Asteroid Pairs.*

It turns out the dynamics of an asteroid pair, consisting of two irregularly shaped asteroids interacting through their gravitational potential, is an example of a full body problem (FBP) in which two or more bodies interact. There is a footnote (page three of the paper) that states: 'as first predicated in James Moriarty's *Dynamics of an Asteroid*'. Somebody has clearly read it.

The National Archives farm out online access of their records to various third parties. For a fee, through one of them, Ancestry. co.uk, you can see birth and death certificates.

Professor Moriarty's year and place of birth are listed on the census return but there is no birth certificate for him in the Archives, even though it should hold the complete parish records for the Highgate area. It is simply not there.

The probability is there will be nothing different when it comes to his death certificate, even though his year of death is known. On the homepage for death certificates issued in 1891 the Archives has a digest of three or four news events from that year. Events striking enough to distract any researcher from a quest for a specific death certificate.

The Great Blizzard of 1891 in the south and west of England killed two hundred and twenty people on land and many more at sea. Extensive snowdrifts on land, vicious storms on the sea off the south coast. Fourteen ships were sunk, including the SS *Utopia*, a steamship built in 1874 by Robert Duncan & Co of Glasgow, heading from the Hook of Holland to England.

It collided with HMS *Anson*. The *Anson* smashed a five-metre hole in the *Utopia*'s hull. The holds were almost immediately flooded, the ship tipped over and within twenty minutes the *Utopia* was swallowed by the sea.

Out of 880 passengers and crew members, 562 died or went missing, presumed dead; 318 survived. The click-through on the homepage is to a facsimile of a whole page of *The Times* given over, in tiny print, to the names of all passengers and crew members in alphabetical order, with an indication after the names about whether they survived, were known to be dead or had gone missing.

Under the letter 'M' a Professor James Moriarty and a Colonel Sebastian Moran are listed as two of the passengers who survived the disaster.

This disaster happened months after the struggle at the Reichenbach Falls. Unsurprisingly, there is no death certificate for a Professor James Moriarty – or any Moriarty – for that year. But then he does appear to have cheated death twice.

But not for long. For the death certificate of a Professor James Moriarty is listed in the following year. On 1 February 1892. The place of death is given as the London Hospital, Whitechapel Road, Whitechapel, E1. The cause of death is given as botulism.

Botulism is something that needs looking up. It's a particularly horrible form of food poisoning caused by the botulinum toxin, the most lethal neurotoxin known. Botulism is deadly to humans and animals if untreated. Death is generally caused by respiratory failure due to paralysis of the respiratory muscles. Not a nice way to go.

The botulinum toxin is produced by the bacterium *clostridium botulinum*, which occurs in soil. People ingest botulinum toxin from food grown in the soil that is contaminated with the bacterium. Intriguingly, in light of Sherlock Holmes's retirement into beekeeping, honey contains it, but it is only lethal in honey to infants.

These days the toxin is more usually linked to a cosmetic procedure that thousands readily submit to. It works by injections that paralyse the muscles that cause frowning or, indeed, any expression of emotion. Wikipedia is not entirely to be trusted, but it says there are four forms of botulinum toxin used commercially for cosmetic procedures for those people who do not wish to show emotion on their faces. The best known is Botox.

Dismissing the notion that Professor Moriarty died from a cosmetic procedure gone wrong, the idea he died from food poisoning is, to be frank, even more bathetic.

So far so intriguing, but how to take these pieces of information further? Well, *The Times* is an invaluable resource at Kew – or online if you are linked to an educational establishment wealthy enough to pay the annual fee for full access to its digitised archive.

Browsing through every edition for, say, the previous three months from the date of Moriarty's death brings hours of fascinating distractions, but also an account, on 18 January 1892, of a world championship chess match in Simpson's chess rooms on the Strand.

In their time together, Sherlock Holmes and Dr Watson repaired regularly to the restaurant at Simpson's-in-the-Strand for good English fare – still today it is celebrated for its roast beef. So perhaps it is no surprise that Dr Watson would attend a chess match there. More surprising is what happened.

Let the newspaper's chess correspondent tell the story, or as much of it as he observed:

> The match between Velikovsky A. K. and Sturgess J. P. was disrupted for a time when a celebrated member of the audience was taken ill. The well-known chronicler of the exploits of Sherlock Holmes, Dr James Watson, collapsed in a booth he was sharing with a companion.
>
> This correspondent became aware of Dr Watson's collapse when he saw his companion trying to revive him. Simpson's staff members quickly came to his aid, as did this correspondent. His companion, who gave no name, explained that they had been watching the tournament and engaging in desultory conversation when the doctor had suddenly slumped forward, unconscious, on the table between them.
>
> Happily, the doctor quickly revived. He could not account

for his collapse – although this correspondent notes the room was very stuffy and overheated with the press of people watching the tournament and the air thick with cigar, cigarette and pipe smoke. Dr Watson asked for his companion – whom he referred to as 'the professor' – but it seemed the man had slipped away. When the match resumed, Velikovsky won.

The professor. Dr Watson and Professor Moriarty together in a year when the good doctor believed Sherlock Holmes – and indeed Moriarty – to be dead? How did that come about? Watson, by his own account in his memoirs of his friend, Holmes, had never met or even seen Moriarty. What to make of this encounter?

A series of clues forming an incomplete narrative. How to complete it? Some might call it inspiration. Researchers – modest creatures on the whole – simply call it doggedness. Looking again at what is in front of you.

The Royal Astronomical Society has its library at Burlington House, along one side of the cobbled courtyard that leads to the Royal Academy. It's a private library and a treasure trove of information about astronomy and astronomers. Its librarians have grown weary of requests from researchers for access to anything they have about or by Professor James Moriarty for the simple reason they have nothing.

However, Hampstead and Highgate have an amateur astronomical society that was founded in the early 1880s. Among the names of the founders the dogged researcher will find the name James Moriarty. Its papers are housed in the archive of Hampstead Library at John Keats' House, just a walk away from the heath. Or, rather, they were housed there. As the library service is dismantled and the branches handed over to volunteers the archive has been deposited at the National Archives for safekeeping.

A good reason to visit Kew. Another relates to that death certificate from the hospital in Whitechapel. Signed by a doctor whose hand is as indecipherable as that of any other doctor. Medical directories from the Victorian era are available online but the London Hospital's archive needs to be consulted by attending in person at Kew.

Kew it is then. There is a pleasant walk in summer along the towpath by the Thames from Hammersmith or Barnes Bridge to the National Archives but a researcher in pursuit of a mystery will use the quickest method: the tube to Kew station and a ten-minute rush through quiet residential streets to the imposing building by the river.

Impatience can also be a virtue. But waiting for medical records and astronomical records to be brought up there are only so many cups of coffee a person can drink.

The astronomical records arrive first. A slim folder. Written in faded black ink on the cover: 'Notes by Professor James Moriarty, January 25, 1892'. Trembling fingers untie the cord that secures the old file. Within are not astronomical tables or records of hours spent with an eye glued to a telescope, but a handwritten account of an encounter in Simpson's chess rooms entitled: *A Further Fragment of Memoir by Professor James Moriarty.*

'You can get help for your dystonia,' the bluff, solid man said. He was wearing a waistcoat that could not conceal his stoutness but there was strength in his shoulders and in the beefy arms that packed the sleeves of his tweed jacket. He had a newspaper under his arm.

I put my finger to my chin and looked up at him. 'Excuse me?'

'Your dystonia.' The man touched his moustache then pointed vaguely in the direction of my head. 'The oscillation.'

I frowned. I don't like people standing over me.

'My head does not oscillate,' I said. I examined him for a moment. 'Do I know you?'

'We have never met,' he said. 'Perhaps it is EHT.'

'I do not know the acronym,' I said. 'Why are you dressed for the country here on the Strand?'

It was his turn to frown, but not about my comment on his clothes.

'Acronym? What is that?'

I tried not to sound supercilious, though everything about this open-faced man irritated me. I indicated the newspaper.

'I thought you a man of letters. But clearly not initial letters. Acronym is a new word for a custom long known in linguistics but never before named. The custom of taking the initial letter of a series of words and making an abbreviation of them.'

'I see,' he said doubtfully.

'From the Greek akros – topmost – and onoma – name,' I said, relishing my pedantry. 'You will recall Edgar Allan Poe used one in his unusually comical story "How To Write A Blackwood Article".'

The man touched his moustache again.

'Why are you here?' I said.

He gestured into the room. 'I am a fan of chess.'

I was sitting in Simpson's chess rooms on the Strand. A game was in progress using the giant chess pieces in the middle of the room. I was sitting in a booth. As often when I concentrate I was unaware of the oscillation of my head. This strange man had diagnosed me correctly. I suffer from dystonic head tremor. Touching my cheek or, as now, cupping my chin in my hand, allayed the symptoms. I was conscious that my head was thrust forward – I had cervical or neck dystonia. A tremulous cervical dystonia is the correct term, I am told.

For a man so proud of his brain – and, believe me, my ego is merited – this thing that my intelligence could not control was irksome beyond imagining. A doctor called Stamford at the London Hospital was doing pioneering work. I intended to look him up.

Alcohol temporarily improves my condition. I took a sip of my wine. A Bordeaux. Indifferent – but then this was London.

He looked at me for longer than seemed polite then showed me the newspaper he had been securing under his arm. It was an old edition of The Times, *the one that recorded the sinking of the ship Moran and I had been travelling on.*

'I thought you dead until I saw an account in The Times *of the sinking of the SS Utopia and your name among the survivors.'*

'Do I know you?' I said again, looking beyond him in case I needed help.

'We have never actually met before,' he said.

He slid into the seat opposite me in the booth – with some difficulty because of his paunch. I frowned.

'If you are here for some kind of revenge for some real or imaginary injury I should advise you not to attempt to remove your service revolver from your pocket,' I said.

'If you have a weapon, you run the same risk,' he said.

I gestured with one hand as I leaned across and touched his neck with the other. As he slumped I murmured: 'My weapon is my knowledge of the workings of everything.'

I had seen stage hypnotists. They were the same as magicians in that they operated by misdirection. In the hypnotists' case it was the pretence that their voice provided the magic when in fact it was the fingers of one hand pressed rapidly against the carotid artery, stopping the flow of blood to the brain, whilst the audience's attention was on whatever flourish the other hand was making.

I reached over and checked his pockets. There were no identifying papers. He carried no service revolver. I looked over at the indifferent chess game. I ignored it and observed the man as he slept, wondering who he might be. I was disturbed when others came to the booth, concerned about him. I slipped away as they attended him.

There is no family history of tremor or dystonia. My two brothers – also called James by our ludicrous parents – suffer no symptoms. And with me it is only the head and only when I am standing. Lying down relieves it. There is no equivalent tremor of the hand, as is often the case.

There the fragment breaks off. Stamford. That name is naggingly familiar and not just because the doctor's signature on Moriarty's death certificate could be interpreted as 'Stamford'.

A request for any files pertaining to Dr Stamford in the London Hospital archives elicits a bulky folder. It has been closed for a hundred years until its release in 2014. It is almost impossible to hide the fact the tremor in one's own hand has got worse, such is the excitement in opening a long-sealed file.

It is a judgement from the British Medical Council striking off Dr Stamford for unprofessional and negligent conduct related to the unexpected and unfortunate death of a patient. Reading through the judgement and an attached handwritten letter from Dr Stamford, it is clear that some dubious behind-the-scenes negotiations took place to prevent Dr Stamford going to prison for manslaughter or to the gallows for the murder of a patient. That patient was Professor James Moriarty.

Google Dr Stamford and you will see that after acting as a dresser at St Bartholomew's Hospital he went on to research a treatment for cervical dystonia. This cure involved the use of botulinum toxin injections to allay the symptoms of dystonia. He was a pioneer in what is now the conventional treatment for the condition. A quick look at the Wikipedia site for botulism confirms that the toxin has proper medical as well as cosmetic uses.

Stamford's official testimony about what happened in surgery with Professor Moriarty in February 1892 is concise to the point of being opaque:

> *I take full responsibility for miscalculating the dose. The patient, Professor James Moriarty, suffered from a severe form of cervical dystonia. The oscillation of his head was severe. I advised him that injecting botulinum toxin would allay his symptoms but that the treatment was still in the research stages. I advised him that calculating the right dosage – based on his age and body weight – was difficult and there was what some might regard as an unacceptable margin of error.*
>
> *Too little and it would have no effect. Too much and he risked death by choking since his respiratory system would be paralysed. He expressed the opinion that since the oscillation of his neck caused him such inconvenience he was willing to take the risk.*
>
> *The appropriate paralysis quickly set in after the intramuscular injection and his head stopped its oscillations. But then it became clear the toxin was continuing its work beyond the intended area. The paralysis spread more extensively than I had anticipated. Professor Moriarty struggled both to breathe*

and speak. There was nothing to be done, no way to stop the lethal work of the toxin. He died within eight minutes of the administration of the dosage.

This testimony was dated February 1892. The appended, handwritten letter was dated May 1894 and is the reason Dr Stamford was struck off. In it he stated:

I took the Hippocratic Oath to save not end life. It weighs heavily on my conscience that I took the life of Professor James Moriarty deliberately. I did this under my own volition. Although my old friend and colleague Dr James Watson was present he was not party to my decision so no blame can be attributed to him.

You may know that at the very start of my career I had been a dresser under Dr Watson at St Bartholomew's Hospital and had been instrumental in bringing him together with my research laboratory acquaintance, Sherlock Holmes, to share lodgings and begin their remarkable career together.

When Professor Moriarty came to me I had already been alerted to the fact he had survived the Reichenbach Falls by Dr Watson, who had seen his name on the list of survivors of the SS Utopia disaster. It enraged me that he had killed such a man as Sherlock Holmes and I decided that I was in a unique position to avenge that great man's death.

On the day of Professor Moriarty's treatment, Dr Watson was present in an adjoining room. Once I had administered the fatal injection, he emerged. Moriarty was surprised to see him again – the two men had met briefly in Simpson's chess rooms – and then became alarmed when Watson identified himself.

He flailed around for a moment but I had taken the precaution of strapping him to the bed on which he lay and the injection soon enough began to take effect and hamper his movements.

As paralysis set in I told him that I had given him a deliberate overdose of botulinum toxin as punishment for his murder of Sherlock Holmes. His eyes bulging, he managed a few words before his vocal cords and respiratory system were totally paralysed.

He said (and it chills me now to think how I dismissed his words as simply those of a desperate man): 'The meddler and I made an agreement. He is not dead.' His mouth contorted horribly as he struggled for breath. We had to lean in to hear Moriarty's final, choked words. 'He will return,' he said. Then he died.

Almost three years later, it fills me with shame that he was telling some form of the truth. As the world knows, Sherlock Holmes has returned in time to participate in the 'Adventure of the Empty House' and solve the mystery of the murder of the Honourable Ronald Adair. As to whether he made an agreement with Professor Moriarty to save both their lives I cannot conjecture. Only he and, perhaps, his chronicler can know the truth of that and it may well be a story for which the world is not yet prepared . . .

CPSIA information can be obtained
at www.ICGtesting.com
Printed in the USA
LVOW12*0522090518
576479LV00004B/34/P